PAUL BOWLES

PAUL BOWLES

THE SHELTERING SKY
LET IT COME DOWN
THE SPIDER'S HOUSE

THE LIBRARY OF AMERICA

The Sheltering Sky copyright 1949 by Paul Bowles. Reprinted by
arrangement with Ecco Press, an imprint of
HarperCollins Publishers, Inc.
Let It Come Down copyright 1952 by Paul Bowles.
Reprinted by permission of Black Sparrow Press.
The Spider's House copyright 1955 by Paul Bowles.
Reprinted by permission of Black Sparrow Press.

The paper used in this publication meets the
minimum requirements of the American National Standard for
Information Sciences—Permanence of Paper for Printed
Library Materials, ANSI Z39.48—1984.

Distributed to the trade in the United States
by Penguin Putnam, Inc.
and in Canada by Penguin Books Canada Ltd.

Library of Congress Catalog Number: 2002019453
For cataloging information, see end of Notes.
ISBN 1–931082–19–7

First Printing
The Library of America—134

Manufactured in the United States of America

Contents

THE SHELTERING SKY

FOR JANE

Tea in the Sahara

"Each man's destiny is personal only insofar as it may
happen to resemble what is already in his memory."
—EDUARDO MALLEA

I

HE AWOKE, opened his eyes. The room meant very little
to him; he was too deeply immersed in the non-being
from which he had just come. If he had not the energy to
ascertain his position in time and space, he also lacked the
desire. He was somewhere, he had come back through vast
regions from nowhere; there was the certitude of an infinite
sadness at the core of his consciousness, but the sadness was
reassuring, because it alone was familiar. He needed no further consolation. In utter comfort, utter relaxation he lay
absolutely still for a while, and then sank back into one of the
light momentary sleeps that occur after a long, profound one.
Suddenly he opened his eyes again and looked at the watch
on his wrist. It was purely a reflex action, for when he saw the
time he was only confused. He sat up, gazed around the
tawdry room, put his hand to his forehead, and sighing
deeply, fell back onto the bed. But now he was awake; in
another few seconds he knew where he was, he knew that the
time was late afternoon, and that he had been sleeping since
lunch. In the next room he could hear his wife stepping about
in her mules on the smooth tile floor, and this sound now
comforted him, since he had reached another level of consciousness where the mere certitude of being alive was not
sufficient. But how difficult it was to accept the high, narrow
room with its beamed ceiling, the huge apathetic designs
stenciled in indifferent colors around the walls, the closed
window of red and orange glass. He yawned: there was no air
in the room. Later he would climb down from the high bed
and fling the window open, and at that moment he would
remember his dream. For although he could not recall a detail

5

of it, he knew he had dreamed. On the other side of the window there would be air, the roofs, the town, the sea. The evening wind would cool his face as he stood looking, and at that moment the dream would be there. Now he only could lie as he was, breathing slowly, almost ready to fall asleep again, paralyzed in the airless room, not waiting for twilight but staying as he was until it should come.

II

On the terrace of the Café d'Eckmühl-Noiseux a few Arabs sat drinking mineral water; only their fezzes of varying shades of red distinguished them from the rest of the population of the port. Their European clothes were worn and gray; it would have been hard to tell what the cut of any garment had been originally. The nearly naked shoe-shine boys squatted on their boxes looking down at the pavement, without the energy to wave away the flies that crawled over their faces. Inside the café the air was cooler but without movement, and it smelled of stale wine and urine.

At the table in the darkest corner sat three Americans: two young men and a girl. They conversed quietly, and in the manner of people who have all the time in the world for everything. One of the men, the thin one with a slightly wry, distraught face, was folding up some large multicolored maps he had spread out on the table a moment ago. His wife watched the meticulous movements he made with amusement and exasperation; maps bored her, and he was always consulting them. Even during the short periods when their lives were stationary, which had been few enough since their marriage twelve years ago, he had only to see a map to begin studying it passionately, and then, often as not, he would begin to plan some new, impossible trip which sometimes eventually became a reality. He did not think of himself as a tourist; he was a traveler. The difference is partly one of time, he would explain. Whereas the tourist generally hurries back home at the end of a few weeks or months, the traveler, belonging no more to one place than to the next, moves slowly, over periods of years, from one part of the earth to another. Indeed, he would have found it difficult to tell, among the many places he had lived, precisely where it was he had felt most at home. Before the war it had been Europe and the Near East, during the war the West Indies and South America. And she had accompanied him without reiterating her complaints too often or too bitterly.

At this point they had crossed the Atlantic for the first time since 1939, with a great deal of luggage and the intention of keeping as far as possible from the places which had been touched by the war. For, as he claimed, another important difference between tourist and traveler is that the former accepts his own civilization without question; not so the traveler, who compares it with the others, and rejects those elements he finds not to his liking. And the war was one facet of the mechanized age he wanted to forget.

In New York they had found that North Africa was one of the few places they could get boat passage to. From his earlier visits, made during his student days in Paris and Madrid, it seemed a likely place to spend a year or so; in any case it was near Spain and Italy, and they could always cross over if it failed to work out. Their little freighter had spewed them out from its comfortable maw the day before onto the hot docks, sweating and scowling with anxiety, where for a long time no one had paid them the slightest attention. As he stood there in the burning sun, he had been tempted to go back aboard and see about taking passage for the continuing voyage to Istanbul, but it would have been difficult to do without losing face, since it was he who had cajoled them into coming to North Africa. So he had cast a matter-of-fact glance up and down the dock, made a few reasonably unflattering remarks about the place, and let it go at that, silently resolving to start inland as quickly as possible.

The other man at the table, when he was not talking, kept whistling aimless little tunes under his breath. He was a few years younger, of sturdier build, and astonishingly handsome, as the girl often told him, in his late Paramount way. Usually there was very little expression of any sort to be found on his smooth face, but the features were formed in such a manner that in repose they suggested a general bland contentment.

They stared out into the street's dusty afternoon glare.

"The war has certainly left its mark here." Small, with blonde hair and an olive complexion, she was saved from prettiness by the intensity of her gaze. Once one had seen her eyes, the rest of the face grew vague, and when one tried to recall her image afterwards, only the piercing, questioning violence of the wide eyes remained.

"Well, naturally. There were troops passing through for a year or more."

"It seems as though there might be some place in the world they could have left alone," said the girl. This was to please her husband, because she regretted having felt annoyed with him about the maps a moment ago. Recognizing the gesture, but not understanding why she was making it, he paid no attention to it.

The other man laughed patronizingly, and he joined in.

"For your special benefit, I suppose?" said her husband.

"For us. You know you hate the whole thing as much as I do."

"What whole thing?" he demanded defensively. "If you mean this colorless mess here that calls itself a town, yes. But I'd still a damned sight rather be here than back in the United States."

She hastened to agree. "Oh, of course. But I didn't mean this place or any other particular place. I meant the whole horrible thing that happens after every war, everywhere."

"Come, Kit," said the other man. "You don't remember any other war."

She paid him no attention. "The people of each country get more like the people of every other country. They have no character, no beauty, no ideals, no culture—nothing, nothing."

Her husband reached over and patted her hand. "You're right. You're right," he said smiling. "Everything's getting gray, and it'll be grayer. But some places'll withstand the malady longer than you think. You'll see, in the Saraha here . . ."

Across the street a radio was sending forth the hysterical screams of a coloratura soprano. Kit shivered. "Let's hurry up and get there," she said. "Maybe we could escape that."

They listened fascinated as the aria, drawing to a close, made the orthodox preparations for the inevitable high final note.

Presently Kit said: "Now that that's over, I've got to have another bottle of Oulmès."

"My God, more of that gas? You'll take off."

"I know, Tunner," she said, "but I can't get my mind off water. It doesn't matter what I look at, it makes me thirsty. For once I feel as if I could get on the wagon and stay there. I can't drink in the heat."

"Another Pernod?" said Tunner to Port.

Kit frowned. "If it were real Pernod—"

"It's not bad," said Tunner, as the waiter set a bottle of mineral water on the table.

"*Ce n'est pas du vrai Pernod?*"

"*Si, si, c'est du Pernod,*" said the waiter.

"Let's have another set-up," Port said. He stared at his glass dully. No one spoke as the waiter moved away. The soprano began another aria.

"She's off!" cried Tunner. The din of a street car and its bell passing across the terrace outside, drowned the music for a moment. Beneath the awning they had a glimpse of the open vehicle in the sunshine as it rocked past. It was crowded with people in tattered clothes.

Port said: "I had a strange dream yesterday. I've been trying to remember it, and just this minute I did."

"No!" cried Kit with force. "Dreams are so dull! Please!"

"You don't want to hear it!" he laughed. "But I'm going to tell it to you *anyway*." The last was said with a certain ferocity which on the surface appeared feigned, but as Kit looked at him she felt that on the contrary he actually was dissimulating the violence he felt. She did not say the withering things that were on the tip of her tongue.

"I'll be quick about it," he smiled. "I know you're doing me a favor by listening, but I can't remember it just thinking about it. It was daytime and I was on a train that kept putting on speed. I thought to myself: 'We're going to plough into a big bed with the sheets all in mountains.'"

Tunner said archly: "Consult Madame La Hiff's *Gypsy Dream Dictionary.*"

"Shut up. And I was thinking that if I wanted to, I could live over again—start at the beginning and come right on up to the present, having exactly the same life, down to the smallest detail."

Kit closed her eyes unhappily.

"What's the matter?" he demanded.

"I think it's extremely thoughtless and egotistical of you to insist this way when you know how boring it is for us."

"But I'm enjoying it so much." He beamed. "And I'll bet Tunner wants to hear it, anyway. Don't you?"

Tunner smiled. "Dreams are my cup of tea. I know my La Hiff by heart."

Kit opened one eye and looked at him. The drinks arrived.

"So I said to myself: 'No! No!' I couldn't face the idea of all those God-awful fears and pains again, *in detail*. And then for no reason I looked out the window at the trees and heard myself say: 'Yes!' Because I knew I'd be willing to go through the whole thing again just to smell the spring the way it used to smell when I was a kid. But then I realized it was too late, because while I'd been thinking 'No!' I'd reached up and snapped off my incisors as if they'd been made of plaster. The train had stopped and I held my teeth in my hand, and I started to sob. You know those terrible dream sobs that shake you like an earthquake?"

Clumsily Kit rose from the table and walked to a door marked *Dames*. She was crying.

"Let her go," said Port to Tunner, whose face showed concern. "She's worn out. The heat gets her down."

III

He sat up in bed reading, wearing only a pair of shorts. The door between their two rooms was open, and so were the windows. Over the town and harbor a lighthouse played its beam in a wide, slow circle, and above the desultory traffic an insistent electric bell shrilled without respite.

"Is that the movie next door?" called Kit.

"Must be," he said absently, still reading.

"I wonder what they're showing."

"What?" He laid down his book. "Don't tell me you're interested in going!"

"No." She sounded doubtful. "I just wondered."

"I'll tell you what it is. It's a film in Arabic called *Fiancée for Rent*. That's what it says under the title."

"It's unbelievable."

"I know."

She wandered into the room, thoughtfully smoking a cigarette, and walked about in a circle for a minute or so. He looked up.

"What is it?" he asked.

"Nothing." She paused. "I'm just a little upset. I don't think you should have told that dream in front of Tunner."

He did not dare say: "Is that why you cried?" But he said: "In *front* of him! I told it *to* him, as much as to you. What's a dream? Good God, don't take everything so seriously! And why shouldn't he hear it? What's wrong with Tunner? We've known him for five years."

"He's such a gossip. You know that. I don't trust him. He always makes a good story."

"But who's he going to gossip with here?" said Port, exasperated.

Kit in turn was annoyed.

"Oh, not here!" she snapped. "You seem to forget we'll be back in New York some day."

"I know, I know. It's hard to believe, but I suppose we will. All right. What's so awful if he remembers every detail and tells it to everybody we know?"

"It's such a humiliating dream. Can't you see?"

"Oh, crap!"

There was a silence.

"Humiliating to whom? You or me?"

She did not answer. He pursued: "What do you mean, you don't trust Tunner? In what way?"

"Oh, I trust him, I suppose. But I've never felt completely at ease with him. I've never felt he was a close friend."

"That's nice, now that we're here with him!"

"Oh, it's all right. I like him very much. Don't misunderstand."

"But you must mean something."

"Of course I mean something. But it's not important."

She went back into her own room. He remained a moment, looking at the ceiling, a puzzled expression on his face.

He started to read again, and stopped.

"Sure you don't want to see *Fiancée for Rent?*"

"I certainly don't."

He closed his book. "I think I'll take a walk for about a half an hour."

He rose, put on a sports shirt and a pair of seersucker trousers, and combed his hair. In her room, she was sitting by the open window, filing her nails. He bent over her and kissed the nape of her neck, where the silky blonde hair climbed upward in wavy furrows.

"That's wonderful stuff you have on. Did you get it here?" He sniffed noisily, with appreciation. Then his voice changed when he said: "But what did you mean about Tunner?"

"Oh, Port! For God's sake, stop *talking* about it!"

"All right, baby," he said submissively, kissing her shoulder. And with an inflection of mock innocence: "Can't I even *think* about it?"

She said nothing until he got to the door. Then she raised her head, and there was pique in her voice: "After all, it's much more your business than it is mine."

"See you soon," he said.

IV

He walked through the streets, unthinkingly seeking the darker ones, glad to be alone and to feel the night air against his face. The streets were crowded. People pushed against him as they passed, stared from doorways and windows, made comments openly to each other about him—whether with sympathy or not he was unable to tell from their faces—and they sometimes ceased to walk merely in order to watch him.

"How friendly are they? Their faces are masks. They all look a thousand years old. What little energy they have is only the blind, mass desire to live, since no one of them eats enough to give him his own personal force. But what do they think of me? Probably nothing. Would one of them help me if I were to have an accident? Or would I lie here in the street until the police found me? What motive could any one of them *have* for helping me? They have no religion left. Are they Moslems or Christians? They don't know. They know money, and when they get it all they want is to eat. But what's wrong with that? Why do I feel this way about them? Guilt at being well fed and healthy among them? But suffering is equally divided among all men; each has the same amount to undergo. . . ." Emotionally he felt that this last idea was untrue, but at the moment it was a necessary belief: it is not always easy to support the stares of hungry people. Thinking that way he could walk on through the streets. It was as if either he or they did not exist. Both suppositions were possible. The Spanish maid at the hotel had said to him that noon: "*La vida es pena.*" "Of course," he had replied, feeling false even as he spoke, asking himself if any American can truthfully accept a definition of life which makes it synonymous with suffering. But at the moment he had approved her sentiment because she was old, withered, so clearly of the people. For years it had been one of his superstitions that reality and true perception were to be found in the conversation of the laboring classes. Even though now he saw clearly that their formulas of thought and speech are as strict and as patterned, and thus as far removed from any profound expression of truth as those of any other class, often he found himself still in the act of waiting, with the unreasoning belief that gems of wisdom might yet issue from their mouths. As he walked along, his nervousness was made manifest to him by the sudden consciousness that he was repeatedly tracing rapid figure-eights with his right index finger. He sighed and made himself stop doing it.

His spirits rose a bit as he came out onto a square that was relatively brightly lighted. The cafés on all four sides of the little plaza had put tables and chairs not only across the sidewalks, but in the street as well, so that it would have been impossible for a vehicle to pass through without upsetting them. In the center of the square was a tiny park adorned by four plane trees that had been trimmed to look like open parasols. Underneath the trees there were at least a dozen dogs of various sizes, milling about in a close huddle, and all barking frantically. He made his way slowly across the square, trying to avoid the dogs. As he moved along cautiously under the trees he became aware that at each step he was crushing something beneath his feet. The ground was covered with large insects; their hard shells broke with little explosions that were quite audible to him even amidst the noise the dogs were making. He was aware that ordinarily he would have experienced a thrill of disgust on contact with such a phenomenon, but unreasonably tonight he felt instead a childish triumph. "I'm in a bad way and so what?" The few scattered people sitting at the tables were for the most part silent, but when they spoke, he heard all three of the town's tongues: Arabic, Spanish and French.

Slowly the street began to descend; this surprised him because he imagined that the entire town was built on the slope facing the harbor, and he had consciously chosen to walk inland rather than toward the waterfront. The odors in the air grew ever stronger. They were varied, but they all represented filth of one sort or another. This proximity with, as it were, a forbidden element, served to elate him. He abandoned himself to the perverse pleasure he found in continuing mechanically to put one foot in front of the other, even though he was quite clearly aware of his fatigue. "Suddenly I'll find myself turning around and going back," he thought. But not until then, because he would not make the decision to do it. The impulse to retrace his steps delayed itself from moment to moment. Finally he ceased being surprised: a faint vision began to haunt his mind. It was Kit, seated by the open window, filing her nails and looking out over the town. And as he found his fancy returning more often, as the minutes went by, to that scene, unconsciously he felt himself the protagonist, Kit the spectator. The validity of his existence at that moment was predicated on the assumption that she had not moved, but was still sitting there. It was as if she could still see him from the window, tiny and far away as he was, walking rhythmically uphill and down, through light and shadow; it was as if only she knew when he would turn around and walk the other way.

The street lights were very far apart now, and the streets had left off being paved. Still there were children in the gutters, playing with the garbage and screeching. A small stone suddenly hit him in the back. He wheeled about, but it was too dark to see where it had come from. A few seconds later another stone, coming from in front of him, landed against his knee. In the dim light, he saw a group of small children scattering before him. More stones came from the other direction, this time without hitting him. When he got beyond, to a point where there was a light, he stopped and tried to watch the two groups in battle, but they all ran off into the dark, and so he started up again, his gait as mechanical and rhythmical as before. A wind that was dry and warm, coming up the street out of the blackness before him, met him head on. He sniffed at the fragments of mystery in it, and again he felt an unaccustomed exaltation.

Even though the street became constantly less urban, it seemed reluctant to give up; huts continued to line it on both sides. Beyond a certain point there were no more lights, and the dwellings themselves lay in darkness. The wind, straight from the south, blew across the barren mountains that were invisible ahead of him, over the vast flat sebkha to the edges of the town, raising curtains of dust that climbed to the crest of the hill and lost themselves in the air above the harbor. He stood still. The last possible suburb had been strung on the street's thread. Beyond the final hut the garbage and rubble floor of the road sloped abruptly downward in three directions. In the dimness below were shallow, crooked canyon-like formations. Port raised his eyes to the sky: the powdery course of the Milky Way was like a giant rift across the heavens that let the faint white light through. In the distance he heard a motorcycle. When its sound was finally gone, there was nothing to hear but an occasional cockcrow, like the highest part of a repeated melody whose other notes were inaudible.

He started down the bank to the right, sliding among the fish skeletons and dust. Once below, he felt out a rock that seemed clean and sat down on it. The stench was overpowering. He lit a match, saw the ground thick with chicken feathers and decayed melon rinds. As he rose to his feet he heard steps above him at the end of the street. A figure stood at the top of the embankment. It did not speak, yet Port was certain that it had seen him, had followed him, and knew he was sitting down there. It lit a cigarette, and for a moment he saw an Arab wearing a chechia on his head. The match, thrown into the air, made a fading parabola, the face disappeared, and only the red point of the cigarette remained. The cock crowed several times. Finally the man cried out.

"*Qu'est-ce ti cherches là?*"

"Here's where the trouble begins," thought Port. He did not move.

The Arab waited a bit. He walked to the very edge of the slope. A dislodged tin can rolled noisily down toward the rock where Port sat.

"*Hé! M'sieu! Qu'est-ce ti vo?*"

He decided to answer. His French was good.

"Who? Me? Nothing."

The Arab bounded down the bank and stood in front of him. With the characteristic impatient, almost indignant gestures he pursued his inquisition. What are you doing here all alone? Where do you come from? What do you want here? Are you looking for something? To which Port answered wearily: Nothing. That way. Nothing. No.

For a moment the Arab was silent, trying to decide what direction to give the dialogue. He drew violently on his cigarette several times until it glowed very bright, then he flicked it away and exhaled the smoke.

"Do you want to take a walk?" he said.

"What? A walk? Where?"

"Out there." His arm waved toward the mountains.

"What's out there?"

"Nothing."

There was another silence between them.

"I'll pay you a drink," said the Arab. And immediately on that: "What's your name?"

"Jean," said Port.

The Arab repeated the name twice, as if considering its merits. "Me," tapping his chest, "Smaïl. So, do we go and drink?"

"No."

"Why not?"

"I don't feel like it."

"You don't feel like it. What do you feel like doing?"

"Nothing."

All at once the conversation began again from the beginning. Only the now truly outraged inflection of the Arab's voice marked any difference: "*Qu'est-ce ti fi là? Qu'est-ce ti cherches?*" Port rose and started to climb up the slope, but it was difficult going. He kept sliding back down. At once the Arab was beside him, tugging at his arm. "Where are you going, Jean?" Without answering Port made a great effort and gained the top. "*Au revoir,*" he called, walking quickly up the middle of the street. He heard a desperate scrambling behind him; a moment later the man was at his side.

"You didn't wait for me," he said in an aggrieved tone.

"No. I said good-bye."

"I'll go with you."

Port did not answer. They walked a good distance in silence. When they came to the first street light, the Arab reached into his pocket and pulled out a worn wallet. Port glanced at it and continued to walk.

"Look!" cried the Arab, waving it in his face. Port did not look.

"What is it?" he said flatly.

"I was in the Fifth Battalion of Sharpshooters. Look at the paper! Look! You'll see!"

Port walked faster. Soon there began to be people in the street. No one stared at them. One would have said that the presence of the Arab beside him made him invisible. But now he was no longer sure of the way. It would never do to let this be seen. He continued to walk straight ahead as if there were no doubt in his mind. "Over the crest of the hill and down," he said to himself, "and I can't miss it."

Everything looked unfamiliar: the houses, the streets, the cafés, even the formation of the town with regard to the hill. Instead of finding a summit from which to begin the downward walk, he discovered that here the streets all led perceptibly upward, no matter which way he turned; to descend he would have had to go back. The Arab walked solemnly along with him, now beside him, now slipping behind when there was not enough room to walk two abreast. He no longer made attempts at conversation; Port noticed with relish that he was a little out of breath.

"I can keep this up all night if I have to," he thought, "but how the hell will I get to the hotel?"

All at once they were in a street which was no more than a passageway. Above their heads the opposite walls jutted out to within a few inches of each other. For an instant Port hesitated: this was not the kind of street he wanted to walk in, and besides, it so obviously did not lead to the hotel. In that short moment the Arab took charge. He said: "You don't know this street? It's called Rue de la Mer Rouge. You know it? Come on. There are *cafés arabes* up this way. Just a little way. Come on."

Port considered. He wanted at all costs to keep up the pretense of being familiar with the town.

"*Je ne sais pas si je veux y aller ce soir,*" he reflected, aloud.

The Arab began to pull Port's sleeve in his excitement. "*Si, si!*" he cried. "*Viens!* I'll pay you a drink."

"I don't drink. It's very late."

Two cats nearby screamed at each other. The Arab made a hissing noise and stamped his feet; they ran off in opposite directions.

"We'll have tea, then," he pursued.

Port sighed. "*Bien,*" he said.

The café had a complicated entrance. They went through a low arched door, down a dim hall into a small garden. The air reeked of lilies, and it was also tinged with the sour smell of drains. In the dark they crossed the garden and climbed a long flight of stone steps. The staccato sound of a hand drum came from above, tapping indolent patterns above a sea of voices.

"Do we sit outside or in?" the Arab asked.

"Outside," said Port. He sniffed the invigorating smell of hashish smoke, and unconsciously smoothed his hair as they arrived at the top of the stairs. The Arab noticed even that small gesture. "No ladies here, you know."

"Oh, I know."

Through a doorway he caught a glimpse of the long succession of tiny, brightly-lit rooms, and the men seated everywhere on the reed matting that covered the floors. They all wore either white turbans or red chechias on their heads, a detail which lent the scene such a strong aspect of homogeneity that Port exclaimed: "Ah!" as they passed by the door. When they were on the terrace in the starlight, with an oud being plucked idly in the dark nearby, he said to his companion: "But I didn't know there was anything like this left in this city." The Arab did not understand. "Like this?" he echoed. "How?"

"With nothing but Arabs. Like the inside here. I thought all the cafés were like the ones in the street, all mixed up; Jews, French, Spanish, Arabs together. I thought the war had changed everything."

The Arab laughed. "The war was bad. A lot of people died. There was nothing to eat. That's all. How would that change the cafés? Oh no, my friend. It's the same as always." A moment later he said: "So you haven't been here since the war! But you were here before the war?"

"Yes," said Port. This was true; he had once spent an afternoon in the town when his boat had made a brief call there.

The tea arrived; they chatted and drank it. Slowly the image of Kit sitting in the window began to take shape again in Port's mind. At first, when he became conscious of it, he felt a pang of guilt. Then his fantasy took a hand, and he saw her face, tight-lipped with fury as she undressed and flung her flimsy pieces of clothing across the furniture. By now she had surely given up waiting and gone to bed. He shrugged his shoulders and grew pensive, rinsing what was left of his tea around and around in the bottom of the glass, and following with his eyes the circular motion he was making.

"You're sad," said Smaïl.

"No, no." He looked up and smiled wistfully, then resumed watching the glass.

"You live only a short time. *Il faut rigoler.*"

Port was impatient; he was not in the mood for café philosophizing.

"Yes, I know," he said shortly, and he sighed. Smaïl pinched his arm. His eyes were shining.

"When we leave here, I'll take you to see a friend of mine."

"I don't want to meet him," said Port, adding: "Thank you anyway."

"Ah, you're really sad," laughed Smaïl. "It's a girl. Beautiful as the moon."

Port's heart missed a beat. "A girl," he repeated automatically, without taking his eyes from the glass. He was perturbed to witness his own interior excitement. He looked at Smaïl.

"A girl?" he said. "You mean a whore."

Smaïl was mildly indignant. "A whore? Ah, my friend, you don't know me. I wouldn't introduce you to that. *C'est de la saloperie, ça!* This is a friend of mine, very elegant, very nice. When you meet her, you'll see."

The musician stopped playing the oud. Inside the café they were calling out numbers for the lotto game: "*Ouahad aou tletine! Arbaine!*"

Port said: "How old is she?"

Smaïl hesitated. "About sixteen. Sixteen or seventeen."

"Or twenty or twenty-five," suggested Port, with a leer.

Again Smaïl was indignant. "What do you mean, twenty-five? I tell you she's sixteen or seventeen. You don't believe me? Listen. You meet her. If you don't like her, you just pay for the tea and we'll go out again. Is that all right?"

"And if I do like her?"

"Well, you'll do whatever you want."

"But I'll pay her?"

"But of course, you'll pay her."

Port laughed. "And you say she's not a whore."

Smaïl leaned over the table towards him and said with a great show of patience: "Listen, Jean. She's a dancer. She only arrived from her bled in the desert a few weeks ago. How can she be a whore if she's not registered and doesn't live in the quartier? Eh? Tell me! You pay her because you take up her time. She dances in the quartier, but she has no room, no bed there. She's not a whore. So now, shall we go?"

Port thought a long time, looked up at the sky, down into the garden, and all around the terrace before answering: "Yes. Let's go. Now."

V

When they left the café it seemed to him that they were going more or less in the same direction from which they had just come. There were fewer people in the streets and the air was cooler. They walked for a good distance through the Casbah, making a sudden exit through a tall gateway onto a high, open space outside the walls. Here it was silent, and the stars were very much in evidence. The pleasure he felt at the unexpected freshness of the air and the relief at being in the open once more, out from under the overhanging houses, served to delay Port in asking the question that was in his mind: "Where are we going?" But as they continued along what seemed a parapet at the edge of a deep, dry moat, he finally gave voice to it. Smaïl replied vaguely that the girl lived with some friends at the edge of town.

"But we're already in the country," objected Port.

"Yes, it's the country," said Smaïl.

It was perfectly clear that he was being evasive now; his character seemed to have changed again. The beginning of intimacy was gone. To Port he was once more the anonymous dark figure that had stood above him in the garbage at the end of the street, smoking a bright cigarette. *You can still break it up. Stop walking. Now.* But the combined even rhythm of their feet on the stones was too powerful. The parapet made a wide curve and the ground below dropped steeply away into a deeper darkness. The moat had ended some hundred feet back. They were now high above the upper end of an open valley.

"The Turkish fortress," remarked Smaïl, pounding on the stones with his heel.

"Listen to me," began Port angrily; "where are we going?" He looked at the rim of uneven black mountains ahead of them on the horizon.

"Down there." Smaïl pointed to the valley. A moment later he stopped walking. "Here are the stairs." They leaned over the edge. A narrow iron staircase was fastened to the side of the wall. It had no railing and led straight downward at a steep angle.

"It's a long way," said Port.

"Ah, yes, it's the Turkish fortress. You see that light down there?" He indicated a faint red glimmer that came and went, almost directly beneath them. "That's the tent where she lives."

"The tent!"

"There are no houses down here. Only tents. There are a lot of them. *On déscend?*"

Smaïl went first, keeping close to the wall. "Touch the stones," he said.

As they approached the bottom, he saw that the feeble glow of light was a dying bonfire built in an open space between two large nomad tents. Smaïl suddenly stopped to listen. There was an indistinguishable murmur of male voices. "*Allons-y,*" he muttered; his voice sounded satisfied.

They reached the end of the staircase. There was hard ground beneath their feet. To his left Port saw the black silhouette of a huge agave plant in flower.

"Wait here," whispered Smaïl. Port was about to light a cigarette; Smaïl hit his arm angrily. "No!" he whispered. "But what is it?" began Port, highly annoyed at the show of secrecy. Smaïl disappeared.

Leaning against the cold rock wall, Port waited to hear a break in the monotonous, low-pitched conversation, an exchange of greetings, but nothing happened. The voices went on exactly as before, an uninterrupted flow of expressionless sounds. "He must have gone into the other tent," he thought. One side of the further tent flickered pink in the light of the bonfire; beyond was darkness. He edged a few steps along the wall, trying to see the entrance of the tent, but it faced in the other direction. Then he listened for the sound of voices there, but none came. For no reason at all he suddenly heard Kit's parting remark as he had left her room: "After all, it's much more your business than it is mine." Even now the words meant nothing in particular to him, but he remembered the tone in which she had said it: she had sounded hurt and rebellious. And it was all about Tunner. He stood up straight. "He's been after her," he whispered aloud. Abruptly he turned and went to the staircase, started up it. After six steps he stopped and looked around. "What can I do

tonight?" he thought. "I'm using this as an excuse to get out
of here, because I'm afraid. What the hell, he'll never get her."

A figure darted out from between the two tents and ran
lightly to the foot of the stairs. "Jean!" it whispered. Port
stood still.

"*Ah! Ti es là!* What are you doing up there? Come on!"

Port walked slowly back down. Smaïl stepped out of his
way, took his arm.

"Why can't we talk?" whispered Port. Smaïl squeezed his
arm. "Shh!" he said into his ear. They skirted the nearer tent,
brushing past a clump of high thistles, and made their way
over the stones to the entrance of the other.

"Take off your shoes," commanded Smaïl, slipping off his
sandals.

"Not a good idea," thought Port. "No," he said aloud.

"Shh!" Smaïl pushed him inside, shoes still on.

The central part of the tent was high enough to stand up
in. A short candle stuck on top of a chest near the entrance
provided the light, so that the nether parts of the tent were in
almost complete darkness. Lengths of straw matting had been
spread on the ground at senseless angles; objects were scattered everywhere in utter disorder. There was no one in the
tent waiting for them.

"Sit down," said Smaïl, acting the host. He cleared the
largest piece of matting of an alarm clock, a sardine can, and
an ancient, incredibly greasy pair of overalls. Port sat down
and put his elbows on his knees. On the mat next to him lay
a chipped enamel bedpan, half filled with a darkish liquid.
There were bits of stale bread everywhere. He lit a cigarette
without offering one to Smaïl, who returned to stand near the
entrance, looking out.

And suddenly she stepped inside—a slim, wild-looking girl
with great dark eyes. She was dressed in spotless white, with a
white turbanlike headdress that pulled her hair tightly backward, accentuating the indigo designs tattooed on her forehead. Once inside the tent, she stood quite still, looking at
Port with something of the expression, he thought, the
young bull often wears as he takes the first few steps into the
glare of the arena. There was bewilderment, fear, and a
passive expectancy in her face as she stared quietly at him.

"Ah, here she is!" said Smaïl, still in a hushed voice. "Her name is Marhnia." He waited a bit. Port rose and stepped forward to take her hand. "She doesn't speak French," Smaïl explained. Without smiling, she touched Port's hand lightly with her own and raised her fingers to her lips. Bowing, she said, in what amounted almost to a whisper: "*Ya sidi, la bess âlik? Eglès, baraka 'laou'fik.*" With gracious dignity and a peculiar modesty of movement, she unstuck the lighted candle from the chest, and walked across to the back of the tent, where a blanket stretched from the ceiling formed a partial alcove. Before disappearing behind the blanket, she turned her head to them, and said, gesturing: "*Agi! Agi menah!*" The two men followed her into the alcove, where an old mattress had been laid on some low boxes in an attempt to make a salon. There was a tiny tea table beside the improvised divan, and a pile of small, lumpy cushions lay on the mat by the table. The girl set the candle down on the bare earth and began to arrange the cushions along the mattress.

"*Essmah!*" she said to Port, and to Smaïl: "*Tsekellem bellatsi.*" Then she went out. He laughed and called after her in a low voice: "*Fhemtek!*" Port was intrigued by the girl, but the language barrier annoyed him, and he was even more irritated by the fact that Smaïl and she could converse together in his presence. "She's gone to get fire," said Smaïl. "Yes, yes," said Port, "but why do we have to whisper?" Smaïl rolled his eyes toward the tent's entrance. "The men in the other tent," he said.

Presently she returned, carrying an earthen pot of bright coals. While she was boiling the water and preparing the tea, Smaïl chatted with her. Her replies were always grave, her voice hushed but pleasantly modulated. It seemed to Port that she was much more like a young nun than a café dancer. At the same time he did not in the least trust her, being content to sit and marvel at the delicate movements of her nimble, henna-stained fingers as she tore the stalks of mint apart and stuffed them into the little teapot.

When she had sampled the tea several times and eventually had found it to her liking, she handed them each a glass, and with a solemn air sat back on her haunches and began to drink hers. "Sit here," said Port, patting the couch beside him. She indicated that she was quite happy where she was, and thanked him politely. Turning her attention to Smaïl, she proceeded to engage him in a lengthy conversation during which Port sipped his tea and tried to relax. He had an oppressive sensation that daybreak was near at hand—surely not more than an hour or so away, and he felt that all this time was being wasted. He looked anxiously at his watch; it had stopped at five minutes of two. But it was still going. Surely it must be later than that. Marhnia addressed a question to Smaïl which seemed to include Port. "She wants to know if you have heard the story about Outka, Mimouna and Aïcha," said Smaïl. "No," said Port. "*Goul lou, goul lou,*" said Marhnia to Smaïl, urging him.

"There are three girls from the mountains, from a place near Marhnia's bled, and they are called Outka, Mimouna and Aïcha." Marhnia was nodding her head slowly in affirmation, her large soft eyes fixed on Port. "They go to seek their fortune in the M'Zab. Most girls from the mountains go to Alger, Tunis, here, to earn money, but these girls want one thing more than everything else. They want to drink tea in the Sahara." Marhnia continued to nod her head; she was keeping up with the story solely by means of the place-names as Smaïl pronounced them.

"I see," said Port, who had no idea whether the story was a humorous one or a tragic one; he was determined to be careful, so that he could pretend to savor it as much as she clearly hoped he would. He only wished it might be short.

"In the M'Zab the men are all ugly. The girls dance in the cafés of Ghardaia, but they are always sad; they still want to have tea in the Sahara." Port glanced again at Marhnia. Her expression was completely serious. He nodded his head again. "So, many months pass, and they are still in the M'Zab, and they are very, very sad, because the men are all so ugly. They are very ugly there, like pigs. And they don't pay enough money to the poor girls so they can go and have tea in the Sahara." Each time he said "Sahara," which he pronounced in the Arabic fashion, with a vehement accent on the first syllable, he stopped for a moment. "One day a Targui comes, he is tall and handsome, on a beautiful mehari; he talks to Outka, Mimouna and Aïcha, he tells them about the desert, down

there where he lives, his bled, and they listen, and their eyes
are big. Then he says: 'Dance for me,' and they dance. Then
he makes love with all three, he gives a silver piece to Outka,
a silver piece to Mimouna, and a silver piece to Aïcha. At
daybreak he gets on his mehari and goes away to the south.
After that they are very sad, and the M'Zabi look uglier than
ever to them, and they only are thinking of the tall Targui
who lives in the Sahara." Port lit a cigarette; then he noticed
Marhnia looking expectantly at him, and he passed her the
pack. She took one, and with a crude pair of tongs elegantly
lifted a live coal to the end of it. It ignited immediately,
whereupon she passed it to Port, taking his in exchange. He
smiled at her. She bowed almost imperceptibly.

"Many months go by, and still they can't earn enough
money to go to the Sahara. They have kept the silver pieces,
because all three are in love with the Targui. And they are
always sad. One day they say: 'We are going to finish like
this—always sad, without ever having tea in the Sahara—so
now we must go anyway, even without money.' And they put
all their money together, even the three silver pieces, and they
buy a teapot and a tray and three glasses, and they buy bus
tickets to El Goléa. And there they have only a little money
left, and they give it all to a bachhamar who is taking his
caravan south to the Sahara. So he lets them ride with his
caravan. And one night, when the sun is going to go down,
they come to the great dunes of sand, and they think: 'Ah,
now we are in the Sahara; we are going to make tea.' The
moon comes up, all the men are asleep except the guard. He
is sitting with the camels playing his flute." Smaïl wriggled his
fingers in front of his mouth. "Outka, Mimouna and Aïcha go
away from the caravan quietly with their tray and their teapot
and their glasses. They are going to look for the highest dune
so they can see all the Sahara. Then they are going to make
tea. They walk a long time. Outka says: 'I see a high dune,'
and they go to it and climb up to the top. Then Mimouna
says: 'I see a dune over there. It's much higher and we can
see all the way to In Salah from it.' So they go to it, and it
is much higher. But when they get to the top, Aïcha
says: 'Look! There's the highest dune of all. We can see to
Tamanrasset. That's where the Targui lives.' The sun came up

and they kept walking. At noon they were very hot. But they came to the dune and they climbed and climbed. When they got to the top they were very tired and they said: 'We'll rest a little and then make tea.' But first they set out the tray and the teapot and the glasses. Then they lay down and slept. And then"—Smaïl paused and looked at Port—"Many days later another caravan was passing and a man saw something on top of the highest dune there. And when they went up to see, they found Outka, Mimouna and Aïcha; they were still there, lying the same way as when they had gone to sleep. And all three of the glasses," he held up his own little tea glass, "were full of sand. That was how they had their tea in the Sahara."

There was a long silence. It was obviously the end of the story. Port looked at Marhnia; she was still nodding her head, her eyes fixed on him. He decided to hazard a remark. "It's very sad," he said. She immediately inquired of Smaïl what he had said. "*Gallik merhmoum bzef,*" translated Smaïl. She shut her eyes slowly and continued to nod her head. "*Ei oua!*" she said, opening them again. Port turned quickly to Smaïl. "Listen, it's very late. I want to arrange a price with her. How much should I give her?"

Smaïl looked scandalized. "You can't do that as if you were dealing with a whore! *Ci pas une putain, je t'ai dit!*"

"But I'll pay her if I stay with her?"

"Of course."

"Then I want to arrange it now."

"I can't do that for you, my friend."

Port shrugged his shoulders and stood up. "I've got to go. It's late."

Marhnia looked quickly from one man to the other. Then she said a word or two in a very soft voice to Smaïl, who frowned but stalked out of the tent yawning.

They lay on the couch together. She was very beautiful, very docile, very understanding, and still he did not trust her. She declined to disrobe completely, but in her delicate gestures of refusal he discerned an ultimate yielding, to bring about which it would require only time. With time he could have had her confidence; tonight he could only have that which had been taken for granted from the beginning. He reflected on this as he lay, looking into her untroubled face, remembered that he was leaving for the south in a day or two, inwardly swore at his luck, and said to himself: "Better half a loaf." Marhnia leaned over and snuffed the candle between her fingers. For a second there was utter silence, utter blackness. Then he felt her soft arms slowly encircle his neck, and her lips on his forehead.

Almost immediately a dog began to howl in the distance. For a while he did not hear it; when he did, it troubled him. It was the wrong music for the moment. Soon he found himself imagining that Kit was a silent onlooker. The fantasy stimulated him—the lugubrious howling no longer bothered him.

Not more than a quarter of an hour later, he got up and peered around the blanket, to the flap of the tent: it was still dark. He was seized with an abrupt desire to be out of the place. He sat down on the couch and began to arrange his clothing. The two arms stole up again, locked themselves about his neck. Firmly he pulled them away, gave them a few playful pats. Only one came up this time; the other slipped inside his jacket and he felt his chest being caressed. Some indefinable false movement there made him reach inside to put his hand on hers. His wallet was already between her fingers. He yanked it away from her and pushed her back down on the mattress. "Ah!" she cried, very loud. He rose and stumbled noisily through the welter of objects that lay between him and the exit. This time she screamed, briefly. The voices in the other tent became audible. With his wallet still in his hand he rushed out, turned sharply to the left and began to run toward the wall. He fell twice, once against a rock and once because the ground sloped unexpectedly down. As he rose the second time, he saw a man coming from one side to cut him off from the staircase. He was limping, but he was nearly there. He did get there. All the way up the stairs it seemed to him that someone immediately behind him would have hold of one of his legs during the next second. His lungs were an enormous pod of pain, would burst instantly. His mouth was open, drawn down at the sides, his teeth clenched, and the air whistled between them as he drew breath. At the top he turned, and seizing a boulder he could not lift, he did lift it, and hurled it down the staircase. Then he breathed deeply and began to run along the parapet. The sky was palpably lighter, an immaculate gray clarity spreading upward from behind the low hills in the east. He could not run very far. His heart was beating in his head and neck. He knew he never could reach the town. On the side of the road away from the valley there was a wall, too high to be climbed. But a few hundred feet farther on, it had been broken down for a short distance, and a talus of stones and dirt made a perfect stile. He cut back inside the wall in the direction from which he had just come, and hurried panting up a gradual side hill studded with the flat stone beds which are Moslem tombstones. Finally he sat down for a minute, his head in his hands, and was conscious of several things at once: the pain of his head and chest, the fact that he no longer held his wallet, and the loud sound of his own heart, which, however, did not keep him from thinking he heard the excited voices of his pursuers below in the road a moment later. He rose and staggered on upward over the graves. Eventually the hill sloped downward in the other direction. He felt a little safer. But each minute the light of day was nearer; it would be easy to spot his solitary figure from a distance, wandering over the hill. He began to run again, downhill, always in the same direction, staggering now and then, never looking up for fear he should fall; this went on for a long time; the graveyard was left behind. Finally he reached a high spot covered with bushes and cactus, but from which he could dominate the entire immediate countryside. He sat down among the bushes. It was perfectly quiet. The sky was white. Occasionally he stood up carefully and peered out. And so it was that when the sun came up he looked between two oleanders and saw it reflected red across the miles of glittering salt sebkha that lay between him and the mountains.

VI

Kit awoke in a sweat with the hot morning sun pouring over her. She stumbled up, closed the curtains, and fell back into bed. The sheets were wet where she had lain. The thought of breakfast turned her stomach. There were days when from the moment she came out of sleep, she could feel doom hanging

over her head like a low rain cloud. Those were difficult days
to live through, not so much because of the sensation of
suspended disaster of which she was acutely conscious then,
but because the customary smooth functioning of her system
of omens was wholly upset. If on ordinary days on her way
out to go shopping she turned her ankle or scraped her shin
on the furniture, it was easy to conclude that the shopping
expedition would be a failure for one reason or another, or
that it might be actually dangerous for her to persist in making it. At least on those days she knew a good omen from a
bad one. But the other days were treacherous, for the feeling
of doom was so strong that it became a hostile consciousness
just behind or beside her, foreseeing her attempts to avoid
flying in the face of the evil omens, and thus all too able to set
traps for her. In this way what at first sight might seem a pro-
pitious sign could easily be nothing more than a kind of bait
to lure her into danger. Then, too, the turned ankle could be
a thing to disregard in such cases, since it had been brought
upon her so that she might abandon her intention of going
out, and thus might be at home when the furnace boiler exploded, the house caught on fire, or someone she particularly
wanted to avoid stopped by to see her. And in her personal
life, in her relationships with her friends, these considerations
reached monstrous proportions. She was capable of sitting all
morning long, attempting to recall the details of a brief scene
or conversation, in order to be able to try out in her mind
every possible interpretation of each gesture or sentence, each
facial expression or vocal inflection, together with their juxta-
positions. A great part of her life was dedicated to the cate-
gorizing of omens. And so it is not surprising that when she
found it impossible to exercise that function, because of her
doubt, her ability to go through the motions of everyday
existence was reduced to a minimum. It was as if she had
been stricken by a strange paralysis. She had no reactions at
all; her entire personality withdrew from sight; she had a
haunted look. On these days of doom friends who knew her
well would say: "Oh, this is one of Kit's *days*." If on these
days she was subdued and seemed most reasonable, it was
only because she was imitating mechanically what she considered rational behavior. One reason she had such a strong

dislike of hearing dreams recounted was that the telling of them brought straightway to her attention the struggle that raged in her—the war between reason and atavism. In intellectual discussions she was always the proponent of scientific method; at the same time it was inevitable that she should regard the dream as an omen.

A further complexity was brought to the situation by the fact that also she lived through still other days when vengeance from above seemed the remotest of possibilities. Every sign was good; an unearthly aura of beneficence glowed from behind each person, object and circumstance. On those days, if she permitted herself to act as she felt, Kit could be quite happy. But of late she had begun to believe that such days, which were rare enough, to be sure, were given her only to throw her off her guard, so that she would not be able to deal with her omens. A natural euphoria was then transformed into a nervous and slightly hysterical peevishness. In conversation repeatedly she would catch herself up, trying to pretend that her remarks had been made in wilful jest, when actually they had been uttered with all the venom of which a foul humor is capable.

She was no more disturbed by other people as such, than the marble statue is by the flies that crawl on it; however, as possible harbingers of undesirable events and wielders of unfavorable influence in her own life, she accorded other people supreme importance. She would say: "Other people rule my life," and it was true. But she allowed them to do it only because her superstitious fancy had invested them with magical importance regarding her own destiny, and never because their personalities awoke any profound sympathy or understanding in her.

A good part of the night she had lain awake, thinking. Her intuition generally let her know when Port was up to something. She told herself always that it did not matter what he did, but she had repeated the statement so often in her mind that long ago she had become suspicious of its truth. It had not been easy thing to accept the fact that she did care. Against her will she forced herself to admit that she still belonged to Port, even though he did not come to claim her—and that she still lived in a world illumined by the distant light of a possible miracle: he might yet return to her. It made her feel abject, and therefore, of course, furious with herself, to realize that everything depended on him, that she was merely waiting for some unlikely caprice on his part, something which might in some unforeseen manner bring him back. She was far too intelligent to make the slightest effort in that direction herself; even the subtlest means would have failed, and to fail would be far worse than never to have tried. It was merely a question of sitting tight, of being there. Perhaps some day he would see her. But in the meantime so many precious months were going past, unused!

Tunner annoyed her because although his presence and his interest in her provided a classical situation which, if ex- ploited, actually might give results where nothing else could, she was for some reason incapable of playing up to him. He bored her; she involuntarily compared him with Port, and always to Port's advantage. As she had been lying thinking in the night she had tried again and again to direct her fantasies in such a way as to make Tunner an object of excitement. Naturally this had been a failure. Nevertheless she had resolved to attempt the building of a more intimate relation- ship with him, despite the fact that even as she had made the decision she was quite aware that not only would it be a thor- oughly unsavory chore for her, but also that she would be doing it, as she always did everything that required a con- scious effort, for Port.

There was a knock at the door into the hall.

"Oh, God, who is it?" Kit said aloud.

"Me." It was Tunner's voice. As usual, he sounded offen- sively chipper. "Are you awake?"

She scrambled about in the bed, making a loud noise that mingled sighs, flapping sheet, and creaking bedspring. "Not very," she groaned, at last.

"This is the best time of day. You shouldn't miss it!" he shouted.

There was a pointed silence, during which she remembered her resolution. In a martyred voice she called: "Just a minute, Tunner."

"Right!" A minute, an hour—he would wait, and show the same good-natured (and false, she thought) smile when he finally was let in. She dashed cold water into her face, rubbed it with a flimsy turkish towel, put on some lipstick and ran a comb through her hair. Suddenly frantic, she began to look about the room for the right bathrobe. Through the partially open door into Port's room she caught sight of his big white terry-cloth robe hanging on the wall. She knocked rapidly on the door as she went in, saw that he was not there, and snatched up the robe. As she pulled the belt about her waist in front of her mirror she reflected with satisfaction that no one ever could accuse her of coquetry in having chosen this particular garment. It came to the floor on her, and she had to roll the sleeves back twice to uncover her hands.

She opened the door.

"Hi!"

There was the smile.

"Hello, Tunner," she said apathetically. "Come in."

He rumpled her hair with his left hand as he walked past her on his way to the window, where he pulled the curtains aside. "You holding a séance in here? Ah, now I can see you." The sharp morning light filled the room, the polished floor-tiles reflecting the sun on the ceiling as if they had been water.

"How are you?" she said vacantly as she stood beside the mirror again, combing her hair where he had tousled it.

"Wonderful." He beamed at her image in the mirror, making his eyes sparkle, and even, she noted with great distaste, moving a certain facial muscle that emphasized the dimples in his cheeks. "He's such a fake," she thought. "What in God's name's he doing here with us? Of course, it's Port's fault. He's the one who encouraged him to drag along."

"What happened to Port last night?" Tunner was saying. "I sort of waited up for him, but he didn't show up."

Kit looked at him. "Waited up for him?" she repeated, incredulous.

"Well, we more or less had a date at our café, you know the one. For a nightcap. But no hide, no hair. I got in bed and read until pretty late. He hadn't come in by three." This was completely false. Actually Tunner had said: "If you go out, look into the Eckmühl; I'll probably be in there." He had gone out shortly after Port, had picked up a French girl and stayed with her at her hotel until five. When he had come back at dawn he had managed to look through the low glass transoms into their rooms, and had seen the empty bed in one and Kit asleep in the other.

"Really?" she said, turning back to the mirror. "He can't have had much sleep, then, because he's already gone out."

"You mean he hasn't come in yet," said Tunner, staring at her intently.

She did not answer. "Will you push that button there, please?" she said presently. "I think I'll have a cup of their chicory and one of those plaster croissants."

When she thought enough time had passed, she wandered into Port's room and glanced at the bed. It had been turned down for the night and not touched since. Without knowing precisely why, she pulled the sheet all the way down and sat on the bed for a moment, pushing dents in the pillows with her hands. Then she unfolded the laid-out pajamas and dropped them in a heap at the foot. The servant knocked at her door; she went back into her room and ordered breakfast. When the servant had left she shut the door and sat in the armchair by the window, not looking out.

"You know," Tunner said musingly, "I've thought a lot about it lately. You're a very curious person. It's hard to understand you."

Kit clicked her tongue with exasperation. "Oh, Tunner! Stop trying to be interesting." Immediately she blamed herself for showing her impatience, and added, smiling: "On you it looks terrible."

His hurt expression quickly changed into a grin. "No, I mean it. You're a fascinating case."

She pursed her lips angrily; she was furious, not so much because of what he was saying, although she considered it all idiotic, but because the idea of having to converse with him at all right now seemed almost more than she could bear. "Probably," she said.

Breakfast arrived. He sat with her while she drank her coffee and ate her croissant. Her eyes had assumed a dreamy expression, and he had the feeling that she had completely forgotten his presence. When she had nearly finished her breakfast, she turned to him and said politely: "Will you excuse me if I eat?"

He began to laugh. She looked startled.

"Hurry up!" he said. "I want to take you out for a walk before it gets too hot. You had a lot of stuff on your list anyway."

"Oh!" she moaned. "I don't feel—" But he cut her short. "Come on, come on. You dress. I'll wait in Port's room. I'll even shut the door."

She could think of nothing to say. Port never gave her orders; he hung back, hoping thereby to discover what she really wanted. He made it more difficult for her, since she seldom acted on her own desires, behaving instead according to her complex system of balancing those omens to be observed against those to be disregarded.

Tunner had already gone into the adjacent room and closed the door. It gratified Kit to think that he would see the disheveled bedclothes. As she dressed she heard him whistling. "A bore, a bore, a bore!" she said under her breath. At that moment the other door opened; Port stood there in the hall, running his left hand through his hair.

"May I come in?" he asked.

She was staring at him.

"Well, obviously. What's the matter with you?"

He still stood there.

"What in God's name's wrong with you?" she said impatiently.

"Nothing." His voice rasped. He strode to the center of the room and pointed to the closed connecting door. "Who's in there?"

"Tunner," she said with unfeigned innocence, as if it were a most natural occurrence. "He's waiting for me while I get dressed."

"What the hell goes on here?"

Kit flushed and turned away vehemently. "Nothing. Nothing," she said quickly. "Don't be crazy. What do you *think* goes on, anyway?"

He did not lower his voice. "I don't know. *I'm* asking *you*."

She pushed him in the chest with her outspread hands and walked toward the door to open it, but he caught her arm and pulled her around.

"Please stop it!" she whispered furiously.

"All right, all right. I'll open the door myself," he said, as if by allowing her to do it he might be running too great a risk.

He went into his room. Tunner was leaning out the window, looking down. He swung around, smiling broadly. "Well, well!" he began.

Port was staring at the bed. "What *is* this? What's the matter with your room that you have to be in here?" he demanded.

But Tunner appeared not to take in the situation at all, or else he refused to admit that there was any. "So! Back from the wars!" he cried. "And do you look it! Kit and I are going for a walk. You probably want some sleep." He dragged Port over in front of the mirror. "Look at yourself!" he commanded. At the sight of his smeared face and red-rimmed eyes, Port wilted.

"I want some black coffee," he grumbled. "And I want to go down and get a shave." Now he raised his voice. "And I wish to hell you'd both get out of here and take your walk." He pushed the wall button savagely.

Tunner gave him a fraternal pat on the back. "See you later, old man. Get some sleep."

Port glared at him as he went out, and sat down on the bed when he had gone. A large ship had just steamed into the harbor; its deep whistle sounded below the street noises. He lay back on the bed, gasping a little. When the knocking came at the door, he never heard it. The servant stuck his head in, said: "*Monsieur*," waited a few seconds, quietly shut the door and went away.

VII

He slept all day. Kit came back at lunch time; she went in softly, and having coughed once to see if he would wake, went to eat without him. Before twilight he awoke, feeling greatly cleansed. He rose and undressed slowly. In the bathroom he drew a hot tub, bathed at length, shaved, and searched for his white bathrobe. He found it in Kit's room, but she was not there. On her table was a variety of groceries she had bought to take on the trip. Most of the items were black-market goods from England, and according to the labels they had been manufactured by appointment to H.M. King George VI. He opened a package of biscuits and began to eat one after another, voraciously. Framed by the window, the town below was growing dim. It was that moment of twilight when light objects seem unnaturally bright, and the others are restfully dark. The town's electricity had not yet been turned on, so that the only lights were those on the few ships anchored in the harbor, itself neither light nor dark—merely an empty area between the buildings and the sky. And to the right were the mountains. The first one coming up out of the sea looked to him like two knees drawn up under a huge sheet. For a fraction of a second, but with such force that he felt the change's impact as a physical sensation, he was somewhere else, it was long ago. Then he saw the mountains again. He wandered downstairs.

They had made a point of not patronizing the hotel bar because it was always empty. Now, going into the gloomy little room, Port was mildly surprised to see sitting alone at the bar a heavy-looking youth with a formless face which was saved from complete non-existence by an undefined brown beard. As he installed himself at the other end, the young man said with a heavy English accent: "*Otro Tio Pepe,*" and pushed his glass toward the barman.

Port thought of the cool subterranean bodegas at Jerez where Tio Pepe of 1842 had been tendered him, and ordered the same. The young man looked at him with a certain curiosity in his eyes, but said nothing. Presently a large, sallow-skinned woman, her hair fiery with henna, appeared in the doorway and squealed. She had the glassy black eyes of a doll; their lack of expression was accentuated by the gleaming make-up around them. The young man turned in her direction.

"Hello, Mother. Come in and sit down."

The woman moved to the youth's side but did not sit. In her excitement and indignation she seemed not to have noticed Port. Her voice was very high. "Eric, you filthy toad!" she cried. "Do you realize I've been looking for you everywhere? I've never seen such behavior! And what are you drinking? What do you *mean* by drinking, after what Doctor Levy told you? You *wretched* boy!"

The young man did not look at her. "Don't scream so, Mother."

She glanced in Port's direction, saw him. "What *is* that you're drinking, Eric?" she demanded again, her voice slightly more subdued, but no less intense.

"It's just sherry, and it's quite delightful. I wish you wouldn't get so upset."

"And who do you think's going to pay for your caprices?" She seated herself on the stool beside him and began to fumble in her bag. "Oh, blast! I've come off without my key," she said. "Thanks to your thoughtlessness. You'll have to let me in through your room. I've discovered the sweetest mosque, but it's covered with brats all shrieking like demons. Filthy little beasts, they are! I'll show it to you tomorrow. Order a glass of sherry for me, if it's dry. I think it might help me. I've felt wretched all day. I'm positive it's the malaria coming back. It's about time for it, you know."

"*Otro Tio Pepe,*" said the youth imperturbably.

Port watched, fascinated as always by the sight of a human being being brought down to the importance of an automaton or a caricature. By whatever circumstances and in whatever manner reduced, whether ludicrous or horrible, such persons delighted him.

The dining room was unfriendly and formal to a degree which is acceptable only when the service is impeccable; this was not the case here. The waiters were impassive and moved slowly. They seemed to have difficulty in understanding the wants even of the French; certainly they showed no sign of interest in pleasing anyone. The two English people were given a table near the corner where Port and Kit were eating; Tunner was out with his French girl.

"Here they are," whispered Port. "Keep an ear open. But try and keep a straight face."

"He looks like a young Vacher," said Kit, leaning far over the table, "the one who wandered across France slicing children into pieces, you remember?"

They were silent a few minutes, hoping to be diverted by the other table, but mother and son appeared to have nothing to say to each other. Finally Port turned to Kit and said: "Oh, while I think of it, what was all that this morning?"

"Do we have to go into it now?"

"No, but I was just asking. I thought maybe you could answer."

"You saw all there was to see."

"I wouldn't ask you if I thought so."

"Oh, can't you see—" Kit began in a tone of exasperation; then she stopped. She was about to say: "Can't you see that I didn't want Tunner to know you hadn't come back last night? Can't you see he'd be interested to know that? Can't you see it would give him just the wedge he's looking for?" Instead she said: "Do we have to discuss it? I told you the whole story when you came in. He came while I was having breakfast and I sent him into your room to wait while I got dressed. Isn't that perfectly proper?"

"It depends on your conception of propriety, baby."

"It certainly does," she said acidly. "You notice I haven't mentioned what *you* did last night."

Port smiled and said smoothly: "You couldn't very well, since you don't know."

"And I don't want to." She was letting her anger show in spite of herself. "You can think whatever you want to think. I don't give a damn." She glanced over at the other table and noticed that the large bright-eyed woman was following what she could of their conversation with acute interest. When that lady saw that Kit was aware of her attention, she turned back to the youth and began a loud monologue of her own.

"This hotel has the most extraordinary plumbing system; the water taps do nothing but sigh and gurgle constantly, no matter how tightly one shuts them off. The stupidity of the French! It's unbelievable! They're all mental defectives. Madame Gautier herself told me they have the lowest national intelligence quotient in the world. Of course, their blood is thin; they've gone to seed. They're all part Jewish or Negro. Look at them!" She made a wide gesture which included the whole room.

"Oh, here, perhaps," said the young man, holding his glass of water up to the light and studying it carefully.

"In France!" the woman cried excitedly. "Madame Gautier told me herself, and I've read it in ever so .many books and papers."

"What revolting water," he murmured. He set the glass on the table. "I don't think I shall drink it."

"What a fearful sissy you are! Stop complaining! I don't want to hear about it! I can't bear to hear any more of your talk about dirt and worms. *Don't* drink it. No one cares whether you do or not. It's frightful for you, anyway, washing everything down with liquids the way you do. Try to grow up. Have you got the paraffin for the Primus, or did you forget that as well as the Vittel?"

The young man smiled with poisonous mock benevolence, and spoke slowly, as if to a backward child: "No, I did not forget the paraffin as well as the Vittel. The tin is in the back of the car. Now, if I may, I think I shall take a little walk." He rose, still smiling most unpleasantly, and moved away from the table.

"Why, you rude puppy! I'll box your ears!" the woman called after him. He did not turn around.

"Aren't they something?" whispered Port.

"Very amusing," said Kit. She was still angry. "Why don't you ask them to join us on our great trek? It's all we'd need."

They ate their fruit in silence.

After dinner, when Kit had gone up to her room, Port wandered around the barren street floor of the hotel, to the writing room with its impossible, dim lights far overhead; to the palm-stuffed foyer where two ancient French women in black sat on the edges of their chairs, whispering to one another; to the front entrance, in which he stood a few minutes staring at a large Mercédès touring car parked opposite; and back to the writing room. He sat down. The sickly light from above scarcely illumined the travel posters on the walls: *Fès la Mystérieuse, Air-France, Visitez l'Espagne*. From a grilled window over his head came hard female voices and the metallic sound of kitchen activities, amplified by the stone walls and tile floors. This room, even more than the others, reminded him of a dungeon. The electric bell of the cinema was audible above all the other noises, a constant, nerveracking background. He went to the writing tables, lifted the blotters, opened the drawers, searching for stationery; there was none. Then he shook the inkwells; they were dry. A violent argument had broken out in the kitchen. Scratching the fleshy parts of his hands, where the mosquitoes had just bitten him, he walked slowly out of the room through the foyer, along the corridor into the bar. Even here the light was weak and distant, but the array of bottles behind the bar formed a focal point of interest for the eyes. He had a slight indigestion— not a sourness, but the promise of a pain which at the moment was only a tiny physical unhappiness in some unlocatable center. The swarthy barman was staring at him expectantly. There was no one else in the room. He ordered a whiskey and sat savoring it, drinking slowly. Somewhere in the hotel a toilet was flushed, making its sounds of choking and regurgitation.

The unpleasant tension inside him was lessening; he felt very much awake. The bar was stuffy and melancholy. It was full of the sadness inherent in all deracinated things. "Since the day the first drink was served at this bar," he thought, "how many moments of happiness have been lived through, here?" The happiness, if there still was any, existed elsewhere: in sequestered rooms that looked onto bright alleys where the cats gnawed fish-heads; in shaded cafés hung with reed matting, where the hashish smoke mingled with the fumes of mint from the hot tea; down on the docks, out at the edge of the sebkha in the tents (he passed over the white image of Marhnia, the placid face); beyond the mountains in the great Sahara, in the endless regions that were all of Africa. But not here in this sad colonial room where each invocation of Europe was merely one more squalid touch, one more visible proof of isolation; the mother country seemed farthest in such a room.

As he sat regularly swallowing small mouthfuls of warm whiskey, he heard footsteps approaching in the corridor. The young Englishman came into the room, and without looking in Port's direction sat down at one of the small tables. Port watched him order a liqueur, and when the barman was back behind the bar, he walked over to the table. "*Pardon, monsieur,*" he said. "*Vous parlez français?*" "*Oui, oui,*" the young man answered, looking startled. "But you also speak English?" pursued Port quickly. "I do," he replied, setting his glass down and staring at his interlocutor in a manner which Port suspected was completely theatrical. His intuition told him that flattery was the surest approach in this case. "Then maybe you can give me some advice," he went on with great seriousness.

The young man smiled weakly. "If it's about Africa, I daresay I can. I've been mucking about here for the past five years. Fascinating place, of course."

"Wonderful, yes."

"You know it?" He looked a bit worried; he wanted so much to be the only traveler.

"Only certain parts," Port reassured him. "I've traveled a good deal in the north and west. Roughly Tripoli to Dakar."

"Dakar's a filthy hole."

"But so are ports all over the world. What I wanted advice about is the exchange. What bank do you think it's best to use? I have dollars."

The Englishman smiled. "I think I'm rather a good person to give you such information. I'm actually Australian myself, but my mother and I live mostly on American dollars." He proceeded to offer Port a complete exposition of the French banking system in North Africa. His voice took on the inflections of an old-fashioned professor; his manner of expressing himself was objectionably pedantic, Port thought. At the same time there was a light in his eyes which not only belied the voice and manner but also managed to annul whatever weight his words might carry. It seemed to Port that the young man was speaking to him rather as if he thought he were dealing with a maniac, as if the subject of conversation had been chosen as one proper to the occasion, one which could be extended for as long a time as necessary, until the patient was calmed.

Port allowed him to continue his discourse, which presently left banking behind and went into personal experiences. This terrain was more fertile; it obviously was where the young man had been heading from the start. Port offered no comments, save for an occasional polite exclamation which helped to give the monologue the semblance of a conversation. He learned that prior to their arrival in Mombasa the young man and his mother, who wrote travel books and illustrated them with her own photographs, had lived for three years in India, where an elder son had died; that the five African years, spent in every part of the continent, had managed to give them both an astonishing list of diseases, and that they still suffered intermittently from most of them. It was difficult, however, to know what to believe and what to discount, since the report was decorated with such remarks as: "At that time I was manager of a large import-export firm in Durban," "The government put me in charge of three thousand Zulus," "In Lagos I bought a command car and drove it through to Casamance," "We were the only whites ever to have penetrated into the region," "They wanted me to be cameraman for the expedition, but there was no one in Cape Town I could trust to keep the studios running properly, and we were making four films at the time." Port began to resent his not knowing better how far to go with his listener, but he let it all pass, and was delighted with the ghoulish pleasure the young man took in describing the dead bodies in the river at Douala, the murders in Takoradi, the self-immolating madman in the market at Gao. Finally the talker leaned back, signaled to the barman to bring him another liqueur, and said: "Ah, yes, Africa's a great place. I wouldn't live anywhere else these days."

"And your mother? Does she feel the same way?"

"Oh, she's in love with it. She wouldn't know what to do if you put her down in a civilized country."

"She writes all the time?"

"All the time. Every day. Mostly about out-of-the-way places. We're about to go down to Fort Charlet. Do you know it?"

He seemed reasonably sure that Port would not know Fort Charlet. "No, I don't," said Port. "But I know where it is. How're you going to get there? There's no service of any kind, is there?"

"Oh, we'll get there. The Touareg will be just Mother's meat. I have a great collection of maps, military and otherwise, which I study carefully each morning before we set out. Then I simply follow them. We have a car," he added, seeing Port's look of bewilderment. "An ancient Mercédès. Powerful old thing."

"Ah, yes, I saw it outside," murmured Port.

"Yes," said the young man smugly. "We always get there."

"Your mother must be a very interesting woman," said Port.

The young man was enthusiastic. "Absolutely amazing. You must meet her tomorrow."

"I should like very much to."

"I've packed her off to bed, but she won't sleep until I get in. We always have communicating rooms, of course, so that unfortunately she knows just when I go to bed. Isn't married life wonderful?"

Port glanced at him quickly, a little shocked at the crudity of his remark, but he was laughing in an open and unaware fashion.

"Yes, you'll enjoy talking with her. Unluckily we have an itinerary which we try to follow exactly. We're leaving tomorrow noon. When are you pulling out of this hellhole?"

"Oh, we've been planning to get the train tomorrow for Boussif, but we're not in any hurry. So we may wait until Thursday. The only way to travel, at least for us, is to go when you feel like going and stay where you feel like staying."

"I quite agree. But surely you don't feel like staying here?"

"Oh, God, no!" laughed Port. "We hate it. But there are three of us, and we just haven't all managed to get up the necessary energy at one time."

"Three of you? I see." The young man appeared to be considering this unexpected news. "I see." He rose and reached in his pocket, pulling out a card which he handed to Port. "I might give you this. My name is Lyle. Well, cheer-o, and I hope you work up the initiative. May see you in the morning." He spun around as if in embarrassment, and walked stiffly out of the room.

Port slipped the card into his pocket. The barman was asleep, his head on the bar. Deciding to have a last drink, he went over and tapped him lightly on the shoulder. The man raised his head with a groan.

VIII

"Where have you been?" said Kit. She was sitting up in bed reading, having dragged the little lamp to the very edge of the night-table. Port moved the table against the bed and pushed the lamp back to a safe distance from the edge. "Guzzling down in the bar. I have a feeling we're going to be invited to drive to Boussif."

Kit looked up, delighted. She hated trains. "Oh, no! Really? How marvelous!"

"But wait'll you hear by whom!"

"Oh God! Not those monsters!"

"They haven't said anything. I just have a feeling they will."

"Oh well, that's absolutely out, of course."

Port went into his room. "I wouldn't worry about it either way. Nobody's said anything. I got a long story from the son. He's a mental case."

"You know I'll worry about it. You *know* how I hate train rides. And you come in calmly and say we may have an invitation to go in a car! You might at least have waited till morning and let me have a decent night's sleep before having to make up my mind which of the two tortures I want."

"Why don't you begin your worrying once we've been asked?"

"Oh, don't be ridiculous!" she cried, jumping out of bed. She stood in the doorway, watching him undress. "Good night," she said suddenly, and shut the door.

Things came about somewhat as Port had imagined they would. In the morning, as he was standing in the window wondering at the first clouds he had seen since mid-Atlantic, a knock came at the door; it was Eric Lyle, his face suffused and puffy from having just awakened.

"Good morning. I say, do forgive me if I've awakened you, but I've something rather important to talk about. May I come in?" He glanced about the room in a strangely surreptitious manner, his pale eyes darting swiftly from object to object. Port had the uncomfortable feeling that he should have put things away and closed all his luggage before letting him in.

"Have you had tea?" said Lyle.

"Yes, only it was coffee."

"Aha!" He edged nearer to a valise, toyed with the straps. "You have some nice labels on your bags." He lifted the leather tag with Port's name and address on it. "Now I see your name. Mr. Porter Moresby." He crossed the room. "You must forgive me if I snoop. Luggage always fascinates me.

May I sit down? Now, look, Mr. Moresby. That *is* you, isn't it? I've been talking at some length with Mother and she agrees with me that it would be much pleasanter for you and Mrs. Moresby—I suppose that's the lady you were with last night—" he paused.

"Yes," said Port.

"—if you both came along with us to Boussif. It's only five hours by car, and the train ride takes ages; something like eleven hours, if I remember. And eleven hours of utter hell. Since the war the trains are completely impossible, you know. We think—"

Port interrupted him. "No, no. We couldn't put you out to that extent. No, no."

"Yes, *yes*," said Lyle archly.

"Besides, we're three, you know."

"Ah, yes, of course," said Lyle in a vague voice. "Your friend couldn't come along on the train, I suppose?"

"I don't think he'd be very happy with the arrangement. Anyway, we couldn't very well go off and leave him."

"I see. That's a shame. We can scarcely take him along, with all the luggage there'd be, you know." He rose, looked at Port with his head on one side like a bird listening for a worm, and said: "Come along with us; do. You can manage it, I know." He went to the door, opened it, and leaned through toward Port, standing on tiptoe. "I'll tell you what. You come by and let me know in an hour. Fifty-three. And I do hope your decision is favorable." Smiling, and letting his gaze wander once more around the room, he shut the door.

Kit literally had not slept at all during the night; at day-break she had dozed off, but her sleep was troubled. She was not in a receptive mood when Port rapped loudly on the communicating door and opened it immediately afterward. Straightway she sat up, holding the sheet high around her neck with her hand, and staring wildly. She relaxed and fell back.

"What *is* it?"

"I've got to talk to you."

"I'm so sleepy."

"We have the invitation to drive to Boussif."

Again she bobbed up, this time rubbing her eyes. He sat on the bed and kissed her shoulder absently. She drew back and looked at him. "From the monsters? Have you accepted?"

He wanted to say "Yes," because that would have avoided a long discussion; the matter would have been settled for her as well as for him.

"Not yet."

"Oh, you'll have to refuse."

"Why? It'll be much more comfortable. And quicker. And certainly safer."

"Are you trying to terrify me so I won't budge out of the hotel?" She looked toward the window. "Why is it so dark out still? What time is it?"

"It's cloudy today for some strange reason."

She was silent; the haunted look came into her eyes.

"They won't take Tunner," said Port.

"Are you stark, raving mad?" she cried. "I wouldn't dream of going without him. Not for a second!"

"Why not?" said Port, nettled. "He could get there all right on the train. I don't know why we should lose a good ride just because he happens to be along. We don't have to stick with him every damned minute, do we?"

"You don't have to; no."

"You mean you do?"

"I mean I wouldn't consider leaving Tunner here and going off in a car with those two. She's an hysterical old hag, and the boy——! He's a real criminal degenerate if I ever saw one. He gives me the creeps."

"Oh, come on!" scoffed Port. "*You* dare use the word hysterical. My God! I wish you could see yourself this minute."

"You do exactly what you like," said Kit, lying back. "I'll go on the train with Tunner."

Port's eyes narrowed. "Well, by God, you can *go* on the train with him, then. And I hope there's a wreck!" He went into his room and dressed.

Kit rapped on the door. "*Entrez*," said Tunner with his American accent. "Well, well, this is a surprise! What's up? To what do I owe this unexpected visit?"

"Oh, nothing in particular," she said, surveying him with a vague distaste which she hoped she managed to conceal. "You and I've got to go alone to Boussif on the train. Port has an invitation to drive there with some friends." She tried to keep her voice wholly inexpressive.

He looked mystified. "What's all this? Say it again slowly. Friends?"

"That's right. Some English woman and her son. They've asked him."

Little by little his face began to beam. This was not false now, she noted. He was just incredibly slow in reacting.

"Well, well!" he said again, grinning.

"What a dolt he is," she thought, observing the utter lack of inhibition in his behavior. (The blatantly normal always infuriated her.) "His emotional maneuvers all take place out in the open. Not a tree or a rock to hide behind."

Aloud she said: "The train leaves at six and gets there at some God-forsaken hour of the morning. But they say it's always late, and that's good, for once."

"So we'll just go together, the two of us."

"Port'll be there long before, so he can get rooms for us. I've got to go now and find a beauty parlor, God forbid."

"What do you need of that?" protested Tunner. "Let well enough alone. You can't improve on nature."

She had no patience with gallantry; nevertheless she smiled at him as she went out. "Because I'm a coward," she thought. She was quite conscious of a desire to pit Tunner's magic against Port's, since Port had put a curse on the trip. And as she smiled she said, as if to nobody: "I think we can avoid the wreck."

"Huh?"

"Oh, nothing. I'll see you for lunch in the dining room at two."

Tunner was the sort of person to whom it would occur only with difficulty that he might be being used. Because he was accustomed to imposing his will without meeting opposition, he had a highly developed and very male vanity which endeared him, strangely enough, to almost everyone. Doubtless the principal reason why he had been so eager to accompany Port and Kit on this trip was that with them as with no one else he felt a definite resistance to his unceasing attempts at moral domination, at which he was forced, when with them, to work much harder; thus unconsciously he was giving his personality the exercise it required. Kit and Port, on the other hand, both resented even the reduced degree to which they responded to his somewhat obvious charm, which was why neither one would admit to having encouraged him to come along with them. There was no small amount of shame involved where they were concerned, since both of them were conscious of all the acting and formula-following in his behavior, and yet to a certain degree both were willingly ensnared by it. Tunner himself was an essentially simple individual irresistibly attracted by whatever remained just beyond his intellectual grasp. Contenting himself with not quite being able to seize an idea was a habit he had acquired in adolescence, and it operated in him now with still greater force. If he could get on all sides of a thought, he concluded that it was an inferior one; there had to be an inaccessible part of it for his interest to be aroused. His attention, however, did not spur him to additional thought. On the contrary, it merely provided him with an emotional satisfaction *vis-à-vis* the idea, making it possible for him to relax and admire it at a distance. At the beginning of his friendship with Port and Kit he had been inclined to treat them with the careful deference he felt was due them, not as individuals, but as beings who dealt almost exclusively with ideas, sacred things. Their discouraging of this tactic had been so categorical that he had been obliged to adopt a new one, in using which he felt even less sure of himself. This consisted of gentle prods, ridicule so faint and unfocused that it always could be given a flattering turn if necessary, and the adoption of an attitude of amused, if slightly pained resignation, that made him feel like the father of a pair of impossibly spoiled prodigies.

Light-hearted now, he moved about the room whistling at the prospect of being alone with Kit; he had decided she needed him. He was not at all sure of being able to convince her that the need lay precisely in the field where he liked to think it did. Indeed, of all the women with whom he hoped some day to have intimate relations he considered Kit the most unlikely, the most difficult. He caught a glimpse of himself as he stood bent over a suitcase, and smiled inscrutably at his image; it was the same smile that Kit thought so false.

At one o'clock he went to Port's room to find the door open and the luggage gone. Two maids were making the bed up with fresh linen. "*Se ha marchao,*" said one. At two he met Kit in the dining room; she was looking exceptionally well groomed and pretty.

He ordered champagne.

"At a thousand francs a bottle!" she remonstrated. "Port would have a fit!"

"Port isn't here," said Tunner.

IX

A few minutes before twelve Port stood outside the entrance of the hotel with all his luggage. Three Arab porters, acting under the direction of young Lyle, were piling bags into the back of the car. The slow-moving clouds above were interspersed now with great holes of deep blue sky; when the sun came through its heat was unexpectedly powerful. In the direction of the mountains the sky was still black and frowning. Port was impatient; he hoped they would get off before Kit or Tunner happened by.

Precisely at twelve Mrs. Lyle was in the lobby complaining about her bill. The pitch of her voice rose and fell in sharp scallops of sound. Coming to the doorway she cried: "Eric, will you come in here and tell this man I did *not* have biscuits yesterday at tea? Immediately!"

"Tell him yourself," said Eric absently. "*Cell-là on va mettre ici en bas,*" he went on to one of the Arabs, indicating a heavy pigskin case.

"You idiot!" She went back in; a moment later Port heard her squealing: "*Non! Non! Thé seulement! Pas gateau!*"

Eventually she appeared again, red in the face, her handbag swinging on her arm. Seeing Port she stood still and called: "Eric!" He looked up from the car, came over and presented Port to his mother.

"I'm very glad you can come with us. It's an added protection. They say in the mountains here it's better to carry a gun. Although I must say I've never seen an Arab I couldn't handle. It's the beastly French one really needs protection from. Filthy lot! Fancy their telling me what I had yesterday for tea. But the insolence! Eric, you coward! You let me do all the fighting at the desk. *You* probably ate the biscuits they were charging me for!"

"It's all one, isn't it?" Eric smiled.

"I should think you'd be ashamed to admit it. Mr. Moresby, look at that hulking boy. He's never done a day's work in his life. I have to pay all his bills."

"Come *on*, Mother! Get in." This was said despairingly.

"What do you mean, *get in*?" Her voice went very high. "Fancy talking to me like that! You need a good slap in the face. That might help you." She climbed into the front of the car. "I've never had such talk from anyone."

"We shall all three sit in front," said Eric. "Do you mind, Mr. Moresby?"

"I'm delighted. I prefer the front," said Port. He was determined to remain wholly on the periphery of this family pattern; the best way of assuring that, he thought, would be to have no visible personality whatever, merely to be civil, to listen. It was likely that this ludicrous wrangling was the only form of conversation these two had ever managed to devise for themselves.

They started up, Eric at the wheel, racing the motor first. The porters shouted: "*Bon voyage!*"

"I noticed several people staring at me when I left," said Mrs. Lyle, settling back. "Those filthy Arabs have done their work here, the same as everywhere else."

"Work? What do you mean?" said Port.

"Why, their spying. They spy on you all the time here, you know. That's the way they make their living. You think you can do anything without their knowing it?" She laughed unpleasantly. "Within an hour all the miserable little touts and undersecretaries at the consulates know everything."

"You mean the British Consulate?"

"*All* the consulates, the police, the banks, everyone," she said firmly.

Port looked at Eric expectantly. "But—"

"Oh, yes," said Eric, apparently happy to reinforce his

mother's statement. "It's a frightful mess. We never have a moment's peace. Wherever we go, they hold back our letters, they try to keep us out of hotels by saying they have no rooms, and when we do get rooms they search them while we're out and steal our things, they get the porters and chambermaids to eavesdrop—"

"But *who?* Who does all this? And why?"

"The Arabs!" cried Mrs. Lyle. "They're a stinking, low race of people with nothing to do in life but spy on others. How else do you think they live?"

"It seems incredible," Port ventured timidly, hoping in this way to call forth more of the same, for it amused him.

"Hah!" she said in a tone of triumph. "It may seem incredible to you because you don't know them, but look out for them. They hate us all. And so do the French. Oh, *they* loathe us!"

"I've always found the Arabs very sympathetic," said Port.

"Of course. That's because they're servile, they flatter you and fawn on you. And the moment your back is turned, off they rush to the consulate."

Said Eric: "Once in Mogador—" His mother cut him short.

"Oh, shut up! Let someone else talk. Do you think anyone wants to hear about your blundering stupidities? If you'd had a little sense you'd not have got into that business. What right did you have to go to Mogador, when I was dying in Fez? Mr. Moresby, I was dying! In the hospital, on my back, with a terrible Arab nurse who couldn't even give a proper injection—"

"She could!" said Eric stoutly. "She gave me at least twenty. You just happened to get infected because your resistance was low."

"*Resistance!*" shrieked Mrs. Lyle. "I refuse to talk any more. Look, Mr. Moresby, at the colors of the hills. Have you ever tried infra-red on landscapes? I took some exceptionally fine ones in Rhodesia, but they were stolen from me by an editor in Johannesburg."

"Mr. Moresby's not a photographer, Mother."

"Oh, be quiet. Would that keep him from knowing about infra-red photography?"

"I've seen samples of it," said Port.

"Well, of course you have. You see, Eric, you simply don't know what you're saying, ever. It all comes from lack of discipline. I only wish you had to earn your living for one day. It would teach you to think before you speak. At this point you're no better than an imbecile."

A particularly arid argument ensued, in which Eric, apparently for Port's benefit, enumerated a list of unlikely sounding jobs he claimed to have held during the past four years, while the mother systematically challenged each item with what seemed convincing proof of its falsity. At each new claim she cried: "What lies! What a liar! You don't even know what the truth is!" Finally Eric replied in an aggrieved tone, as if capitulating: "You'd never let me stick at any work, anyway. You're terrified that I might become independent."

Mrs. Lyle cried: "Look, look! Mr. Moresby! That sweet burro! It reminds me of Spain. We just spent two months there. It's a horrible country," (she pronounced it *hawibble*) "all soldiers and priests and Jews."

"Jews?" echoed Port incredulously.

"Of course. Didn't you know? The hotels are full of them. They run the country. From behind the scenes, of course. The same as everywhere else. Only in Spain they're very clever about it. They will *not* admit to being Jewish. In Córdoba—this will show you how wily and deceitful they are. In Córdoba I went through a street called Judería. It's where the synagogue is. Naturally it's positively teeming with Jews— a typical ghetto. But do you think one of them would admit it? Certainly not! They all shook their fingers back and forth in front of my face, and shouted: '*Católico! Católico!*' at me. But fancy that, Mr. Moresby, their claiming to be Roman Catholics. And when I went through the synagogue the guide kept insisting that no services had been held in it since the fifteenth century! I'm afraid I was dreadfully rude to him. I burst out laughing in his face."

"What did he say?" Port inquired.

"Oh, he merely went on with his lecture. He'd learned it by rote, of course. He did stare. They all do. But I think he respected me for not being afraid. The ruder you are to them the more they admire you. I showed him I knew he was telling me the most fearful lot of lies. Catholics! I daresay they think that makes them superior. It was too funny, when they were all most Jewy; one had only to look at them. Oh, I know Jews. I've had too many vile experiences with them not to know them."

The novelty of the caricature was wearing off. Port was beginning to feel smothered sitting there between them; their obsessions depressed him. Mrs. Lyle was even more objectionable than her son. Unlike him, she had no exploits, imaginary or real, to recount; her entire conversation consisted of descriptions in detail of the persecutions to which she believed she had been subjected, and of word-by-word accounts of the bitter quarrels in which she had been engaged with those who harassed her. As she spoke, her character took shape before him, although already he was far less inclined to be interested in it. Her life had been devoid of personal contacts, and she needed them. Thus she manufactured them as best she could; each fight was an abortive attempt at establishing some kind of human relationship. Even with Eric, she had come to accept the dispute as the natural mode of talking. He decided that she was the loneliest woman he had ever seen, but he could not care very much.

He ceased listening. They had left the town, traversed the valley, and were climbing a large, bare hill on the other side. As they swung around one of the many S-curves, he realized with a start that he was looking straight at the Turkish fortress, small and perfect as a toy at this distance, on the opposite side of the valley. Under the wall, scattered about on the yellow earth, were several tiny black tents; which one he had been in, which one was Marhnia's, he could not say, for the staircase was not visible from here. And there she was, doubtless, somewhere below in the valley, having her noonday sleep in the airless heat of a tent, alone or with a lucky Arab friend—not Smaïl, he thought. They turned again, mounting ever higher; there were cliffs above them. By the road sometimes were high clumps of dead thistle plants, coated with white dust, and from the plants the locusts called, a high, unceasing scream like the sound of heat itself. Again and again the valley came into view, always a little smaller, a little farther away, a little less real. The Mercédès roared like a plane; there was no muffler on the exhaust pipe.

"You can't read in this light," he said.

"I'm just looking at pictures."

"Oh."

"You'll excuse me, won't you? In a minute I won't even be able to do this much. I'm a little nervous on trains."

"Go right ahead," he said.

They had brought a cold supper with them, put up by the hotel. From time to time Tunner eyed the basket speculatively. Finally she looked up and caught him at it. "Tunner! Don't tell me you're hungry!" she cried.

"Only my tapeworm."

"You're revolting." She lifted the basket, glad to be able to engage in any manual activity. One by one she pulled out the thick sandwiches, separately wrapped in flimsy paper napkins.

"I told them not to give us any of that lousy Spanish ham. It's raw, and you can *really* get worms from it. I'm sure some of these are made of it, though. I think I can smell it. They always think you're talking just to hear the sound of your voice."

"I'll eat the ham if there is any," said Tunner. "It's good stuff, if I remember."

"Oh, it tastes all right." She brought out a package of hard-boiled eggs, wrapped with some very oily black olives. The train shrieked and plunged into a tunnel. Kit hastily put the eggs into the basket and looked apprehensively at the window. She could see the outline of her face reflected in the glass, pitilessly illumined by the feeble glare from overhead. The stench of coal smoke increased each second; she could feel it constricting her lungs.

"Phew!" Tunner choked.

She sat still, waiting. If the accident were going to come, it would probably be either in a tunnel or on a trestle. "If I could only be sure it would happen tonight," she thought. "I could relax. But the uncertainty. You never know, so you always wait."

Presently they emerged, breathed again. Outside, over the miles of indistinct rocky land, the mountains loomed, jet-black. Above their sharp crests what little light was left in the sky came from between heavy threatening clouds.

"How about those eggs?"

"Oh!" She handed him the whole package.

"I don't want 'em all!"

"You must eat them," she said, making a great effort to be present, to take part in the little life going on inside the creaking wooden walls of the car. "I only want some fruit. And a sandwich."

But she found the bread hard and dry; she had difficulty chewing it. Tunner was busy leaning over, dragging out one of his valises from under the seat. She slipped the uneaten sandwich into the space between her seat and the window.

He sat up, his face triumphant, holding a large dark bottle; fished in his pocket a moment, and brought out a corkscrew.

"What is it?"

"You guess," he said grinning.

"Not—champagne!"

"The first time."

In her nervousness she reached out and clasped his head in her two hands, kissing him noisily on the forehead.

"You *darling*!" she cried. "You're marvelous!"

He tugged at the cork; there was a pop. A haggard woman in black passed along the corridor and stared in at them. Holding the bottle in his hand, Tunner rose and drew the shades. Kit watched him, thinking: "He's very different from Port. Port would never have done this."

And as he poured it out into the plastic traveling cups, she continued to debate with herself. "But it means nothing except that he spent the money. It's something bought, that's all. Still, being willing to spend the money. . . . And having thought of it, more than anything."

They touched cups in a toast. There was no familiar clink—only a dead paper-like sound. "Here's to Africa," said Tunner, suddenly bashful. He had meant to say: "Here's to tonight."

"Yes."

She looked at the bottle where he had set it on the floor. Characteristically, she decided at once that it was the magic object which was going to save her, that through its power she might escape the disaster. She drained her cup. He refilled it.

"We must make it last," she cautioned, suddenly fearful lest the magic give out.

"You think so? Why?" He pulled out the valise and opened it again. "Look." There were five more bottles. "That's why I made such a fuss about carrying this bag myself," he said, smiling to make his dimples deep. "You probably thought I was nuts."

"I didn't notice," she said faintly, not even noticing the dimples she disliked so strongly. The sight of so much magic had somewhat overcome her.

"So, drink up. Fast and furious."

"Don't you worry about me," she laughed. "I don't need any exhortations." She felt absurdly happy—much too happy for the occasion, she reminded herself. But it was always a pendulum; in another hour she would be back where she had been a minute ago.

The train came slowly to a stop. Beyond the window it was black night; there was not a light to be seen. Somewhere outside, a voice was singing a strange, repetitious melody. Always beginning high and wandering downward until the breath gave out, only to recommence again at the top of the scale, the song had the pattern of a child's weeping.

"Is that a man?" said Kit incredulously.

"Where?" said Tunner, looking around.

"Singing."

He listened a moment. "Hard to tell. Drink up."

She drank, and smiled. Soon she was staring out the window at the black night. "I think I was never meant to live," she said ruefully.

He looked worried. "Now see here, Kit. I know you're nervous. That's why I brought the fizz-water along. But you've just got to calm down. Take it easy. Relax. Nothing's that important, you know. Who was it said—"

"No. That's something I don't want," she interrupted. "Champagne, yes. Philosophy, no. And I think you were incredibly sweet to have thought of it, especially now that I see why you brought it along."

He stopped chewing. His face changed expression; his eyes grew a little bit hard. "What do you mean?"

"Because you realized I was a nervous fool on trains. And you couldn't possibly have done anything I'd have appreciated more."

He chewed again, and grinned. "Oh, forget it. I'm doing all right by it, too, you may have noticed. So here's to good old Mumm!" He uncorked the second bottle. Painfully the train started up again.

The fact that they were moving once more exhilarated her. "*Dime ingrato, porqué me abandonaste, y sola me dejaste . . .*" she sang.

"More?" He held the bottle.

"*Claro que sí,*" she said, downing it at one gulp, and stretching forth her cup again, immediately.

The train jolted along, stopping every little while, each time in what looked like empty countryside. But always there were voices out beyond in the darkness, shouting in the guttural mountain tongue. They completed their supper; as Kit was eating her last fig, Tunner bent over to pull out another bottle from the valise. Without quite knowing what she was doing, she reached into the space where she had hidden her sandwich, drew it out and stuffed it into her handbag on top of her compact. He poured her some champagne.

"The champagne's not as cool as it was," she said, sipping it.

"Can't have everything."

"Oh, but I love it! I don't mind it warm. You know, I think I'm getting quite high."

"Bah! Not on the little bit you've had." He laughed.

"Oh, you don't know me! When I'm nervous or upset, right off I'm high."

He looked at his watch. "Well, we've got another eight hours at least. We might as well dig in. Is it all right with you if I change seats and sit with you?"

"Of course. I asked you to when we first got on, so you wouldn't have to ride backwards."

"Fine." He rose, stretched, yawned, and sat down beside her very hard, bumping against her. "I'm sorry," he said. "I miscalculated the beast's gyrations. God, what a train." His right arm went around her, and he pulled her toward him a little. "Lean against me. You'll be more comfortable. Relax! You're all tense and tight."

"Tight, yes! I'm afraid so." She laughed; to her it sounded like a titter. She reclined partially against him, her head on his shoulder. "This should make me feel comfortable," she was thinking, "but it only makes everything worse. I'm going to jump out of my skin."

For a few minutes she made herself sit there without moving. It was difficult not to be tense, because it seemed to her that the motion of the train kept pushing her toward him. Slowly she felt the muscles of his arm tightening around her waist. The train came to a halt. She bounded up, crying: "I want to go to the door and see what it looks like outside."

He rose, put his arm around her again, held it there with insistence, and said: "You know what it looks like. Just dark mountains."

She looked up into his face. "I know. Please, Tunner." She wriggled slightly, and felt him let go. At that moment the door into the corridor opened, and the ravaged-looking woman in black made as if to enter the compartment.

"*Ah, pardon. Je me suis trompée,*" she said, scowling balefully, and going on without shutting the door behind her.

"What does that old harpy want?" said Tunner.

Kit walked to the doorway, stood in it, and said loudly: "She's just a *voyeuse*." The woman, already halfway down the corridor, turned furiously and glared at her. Kit was delighted. The satisfaction she derived from knowing that the woman had heard the word struck her as absurd. Yet there it was, a strong, exultant force inside her. "A little more and I'll be hysterical. And then Tunner *will* be helpless!"

In normal situations she felt that Port was inclined to lack understanding, but in extremities no one else could take his place; in really bad moments she relied on him utterly, not because he was an infallible guide under such circumstances, but because a section of her consciousness annexed him as a buttress, so that in part she identified herself with him. "And Port's not here. So no hysteria, please." Aloud she said: "I'll be right back. Don't let the witch in."

"I'll come with you," he said.

"Really, Tunner," she laughed. "I'm afraid where I'm going you'd be just a little in the way."

He strove not to show his embarrassment. "Oh! Okay. Sorry."

The corridor was empty. She tried to see out the windows,

but they were coated with dust and fingermarks. Up ahead she could hear the noise of voices. The doors onto the quai were closed. She went into the next coach; it was marked "II," and it was more brightly lighted, more populous, much shabbier. At the other end she met people coming into the car from outside. She crowded past them, got off and walked along the ground toward the front of the train. The fourth-class passengers, all native Berbers and Arabs, were milling about in the midst of a confusion of bundles and boxes, piled on the dirt platform under the faint light of a bare electric bulb. A sharp wind swept down from the nearby mountains. Quickly she slipped in among the people and climbed aboard.

As she entered the car, her first impression was that she was not on the train at all. It was merely an oblong area, crowded to bursting with men in dun-colored burnouses, squatting, sleeping, reclining, standing, and moving about through a welter of amorphous bundles. She stood still an instant taking in the sight; for the first time she felt she was in a strange land. Someone was pushing her from behind, obliging her to go on into the car. She resisted, seeing no place to move to, and fell against a man with a white beard, who stared at her sternly. Under his gaze she felt like a badly behaved child. "*Pardon, monsieur,*" she said, trying to bend out of the way in order to avoid the growing pressure from behind. It was useless; she was impelled forward in spite of all her efforts, and staggering over the prostrate forms and the piles of objects, she moved into the middle of the car. The train lurched into motion. She glanced around a little fearfully. The idea occurred to her that these were Moslems, and that the odor of alcohol on her breath would scandalize them almost as much as if she were suddenly to remove all her clothing. Stumbling over the crouched figures, she worked her way to one side of the windowless wall and leaned against it while she took out a small bottle of perfume from her bag and rubbed it over her face and neck, hoping it would counteract, or at least blend with, whatever alcoholic odor there might be about her. As she rubbed, her fingers struck a small, soft object on the nape of her neck. She looked: it was a yellow louse. She had partly crushed it. With disgust she wiped her finger against the wall. Men were looking at her, but with neither sympathy nor antipathy. Nor even with curiosity, she thought. They had the absorbed and vacant expression of the man who looks into his handkerchief after blowing his nose. She shut her eyes for a moment. To her surprise she felt hungry. She took the sandwich out and ate it, breaking off the bread in small pieces and chewing them violently. The man leaning against the wall beside her was also eating—small dark objects which he kept taking out of the hood of his garment and crunching noisily. With a faint shudder she saw that they were red locusts with the legs and heads removed. The babble of voices which had been constant suddenly ceased; people appeared to be listening. Above the rumbling of the train and the rhythmical clacking of the wheels over the rails she could hear the sharp, steady sound of rain on the tin roof of the car. The men were nodding their heads; conversation started up again. She determined to fight her way back to the door in order to be able to get down at the next stop. Holding her head slightly lowered in front of her, she began to burrow wildly through the crowd. There were groans from below as she stepped on sleepers, there were exclamations of indignation as her elbows came in contact with faces. At each step she cried: "*Pardon! Pardon!*" She had got herself wedged into a corner at the end of the car. Now all she needed was to get to the door. Barring her way was a wild-faced man holding a severed sheep's head, its eyes like agate marbles staring from their sockets. "Oh!" she moaned. The man looked at her stolidly, making no movement to let her by. Using all her strength, she fought her way around him, rubbing her skirt against the bloody neck as she squeezed past. With relief she saw that the door onto the platform was open; she would have only to get by those who filled the entrance. She began her cries of "*Pardon!*" once more, and charged through. The platform itself was less crowded because the cold rain was sweeping across it. Those sitting there had their heads covered with the hoods of their burnouses. Turning her back to the rain she gripped the iron railing and looked directly into the most hideous human face she had ever seen. The tall man wore cast-off European clothes, and a burlap bag over his head like a haïk. But where his nose should have been was a dark triangular abyss, and the strange flat lips were white. For no reason at all she thought of a lion's muzzle; she could not take her eyes away from it. The man seemed neither to see her nor to feel the rain; he merely stood there. As she stared she found herself wondering why it was that a diseased face, which basically means nothing, should be so much more horrible to look at than a face whose tissues are healthy but whose expression reveals an interior corruption. Port would say that in a non-materialistic age it would not be thus. And probably he would be right.

She was drenched through and shivering, but she still held on to the cold metal railing and looked straight ahead of her—sometimes into the face, and sometimes to one side into the gray, rain-filled air of the night behind it. It was a *tête-à-tête* which would last until they came to a station. The train was laboring slowly, noisily, up a steep grade. From time to time, in the middle of the shaking and racket, there was a hollow sound for a few seconds as it crossed a short bridge or a trestle. At such moments it seemed to her that she was moving high in the air and that far below there was water rushing between the rocky walls of the chasms. The driving rain continued. She had the impression of living a dream of terror which refused to come to a finish. She was not conscious of time passing; on the contrary, she felt that it had stopped, that she had become a static thing suspended in a vacuum. Yet underneath was the certainty that at a given moment it would no longer be this way—but she did not want to think of that, for fear that she should become alive once more, that time should begin to move again and that she should be aware of the endless seconds as they passed.

And so she stood unmoving, always shivering, holding herself very erect. When the train slowed down and came to a stop, the lion-faced man was gone. She got off and hurried through the rain, back toward the end of the train. As she climbed into the second-class carriage, she remembered that he had stepped aside like any normal man, to let her pass. She began to laugh to herself, quietly. Then she stood still. There were people in the corridor, talking. She turned and went back to the toilet, locked herself in, and began to make up by the flickering lantern overhead, looking into the small oval mirror above the washstand. She was still trembling with cold, and water ran down her legs onto the floor. When she felt she could face Tunner again, she went out, down the corridor, and crossed over into the first-class coach. The door of their compartment was open. Tunner was staring moodily out the window. He turned as she went in, and jumped up.

"My God, Kit! Where have you been?"

"In the fourth-class carriage." She was shaking violently, so that it was impossible for her to sound nonchalant, as she had intended.

"But look at you! Come in here." His voice was suddenly very serious. He pulled her firmly into the compartment, shut the door, helped her to sit down, and immediately began to go through his luggage, taking things out and laying them on the seat. She watched him in a stupor. Presently he was holding two aspirin tablets and a plastic cup in front of her face. "Take these," he commanded. The cup contained champagne. She did as she was told. Then he indicated the flannel bathrobe on the seat across from her. "I'm going out into the passageway here, and I want you to take off every stitch you have on, and put on that. Then you rap on the door and I'll come in and massage your feet. No excuses, now. Just do it." He went out and rolled the door shut after him.

She pulled down the shades at the outside windows and did as he had told her. The robe was soft and warm; she sat huddled in it on the seat for a while, her legs drawn up under her. And she poured herself three more cups of champagne, drinking them quickly one after the other. Then she tapped softly on the glass. The door opened a little. "All clear?" said Tunner.

"Yes, yes. Come in."

He sat down opposite her. "Now, stick your foot out here. I'm going to give them an alcohol rub. What's the matter with you, anyway? Are you crazy? Want to get pneumonia? What happened? Why were you so long? You had me nuts here, running up and down the place, in and out of cars asking everybody if they'd seen you. I didn't know *where* the hell you'd gone to."

"I told you I was in the fourth-class with the natives. I couldn't get back because there's no bridge between the cars. That feels wonderful. You'll wear yourself out."

He laughed, and rubbed more vigorously. "Never have yet."

When she was completely warm and comfortable he reached up and turned the lantern's wick very low. Then he moved across and sat beside her. The arm went around her, the pressure began again. She could think of nothing to say to stop him.

"You all right?" he asked softly, his voice husky.

"Yes," she said.

A minute later she whispered nervously: "No, no, no! Someone may open the door."

"No one's going to open the door." He kissed her. Over and over in her head she heard the slow wheels on the rails saying: "Not *now* not now, not *now* not now . . ." And underneath she imagined the deep chasms in the rain, swollen with water. She reached up and caressed the back of his head, but she said nothing.

"Darling," he murmured. "Just be still. Rest."

She could no longer think, nor were there any more images in her head. She was aware only of the softness of the woolen bathrobe next to her skin, and then of the nearness and warmth of a being that did not frighten her. The rain beat against the window panes.

XI

The roof of the hotel in the early morning, before the sun had come from behind the nearby mountainside, was a pleasant place for breakfast. The tables were set out along the edge of the terrace, overlooking the valley. In the gardens below, the fig trees and high stalks of papyrus moved slightly in the fresh morning wind. Further down were the larger trees where the storks had made their huge nests, and at the bottom of the slope was the river, running with thick red water. Port sat drinking his coffee, enjoying the rain-washed smell of the mountain air. Just below, the storks were teaching their young to fly; the rachet-like croaking of the older birds was mingled with shrill cries from the fluttering young ones.

As he watched, Mrs. Lyle came through the doorway from downstairs. It seemed to him that she looked unusually distraught. He invited her to sit with him, and she ordered her tea from an old Arab waiter in a shoddy rose-colored uniform.

"Gracious! Aren't we ever picturesque!" she said.

Port called her attention to the birds; they watched them until her tea was brought.

"Tell me, has your wife arrived safely?"

"Yes, but I haven't seen her. She's still asleep."

"I should think so, after that damnable trip."

"And your son. Still in bed?"

"Good heavens, no! He's gone off somewhere, to see some caïd or other. That boy has letters of introduction to Arabs in every town of North Africa, I expect." She became pensive. After a moment she said, looking at him sharply: "I do hope you don't go near them."

"Arabs, you mean? I don't know any personally. But it's rather hard not to go near them, since they're all over the place."

"Oh, I'm talking about social contact with them. Eric's an absolute fool. He wouldn't be ill today if it hadn't been for those filthy people."

"Ill? He looks well enough to me. What's wrong with him?"

"He's very ill." Her voice sounded distant; she looked down toward the river. Then she poured herself some more tea, and offered Port a biscuit from a tin she had brought upstairs with her. Her voice more definite, she continued. "They're all contaminated, you know, of course. Well, that's it. And I've been having the most *beastly* time trying to make him get proper treatment. He's a young idiot."

"I don't think I quite understand," said Port.

"An infection, an infection," she said impatiently. "Some filthy swine of an Arab woman," she added, with astonishing violence.

"Ah," said Port, noncommittal.

Now she sounded less sure of herself. "I've been told that such infections can even be transmitted among men directly. Do you believe that, Mr. Moresby?"

"I really don't know," he answered, looking at her in some surprise. "There's so much uninformed talk about such things. I should think a doctor would know best."

She passed him another biscuit. "I don't blame you for not wanting to discuss it. You must forgive me."

"Oh, I have no objection at all," he protested. "But I'm not a doctor. You understand."

She seemed not to have heard him. "It's disgusting. You're quite right."

Half of the sun was peering from behind the rim of the mountain; in another minute it would be hot. "Here's the sun," said Port. Mrs. Lyle gathered her things together.

"Shall you be staying long in Boussif?" she asked.

"We have no plans at all. And you?"

"Oh, Eric has some mad itinerary worked out. I believe we go on to Aïn Krorfa tomorrow morning, unless he decides to leave this noon and spend the night in Sfissifa. There's supposed to be a fairly decent little hotel there. Nothing so grand as this, of course."

Port looked around at the battered tables and chairs, and smiled. "I don't think I'd want anything much less grand than this."

"Oh, but my dear Mr. Moresby! This is positively luxurious. This is the best hotel you'll find between here and the Congo. There's nothing after this with running water, you know. Well, we shall see you before we go, in any case. I'm being baked by this horrible sun. Please say good morning to your wife for me." She rose and went downstairs.

Port hung his coat on the back of the chair and sat a while, pondering the unusual behavior of this eccentric woman. He could not bring himself to attribute it to mere irresponsibility or craziness; it seemed much more likely that her deportment was a roundabout means of communicating an idea she dared not express directly. In her own confused mind the procedure was apparently logical. All he could be certain of was that her basic motivation was fear. And Eric's was greed; of that also he was sure. But the compound made by the two together continued to mystify him. He had the impression that the merest indication of a design was beginning to take shape; what the design was, what it might end by meaning, all that was still wholly problematical. He guessed however that at the moment mother and son were working at cross-purposes. Each had a reason for being interested in his presence, but the reasons were not identical, nor even complementary, he thought.

He consulted his watch: it was ten-thirty. Kit would probably not be awake yet. When he saw her he intended to discuss the matter with her, if she were not still angry with him. Her ability to decipher motivations was considerable. He decided to take a walk around the town. Stopping off in his room, he left his jacket there and picked up his sun glasses. He had reserved the room across the hall for Kit. As he went out he put his ear against the door of her room and listened; there was no sound within.

Boussif was a completely modern town, laid out in large square blocks, with the market in the middle. The unpaved streets, lined for the most part with box-shaped one-story buildings, were filled with a rich red mud. A steady procession of men and sheep moved through the principal thoroughfare toward the market, the men walking with the hoods of their burnouses drawn up over their heads against the sun's fierce attack. There was not a tree to be seen anywhere. At the ends of the transversal streets the bare wasteland sloped slowly upward to the base of the mountains, which were raw, savage rock without vegetation. Except for the faces he found little of interest in the enormous market. At one end there was a tiny café with one table set outside under a cane trellis. He sat down and clapped his hands twice. "*Ouahad atai*," he called; that much Arabic he remembered. While he sipped the tea, which he noticed was made with dried mint leaves instead of fresh, he observed that the same ancient bus kept passing the café, sounding its horn insistently. He watched it as it went by. Filled with native passengers, it made the tour of the market again and again, the boy on the back platform pounding its resonant tin body rhythmically, and shouting: "*Arfâ! Arfâ! Arfâ! Arfâ!*" without stopping.

He sat there until lunchtime.

XII

The first thing Kit knew when she awoke was that she had a bad hangover. Then she noticed the bright sun shining into the room. What room? It was too much effort for her to think

back. Something moved at her side on the pillow. She rolled
her eyes to the left, and saw a shapeless dark mass beside her
head. She cried out and sprang up, but even as she did so she
knew it was only Tunner's black hair. In his sleep he stirred,
and stretched out his arm to embrace her. Her head pounding
painfully, she jumped out of bed and stood staring at him.
"My God!" she said aloud. With difficulty she aroused him,
made him get up and dress, forced him out into the hall with
all his luggage, and quickly locked the door after him. Then,
before he had thought of finding a boy to help him with the
bags, while he was still standing there stupidly, she opened the
door and made a whispered demand for a bottle of champagne. He got one out, passed it in to her, and she shut the
door again. She sat down on the bed and drank the whole
bottle. Her need for the drink was partly physical, but particularly she felt she could not face Port until she had engaged in
an inner dialogue from which she might emerge in some measure absolved for last night. She also hoped the champagne
would make her ill, so that she could have a legitimate reason
for staying in bed all day. It had quite the opposite effect: no
sooner had she finished it than her hangover was gone, and
she felt slightly tipsy, but very well. She went to the window
and looked out onto the glaring courtyard where two Arab
women were washing clothes in a large stone basin, spreading
them out over the bushes to dry in the sun. She turned
quickly and unpacked her overnight case, scattering the objects about the room. Then she began a careful search for any
trace of Tunner that might be left in the room. A black hair
on the pillow caused her heart to skip a beat; she dropped it
out the window. Meticulously she made the bed, spread the
woolen cover over it. Next she called the maid and asked her
to have the fathma come and wash the floor. That way, if Port
should arrive soon, it would look as though the maid had already finished the room. She dressed and went downstairs.
The fathma's heavy bracelets jangled as she scrubbed the tiles.

When he got back to the hotel Port knocked on the door
of the room opposite his. A male voice said: "*Entrez,*" and he
walked in. Tunner had partially undressed and was unpacking
his valises. He had not thought to unmake the bed, but Port
did not notice this.

"What the hell!" said Port. "Don't tell me they've given Kit the lousy back room I reserved for you."

"I guess they must have. But thanks anyway." Tunner laughed.

"You don't mind changing, do you?"

"Why? Is the other room so bad? No, I don't mind. It just seems like a lot of damned nonsense for just a day. No?"

"Maybe it'll be more than a day. Anyway, I'd like Kit to be here across from me."

"Of course. Of course. Better let her know too, though. She's probably in the other room there in all innocence, thinking it's the best in the hotel."

"It's not a bad room. It's just on the back, that's all. It was all they had yesterday when I reserved them."

"Righto. We'll get one of these monkeys to make the shift for us."

At lunch the three were reunited. Kit was nervous; she talked steadily, mainly about post-war European politics. The food was bad, so that none of them was in a very pleasant humor.

"Europe has destroyed the whole world," said Port. "Should I be thankful to it and sorry for it? I hope the whole place gets wiped off the map." He wanted to cut short the discussion, to get Kit aside and talk with her privately. Their long, rambling, supremely personal conversations always made him feel better. But she hoped particularly to avoid just such a *tête-à-tête*.

"Why don't you extend your good wishes to all humanity, while you're at it?" she demanded.

"Humanity?" cried Port. "What's that? Who is humanity? I'll tell you. Humanity is everyone but one's self. So of what interest can it possibly be to anybody?"

Tunner said slowly: "Wait a minute. Wait a minute. I'd like to take issue with you on that. I'd say humanity *is* you, and that's just what makes it interesting."

"Good, Tunner!" cried Kit.

Port was annoyed. "What rot!" he snapped. "You're never humanity; you're only your own poor hopelessly isolated self." Kit tried to interrupt. He raised his voice and went on. "I don't have to justify my existence by any such primitive means. The fact that I breathe is my justification. If humanity doesn't consider that a justification, it can do what it likes to me. I'm not going to carry a passport to existence around with me, to prove I have the right to be here! I'm here! I'm in the world! But my world's not humanity's world. It's the world as *I* see it."

"Don't yell," said Kit evenly. "If that's the way you feel, it's all right with me. But you ought to be bright enough to understand that not everybody feels the same way."

They got up. The Lyles smiled from their corner as the trio left the room.

Tunner announced: "I'm off for a siesta. No coffee for me. See you later."

When Port and Kit stood alone in the hall, he said to her: "Let's have coffee out in the little café by the market."

"Oh, please!" she protested. "After that leaden meal? I couldn't ever walk anywhere. I'm still exhausted from the trip."

"All right; up in my room?"

She hesitated. "For a few minutes. Yes, I'd love it." Her voice did not sound enthusiastic. "Then I'm going to have a nap, too."

Upstairs they both stretched out on the wide bed and waited for the boy to arrive with the coffee. The curtains were drawn, but the insistent light filtered through them, giving objects in the room a uniform, pleasant rose color. It was very quiet outside in the street; everything but the sun was having a siesta.

"What's new?" said Port.

"Nothing, except as I told you, I'm worn out from the train trip."

"You could have come with us in the car. It was a fine ride."

"No, I couldn't. Don't start that again. Oh, I saw Mr. Lyle this morning downstairs. I still think he's a monster. He insisted on showing me not only his own passport, but his mother's, too. Of course they were both crammed with stamps and visas. I told him you'd want to see them, that you liked that sort of thing more than I did. She was born in Melbourne in 1899 and he was born in 1925, I don't remember where. Both British passports. So there's all your information."

Port glanced sideways at her admiringly. "God, how did you get all that without letting him see you staring?"

"Just shuffling the pages quickly. And she's down as a journalist and he as a student. Isn't that ridiculous? I'm sure he never opened a book in his life."

"Oh, he's a halfwit," said Port absently, taking her hand and stroking it. "Are you sleepy, baby?"

"Yes, terribly, and I'm only going to take a tiny sip of coffee because I don't want to get waked up. I want to sleep."

"So do I, now that I'm lying down. If he doesn't come in a minute I'll go down and cancel the order."

But a knock came at the door. Before they had time to reply, it was flung open, and the boy advanced bearing a huge copper tray. "*Deux cafés,*" he said grinning.

"Look at that mug," said Port. "He thinks he's come in on a hot romance."

"Of course. Let the poor boy think it. He has to have some fun in life."

The Arab set the tray down discreetly by the window and tiptoed out of the room, looking back once over his shoulder at the bed, almost wistfully, it seemed to Kit. Port got up and brought the tray to the bed. As they had their coffee he turned to her suddenly.

"Listen!" he cried, his voice full of enthusiasm.

Looking at him, she thought: "How like an adolescent he is."

"Yes?" she said, feeling like a middle-aged mother.

"There's a place that rents bicycles near the market. When you wake up, let's hire a couple and go for a ride. It's fairly flat all around Boussif."

The idea appealed to her vaguely, although she could not imagine why.

"Perfect!" she said. "I'm sleepy. You can wake me at five, if you think of it."

XIII

They rode slowly out the long street toward the cleft in the low mountain ridge south of the town. Where the houses ended the plain began, on either side of them, a sea of stones. The air was cool, the dry sunset wind blew against them.

Port's bicycle squeaked slightly as he pedaled. They said nothing, Kit riding a little ahead. In the distance, behind them, a bugle was being blown; a firm, bright blade of sound in the air. Even now, when it would be setting in a half-hour or so, the sun burned. They came to a village, went through it. The dogs barked wildly and the women turned away, covering their mouths. Only the children remained as they were, looking, in a paralysis of surprise. Beyond the village, the road began to rise. They were aware of the grade only from their pedaling; to the eye it looked flat. Soon Kit was tired. They stopped, looked back across the seemingly level plain to Boussif, a pattern of brown blocks at the base of the mountains. The breeze blew harder.

"It's the freshest air you'll ever smell," said Port.

"It's wonderful," said Kit. She was in a dreamy, amiable state of mind, and she did not feel talkative.

"Shall we try and make the pass there?"

"In a minute. I just want to catch my breath."

Presently they started out again, pedaling determinedly, their eyes on the gap in the ridge ahead. As they approached it, already they could see the endless flat desert beyond, broken here and there by sharp crests of rock that rose above the surface like the dorsal fins of so many monstrous fish, all moving in the same direction. The road had been blasted through the top of the ridge, and the jagged boulders had slid down on both sides of the cut. They left the bicycles by the road and started to climb upward among the huge rocks, toward the top of the ridge. The sun was at the flat horizon; the air was suffused with redness. As they stepped around the side of a boulder they came all at once on a man, seated with his burnous pulled up about his neck—so that he was stark naked from the shoulders down—deeply immersed in the business of shaving his pubic hair with a long pointed knife. He glanced up at them with indifference as they passed before him, immediately lowering his head again to continue the careful operation.

Kit took Port's hand. They climbed in silence, happy to be together.

"Sunset is such a sad hour," she said, presently.

"If I watch the end of a day—any day—I always feel it's the end of a whole epoch. And the autumn! It might as well be the end of everything," he said. "That's why I hate cold countries, and love the warm ones, where there's no winter, and when night comes you feel an opening up of the life there, instead of a closing down. Don't you feel that?"

"Yes," said Kit, "but I'm not sure I prefer the warm countries. I don't know. I'm not sure I don't feel that it's wrong to try to escape the night and winter, and that if you do you'll have to pay for it somehow."

"Oh, Kit! You're really crazy." He helped her up the side of a low cliff. The desert was directly below them, much farther down than the plain from which they had just climbed.

She did not answer. It made her sad to realize that in spite of their so often having the same reactions, the same feelings, they never would reach the same conclusions, because their respective aims in life were almost diametrically opposed.

They sat down on the rocks side by side, facing the vastness below. She linked her arm through his and rested her head against his shoulder. He only stared straight before him, sighed, and finally shook his head slowly.

It was such places as this, such moments that he loved above all else in life; she knew that, and she also knew that he loved them more if she could be there to experience them with him. And although he was aware that the very silences and emptinesses that touched his soul terrified her, he could not bear to be reminded of that. It was as if always he held the fresh hope that she, too, would be touched in the same way as he by solitude and the proximity to infinite things. He had often told her: "It is your only hope," and she was never sure what he meant. Sometimes she thought he meant that it was *his* only hope, that only if she were able to become as he was, could he find his way back to love, since love for Port meant loving her—there was no question of anyone else. And now for so long there had been no love, no possibility of it. But in spite of her willingness to become whatever he wanted her to become, she could not change that much: the terror was always there inside her ready to take command. It was useless to pretend otherwise. And just as she was unable to shake off the dread that was always with her, he was unable to break out of the cage into which he had shut himself, the cage he had built long ago to save himself from love.

She pinched his arm. "Look there!" she whispered. Only a few paces from them, atop a rock, sitting so still that they had not noticed him, was a venerable Arab, his legs tucked under him, his eyes shut. At first it seemed as though he might be asleep, in spite of his erect posture, since he made no sign of being conscious of their presence. But then they saw his lips moving ever so little, and they knew he was praying.

"Do you think we should watch like this?" she said, her voice hushed.

"It's all right. We'll just sit here quietly." He put his head in her lap and lay looking up at the clear sky. Over and over, very lightly, she stroked his hair. The wind from the regions below gathered force. Slowly the sky lost its intensity of light. She glanced up at the Arab; he had not moved. Suddenly she wanted to go back, but she sat perfectly still for a while looking tenderly down at the inert head beneath her hand.

"You know," said Port, and his voice sounded unreal, as voices are likely to do after a long pause in an utterly silent spot, "the sky here's very strange. I often have the sensation when I look at it that it's a solid thing up there, protecting us from what's behind."

Kit shuddered slightly as she said: "From what's behind?"

"Yes."

"But what *is* behind?" Her voice was very small.

"Nothing, I suppose. Just darkness. Absolute night."

"*Please* don't talk about it now." There was agony in her entreaty. "Everything you say frightens me, up here. It's getting dark, and the wind is blowing, and I can't stand it."

He sat up, put his arms about her neck, kissed her, drew back and looked at her, kissed her again, drew back again, and so on, several times. There were tears on her cheeks. She smiled forlornly as he rubbed them away with his forefingers.

"You know what?" he said with great earnestness. "I think we're both afraid of the same thing. And for the same reason. We've never managed, either one of us, to get all the way into life. We're hanging on to the outside for all we're worth, convinced we're going to fall off at the next bump. Isn't that true?"

She shut her eyes for a moment. His lips on her cheek had awakened the sense of guilt, and it swept over her now in a great wave that made her dizzy and ill. She had spent her siesta trying to wipe her conscience clean of the things that had happened the night before, but now she was clearly aware that she had not been able to do it, and that she never would be able to do it. She put her hand to her forehead, holding it there. At length she said: "But if we're not in, then we *are* more likely to—fall off."

She had hoped he would offer some argument to this, that he would find his own analogy faulty, perhaps—that some consolation would be forthcoming. All he said was: "I don't know."

The light was growing palpably dimmer. Still the old Arab sat buried in his prayers, severe and statue-like in the advancing dusk. It seemed to Port that behind them, back on the plain, he could hear one long-drawn-out bugle note, but it went on and on. No man could hold his breath that long: it was his imagination. He took her hand and pressed it. "We must go back," he whispered. Quickly they rose and went leaping over the rocks down to the road. The bicycles were there where they had left them. They coasted silently back toward the town. The dogs in the village set up a clamor as they sped past. At the market place they left the bicycles, and walked slowly through the street that led to the hotel, head on into the parade of men and sheep that continued its steady advance into the town, even at night.

All the way back to town Kit had been turning an idea over and over in her head: "Somehow Port knows about Tunner and me." At the same time she did not believe he was conscious of knowing it. But with a deeper part of his intelligence she was certain he felt the truth, felt what had happened. As they walked along the dark street she was almost tempted to ask him how he knew. She was curious about the functioning of a purely animal sense like that, in a man as complex as Port. But it would have done no good; as soon as he had been made aware of his knowledge he would have decided to be furiously jealous, immediately there would have been a scene, and all the implicit tenderness between them would have vanished, perhaps never to be recovered. To have not even that tenuous communion with him would be unbearable.

Port did a curious thing when dinner was over. Alone he went out to the market, sat in the café for a few minutes watching the animals and men by the flickering carbide lamps, and on passing the open door of the shop where he had rented the bicycles, went in. There he asked for a bicycle equipped with a headlight, told the man to wait for him until he returned, and quickly rode off in the direction of the gap. Up there among the rocks it was cold, the night wind blew. There was no moon; he could not see the desert in front of him, down below—only the hard stars above that flared in the sky. He sat on the rock and let the wind chill him. Riding down to Boussif he realized he never could tell Kit that he had been back there. She would not understand his having wanted to return without her. Or perhaps, he reflected, she would understand it too well.

XIV

Two nights later they got on the bus for Aïn Krorfa, having chosen the night car to avoid the heat, which is oppressive along that route. Somehow, too, the dust seems less heavy when one cannot see it. Daytime, as the bus makes its way across this part of the desert, winding down and up through the small canyons, one watches the trail of dust that rises in the car's wake, sometimes breathing it in when the road doubles back on itself sharply. The fine powder piles up on every surface which is anywhere near to being horizontal, and this includes the wrinkles in the skin, the eyelids, the insides of the ears, and even, on occasions, hidden spots like the navel. And by day, unless the traveler is accustomed to such quantities of dust, he is supremely conscious of its presence, and is likely to magnify the discomfort it causes him. But at night, because the stars are bright in the clear sky, he has the impression, so long as he does not move, that there is no dust. The steady hum of the motor lulls him into a trance-like state in which his entire attention goes to watching the road move endlessly toward him as the headlights uncover it. That is, until he falls asleep, to be awakened later by the stopping of the bus at some dark, forsaken bordj, where he gets out chilled and stiff, to drink a glass of sweet coffee inside the gates.

Having reserved their places in advance, they had been able to get the most desirable seats in the bus, which were those in front with the driver. There was less dust here, and the heat from the motor, although excessive and a bit uncomfortable for the feet, was welcome by eleven o'clock, when the warmth of the day had totally disappeared and they became conscious of the dry, intense cold that always comes at night in this high region. And so all three of them were squeezed together with the driver, on the front seat. Tunner, who sat by the door, seemed to be asleep. Kit, with her head resting heavily against Port's arm, stirred a little now and then, but her eyes were closed. Straddling the emergency brake, and with his ribs continually being prodded by the driver's elbow as he steered, Port had by far the least comfortable spot, and consequently he was wide awake. He sat staring ahead through the windshield at the flat road that kept coming on, always toward him, and always being devoured by the headlights. Whenever he was en route from one place to another, he was able to look at his life with a little more objectivity than usual. It was often on trips that he thought most clearly, and made the decisions that he could not reach when he was stationary.

Since the day he and Kit had gone bicycling together he had felt a definite desire to strengthen the sentimental bonds between them. Slowly it was assuming an enormous importance to him. At times he said to himself that subconsciously he had had that in mind when he had conceived this expedition with Kit from New York into the unknown; it was only at the last minute that Tunner had been asked to come along, and perhaps that, too, had been subconsciously motivated, but out of fear; for much as he desired the rapprochement, he knew that also he dreaded the emotional responsibilities it would entail. But now, here in this distant and unconnected part of the world, the longing for closer ties with her was proving stronger than the fear. To forge such a bond required that they be alone together. The last two days at Boussif had been agonizing ones. It was almost as if Tunner had been aware of Port's desire and were determined to frustrate it. He had been present with them all day and half the night, ceaselessly talking, and apparently without a wish in the world save that of sitting with them, eating with them, taking walks with them, and even going with them to Kit's room at night, when of all times Port wanted to be alone with her, and standing for an hour or so in the doorway making pointless conversation. (It occurred to him, naturally, that Tunner might still have hopes of getting his way with her. The exaggerated attention he paid her, the banal flattery which was supposed to pass for gallantry, made him think this likely; but because Port ingenuously believed that his own feeling for Kit was identical in every respect with hers for him, he remained convinced that never under any circumstances would she yield to a person like Tunner.)

The only time he had succeeded in getting Kit out of the hotel alone had been while Tunner was still having his siesta, and then they had gone a scant hundred yards down the street and run into Eric Lyle, who straightway had announced that he would be delighted to accompany them on their walk. This he had done, to Port's silent fury, and Kit's visible disgust; indeed, Kit had been so annoyed by his presence that she had scarcely sat down at the café in the market when she had complained of a headache and rushed back to the hotel, leaving Port to cope with Eric. The objectionable youth was looking particularly pale and pimply in a flamboyant shirt decorated with giant tulips. He had bought the material, he said, in the Congo.

Once alone with Port, he had had the effrontery to ask him to lend him ten thousand francs, explaining that his mother was eccentric about money, and often flatly refused for weeks at a time to give him any.

"Not a chance. Sorry," Port had said, determining to be adamant. The sum had gradually been reduced, until at last he had remarked wistfully: "Even five hundred francs would keep me in smokes for a fortnight."

"I never lend anyone money," Port had explained with annoyance.

"But you will me." His voice was of honey.

"I will not."

"I'm not one of those stupid English who think all Americans have pots of money. It isn't that at all. But my mother's mad. She simply refuses to give me money. What am I to do?"

"Since he has no shame," thought Port, "I'll have no mercy." So he said: "The reason I won't lend you money is that I know I'll never get it back, and I haven't enough to give away. You see? But I'll give you three hundred francs. Gladly. I notice you smoke the *tabac du pays*. Fortunately it's very cheap."

In Oriental fashion Eric had bowed his head in agreement. Then he held forth his hand for the money. It made Port uncomfortable even now to recall the scene. When he had got back to the hotel he had found Kit and Tunner drinking beer together in the bar, and since then he had not had her to himself a minute, save the night before, when she had bidden him good night in the doorway. It did not make it easier for him, the fact that he suspected she was trying to keep from being alone with him.

"But there's plenty of time," he said to himself. "The only thing is, I must get rid of Tunner." He was pleased to have reached at last a definite decision. Perhaps Tunner would take a hint and leave of his own accord; if not, they would have to leave him. Either way, it must be done, and immediately, before they found a place they wanted to stay in long enough for Tunner to begin using it as a mail address.

He could hear the heavy valises sliding about on the top of the bus above his head; with conveyances no better than this he wondered if they had been wise to bring so much. However, it was too late now to do anything about it. There would be no place along the way where they could leave anything, because it was more than likely they would be coming back by some other route, if, indeed, they returned to the Mediterranean coast at all. For he had hopes of being able to continue southward; only, since no data on transportation and lodging facilities ahead of them were available, they would have to take their chances on what each place had to offer, hoping at best to gather some information each time about the next town, as they moved along. It was merely that the institution of tourist travel in this part of the world, never well developed in any case, had been, not interrupted, but utterly destroyed by the war. And so far there had been no tourists to start it up again. In a sense this state of affairs pleased him, it made him feel that he was pioneering—he felt more closely identified with his great-grandparents, when he was rolling along out here in the desert than he did sitting at home looking out over the reservoir in Central Park—but at the same time he wondered how seriously one ought to take the travel bulletins in their attempts to discourage such pioneering: "At present travelers are strongly advised not to undertake land trips into the interiors of French North Africa, French West Africa, or French Equatorial Africa. As more is learned on the subject of touristic conditions in this part of the world, such information will be made available to the public." He had not shown any such paragraphs to Kit while he was making his campaign speeches for Africa as against Europe. What he had shown her was a carefully chosen collection of photographs he had brought back from previous trips: views of oases and markets, as well as attractive vistas of the lobbies and gardens of hotels which no longer operated. So far she was being quite sensible—she had not objected once to the accommodations—but Mrs. Lyle's vivid warning worried him a little. It would not be amusing for very long to sleep in dirty beds, eat inedible meals, and wait an hour or so every time one wanted to wash one's hands.

The night went by slowly; yet to Port, watching the road was hypnotic rather than monotonous. If he had not been journeying into regions he did not know, he would have found it insufferable. The idea that at each successive moment he was deeper into the Sahara than he had been the moment before, that he was leaving behind all familiar things, this constant consideration kept him in a state of pleasurable agitation.

Kit moved from time to time, lifted her head, and murmuring something unintelligible, let it fall back against him. Once she shifted and allowed it to fall in the other direction, against Tunner who gave no sign of being awake. Firmly Port grasped her arm and pulled her around so that she leaned once more upon his shoulder. About once every hour he and the chauffeur had a cigarette together, but otherwise they engaged in no words. At one point, waving his hands toward the dark, the chauffeur said: "Last year they say they saw a lion around here. The first time in years. They say it ate a lot of sheep. It was probably a panther, though."

"Did they catch it?"

"No. They're all afraid of lions."

"I wonder what became of it."

The driver shrugged his shoulders and lapsed into the silence he obviously preferred. Port was pleased to hear the beast had not been killed.

Just before dawn, at the coldest time of the night, they came to a bordj, bleak and austere in the windswept plain. Its single gate was opened, and more asleep than awake, the three staggered in, following the crowd of natives from the back of the bus. The vast courtyard was packed with horses, sheep and men. Several fires blazed; the red sparks flew wildly in the wind.

On a bench near the entrance of the room where the coffee was served there were five falcons, each with a black leather mask over its head, and each fastened to a peg in the bench by a delicate chain attached to its leg. They all perched in a row, quite unmoving, as if they had been mounted and ranged there by a taxidermist. Tunner became quite excited about them and rushed around inquiring if the birds were for sale. His questions were answered by polite stares. Finally he returned to the table looking somewhat confused, and sat down saying: "No one seems to know who they belong to."

Port snorted. "You mean nobody understood anything you said. What the hell would you want with them anyway?"

Tunner reflected a second. Then he laughed and said: "I don't know. I liked them, that's all."

When they went out again, the first signs of light were pushing up from behind the plain. And now it was Port's turn to sit by the door. By the time the bordj had become only a tiny white box far behind them, he was asleep. In this way he missed the night's grand finale: the shifting colors that played on the sky from behind the earth before the rising of the sun.

XV

Even before before Aïn Krorfa was in sight, the flies had made their presence known. As the first straggling oases appeared and the road darted between the high mud walls of the outlying settlements, all at once the bus was mysteriously full of them—small, grayish and tenacious. Some of the Arabs remarked about them, and covered their heads; the rest seemed not to be conscious of them. The driver said: "*Ah, les salauds! On voit bien que nous sommes à Aïn Krorfa!*"

Kit and Tunner went into a frenzy of activity, waving their arms about, fanning their faces, and blowing sideways frantically to drive the insects off their cheeks and noses, all of which was next to useless. They clung with surprising determination, and had practically to be lifted off; at the last instant they would rise swiftly, and then descend almost simultaneously to the same spot.

"We're being attacked!" cried Kit.

Tunner set about fanning her with a piece of newspaper. Port was still asleep by the door; the corners of his mouth bristled with flies.

"They stick when it's cool," said the driver. "Early in the morning you can't get rid of them."

"But where do they come from?" demanded Kit.

The outraged tone of her voice made him laugh.

"This is nothing," he said, with a deprecatory wave of the hand. "You must see them in the town. Like black snow, over everything."

"When will there be a bus leaving?" she said.

"You mean back to Boussif? I go back tomorrow."

"No, no! I mean toward the south."

"Ah, that! You must ask in Aïn Krorfa. I know only about the Boussif service. I think they have a line that makes Bou Noura once a week, and you can always get a ride on a produce truck to Messad."

"Oh, I don't want to go there," said Kit. She had heard Port say Messad was of no interest.

"Well, I do," interrupted Tunner in English with some force. "Wait a week in a place like this? My God, I'd be dead!"

"Don't get excited. You haven't seen it yet. Maybe the driver's just having us on, as Mr. Lyle would say. Besides, it probably wouldn't be a week, the bus to Bou Noura. It might be leaving tomorrow. It could even be today, as far as that goes."

"No," Tunner said obstinately. "One thing I can't stand is filth."

"Yes, you're a real American, I know." She turned her head to look at him, and he felt she was making fun of him. His face grew red.

"You're damned right."

Port awoke. His first gesture was to drive away the flies from his face. He opened his eyes and stared out the window at the increasing vegetation. High palms shot up behind the walls; beneath them in a tangled mass were the oranges, figs and pomegranates. He opened the window and leaned out to sniff the air. It smelled of mint and woodsmoke. A wide river-bed lay ahead; there was even a meandering stream of water in the middle of it. And on each side of the road, and of all the roads that branched from it, were the deep seguias running with water that is the pride of Aïn Krorfa. He withdrew his head and said good morning to his companions. Mechanically he kept brushing away the insistent flies. It was not until several minutes later that he noticed Kit and Tunner doing the same thing. "What are all these flies?" he demanded.

Kit looked at Tunner and laughed. Port felt that they had a secret between them. "I was wondering how long it would be before you discovered them," she said.

Again they discussed the flies, Tunner calling upon the driver to attest to their number in Aïn Krorfa—this for Port's benefit, because he hoped to gain a recruit for his projected exodus to Messad—and Kit repeating that it would be only logical to examine the town before making any decisions. So far she found it the only visually attractive place she had seen since arriving in Africa.

This pleasant impression, however, was based wholly upon her appreciation of the verdure she could not help noticing behind the walls as the bus sped onward toward the town; the town itself, once they had arrived, seemed scarcely to exist. She was disappointed to see that it rather resembled Boussif, save that it appeared to be much smaller. What she could see of it was completely modern and geometrically laid out, and had it not been for the fact that the buildings were white instead of brown, and for the sidewalks bordering the principal street, which lay in the shadows of projecting arcades, she easily could have thought herself still in the other town. Her first

view of the Grand Hotel's interior quite unnerved her, but
Tunner was present and she felt impelled to sustain her position as one who had the right to twit him about his fastidiousness.

"Good heavens, what a mess!" she exclaimed; actually her
epithet fell far short of describing what she really felt about
the patio they had just entered. The simple Tunner was horrified. He merely looked, taking in each detail as it reached his
gaze. As for Port, he was too sleepy to see much of anything,
and he stood in the entrance, waving his arms around like a
windmill in an attempt to keep the flies away from his face.

Originally having been built to shelter an administrative office of the colonial government, the building since had fallen
on evil days. The fountain which at one time had risen from
the basin in the center of the patio was gone, but the basin remained. In it reposed a small mountain of reeking garbage,
and reclining on the sides of the mountain were three screaming, naked infants, their soft formless bodies troubled with
bursting sores. They looked human there in their helpless
misery, but somehow not quite so human as the two pink
dogs lying on the tiles nearby—pink because long ago they
had lost all their hair, and their raw, aged skin lay indecently
exposed to the kisses of the flies and sun. One of them feebly
raised its head an inch or so off the floor and looked at the
newcomers vacantly through its pale yellow eyes; the other
did not move. Behind the columns which formed an arcade at
one side were a few amorphous and useless pieces of furniture
piled on top of each other. A huge blue and white agateware
pitcher stood near the central basin. In spite of the quantity
of garbage in the patio, the predominating odor was of the
latrine. Above the crying of the babies there was the shrill
sound of women's voices in dispute, and the thick noise of a
radio boomed in the background. For a brief instant a woman
appeared in a doorway. Then she shrieked and immediately
disappeared again. In the interior there were screams and
giggles; one woman began to cry out: "Yah, Mohammed!"
Tunner swung about and went into the street, where he
joined the porters who had been told to wait outside with the
luggage. Port and Kit stood quietly until the man called
Mohammed appeared: he was wrapping a long scarlet sash

around and around his waist; the end still trailed along the floor. In the course of the conversation about rooms, he kept insisting that they take one room with three beds—it would be cheaper for them and less work for the maids.

"If I could only get out of here," Kit thought, "before Port arranges something with him!" But her sense of guilt expressed itself in allegiance; she could not go out into the street because Tunner was there and she would appear to be choosing sides. Suddenly she, too, wished Tunner were not with them. She would feel much freer in expressing her own preferences. As she had feared, Port went upstairs with the man, returning presently to announce that the rooms were not really bad at all.

They engaged three smelly rooms, all giving onto a small court whose walls were bright blue. In the center of the court was a dead fig tree with masses of barbed wire looped from its branches. As Kit peered from the window a hungry-looking cat with a tiny head and huge ears walked carefully across the court. She sat down on the great brass bed, which, besides the jackal skin on the floor by it, was the only furnishing in the room. She could scarcely blame Tunner for having refused at first even to look at the rooms. But as Port said, one always ends by getting used to anything, and although at the moment Tunner was inclined to be a little unpleasant about it, by night he would probably have grown accustomed to the whole gamut of incredible odors.

At lunch they sat in a bare, well-like room without windows, where the temptation was to whisper, since the spoken word was attended by distorting echoes. The only light came from the door into the main patio. Port clicked the switch of the overhead electric bulb: nothing happened. The barefoot waitress giggled. "No light," she said, setting their soup on the table.

"All right," said Tunner, "we'll eat in the patio."

The waitress rushed out of the room and returned with Mohammed, who frowned but set about helping them move the table and chairs out under the arcade.

"Thank heavens they're Arabs, and not French," said Kit. "Otherwise it would have been against the rules to eat out here."

"If they were French we could eat inside," said Tunner.

They lighted cigarettes in the hope of counteracting some of the stench that occasionally was wafted toward them from the basin. The babies were gone; their screams came from an inner room now.

Tunner stopped eating his soup and stared at it. Then he pushed his chair back and threw his napkin onto the table. "Well, by God in heaven, this may be the only hotel in town, but I can find better food than this in the market. Look at the soup! It's full of corpses."

Port examined his bowl. "They're weevils. They must have been in the noodles."

"Well, they're in the soup now. It's thick with 'em. You all can eat here at Carrion Towers if you like. I'm going to dig up a native restaurant."

"So long," said Port. Tunner went out.

He returned an hour later, less belligerent and slightly crestfallen. Port and Kit were still in the patio, sitting over coffee and waving away flies.

"How was it? Did you find anything?" they asked.

"The food? Damned good." He sat down. "But I can't get any information on how to get out of this place."

Port, whose opinion of his friend's mastery of the French language had never been high, said: "Oh." A few minutes later he got up and went out into the town to collect by himself whatever bits of knowledge he could relating to the transportation facilities of the region. The heat was oppressive, and he had not eaten well. In spite of these things he whistled as he walked along under the deserted arcades, because the idea of getting rid of Tunner made him unaccountably lively. Already he was noticing the flies less.

Late in the afternoon a large automobile drew up in front of the hotel entrance. It was the Lyles' Mercédès.

"Of all the utterly idiotic things to have done! To try to find some lost village no one ever heard of!" Mrs. Lyle was saying. "You nearly made me miss tea. I suppose you'd have thought that amusing. Now drive away these wretched brats and come in here. Mosh! Mosh!" she cried, suddenly charging at a group of native youngsters who had approached the car. "Mosh! *Imshi!*" She raised her handbag in a menacing gesture; the bewildered children slowly backed away from her.

"I must find the right term to get rid of them with here," said Eric, jumping out and slamming the door. "It's no use saying you'll get the police. They don't know what that is."

"What nonsense! Police indeed! Never threaten natives with the local authorities. Remember, we don't recognize French sovereignty here."

"Oh, that's in the Rif, Mother, and it's Spanish sovereignty."

"Eric! Will you be quiet? Don't you think I know what Madame Gautier told me? What do you *mean*?" She stopped as she saw the table under the arcade, still laden with the dirty dishes and glasses left by Port and Kit. "Hello! Someone else has arrived," she said in a tone that denoted the greatest interest. She turned accusingly to Eric. "And they've eaten outside! I told you we could have eaten outside, if you'd only insisted a bit. The tea's in your room. Will you bring it down? I must see about that putrid fire in the kitchen. And get out the sugar and open a new tin of biscuits."

As Eric returned through the patio with the box of tea, Port came in the door from the street.

"Mr. Moresby!" he cried. "What a pleasant surprise!"

Port tried to keep his face from falling. "Hello," he said. "What are you doing here? I thought I'd recognized your car outside."

"Just one second. I've got to deliver this tea to Mother. She's in the kitchen waiting for it." He rushed through the side door, stepping on one of the obscene dogs that lay exhausted just inside in the dark. It yelped lengthily. Port hurried upstairs to Kit and imparted the latest bad news to her. A minute later Eric pounded on the door. "I say, do have tea with us in ten minutes in room eleven. How nice to see you, Mrs. Moresby."

Room eleven was Mrs. Lyle's, longer but no less bare than the others, and directly over the entrance. While she drank her tea, she kept rising from the bed where everyone was sitting for lack of chairs, going to the window and crying "Mosh! Mosh!" into the street.

Presently Port could no longer contain his curiosity. "What is that strange word you're calling out the window, Mrs. Lyle?"

"I'm driving those thieving little niggers away from my car."

"But what are you saying to them? Is it Arabic?"

"It's French," she said, "and it means get out."

"I see. Do they understand it?"

"They'd jolly well better. More tea, Mrs. Moresby!"

Tunner had begged off, having heard enough about the Lyles from Kit's description of Eric. According to Mrs. Lyle, Aïn Krorfa was a charming town, especially the camel market, where there was a baby camel they must photograph. She had taken several shots of it that morning. "It's too sweet," she said. Eric sat devouring Port with his eyes. "He wants more money," Port thought. Kit noticed his extraordinary expression, too, but she put a different interpretation on it.

When tea was over, and they were taking their leave, since they seemed to have exhausted all the possible subjects for conversation, Eric turned to Port. "If I don't see you at dinner, I'll drop in on you tonight afterward. What time do you go to bed?"

Port was vague. "Oh, any time, more or less. We'll probably be out fairly late looking around the town."

"Righto," said Eric, patting his shoulder affectionately as he shut the door.

When they got back to Kit's room she stood gazing out the window at the skeletal fig tree. "I wish we'd gone to Italy," she said. Port looked up quickly. "Why do you say that? Is it because of them, because of the hotel?"

"Because of everything." She turned toward him, smiling. "But I don't really mean it. This is just the right hour to go out. Let's."

Aïn Krorfa was beginning to awaken from its daily sun-drugged stupor. Behind the fort, which stood near the mosque on a high rocky hill that rose in the very middle of the town, the streets became informal, there were vestiges of the original haphazard design of the native quarter. In the stalls, whose angry lamps had already begun to gutter and flare, in the open cafés where the hashish smoke hung in the air, even in the dust of the hidden palm-bordered lanes, men squatted, fanning little fires, bringing their tin vessels of water to a boil, making their tea, drinking it.

"Teatime! They're really Englishmen dressed for a masquerade," said Kit. She and Port walked very slowly, hand in hand, perfectly in tune with the soft twilight. It was an evening that suggested languor rather than mystery.

They came to the river, here merely a flat expanse of white sand stretching away in the half light, and followed it a while until the sounds of the town became faint and high in the distance. Out here the dogs barked behind the walls, but the walls themselves were far from the river. Ahead of them a fire burned; seated by it was a solitary man playing a flute, and beyond him in the shifting shadows cast by the flames, a dozen or so camels rested, chewing solemnly on their cuds. The man looked toward them as they passed, but continued his music.

"Do you think you can be happy here?" asked Port in a hushed voice.

Kit was startled. "Happy? Happy? How do you mean?"

"Do you think you'll like it?"

"Oh, I don't know!" she said, with an edge of annoyance in her voice. "How can I tell? It's impossible to get into their lives, and know what they're really thinking."

"I didn't ask you that," Port remarked, nettled.

"You should have. That's what's important here."

"Not at all," he said. "Not for me. I feel that this town, this river, this sky, all belong to me as much as to them."

She felt like saying: "Well, you're crazy," but she confined herself to: "How strange."

They circled back toward the town, taking a road that led between garden walls.

"I wish you wouldn't ask me such questions," she said suddenly. "I can't answer them. How could I say: yes, I'm going to be happy in Africa? I like Aïn Krorfa very much, but I can't tell whether I want to stay a month or leave tomorrow."

"You couldn't leave tomorrow, for that matter, even if you did want to, unless you went back to Boussif. I found out about the buses. It's four days before the one for Bou Noura leaves. And it's forbidden to get rides on trucks to Messad now. They have soldiers who check along the way. There's a heavy fine for the drivers."

"So we're stuck in the Grand Hotel."

"*With* Tunner," thought Port. Aloud: "*With* the Lyles."

"God forbid," Kit murmured.

"I wonder how long we've got to keep on running into them. I wish to hell they'd either get ahead of us once and for all, or let us get ahead of them and stay there."

"Things like that have to be arranged," said Kit. She, too, was thinking of Tunner. It seemed to her that if presently she were not going to have to sit opposite him over a meal, she could relax completely now, and live in the moment, which was Port's moment. But it seemed useless even to try, if in an hour she was going to be faced with the living proof of her guilt.

It was completely dark when they got back to the hotel. They ate fairly late, and after dinner, since no one felt like going out, they went to bed. This process took longer than usual because there was only one wash basin and water pitcher—on the roof at the end of the corridor. The town was very quiet. Some café radio was playing a transcription of a record by Abd-el-Wahab: a dirge-like popular song called: *I Am Weeping Upon Your Grave*. Port listened to the melancholy notes as he washed; they were broken into by nearby outbursts of dogs barking.

He was already in bed when Eric tapped on his door. Unfortunately he had not turned off his light, and for fear that it showed under the door he did not dare pretend to be asleep. The fact that Eric tiptoed into the room, a conspiratorial look on his face, displeased him. He pulled his bathrobe on.

"What's the matter?" he demanded. "Nobody's asleep."

"I hope I'm not disturbing you, old man." As always, he appeared to be talking to the corners of the room.

"No, no. But it's lucky you came when you did. Another minute and my light would have been out."

"Is your wife asleep?"

"I believe she's reading. She usually does before she goes to sleep. Why?"

"I wondered if I might have that novel she promised me this afternoon."

"When, now?" He passed Eric a cigarette and lit one himself.

"Oh, not if it will disturb her."

"Tomorrow would be better, don't you think?" said Port, looking at him.

"Right you are. What I actually came about was that money—" He hesitated.

"Which?"

"The three hundred francs you lent me. I want to give them back to you."

"Oh, that's quite all right." Port laughed, still looking at him. Neither one spoke for a moment.

"Well, of course, if you like," Port said finally, wondering if by any unlikely chance he had misjudged the youth, and somehow feeling more convinced than ever that he had not.

"Ah, excellent," murmured Eric, fumbling about in his coat pocket. "I don't like to have these things on my conscience."

"You didn't need to have it on your conscience, because if you'll remember, I gave it to you. But if you'd rather return it, as I say, naturally, that's fine with me."

Eric had finally extracted a worn thousand-franc note, and held it forth with a faint, propitiatory smile. "I hope you have change for this," he said, finally looking into Port's face, but as though it were costing him a great effort. Port sensed that this was the important moment, but he had no idea why. "I don't know," he said, not taking the proffered bill. "Do you want me to look?"

"If you could." His voice was very low. As Port clumsily got out of bed and went to the valise where he kept his money and documents, Eric seemed to take courage.

"I do feel like a rotter, coming here in the middle of the night and bothering you this way, but first of all I want to get this off my mind, and besides, I need the change badly, and they don't seem to have any here in the hotel, and Mother and I are leaving first thing in the morning for Messad and I was afraid I might not see you again—"

"You are? Messad?" Port turned, his wallet in his hand. "Really? Good Lord! And our friend Mr. Tunner wants so much to go!"

"Oh?" Eric stood up slowly. "Oh?" he said again. "I daresay we could take him along." He looked at Port's face and saw it brighten. "But we're leaving at daybreak. You'd better go immediately and tell him to be ready downstairs at six-thirty. We've ordered tea for six o'clock. You'd better have him do likewise."

"I'll do that," said Port, slipping his wallet into his pocket. "I'll also ask him for the change, which I don't seem to have."

"Good. Good," Eric said with a smile, sitting down again on the bed.

Port found Tunner naked, wandering distractedly around his room with a DDT bomb in his hand. "Come in," he said. "This stuff is no good."

"What have you got?"

"Bedbugs, for one thing."

"Listen. Do you want to go to Messad tomorrow morning at six-thirty?"

"I want to go tonight at *eleven*-thirty. Why?"

"The Lyles will drive you."

"And then what?"

Port improvised. "They'll be coming back here in a few days and going straight on to Bou Noura. They'll take you down and we'll be there expecting you. Lyle's in my room now. Do you want to talk with him?"

"No."

There was a silence. The electric light suddenly went off, then came on, a feeble orange worm inside the bulb, so that the room looked as if it were being viewed through heavy black glasses. Tunner glanced at his disordered bed and shrugged. "What time did you say?"

"Six-thirty they're going."

"Tell him I'll be down at the door." He frowned at Port, a faint suspicion in his face. "And you. Why aren't you going?"

"They'll only take one," he lied, "and besides, I like it here."

"You won't once you've gotten into your bed," said Tunner bitterly.

"You'll probably have them in Messad too," Port suggested. He felt safe now.

"I'll take my chances on any hotel after this one."

"We'll look for you in a few days in Bou Noura. Don't crash any harems."

He shut the door behind him and went back to his room. Eric was still sitting in the same position on the bed, but he had lighted another cigarette.

"Mr. Tunner is delighted, and'll meet you at six-thirty down at the door. Oh, damn! I forgot to ask him about the change for your thousand francs." He hesitated, about to go back out.

"Don't bother, please. He can change it for me tomorrow on the way, in case I need it changed."

Port opened his mouth to say: "But I thought you wanted to pay me back the three hundred." He thought better of it. Now that the thing was settled, it would be tragic to risk a slip-up, just for a few francs. So he smiled and said: "Surely. Well, I hope we'll see you when you come back."

"Yes, indeed," smiled Eric, looking at the floor. He got up suddenly and went to the door. "Good night."

"Good night."

Port locked the door after him and stood by it, musing. Eric's behavior had impressed him as being unusually eccentric, yet he still suspected that it was explainable. Being sleepy, he turned off what remained of the light and got into bed. The dogs barked in chorus, far and nearby, but he was not molested by vermin.

That night he awoke sobbing. His being was a well a thousand miles deep; he rose from the lower regions with a sense of infinite sadness and repose, but with no memory of any dream save the faceless voice that had whispered: "The soul is the weariest part of the body." The night was silent, save for a small wind that blew through the fig tree and moved the loops of wire hanging there. Back and forth they rubbed, creaking ever so slightly. After he had listened a while, he fell asleep.

XVI

Kit sat up in bed, her breakfast tray on her knees. The room was lighted by the reflection of the sun on the blue wall outside. Port had brought her her breakfast, having decided after observing their behavior that the servants were incapable of carrying out any orders whatever. She had eaten, and now was thinking of what he had told her (with ill-concealed relish) about having got rid of Tunner. Because she, too, had secretly wished him gone, it seemed to her a doubly ignoble thing to have done. But why? He had gone of his own free will. Then she realized that intuitively she already was aware of Port's next move: he would contrive to miss connections with Tunner at Bou Noura. She could tell by his behavior, in spite of whatever he said, that he had no intention of meeting him there. That was why it seemed unkind. The deceit of the maneuver, if she were correct, was too bald; she determined not to be a party to it. "Even if Port runs out on him, I'll stay and meet him." She reached over and set the tray on the jackal skin; badly cured, the pelt gave off a sour odor. "Or am I only trying to go on punishing myself by seeing Tunner in front of me every day?" she wondered. "Would it be better really to get rid of him?" If only it were possible to dig behind the coming weeks and know! The clouds above the mountains had been a bad sign, but not in the way she had imagined. Instead of the wreck there had been another experience which perhaps would prove more disastrous in its results. As usual she was being saved up for something worse than she expected. But she did not believe it was to be Tunner, so that it really was not important how she behaved now with regard to him. The other omens indicated a horror more vast, and surely ineluctable. Each escape merely made it possible for her to advance into a region of heightened danger. "In that case," she thought, "why not give in? And if I should give in, how would I behave? Exactly the same as now." So that giving in or not giving in had nothing to do with her problem. She was pushing against her own existence. All she could hope to do was eat, sleep and cringe before her omens.

She spent most of the day in bed reading, getting dressed only to have lunch with Port down in the stinking patio under the arcade. Immediately on returning to her room she pulled her clothes off. The room had not been made up. She straightened the bedsheet and lay down again. The air was dry, hot, breathless. During the morning Port had been out in the town. She wondered how he could support the sun, even with his helmet; it made her ill to be in it even for five minutes. His was not a rugged body, yet he had wandered for hours in the oven-like streets and returned to eat heartily of the execrable food. And he had unearthed some Arab who expected them both to tea at six. He had impressed it upon her that on no account must they be late. It was typical of him to insist upon punctuality in the case of an anonymous shopkeeper in Aïn Krorfa, when with his friends and with her he behaved in a most cavalier fashion, arriving at his appointments indifferently anywhere from a half-hour to two hours after the specified time.

The Arab's name was Abdeslam ben Hadj Chaoui; they called for him at his leather shop and waited for him to close and lock the front of it. He led them slowly through the twisting streets as the muezzin called, talking all the while in flowery French, and addressing himself principally to Kit.

"How happy I am! This is the first time I have the honor to invite a lady, and a gentleman, from New York. How I should like to go and see New York! What riches! Gold and silver everywhere! *Le grand luxe pour tout le monde,* ah! Not like Aïn Krorfa—sand in the streets, a few palms, hot sun, sadness always. It is a great pleasure for me to be able to invite a lady from New York. And a gentleman. New York! What a beautiful word!" They let him talk on.

The garden, like all the gardens in Aïn Krorfa, was really an orchard. Under the orange trees were small channels running with water fed from the well, which was built up on an artificial plateau at one end. The highest palms stood at the opposite end, near the wall that bordered the river-bed, and underneath one of these a great red and white wool rug was spread out. There they sat while a servant brought fire and the apparatus for making tea. The air was heavy with the odor of the spearmint that grew beside the water channels.

"We shall talk a little, while the water boils," said their host, smiling beneficently from one to the other. "We plant the male palm here because it is more beautiful. In Bou Noura they think only of money. They plant the female. You know how *they* look? They are short and fat, they give many dates, but the dates are not even good, not in Bou Noura!" He laughed with quiet satisfaction. "Now you see how stupid the people are in Bou Noura!"

The wind blew and the palm trunks slowly moved with it, their lofty tops swaying slightly in a circular motion. A young man in a yellow turban approached, greeted them gravely, and seated himself a little in the background, at the edge of the rug. From under his burnous he brought forth an oud, whose strings he began to pluck casually, looking off under the trees all the while. Kit drank her tea in silence, smiling from time to time at M. Chaoui's remarks. At one point she asked Port in English for a cigarette, but he frowned, and she understood that it would shock the others to see a lady smoke. And so she sat drinking the tea, feeling that what she saw and heard around her was not really happening, or if it were, she was not really there herself. The light was fading; little by little the pots of coals became the eyes' natural focusing point. Still the lute music went on, a patterned background for the aimless talk; listening to its notes was like watching the smoke of a cigarette curl and fold in untroubled air. She had no desire to move, speak, or even think. But suddenly she was cold. She interrupted the conversation to say so. M. Chaoui was not pleased to hear it; he considered it a piece of incredible rudeness. He smiled, and said: "Ah, yes. Madame is blonde. The blondes are like the seguia when it has no water in it. The Arabs are like the seguias of Aïn Krorfa. The seguias of Aïn Krorfa are always full. We have flowers, fruit, trees."

"Yet you say Aïn Krorfa is sad," said Port.

"Sad?" repeated M. Chaoui with astonishment. "Aïn Krorfa is never sad. It is peaceful and full of joy. If one offered me twenty million francs and a palace, I would not leave my native land."

"Of course," Port agreed, and seeing that his host no longer desired to sustain the conversation, he said: "Since Madame is cold, we must go, but we thank you a thousand times. It has been a great privilege for us to be allowed to come to this exquisite garden."

M. Chaoui did not rise. He nodded his head, extended his hand, said: "Yes, yes. Go, since it is cold."

Both guests offered florid apologies for their departure: it could not be said that they were accepted with very good grace. "Yes, yes, yes," said M. Chaoui. "Another time perhaps it will be warmer."

Port restrained his mounting anger, which, even as he was feeling it, made him annoyed with himself.

"*Au 'voir, cher monsieur,*" Kit suddenly said in a childish treble. Port pinched her arm. M. Chaoui had noticed nothing extraordinary; indeed, he unbent sufficiently to smile once more. The musician, still strumming on his lute, accompanied them to the gate, and solemnly said: "*B'slemah*" as he closed it after them.

The road was almost dark. They began to walk quickly.

"I hope you're not going to blame me for that," began Kit defensively.

Port slipped his arm around her waist. "Blame you! Why? How could I? And what difference does it make, anyway?"

"Of course it makes a difference," she said. "If it doesn't, what was the point of seeing the man in the first place?"

"Oh, *point!* I don't suppose there was any particular point. I thought it would be fun. And I still think it was; I'm glad we went."

"So am I, in a way. It gave me a first-hand opportunity of seeing what the conversations are going to be like here—just how unbelievably superficial they can be."

He let go of her waist. "I disagree. You don't say a frieze is superficial just because it has only two dimensions."

"You do if you're accustomed to having conversation that's something more than decoration. I don't think of conversation as a frieze, myself."

"Oh, nonsense! It's just another way of living they have, a completely different philosophy."

"I know that," she said, stopping to shake sand from her shoe. "I'm just saying I could never live with it."

He sighed: the tea-party had accomplished exactly the contrary to what he had hoped it might. She sensed what was in his mind, and presently she said: "Don't think about me. Whatever happens, I'll be all right if I'm with you. I enjoyed it tonight. Really." She pressed his hand. But this was not quite what he wanted; resignation was not enough. He returned her pressure halfheartedly.

"And what was that little performance of yours at the end?"
he asked a moment later.

"I couldn't help it. He was being so ridiculous."

"It's not a good idea generally to make fun of your host,"
he said coldly.

"Oh, bah! If you noticed, he loved it. He thought I was
being deferential."

They ate quietly in the nearly-dark patio. Most of the
garbage had been cleared away, but the stench of the latrines
was as strong as ever. After dinner they went to their rooms
and read.

The next morning, when he took breakfast to her, he said:
"I nearly paid you a visit last night. I couldn't seem to sleep.
But I was afraid of waking you."

"You should have rapped on the wall," she said. "I'd have
heard you. I was probably awake."

All that day he was unaccountably nervous; he attributed it
to the seven glasses of strong tea he had drunk in the garden.
Kit, however, had drunk as much as he, and she seemed not
in the least nervous. In the afternoon he walked by the river,
watched the Spahis training on their perfect white horses,
their blue capes flying behind in the wind. Since his agitation
appeared to be growing rather than diminishing with the passage of time, he set himself the task of tracing it to its source.
He walked along with his head bent over, seeing nothing but
the sand and glistening pebbles. Tunner was gone, Kit and he
were alone. Everything now depended on him. He could
make the right gesture, or the wrong one, but he could not
know beforehand which was which. Experience had taught
him that reason could not be counted on in such situations.
There was always an extra element, mysterious and not quite
within reach, that one had not reckoned with. One had to
know, not deduce. And he did not have the knowledge. He
glanced up; the river-bed had become enormously wide, the
walls and gardens had receded into the distance. Out here
there was no sound but the wind blowing around his head on
its way from one part of the earth to another. Whenever the
thread of his consciousness had unwound too far and got tangled, a little solitude could wind it quickly back. His state of
nervousness was remediable in that it had to do only with

himself: he was afraid of his own ignorance. If he desired to cease being nervous he must conceive a situation for himself in which that ignorance had no importance. He must behave as if there was no question of his having Kit, ever again. Then, perhaps, out of sheer inattention, automatically, it could happen. But should his principal concern at the moment be the purely egocentric one of ridding himself of his agitation, or the accomplishment of his original purpose in spite of it? "I wonder if after all I'm a coward?" he thought. Fear spoke; he listened and let it persuade—the classical procedure. The idea saddened him.

Not far away, on a slight elevation at a point where the river's course turned sharply, was a small ruined building, without a roof, so old that a twisted tree had grown up inside it, covering the area within the walls with its shade. As he passed nearer to it and could see inside, he realized that the lower branches were hung with hundreds of rags, regularly torn strips of cloth that had once been white, all moving in the same direction with the wind. Faintly curious, he climbed the bank and went to investigate, but on approaching he saw that the ruin was occupied: an old, old man sat beneath the tree, his thin brown arms and legs bound with ancient bandages. Around the base of the trunk he had built a shelter; it was clear to see that he lived there. Port stood looking at him a long time, but he did not lift his head.

Going more slowly, he continued. He had brought with him some figs, which he now pulled out and devoured. When he had followed the river's complete turning, he found himself facing the sun in the west, looking up a small valley that lay between two gently graded, bare hills. At the end was a steeper hill, reddish in color, and in the side of the hill was a dark aperture. He liked caves, and was tempted to set out for it. But distances here were deceptive, and there might not be time before dark; besides, he did not feel the necessary energy inside him. "Tomorrow I'll come earlier and go up," he said to himself. He stood looking up the valley a little wistfully, his tongue seeking the fig seeds between his teeth, with the small tenacious flies forever returning to crawl along his face. And it occurred to him that a walk through the countryside was a sort of epitome of the passage through life itself. One never took the time to savor the details; one said: another day, but always with the hidden knowledge that each day was unique and final, that there never would be a return, another time.

Under his sun helmet his head was perspiring. He removed the helmet with its wet leather band, and let the sun dry his hair for a moment. Soon the day would be finished, it would be dark, he would be back at the foul-smelling hotel with Kit, but first he must decide what course to take. He turned and walked back toward the town. When he came opposite the ruin, he peered inside. The old man had moved; he was seated just inside what had once been the doorway. The sudden thought struck him that the man must have a disease. He hastened his step and, absurdly enough, held his breath until he was well past the spot. As he allowed the fresh wind to enter his lungs again, he knew what he would do: he would temporarily abandon the idea of getting back together with Kit. In his present state of disquiet he would be certain to take all the wrong turnings, and would perhaps lose her for good. Later, when he least expected it, the thing might come to pass of its own accord. The rest of his walking was done at a brisk pace, and by the time he was back in the streets of Aïn Krorfa he was whistling.

They were having dinner. A traveling salesman eating inside in the dining room had brought a portable radio with him and was tuned in to Radio Oran. In the kitchen a louder radio was playing Egyptian music.

"You can put up with this sort of thing for just so long. Then you go crazy," said Kit. She had found patches of fur in her rabbit stew, and unfortunately the light in that part of the patio was so dim that she had not made the discovery until after she had put the food into her mouth.

"I know," said Port absently. "I hate it as much as you."

"No, you don't. But I think you would if you didn't have me along to do your suffering for you."

"How can you say that? You know it's not so." He toyed with her hand: having made his decision he felt at ease with her. She, however, seemed unexpectedly irritable.

"Another town like this will fix me up fine," she said. "I shall simply go back and take the first boat out for Genoa or

Marseille. This hotel's a nightmare, a *nightmare!*" After Tunner's departure she had vaguely expected a change in their relationship. The only difference his absence made was that
now she could express herself clearly, without fear of seeming
to be choosing sides. But rather than make any effort to ease
whatever small tension might arise between them, she determined on the contrary to be intransigent about everything. It
could come about now or later, that much-awaited reunion,
but it must be all his doing. Because neither she nor Port had
ever lived a life of any kind of regularity, they both had made
the fatal error of coming hazily to regard time as non-
existent. One year was like another year. Eventually everything would happen.

XVII

The following night, which was the eve of their departure for
Bou Noura, they had dinner early, and Kit went up to her
room to pack. Port sat on at their dark table under the arcades, until the other diners inside had finished. He went into
the empty dining room and wandered about aimlessly, looking at the proud proofs of civilization: the varnished tables
covered with sheets of paper instead of tablecloths, the heavy
glass salt shakers, and the opened bottles of wine with the
identifying napkins tied around their necks. One of the pink
dogs came crawling into the room from the kitchen, and seeing him, continued to the patio, where it lay down and sighed
deeply. He walked through the door into the kitchen. In the
center of the room, under the one weak light bulb, stood
Mohammed holding a large butcher's knife with its point
sticking in the table. Under the point was a cockroach, its legs
still feebly waving. Mohammed regarded the insect studiously.
He looked up and grinned.
"Finished?" he asked.
"What?" said Port.
"Finished with dinner?"
"Oh, yes."
"Then I'll lock the dining room." He went and moved
Port's table back into the room, turned off the lights and

locked both doors. Then he put out the light in the kitchen. Port moved into the patio. "Going home to sleep?" he inquired.

Mohammed laughed. "Why do you think I work all day? Just to go home to sleep? Come with me. I'll show you the best place in Aïn Krorfa."

Port walked with him out into the street, where they conversed for a few minutes. Then they moved off down the street together.

The house was several houses, all with a common entrance through a large tiled courtyard. And each house had several rooms, all very small, and, with the exception of those on the ground floor, all at varying levels. As he stood in the courtyard in the faint light that was a blend of carbide-lamp glare and starlight, all the bright little boxlike interiors looked like so many ovens around him. Most of them had their door or windows open, and were filled to bursting with men and girls, both sexes uniformly dressed in flowing white garments. It looked festive, and it exhilarated him to see it; certainly he had no feeling that it was a vicious place, even though at first he tried hard to see it as such.

They went to the door of a room opposite the entrance, and Mohammed peered in, saluting certain of the men sitting inside on the couches along the walls. He entered, motioning to Port to follow him. Room was made for them, and they sat down with the others. A boy took their order for tea and quickly ran out of the room across the court. Mohammed was soon engaged in conversation with a man sitting nearby. Port leaned back and watched the girls as they drank tea and chatted with the men, sitting opposite them on the floor; he was waiting for a licentious gesture, at least a hint of a leer. None was forthcoming.

For some reason which he was unable to fathom, there were a good many small children running about the establishment. They were well behaved and quiet as they played in the gloomy courtyard, exactly as if it had belonged to a school instead of a brothel. Some of them wandered inside the rooms, where the men took them on their laps and treated them with the greatest affection, patting their cheeks and allowing them occasional puffs on their cigarettes. Their

collective disposition toward contentment might easily be
due, he thought, to the casual benevolence of their elders. If
one of the younger ones began to shed tears, the men
laughed and waved it away; it soon stopped.

A fat black police dog waddled in and out of the rooms,
sniffing shoes; it was the object of everyone's admiration.
"The most beautiful dog in Aïn Krorfa," said Mohammed as
it appeared panting in the doorway near them. "It belongs to
Colonel Lefilleul; he must be here tonight."

When the boy returned with the tea he was accompanied
by another, not more than ten years old, but with an ancient,
soft face. Port pointed him out to Mohammed and whispered
that he looked ill.

"Oh, no! He's a singer." He signaled to the child, who began to clap his hands in syncopated rhythm and utter a long
repetitious lament built on three notes. To Port it seemed utterly incongruous and a little scandalous, hearing this recent
addition to humanity produce a music so unchildlike and
weary. While he was still singing, two girls came over and
greeted Mohammed. Without any formalities he made them
sit down and pour the tea. One was thin with a salient nose,
and the other, somewhat younger, had the apple-like cheeks
of a peasant; both bore blue tattoo marks on the foreheads
and chins. Like all the women, their heavy robes were
weighted down with an assortment of even heavier silver jewelry. For no particular reason neither one appealed to Port's
fancy. There was something vaguely workaday about both of
them; they were very much present. He could appreciate now
what a find Marhnia had been, her treachery notwithstanding.
He had not seen anyone here with half her beauty or style.
When the child stopped singing Mohammed gave him some
coins; he looked at Port expectantly as well, but Mohammed
shouted at him, and he ran out. There was music in the next
room: the sharp reedy rhaïta and the dry drums beneath.
Since the two girls bored him, Port excused himself and went
into the courtyard to listen.

In front of the musicians in the middle of the floor a girl
was dancing, if indeed the motions she made could properly
be called a dance. She held a cane in her two hands, behind
her head, and her movements were confined to her agile

neck and shoulders. The motions, graceful and of an impu-
dence verging on the comic, were a perfect translation into
visual terms of the strident and wily sounds of the music.
What moved him, however, was not the dance itself so much
as the strangely detached, somnambulistic expression of the
girl. Her smile was fixed, and, one might have added, her
mind as well, as if upon some object so remote that only she
knew of its existence. There was a supremely impersonal disdain in the unseeing eyes and the curve of the placid lips.
The longer he watched, the more fascinating the face became; it was a mask of perfect proportions, whose beauty ac-
crued less from the configuration of features than from the
meaning that was implicit in their expression—meaning, or
the withholding of it. For what emotion lay behind the face
it was impossible to tell. It was as if she were saying: "A
dance is being done. I do not dance because I am not here.
But it is my dance." When the piece drew to its conclusion
and the music had stopped, she stood still for a moment,
then slowly lowered the cane from behind her head, and tapping vaguely on the floor a few times, turned and spoke to
one of the musicians. Her remarkable expression had not
changed in any respect. The musician rose and made room
for her on the floor beside him. The way he helped her to sit
down struck Port as peculiar, and all at once the realization
came to him that the girl was blind. The knowledge hit him
like an electric shock; he felt his heart leap ahead and his
head grow suddenly hot.

Quickly he went back into the other room and told Mohammed he must speak with him alone. He hoped to get him
into the courtyard so as not to be obliged to go through his
explanation in front of the girls, even though they spoke no
French. But Mohammed was disinclined to move. "Sit down,
my dear friend," he said, pulling at Port's sleeve. Port, however, was far too concerned lest his prey escape him to bother
being civil. "*Non, non, non!*" he cried. "*Viens vite!*" Mohammed shrugged his shoulders in deference to the two girls,
rose and accompanied him into the courtyard, where they
stood by the wall under the light. Port asked him first if the
dancing girls were available, and felt his spirits fall when Mohammed told him that many of them had lovers, and that in

such cases they merely lived in the house as registered prostitutes, using it only as a home, and without engaging in the profession at all. Naturally those with lovers were given a wide berth by everyone else. "*Bsif! Forcément!* Throats are sliced for that," he laughed, his brilliant red gums gleaming like a dentist's model in wax. This was an angle Port had not considered. Still, the case merited a determined effort. He drew Mohammed over near the door of the adjacent cubicle, in which she sat, and pointed her out to him.

"Find out for me about that one there," he said. "Do you know her?"

Mohammed looked. "No," he said at length. "I will find out. If it can be arranged, I myself will arrange it and you pay me a thousand francs. That will be for her, and enough for me to buy coffee and breakfast."

The price was too high for Aïn Krorfa, and Port knew it. But this seemed to him a poor time to begin bargaining, and he accepted the arrangement, going back, as Mohammed bade him do, into the first room and sitting down again with the two dull girls. They were now engaged in a very serious conversation with each other, and scarcely noticed his arrival. The room buzzed with talk and laughter; he sat back and listened to the sound of it; even though he could not understand a word of what was being said he enjoyed studying the inflections of the language.

Mohammed was out of the room for quite a while. It began to be late, the number of people sitting about gradually diminished as the customers either retired to inner chambers or went home. The two girls sat on, talking, interspersing their words now with occasional fits of laughter in which they held onto one another for mutual support. He wondered if he ought to go in search of Mohammed. He tried to sit quietly and be part of the timelessness of the place, but the occasion scarcely lent itself to that kind of imaginative play. When he finally did go into the courtyard to look for him, he immediately caught sight of him in an opposite room, reclining on a couch smoking a hashish pipe with some friends. He went across and called to him, remaining outside because he did not know the etiquette of the hashish chamber. It appeared, however, that there was none.

"Come in," said Mohammed from the cloud of pungent smoke. "Have a pipe."

He went in, greeted the others, and said in a low voice to Mohammed: "And the girl?"

Mohammed looked momentarily blank. Then he laughed: "Ah, that one? You have bad luck, my friend. You know what she has? She is blind, the poor thing."

"I know, I know," he said impatiently, and with mounting apprehension.

"Well, you don't want her, do you? She is blind!"

Port forgot himself. "*Mais bien sûr que je la veux!*" he shouted. "Of course I do! Where is she?"

Mohammed raised himself a little on one elbow. "Ah!" he grunted. "By now, I wonder! Sit down here and have a pipe. It's among friends."

Port turned on his heel in a rage and strode out into the court, where he made a systematic search of the cubicles from one side of the entrance to the other. But the girl was gone. Furious with disappointment, he walked through the gate into the dark street. An Arab soldier and a girl stood just outside the portal, talking in low tones. As he went past them he stared intently into her face. The soldier glared at him, but that was all. It was not she. Looking up and down the ill-lit street, he could discern two or three white-robed figures in the distance to the left and to the right. He started walking, viciously kicking stones out of his path. Now that she was gone, he was persuaded, not that a bit of enjoyment had been denied him, but that he had lost love itself. He climbed the hill and sat down beside the fort, leaning against the old walls. Below him were the few lights of the town, and beyond was the inevitable horizon of the desert. She would have put her hands up to his coat lapels, touched his face tentatively, run her sensitive fingers slowly along his lips. She would have sniffed the brilliantine in his hair and examined his garments with care. And in bed, without eyes to see beyond the bed, she would have been completely there, a prisoner. He thought of the little games he would have played with her, pretending to have disappeared when he was really still there; he thought of the countless ways he could have made her grateful to him. And always in conjunction with his fantasies he saw the imperturbable, faintly questioning face in its masklike symmetry. He felt a sudden shudder of self pity that was almost pleasurable, it was such a complete expression of his mood. It was a physical shudder; he was alone, abandoned, lost, hopeless, cold. Cold especially—a deep interior cold nothing could change. Although it was the basis of his unhappiness, this glacial deadness, he would cling to it always, because it was also the core of his being; he had built the being around it.

But at the moment he felt bodily cold, too, and this was strange because he had just climbed the hill fast and was still panting a little. Seized by a sudden fear, akin to the terror of the child when it brushes against an unidentifiable object in the dark, he jumped up and ran along the crest of the hill until he came to the path that led below to the market place. Running assuaged his fear, but when he stopped and looked down at the ring of lights around the market he still felt the cold, like a piece of metal inside him. He ran on down the hill, deciding to go to the hotel and get the whiskey in his room, and since the kitchen was locked, take it back to the brothel where he could make himself a hot grog with some tea. As he went into the patio he had to step over the watchman lying across the threshold. The man raised himself slightly and called out: "*Echkoun? Qui?*"

"*Numéro vingt!*" he cried, hurrying through the foul smells.

No light came from under Kit's door. In his room he took up the bottle of whiskey and looked at his watch, which out of caution he had left behind on the night table. It was three-thirty. He decided that if he walked quickly he could get there and be back in his room by half-past four, unless they had let the fires go out.

The watchman was snoring when he went out into the street. There he forced himself to take strides so long that the muscles of his legs rebelled, but the exercise failed to mitigate the chill he felt everywhere within him. The town seemed completely asleep. No music was audible as he approached the entrance of the house. The courtyard was totally dark and so were most of the rooms. A few of them, however, were still open and had lights. Mohammed was there, stretched out, talking with his friends.

"Well, did you find her?" he said as Port entered the room. "What are you carrying there?" Port held up the bottle, smiling faintly.

Mohammed frowned. "You don't want that, my friend. That's very bad. It turns your head." He made spiral gestures with one hand and tried to wrest the bottle away from Port with the other. "Have a pipe with me," he urged. "It's better. Sit down."

"I'd like more tea," said Port.

"It's too late," said Mohammed with great assurance.

"Why?" Port asked stupidly. "I must."

"Too late. No fire," Mohammed announced, with a certain satisfaction. "After one pipe you forget you wanted tea. In any case you have already drunk tea."

Port ran out into the courtyard and clapped his hands loudly. Nothing happened. Thrusting his head into one of the cubicles where he saw a woman seated, he asked in French for tea. She stared at him. He asked in his halting Arabic. She answered that it was too late. He said. "A hundred francs." The men murmured among themselves; a hundred francs seemed an interesting and reasonable offer, but the woman, a plump, middle-aged matron, said: "No." Port doubled his offer. The woman rose and motioned him to accompany her. He walked behind her, beneath a curtain hung across the back wall of the room, and through a series of tiny, dark cells, until finally they were out under the stars. She stopped and indicated that he was to sit on the ground and wait for her. A few paces from him she disappeared into a separate hut, where he heard her moving about. Nearer still to him in the dark an animal of some sort was sleeping; it breathed heavily and stirred from time to time. The ground was cold and he began to shiver. Through the breaks in the wall he saw a flicker of light. The woman had lighted a candle and was breaking bundles of twigs. Presently he heard them crackling in flames as she fanned the fire.

The first cock was crowing when she finally came out of the shack with the pot of coals. She led the way, sparks trailing behind her, into one of the dark rooms through which they had passed, and there she set it down and put the water to boil. There was no light but the red glow of the burning charcoal. He squatted before the fire holding his hands fan-wise for the warmth. When the tea was ready to drink, she pushed him gently back until he found himself against a mattress. He sat on it; it was warmer than the floor. She handed him a glass. "*Meziane, skhoun b'zef,*" she croaked, peering at him in the fading light. He drank half a glassful and filled it to the top with whiskey. After repeating the process, he felt better. He relaxed a bit and had another. Then for fear he should begin to sweat, he said: "*Baraka,*" and they went back to the room where the men lay smoking.

Mohammed laughed when he saw them. "What have you been doing?" he said accusingly. He rolled his eyes toward the woman. Port felt a little sleepy now and thought only of getting back to the hotel and into bed. He shook his head. "Yes, yes," insisted Mohammed, determined to have his joke. "I know! The young Englishman who went to Messad the other day, he was like you. Pretending always to be innocent. He pretended the woman was his mother, that he never would go near her, but I caught them together."

Port did not answer immediately. Then he jumped, and cried: "What!"

"Of course! I opened the door of room eleven, and there they are in the bed. Naturally. You believed him when he said she was his mother?" he added, noticing Port's incredulous expression. "You should have seen what I saw when I opened the door. Then you would know what a liar he was! Just because the lady is old, that does not stop her. No, no, no! Nor the man. So I say, what have you been doing with *her*. No?" He went on laughing.

Port smiled and paid the woman, saying to Mohammed: "Look. You see, I'm paying only the two hundred francs I promised for the tea. You see?"

Mohammed laughed louder. "Two hundred francs for tea! Too much for such old tea! I hope you had two glasses, my friend."

"Good night," said Port to the room in general, and he went out into the street.

BOOK TWO

The Earth's Sharp Edge

"'Good-bye,' says the dying man to the mirror they hold in front of him. 'We won't be seeing each other any more.'"—*Valéry*

XVIII

As COMMANDER of the military post of Bou Noura, Lieutenant d'Armagnac found the life there full if somewhat unvaried. At first there had been the novelty of his house; his books and furniture had been sent down from Bordeaux by his family, and he had experienced the pleasure of seeing them in new and unlikely surroundings. Then there had been the natives. The lieutenant was intelligent enough to insist on allowing himself the luxury of not being snobbish about the indigenous population. His overt attitude toward the people of Bou Noura was that they were an accessible part of a great, mysterious tribe from whom the French could learn a great deal if they only would take the trouble. And since he was an educated man, the other soldiers at the post, who would have enjoyed seeing all the natives put behind barbed wire and left there to rot in the sun (". . . *comme on a fait en Tripolitaine*"), did not hold his insanely benevolent attitude against him, contenting themselves by saying to one another that some day he would come to his senses and realize what worthless scum they really were. The lieutenant's true enthusiasm for the natives had lasted three years. About the time he had grown tired of his half-dozen or so Ouled Naïl mistresses, the period of his great devotion to the Arabs came to an end. It was not that he became any less objective in meting out justice to them; it was rather that he suddenly ceased thinking about them and began taking them for granted.

That same year he had gone back to Bordeaux for a six weeks' stay. There he had renewed his acquaintance with a young lady whom he had known since adolescence; but she had acquired a sudden and special interest for him by declaring, as he was about to leave for North Africa to resume his duties, that she could imagine nothing more wonderful and desirable than the idea of spending the rest of her life in the Sahara, and that she considered him the luckiest of men to be on his way back there. A correspondence had ensued, and letters had gone back and forth between Bordeaux and Bou Noura. Less than a year later he had gone to Algiers and met her as she got off the boat. The honeymoon had been spent in a little bougainvillaea-covered villa up at Mustapha-Supérieur (it had rained every day), after which they had returned together to the sunlit rigors of Bou Noura.

It was impossible for the lieutenant to know how nearly her preconceived notion of the place had coincided with what she had discovered to be its reality; he did not know whether she was going to like it or not. At the moment she was already back in France waiting for their first child to be born. Soon she would return and they would be better able to tell.

At present he was bored. After Mme. D'Armagnac had left, the lieutenant had attempted to pick up his old life where he had broken it off, but he found the girls of the Bou Noura quartier exasperatingly uncomplicated after the more evolved relationship to which he latterly had become accustomed. Thus he had occupied himself with building an extra room onto his house to surprise his wife on her return. It was to be an Arab salon. Already he was having the coffee table and couches built, and he had bought a beautiful, large cream-colored wool rug for the wall, and two sheepskins for the floor. It was during the fortnight when he was arranging this room that the trouble began.

The trouble, while it was nothing really serious, had managed to interfere with his work, a fact which could not be overlooked. Moreover, being an active man, he was always bored when he was confined to his bed, and he had been there for several days. Actually it had been a question of bad luck; if only someone else had happened on it—a native, for instance, or even one of his inferiors—he would not have been obliged to give the thing so much attention. But he had had the misfortune to discover it himself one morning while making his semi-weekly tour of inspection of the villages. Thereby it became official and important. It had been just outside the walls of Igherm, which he always visited directly after Tolfa, passing on foot through the cemetery and then climbing the hill; from the big gate of Igherm he could see the valley below where a soldier from the Poste waited in a truck to pick him up and carry him on to Beni Isguen, which was too far to walk. As he had been about to go through the gate into the village, his attention had been drawn by something which ought to have looked perfectly normal. A dog was running along with something in its mouth, something large and suspiciously pink, part of which dragged along the ground. But he had stared at the object.

Then he had made a short walk along the outside of the wall and had met two other dogs coming toward him with similar prizes. Finally he had come upon what he was looking for: it was only an infant, and in all likelihood it had been killed that morning. Wrapped in the pages of some old numbers of *L'Echo d'Alger*, it had been tossed into a shallow ditch. After questioning several people who had been outside the gate that morning he was able to ascertain that a certain Yamina ben Rhaïssa had been seen shortly after sunrise entering the gate, and that this was not a regular occurrence. He had no difficulty in locating Yamina; she lived nearby with her mother. At first she had denied hysterically all knowledge of the crime, but when he had taken her alone out of the house to the edge of the village and had talked with her in what he considered a "reasonable" fashion for five minutes she had calmly told him the entire story. Not the least surprising part of her tale was the fact that she had been able to conceal her pregnancy from her mother, or so she said. The lieutenant had been inclined to disbelieve this until he reflected upon the number of undergarments worn by the women of the region; then he decided that she was telling the truth. She had got the older woman out of the house by means of a stratagem, had given birth to the infant, strangled it and deposited it outside the gate wrapped in newspaper. By the time her mother had returned, she was already washing the floor.

Yamina's principal interest at this point seemed to be in finding out from the lieutenant the names of the persons who had made it possible for him to find her. She was intrigued by his swift detection of her act, and she told him so.

This primitive insouciance rather amused him, and for a quarter of an hour or so he actually allowed himself to consider how he could best arrange to spend the night with her. But by the time he had made her walk with him down the hill to the road where the truck was waiting, already he viewed his fantasies of a few minutes back with astonishment. He canceled the visit to Beni Isguen and took the girl straight to his headquarters. Then he remembered the infant. Seeing that Yamina was safely locked up, he hurried with a soldier to the spot and collected for evidence what small parts of the body were still left. It was on the basis of these few bits of flesh that Yamina was installed in the local prison, pending removal to Algiers for trial. But the trial never took place. During the third night of her imprisonment a gray scorpion, on its way along the earthen floor of her cell, discovered an unexpected and welcome warmth in one corner, and took refuge there. When Yamina stirred in her sleep, the inevitable occurred. The sting entered the nape of her neck; she never recovered consciousness. The news of her death quickly spread around the town, with the detail of the scorpion missing from the telling of it, so that the final and, as it were, official native version was that the girl had been assaulted by the entire garrison, including the lieutenant, and thereafter conveniently murdered. Naturally, it was not everyone who lent complete credence to the tale, but there was the indisputable fact that she had died while in French custody. Whatever the natives believed, the prestige of the lieutenant went into a definite decline.

The lieutenant's sudden unpopularity had immediate results: the workmen failed to appear at his house in order to continue the construction of the new salon. To be sure, the mason did arrive, only to sit in the garden all morning with Ahmed the houseboy, trying to persuade him (and in the end successfully) not to remain another day in the employ of such a monster. And the lieutenant had the quite correct impression that they were going out of their way to avoid meeting him in the street. The women especially seemed to fear his presence. When the news got around that he was in the neighborhood the streets cleared of themselves; all he heard as he walked along was the bolting of doors. If men passed it was with their eyes averted. These things constituted a blow to his prestige as an administrator, but they affected him rather less than the discovery, made the very day he took to his bed with a singular combination of cramps, dizziness and nausea, that his cook, who for some reason had stayed on with him, was a first cousin of the late Yamina.

The arrival of a letter from his commanding officer in Algiers made him no happier. There was no question, it said, of the justice of his procedure: the bits of evidence were in a jar of formaldehyde at the Tribunal of Bou Noura, and the girl had confessed. But it did criticize the lieutenant's negligence, and, which was more painful to him, it raised the question of his fitness to deal with the "native psychology."

He lay in his bed and looked at the ceiling; he felt weak and unhappy. It was nearly time for Jacqueline to come and prepare him his noonday consommé. (At the first cramp he had immediately got rid of his cook; he knew that much about dealing with the native psychology.) Jacqueline had been born in Bou Noura of an Arab father—at least, so it was said, and from her features and complexion it was easy to believe—and a French mother who had died shortly after her birth. What the Frenchwoman had been doing in Bou Noura all alone no one ever knew. But it was all in the distant past; Jacqueline had been taken in by the Pères Blancs and raised in the Mission. She knew all the songs the Fathers labored so diligently to teach the children—indeed, she was the only one who did know them. Besides learning to sing and pray she had also learned how to cook, which last talent proved to be a true blessing for the Mission since the unfortunate Fathers had been living on the local cuisine for many years and all suffered with their livers. When Father Lebrun had learned of the lieutenant's dilemma he straightway had volunteered to send Jacqueline to replace his cook and prepare him two simple meals a day. The Father had come himself the first day, and after looking at the lieutenant had decided that there would be no danger in letting her visit him, at least for a few days. He relied upon Jacqueline to warn him of her patient's progress, because once he was on the road to recovery, the lieutenant's behavior could no longer be counted on. He had said, looking down at him as he lay in his tousled bed: "I leave her in your hands, and you in God's." The lieutenant had understood what he meant, and he had tried to smile, but he felt too sick. Still, now as he thought of it he smiled, since he considered Jacqueline a wretched, skinny thing at whom no one would look twice.

She was late that noon, and when she arrived she was in a breathless state because Corporal Dupeyrier had stopped her near the Zaouia and given her a very important message for him. It was a matter of a foreigner, an American, who had lost his passport.

"An American?" echoed the lieutenant. "In Bou Noura?" Yes, said Jacqueline. He was here with his wife, they were at Abdelkader's pension, (which was the only place they could have been, since it was the only hostelry of any sort in the region), and they had already been in Bou Noura several days. She had even seen the gentleman: a young man.

"Well," said the lieutenant, "I'm hungry. How about a little rice today? Have you time to prepare it?"

"Ah, yes, monsieur. But he told me to tell you that it is important you see the American today."

"What are you talking about? Why should I see him? I can't find his passport for him. When you go back to the Mission, pass by the Poste and tell Corporal Dupeyrier to tell the American he must go to Algiers, to his consul. If he doesn't already know it," he added.

"*Ah, ce n'est pas pour ça!* It's because he accused Monsieur Abdelkader of stealing the passport."

"What?" roared the lieutenant, sitting up.

"Yes. He went yesterday to file a complaint. And Monsieur Abdelkader says that you will oblige him to retract it. That's why you must see him today." Jacqueline, obviously delighted with the degree of his reaction, went into the kitchen and began to rattle the utensils loudly. She was carried away by the idea of her importance.

The lieutenant slumped back into his bed and fell to worrying. It was imperative that the American be induced to withdraw his accusation, not only because Abdelkader was an old friend of his, and was quite incapable of stealing anything whatever, but particularly because he was one of the best known and highly esteemed men of Bou Noura. As proprietor of the inn he maintained close friendships with the chauffeurs of all the buses and trucks that passed through the territory; in the Sahara these are important people. Assuredly there was not one of them who at one time or another had not asked for, and received, credit from Abdelkader on his meals and lodgings; most of them had even borrowed money from him. For an Arab he was amazingly trusting and easy-going about money, both with Europeans and with his compatriots, and everyone liked him for it. Not only was it unthinkable that he should have stolen the passport—it was just as unthinkable that he should be formally accused of such a thing. For that reason the corporal was right. The complaint must be re-tracted immediately. "Another stroke of bad luck," he thought. "Why must it be an American?" With a Frenchman he would have known how to go about persuading him to do it without any unpleasantness. But with an American! Already he could see him: a gorilla-like brute with a fierce frown on his face, a cigar in the corner of his mouth, and probably an automatic in his hip pocket. Doubtless no complete sentences would pass between them because neither one would be able to understand enough of the other's language. He began try-ing to recall his English: "Sir, I must to you, to pray that you will—" "My dear sir, please I would make to you remark—" Then he remembered having heard that Americans did not speak English in any case, that they had a patois which only they could understand among themselves. The most unpleas-ant part of the situation to him was the fact that he would be in bed, while the American would be free to roam about the room, would enjoy all the advantages, physical and moral.

He groaned a little as he sat up to eat the soup Jacqueline had brought him. Outside the wind was blowing and the dogs of the nomad encampment up the road were barking; if the sun had not been shining so brightly that the moving palm branches by the window gleamed like glass, for a mo-ment he would have said it was the middle of the night—the sounds of the wind and the dogs would have been exactly the same. He ate his lunch; when Jacqueline was ready to leave he said to her: "You will go to the Poste and tell Corporal

Dupeyrier to bring the American here at three o'clock. He himself is to bring him, remember."

"*Oui, oui,*" she said, still in a state of acute pleasure. If she had missed out on the infanticide, at least she was in on the new scandal at the start.

XIX

Precisely at three o'clock Corporal Dupeyrier ushered the American into the lieutenant's salon. The house was absolutely silent. "*Un moment,*" said the corporal, going to the bedroom door. He knocked, opened it, the lieutenant made a sign with his hand, and the corporal relayed the command to the American, who walked into the bedroom. The lieutenant saw what he considered to be a somewhat haggard adolescent, and he immediately decided that the young man was slightly peculiar, since in spite of the heat he was wearing a heavy turtle-neck sweater and a woolen jacket.

The American advanced to the bedside and, offering his hand, spoke in perfect French. The lieutenant's initial surprise at his appearance turned to delight. He had the corporal draw up a chair for his guest and asked him to be seated. Then he suggested that the corporal go on back to the Poste; he had decided he could handle the American by himself. When they were alone he offered him a cigarette and said: "It seems you have lost your passport."

"That's exact," replied Port.

"And you believe it was stolen—not lost?"

"I *know* it was stolen. It was in a valise I always keep locked."

"Then how could it have been stolen from the valise?" said the lieutenant, laughing with an air of triumph. "Always is not quite the word."

"It could have been," pursued Port patiently, "because I left the valise open yesterday for a minute when I went out of my room to the bathroom. It was a foolish thing to do, but I did it. And when I returned to my door the proprietor was standing outside it. He claimed he had been knocking because lunch was ready. Yet he had never come himself before; it was always one of the boys. The reason I am sure it was the proprietor is that yesterday is the only time I have ever left the valise open when I have been out of the room, even for an instant. It seems clear to me."

"*Pardon.* Not to me. Not at all. Shall we make a detective story out of it? When is the last time you saw your passport?"

Port thought for a moment. "When I arrived in Aïn Krorfa," he said finally.

"Aha!" cried the lieutenant. "In Aïn Krorfa! And yet you accuse Monsieur Abdelkader, without hesitating. How do you explain that?"

"Yes, I accuse him," Port said stubbornly, nettled by the lieutenant's voice. "I accuse him because logic indicates him as the only possible thief. He's absolutely the only native who had access to the passport, the only one for whom it would have been physically possible."

Lieutenant d'Armagnac raised himself a little higher in bed. "And why precisely do you demand it be a native?"

Port smiled faintly. "Isn't it reasonable to suppose it was a native? Apart from the fact that no one else had the opportunity to take it, isn't it the sort of thing that would naturally turn out to have been done by a native—charming as they may be?"

"No, monsieur. To me it seems just the kind of thing that would *not* have been done by a native."

Port was taken aback. "Ah, really?" he said. "Why? Why do you say that?"

The lieutenant said: "I have been with the Arabs a good many years. Of course they steal. And Frenchmen steal. And in America you have gangsters, I believe?" He smiled archly. Port was impassive: "That was a long time ago, the era of gangsters," he said. But the lieutenant was not discouraged. "Yes, everywhere people steal. And here as well. However, the native here," he spoke more slowly, emphasizing his words, "takes only money or an object he wants for himself. He would never take anything so complicated as a passport."

Port said: "I'm not looking for motives. God knows *why* he took it." His host cut him short. "But I *am* looking for motives!" he cried. "And I see no reason for believing that any native has gone to the trouble of stealing your passport. Certainly not in Bou Noura. And I doubt very much in Aïn

Krorfa. One thing I can assure you, Monsieur Abdelkader did not take it. You can believe that."

"Oh?" said Port, unconvinced.

"Never. I have known him for several years—"

"But you have no more proof that he didn't than I have that he did!" Port exclaimed, annoyed. He turned up his coat collar and huddled in his chair.

"You aren't cold, I hope?" said the lieutenant in surprise.

"I've been cold for days," answered Port, rubbing his hands together.

The lieutenant looked at him closely for an instant. Then he went on: "Will you do me a favor if I do you one in return?"

"I suppose so. What?"

"I should be greatly obliged if you would withdraw your complaint against Monsieur Abdelkader at once—today. And I will try one thing to get you your passport back. *On ne sait jamais.* It may be successful. If your passport has been stolen, as you say, the only place for it logically to be now is Messad. I shall telegraph Messad to have a thorough search made of the Foreign Legion barracks."

Port was sitting quite still, looking straight ahead of him. "Messad," he said.

"You were not there, too, were you?"

"No, no!" There was a silence.

"And so, are you going to do me this favor? I shall have an answer for you as soon as the search has been carried out."

"Yes," said Port. "I'll go this afternoon. Tell me: there is a market for such things at Messad, then?"

"But of course. Passports bring high prices in Legion posts. Especially an American passport! *Oh, là là!*" The lieutenant's spirits were soaring: he had attained his object; this could off-set, at least partially, the damaging effects of the Yamina case to his prestige. "*Tenez,*" he said, pointing to a cupboard in the corner, "you are cold. Will you hand me that bottle of cognac over there? We shall each have a swallow." It was not at all what Port wanted, but he felt he scarcely could refuse the hospitable gesture.

Besides, what did he want? He was not sure, but he thought it was merely to sit quietly in a warm, interior place

for a long time. The sun made him feel colder, made his head
burn, seem enormous and top-heavy. If he had not had his
normal appetite he would have suspected that perhaps he was
not well. He sipped the cognac, wondering if it would make
him warmer, or if he would regret having drunk it, for the
heartburn it sometimes produced in him. The lieutenant appeared to have divined his thoughts, for he said presently:
"It's fine old cognac. It won't hurt you."

"It's excellent," he replied, choosing to ignore the latter
part of the remark.

The lieutenant's impression that here was a young man un-
healthily preoccupied with himself was confirmed by Port's
next words. "It's strange," he said with a deprecatory smile,
"how, ever since I discovered that my passport was gone, I've
felt only half alive. But it's a very depressing thing in a place
like this to have no proof of who you are, you know."

The lieutenant stretched forth the bottle, which Port declined. "Perhaps after my little investigation in Messad you
will recover your identity," he laughed. If the American
wished to extend him such confidences, he was quite willing
to be his confessor for the moment.

"You are here with your wife?" asked the lieutenant. Port
assented absently. "That's it," said the lieutenant to himself.
"He's having trouble with his wife. Poor devil!" It occurred
to him that they might go together to the quartier. He enjoyed showing it off to strangers. But as he was about to say:
"Fortunately my wife is in France—" he remembered that
Port was not French; it would not be advisable.

While he was considering this, Port rose and politely took
his leave—a little abruptly, it is true, but he could hardly be
expected to remain by the bedside the whole afternoon. Besides, he had promised to stop by and withdraw the complaint
against Abdelkader.

As he walked along the hot road toward the walls of Bou
Noura he kept his head down, seeing nothing but the dust
and the thousands of small sharp stones. He did not look up
because he knew how senseless the landscape would appear. It
takes energy to invest life with meaning, and at present this
energy was lacking. He knew how things could stand bare,
their essence having retreated on all sides to beyond the

horizon, as if impelled by a sinister centrifugal force. He did not want to face the intense sky, too blue to be real, above his head, the ribbed pink canyon walls that lay on all sides in the distance, the pyramidal town itself on its rocks, or the dark spots of oasis below. They were there, and they should have pleased his eye, but he did not have the strength to relate them, either to each other or to himself; he could not bring them into any focus beyond the visual. So he would not look at them.

On arriving back at the pension, he stopped by the little room that served as office, and found Abdelkader seated in a dark corner on the divan, playing dominoes with a heavily turbaned individual. "Good day, monsieur," said Port. "I have been to the authorities and withdrawn the accusation."

"Ah, my lieutenant has arranged it," murmured Abdelkader.

"Yes," said Port, although he was vexed to see that no credit was to be given him for acceding to Lieutenant d'Armagnac's wishes.

"*Bon, merci.*" Abdelkader did not look up again, and Port went on upstairs to Kit's room.

There he found that she had ordered all her luggage brought up and was unpacking it. The room looked like a bazaar: there were rows of shoes on the bed, evening gowns had been spread out over the footboard as if for a window display, and bottles of cosmetics and perfumes lined the night table.

"What in God's name are you doing?" he cried.

"Looking at my things," she said innocently. "I haven't seen them in a long time. Ever since the boat I've been living in one bag. I'm so sick of it. And when I looked out that window after lunch," she became more animated as she pointed to the window that gave onto the empty desert, "I felt I'd simply die if I didn't see something civilized soon. Not only that. I'm having a Scotch sent up and I'm opening my last pack of Players."

"You *must* be in a bad way," he said.

"Not at all," she retorted, but a bit too energetically. "It'd be abnormal if I were able to adapt myself too quickly to all this. After all, I'm still an American, you know. And I'm not even trying to be anything else."

"Scotch!" Port said, thinking aloud. "There's no ice this side of Boussif. And no soda either, I'll bet."

"I want it neat." She slipped into a backless gown of pale blue satin and went to make up in the mirror that hung on the back of the door. He decided that she should be humored; in any case it amused him to watch her building her pathetic little fortress of Western culture in the middle of the wilderness. He sat down on the floor in the center of the room and watched her with pleasure as she flitted about, choosing her slippers and trying on bracelets. When the servant knocked, Port himself went to the door and in the hall took the tray from his hands, bottle and all.

"Why didn't you let him in?" demanded Kit, when he had closed the door behind him.

"Because I didn't want him running downstairs with the news," he said, setting the tray on the floor and sitting down again beside it.

"What news?"

He was vague. "Oh, that you have fancy clothes and jewelry in your bags. It's the sort of thing that would go on ahead of us wherever we went, down here. Besides," he smiled at her, "I'd rather they didn't get a look at how pretty you can be."

"Well, really, Port! Make up your mind. Is it me you're trying to protect? Or do you think they'll add ten francs on to the bill downstairs?"

"Come here and have your lousy French whiskey. I want to tell you something."

"I will not. You'll bring it to me like a gentleman." She made room among the objects on the bed and sat down.

"Fine." He poured her a good-sized drink and took it to her.

"You're not having any?" she said.

"No. I had some cognac at the lieutenant's house, and it didn't do any good. I'm as chilly as ever. But I have news, and that's what I wanted to tell you. There's not much doubt that Eric Lyle stole my passport." He told her about the passport market for legionnaires at Messad. In the bus coming from Aïn Krorfa he had already informed her of Mohammed's discovery. She, showing no surprise, had repeated her story of having seen their passports, so that there was no doubt of their being mother and son. Nor was she surprised now. "I suppose he felt that since I'd seen theirs, he had a right to see yours," she said. "But how'd he get it? When'd he get it?"

"I know just when. The night he came to my room in Aïn Krorfa and wanted to give me back the francs I'd let him have. I left my bag open and him in the room while I went in to see Tunner, because I had my wallet with me and it certainly never occurred to me the louse was after my passport. But beyond a doubt that's what happened to it. The more I think about it the surer I am. Whether they find out anything at Messad or not, I'm convinced it was Lyle. I think he intended to steal it the first time he ever saw me. After all, why not? Easy money, and his mother never gives him any."

"I think she does," said Kit, "on certain conditions. And I think he hates all that, and is only looking for a chance to escape, and will hook up with anybody, do anything, rather than that. And I think she's quite aware of it and is terrified he'll go, and will do everything she can to prevent his getting intimate with anybody. Remember what she told you about his being 'infected.'"

Port was silent. "My God! What a mess I got Tunner into!" he said after a moment.

Kit laughed. "What do you mean? He'll weather it. It'll be good for him. Besides, I can't see him being very friendly with either one of them."

"No." He poured himself a drink. "I shouldn't do this," he said. "It'll mess me up inside, with the cognac. But I can't let you sit there and go away by yourself, float off on a few drinks."

"You know I'm delighted to have company, but won't it make you sick?"

"I already feel sick," he exclaimed. "I can't go on forever taking precautions just because I'm cold all the time. Anyway, I think as soon as we get to El Ga'a I'll be better. It's a lot warmer there, you know."

"Again? We only just got *here*."

"But you can't deny it's chilly here at night."

"I certainly do deny it. But that's all right. If we've got to go to El Ga'a, then let's go, by all means, but let's go soon, and stay awhile."

"It's one of the great Saharan cities," he said, as if he were holding it up for her to see.

"You don't have to sell it to me," she said. "And even if you did, that wouldn't be the way. You know that means very little to me. El Ga'a, Timbuctoo, it's all the same to me, more or less; all equally interesting, but not anything I'm going to go mad about. But if you'll be happier there—I mean healthier—we should go, by all means." She made a nervous gesture with her hand, in the hope of driving away an insistent fly.

"Oh. You think my complaint is mental. You said happier."

"I don't think anything because I don't know. But it seems awfully peculiar to me that anybody should be constantly cold in September in the Sahara desert."

"Well, it'll have to seem peculiar," he said with annoyance. Then he suddenly exclaimed: "These flies have claws! They're enough to drive you completely off your balance. What do they want, to crawl down your throat?" He groaned and rose to his feet; she looked at him expectantly. "I'll fix it so we'll be safe from them. Get up." He burrowed into a valise and presently pulled out a folded bundle of netting. At his suggestion Kit cleared the bed of her clothing. Over the headboard and footboard he spread the net, remarking that there was no good reason why a mosquito net could not become a fly net. When it was well fastened they slid underneath with the bottle and lay there quietly as the afternoon wore on. By twilight they were pleasantly drunk, disinclined to move out from under their tent. Perhaps it was the sudden appearance of the stars in the square of sky framed by the window, which helped to determine the course of their conversation. Each moment, as the color deepened, more stars came to fill the spaces which up until then had been empty. Kit smoothed her gown at the hips and said: "When I was young—"

"How young?"

"Before I was twenty, I mean, I used to think that life was a thing that kept gaining impetus. It would get richer and deeper each year. You kept learning more, getting wiser, having more insight, going further into the truth—" She hesitated.

Port laughed abruptly. "And now you know it's not like that. Right? It's more like smoking a cigarette. The first few puffs it tastes wonderful, and you don't even think of its ever being used up. Then you begin taking it for granted. Suddenly you realize it's nearly burned down to the end. And then's when you're conscious of the bitter taste."

"But I'm always conscious of the unpleasant taste *and* of the end approaching," she said.

"Then you should give up smoking."

"How mean you are!" she cried.

"I'm not mean!" he objected, almost upsetting his glass as he raised himself on his elbow to drink. "It seems logical, doesn't it? Or I suppose living's a habit like smoking. You keep saying you're going to give it up, but you go right on."

"*You* don't even threaten to stop, as far as I can see," she said accusingly.

"Why should I? I want to go on."

"But you complain so all the time."

"Oh, not about life; only about human beings."

"The two can't be considered separately."

"They certainly can. All it takes is a little effort. Effort, effort! Why won't anybody make any? I can imagine an absolutely different world. Just a few misplaced accents."

"I've heard it all for years," said Kit. She sat up in the near-dark, cocked her head and said: "Listen!"

Somewhere outside, not far away, perhaps in the market place, an orchestra of drums was playing, little by little gathering up the loose strands of rhythmic force into one mighty compact design which already was revolving, a still imperfect wheel of heavy sounds, lumbering ahead toward the night. Port was silent awhile, and said in a whisper: "That, for instance."

"I don't know," said Kit. She was impatient. "I know I don't feel any part of those drums out there, however much I may admire the sounds they make. And I don't see any reason why I should *want* to feel a part of them." She thought that such a straightforward declaration would put a quick end to the discussion, but Port was stubborn that evening.

"I know, you never like to talk seriously," he said, "but it won't hurt you for once."

She smiled scornfully, since she considered his vague generalities the most frivolous kind of chatter—a mere vehicle for his emotions. According to her, at such times there was no question of his meaning or not meaning what he said, because he did not know really what he was saying. So she said banteringly: "What's the unit of exchange in this different world of yours?"

He did not hesitate. "The tear."

"It isn't fair," she objected. "Some people have to work very hard for a tear. Others can have them just for the thinking."

"What system of exchange *is* fair?" he cried, and his voice sounded as if he were really drunk. "And whoever invented the concept of fairness, anyway? Isn't everything easier if you simply get rid of the idea of justice altogether? *You* think the quantity of pleasure, the degree of suffering is constant among all men? It somehow all comes out in the end? You think that? If it comes out even it's only because the final sum is zero."

"I suppose that's a comfort to you," she said, feeling that if the conversation went on she would get really angry.

"None at all. Are you crazy? I have no interest in knowing the final figure. But I am interested in all the complicated processes that make it possible to get that result inevitably, no matter what the original quantity was."

"The end of the bottle," she murmured. "Perhaps a perfect zero is something to reach."

"Is it all gone? Hell. But we don't reach it. It reaches us. It's not the same thing."

"He's really drunker than I am," she thought. "No, it isn't," she agreed.

And as he was saying: "You're damned right," and flopping violently over to lie on his stomach, she went on thinking of what a waste of energy all this talk was, and wondering how she could stop him from working himself up into an emotional state.

"Ah, I'm disgusted and miserable!" he cried in a sudden burst of fury. "I should never take a drop because it always knocks me out. But it's not weakness the way it is with you. Not at all. It takes more will power for me to make myself take a drink than it does for you not to. I hate the results and I always remember what they'll be."

"Then why do you do it? Nobody asks you to."

"I told you," he said. "I wanted to be with you. And besides, I always imagine that somehow I'll be able to penetrate to the interior of somewhere. Usually I get just about to the suburbs and get lost. I don't think there *is* any interior to get to any more. I think all you drinkers are victims of a huge mass hallucination."

"I refuse to discuss it," said Kit haughtily, climbing down from the bed and struggling her way through the folds of netting that hung to the floor.

He rolled over and sat up.

"I know why I'm disgusted," he called after her. "It's something I ate. Ten years ago."

"I don't know what you're talking about. Lie down again and sleep," she said, and went out of the room.

"I do," he muttered. He crawled out of the bed and went to stand in the window. The dry desert air was taking on its evening chill, and the drums still sounded. The canyon walls were black now, the scattered clumps of palms had become invisible. There were no lights; the room faced away from the town. And this was what he meant. He gripped the window-sill and leaned out, thinking: "She doesn't know what I'm talking about. It's something I ate ten years ago. Twenty years ago." The landscape was there, and more than ever he felt he could not reach it. The rocks and the sky were everywhere, ready to absolve him, but as always he carried the obstacle within him. He would have said that as he looked at them, the rocks and the sky ceased being themselves, that in the act of passing into his consciousness, they became impure. It was slight consolation to be able to say to himself: "I am stronger than they." As he turned back into the room, something bright drew his eye to the mirror on the open door of the wardrobe. It was the new moon shining in through the other window. He sat down on the bed and began to laugh.

XX

Port spent the next two days trying assiduously to gather information about El Ga'a. It was astonishing how little the people of Bou Noura knew about the place. Everyone seemed in agreement that it was a large city—always it was spoken of with a certain respect—that it was far away, that the climate was warmer, and the prices high. Beyond this, no one appeared able to give any description of it, not even the men who had been there, such as the bus driver he spoke with, and the cook in the kitchen. One person who could have given him a somewhat fuller report on the town was Abdelkader, but intercourse between him and Port had been reduced to mere grunts of recognition. When he considered it, he realized now that it rather suited his fancy to be going off with no proof of his identity to a hidden desert town about which no one could tell him anything. So that he was not so much moved as he might have been when on meeting Corporal Dupeyrier in the street and mentioning El Ga'a to him, the corporal said: "But Lieutenant d'Armagnac has spent many months there. He can tell you everything you want to know." Only then did he understand that he really wanted to know nothing about El Ga'a beyond the fact that it was isolated and unfrequented, that it was precisely those things he had been trying to ascertain about it. He determined not to mention the town to the lieutenant, for fear of losing his preconceived idea of it.

The same afternoon Ahmed, who had reinstated himself in the lieutenant's service, appeared at the pension and asked for Port. Kit, in bed reading, told the servant to send the boy to the hammam, where Port had gone to bask in the steam room in the hope of thawing out his chill once and for all. He was lying almost asleep in the dark, on a hot, slippery slab of rock, when an attendant came and roused him. With a wet towel around him he went to the entrance door. Ahmed stood there scowling; he was a light Arab boy from the ereg, and his face had the tell-tale, fiery gashes halfway down each cheek which debauchery sometimes makes in the soft skin of those too young to have pouches and wrinkles.

"The lieutenant wants you right away," said Ahmed.

"Tell him in an hour," Port said, blinking at the light of day.

"Right away," repeated Ahmed stolidly. "I wait here."

"Oh, he gives orders!" He went back inside and had a pail of cold water thrown over him—he would have liked more of it, but water was expensive here, and each pailful was a supplementary charge—and a quick massage before he dressed. It seemed to him that he felt a little better as he stepped out into the street. Ahmed was leaning against the wall talking with a friend, but he sprang to attention at Port's appearance, and kept a few paces behind him all the way to the lieutenant's house.

Dressed in an ugly bathrobe of wine-colored artificial silk, the lieutenant sat in his salon smoking.

"You will pardon me if I remain seated," he said. "I am much better, but I feel best when I move least. Sit down. Will you have sherry, cognac or coffee?"

Port murmured that coffee would please him most. Ahmed was sent to prepare it.

"I don't mean to detain you, monsieur. But I have news for you. Your passport has been found. Thanks to one of your compatriots, who had also discovered his passport missing, a search had already been instigated before I got in contact with Messad. Both documents had been sold to legionnaires. But fortunately both have been recovered." He fumbled in his pocket and brought out a slip of paper. "This American, whose name is Tunner, says he knows you and is coming here to Bou Noura. He offers to bring your passport with him, but I must have your consent before notifying the authorities there to give it to him. Do you give your consent? Do you know this Monsieur Tunner?"

"Yes, yes," said Port absently. The idea horrified him; faced with Tunner's imminent arrival, he was appalled to realize that he had never expected really to see him again. "When is he coming?"

"I believe immediately. You are not in a hurry to leave Bou Noura?"

"No," said Port, his mind darting back and forth like a cornered animal, trying to remember what day the bus left for the south, what day it was then, how long it would take for Tunner to get from Messad. "No, no. I am not pressed for time." The words sounded ridiculous as he said them. Ahmed came in silently with a tray bearing two small tin canisters with steam rising from them. The lieutenant poured a glass of coffee from each and handed one to Port, who took a sip and sat back in his chair.

"But I do hope to get eventually to El Ga'a," he went on, in spite of himself.

"Ah, El Ga'a. You will find it very impressive, very picturesque, and very hot. It was my first Saharan post. I know every alley. It's a vast city, perfectly flat, not too dirty, but rather dark because the streets are built through the houses, like tunnels. Quite safe. You and your wife can wander wherever you please. It's the last town of any size this side of the Soudan. And that's a great distance away, the Soudan. *Oh, là, là!*"

"I suppose there's a hotel in El Ga'a?"

"Hotel? A kind of hotel," laughed the lieutenant. "You will find rooms with beds in them, and it may be clean. It is not so dirty in the Sahara as people say. The sun is a great purifier. With even a minimum of hygiene the people could be healthy here. But of course there is not that minimum. Unfortunately for us, *d'ailleurs.*"

"No. Yes, unfortunately," said Port. He could not bring himself back to the room and the conversation. He had just realized that the bus left that very night, and there would not be another for a week. Tunner would be there by then. With that realization, his decision seemed to have come automatically. Certainly he was not conscious of having made it, but a moment later he relaxed and began to question the lieutenant on the details of his daily life and work in Bou Noura. The lieutenant looked pleased; one by one the inevitable anecdotes of the colonist came out, all having to do with the juxtaposition, sometimes tragic, but usually ludicrous, of the two incongruous and incompatible cultures. Finally Port rose. "It's too bad," he said with a note of sincerity in his voice, "that I shan't be staying here longer."

"But you will be here several days more. I count absolutely on seeing you and Madame before your departure. In another two or three days I shall be completely well. Ahmed will let you know when and call for you. So, I shall notify Messad to give your passport to Monsieur Tunner." He rose, extended his hand; Port went out.

He walked through the little garden planted with stunted palms, and out the gate into the dusty road. The sun had set, and the sky was rapidly cooling. He stood still a moment looking upward, almost expecting to hear the sky crack as the nocturnal chill pressed against it from outside. Behind him in the nomad encampment the dogs barked in chorus. He began to walk quickly, to be out of their hearing as soon as he could. The coffee had accelerated his pulse to an unusual degree, or else it was his nervousness at the thought of missing the bus to El Ga'a. Entering the town gate, he turned immediately to the left and went down the empty street to the offices of the Transports Généraux.

The office was stuffy, without light. In the dimness behind the counter on a pile of burlap sacks sat an Arab, half asleep. Immediately Port said: "What time does the bus leave for El Ga'a?"

"Eight o'clock, monsieur."

"Are there seats still?"

"Oh, no. Three days ago they were all sold."

"*Ah, mon dieu!*" cried Port; his entrails seemed to grow heavier. He gripped the counter.

"Are you sick?" said the Arab, looking at him, and his face showed a little interest.

"Sick," thought Port. And he said: "No, but my wife is very sick. She must get to El Ga'a by tomorrow." He watched the Arab's face closely, to see if he were capable of believing such an obvious lie. Apparently here it was as logical for an ailing person to go away from civilization and medical care as to go in the direction of it, for the Arab's expression slowly changed to one of understanding and sympathy. Still, he raised his hands in a gesture that denoted his inability to help.

But already Port had pulled out a thousand-franc note and spread it on the counter with determination.

"You will have to give us two seats tonight," he said firmly. "This is for you. You persuade someone to go next week." Out of courtesy he did not suggest that the persuasion be used on two natives, although he knew that would be the case. "How much is the passage to El Ga'a?" He drew out more money.

The Arab rose to his feet and stood scratching his turban deliberately. "Four hundred and fifty francs each," he answered, "but I don't know—"

Port laid another twelve hundred francs before him and

said: "That's nine hundred. And twelve hundred and fifty for you, after you take out for the tickets." He saw that the man's decision had been made. "I shall bring the lady at eight o'clock."

"Half-past seven," said the Arab, "for the luggage."

Back at the pension, in his excitement, he rushed into Kit's room without knocking. She was dressing, and cried with indignation: "Really, have you lost your mind?"

"Not at all," he said. "Only I hope you can travel in that dress."

"What do you mean?"

"We have seats on the bus tonight at eight."

"Oh, no! Oh, my God! For where? El Ga'a?" He nodded and there was a silence. "Oh, well," she said finally. "It's all the same to me. You know what you want. But it's six now. All these grips—"

"I'll help you." There was a febrile eagerness in his manner now that she could not help observing. She watched him pulling her clothes out of the wardrobe and sliding them off the hangers with staccato gestures; his behavior struck her as curious, but she said nothing. When he had done all he could in her room he went into his own, where he packed his valises in ten minutes and dragged them out into the corridor himself. Then he ran downstairs and she heard him talking excitedly to the boys. At quarter of seven they sat down to their dinner. In no time he had finished his soup.

"Don't eat so fast. You'll have indigestion," Kit warned him.

"We've got to be at the bus office at seven-thirty," he said, clapping his hands for the next course.

"We'll make it, or they'll wait for us."

"No, no. There'll be trouble about the seats."

While they were still eating their cornes de gazelle he demanded the hotel bill and paid it.

"Did you see Lieutenant d'Armagnac?" she asked, as he was waiting for his change.

"Oh, yes."

"But no passport?"

"Not yet," he said, adding: "Oh, I don't think they'll ever find it. How could you expect them to? It's probably been sent off up to Algiers or Tunis by now."

"I still think you should have wired the consul from here."

"I can send a letter from El Ga'a by the same bus we go down in, when it makes the return trip. It'll only be two or three days later."

"I don't understand you," said Kit.

"Why?" he asked innocently.

"I don't understand anything. Your sudden indifference. Even this morning you were in the most awful state about not having any passport. Anyone would have thought you couldn't live another day without it. And now another few days make no difference. You *will* admit there's no connection?"

"You *will* admit they don't make much difference?"

"I will not. They might easily. And that's not my point. Not at all," she said, "and you know it."

"The main point right now is that we catch the bus." He jumped up and ran out to where Abdelkader was still trying to make change for him. Kit followed a moment later. By the flare of the tiny carbide lamps that swung on long wires from the ceiling the boys were bringing down the bags. It was a procession down the staircase; there were six boys, all laden with luggage. A small army of village gamins had gathered outside the door in the dark, with the tacit hope of being allowed to carry something along to the bus terminal.

Abdelkader was saying: "I hope you will like El Ga'a."

"Yes, yes," Port answered, putting his change into various pockets. "I hope I did not upset you too much with my troubles."

Abdelkader looked away. "Ah, that," he said. "It is better not to speak of it." The apology was too offhand; he could not accept it.

The night wind had risen. Windows and shutters were banging upstairs. The lamps rocked back and forth, sputtering.

"Perhaps we shall see you on our return trip," insisted Port.

Abdelkader should have answered: "*Incha'allah.*" He merely looked at Port, sadly but with understanding. For a moment it seemed that he was about to say something; then he turned his head away. "Perhaps," he said finally, and when he turned back his lips were fixed in a smile—a smile that Port felt was not directed at him, did not even show consciousness of him. They shook hands and he hurried over to Kit, standing in the doorway carefully making up under the moving light of the lamp, while the curious young faces outside were upturned, following each movement of her fingers as she applied the lipstick.

"Come on!" he cried. "There's no time for that."

"I'm all done," she said, swinging around so he should not jostle her as she completed her handiwork. She dropped her lipstick into her bag and snapped it shut.

They went out. The road to the bus station was dark; the new moon gave no light. Behind them a few of the village urchins still straggled hopefully, most of them having given up when they saw the entire staff of the pension's boys accompanying the travelers.

"Too bad it's windy," said Port. "That means dust."

Kit was indifferent to the dust. She did not answer. But she noticed the unusual inflection in his speaking: he was unaccountably exhilarated.

"I only hope there are no mountains to cross," she said to herself, wishing again, but more fervently now, that they had gone to Italy, or any small country with boundaries, where the villages had churches and one went to the station in a taxi or a carriage, and could travel by daylight. And where one was not inevitably on display every time one stirred out of the hotel.

"Oh, my God, I forgot!" Port cried. "You're a very sick woman." And he explained how he had got the seats. "We're almost there. Let me put my arm around your waist. You walk as though you had a pain. Shuffle a little."

"This is ridiculous," she said crossly. "What'll our boys think?"

"They're too busy. You've turned your ankle. Come on. Drag a bit. Nothing simpler." He pulled her against him as they walked along.

"And what about the people whose seats we're usurping?"

"What's a week to them? Time doesn't exist for them."

The bus was there, surrounded by shouting men and boys. The two went into the office, Kit walking with a certain real difficulty caused by the force with which Port was pressing her toward him. "You're hurting me. Let up a little," she whispered. But he continued to constrict her waist tightly, and they arrived at the counter. The Arab who had sold him the tickets said: "You have numbers twenty-two and twenty-three. Get in and take your seats quickly. The others don't want to give them up."

The seats were near the back of the bus. They looked at each other in dismay; it was the first time they had not sat in front with the driver.

"Do you think you can stand it?" he asked her.

"If you can," she said.

And as he saw an elderly man with a gray beard and a high yellow turban looking in through the window with what seemed to him a reproachful expression, he said: "Please lie back and be fatigued, will you? You've got to carry this off to the end."

"I hate deceit," she said with great feeling. Then suddenly she shut her eyes and looked quite ill. She was thinking of Tunner. In spite of the firm resolution she had made in Aïn Krorfa to stay behind and meet him according to their agreement, she was letting Port spirit her off to El Ga'a without even leaving a note of explanation. Now that it was too late to change the pattern of her behavior, suddenly it seemed incredible to her that she had allowed herself to do such a thing. But a second later she said to herself that if this was an unpardonable act of deceit toward Tunner, how much graver was the deception she still practiced with Port in not telling him of her infidelity. Immediately she felt fully justified in leaving; nothing Port asked of her could be refused at this point. She let her head fall forward contritely.

"That's right," said Port encouragingly, pinching her arm. He scrambled over the bundles that had just been piled into the aisle and got out to see that all the luggage was on top. When he got back in, Kit was still in the same attitude.

There were no difficulties. As the motor started up, Port glanced out and saw the old man standing beside a younger one. They were both close to the windows, looking wistfully in. "Like two children," he thought, "who aren't being allowed to go on a picnic with the family."

When they started to move, Kit sat up straight and began to whistle. Port nudged her uneasily.

"It's all over," she said. "You don't think I'm going to go on playing sick all the way, I hope? Besides, you're mad. No one's paying the slightest attention to us." This was true. The bus was full of lively conversation; their presence seemed quite unnoticed.

The road was bad almost immediately. At each bump Port slid down lower in his seat. Noticing that he made no effort to avoid slipping more, Kit said at length: "Where are you going? On to the floor?" When he answered, he said only: "What?" and his voice sounded so strange that she turned sharply and tried to see his face. The light was too dim. She could not tell what expression was there.

"Are you asleep?" she asked him.

"No."

"Is anything wrong? Are you cold? Why don't you spread your coat over you?"

This time he did not answer.

"Freeze, then," she said, looking out at the thin moon, low in the sky.

Some time later the bus began a slow, laborious ascent. The fumes from the exhaust grew heavy and acrid; this, combined with the intense noise of the grinding motor and the constantly increasing cold, served to jar Kit from the stupor into which she had sunk. Wide awake, she looked around the indistinct interior of the bus. The occupants all appeared to be asleep; they were resting at unlikely angles, completely rolled in their burnouses, so that not even a finger or a nose was visible. A slight movement beside her made her look down at Port, who had slid so low in his seat that he now was resting on the middle of his spine. She decided to make him sit up, and tapped him vigorously on the shoulder. His only reply was a slight moan.

"Sit up," she said, tapping again. "You'll ruin your back."

This time he groaned: "Oh-h-h!"

"Port, for heaven's sake, sit up," she said nervously. She began to tug at his head, hoping to rouse him enough to start him into making some effort himself.

"Oh, God!" he said, and he slowly wormed his way backward up onto the seat. "Oh, God!" he repeated when he was sitting up finally. Now that his head was near her, she realized that his teeth were chattering.

"You've got a chill!" she said furiously, although she was furious with herself rather than with him. "I told you to cover up, and you just sat there like an idiot!"

He made no reply, merely sat quite still, his head bent forward and bouncing up and down against his chest with the pitching of the bus. She reached over and pulled at his coat, managing little by little to extricate it from under him where he had thrown it on the seat. Then she spread it over him, tucking it down at the sides with a few petulant gestures. On the surface of her mind, in words, she was thinking: "Typical of him, to be dead to the world, when I'm wide awake and bored." But the formation of the words was a screen to hide the fear beneath—the fear that he might be really ill. She looked out at the wind-swept emptiness. The new moon had slipped behind the earth's sharp edge. Here in the desert, even more than at sea, she had the impression that she was on the top of a great table, that the horizon was the brink of space. She imagined a cube-shaped planet somewhere above the earth, between it and the moon, to which somehow they had been transported. The light would be hard and unreal as it was here, the air would be of the same taut dryness, the contours of the landscape would lack the comforting terrestrial curves, just as they did all through this vast region. And the silence would be of the ultimate degree, leaving room only for the sound of the air as it moved past. She touched the windowpane; it was ice cold. The bus bumped and swayed as it continued upward across the plateau.

XXI

It was a long night. They came to a bordj built into the side of a cliff. The overhead light was turned on. The young Arab just in front of Kit, turning around and smiling at her as he lowered the hood of his burnous, pointed at the earth several times and said: "*Hassi Inifel!*"

"*Merci*," she said, and smiled back. She felt like getting out, and turned to Port. He was doubled up under his coat; his face looked flushed.

"Port," she began, and was surprised to hear him answer immediately. "Yes?" His voice sounded wide awake.

"Let's get out and have something hot. You've slept for hours."

Slowly he sat up. "I haven't slept at all, if you want to know."

She did not believe him. "I see," she said. "Well, do you want to go inside? I'm going."

"If I can. I feel terrible. I think I have grippe or something."

"Oh, nonsense! How could you? You probably have indigestion from eating dinner so fast."

"You go on in. I'll feel better not moving."

She climbed out and stood a moment on the rocks in the wind, taking deep breaths. Dawn was nowhere in sight.

In one of the rooms near the entrance of the bordj there were men singing together and clapping their hands quickly in complex rhythm. She found coffee in a smaller room nearby, and sat down on the floor, warming her hands over the clay vessel of coals. "He *can't* get sick here," she thought. "Neither of us can." There was nothing to do but refuse to be sick, once one was this far away from the world. She went back out and looked through the windows of the bus. Most of the passengers had remained asleep, wrapped in their burnouses. She found Port, and tapped on the glass. "Port!" she called. "Hot coffee!" He did not stir.

"Damn him!" she thought. "He's trying to get attention. He *wants* to be sick!" She climbed aboard and worked her way back to his seat, where he lay inert.

"Port! Please come and have some coffee. As a favor to me." She cocked her head and looked at his face. Smoothing his hair she asked: "Do you feel sick?"

He spoke into his coat. "I don't want anything. Please. I don't want to move."

She disliked to humor him; perhaps by waiting on him she would be playing right into his hands. But in the event he had been chilled he should drink something hot. She determined to get the coffee into him somehow. So she said: "Will you drink it if I bring it to you?"

His reply was a long time in coming, but he finally said: "Yes."

The driver, an Arab who wore a visored cap instead of a turban, was already on his way out of the bordj as she rushed in. "Wait!" she said to him. He stood still and turned around, looking her up and down speculatively. He had no one to whom he could make any remarks about her, since there were no Europeans present, and the other Arabs were not from the city, and would have failed completely to understand his obscene comments.

Port sat up and drank the coffee, sighing between swallows.

"Finished? I've got to give the glass back."

"Yes." The glass was relayed through the bus to the front, where a child waited for it, peering anxiously back lest the bus start up before he had it in his hands.

They moved off slowly across the plateau. Now that the doors had been open, it was colder inside.

"I think that helped," Port said. "Thanks an awful lot. Only I *have* got something wrong with me. God knows I never felt quite like this before. If I could only be in bed and lie out flat, I'd be all right, I think."

"But what do you think it *is?*" she said, suddenly feeling them all there in full force, the fears she had been holding at bay for so many days.

"You tell *me.* We don't get in till noon, do we? What a mess, what a mess!"

"Try and sleep, darling." She had not called him that in at least a year. "Lean over, way over, this way, put your head here. Are you warm enough?" For a few minutes she tried to break the jolts of the bus for him by posting with her body against the back of the seat, but her muscles soon tired; she leaned back and relaxed, letting his head bounce up and down on her breast. His hand in her lap sought hers, found it, held it tightly at first, then loosely. She decided he was asleep, and shut her eyes, thinking: "Of course, there's no escape now. I'm here."

At dawn they reached another bordj standing on a perfectly flat expanse of land. The bus drove through the entrance into a court, where several tents stood. A camel peered haughtily through the window beside Kit's face. This time everyone got out. She woke Port. "Want some breakfast?" she said.

"Believe it or not, I'm a little hungry."

"Why shouldn't you be?" she said brightly. "It's nearly six o'clock."

They had more of the sweet black coffee, and some hard-boiled eggs, and dates. The young Arab who had told her the name of the other bordj walked by as they sat on the floor eating. Kit could not help noticing how unusually tall he was, what an admirable figure he cut when he stood erect in his flowing white garment. To efface her feeling of guilt at having thought anything at all about him, she felt impelled to bring him to Port's attention.

"Isn't that one striking!" she heard herself saying, as the Arab moved from the room. The phrase was not at all hers, and it sounded completely ridiculous coming out of her mouth; she waited uneasily for Port's reaction. But Port was holding his hand over his abdomen; his face was white.

"What is it?" she cried.

"Don't let the bus go," he said. He rose unsteadily to his feet and left the room precipitately. Accompanied by a boy he stumbled across the wide court, past the tents where fires burned and babies cried. He walked doubled over, holding his head with one hand and his belly with the other.

In the far corner was a little stone enclosure like a gun-turret, and the boy pointed to it. "*Daoua,*" he said. Port went up the steps and in, slamming the wooden door after him. It stank inside, and it was dark. He leaned back against the cold stone wall and heard the spiderwebs snap as his head touched them. The pain was ambiguous: it was a violent cramp and a mounting nausea, both at once. He stood still for some time, swallowing hard and breathing heavily. What faint light there was in the chamber came up through the square hole in the floor. Something ran swiftly across the back of his neck. He moved away from the wall and leaned over the hole, pushing with his hands against the other wall in front of him. Below were the fouled earth and spattered stones, moving with flies. He shut his eyes and remained in that expectant position for some minutes, groaning from time to time. The bus driver began to blow his horn; for some reason the sound increased his anguish. "Oh, God, shut up!" he cried aloud, groaning immediately afterward.

But the horn continued, mixing short blasts with long ones. Finally came the moment when the pain suddenly seemed to have lessened. He opened his eyes, and made an involuntary movement upward with his head, because for an instant he thought he saw flames. It was the red rising sun shining on the rocks and filth beneath. When he opened the door Kit and the young Arab stood outside; between them they helped him out to the waiting bus.

As the morning passed, the landscape took on a gaiety and softness that were not quite like anything Kit had ever seen. Suddenly she realized that it was because in good part sand had replaced rock. And lacy trees grew here and there, especially in the spots where there were agglomerations of huts, and these spots became more frequent. Several times they came upon groups of dark men mounted on mehara. These held the reins proudly, their kohl-farded eyes were fierce above the draped indigo veils that hid their faces.

For the first time she felt a faint thrill of excitement. "It *is* rather wonderful," she thought, "to be riding past such people in the Atomic Age."

Port reclined in his seat, his eyes shut. "Just forget I'm here," he had said when they left the bordj, "and I'll be better able to do the same thing. It's only a few hours more—then bed, thank God."

The young Arab spoke just enough French to be undaunted by the patent impossibility of his engaging in an actual conversation with Kit. It appeared that in his eyes a noun alone or a verb uttered with feeling was sufficient, and she seemed to be of the same mind. He told her, with the usual Arab talent for making a legend out of a mere recounting of facts, about El Ga'a and its high walls with their gates that shut at sunset, its quiet dark streets and its great market where men sold many things that came from the Soudan and from even farther away: salt bars, ostrich plumes, gold dust, leopard skins—he enumerated them in a long list, unconcernedly using the Arabic term for a thing when he did not know the French. She listened with complete attention, hypnotized by the extraordinary charm of his face and his voice, and fascinated as well by the strangeness of what he was talking about, the odd way he was saying it.

The terrain now was a sandy wasteland, strewn with occasional tortured bushlike trees that crouched low in the virulent sunlight. Ahead, the blue of the firmament was turning white with a more fierce glare than she had thought possible: it was the air over the city. Before she knew it, they were riding along beside the gray mud walls. The children cried out as the bus went past, their voices like bright needles. Port's eyes were still shut; she decided not to disturb him until they had arrived. They turned sharply to the left, making a cloud of dust, and went through a big gate into an enormous open square—a sort of antechamber to the city, at the end of which was another gate, even larger. Beyond that the people and animals disappeared into darkness. The bus stopped with a jolt and the driver got out abruptly and walked away with the air of wishing to have nothing further to do with it. Passengers still slept, or yawned and began looking about for their belongings, most of which were no longer in the places where they had put them the night before.

Kit indicated by word and gesture that she and Port would stay where they were until everyone else had left the vehicle. The young Arab said that in that event he would, too, because she would need him to help take Port to the hotel. As they sat there waiting for the leisurely travelers to get down, he explained that the hotel was across the town on the side by the fort, since it was operated exclusively for the few officers who did not have homes, it being very rare that anyone arriving by bus had need of a hotel.

"You are very kind," she said, sitting back in her seat.

"Yes, madame." His face expressed nothing but friendly solicitousness, and she trusted him implicitly.

When at last the bus was empty save for the débris of pomegranate peel and date pits on the floor and seats, he got out and called a group of men to carry the bags.

"We're here," said Kit in a loud voice. Port stirred, opened his eyes, and said: "I finally slept. What a hellish trip. Where's the hotel?"

"It's somewhere around," she said vaguely; she did not like to tell him that it was on the other side of the city.

He sat up slowly. "God, I hope it's near. I don't think I can make it if it isn't. I feel like hell. I really feel like hell."

"There's an Arab here who's helping us. He's taking us there. It seems it isn't right here by the terminal." She felt better letting him discover the truth about the hotel from the Arab; that way she would remain uninvolved in the matter, and whatever resentment Port might feel would not be directed against her.

Outside in the dust was the disorder of Africa, but for the first time without any visible sign of European influence, so that the scene had a purity which had been lacking in the other towns, an unexpected quality of being complete which dissipated the feeling of chaos. Even Port, as they helped him out, noticed the unified aspect of the place. "It's wonderful here," he said, "what I can see of it, anyway."

"What you can see of it!" echoed Kit. "Is something wrong with your eyes?"

"I'm dizzy. It's a fever, I know that much."

She felt his forehead, and said nothing but: "Well, let's get out of this sun."

The young Arab walked on his left and Kit on his right; each had a supporting arm about him. The porters had gone on ahead.

"The first decent place," said Port bitterly, "and I have to feel like this."

"You're going to stay in bed until you're absolutely well. We'll have plenty of time to explore later."

He did not answer. They went through the inner gate and straightway plunged into a long, crooked tunnel. Passersby brushed against them in the dark. People were sitting along the walls at the sides, from where muffled voices rose, chanting long repetitious phrases. Soon they were in the sunlight once more, then there was another stretch of darkness where the street burrowed through the thick-walled houses.

"Didn't he tell you where it was? I can't take much more of this," Port said. He had not once addressed the Arab directly.

"Ten, fifteen minutes," said the young Arab.

He still disregarded him. "It's out of the question," he told Kit, gasping a little.

"My dear boy, you've *got* to go. You can't just sit down in the street here."

"What is it?" said the Arab, who was watching their faces. And on being told, he hailed a passing stranger and spoke with him briefly. "There is a fondouk that way." He pointed. "He can—" He made a gesture of sleeping, his hand against his cheek. "Then we go hotel and get men and *rfed, très bien!*" He made as if to sweep Port off his feet and carry him in his arms.

"No, no!" cried Kit, thinking he really was about to pick him up.

He laughed and said to Port: "You want to go there?"

"Yes."

They turned around and made their way back through a part of the interior labyrinth. Again the young Arab spoke with someone in the street. He turned back to them smiling. "The end. The next dark place."

The fondouk was a small, crowded and dirty version of any one of the bordjes they had passed through during the recent weeks, save that the center was covered with a latticework of reeds as a protection from the sun. It was filled with country folk and camels, all of them reclining together on the ground. They went in and the Arab spoke with one of the guardians, who cleared the occupants from a stall at one side and piled fresh straw in its corner for Port to lie down on. The porters sat on the luggage in the courtyard.

"I can't leave here," said Kit, looking about the filthy cubicle. "Move your hand!" It lay on some camel dung, but he left it there. "Go on, please. *Now*," he said. "I'll be all right until you get back. But Hurry. Hurry!"

She cast a last anguished glance at him and went out into the court, followed by the Arab. It was a relief to her to be able to walk quickly in the street.

"*Vite! Vite!*" she kept repeating to him, like a machine. They panted as they went along, threading their way through the slow-moving crowd, down into the heart of the city and out on the other side, until they saw the hill ahead with the fort on it. This side of the town was more open than the other, consisting in part of gardens separated from the streets by high walls, above which rose an occasional tall black cypress. At the end of a long alley there was an almost unnoticeable wooden plaque painted with the words: *Hôtel du Ksar*, and an arrow pointing left. "Ah!" cried Kit. Even here at the edge of town it was still a maze; the streets were constructed in such a way that each stretch seemed to be an impasse with walls at the end. Three times they had to turn back and retrace their steps. There were no doorways, no stalls, not even any passersby—only the impassive pink walls baking in the breathless sunlight.

At last they came upon a tiny, but well-bolted door in the middle of a great expanse of wall. *Entrée de l'Hôtel*, said the sign above it. The Arab knocked loudly.

A long time passed and there was no answer. Kit's throat was painfully dry; her heart was still beating very fast. She shut her eyes and listened. She heard nothing.

"Knock again," she said, reaching up to do it herself. But his hand was still on the knocker, and he pounded with greater energy than before. This time a dog began to bark somewhere back in the garden, and as the sound gradually came closer it was mingled with cries of reproof. "*Askout!*" cried the woman indignantly, but the animal continued to bark. Then there was a period during which an occasional stone bumped on the ground, and the dog was quiet. In her impatience Kit pushed the Arab's hand away from the knocker and started an incessant hammering, which she did not stop until the woman's voice was on the other side of the door, screaming: "*Echkoun? Echkoun?*"

The young Arab and the woman engaged in a long argument, he making extravagant gestures while he demanded she open the door, and she refusing to touch it. Finally she went away. They heard her slippered feet shuffling along the path, then they heard the dog bark again, the woman's reprimands, followed by yelps as she struck it, after which they heard nothing.

"What is it?" cried Kit desperately. "*Pourquoi on ne nous laisse pas entrer?*"

He smiled and shrugged his shoulders. "Madame is coming," he said.

"Oh, good God!" she said in English. She seized the knocker and hammered violently with it, at the same time kicking the base of the door with all her strength. It did not budge. Still smiling, the Arab shook his head slowly from side to side. "*Peut pas,*" he told her. But she continued to pound. Even though she knew she had no reason to be, she was furious with him for not having been able to make the woman open the door. After a moment she stopped, with the sensation that she was about to faint. She was shaking with fatigue, and her mouth and throat felt as though they were made of tin. The sun poured down on the bare earth; there was not a square inch of shadow, save at their feet. Her mind went back to the many times when, as a child, she had held a reading glass over some hapless insect, following it along the ground in its frenzied attempts to escape the increasingly accurate focusing of the lens, until finally she touched it with the blinding pinpoint of light, when as if by magic it ceased running, and she watched it slowly wither and begin to smoke. She felt that if she looked up she would find the sun grown to monstrous proportions. She leaned against the wall and waited.

Eventually there were steps in the garden. She listened to their sound grow in clarity and volume, until they came right up to the door. Without even turning her head she waited for it to be opened; but that did not happen.

"*Qui est là?*" said a woman's voice.

Out of fear that the young Arab would speak and perhaps be refused entrance for being a native, Kit summoned all her strength and cried: "*Vous êtes la propriétaire?*"

There was a short silence. Then the woman, speaking with a Corsican or Italian accent, began a voluble entreaty: "*Ah, madame, allez vous en, je vous en supplie!* . . . *Vous ne pouvez pas entrer ici!* I regret! It is useless to insist. I cannot let you in! No one has been in or out of the hotel for more than a week! It is unfortunate, but you cannot enter!"

"But, madame," Kit cried, almost sobbing, "my husband is very ill!"

"*Aïe!*" The woman's voice rose in pitch and Kit had the impression that she had retreated several steps into the garden; her voice, a little further away, now confirmed it. "*Ah, mon dieu!* Go away! There is nothing I can do!"

"But where?" screamed Kit. "Where can I go?"

The woman already had started back through the garden. She stopped to cry: "Away from El Ga'a! Leave the city! You cannot expect me to let you in. So far we are free of the epidemic, here in the hotel."

The young Arab was trying to pull Kit away. He had understood nothing except that they were not to be let in. "Come. We find fondouk," he was saying. She shook him off, cupped her hands, and called: "Madame, what epidemic?"

The voice came from still farther away. "But, meningitis. You did not know? *Mais oui, madame! Partez! Partez!*" The sound of her hurried footsteps became fainter, was lost. Around the corner of the passageway a blind man had appeared, and was advancing toward them slowly, touching the wall as he moved. Kit looked at the young Arab; her eyes had opened very wide. She was saying to herself: "This is a crisis. There are only a certain number of them in life. I must be calm, and think." He, seeing her staring eyes, and still understanding nothing, put his hand comfortingly on her shoulder and said: "Come." She did not hear him, but she let him pull her away from the wall just before the blind man reached them. And he led her along the street back into the town, as she kept thinking: "This is a crisis." The sudden darkness of a tunnel broke into her self-imposed hypnosis. "Where are we going?" she said to him. The question pleased him greatly; into it he read a recognition of her reliance upon him. "Fondouk," he replied, but some trace of his triumph must have been implicit in the utterance of his word, for she stopped walking and stepped away from him. "*Balak!*" cried a voice beside her, and she was jolted by a man carrying a bundle. The young Arab reached out and gently pulled her toward him. "The fondouk," she repeated vaguely. "Ah, yes." They resumed walking.

In his noisy stable Port seemed to be asleep. His hand still rested on the patch of camel dung—he had not moved at all. Nevertheless he heard them enter and stirred a little to show them he was conscious of their presence. Kit crouched in the straw beside him and smoothed his hair. She had no idea what she was going to say to him, nor, of course, what they were going to do, but it comforted her to be this near to him. For a long time she squatted there, until the position became too painful. Then she stood up. The young Arab was sitting on the ground outside the door. "Port has not said a word," she thought, "but he is expecting the men from the hotel to come and carry him there." At this moment the most difficult part of her task was having to tell him that there was nowhere for him to stay in El Ga'a; she determined not to tell him. At the same time her course of action was decided for her. She knew just what she would do.

And it was all done quickly. She sent the young Arab to the market. Any car, any truck, any bus would do, she had said to him, and price meant nothing. This last enjoinder was wasted on him, of course—he spent nearly an hour haggling over the price three people would pay to be taken in the back of a produce truck that was going to a place called Sbâ that afternoon. But when he came back it was arranged. Once the truck was loaded, the driver would call with it at the New Gate, which was the gate nearest to the fondouk, and would send his mechanic-copain to let them know he was waiting for them, and to recruit the men necessary for carrying Port through the town to the vehicle. "It is good luck," said the young Arab. "Two times one month they go to Sbâ." Kit thanked him. During all the time of his absence Port had not stirred, and she had not dared attempt to rouse him. Now she knelt down with her mouth close to his ear and began to repeat his name softly from time to time. "Yes, Kit," he finally said, his voice very faint. "How are you?" she whispered.

He waited a good while before answering. "Sleepy," he said.

She patted his head. "Sleep a while longer. The men will be here in a little while."

But they did not come until nearly sunset. Meanwhile the young Arab had gone to fetch a bowl of food for Kit. Even with her ravenous appetite, she could hardly manage to swallow what he brought her: the meat consisted of various unidentifiable inner organs fried in deep fat, and there were some rather hard quinces cut in halves, cooked in olive oil. There was also bread, and it was of this that she ate most copiously. When the light already was fading, and the people outside in the courtyard were beginning to prepare their evening meal, the mechanic arrived with three fierce-looking Negroes. None of them spoke any French. The young Arab pointed Port out to them, and they unceremoniously lifted

him up from his bed of straw and carried him out into the
street, Kit following as near to his head as possible, to see that
they did not let it fall too low. They walked quickly along the
darkening passageways, through the camel and goat market,
where there was no sound now but the soft bells worn by
some of the animals. And soon they were outside the walls of
the city, and the desert was dark beyond the headlights of the
waiting truck.

"Back. He goes in back," said the young Arab to her by
way of explanation, as the three let their burden fall limply on
the sacks of potatoes. She handed him some money and asked
him to settle with the Soudanese and the porters. It was not
enough; she had to give him more. Then they went away. The
chauffeur was racing the motor, the mechanic hopped into
the front seat beside him and shut the door. The young Arab
helped her up into the back, and she stood there leaning over
a stack of wine cases looking down at him. He made as if to
jump in with her, but at that instant the truck started to
move. The young Arab ran after it, surely expecting Kit to call
out to the driver to stop, since he had every intention of accompanying her. Once she had caught her balance, however,
she deliberately crouched low and lay down on the floor
among the sacks and bundles, near Port. She did not look out
until they were miles into the desert. Then she looked with
fear, lifting her head and peering quickly as if she expected to
see him out there in the cold wasteland, running along the
trail behind the truck after her.

The truck rode more easily than she had expected, perhaps
because the trail was smooth and there were few curves; the
way seemed to lie through a straight, endless valley on each
side of which in the distance were high dunes. She looked up
at the moon, still tiny, but visibly thicker than last night. And
she shivered a little, laying her handbag on her bosom. It gave
her momentary pleasure to think of that dark little world, the
handbag smelling of leather and cosmetics, that lay between
the hostile air and her body. Nothing was changed in there;
the same objects fell against each other in the same limited
chaos, and the names were still there, still represented the
same things. Mark Cross, Caron, Helena Rubinstein. "Helena
Rubinstein," she said aloud, and it made her laugh. "I'm

going to be hysterical in one minute," she said to herself. She clutched one of Port's inert hands and squeezed the fingers as hard as she could. Then she sat up and devoted all her attention to kneading and massaging the hand, in the hope of feeling it grow warmer under her pressure. A sudden terror swept over her. She put her hand on his chest. Of course, his heart was beating. But he seemed cold. Using all her energy, she pushed his body over onto its side, and stretched herself out behind him, touching him at as many points as possible, hoping in this way to keep him warm. As she relaxed, it struck her that she herself had been cold and that she felt more comfortable now. She wondered if subconsciously part of her desire in lying beside Port had been to warm herself. "Probably, or I never should have thought of it." She slept a little.

And awoke with a start. It was natural, now her mind was clear, that there should be a horror. She tried to keep from thinking what it was. Not Port. That had been going on for a long time now. A new horror, connected with sunlight, dust. . . . She looked away with all her power as she felt her mind being swept into contact with the idea. In a split second it would no longer be possible not to know what it was. . . . There! Meningitis!

The epidemic was in El Ga'a and she had been exposed to it. In the hot tunnels of the streets she had breathed in the poisoned air, she had nestled in the contaminated straw at the fondouk. Surely by now the virus had lodged within her and was multiplying. At the thought of it she felt her back grow stiff. But Port could not be suffering from meningitis: he had been cold since Aïn Krorfa, and he had probably had a fever since the first days in Bou Noura, if they only had had the intelligence between them to find out. She tried to recall what she knew about symptoms, not only of meningitis, but of the other principal contagious diseases. Diphtheria began with a sore throat, cholera with diarrhea, but typhus, typhoid, the plague, malaria, yellow fever, kala azar—as far as she knew they all began with fever and malaise of one sort or another. It was a toss-up. "Perhaps it's amoebic dysentery combined with a return of malaria," she reasoned. "But whatever it is, it's already there in him, and nothing I do or don't do can change the outcome of it." She did not want to feel in any way responsible; that would have been too much to bear at this point. As it was, she felt that she was holding up rather well. She remembered stories of horror from the war, stories whose moral always turned out to be: "One never knows what a person is made of until the moment of stress; then often the most timorous person turns out to be the bravest." She wondered if she were being brave, or just resigned. Or cowardly, she added to herself. That, too, was possible, and there was no way of knowing. Port could never tell her because he knew even less about it. If she nursed him and got him through whatever he had, he doubtless would tell her she had been brave, a martyr, and many other things, but that would be out of gratitude. And then she wondered why she wanted to know—it seemed rather a frivolous consideration at the moment.

The truck roared on and on. Fortunately the back was completely open, or the exhaust fumes would have been troublesome. As it was, she caught a sharp odor now and then, but in the following instant it was dissipated in the cold night air. The moon set, the stars were there, she had no idea how late it was. The noise of the motor drowned out the sound of whatever conversation there may have been in front between the driver and the mechanic, and made it impossible for her to communicate with them. She put her arms about Port's waist, and hugged him closer for warmth. "Whatever he has, he's breathing it away from me," she thought. In her moments of sleep she burrowed with her legs beneath the sacks to keep warm; their weight sometimes woke her, but she preferred the pressure to the cold. She had put some empty sacks over Port's legs. It was a long night.

XXII

As he lay in the back of the truck, protected somewhat from the cold by Kit, now and then he was aware of the straight road beneath him. The twisting roads of the past weeks became alien, faded from his memory; it had been one strict, undeviating course inland to the desert, and now he was very nearly at the center.

How many times his friends, envying him his life, had said to him: "Your life is so simple." "Your life seems always to go

in a straight line." Whenever they had said the words he heard
in them an implicit reproach: it is not difficult to build a
straight road on a treeless plain. He felt that what they really
meant to say was: "You have chosen the easiest terrain." But if
they elected to place obstacles in their own way—and they so
clearly did, encumbering themselves with every sort of unnecessary allegiance—that was no reason why they should object
to his having simplified his life. So it was with a certain annoyance that he would say: "Everyone makes the life he wants.
Right?" as though there were nothing further to be said.

The immigration authorities at his disembarkation had not
been satisfied to leave a blank after the word *Profession* on
their papers as he had done in his passport. (That passport,
official proof of his existence, racing after him, somewhere behind in the desert!) They had said: "Surely monsieur must do
something." And Kit, seeing that he was about to contest the
point, had interposed quickly: "Ah, yes. Monsieur is a writer,
but he is modest!" They had laughed, filled in the space with
the word *écrivain*, and made the remark that they hoped he
would find inspiration in the Sahara. For a while he had been
infuriated by their stubbornness in insisting upon his having a
label, an *état-civil.* Then for a few hours the idea of his actually writing a book had amused him. A journal, filled in each
evening with the day's thoughts, carefully seasoned with local
color, in which the absolute truth of the theorem he would
set forth in the beginning—namely, that the difference between something and nothing is nothing—should be clearly
and calmly demonstrated. He had not even mentioned the
idea to Kit; she surely would have killed it with her enthusiasm. Since the death of his father he no longer worked at anything, because it was not necessary, but Kit constantly held
the hope that he would begin again to write—to write no
matter what, so long as he worked at it. "He's a *little* less in-
supportable when he's working," she explained to others, and
by no means totally in jest. And when he saw his mother,
which was seldom, she too would say: "Been working?" and
look at him with her large sad eyes. He would reply: "Nope,"
and look back at her insolently. Even as they were driving to
the hotel in the taxi, with Tunner saying: "What a hellhole"
as he saw the miserable streets, he had been thinking that Kit

would be too delighted at the prospect; it would have to be done in secret—it was the only way he would be able to carry it off. But then when he had got settled in the hotel, and they had started their little pattern of café life at the Eckmühl-Noiseux, there had been nothing to write about—he could not establish a connection in his mind between the absurd trivialities which filled the day and the serious business of putting words on paper. He thought it was probably Tunner who prevented him from being completely at ease. Tunner's presence created a situation, however slight, which kept him from entering into the reflective state he considered essential. As long as he was living his life, he could not write about it. Where one left off, the other began, and the existence of circumstances which demanded even the vaguest participation on his part was sufficient to place writing outside the realm of possibility. But that was all right. He would not have written well, and so he would have got no pleasure from it. And even if what he might have written had been good, how many people would have known it? It was all right to speed ahead into the desert leaving no trace.

Suddenly he remembered that they were on their way to the hotel in El Ga'a. It was another night and they had not yet arrived; there was a contradiction somewhere, he knew, but he did not have the energy to look for it. Occasionally he felt the fever rage within him, a separate entity; it gave him the image of a baseball player winding up, getting ready to pitch. And he was the ball. Around and around he went, then he was flung into space for a while, dissolving in flight.

They stood over him. There had been a long struggle, and he was very tired. Kit was one; the other was a soldier. They were talking, but what they said meant nothing. He left them there standing over him, and went back where he had come from.

"He will be as well off here as anywhere else this side of Sidi-bel-Abbès," said the soldier. "With typhoid all you can do, even in a hospital, is to keep the fever as low as possible, and wait. We have little here in Sbâ in the way of medicine, but these"—he pointed to a tube of pills that lay on an overturned box by the cot—"will bring the fever down, and that is already a great deal."

Kit did not look at him. "And peritonitis?" she said in a low voice.

Captain Broussard frowned. "Do not look for complications, madame," he said severely. "It is always bad enough without that. Yes, of course, peritonitis, pneumonia, heart stoppage, who knows? And you, too, maybe you have the famous El Ga'a meningitis that Madame Luccioni was kind enough to warn you about. *Bien sûr!* And maybe there are fifty cases of cholera here in Sbâ at this moment. I would not tell you even if there were."

"Why not?" she said, finally looking up.

"It would be absolutely useless; and besides, it would lower your morale. No, no. I would isolate the sick, and take measures to prevent the spread of the disease, nothing more. What we have in our hands is always enough. We have a man here with typhoid. We must bring down the fever. That is all. And these stories of peritonitis for him, meningitis for you, do not interest me in the least. You must be realistic, madame. If you stray outside that, you do harm to everyone. You have only to give him his pills every two hours, and try to make him take as much soup as possible. The cook's name is Zina. It would be prudent to be in the kitchen with her now and then to be sure there is always a fire and a big pot of soup constantly hot and ready. Zina is magnificent; she has cooked for us twelve years. But all natives need to be watched, always. They forget. And now, madame, if you will pardon me, I shall get back to my work. One of the men will bring you the mattress I promised you from my house, this afternoon. It will not be very comfortable, doubtless, but what can you expect—you are in Sbâ, not in Paris." He turned in the doorway. "*Enfin, madame, soyez courageuse!*" he said, frowning again, and went out.

Kit stood unmoving, and slowly looked about the bare little room with the door on one side, and a window on the other. Port lay on the rickety cot, facing the wall, breathing regularly with the sheet pulled up around his head. This room was the hospital of Sbâ; it had the one available bed in the town, with real sheets and blankets, and Port was in it only because no member of the military force happened to be ill at the moment. A mud wall came halfway up the window outside, but above that the sky's agonizing light poured in. She took the extra sheet the captain had given her for herself, folded it into a small square the size of the window, got a box of thumbtacks out of Port's luggage, and covered the open space. Even as she stood in the window she was struck with the silence of the place. She could have thought there was not a living being within a thousand miles. The famous silence of the Sahara. She wondered if as the days went by each breath she took would sound as loud to her as it did now, if she would get used to the ridiculous noise her saliva made as she swallowed, and if she would have to swallow as often as she seemed to be doing at the moment, now that she was so conscious of it.

"Port," she said, very softly. He did not stir. She walked out of the room into the blinding light of the courtyard with its floor of sand. There was no one in sight. There was nothing but the blazing white walls, the unmoving sand at her feet and the blue depths of the sky above. She took a few steps, and feeling a little ill, turned and went back into the room. There was not a chair to sit on—only the cot and the little box beside it. She sat down on one of the valises. A tag hung from the handle by her hand. *Wanted on Voyage*, it said. The room had the utterly noncommittal look of a storeroom. With the luggage in the middle of the floor there was not even space for the mattress they were going to bring; the bags would have to be piled in one huge heap in a corner. She looked at her hands, she looked at her feet in their lizard-skin pumps. There was no mirror in the room; she reached across to another valise and seized her handbag, pulling out her compact and lipstick. When she opened the compact she discovered there was not enough light to see her face in its little mirror. Standing in the doorway, she made up slowly and carefully.

"Port," she said again, as softly as before. He went on breathing. She locked her handbag into a valise, looked at her wristwatch, and stepped forth once more into the bright courtyard, this time wearing dark glasses.

Dominating the town, the fort sat astride a high hill of sand, a succession of scattered buildings protected by a wandering outer rampart. It was a separate town, alien to the

surrounding landscape and candidly military in aspect. The
native guards at the gate looked at her with interest as she
went through. The town, sand-color, was spread out below
with its single-storied, flat-roofed houses. She turned in the
other direction and skirted the wall, climbing for a brief distance until she was at the top of the hill. The heat and the
light made her slightly dizzy, and the sand kept filling her
shoes. From this point she could hear the clear, high-pitched
sounds of the town below; children's voices and dogs barking. In all directions, where the earth and sky met, there was
a faint, rapidly pulsating haze.

"Sbâ," she said aloud. The word meant nothing to her; it
did not even represent the haphazard collection of formless
huts below. When she returned to the room someone had left
a mammoth white china chamber-pot in the middle of the
floor. Port was lying on his back, looking up at the ceiling,
and he had pushed the covers off.

She hurried to the cot and pulled them up over him. There
was no way of tucking him in. She took his temperature: it
had fallen somewhat.

"This bed hurts my back," he said unexpectedly, gasping a
little. She stepped back and surveyed the cot: it sagged heavily between the head and the foot.

"We'll fix that in a little while," she said. "Now, be good
and keep covered up."

He looked at her reproachfully. "You don't have to talk to
me as if I were a child," he said. "I'm still the same person."

"It's just automatic, I suppose, when people are sick," she
said, laughing uncomfortably. "I'm sorry."

He still looked at her. "I don't have to be humored in any
way," he said slowly. Then he shut his eyes and sighed deeply.

When the mattress arrived, she had the Arab who had
brought it go and get another man. Together they lifted Port
off the cot and laid him onto the mattress which was spread
on the floor. Then she had them pile some of the valises on
the cot. The Arabs went out.

"Where are you going to sleep?" asked Port.

"On the floor here beside you," she said.

He did not ask her any more. She gave him his pills and
said: "Now sleep." Then she went out to the gate and tried

to speak with the guards; they did not understand any French, and kept saying: "*Non, m'si.*" As she was gesticulating with them, Captain Broussard appeared in a nearby doorway and looked at her with a certain suspicion in his eyes. "Do you want something, madame?" he said.

"I want someone to go with me to the market and help me buy some blankets," said Kit.

"*Ah, je regrette, madame,*" he said. "There is no one in the post here who could render you that service, and I do not advise you to go alone. But if you like I can send you blankets from my quarters."

Kit was effusive in her thanks. She went back into the inner courtyard and stood a moment looking at the door of the room, loath to enter. "It's a prison," she thought. "I'm a prisoner here, and for how long? God knows." She went in, sat down on a valise just inside the door, and stared at the floor. Then she rose, opened a bag, pulled out a fat French novel she had bought before leaving for Boussif, and tried to read. When she had got to the fifth page, she heard someone coming through the courtyard. It was a young French soldier carrying three camel blankets. She got up and stepped aside for him to enter, saying: "*Ah, merci. Comme vous êtes aimable!*" But he stood still just outside the door, holding his arm out toward her for her to take the blankets. She lifted them off and laid them on the floor at her feet. When she looked up he already had started away. She stared after him an instant, vaguely perplexed, and then set about collecting various odd pieces of clothing from among her effects, which could serve as a foundation to place underneath the blankets. She finally arranged her bed, lay down on it, and was pleasantly surprised to find it comfortable. All at once she felt an overwhelming desire to sleep. It would be another hour and a half before she must give Port his medicine. She closed her eyes and for a moment was in the back of the truck on her way from El Ga'a to Sbâ. The sensation of motion lulled her, and she immediately fell asleep.

She was awakened by feeling something brush past her face. She started up, saw that it was dark and that someone was moving about in the room. "Port!" she cried. A woman's voice said: "*Voici mangi, madame.*" She was standing directly above her. Someone came through the courtyard silently bearing a carbide lamp. It was a small boy, who walked to the door, reached in, and set the light down on the floor. She looked up and saw a large-boned old woman with eyes that were still beautiful. "This is Zina," she thought, and she called her by name. The woman smiled, and stooped down, putting the tray on the floor by Kit's bed. Then she went out.

It was difficult to feed Port; much of the soup ran over his face and down his neck. "Maybe tomorrow you'll feel like sitting up to eat," she said as she wiped his mouth with a handkerchief. "Maybe," he said feebly.

"Oh, my God!" she cried. She had overslept; the pills were long overdue. She gave them to him and had him wash them down with a swallow of tepid water. He made a face. "The water," he said. She sniffed the carafe. It reeked of chlorine. She had put the Halazone tablets in twice by mistake. "It won't hurt you," she said.

She ate her food with relish; Zina was quite a good cook. While she was still eating, she looked over at Port and saw that he was already asleep. The pills seemed each time to have that effect. She thought of taking a short walk after the meal, but she was afraid that Captain Broussard might have given orders to the guards not to let her pass. She went out into the courtyard and walked around it several times, looking up at the stars. An accordion was being played somewhere at the other end of the fort; its sound was very faint. She went into the room, shut the door, locked it, undressed, and lay on her blankets beside Port's mattress, pulling the lamp over near her head so she could read. But the light was not strong enough, and it moved too much, so that her eyes began to hurt, and the smell of it disgusted her. Reluctantly she blew out the flame, and the room fell back into the profoundest darkness. She had scarcely lain down before she sprang up again, and began to scrabble about the floor with her hand, searching for matches. She lit the lamp, which seemed to be smelling stronger than ever since she had blown it out, and said to herself, but moving her lips: "Every two hours. Every two hours."

In the night she awoke sneezing. At first she thought it was the odor of the lamp, but then she put her hand to her face, and felt the grit on her skin. She moved her fingers along the pillow: it was covered with a coating of dust. Then she became conscious of the noise of the wind outside. It was like the roar of the sea. Fearful of waking Port, she tried to stifle the sneeze that was on its way; her effort was unsuccessful. She got up. It seemed cold in the room. She spread Port's bathrobe over him. Then she got two large handkerchiefs out of a suitcase and tied one over the lower part of her face, bandit-fashion. The other one she intended to arrange for Port when she woke him up to give him his pills. It would be only another twenty minutes. She lay down, sneezing again as a result of the dust raised by moving the blankets. She lay perfectly still listening to the fury of the wind as it swept by outside the door.

"Here I am, in the middle of horror," she thought, attempting to exaggerate the situation, in the hope of convincing herself that the worst had happened, was actually there with her. But it would not work. The sudden arrival of the wind was a new omen, connected only with the time to come. It began to make a singular, animal-like sound beneath the door. If she could only give up, relax, and live in the perfect knowledge that there was no hope. But there was never any knowing or any certitude; the time to come always had more than one possible direction. One could not even give up hope. The wind would blow, the sand would settle, and in some as yet unforeseen manner time would bring about a change which could only be terrifying, since it would not be a continuation of the present.

She remained awake the rest of the night, giving Port his pills regularly, and trying to relax in the periods between. Each time she woke him he moved obediently and swallowed the water and the tablet proffered him without speaking or even opening his eyes. In the pale, infected light of daybreak she heard him begin to sob. Electrified, she sat up and stared at the corner where his head lay. Her heart was beating very fast, activated by a strange emotion she could not identify. She listened a while, decided it was compassion she felt, and leaned nearer to him. The sobs came up mechanically, like hiccups or belches. Little by little the sensation of excitement died away, but she remained sitting up, listening intently to the two sounds together: the sobs inside the room and the wind without. Two impersonal, natural sounds. After a sudden, short silence she heard him say, quite distinctly: "Kit. Kit." As her eyes grew wide she said: "Yes?" But he did not answer. After a long time, clandestinely, she slid back down under the blanket and fell asleep for a while. When she awoke the morning had really begun. The inflamed shafts of distant sunlight sifted down from the sky along with the air's fine grit; the insistent wind seemed about to blow away what feeble strands of light there were.

She arose and moved about the room stiffly in the cold, trying to raise as little dust as possible while she made her toilet. But the dust lay thick on everything. She was conscious of a defect in her functioning—it was as if an entire section of her mind were numb. She felt the lack there: an enormous blind spot inside her—but she could not locate it. And as if from a distance she watched the fumbling gestures her hands made as they came in contact with the objects and the garments. "This has got to stop," she said to herself. "This has got to stop." But she did not know quite what she meant. Nothing could stop; everything always went on.

Zina arrived, completely shrouded in a great white blanket, and slamming the door behind her against the blast, drew forth from beneath the folds of her clothing a small tray which bore a teapot and a glass. "*Bonjour, madame. R'mleh bzef,*" she said, with a gesture toward the sky, and set the tray on the floor beside the mattress.

The hot tea gave her a little strength; she drank it all and sat a while listening to the wind. Suddenly she realized that there was nothing for Port. Tea would not be enough for him. She decided to go in search of Zina to see if there was any way of getting him some milk. She went out and stood in the courtyard, calling: "Zina! Zina!" in a voice rendered feeble by the wind's fury, grinding the sand between her teeth as she caught her breath.

No one appeared. After stumbling into and out of several empty niche-like rooms, she discovered a passageway that led to the kitchen. Zina was there squatting on the floor, but Kit could not make her understand what she wanted. With motions the old woman indicated that she would presently fetch

Captain Broussard and send him to the room. Back in the semi-darkness she lay down on her pallet, coughing and rubbing away from her eyes the sand that had gathered on her face. Port was still sleeping.

She herself was almost asleep when the captain came in. He removed the hood of his camel's-hair burnous from around his face, and shook it, then he shut the door behind him and squinted about in the obscurity. Kit stood up. The expected queries and responses regarding the state of the patient were made. But when she asked him about the milk he merely looked at her pityingly. All canned milk was rationed, and that only to women with infants. "And the sheep's milk is always sour and undrinkable in any case," he added. It seemed to Kit that each time he looked at her it was as if he suspected her of harboring secret and reprehensible motives. The resentment she felt at his accusatory gaze helped her to regain a little of her lost sense of reality. "I'm sure he doesn't look at everybody that way," she thought. "Then why me? Damn his soul!" But she felt too utterly dependent upon the man to allow herself the satisfaction of letting him perceive anything of her reactions. She stood, trying to look forlorn, with her right hand outstretched above Port's head in a compassionate gesture, hoping the captain's heart might be moved; she was convinced that he could get her all the canned milk she wanted, if he chose.

"Milk is completely unnecessary for your husband in any case, madame," he said dryly. "The soup I have ordered is quite sufficient, and more digestible. I shall have Zina bring a bowl immediately." He went out; the sand-laden wind still roared.

Kit spent the day reading and seeing to it that Port was dosed and fed regularly. He was utterly disinclined to speak; perhaps he did not have the strength. While she was reading, sometimes she forgot the room, the situation, for minutes at a time, and on each occasion when she raised her head and remembered again, it was like being struck in the face. Once she almost laughed, it seemed so ridiculously unlikely. "Sbâ," she said, prolonging the vowel so that it sounded like the bleat of a sheep.

Toward late afternoon she tired of her book and stretched out on her bed, carefully, so as not to disturb Port. As she turned toward him, she realized with a disagreeable shock that his eyes were open, looking at her across the few inches of bedding. The sensation was so violently unpleasant that she sprang up, and staring back at him, said in a tone of forced solicitude: "How do you feel?" He frowned a little, but did not reply. Falteringly she pursued. "Do you think the pills help? At least they seem to bring the fever down a bit." And now, surprisingly enough, he answered, in a soft but clear voice. "I'm very sick," he said slowly. "I don't know whether I'll come back."

"Back?" she said stupidly. Then she patted his hot forehead, feeling disgusted with herself even as she uttered the words: "You'll be all right."

All at once she decided she must get out of the room for a while before dark—even if just for a few minutes. A change of air. She waited until he had closed his eyes. Then without looking at him again for fear she would see them open once more, she got up quickly and stepped out into the wind. It seemed to have shifted a little, and there was less sand in the air. Even so, she felt the sting of the grains on her cheeks. Briskly she walked out beneath the high mud portal, not looking at the guards, not stopping when she reached the road, but continuing downward until she came to the street that led to the market place. Down there the wind was less noticeable. Apart from an inert figure lying here and there entirely swathed in its burnous, the way was empty. As she moved along through the soft sand of the street, the remote sun fell rapidly behind the flat hammada ahead, and the walls and arches took on their twilight rose hue. She was a little ashamed of herself for having given in to her nervous impatience to be out of the room, but she banished the sentiment by arguing with herself that nurses, like everyone else, must rest occasionally.

She came to the market, a vast, square, open space enclosed on all four sides by whitewashed arcades whose innumerable arches made a monotonous pattern whichever way she turned her head. A few camels lay grumbling in the center, a few palm-branch fires flared, but the merchants and their wares were gone. Then she heard the muezzins calling in three distinct parts of the town, and saw those men who were left begin their evening prayer. Crossing the market, she wandered into a side street with its earthen buildings all orange in the momentary glow. The little shop doors were closed—all but one, in front of which she paused an instant, peering in vaguely. A man wearing a beret crouched inside over a small fire built in the middle of the floor, holding his hands fanwise almost in the flames. He glanced up and saw her, then rising, he came to the door. "*Entrez, madame,*" he said, making a wide gesture. For lack of anything else to do, she obeyed. It was a tiny shop; in the dimness she could see a few bolts of white cloth lying on the shelves. He fitted a carbide lamp together, touched a match to the spout, and watched the sharp flame spring up. "Daoud Zozeph," he said, holding forth his hand. She was faintly surprised: for some reason she had thought he was French. Certainly he was not a native of Sbâ. She sat on the stool he offered her, and they talked a few minutes. His French was quite good, and he spoke it gently in a tone of obscure reproof. Suddenly she realized he was a Jew. She asked him; he seemed astonished and amused at her question. "Of course," he said. "I stay open during the hour of prayer. Afterward there are always a few customers." They spoke of the difficulties of being a Jew here in Sbâ, and then she found herself telling him of her predicament, of Port who lay alone up in the Poste Militaire. He leaned against the counter above her, and it seemed to her that his dark eyes glowed with sympathy. Even this faint impression, unconfirmed as it was, made her aware for the first time of how cruelly lacking in that sentiment was the human landscape here, and of how acutely she had been missing it without realizing she was missing it. And so she talked on and on, even going into her feeling about omens. She stopped abruptly, looked at him a little fearfully, and laughed. But he was very serious; he seemed to understand her very well. "Yes, yes," he said, stroking his beardless chin meditatively. "You are right about all that."

Logically she should not have found such a statement reassuring, but the fact that he agreed with her she found deliciously comforting. However, he continued: "The mistake you make is in being afraid. That is the great mistake. The signs are given us for our good, not for our harm. But when you are afraid you read them wrong and make bad things where good ones were meant to be."

"But I *am* afraid," protested Kit. "How can I change that? It's impossible."

He looked at her and shook his head. "That is not the way to live," he said.

"I know," she said sadly.

An Arab entered the shop, bade her good evening, and purchased a pack of cigarettes. As he went out the door, he turned and spat just inside it on the floor. Then he gave a disdainful toss of his burnous over his shoulder and strode away. Kit looked at Daoud Zozeph.

"Did he spit on purpose?" she asked him.

He laughed. "Yes. No. Who knows? I have been spat upon so many thousand times that I do not see it when it happens. You see! You should be a Jew in Sbâ, and you would learn not to be afraid! At least you would learn not to be afraid of God. You would see that even when God is most terrible, he is never cruel, the way men are."

Suddenly what he was saying sounded ridiculous. She rose, smoothed her skirt, and said she must be going.

"One moment," he said, going behind a curtain into a room beyond. He returned presently with a small parcel. Behind the counter he resumed the anonymous air of a shopkeeper. He handed the parcel across to her, saying quietly: "You said you wanted to give your husband milk. Here are two cans. They were the ration for our baby." He raised his hand as she tried to interrupt. "But it was born dead, last week, too soon. Next year if we have another we can get more."

Seeing Kit's look of anguish, he laughed: "I promise you," he said, "as soon as my wife knows, I will apply for the coupons. There will be no trouble. *Allons!* What are you afraid of now?" And as she still stood looking at him, he raised the parcel in the air and presented it again with such an air of finality that automatically she took hold of it. "This is one of those occasions where one doesn't try to put into words what one feels," she said to herself. She thanked him saying that her husband would be very happy, and that she hoped they would meet again in a few days. Then she went out. With the coming of night, the wind had risen somewhat. She shivered climbing the hill on the way to the fort.

The first thing she did on arriving back in the room was to light the lamp. Then she took Port's temperature: she was horrified to find it higher. The pills were no longer working. He looked at her with an unaccustomed expression in his shining eyes.

"Today's my birthday," he murmured.

"No, it isn't," she said sharply; then she reflected an instant, and asked with feigned interest: "Is it, really?"

"Yes. This was the one I've been waiting for."

She did not ask him what he meant. He went on: "Is it beautiful out?"

"No."

"I wish you could have said yes."

"Why?"

"I'd have liked it to be beautiful out."

"I suppose you could call it beautiful, but it's just a little unpleasant to walk in."

"Ah, well, we're not out in it," he said.

The quietness of this dialogue made more monstrous the groans of pain which an instant later issued from within him. "What is it?" she cried in a frenzy. But he could not hear her. She knelt on her mattress and looked at him, unable to decide what to do. Little by little he grew silent, but he did not open his eyes. For a while she studied the inert body as it lay there beneath the covers, which rose and fell slightly with the rapid respiration. "He's stopped being human," she said to herself. Illness reduces man to his basic state: a cloaca in which the chemical processes continue. The meaningless hegemony of the involuntary. It was the ultimate taboo stretched out there beside her, helpless and terrifying beyond all reason. She choked back a wave of nausea that threatened her for an instant.

There was a knocking at the door: it was Zina with Port's soup, and a plate of couscous for her. Kit indicated that she wanted her to feed the invalid; the old woman seemed delighted, and began to try to coax him into sitting up. There was no response save a slight acceleration in his breathing. She was patient and persevering, but to no avail. Kit had her take the soup away, deciding that if he wanted nourishment later she would open one of the tins of milk and mix it with hot water for him.

The wind was blowing again, but without fury, and from the other direction. It moaned spasmodically through the cracks around the window, and the folded sheet moved a bit now and then. Kit stared at the spurting white flame of the lamp, trying to conquer her powerful desire to run out of the room. It was no longer the familiar fear that she felt—it was a steadily mounting sentiment of revulsion.

But she lay perfectly still, blaming herself and thinking: "If I feel no sense of duty toward him, at least I can act as if I did." At the same time there was an element of self-chastisement in her immobility. "You're not even to move your foot if it falls asleep. And I hope it hurts." Time passed, expressed in the low cry of the wind as it sought to enter the room, the cry rising and falling in pitch but never quite ceasing. Unexpectedly Port breathed a profound sigh and shifted his position on the mattress. And incredibly, he began to speak.

"Kit." His voice was faint but in no way distorted. She held her breath, as if her least movement might snap the thread that held him to rationality.

"Kit."

"Yes."

"I've been trying to get back. Here." He kept his eyes closed.

"Yes—"

"And now I am."

"Yes!"

"I wanted to talk to you. There's nobody here?"

"No, no!"

"Is the door locked?"

"I don't know," she said. She bounded up and locked it, returning to her pallet, all in the same movement. "Yes, it's locked."

"I wanted to talk to you."

She did not know what to say. She said: "I'm glad."

"There are so many things I want to say. I don't know what they are. I've forgotten them all."

She patted his hand lightly. "It's always that way."

He lay silent a moment.

"Wouldn't you like some warm milk?" she said cheerfully.

He seemed distraught. "I don't think there's time. I don't know."

"I'll fix it for you," she announced, and she sat up, glad to be free.

"Please stay here."

She lay down again, murmuring: "I'm so glad you feel better. You don't know how different it makes *me* feel to hear you talk. I've been going crazy here. There's not a soul around—" She stopped, feeling the momentum of hysteria begin to gather in the background. But Port seemed not to have heard her.

"Please stay here," he repeated, moving his hand uncertainly along the sheet. She knew it was searching for hers, but she could not make herself reach out and let it take hold. At the same moment she became aware of her refusal, and the tears came into her eyes—tears of pity for Port. Still she did not move.

Again he sighed. "I feel very sick. I feel awful. There's no reason to be afraid, but I am. Sometimes I'm not here, and I don't like that. Because then I'm far away and all alone. No one could ever get there. It's too far. And there I'm alone."

She wanted to stop him, but behind the stream of quiet words she heard the entreaty of a moment back: "Please stay here." And she did not have the strength to stop him unless she got up and moved about. But his words made her miserable; it was like hearing him recount one of his dreams—worse, even.

"So alone I can't even remember the idea of not being alone," he was saying. His fever would go up. "I can't even think what it would be like for there to be someone else in the world. When I'm there I can't remember being here; I'm just afraid. But here I can remember being there. I wish I could stop remembering it. It's awful to be two things at once. You know that, don't you?" His hand sought hers desperately. "You do know that? You understand how awful it is? You've got to." She let him take her hand, pull it towards his mouth. He rubbed his rough lips along it with a terrible avidity that shocked her; at the same time she felt the hair at the back of her head rise and stiffen. She watched his lips opening and shutting against her knuckles, and felt the hot breath on her fingers.

"Kit, Kit. I'm afraid, but it's not only that. Kit! All these years I've been living for you. I didn't know it, and now I do. I do know it! But now you're going away." He tried to roll over and lie on top of her arm; he clutched her hand always tighter.

"I'm not!" she cried.

His legs moved spasmodically.

"I'm right here!" she shouted, even louder, trying to imagine how her voice sounded to him, whirling down his own dark halls toward chaos. And as he lay still for a while, breathing violently, she began to think: "He says it's more than just being afraid. But it isn't. He's never lived for me. Never. Never." She held to the thought with an intensity that drove it from her mind, so that presently she found herself lying taut in every muscle without an idea in her head, listening to the wind's senseless monologue. For a time this went on; she did not relax. Then little by little she tried to draw her hand away from Port's desperate grasp. There was a sudden violent activity beside her, and she turned to see him partially sitting up.

"Port!" she cried, pushing herself up and putting her hands on his shoulders. "You've got to lie down!" She used all her strength; he did not budge. His eyes were open and he was looking at her. "Port!" she cried again in a different voice. He raised one hand and took hold of her arm.

"But Kit," he said softly. They looked at each other. She made a slight motion with her head, letting it fall onto his chest. Even as he glanced down at her, her first sob came up, and the first cleared the passage for the others. He closed his eyes again, and for a moment had the illusion of holding the world in his arms—a warm world all tropics, lashed by storm. "No, no, no, no, no, no, no," he said. It was all he had the strength to say. But even if he had been able to say more, still he would have said only: "No, no, no, no."

It was not a whole life whose loss she was mourning there in his arms, but it was a great part of one; above all it was a part whose limits she knew precisely, and her knowledge augmented the bitterness. And presently within her, deeper than the weeping for the wasted years, she found a ghastly dread all formed and growing. She raised her head and looked up at him with tenderness and terror. His head had dropped to one side; his eyes were closed. She put her arms around his neck and kissed his forehead many times. Then, half-pulling and half-coaxing, she got him back down into bed and covered him. She gave him his pill, undressed silently and lay down facing him, leaving the lamp burning so she could see him as she fell asleep. The wind at the window celebrated her dark sensation of having attained a new depth of solitude.

XXIII

"More wood!" shouted the lieutenant, looking into the fireplace where the flames were dying down. But Ahmed refused to be prodigal with the wood, and brought in another small armful of the meager, gnarled branches. He remembered the early mornings of bitter cold when his mother and sister had got up long before dawn to set out across the high dunes toward Hassi Mokhtar; he remembered their return when the sun would be setting, and their faces, seamed with fatigue, as they came into the courtyard bent over double beneath their loads. The lieutenant would often throw on the fire as much wood as his sister had used to gather in the entire day, but *he* would not do it; he always brought in a scant amount. The lieutenant was quite aware that this was sheer recalcitrance on Ahmed's part. He considered it a senseless but unalterable eccentricity.

"He's a crazy boy," said Lieutenant d'Armagnac, sipping his vermouth-cassis, "but honest and faithful. Those are the prime qualities to look for in a servant. Even stupidity and stubbornness are acceptable, if he has the others. Not that Ahmed is stupid, by any means. Sometimes he has a better intuition than I. In the case of your friend, for instance. The last time he came to see me here at my house, I invited him and his wife for dinner. I told him I would send Ahmed to let him know exactly which day it would be. I was ill at the time. I think my cook had been trying to poison me. You understand everything I am saying, monsieur?"

"*Oui, oui,*" said Tunner, whose ear was superior to his tongue. He was following the lieutenant's conversation with only a slight amount of difficulty.

"After your friend had left, Ahmed said to me: 'He will never come.' I said: 'Nonsense. Of course he will, and with his wife.' 'No,' said Ahmed. 'I can tell by his face. He has no intention of coming.' And you see he was right. That very evening they both left for El Ga'a. I heard only the next day. It's astonishing, isn't it?"

"*Oui*," said Tunner again; he was sitting forward in his chair, his hands on his knees, looking very serious.

"Ah, yes," yawned his host, rising to throw more wood on the fire. "A surprising people, the Arabs. Of course here there's a very heavy admixture of Soudanese, from the time of slavery—"

Tunner interrupted him. "But you say they're not in El Ga'a now?"

"Your friends? No. They've gone to Sbâ, as I told you. The Chef de Poste there is Captain Broussard; he is the one who telegraphed me about the typhoid. You'll find him a bit curt, but he's a fine man. Only the Sahara does not agree with him. Some it does, some not. Me, for example, I'm in my element here."

Again Tunner interrupted. "How soon do you think I can be in Sbâ?"

The lieutenant laughed indulgently. "*Vous êtes bien pressé!* But there's no hurry with typhoid. It will be several weeks before your friend will care whether he sees you or not. And he will not be needing that passport in the meantime! So you can take your time." He felt warmly toward this American, whom he found much more to his liking than the first. The first had been furtive, had made him vaguely uneasy (but perhaps that impression had been due to his own state of mind at the time). In any case, in spite of Tunner's obvious haste to leave Bou Noura, he found him a sympathetic companion, and he hoped to persuade him to stay a while.

"You will remain for dinner?" said the lieutenant.

"Oh," said Tunner distraughtly. "Thank you very much."

First of all there was the room. Nothing could change the hard little shell of its existence, its white plaster walls and its faintly arched ceiling, its concrete floor and its windows across which a sheet had been tacked, folded over many times to keep out the light. Nothing could change it because that was all there was of it, that and the mattress on which he lay. When from time to time a gust of clarity swept down upon him, and he opened his eyes and saw what was really there, and knew where he really was, he fixed the walls, the ceiling and the floor in his memory, so that he could find his way back next time. For there were so many other parts of the world, so many other moments in time to be visited; he never was certain that the way back would really be there. Counting was impossible. How many hours he had been like this, lying on the burning mattress, how many times he had seen Kit stretched out on the floor nearby, had made a sound and seen her turn over, get up and then come toward him to give him water—things like that he could not have told, even if he had thought to ask them of himself. His mind was occupied with very different problems. Sometimes he spoke aloud, but it was not satisfying; it seemed rather to hold back the natural development of the ideas. They flowed out through his mouth, and he was never sure whether they had been resolved in the right words. Words were much more alive and more difficult to handle, now; so much so that Kit did not seem to understand them when he used them. They slipped into his head like the wind blowing into a room, and extinguished the frail flame of an idea forming there in the dark. Less and less he used them in his thinking. The process became more mobile; he followed the course of thoughts because he was tied on behind. Often the way was vertiginous, but he could not let go. There was no repetition in the landscape; it was always new territory and the peril increased constantly. Slowly, pitilessly, the number of dimensions was lessening. There were fewer directions in which to move. It was not a clear process, there was nothing definite about it so that he could say: "Now up is gone." Yet he had witnessed occasions when two different dimensions had deliberately, spitefully, merged their identities, as if to say to him: "Try and tell which is which." His reaction was always the same: a sensation in which the outer parts of his being rushed inward for protection, the same movement one sometimes sees in a kaleidoscope on turning it very slowly, when the parts of the design fall headlong into the center. But the center! Sometimes it was gigantic, painful, raw and false, it extended from one side of creation to the other, there was no telling where it was; it was everywhere. And sometimes it would disappear, and the other center, the true one, the tiny burning black point, would be there in its place, unmoving and impossibly sharp, hard and distant. And each center he called "That." He knew one from the other, and which was the true, because when for a few minutes sometimes he actually came back to the room and saw it, and saw Kit, and said to himself: "I am in Sbâ," he could remember the two centers and distinguish between them, even though he hated them both, and he knew that the one which was only *there* was the true one, while the other was wrong, wrong, wrong.

It was an existence of exile from the world. He never saw a human face or figure, nor even an animal; there were no familiar objects along the way, there was no ground below, nor sky above, yet the space was full of things. Sometimes he saw them, knowing at the same time that really they could only be heard. Sometimes they were absolutely still, like the printed page, and he was conscious of their terrible invisible motion underneath, and of its portent to him because he was alone. Sometimes he could touch them with his fingers, and at the same time they poured in through his mouth. It was all utterly familiar and wholly horrible—existence unmodifiable, not to be questioned, that must be borne. It would never occur to him to cry out.

The next morning the lamp had still been burning and the wind had gone. She had been unable to rouse him to give him his medicine, but she had taken his temperature through his half-open mouth: it had gone much higher. Then she had rushed out to find Captain Broussard, had brought him to the bedside where he had been noncommittal, trying to reassure her without giving her any reason for hope. She had passed the day sitting on the edge of her pallet in an attitude of despair, looking at Port from time to time, hearing his labored breathing and seeing him twist in the throes of an inner torment. Nor could Zina tempt her with food.

When night came and Zina reported that the American lady still would not eat, Captain Broussard decided upon a simple course of action. He went to the room and knocked on the door. After a short interval he heard Kit say: "*Qui est là?*" Then she opened the door. She had not lighted the lamp; the room was black behind her.

"Is it you, madame?" He tried to make his voice pleasant.

"Yes."

"Could you come with me a moment? I should like to speak with you."

She followed him through several courtyards into a brightly lighted room with a blazing fireplace at one end. There was a profusion of native rugs which covered the walls, the divans and the floor. At the far end was a small bar attended by a tall black Soudanese in a very white turban and jacket. The captain gestured nonchalantly toward her.

"Will you take something?"

"Oh, no. Thank you."

"A little apéritif."

Kit was still blinking at the light. "I couldn't," she said.

"You'll have a Cinzano with me." He signaled to his barman. "*Deux Cinzanos.* Come, come, sit down, I beg you. I shall not detain you long."

Kit obeyed, took the glass from the proffered tray. The taste of the wine pleased her, but she did not want to be pleased, she did not want to be ripped from her apathy. Besides, she was still conscious of the peculiar light of suspicion in the captain's eyes when he looked at her. He sat studying her face as he sipped his drink: he had about come to the decision that she was not exactly what he had taken her for at first, that perhaps she really was the sick man's wife after all.

"As Chef de Poste," he said, "I am more or less obliged to verify the identity of the persons who pass through Sbâ. Of course the arrivals are very infrequent. I regret having to trouble you at such a time, naturally. It is merely a question of seeing your identity papers. Ali!" The barman stepped silently to their chairs and refilled the glasses. Kit did not reply for a moment. The apéritif had made her violently hungry.

"I have my passport."

"Excellent. Tomorrow I shall send for both passports and return them to you within the hour."

"My husband has lost his passport. I can only give you mine."

"*Ah, ça!*" cried the captain. It was as he had expected, then.

He was furious; at the same time he felt a certain satisfaction in the reflection that his first impression had been correct. And how right he had been to forbid his inferior officers to have anything to do with her. He had expected just something of this sort, save that in such cases it was usually the woman's papers which were difficult to get hold of, rather than the man's.

"Madame," he said, leaning forward in his seat, "please understand that I am in no way interested in probing matters which I consider strictly personal. It is merely a formality, but one which must be carried out. I must see both passports. The names are a matter of complete indifference to me. But two people, two passports, no? Unless you have one together."

Kit thought he had not heard her correctly. "My husband's passport was stolen in Aïn Krorfa."

The captain hesitated. "I shall have to report this, of course. To the commander of the territory." He rose to his feet. "You yourselves should have reported it as soon as it happened." He had had the servant lay a place at table for Kit, but now he did not want to eat with her.

"Oh, but we did. Lieutenant d'Armagnac at Bou Noura knows all about it," said Kit, finishing her glass. "May I have a cigarette, please?" He gave her a Chesterfield, lighted it for her, and watched her inhale. "My cigarettes are all gone." She smiled, her eyes on the pack he held in his hand. She felt better, but the hunger inside her was planting its claws deeper each minute. The captain said nothing. She went on. "Lieutenant d'Armagnac did everything he could for my husband to try and get it back from Messad."

The captain did not believe a word she was saying; he considered it all an admirable piece of lying. He was convinced now that she was not only an adventuress, but a truly suspicious character. "I see," he said, studying the rug at his feet. "Very well, madame. I shall not detain you now."

She rose.

"Tomorrow you will give me your passport, I shall prepare my report and we shall see what the outcome will be." He escorted her back to the room and returned to eat alone, highly annoyed with her for having insisted upon trying to deceive him. Kit stood in the dark room a second, reopened the door slightly and watched the glow cast on the sand by his flashlight disappear. Then she went in search of Zina, who fed her in the kitchen.

When she had finished eating she went to the room and lighted the lamp. Port's body squirmed and his face protested against the sudden light. She put the lamp in a corner behind some valises and stood a while in the middle of the room thinking of nothing. A few minutes later she took up her coat and went out into the courtyard.

The roof of the fort was a great, flat, irregularly shaped mud terrace whose varying heights were a projection, as it were, of the uneven ground below. The ramps and staircases between the different wings were hard to see in the dark. And although there was a low wall around the outer edge, the innumerable courtyards were merely open wells to be skirted with caution. The stars gave enough light to protect her against mishaps. She breathed deeply, feeling rather as if she were on shipboard. The town below was invisible—not a light showed—but to the north glimmered the white ereg, the vast ocean of sand with its frozen swirling crests, its unmoving silence. She turned slowly about, scanning the horizon. The air, doubly still now after the departure of the wind, was like something paralyzed. Whichever way she looked, the night's landscape suggested only one thing to her: negation of movement, suspension of continuity. But as she stood there, momentarily a part of the void she had created, little by little a doubt slipped into her mind, the sensation came to her, first faint, then sure, that some part of this landscape was moving even as she looked at it. She glanced up and grimaced. The whole, monstrous star-filled sky was turning sideways before her eyes. It looked still as death, yet it moved. Every second an invisible star edged above the earth's line on that side, and another fell below on the opposite side. She coughed self-consciously, and started to walk again, trying to remember how much she disliked Captain Broussard. He had not even offered her a pack of cigarettes, in spite of her overt remark. "Oh, God," she said aloud, wishing she had not finished her last Players in Bou Noura.

*

He opened his eyes. The room was malignant. It was empty. "Now, at last, I must fight against this room." But later he had a moment of vertiginous clarity. He was at the edge of a realm where each thought, each image, had an arbitrary existence, where the connection between each thing and the next had been cut. As he labored to seize the essence of that kind of consciousness, he began to slip back into its precinct without suspecting that he was no longer wholly outside in the open, no longer able to consider the idea at a distance. It seemed to him that here was an untried variety of thinking, in which there was no necessity for a relationship with life. "The thought in itself," he said—a gratuitous fact, like a painting of pure design. They were coming again, they began to flash by. He tried to hold one, believed he had it. "But a thought of what? What is it?" Even then it was pushed out of the way by the others crowding behind it. While he succumbed, struggling, he opened his eyes for help. "The room! The room! Still here!" It was in the silence of the room that he now located all those hostile forces; the very fact that the room's inert watchfulness was on all sides made him distrust it. Outside himself, it was all there was. He looked at the line made by the joining of the wall and the floor, endeavored to fix it in his mind, that he might have something to hang on to when his eyes should shut. There was a terrible disparity between the speed at which he was moving and the quiet immobility of that line, but he insisted. So as not to go. To stay behind. To overflow, take root in what would stay here. A centipede can, cut into pieces. Each part can walk by itself. Still more, each leg flexes, lying alone on the floor.

There was a screaming sound in each ear, and the difference between the two pitches was so narrow that the vibration was like running his fingernail along the edge of a new dime. In front of his eyes clusters of round spots were being born; they were the little spots that result when a photographic cut in a newspaper is enlarged many times. Lighter agglomerations, darker masses, small regions of uninhabited space here and there. Each spot slowly took on a third dimension. He tried to recoil from the expanding globules of matter. Did he cry out? Could he move?

The thin distance between the two high screams became narrower, they were almost one; now the difference was the edge of a razor blade, poised against the tips of each finger. The fingers were to be sliced longitudinally.

A servant traced the cries to the room where the American lay. Captain Broussard was summoned. He walked quickly to the door, pounded on it, and hearing nothing but the continued yelling within, stepped into the room. With the aid of the servant, he succeeded in holding Port still enough to give him an injection of morphine. When he had finished, he glared about the room in an access of rage. "And that woman!" he shouted. "Where in the name of God is she?"

"I don't know, my Captain," said the servant, who thought the question had been addressed to him.

"Stay here. Stand by the door," growled the captain. He was determined to find Kit, and when he found her he was going to tell her what he thought of her. If necessary, he would place a guard outside the door, and force her to stay inside to watch the patient. He went first to the main gate, which was locked at night so that no guard was necessary. It stood open. "*Ah, ça, par exemple!*" he cried, beside himself. He stepped outside, and saw nothing but the night. Going within, he slammed the high portal shut and bolted it savagely. Then he went back to the room and waited while the servant fetched a blanket, and instructed him to stay there until morning. He returned to his quarters and had a glass of cognac to calm his fury before trying to sleep.

As she paced back and forth on the roof, two things happened at once. On one side the large moon swiftly rose above the edge of the plateau, and on the other, in the distant air, an almost imperceptible humming sound became audible, was lost, became audible again. She listened: now it was gone, now it was a little stronger. And so it continued for a long time, disappearing, and coming back always a bit nearer. Now, even though it was still far away, the sound was quite recognizable as that of a motor. She could hear the shifts of speed as it climbed a slope and reached level ground again. Twenty kilometers down the trail, they had told her, you can hear a truck coming. She waited. Finally, when it seemed that the vehicle must already be in the town, she saw a tiny portion of rock far out on the hammada being swept by the headlights as the truck made a curve in its descent toward the oasis. A moment later she saw the two points of light. Then they were lost for a while behind the rocks, but the motor grew ever louder. With the moon casting more light each minute, and the truck bringing people to town, even if the people were anonymous figures in white robes, the world moved back into the realm of the possible. Suddenly she wanted to be present at the arrival down in the market. She hurried below, tiptoed through the courtyards, managed to open the heavy gate, and began to run down the side of the hill toward the town. The truck was making a great racket as it went along between the high walls in the oasis; as she came opposite the mosque it nosed above the last rise on its way up into the town. There were a few ragged men standing at the entrance of the market place. When the big vehicle roared in and stopped, the silence that followed lasted only a second before the excited voices began, all at once.

She stood back and watched the laborious getting-down of the natives and the leisurely unloading of their possessions: camel saddles that shone in the moonlight, great formless bundles done up in striped blankets, coffers and sacks, and two gigantic women so fat they could barely walk, their bosoms, arms and legs weighted down with pounds of massive silver ornaments. And all these possessions, with their owners, presently disappeared behind the dark arcades and went out of hearing. She moved around so she could see the front end of the truck, where the chauffeur and mechanic and a few other men stood in the glare of the headlights talking. She heard French being spoken—bad French—as well as Arabic. The chauffeur reached in and switched off the lights; the men began to walk slowly up into the market place. No one seemed to have noticed her. She stood still a moment, listening.

She cried: "Tunner!"

One of the figures in a burnous stopped, came running back. On its way, it called: "Kit!" She ran a few steps, saw the other man turning to look, and was being smothered in Tunner's burnous as he hugged her. She thought he would never let go, but he did, and said: "So you're really here!" Two of the men had come over. "Is this the lady you were looking for?" said one. "*Oui, oui!*" Tunner cried, and they said good night.

They stood alone in the market place. "But this is wonderful, Kit!" he said. She wanted to speak, but she felt that if she tried, her words would turn to sobs, so she nodded her head and automatically began to pull him along toward the little public garden by the mosque. She felt weak; she wanted to sit down.

"My stuff is locked in the truck for the night. I didn't know where I'd be sleeping. God, what a trip from Bou Noura! Three blowouts on the way, and these monkeys think changing a tire should always take a couple of hours at least." He went into details. They had reached the entrance to the garden. The moon shone like a cold white sun; the spearlike shadows of the palm branches were black on the sand, a sharp unvaried pattern along the garden walk.

"But let's see you!" he cried, spinning her around so the moon's light struck her face. "Ah, poor Kit! It must have been hell!" he murmured, as she squinted up into the brightness, her features distorted by the imminent outbreaking of tears.

They sat on a concrete bench and she wept for a long time, her face buried in his lap, rubbing the rough wool of the burnous. From time to time he uttered consoling words, and as he found her shivering, he enveloped her in one great wing of the robe. She hated the salt sting of the tears, and even more she hated the ignominy of her being there, demanding comfort of Tunner. But she could not, could not stop; the longer she continued to sob, the more clearly she sensed that this was a situation beyond her control. She was unable to sit up, dry her tears, and make an attempt to extricate herself from the net of involvement she felt being drawn around her. She did not want to be involved again: the taste of guilt was still strong in her memory. Yet she saw nothing ahead of her but Tunner's will awaiting her signal to take command. And she would give the signal. Even as she knew this she was aware of a pervading sense of relief, to struggle against which would have been unthinkable. What delight, not to be responsible—not to have to decide anything of what was to happen! To know, even if there was no hope, that no action one might take or fail to take could change the outcome in the slightest degree—that it was impossible to be at fault in any way, and thus impossible to feel regret, or, above all, guilt. She realized the absurdity of still hoping to attain such a state permanently, but the hope would not leave her.

The street led up a steep hill where the hot sun was shining, the sidewalks were crowded with pedestrians looking in the shop windows. He had the feeling there was traffic in the side streets, but the shadows there were dark. An attitude of expectancy was growing in the crowd; they were waiting for something. For what, he did not know. The entire afternoon was tense, poised, ready to fall. At the top of the street a huge automobile suddenly appeared, glistening in the sunlight. It came careening over the crest and down the hill, swerving savagely from one curb to the other. A great yell rose up from the crowd. He turned and frantically sought a doorway. At the corner there was a pastry shop, its windows full of cakes and meringues. He fumbled along the wall. If he could reach the door. . . . He wheeled, stood transfixed. In the tremendous flash of sunlight reflected from the glass as it splintered he saw the metal pinning him to the stone. He heard his own ridiculous cry, and felt his bowels pierced through. As he tried to topple over, to lose consciousness, he found his face a few inches from a row of pastries, still intact on their paper-covered shelf.

They were a row of mud wells in the desert. But how near were they? He could not tell: the debris had pinned him to the earth. The pain was all of existence at that moment. All the energy he could exert would not budge him from the spot where he lay impaled, his bleeding entrails open to the sky. He imagined an enemy arriving to step into his open belly. He imagined himself rising, running through the twisting alleys between the walls. For hours in all directions in the alleys, with never a door, never the final opening. It would get dark, they would be coming nearer, his breath would be failing. And when he willed it hard enough, the gate would appear, but even as he rushed panting through it, he would realize his terrible mistake.

Too late! There was only the endless black wall rising ahead
of him, the rickety iron staircase he was obliged to take,
knowing that above, at the top, they were waiting with the
boulder poised, ready to hurl it when he came near enough.
And as he got close to the top it would come hurtling down
at him, striking him with the weight of the entire world. He
cried out again as it hit, holding his hands over his abdomen
to protect the gaping hole there. He ceased imagining and lay
still beneath the rubble. The pain could not go on. He
opened his eyes, shut his eyes, saw only the thin sky stretched
across to protect him. Slowly the split would occur, the sky
draw back, and he would see what he never had doubted lay
behind advance upon him with the speed of a million winds.
His cry was a separate thing beside him in the desert. It went
on and on.

The moon had reached the center of the sky when they arrived at the fort and found the gate locked. Holding Tunner's
hand, Kit looked up at him. "What'll we do?"
He hesitated, and pointed to the mountain of sand above
the fort. They climbed slowly upward along the dunes. The
cold sand filled their shoes: they took them off and continued. Up here the brightness was intense; each grain of sand
sent out a fragment of the polar light shed from above. They
could not walk side by side—the ridge of the highest dune
was too steep. Tunner draped his burnous around Kit's shoulders and went ahead. The crest was infinitely higher and further away than they had imagined. When finally they climbed
atop it, the ereg with its sea of motionless waves lay all about
them. They did not stop to look: absolute silence is too powerful once one has trusted oneself to it for an instant, its spell
too difficult to break.
"Down here!" said Tunner.
They let themselves slide forward into a great moonlit cup.
Kit rolled over and the burnous slipped off; he had to dig
into the sand and climb back after it. He tried to fold it and
throw it down at her playfully, but it fell halfway. She let herself roll to the bottom and lay there waiting. When he came
down he spread the wide white garment out on the sand.
They stretched out on it side by side and pulled the edges up

around them. What conversation had eventually taken place down in the garden had centered about Port. Now Tunner looked at the moon. He took her hand.

"Do you remember our night on the train?" he said. As she did not reply, he feared he had made a tactical error, and went on quickly: "I don't think a drop of rain has fallen since that night, anywhere on the whole damned continent."

Still Kit made no answer. His mention of the night ride to Boussif had evoked the wrong memories. She saw the dim lamps swinging, smelled the coal gas, and heard the rain on the windows. She remembered the confused horror of the freight car full of natives; her mind refused to continue further.

"Kit. What's the matter?"

"Nothing. You know how I am. Really, nothing's wrong." She pressed his hand.

His voice became faintly paternal. "He's going to be all right, Kit. Only some of it's up to you, you know. You've got to keep in good shape to take care of him. Can't you see that? And how can you take care of him if you get sick?"

"I know, I know," she said.

"Then I'd have two patients on my hands—"

She sat up. "What hypocrites we are, both of us!" she cried. "You know damned well I haven't been near him for hours. How do we know he's not already dead? He could die there all alone! We'd never know. Who could stop him?"

He caught her arm, held it firmly. "Now, wait a minute, will you? Just for the record, I want to ask you: who could stop him even if we were both there beside him? Who?" He paused. "If you're going to take the worst possible view of everything, you might as well follow it through with a little logic at least, girl. But he's not going to die. You shouldn't even think of it. It's crazy." He shook her arm slowly, as one does to awaken a person from a deep sleep. "Just be sensible. You can't get in to him until morning. So relax. Try and get a little rest. Come on."

As he coaxed, she suddenly burst into tears once again, throwing both arms around him desperately. "Oh, Tunner! I love him so much!" she sobbed, clinging ever more tightly. "I love him! I love him!"

In the moonlight he smiled.

*

His cry went on through the final image: the spots of raw bright blood on the earth. Blood on excrement. The supreme moment, high above the desert, when the two elements, blood and excrement, long kept apart, merge. A black star appears, a point of darkness in the night sky's clarity. Point of darkness and gateway to repose. Reach out, pierce the fine fabric of the sheltering sky, take repose.

XXIV

She opened the door. Port lay in a strange position, his legs wound tightly in the bedcovers. That corner of the room was like a still photograph suddenly flashed on the screen in the middle of the stream of moving images. She shut the door softly, locked it, turned again toward the corner, and walked slowly over to the mattress. She held her breath, bent over, and looked into the meaningless eyes. But already she knew, even to the convulsive lowering of her hand to the bare chest, even without the violent push she gave the inert torso immediately afterward. As her hands went to her own face, she cried: "No!" once—no more. She stood perfectly still for a long, long time, her head raised, facing the wall. Nothing moved inside her; she was conscious of nothing outside or in. If Zina had come to the door it is doubtful whether she would have heard the knock. But no one came. Below in the town a caravan setting out for Atar left the market place, swayed through the oasis, the camels grumbling, the bearded black men silent as they walked along thinking of the twenty days and nights that lay ahead, before the walls of Atar would rise above the rocks. A few hundred feet away in his bedroom Captain Broussard read an entire short story in a magazine that had arrived that morning in his mail, brought by last night's truck. In the room, however, nothing happened.

Much later in the morning, probably out of sheer fatigue, she began to walk in a small orbit in the middle of the room, a few steps one way and a few the other. A loud knock on the door interrupted this. She stood still, staring toward the door. The knock was repeated. Tunner's voice, carefully lowered, said: "Kit?" Again her hands rose to cover her face, and she remained standing that way during the rest of the time he stayed outside the door, now rapping softly, now faster and nervously, now pounding violently. When there was no more sound, she sat down on her pallet for a while, presently lying out flat with her head on the pillow as if to sleep. But her eyes remained open, staring upward almost as fixedly as those beside her. These were the first moments of a new existence, a strange one in which she already glimpsed the element of timelessness that would surround her. The person who frantically has been counting the seconds on his way to catch a train, and arrives panting just as it disappears, knowing the next one is not due for many hours, feels something of the same sudden surfeit of time, the momentary sensation of drowning in an element become too rich and too plentiful to be consumed, and thereby made meaningless, non-existent. As the minutes went by, she felt no impulse to move; no thought wandered near her. Now she did not remember their many conversations built around the idea of death, perhaps because no idea about death has anything in common with the presence of death. She did not recall how they had agreed that one can *be* anything but *dead*, that the two words together created an antinomy. Nor did it occur to her how she once had thought that if Port should die before she did, she would not really believe he was dead, but rather that he had in some way gone back inside himself to stay there, and that he never would be conscious of her again; so that in reality it would be she who would have ceased to exist, at least to a great degree. She would be the one who had entered partially into the realm of death, while he would go on, an anguish inside her, a door left unopened, a chance irretrievably lost. She had quite forgotten the August afternoon only a little more than a year ago, when they had sat alone out on the grass beneath the maples, watching the thunderstorm sweep up the river valley toward them, and death had become the topic. And Port had said: "Death is always on the way, but the fact that you don't know when it will arrive seems to take away from the finiteness of life. It's that terrible precision that we hate so much. But because we don't know, we get to think of life as an inexhaustible well. Yet everything happens only a certain number of times, and a very small number, really. How many more times will you remember a certain afternoon of your childhood, some afternoon that's so deeply a part of your being that you can't even conceive of your life without it? Perhaps four or five times more. Perhaps not even that. How many more times will you watch the full moon rise? Perhaps twenty. And yet it all seems limitless." She had not listened at the time because the idea had depressed her; now if she had called it to mind it would have seemed beside the point. She was incapable now of thinking about death, and since death was there beside her, she thought of nothing at all.

And yet, deeper than the empty region which was her consciousness, in an obscure and innermost part of her mind, an idea must already have been in gestation, since when in the late afternoon Tunner came again and hammered on the door, she got up, and standing with her hand on the knob, spoke: "Is that you, Tunner?"

"For God's sake, where were you this morning?" he cried.

"I'll see you tonight about eight in the garden," she said, speaking as low as possible.

"Is he all right?"

"Yes. He's the same."

"Good. See you at eight." He went away.

She glanced at her watch: it was quarter of five. Going to her overnight bag, she set to work removing all the fittings; one by one, brushes, bottles and manicuring implements were laid on the floor. With an air of extreme preoccupation she emptied her other valises, choosing here and there a garment or object which she carefully packed into the small bag. Occasionally she stopped moving and listened: the only sound she could hear was her own measured breathing. Each time she listened she seemed reassured, straightway resuming her deliberate movements. In the flaps at the sides of the bag she put her passport, her express checks and what money she had. Soon she went to Port's luggage and searched awhile among the clothing there, returning to her little case with a good many more thousand-franc notes which she stuffed in wherever she could.

The packing of the bag took nearly an hour. When she had finished, she closed it, spun the combination lock, and went to the door. She hesitated a second before turning the key.

The door open, the key in her hand, she stepped out into the courtyard with the bag and locked the door after her. She went to the kitchen, where she found the boy who tended the lamps sitting in a corner smoking.

"Can you do an errand for me?" she said.

He jumped to his feet smiling. She handed him the bag and told him to take it to Daoud Zozeph's shop and leave it, saying it was from the American lady.

Back in the room she again locked the door behind her and went over to the little window. With a single motion she ripped away the sheet that covered it. The wall outside was turning pink as the sun dropped lower in the sky; the pinkness filled the room. During all the time she had been moving about packing she had not once glanced downward at the corner. Now she knelt and looked closely at Port's face as if she had never seen it before. Scarcely touching the skin, she moved her hand along the forehead with infinite delicacy. She bent over further and placed her lips on the smooth brow. For a while she remained thus. The room grew red. Softly she laid her cheek on the pillow and stroked his hair. No tears flowed; it was a silent leave-taking. A strangely intense buzzing in front of her made her open her eyes. She watched fascinated while two flies made their brief, frantic love on his lower lip.

Then she rose, put on her coat, took the burnous which Tunner had left with her, and without looking back went out the door. She locked it behind her and put the key into her handbag. At the big gate the guard made as if to stop her. She said good evening to him and pushed by. Immediately afterward she heard him call to another in an inner room nearby. She breathed deeply and walked ahead, down toward the town. The sun had set; the earth was like a single ember alone on the hearth, rapidly cooling and growing black. A drum beat in the oasis. There would probably be dancing in the gardens later. The season of feasts had begun. Quickly she descended the hill and went straight to Daoud Zozeph's shop without once looking around.

She went in. Daoud Zozeph stood behind the counter in the fading light. He reached across and shook her hand.

"Good evening, madame."

"Good evening."

"Your valise is here. Shall I call a boy to carry it for you?"

"No, no," she said. "At least, not now. I came to talk to you." She glanced around at the doorway behind her; he did not notice.

"I am delighted," he said. "One moment. I shall get you a chair, madame." He brought a small folding chair around from behind the counter and placed it beside her.

"Thank you," she said, but she remained standing. "I wanted to ask you about trucks leaving Sbâ."

"Ah, for El Ga'a. We have no regular service. One came last night and left again this afternoon. We never know when the next will come. But Captain Broussard is always notified at least a day in advance. He could tell you better than anyone else."

"Captain Broussard. Ah, I see."

"And your husband. Is he better? Did he enjoy the milk?"

"The milk. Yes, he enjoyed it," she said slowly, wondering a little that the words could sound so natural.

"I hope he will soon be well."

"He is already well."

"Ah, *hamdoul'lah!*"

"Yes." And starting afresh, she said: "Monsieur Daoud Zozeph, I have a favor to ask of you."

"Your favor is granted, madame," he said gallantly. She felt that he had bowed in the darkness.

"A great favor," she warned.

Daoud Zozeph, thinking that perhaps she wanted to borrow money, began to rattle objects on the counter, saying: "But we are talking in the dark. Wait. I shall light a lamp."

"No! Please!" exclaimed Kit.

"But we don't see each other!" he protested.

She put her hand on his arm. "I know, but don't light the lamp, please. I want to ask you this favor immediately. May I spend the night with you and your wife?"

Daoud Zozeph was completely taken aback—both astonished and relieved. "Tonight?" he said.

"Yes."

There was a short silence.

"You understand, madame, we should be honored to have you in our house. But you would not be comfortable. You know, a house of poor people is not like a hotel or a poste militaire. . . ."

"But since I ask you," she said reproachfully, "that means I don't care. You think that matters to me? I have been sleeping on the floor here in Sbâ."

"Ah, that you would not have to do in my house," said Daoud Zozeph energetically.

"But I should be delighted to sleep on the floor. Anywhere. It doesn't matter."

"Ah, no! No, madame! Not on the floor! *Quand-même!*" he objected. And as he struck a match to light the lamp, she touched his arm again.

"*Ecoutez, monsieur,*" she said, her voice sinking to a conspiratorial whisper, "my husband is looking for me, and I don't want him to find me. We have had a misunderstanding. I don't want to see him tonight. It's very simple. I think your wife would understand."

Daoud Zozeph laughed. "Of course! Of course!" Still laughing, he closed the door into the street, bolted it, and struck a match, holding it high in the air. Lighting matches all the way, he led her through a dark inner room and across a small court. The stars were above. He paused in front of a door. "You can sleep here." He opened the door and stepped inside. Again a match flared: she saw a tiny room in disorder, its sagging iron bed covered with a mattress that vomited excelsior.

"This is not your room, I hope?" she ventured, as the match went out.

"Ah, no! We have another bed in our room, my wife and I," he answered, a note of pride in his voice. "This is where my brother sleeps when he comes from Colomb-Béchar. Once a year he visits me for a month, sometimes longer. Wait. I shall bring a lamp." He went off, and she heard him talking in another room. Presently he returned with an oil lamp and a small tin pail of water.

With the arrival of the light, the room took on an even more piteous aspect. She had the feeling that the floor had never yet been swept since the day the mason had finished piling the mud on the walls, the ubiquitous mud that dried, crumbled, and fell in a fine powder day and night. . . . She glanced up at him and smiled.

"My wife wants to know if you like noodles," said Daoud Zozeph.

"Yes, of course," she answered, trying to look into the peeling mirror over the washstand. She could see nothing at all.

"*Bien.* You know, my wife speaks no French."

"Really. You will have to be my interpreter."

There was a dull knocking, out in the shop. Daoud Zozeph excused himself and crossed the court. She shut the door, found there was no key, stood there waiting. It would have been so easy for one of the guards at the fort to follow her. But she doubted that they had thought of it in time. She sat down on the outrageous bed and stared at the wall opposite. The lamp sent up a column of acrid smoke.

The evening meal at Daoud Zozeph's was unbelievably bad. She forced down the amorphous lumps of dough fried in deep fat and served cold, the pieces of cartilaginous meat, and the soggy bread, murmuring vague compliments which were warmly received, but which led her hosts to press more of the food upon her. Several times during the meal she glanced at her watch. Tunner would be waiting in the public garden now, and when he left there he would go up to the fort. At that moment the trouble would begin; Daoud Zozeph could not help hearing of it tomorrow from his customers.

Madame Daoud Zozeph gestured vigorously for Kit to continue eating; her bright eyes were fixed on her guest's plate. Kit looked across at her and smiled.

"Tell madame that because I am a little upset now I am not very hungry," she said to Daoud Zozeph, "but that I should like to have something in my room to eat later. Some bread would be perfect."

"But of course. Of course," he said.

When she had gone to her room, Madame Daoud Zozeph brought her a plate piled high with pieces of bread. She thanked her and said good night, but her hostess was not inclined to leave, making it clear that she was interested in seeing the interior of the traveling case. Kit was determined not to open it in front of her; the thousand-franc notes would quickly become a legend in Sbâ. She pretended not to understand, patted the case, nodded and laughed. Then she turned again toward the plate of bread and repeated her thanks. But

Madame Daoud Zozeph's eyes did not leave the valise. There was a screeching and fluttering of wings outside in the court. Daoud Zozeph appeared carrying a fat hen, which he set down in the middle of the floor.

"Against the vermin," he explained, pointing at the hen.

"Vermin?" echoed Kit.

"If a scorpion shows its head anywhere along the floor—tac! She eats it!"

"Ah!" She fabricated a yawn.

"I know madame is nervous. With our friend here she will feel better."

"This evening," she said, "I am so sleepy that nothing could make me nervous."

They shook hands solemnly. Daoud Zozeph pushed his wife out of the room and shut the door. The hen scratched a minute in the dust, then scrambled up onto the rung of the washstand and remained motionless. Kit sat on the bed looking into the uneven flame of the lamp; the room was full of its smoke. She felt no anxiety—only an overwhelming impatience to put all this ludicrous décor behind her, out of her consciousness. Rising, she stood with her ear against the door. She heard the sound of voices, now and then a distant thud. She put on her coat, filled the pockets with pieces of bread, and sat down again to wait.

From time to time she sighed deeply. Once she got up to turn down the wick of the lamp. When her watch said ten o'clock, she went again to the door and listened. She opened it: the court glowed with reflected moonlight. Stepping back inside, she picked up Tunner's burnous and flung it under the bed. The resultant swirl of dust almost made her sneeze. She took her handbag and the valise and went out, taking care to shut the door after her. On her way through the inner room of the shop she stumbled over something and nearly lost her balance. Going more slowly, she moved ahead into the shop, around the end of the counter, feeling lightly along its top with the fingers of her left hand as she went. The door had a simple bolt which she drew back with difficulty; eventually it made a heavy metallic noise. Quickly she swung the door open and went out.

The light of the moon was violent—walking along the white street in it was like being in the sunlight. "Anyone could see me." But there was no one. She walked straight to the edge of town, where the oasis straggled over into the courtyards of the houses. Below, in the wide black mass formed by the tops of the palms, the drums were still going. The sound came from the direction of the ksar, the Negro village in the middle of the oasis.

She turned into a long, straight alley bordered by high walls. On the other side of them the palms rustled and the running water gurgled. Occasionally there was a white pile of dried palm branches stacked against the wall; each time she thought it was a man sitting in the moonlight. The alley swerved toward the sound of the drums, and she came out upon a square, full of little channels and aqueducts running paradoxically in all directions; it looked like a very complex toy railway. Several walks led off into the oasis from here. She chose the narrowest, which she thought might skirt the ksar rather than lead to it, and went on ahead between the walls. The path turned this way and that.

The sound of the drums was louder: now she could hear voices repeating a rhythmical refrain, always the same. They were men's voices, and there seemed to be a great many of them. Sometimes, when she reached the heavy shadows, she stopped and listened, an inscrutable smile on her lips.

The little bag was growing heavy. More and more frequently she shifted it from one hand to the other. But she did not want to stop and rest. At each instant she was ready to turn around and go back to look for another alley, in case she should come out all at once from between the walls into the middle of the ksar. The music seemed quite nearby at times, but it was hard to tell with all the twisting walls and trees in between. Occasionally it sounded almost at hand, as if only a wall and a few hundred feet of garden separated her from it, and then it retreated into the distance and was nearly covered by the dry sound of the wind blowing through the palm leaves.

And the liquid sound of the rivulets on all sides had their effect without her knowing it: she suddenly felt dry. The cool moonlight and the softly moving shadows through which she passed did much to dispel the sensation, but it seemed to her that she would be completely content only if she could have water all around her. All at once she was looking through a

wide break in the wall into a garden; the graceful palm trunks
rose high into the air from the sides of a wide pool. She stood
staring at the calm dark surface of water; straightway she
found it impossible to know whether she had thought of
bathing just before or just after seeing the pool. Whichever it
was, there was the pool. She reached through the aperture in
the crumbling wall and set down her bag before climbing
across the pile of dirt that lay in her way. Once in the garden
she found herself pulling off her clothes. She felt a vague
surprise that her actions should go on so far ahead of her
consciousness of them. Every moment she made seemed the
perfect expression of lightness and grace. "Look out," said a
part of her. "Go carefully." But it was the same part of her
that sent out the warning when she was drinking too much.
At this point it was meaningless. "Habit," she thought.
"Whenever I'm about to be happy I hang on instead of letting go." She kicked off her sandals and stood naked in the
shadows. She felt a strange intensity being born within her. As
she looked about the quiet garden she had the impression
that for the first time since her childhood she was seeing objects clearly. Life was suddenly there, she was in it, not looking through the window at it. The dignity that came from
feeling a part of its power and grandeur, that was a familiar
sensation, but it was years ago that she had last known it. She
stepped out into the moonlight and waded slowly toward the
center of the pool. Its floor was slippery with clay; in the middle the water came to her waist. As she immersed herself completely, the thought came to her: "I shall never be hysterical
again." That kind of tension, that degree of caring about herself, she felt she would never attain them any more in her life.

She bathed lengthily; the cool water on her skin awakened
an impulse to sing. Each time she bent to get water between
her cupped palms she uttered a burst of wordless song. Suddenly she stopped and listened. She no longer heard the
drums—only the drops of water falling from her body into
the pool. She finished her bath in silence, her access of high
spirits gone; but life did not recede from her. "It's here to
stay," she murmured aloud, as she walked toward the bank.
She used her coat as a towel, hopping up and down with cold
as she dried herself. While she dressed she whistled under her

breath. Every so often she stopped and listened for a second, to see if she could hear the sound of voices, or the drums starting up again. The wind came by, up there above her head, in the tops of the trees, and there was the faint trickle of water somewhere nearby. Nothing more. All at once she was seized with the suspicion that something had happened behind her back, that time had played a trick on her: she had spent hours in the pool instead of minutes, and never realized it. The festivities in the ksar had come to an end, the people had dispersed, and she had not even been conscious of the cessation of the drums. Absurd things like that did happen, sometimes. She bent to take her wrist watch from the stone where she had laid it. It was not there; she could not verify the hour. She searched a bit, already convinced that she would never find it: its disappearance was a part of the trick. She walked lightly over to the wall and picked up her valise, flung her coat over her arm, and said aloud to the garden: "You think it matters to me?" And she laughed before climbing back across the broken wall.

Swiftly she walked along, focusing her mind on that feeling of solid delight she had recaptured. She had always known it was there, just behind things, but long ago she had accepted not having it as a natural condition of life. Because she had found it again, the joy of being, she said to herself that she would hang on to it no matter what the effort entailed. She pulled a piece of bread from the pocket of her coat and ate it voraciously.

The alley grew wide, its wall receding to follow the line of vegetation. She had reached the oued, at this point a flat open valley dotted with small dunes. Here and there a weeping tamarisk tree lay like a mass of gray smoke along the sand. Without hesitating she made for the nearest tree and set her bag down. The feathery branches swept the sand on all sides of the trunk—it was like a tent. She put on her coat, crawled in, and pulled the valise in after her. In no time at all she was asleep.

XXV

Lieutenant d'Armagnac stood in his garden supervising Ahmed and several native masons in the work of topping the high enclosing wall with a crown of broken glass. A hundred times his wife had suggested this added protection for their dwelling, and he like a good colonial had promised but not performed; now that she was returning from France he would have it ready for her as one more pleasant surprise. Everything was going well: the baby was healthy, Mme. d'Armagnac was happy, and he would go up to Algiers at the end of the month to meet them. At the same time they would spend a happy few days in some good little hotel there—a sort of second honeymoon—before returning to Bou Noura.

It was true that things were going well only in his own little cosmos; he pitied Captain Broussard down in Sbâ and thought with an inward shudder that but for the grace of God all that trouble would have fallen upon him. He had even urged the travelers to stay on in Bou Noura; at least he was able to feel blameless on that score. He had not known the American was ill, so that it was not his fault the man had gone on and died in Broussard's territory. But of course death from typhoid was one thing and the disappearance of a white woman into the desert was another; it was the latter which was making all the trouble. The terrain around Sbâ was not favorable to the success of searching parties conducted in jeeps; besides, there were only two such vehicles in the region, and the expeditions had not been inaugurated immediately because of the more pressing business of the dead American at the fort. And everyone had imagined that she would be found somewhere in the town. He regretted not having met the wife. She sounded amusing—a typical, high-spirited American girl. Only an American could do anything so unheard-of as to lock her sick husband into a room and run off into the desert, leaving him behind to die alone. It was inexcusable, of course, but he could not be really horrified at the idea, as it seemed Broussard was. But Broussard was a Puritan. He was easily scandalized, and unpleasantly irreproachable in his own behavior. He had probably hated the girl because she was attractive and had disturbed his poise; that would be difficult for Broussard to forgive.

He wished again that he could have seen the girl before she had so successfully vanished from the face of the earth. At the same time he felt mixed emotions regarding the recent return of the third American to Bou Noura: he liked the man personally, but he hoped to avoid involvement in the affair, he wanted no part of it. Above all he prayed that the wife would not turn up in his territory, now that she was practically a cause célèbre. There was the likelihood that she, too, would be ill, and the curiosity he felt to see her was outweighed by the dreaded prospect of complications in his work and reports to be made out. "*Pourvu qu'ils la trouvent là-bas!*" he thought ardently.

There was a knock at the gate. Ahmed swung it open. The American stood there; he came each day in the hope of getting news, and each day he looked more despondent at hearing that none had been received. "I knew the other one was having trouble with his wife, and *this* was the trouble," said the lieutenant to himself when he glanced up and saw Tunner's unhappy face.

"*Bonjour, monsieur,*" he said jovially, advancing upon his guest. "Same news as always. But that can't continue forever."

Tunner greeted him, nodding his head understandingly on hearing what he had expected to hear. The lieutenant allowed the intervention of a silence proper to the occasion, then he suggested that they repair to the salon for their usual cognac. In the short while he had been waiting here at Bou Noura, Tunner had come to rely on these morning visits to the lieutenant's house as a necessary stimulus for his morale. The lieutenant was sanguine by nature, his conversation was light and his choice of words such that he was easily understandable. It was agreeable to sit in the bright salon, and the cognac fused these elements into a pleasant experience whose regular recurrence prevented his spirits from sinking all the way into the well of despair.

His host called to Ahmed, and led the way into the house. They sat facing each other.

"Two weeks more and I shall be a married man again," said the lieutenant, beaming at him, and thinking that perhaps he might yet show the Ouled Naïl girls to an American.

"Very good, very good." Tunner was distraught. God help poor Madame d'Armagnac, he thought gloomily, if she had to spend the rest of her life here. Since Port's death and Kit's disappearance he hated the desert: in an obscure fashion he felt that it had deprived him of his friends. It was too powerful an entity not to lend itself to personification. The desert—its very silence was like a tacit admission of the half-conscious presence it harbored. (Captain Broussard had told him, one night when he was in a talkative mood, that even the Frenchmen who accompanied the peloton into the wilderness there managed to see djnoun, even though out of pride they refused to believe in them.) And what did this mean, save that such things were the imagination's simple way of interpreting that presence?

Ahmed brought in the bottle and the glasses. They drank for a moment in silence; then the lieutenant remarked, as much to break the silence as for any other reason: "Ah, yes. Life is amazing. Nothing ever happens the way one imagines it is going to. One realizes that most clearly here; all your philosophic systems crumble. At every turn one finds the unexpected. When your friend came here without his passport and accused poor Abdelkader, who ever would have thought that this short time later such a thing would have happened to him?" Then, thinking that his sequence of logic might be misinterpreted, he added: "Abdelkader was very sorry to hear of his death. He bore him no grudge, you know."

Tunner seemed not to be listening. The lieutenant's mind ambled off in another direction. "Tell me," he said, curiosity coloring his voice, "did you ever manage to convince Captain Broussard that his suspicions about the lady were unfounded? Or does he still think they were not married? In his letter to me he said some very unkind things about her. You showed him Monsieur Moresby's passport?"

"What?" said Tunner, knowing he was going to have trouble with his French. "Oh, yes. I gave it to him to send to the Consul in Algiers with his report. But he never believed they were married, because Mrs. Moresby promised to give him her passport, and in place of that, ran away. So he had no idea who she really was."

"But they were husband and wife," pursued the lieutenant softly.

"Of course. Of course," said Tunner with impatience, feeling that for him even to engage in such a conversation was disloyal.

"And even if they had not been, what difference?" He poured them each another drink, and seeing that his guest was disinclined to continue that conversation, he went on to another which might be less painful in its associations. Tunner, however, followed the new one with almost as little enthusiasm. At the back of his mind he kept reliving the day of the burial in Sbâ. Port's death had been the only truly unacceptable fact in his life. Even now he knew that he had lost a great deal, that Port really had been his closest friend (how had he failed to recognize that before?), but he felt that it would be only later, when he had come to the full acceptance of the fact of his death, that he would be able to begin reckoning his loss in detail.

Tunner was sentimental, and in accordance with this trait, his conscience troubled him for not having offered more vigorous opposition to Captain Broussard's insistence upon a certain amount of religious ceremony during the burial. He had the feeling that he had been cowardly about it; he was certain that Port would have despised the inclusion of such nonsense on that occasion and would have relied upon his friend to see that it was not carried through. To be sure, he had protested beforehand that Port was not a Catholic—was not even, strictly speaking, a Christian, and consequently had the right to be spared such goings-on at his own funeral. But Captain Broussard had replied with heat: "I have only your word for all this, monsieur. And you were not with him when he died. You have no idea what his last thoughts were, what his final wishes may have been. Even if you were willing to take upon yourself such an enormous responsibility as to pretend to know such a thing, I could not let you do it. I am a Catholic, monsieur, and I am also in command here." And Tunner had given in. So that instead of being buried anonymously and in silence out on the hammada or in the ereg, where surely he would have wished to be put, Port had been laid to rest officially in the tiny Christian cemetery behind the fort, while phrases in Latin were spoken. To Tunner's sentimental mind it had seemed grossly unfair, but he had seen no way of preventing it. Now he felt that he had been weak and somehow unfaithful. At night when he lay awake thinking about it, it had even occurred to him that he might go all the way back to Sbâ and, waiting for the right moment, break into the cemetery and destroy the absurd little cross they had put over the grave. It was the sort of gesture which would have made him happier, but he knew he never would make it.

Instead, he told himself, he would be practical, and the important thing now was to find Kit and get her back to New York. In the beginning he had felt that in some way the whole business of her vanishing was a nightmarish practical joke, that at the end of a week or so she would surely have reappeared, just as she had on the train ride to Boussif. And so he had determined to wait until she did. Now that time had elapsed and there was still no sign of her, he understood that he would wait much longer—indefinitely if necessary.

He put his glass on the coffee table beside him. Giving voice to his thoughts, he said: "I'm going to stay here until Mrs. Moresby is found." And he asked himself why he was being so stubborn about it, why Kit's return obsessed him so utterly. Assuredly he was not in love with the poor girl. His overtures to her had been made out of pity (because she was a woman) and out of vanity (because he was a man), and the two feelings together had awakened the acquisitive desire of the trophy collector, nothing more. In fact, at this point, he realized that unless he thought carefully he was inclined to pass over the entire episode of intimacy between them, and to consider Kit purely in terms of their first meeting, when she and Port had impressed him so deeply as being the two people in the world he had wanted to know. It was less of a strain on his conscience that way; for more than once he had asked himself what had happened that crazy day at Sbâ when she had refused to open the door of the sick chamber, and whether or not she had told Port of her infidelity. Fervently he hoped not; he did not want to think of it.

"Yes," said Lieutenant d'Armagnac. "You can't very well go back to New York and have all your friends ask: 'What have you done with Mrs. Moresby?' That would be very embarrassing."

Inwardly Tunner winced. He definitely could not. Those who knew the two families might already be asking it of each other (since he had sent Port's mother both items of unfortunate news in two cables separated in time by three days, in the hope that Kit would turn up), but they were there and he was here, and he did not have to face them when they said:

"So both Port and Kit are gone!" It was the sort of thing that never did, couldn't, happen, and if he remained here in Bou Noura long enough he knew she would be unearthed.

"Very embarrassing," he agreed, laughing uncomfortably. Even Port's death by itself would be difficult enough to account for. There would be those who would say: "For God's sake, couldn't you have gotten him into a plane and up to a hospital somewhere, at least as far as Algiers? Typhoid's not that quick, you know." And he would have to admit that he had left them and gone off by himself, that he hadn't been able to "take" the desert. Still, he could envisage all that without too much misery; Port had neglected to be immunized against any sort of disease before leaving. But to go back leaving Kit lost was unthinkable from every point of view.

"Of course," ventured the lieutenant, again remembering the possible complications should the lost American lady turn up in anything but perfect condition, and then be moved to Bou Noura because of Tunner's presence there, "your staying or not staying will have nothing to do with her being found." He felt ashamed as soon as he heard the words come out of his mouth, but it was too late; they had been spoken.

"I know, I know," said Tunner vehemently. "But I'm going to stay." There was no more to be said about it; Lieutenant d'Armagnac would not raise the question again.

They talked on a little while. The lieutenant brought up the possibility of a visit some evening to the quartier réservé. "One of these days," said Tunner dispassionately.

"You need a little relaxation. Too much brooding is bad. I know just the girl—" He stopped, remembering from experience that explicit suggestions of that nature generally destroy the very interest they are meant to arouse. No hunter wants his prey chosen and run to earth for him, even if it means the only assurance of a kill.

"Good. Good," said Tunner absently.

Soon he rose and took his leave. He would return tomorrow morning and the next, and every morning after that, until one day Lieutenant d'Armagnac would meet him at the door with a new light in his eyes, and say to him: "*Enfin, mon ami!* Good news at last!"

In the garden he looked down at the bare, baked earth. The huge red ants were rushing along the ground waving their front legs and mandibles belligerently in the air. Ahmed shut the gate behind him, and he walked moodily back to the pension.

He would have his lunch in the hot little dining room next to the kitchen, making the meal more digestible by drinking a whole bottle of vin rosé. Then stupefied by the wine and the heat he would go upstairs to his room, undress, and throw himself on his bed, to sleep until the sun's rays were more oblique and the countryside had lost some of the poisonous light that came out of its stones at midday. Walks to towns round about were pleasant: there were bright Igherm on the hill, the larger community of Beni Isguen down the valley, Tadjmout with its terraced pink and blue houses, and there was always the vast palmeraie where the town dwellers had built their toylike country palaces of red mud and pale palm thatch, where the creak of the wells was constant, and the sound of the water gurgling in the narrow aqueducts belied the awful dryness of the earth and air. Sometimes he would merely walk to the great market place in Bou Noura itself, and sit along the side under the arcades, following the progress of some interminable purchase; both buyer and seller employed every histrionic device short of actual tears, in their struggle to lower and raise the price. There were days when he felt contempt for these absurd people; they were unreal, not to be counted seriously among the earth's inhabitants. These were the same days he was so infuriated by the soft hands of the little children when they unconsciously clutched at his clothing and pushed against him in a street full of people. At first he had thought they were pickpockets, and then he had realized they were merely using him for leverage to propel themselves along more quickly in the crowd, as if he had been a tree or a wall. He was even more annoyed then, and pushed them away violently; there was not one among them who was free of scrofula, and most were completely bald, their dark skulls covered with a crust of sores and an outer layer of flies.

But there were other days when he felt less nervous, sat watching the calm old men walk slowly through the market, and said to himself that if he could muster that much dignity when he got to be their age he would consider that his life had been well spent. For their mien was merely a natural concomitant of inner well-being and satisfaction. Without thinking too much about it, eventually he came to the conclusion that their lives must have been worth living.

In the evenings he sat in the salon playing chess with Abdelkader, a slow-moving but by no means negligible adversary. The two had become firm friends as a result of these nightly sessions. When the boys had put out all the lamps and lanterns of the establishment except the one in the corner where they sat at the chessboard, and they were the only two left awake, they would sometimes have a Pernod together, Abdelkader smiling like a conspirator afterward as he got up to wash the glasses himself and put them away; it would never do for anyone to know he had taken a drink of something alcoholic. Tunner would go off up to bed and sleep heavily. He would awaken at sunrise thinking: "Perhaps today—" and by eight he would be on the roof in shorts taking a sunbath; he had his breakfast brought up there each day and drank his coffee while studying French verbs. Then the itch for news would grow too strong; he would have to go and make his morning inquiry.

The inevitable happened: after having made innumerable side-trips from Messad the Lyles came to Bou Noura. Earlier in the same day a party of Frenchmen had arrived in an old command car and taken rooms at the pension. Tunner was at lunch when he heard the familiar roar of the Mercédès. He grimaced: it would be a bore to have those two around the place. He was not in a mood to force himself to politeness. With the Lyles he had never established any more than a passing acquaintanceship, partly because they had left Messad only two days after taking him there, and partly because he had no desire to push the relationship any further than it had gone. Mrs. Lyle was a sour, fat, gabby female, and Eric her spoiled sissy brat grown up; those were his sentiments, and he did not think he would change them. He had not connected Eric with the episode of the passports; he supposed they had been stolen simultaneously in the Aïn Krorfa hotel by some native who had connections with the shady elements that pandered to the Legionnaires in Messad.

Now in the hall he heard Eric say in a hushed voice: "Oh, I say, Mother, what next? That Tunner person is still mucking about here." Evidently he was looking at the room slate over the desk. And in a stage whisper she admonished him: "Eric! You fool! Shut up!" He drank his coffee and went out the side door into the stifling sunlight, hoping to avoid them and get up to his rooms while they were having lunch. This he accomplished. In the middle of his siesta there was a knock on the door. It took him a while to get awake. When he opened, Abdelkader stood outside, an apologetic smile on his face.

"Would it disturb you very much to change your room?" he asked.

Tunner wanted to know why.

"The only rooms free now are the two on each side of you. An English lady has arrived with her son, and she wants him in the room next to her. She's afraid to be alone."

This picture of Mrs. Lyle, drawn by Abdelkader, did not coincide with his own conception of her. "All right," he grumbled. "One room's like another. Send the boys up to move me." Abdelkader patted him on the shoulder with an affectionate gesture. The boys arrived, opened the door between his room and the next, and began to effect the change. In the middle of the moving Eric stepped into the room that was being vacated. He stopped short on catching sight of Tunner.

"Aha!" he exclaimed. "Fancy bumping into you, old man! I expected you'd be down in Timbuctoo by now."

Tunner said: "Hello, Lyle." Now that he was face to face with Eric, he could hardly bring himself to look at him or touch his hand. He had not realized the boy disgusted him so deeply.

"Do forgive this silly whim of Mother's. She's just exhausted from the trip. It's a ghastly lap from Messad here, and she's in a fearful state of nerves."

"That's too bad."

"You understand our putting you out."

"Yes, yes," said Tunner, angry to hear it phrased this way. "When you leave I'll move back in."

"Oh, quite. Have you heard from the Moresbys recently?"

Eric, when he looked at all into the face of the person with whom he was speaking, had a habit of peering closely, as if he placed very little importance on the words that were said, and was trying instead to read between the lines of the conversation, to discover what the other really meant. It seemed to Tunner now that he was observing him with more than a usual degree of attention.

"Yes," said Tunner forcefully. "They're fine. Excuse me. I think I'll go and finish the nap I was taking." Stepping through the connecting door he went into the next room. When the boys had carried everything in there he locked the door and lay on the bed, but he could not sleep.

"God, what a slob!" he said aloud, and then, feeling angry with himself for having capitulated: "Who the hell do they think they are?" He hoped the Lyles would not press him for news of Kit and Port; he would be forced to tell them, and he did not want to. As far as they were concerned, he hoped to keep the tragedy private; their kind of commiseration would be unbearable.

Later in the afternoon he passed by the salon. The Lyles sat in the dim subterranean light clinking their teacups. Mrs. Lyle had spread out some of her old photographs, which were propped against the stiff leather cushions along the back of the divan; she was offering one to Abdelkader to hang beside the ancient gun that adorned the wall. She caught sight of Tunner poised hesitantly in the doorway, and rose in the gloom to greet him.

"Mr. Tunner! How delightful! And what a surprise to see you! How fortunate you were, to leave Messad when you did. Or wise—I don't know which. When we got back from all our touring about, the climate there was positively beastly! Oh, horrible! And of course I got my malaria and had to take to bed. I thought we should never get away. And Eric of course made things more difficult with his silly behavior."

"It's nice to see you again," said Tunner. He thought he had made his final adieux back in Messad, and now discovered he had very little civility left to draw upon.

"We're motoring out to some very old Garamantic ruins tomorrow. You must come along. It'll be quite thrilling."

"That's very kind of you, Mrs. Lyle—"

"Come and have tea!" she cried, seizing his sleeve.

But he begged off, and went out to the palmeraie and walked for miles between the walls under the trees, feeling that he never would get out of Bou Noura. For no reason, the likelihood of Kit's turning up seemed further removed than ever, now that the Lyles were around. He started back at sunset, and it was dark by the time he arrived at the pension. Under his door a telegram had been pushed; the message was written in lavender ink in an almost illegible hand. It was from the American Consul at Dakar, in answer to one of his many wires: NO INFORMATION REGARDING KATHERINE MORESBY WILL ADVISE IF ANY RECEIVED. He threw it into the wastebasket and sat down on a pile of Kit's luggage. Some of the bags had been Port's; now they belonged to Kit, but they were all in his room, waiting.

"How much longer can all this go on?" he asked himself. He was out of his element here; the general inaction was telling on his nerves. It was all very well to do the right thing and wait for Kit to appear somewhere out of the Sahara, but suppose she never did appear? Suppose—the possibility had to be faced—she were already dead? There would have to be a limit to his waiting, a final day after which he would no longer be there. Then he saw himself walking into Hubert David's apartment in East Fifty-fifth Street, where he had first met Port and Kit. All their friends would be there: some would be noisily sympathetic; some would be indignant; some just a little knowing and supercilious, saying nothing but thinking a lot; some would consider the whole thing a gloriously romantic episode, tragic only in passing. But he did not want to see any of them. The longer he stayed here the more remote the incident would become, and the less precise the blame that might attach to him—that much was certain.

That evening he enjoyed his chess game less than usual. Abdelkader saw that he was preoccupied and suddenly suggested they stop playing. He was glad of the opportunity to get to sleep early, and he found himself hoping that the bed in his new room would not prove to have something wrong with it. He told Abdelkader he would see him in the morning, and slowly mounted the stairs, feeling certain now that he would be staying in Bou Noura all winter. Living was cheap; his money would hold out.

The first thing he noticed on stepping into his room was the open communicating door. The lamps were lighted in both rooms, and there was a smaller, more intense light moving beside his bed. Eric Lyle stood there on the far side of the bed, a flashlight in his hand. For a second neither one moved. Then Eric said, in a voice trying to sound sure of itself: "Yes? Who is it?"

Tunner shut the door behind him and walked toward the bed; Eric backed against the wall. He turned the flashlight in Tunner's face.

"Who— Don't tell me I'm in the wrong room!" Eric laughed feebly; nevertheless the sound of it seemed to give him courage. "By the look of your face I expect I am! How awful! I just came in from outside. I thought everything looked a bit odd." Tunner said nothing. "I must have come automatically to this room because my things had been in it this noon. Good God! I'm so fagged I'm scarcely conscious."

It was natural for Tunner to believe what people told him; his sense of suspicion was not well developed, and even though it had been aroused a moment ago he had been allowing himself to be convinced by this pitiful monologue. He was about to say: "That's all right," when he glanced down at the bed. One of Port's small overnight cases lay there open; half of its contents had been piled beside it on the blanket.

Slowly Tunner looked up. At the same time he thrust his neck forward in a way that sent a thrill of fear through Eric, who said apprehensively: "Oh!" Taking four long steps around the foot of the bed he reached the corner where Eric stood transfixed.

"*You* God-damned little son of a bitch!" He grabbed the front of Eric's shirt with his left hand and rocked him back and forth. Still holding it, he took a step sideways to a comfortable distance and swung at him, not too hard. Eric fell back against the wall and remained leaning there as if he were completely paralyzed, his bright eyes on Tunner's face. When it became apparent that the youth was not going to react in any other way, Tunner stepped toward him to pull him upright, perhaps to take another swing at him, depending on how he felt the next second. As he seized his clothing, a sob came in the middle of Eric's heavy breathing, and never shifting his piercing gaze, he said in a low voice, but distinctly: "Hit me."

The words enraged Tunner. "*With* pleasure," he replied, and did so, harder than before—a good deal harder, it seemed, since Eric slumped to the floor and did not move. He looked down at the full, white face with loathing. Then he put the things back into the valise, shut it, and stood still, trying to collect his thoughts. After a moment Eric stirred, groaned. He pulled him up and propelled him toward the door, where he gave him a vicious shove into the next room. He slammed the door, and locked it, feeling slightly sick. Anyone's violence upset him—his own most of all.

The next morning the Lyles were gone. The photograph, a study in sepia of a Peulh water carrier with the famous Red Mosque of Djenné in the background, remained tacked on the salon wall above the divan all winter.

BOOK THREE

The Sky

"From a certain point onward there is no
longer any turning back. That is the point
that must be reached."

—KAFKA

XXVI

WHEN she opened her eyes she knew immediately where
she was. The moon was low in the sky. She pulled her
coat around her legs and shivered slightly, thinking of nothing. There was a part of her mind that ached, that needed
rest. It was good merely to lie there, to exist and ask no questions. She was sure that if she wanted to, she could begin remembering all that had happened. It required only a small
effort. But she was comfortable there as she was, with that
opaque curtain falling between. She would not be the one to
lift it, to gaze down into the abyss of yesterday and suffer
again its grief and remorse. At present, what had gone before
was indistinct, unidentifiable. Resolutely she turned her mind
away, refusing to examine it, bending all her efforts to putting
a sure barrier between herself and it. Like an insect spinning
its cocoon thicker and more resistant, her mind would go on
strengthening the thin partition, the danger spot of her being.

She lay quietly, her feet drawn up under her. The sand was
soft, but its coldness penetrated her garments. When she felt
she could no longer bear to go on shivering, she crawled out
from under her protecting tree and set to striding back and
forth in front of it in the hope of warming herself. The air was
dead; not a breath stirred, and the cold grew by the minute. She
began to walk farther afield, munching bread as she went. Each
time she returned to the tamarisk tree she was tempted to slide
back down under its branches and sleep. However, by the time
the first light of dawn appeared, she was wide awake and warm.

The desert landscape is always at its best in the half-light
of dawn or dusk. The sense of distance lacks: a ridge nearby

can be a far-off mountain range, each small detail can take on the importance of a major variant on the countryside's repetitious theme. The coming of day promises a change; it is only when the day has fully arrived that the watcher suspects it is the same day returned once again—the same day he has been living for a long time, over and over, still blindingly bright and untarnished by time. Kit breathed deeply, looked around at the soft line of the little dunes, at the vast pure light rising up from behind the hammada's mineral rim, at the forest of palms behind her still immersed in night, and knew that it was not the same day. Even when it grew entirely light, even when the huge sun shot up, and the sand, trees and sky gradually resumed their familiar daytime aspect, she had no doubts whatever about its being a new and wholly separate day.

A caravan comprising two dozen or more camels laden with bulging woolen sacks appeared coming down the oued toward her. There were several men walking beside the beasts. At the rear of the procession were two riders mounted on their high meharis, whose nose rings and reins gave them an even more disdainful expression than that of the ordinary camels ahead. Even as she saw these two men she knew that she would accompany them, and the certainty gave her an unexpected sense of power: instead of feeling the omens, she now would make them, *be* them herself. But she was only faintly astonished at her discovery of this further possibility in existence. She stepped out into the path of the oncoming procession and called to it, waving her arms in the air. And before the animals had stopped walking, she rushed back to the tree and dragged out her valise. The two riders looked at her and at each other in astonishment. They drew up their respective mehara and leaned forward, staring down at her in fascinated curiosity.

Because each of her gestures was authoritative, an outward expression of utter conviction, betraying no slightest sign of hesitation, it did not occur to the masters of the caravan to interfere as she passed the valise to one of the men on foot and motioned to him to tie it atop the sacks on the nearest pack camel. The man glanced back at his masters, saw no expression on their faces indicating opposition to her command,

and made the complaining animal kneel and receive the extra burden. The other camel drivers looked on in silence as she walked back to the riders and stretching her arms up toward the younger of the two, said to him in English: "Is there room for me?"

The rider smiled. Grumbling mightily, his mehari was brought to its knees; she seated herself sideways, a few inches in front of the man. When the animal rose, he was obliged to hold her on by passing one arm around her waist, or she would have fallen off. The two riders laughed a bit, and exchanged a few brief remarks as they started on their way along the oued.

After a certain length of time they left the valley and turned across a wide plantless region strewn with stones. The yellow dunes lay ahead. There was the heat of the sun, the slow climbing to the crests and the gentle going down into the hollows, over and over—and the lively, insistent pressure of his arm about her. She raised no problem for herself; she was content to be relaxed and to see the soft unvaried landscape going by. To be sure, several times it occurred to her that they were not really moving at all, that the dune along whose sharp rim they were now traveling was the same dune they had left behind much earlier, that there was no question of going anywhere since they were nowhere. And when these sensations came to her they started an ever so slight stirring of thought. "Am I dead?" she said to herself, but without anguish, for she knew she was not. As long as she could ask herself the question: "Is there anything?" and answer: "Yes," she could not be dead. And there were the sky, the sun, the sand, the slow monotonous motion of the mehari's pace. Even if the moment came, she reflected at last, when she no longer could reply, the unanswered question would still be there before her, and she would know that she lived. The idea comforted her. Then she felt exhilarated; she leaned back against the man and became conscious of her extreme discomfort. Her legs must have been asleep for a long time. Now the rising pain made her embark on a ceaseless series of shiftings. She hitched and wriggled. The rider increased the pressure of his enfolding arm and said a few words to his companion; they both chuckled.

At the hour when the sun shone its hottest, they came within sight of an oasis. The dunes here leveled off to make the terrain nearly flat. In a landscape made gray by too much light, the few hundred palms at first were no more than a line of darker gray at the horizon—a line which varied in thickness as the eye beheld it, moving like a slow-running liquid: a wide band, a long gray cliff, nothing at all, then once more the thin penciled border between the earth and the sky. She watched the phenomenon dispassionately, extracting a piece of bread from the pocket of her coat which lay spread across the ungainly shoulders of the mehari. The bread was completely dry.

"*Stenna, stenna. Chouia, chouia,*" said the man.

Soon a solitary thing detached itself from the undecided mass on the horizon, rising suddenly like a djinn into the air. A moment later it subsided, shortened, was merely a distant palm standing quite still on the edge of the oasis. Quietly they continued another hour or so, and presently they were among the trees. The well was enclosed by a low wall. There were no people, no signs of people. The palms grew sparsely; their branches, still more gray than green, shone with a metallic glister and gave almost no shade. Glad to rest, the camels remained lying down after the packs had been removed. From the bundles the servants took huge striped rugs, a nickel tea service, paper parcels of bread, dates and meat. A black goatskin canteen with a wooden faucet was brought out, and the three drank from it; the well water was considered satisfactory for the camels and drivers. She sat on the edge of the rug, leaning against a palm trunk, and watched the leisurely preparations for the meal. When it was ready she ate heartily and found everything delicious; still she did not down enough to please her two hosts, who continued to force food upon her long after she could eat no more.

"*Smitsek? Kuli!*" they would say to her, holding small bits of food in front of her face; the younger tried to push dates between her teeth, but she laughed and shook her head, letting them fall onto the rug, whereupon the other quickly seized and ate them. Wood was brought from the packs and a fire was built so the tea could be brewed. When all this was done—the tea drunk, remade and drunk again—it was mid-afternoon. The sun still burned in the sky.

Another rug was spread beside the two supine meharis, and the men motioned to her to lie down there with them in the shade cast by the animals. She obeyed, and stretched out in the spot they indicated, which was between them. The younger one promptly seized her and held her in a fierce embrace. She cried out and attempted to sit up, but he would not let her go. The other man spoke to him sharply and pointed to the camel drivers, who were seated leaning against the wall around the well, attempting to hide their mirth.

"*Luh, Belqassim! Essbar!*" he whispered, shaking his head in disapproval, and running his hand lovingly over his black beard. Belqassim was none too pleased, but having as yet no beard of his own, he felt obliged to subscribe to the other's sage advice. Kit sat up, smoothed her dress, looked at the older man and said: "Thank you." Then she tried to climb over him so that he would lie between her and Belqassim; roughly he pushed her back down on the rug and shook his head. "*Nassi,*" he said, signaling that she sleep. She shut her eyes. The hot tea had made her drowsy, and since Belqassim gave no further sign of intending to bother her, she relaxed completely and fell into a heavy slumber.

She was cold. It was dark, and the muscles of her back and legs ached. She sat up, looked about, saw that she was alone on the rug. The moon had not yet risen. Nearby the camel drivers were building a fire, throwing whole palm branches into the already soaring flames. She lay down again and faced the sky above her, seeing the high palms flare red each time a branch was added to the blaze.

Presently the older man stood at the side of the rug, motioning to her to get up. She obeyed, followed him across the sand a short way to a slight depression behind a clump of young palms. There Belqassim was seated, a dark form in the center of a white rug, facing the side of the sky where it was apparent that the moon would shortly rise. He reached out and took hold of her skirt, pulling her quickly down beside him. Before she could attempt to rise again she was caught in his embrace. "No, no, no!" she cried as her head was tilted backward and the stars rushed across the black space above. But he was there all around her, more powerful by far; she could make no movement not prompted by his will. At first she was stiff, gasping angrily, grimly trying to fight him, although the battle went on wholly inside her. Then she realized her helplessness and accepted it. Straightway she was conscious only of his lips and the breath coming from between them, sweet and fresh as a spring morning in childhood. There was an animal-like quality in the firmness with which he held her, affectionate, sensuous, wholly irrational—gentle but of a determination that only death could gainsay. She was alone in a vast and unrecognizable world, but alone only for a moment; then she understood that this friendly carnal presence was there with her. Little by little she found herself considering him with affection: everything he did, all his overpowering little attentions were for her. In his behavior there was a perfect balance between gentleness and violence that gave her particular delight. The moon came up, but she did not see it.

"*Yah, Belqassim!*" cried a voice impatiently. She opened her eyes: the other man was standing above them, looking down at them. The moon shone full into his eagle-like face. An unhappy intuition whispered to her what would occur. Desperately she clung to Belqassim, covering his face with kisses. But a moment later she had with her a different animal, bristling and alien, and her weeping passed unnoticed. She kept her eyes open, staring at Belqassim who leaned idly against a nearby tree, his sharp cheekbones carved brightly by the moonlight. Again and again she followed the line of his face from his forehead down to his fine neck, exploring the deep shadows in search of his eyes, hidden in the darkness. At one point she cried aloud, and then she sobbed a little because he was so near and she could not touch him.

The man's caresses were brusque, his motions uncouth, unacceptable. At last he rose. "*Yah latif! Yah latif!*" he muttered, slowly walking away. Belqassim chuckled, stepped over and threw himself down at her side. She tried to look reproachful, but she knew beforehand that it was hopeless, that even had they had a language in common, he never could understand her. She held his head between her hands. "Why did you let him?" she could not help saying.

"*Habibi,*" he murmured, stroking her cheek tenderly.

Again she was happy for a while, floating on the surface of time, conscious of making the gestures of love only after she had discovered herself in the act of making them. Since the beginning of all things each motion had been waiting to be born, and at last was coming into existence. Later, as the round moon, mounting, grew smaller in the sky, she heard the sound of flutes by the fire. Presently the older merchant appeared again and called peevishly to Belqassim, who answered him with the same ill humor.

"*Baraka!*" said the other, going away again. A few moments later Belqassim sighed regretfully and sat up. She made no effort to hold him. Presently she also rose and walked toward the fire, which had died down and was being used to roast some skewers of meat. They ate quietly without conversation, and shortly afterward the packs were closed and piled onto the camels. It was nearly the middle of the night when they set out, doubling back on their tracks to the high dunes, where they continued in the direction they had been traveling the previous day. This time she wore a burnous that Belqassim had tossed to her as they were about to start. The night was cold and miraculously clear.

They continued until mid-morning, stopping at a place in the high dunes that had not a sign of vegetation. Again they slept through the afternoon, and again the double ritual of love was observed at a distance from the camping site when dark had fallen.

And so the days went by, each one imperceptibly hotter than the one before it, as they moved southward across the desert. Mornings—the painful journey under the unbearable sun; afternoons—the soft hours beside Belqassim (the short interlude with the other no longer bothered her, since Belqassim always stood by); and nights—the setting forth under the now waning moon, toward other dunes and other plains, each more distant than the last and yet indistinguishable from it.

But if the surroundings seemed always the same, there were certain changes appearing in the situation that existed among the three of them: the ease and lack of tension in their uncomplicated relationship began to be troubled by a noticeable want of good feeling on the part of the older man. He and Belqassim had endless argumentative discussions in the hot afternoons when the camel drivers were sleeping. She also would have liked to take advantage of the hour, but they kept

her awake, and although she could not understand a word
they said, it seemed to her that the older man was warning
Belqassim against a course of action upon which the latter
was stubbornly determined. In a perfect orgy of excitement
he would go through a lengthy mimicry in which a group of
people successively registered astonishment, indignant disapproval and rage. Belqassim would smile indulgently and shake
his head with patient disagreement; there was something
both intransigent and self-assured about his attitude in the
matter that infuriated the other, who, each time it seemed
that further expostulation would be useless, got up and took
a few steps away, only to turn a moment later and renew the
attack. But it was quite clear that Belqassim had made up his
mind, that no threat or prophecy of which his companion
was capable would succeed in altering the decision he had
made. At the same time Belqassim was adopting an increasingly proprietary attitude toward Kit. Now he made it understood that he suffered the other to take his brief nightly
pleasure with her only because he was being exceptionally
generous. Each evening she expected that he finally would
refuse to yield her up, fail to rise and walk over to lean
against a tree when the other approached. And indeed, he
had taken to grumbling objections when that moment arrived, but still he let his friend have her, and she supposed
that it was a gentleman's agreement, made for the duration of
the voyage.

During the middle of the day it was no longer the sun
alone that persecuted from above—the entire sky was like a
metal dome grown white with heat. The merciless light
pushed down from all directions; the sun was the whole sky.
They took to traveling only at night, setting out shortly after
twilight and halting at the first sign of the rising sun. The
sand had been left far behind, and so had the great dead stony
plains. Now there was a gray, insect-like vegetation everywhere, a tortured scrub of hard shells and stiff hairy spines
that covered the earth like an excrescence of hatred. The
ashen landscape as they moved through it was flat as a floor.
Day by day the plants grew higher, and the thorns that
sprouted from them stronger and more cruel. Now some
reached the stature of trees, flat-topped and wide, and always

defiant, but a puff of smoke would have afforded as much
protection from the sun's attack. The nights were moonless
and much warmer. Sometimes as they advanced across the
dark countryside there was the startled sound of beasts fleeing
from their path. She wondered what she would have seen if it
had been daylight, but she did not feel any real danger. At
this point, apart from a gnawing desire to be close to Belqassim all the time, it would have been hard for her to know
what she did feel. It was so long since she had canalized her
thoughts by speaking aloud, and she had grown accustomed
to acting without the consciousness of being in the act. She
did only the things she found herself already doing.

One night, having stopped the caravan to go into the
bushes for a necessary moment, and seeing the outline of a
large animal in the dimness near her, she cried out, and was
joined instantly by Belqassim, who consoled her and then
forced her savagely to the ground where he made unexpected
love to her while the caravan waited. She had the impression,
notwithstanding the painful thorns that remained in various
parts of her flesh, that this was a usual occurrence, and she
suffered calmly the rest of the night. The next day the thorns
were still there and the places had festered, and when Belqassim undressed her he saw the red welts and was angry because
they marred the whiteness of her body, thus diminishing
greatly the intensity of his pleasure. Before he would have
anything to do with her, she was forced to undergo the excruciating extraction of every thorn. Then he rubbed butter
all over her back and legs.

Now that their love making was carried on in the daytime,
each morning when it was definitely over, he left the blanket
where she lay and took a gourba of water with him to a spot
a few yards distant, where he stood in the early sunlight and
bathed assiduously. Afterwards she, too, would fetch a gourba
and carry it as far away as she could, but often she found herself washing in full view of the entire camp, because there was
nothing behind which she could conceal herself. But the
camel drivers paid her no more attention at such moments
than did the camels themselves. For all that she was a topic of
intense interest and constant discussion among them, she remained a piece of property that belonged to their masters, as

private and inviolable as the soft leather pouches full of silver these latter carried slung across their shoulders.

At last there came a night when the caravan turned into a well trodden road. In the distance ahead a fire blazed; when they came abreast of it they saw men and camels sleeping. Before dawn they stopped outside a village and ate. When morning came, Belqassim went on foot into the town, returning some time later with a bundle of clothing. Kit was asleep, but he woke her and spread the garments out on the blanket in the ambiguous shadow of the thorn trees, indicating that she undress and put them on. She was pleased to lay aside her own clothes, which were in an unrecognizable state of dishevelment at this point, and it was with growing delight that she pulled on the full soft trousers and got into the loose vests and the flowing robe. Belqassim watched her closely when she had finished and was walking about. He beckoned her to him, took up a long white turban and wound it around her head, hiding her hair completely. Then he sat back and watched her some more. He frowned, called her to him again and produced a woolen sash with which he bound the upper part of her body tightly, pressing it against her bare skin directly under her arms and tying it firmly in the back. She felt a certain difficulty in breathing, and wanted him to take it off, but he shook his head. Suddenly she understood that these were men's garments and that she was being made to look like a man. She began to laugh; Belqassim joined her in her merriment, and made her walk back and forth in front of him several times; each time she passed he patted her on the buttocks with satisfaction. Her own clothes they left there in the bushes, and when an hour or so later Belqassim discovered that one of the camel drivers had appropriated them, presumably with the intention of selling them as they passed through the village presently, he was very angry, and wrenched them away from the man, bidding him dig a shallow hole and bury them then and there while he watched.

She went to the camels and opened her bag for the first time, looked into the mirror on the inside of the lid, and discovered that with the heavy tan she had acquired during the past weeks she looked astonishingly like an Arab boy. The idea amused her. While she was still trying to see the ensemble effect in the small glass, Belqassim came up, and seizing her, bore her off bodily to the blanket where he showered kisses and caresses upon her for a long time, calling her "Ali" amid peals of delighted laughter.

The village was an agglomeration of round mud huts with thatched roofs; it seemed strangely deserted. The three left the camels and drivers at the entrance and went on foot to the small market, where the older man bought several packets of spices. It was unbelievably hot; the rough wool against her skin and the tightness with which the sash was bound about her chest made her feel that at any moment she would collapse into the dust. The people squatting in the market were all very black, and most of them had old, lifeless faces. When a man addressed himself to Kit, holding up a pair of used sandals (she was barefoot), Belqassim pushed forward and answered for her, indicating with accompanying gestures that the young man with him was not in his right mind and must not be bothered or spoken to. This explanation was given several times during their walk through the village; everyone accepted it without comment. At one point an aged woman whose face and hands were partially devoured by leprosy reached up and seized Kit's clothing, asking alms. She glanced down, shrieked, and clutched at Belqassim for protection. Brutally he pushed her away from him, so that she fell against the beggar; at the same time he poured forth a flood of scornful invective at her, spitting furiously on the ground when he had finished. The onlookers seemed amused; but the older man shook his head, and later when they were back at the edge of the town with the camels, he began to berate Belqassim, pointing wrathfully at each item of Kit's disguise. Still Belqassim only smiled and answered in monosyllables. But this time the other's anger was unappeasable, and she had the impression that he was delivering a final warning which he knew to be futile, that henceforth he would consider the matter outside the domain of his interest. And sure enough, neither that day or the next did he have anything to do with her.

They started at dusk. Several times during the night they met processions of men and oxen, and they passed through two smaller villages where fires burned in the streets. The following day while they rested and slept there was a constant stream of traffic moving along the road. That evening they set out even before the sun had set. By the time the moon was well up in the sky they had arrived at the top of a slight eminence from which they could see, spread out not far below, the fires and lights of a great flat city. She listened to the men's conversation, hoping to discover its name, but without success.

An hour or so later they passed through the gate. The city was silent in the moonlight, and the wide streets were deserted. She realized that the fires she had seen from the distance had been outside the town, along the walls where the travelers encamped. But here within, all was still, everyone slept behind the high, fortress-like façades of the big houses. Yet when they turned into an alley and dismounted to the sound of the mehara growling in chorus, she also heard drums not far away.

A door was opened, Belqassim disappeared into the dark, and soon there was life stirring within the house. Servants arrived, each one carrying a carbide lamp which he set down among the packs being removed from the camels. Soon the entire alley had the familiar aspect of a camp in the desert. She leaned against the front of the house near the door and watched the activity. Suddenly she saw her valise among the sacks and rugs. She stepped over and took it. One of the men eyed her distrustfully and said something to her. She returned to her vantage point with the bag. Belqassim did not reappear from inside for a long time. When he came out he turned directly to her, took her arm, and led her into the house.

Later when she was alone in the dark she remembered a chaos of passageways, stairways and turnings, of black spaces beside her suddenly lighted for an instant by the lamp Belqassim carried, of wide roofs where goats wandered in the moonlight, of tiny courtyards, and of places where she had to stoop to pass through and even then felt the fringe of loose fibres hanging from the palmwood beams brushing the turban on her head. They had gone up and down, to the left and to the right, and, she thought, through innumerable houses. Once she had seen two women in white squatting in the corner of a room by a small fire while a child stood by stark naked, fanning it with a bellows. Always there had been

the hard pressure of Belqassim's hand on her arm as, in haste
and with a certain apprehension it seemed to her, he guided
her through the maze, deeper and deeper into the immense
dwelling. She carried her bag; it bumped against her legs and
against the walls. Finally they had crossed a very short stretch
of open roof, climbed a few uneven dirt steps, and after he
had inserted a key and pulled open a door, they had bent
over and entered a small room. And here he had set the light
down on the floor, turned without speaking a word, and
gone out again, locking the door behind him. She had heard
six retreating footsteps and the striking of a match, and that
was all. For a long time she had stood hunched over (for the
ceiling was too low for her to stand upright), listening to the
silence that swarmed around her, profoundly troubled without knowing why, vaguely terrified, but for no reason she
could identify. It was more as though she had been listening
to herself, waiting for something to happen in a place she had
somehow forgotten, yet dimly felt was still there with her.
But nothing happened; she could not even hear her heart
beat. There was only the familiar, faint hissing sound in her
ears. When her neck grew tired of its uncomfortable position
she sat down on the mattress at her feet and pulled small
tufts of wool out of the blanket. The mud walls, smoothed
by the palm of the mason's hand, had a softness that attracted her eye. She sat gazing at them until the fire of the
lamp weakened, began to flutter. When the little flame had
given its final gasp, she pulled up the blanket and lay down,
feeling that something was wrong. Soon, in the darkness, far
and near, the cocks began to crow, and the sound made her
shiver.

XXVII

The limpid, burning sky each morning when she looked out
the window from where she lay, repeated identically day after
day, was part of an apparatus functioning without any relationship to her, a power that had gone on, leaving her far behind.
One cloudy day, she felt, would allow her to catch up with
time. But there was always the immaculate, vast clarity out
there when she looked, unchanging and pitiless above the city.

By her mattress was a tiny square window with iron grill-work across the opening; a nearby wall of dried brown mud cut off all but a narrow glimpse of a fairly distant section of the city. The chaos of cubical buildings with their flat roofs seemed to go on to infinity, and with the dust and heat-haze it was hard to tell just where the sky began. In spite of the glare the landscape was gray—blinding in its brilliancy, but gray in color. In the early morning for a short while the steel-yellow sun glittered distantly in the sky, fixing her like a ser-pent's eye as she sat propped up against the cushions staring out at the rectangle of impossible light. Then when she would look back at her hands, heavy with the massive rings and bracelets Belqassim had given her, she could hardly see them for the dark, and it would take a while for her eyes to grow used to the reduced interior light. Sometimes on a far-off roof she could distinguish minute human figures moving in silhou-ette against the sky, and she would lose herself in imagining what they saw as they looked out over the endless terraces of the city. Then a sound near at hand would rouse her; quickly she would pull off the silver bracelets and drop them into her valise, waiting for the footsteps to approach up the stairs, and for the key to be turned in the lock. An ancient Negro slave woman with a skin like an elephant's hide brought her food four times a day. At each meal, before she arrived bearing the huge copper tray, Kit could hear her wide feet slapping the earthen roof and the silver bangles on her ankles jangling. When she came in, she would say solemnly: "*Sbalkheir,*" or "*Msalkheir,*" close the door, hand Kit the tray, and crouch in the corner staring at the floor while she ate. Kit never spoke to her, for the old woman, along with everyone else in the house with the exception of Belqassim, was under the impression that the guest was a young man; and Belqassim had portrayed for her in vivid pantomime the reactions of the feminine mem-bers of the household should they discover otherwise.

She had not yet learned his language; indeed, she did not consider making the effort. But she had grown used to the in-flection of his speech and to the sound of certain words, so that with patience he could make her understand any idea that was not too complicated. She knew, for instance, that the house belonged to Belqassim's father; that the family came

from the north, from Mecheria, where they had another
house; and that Belqassim and his brothers took turns con-
ducting caravans back and forth between points in Algeria
and the Soudan. She also knew that Belqassim, in spite of his
youth, had a wife in Mecheria and three here in the house,
and that with his own wives and those of his father and his
brothers, there were twenty-two women living in the establishment, exclusive of the servants. And these must never suspect that Kit was anything but an unfortunate young traveler
rescued by Belqassim as he was dying of thirst, and still not
fully recovered from the effects of his ordeal.

Belqassim came to visit her at mid-afternoon each day and
stayed until twilight; it would occur to her when he had left
and she lay alone in the evening, remembering the intensity
and insistence of his ardor, that the three wives must certainly
be suffering considerable neglect, in which case they must already be both suspicious and jealous of this strange young
man who for such a long time had been enjoying the hospitality of the house and the friendship of their husband. But
since she lived now solely for those few fiery hours spent each
day beside Belqassim, she could not bear to think of warning
him to be less prodigal of his love with her in order to allay
their suspicion. What she did not guess was that the three
wives were not being neglected at all, and that even if such
had been the case, and they had believed a boy to be the
cause of it, it never would have occurred to them to be jealous of him. So that it was out of pure curiosity that they sent
little Othman, a Negro urchin who often ran about the house
without a stitch of clothing on him, to spy on the young
stranger and report to them what he looked like.

Frog-faced Othman accordingly installed himself in the
niche under the small stairway leading from the roof to the
high room. The first day he saw the old slave woman carrying
trays up and down, and he saw Belqassim going to visit in the
afternoon and coming away again much later adjusting his
robes, so that he was able to tell the wives how long their
husband had spent with the stranger and what he thought
was going on. But that was not what they wanted to know;
they were interested in the stranger himself—was he tall and
did he have light skin? The excitement they felt at having an

unknown young man living in the house, particularly if their
husband were sleeping with him, was more than they could
endure. That he was handsome and desirable they did not
doubt for an instant, otherwise Belqassim would not keep
him there.

The next morning after the old slave had carried the breakfast tray down, Othman crawled out of his niche and rapped
gently on the door. Then he turned the key and stood there
in the open doorway with a carefully studied expression of
forlorn pertness on his small black face. Kit laughed. The
small naked being with the protruding stomach and the ill-
matched head struck her as ridiculous. The sound of her voice
was not lost on little Othman, who nevertheless grinned and
pretended suddenly to be overcome by a paroxysm of shyness.
She wondered if Belqassim would mind if a child like this
were to come into the room; at the same time she found herself beckoning to him. Slowly he advanced, head down, finger
in mouth, his huge pop-eyes rolled far upward, fixed on hers.
She stepped across the room and closed the door behind him.
In no time at all he was giggling, turning somersaults, singing
silly, pantomimic songs, and in general acting the fool to be-
guile her. She was careful not to speak, but she could not help
laughing from time to time, and this disturbed her a little, because her intuition had begun to whisper to her that there
was something factitious about his gaiety, something faintly
circumspect in the growing intimacy of his regard; his antics
amused her but his eyes alarmed her. Now he was walking on
his hands. When he stood upright again he flexed his arms
like a gymnast. Without warning he sprang to her side where
she sat on the mattress, pinched her biceps under their robes,
and said innocently: "*Deba, enta,*" indicating that the young
guest was to exhibit his prowess as well. She was suddenly
wholly suspicious; she pushed his lingering hand away, at the
same time feeling his little arm brush deliberately across her
breast. Furious and frightened, she tried to hold his gaze and
read his thoughts; he was still laughing and urging her to
stand up and perform. But the fear in her was like a mad motor that had started up. She looked at the grimacing reptilian
face with increasing terror. The emotion was a familiar feeling
to have there inside her; the overwhelming memory of her

intimacy with it cut her off from all sense of reality. She sat there, frozen inside her skin, knowing all at once that she did not know anything—neither where nor what she was; there was a slight, impossible step that must be taken toward one side or the other before she could be back in focus.

Perhaps she sat staring at the wall too long to please Othman, or perhaps he, having made his great discovery, felt no need of providing her with further entertainment: after a few desultory dance steps he began backing toward the door, still keeping his eyes unflinchingly fixed on hers, as if his distrust of her were so great that he believed her capable of any treachery. When he reached the doorway, he felt softly behind his back for the latch, swiftly stepped out, slammed the door shut and locked it.

The slave brought her the noonday meal, but she still sat unmoving, eyes unseeing. The old woman held up morsels of food before her face, tried to push them into her mouth. Then she went out to look for Belqassim, to tell him that the young gentleman was ill or bewitched, and would not eat. But Belqassim was lunching that day at the home of a leather merchant at the far end of the city, so she could not reach him. Deciding to take matters into her own hands, she went to her quarters off a courtyard near the stables, and prepared a small bowl of goat's butter and powdered camel dung which she mixed carefully with a pestle. This done, she made a ball of half of it and swallowed it without chewing it. With the rest she anointed the two thongs of a long leather whip she kept by her pallet. Carrying the whip she returned to the room where Kit still sat motionless on her mattress. When she had shut the door behind her she stood a while gathering her forces, and presently she broke into a monotonous, whining song, flourishing the serpentine lash slowly in the air as she chanted, watching Kit's paralyzed countenance for a sign of awareness. After a few minutes, seeing that none was forthcoming, she moved closer to the mattress and brandished the whip above her head; at the same time she began to move her feet in a slow, shuffling step that made the heavy bands of silver on her ankles ring in a rhythmical accompaniment to her song. Soon the sweat ran down the furrows of her black face, dripped onto her garments and onto the dry earthen floor

where each drop slowly spread to make a large round spot.
Kit sat, conscious of her presence and her musty odor, conscious of the heat and the song in the room, but none of it
was anything that had to do with her—it was all like a distant,
fleeting memory, far on the outside. Suddenly the old woman
brought the whip down across her face with a quick, light
gesture. The lithe greased leather wrapped itself around her
head for the fraction of a second, stinging the skin of her
cheek. She sat still. A few seconds later she slowly raised
her hand to her face, and at the the same time she gave a
slight scream, not loud, but unmistakably a sound made by
a woman. The old slave watched fearfully, perplexed; clearly
the young man was under a very serious spell. She stood
looking as Kit fell back on the mattress and surrendered herself to a long fit of crying.

At this point the old woman heard steps on the stairs.
Terrified that Belqassim was returning and would punish her
for meddling, she dropped the whip and turned toward the
door. It opened, and one after the other the three wives of
Belqassim strode into the room, bending their heads slightly
forward to avoid scraping them on the ceiling. Paying no attention to the old woman, they rushed as one person to the
mattress and threw themselves upon Kit's prostrate form,
wrenching the turban from her head and ripping her garments open by sheer force, so that all at once the upper part
of her body was entirely unclothed. The onslaught was so
unexpected and so violent that the thing was accomplished in
a very few seconds; Kit did not know what was happening.
Then she felt the whip strike across her breasts. As she
screamed she reached out and grasped a head that bobbed in
front of her. She felt the hair, the soft features of the face beneath her clenched fingers. With all her might she pulled it
downward and tried to rip the thing to shreds, but it would
not tear; it merely became wet. The whip was making streaks
of fire across her shoulders and back. Someone else was
screaming now, and shrill voices were crying out. There was
the weight of a body against her face. She bit into soft flesh.
"Thank God I have good teeth," she thought, and she saw
the words of the sentence printed in front of her as she
clamped her jaws together, felt her teeth sinking into the mass

of flesh. The sensation was delicious. She tasted the warm salt blood on her tongue, and the pain of the blows receded. There were many people in the room; the air was a jumble of sobs and screeches. Above the noise she heard Belqassim's voice shout furiously. Knowing now that he was there, she relaxed the grip of her jaws, and received a violent blow in the face. The sounds sped away and she was alone in the dark for a while, thinking she was humming a little song that Belqassim often had sung to her.

Or was it his voice, was she lying with her head in his lap, with her arms stretching upward to draw his face down to hers? Had there been a quiet night in between, or several nights, before she was sitting cross-legged in the large room lighted by many candles, in a gold dress, surrounded by all these sullen-faced women? How long would they keep filling her glass with tea as she sat there alone with them? But Belqassim was there; his eyes were grave. She watched him: in the static posture of a character in a dream he removed the jewelry from around the necks of the three wives, turning repeatedly to place the pieces gently in her lap. The gold brocade was weighted down with the heavy metal. She stared at the bright objects and then at the wives, but they kept their eyes on the floor, refusing to look up at all. Beyond the balcony in the court below, the sound of men's voices constantly augmented, the music began, and the women around her all screamed together in her honor. Even as Belqassim sat before her fastening the jewelry about her neck and bosom she knew that all the women hated her, and that he never could protect her from their hatred. Today he punished his wives by taking another woman and humiliating them before her, but the other somber woman-faces around her, even the slaves looking in from the balcony, would be waiting from this moment on, to savor her downfall.

As Belqassim fed her a cake, she sobbed and choked, showering crumbs into his face. "*G igherdh ish'ed our illi,*" sang the musicians below, over and over, while the rhythm of the hand drum changed, slowly closing in upon itself to form a circle from which she would not escape. Belqassim was looking at her with mingled concern and disgust. She coughed lengthily in the midst of her sobbing. The kohl

from her eyes was streaking her face, her tears were wetting
the marriage robe. The men laughing in the court below
would not save her, Belqassim would not save her. Even now
he was angry with her. She hid her face in her hands and she
felt him seize her wrists. He was talking to her in a whisper,
and the incomprehensible words made hissing sounds. Violently he pulled her hands away and her head fell forward.
He would leave her alone for an hour, and the three would
be waiting. Already they were thinking in unison; she could
follow the vengeful direction of their thoughts as they sat
there opposite her, refusing to look up. She cried out and
struggled to rise to her feet, but Belqassim shoved her back
fiercely. A huge black woman tottered across the room and
seated herself against her, putting her massive arm around
her and pinning her against the pile of cushions on the other
side. She saw Belqassim leave the room; straightway she unhooked what necklaces and brooches she could; the black
woman did not notice the movements of her hands. When
she had several pieces in her lap she tossed them to the three
sitting across from her. There was an outcry from the other
women in the room; a slave went running in search of
Belqassim. In no time he was back, his face dark with rage.
No one had moved to touch the pieces of jewelry, which still
lay in front of the three wives on the rug. ("*G igherdh ish'ed
our illi*," insisted the song sadly.) She saw him stoop to pick
them up, and she felt them strike her face and roll down
upon the front of her dress.

Her lip was cut; the sight of the blood on her finger fascinated her and she sat quietly for a long time, conscious only
of the music. Sitting quietly seemed to be the best way to
avoid more pain. If there was to be pain in any case, the only
way of living was to find the means of keeping it away as long
as possible. No one hurt her now that she was sitting still.
The woman's fat black hands bedecked her with the necklaces
and charms once more. Someone passed her a glass of very
hot tea, and someone else held a plate of cakes before her.
The music went on, the women regularly punctuated its ca-
dences with their yodeling screams. The candles burned
down, many of them went out, and the room grew gradually
darker. She dozed, leaning against the black woman.

Much later in the darkness she climbed up the four steps into an enormous enclosed bed, smelling the cloves with which its curtains had been scented, and hearing Belqassim's heavy breathing behind her as he held her arm to guide her there. Now that he owned her completely, there was a new savageness, a kind of angry abandon in his manner. The bed was a wild sea, she lay at the mercy of its violence and chaos as the heavy waves toppled upon her from above. Why, at the height of the storm, did two drowning hands press themselves tighter and tighter about her throat? Tighter, until even the huge gray music of the sea was covered by a greater, darker noise—the roar of nothingness the spirit hears as it approaches the abyss and leans over.

Afterwards, she lay wakeful in the sweet silence of the night, breathing softly while he slept. The following day she spent in the intimacy of the bed, with the curtains drawn. It was like being inside of a great box. During the morning Belqassim dressed and went out; the fat woman of the night before bolted the door after him and sat on the floor leaning against it. Each time the servants brought food, drink or washing water the woman rose with incredible slowness, panting and grunting, to pull open the big door.

The food disgusted her: it was tallowy, cloying and soft—not at all like what she had been eating in her room on the roof. Some of the dishes seemed to consist principally of lumps of half-cooked lamb fat. She ate very little, and saw the servants look at her disapprovingly when they came to collect the trays. Knowing that for the moment she was safe, she felt almost calm. She had her little valise brought her, and in the privacy of the bed she set it on her knees and opened it to examine the objects inside. Automatically she used her compact, lipstick and perfume; the folded thousand-franc notes fell out onto the bed. For a long time she stared at the other articles: small white handkerchiefs, shiny nail scissors, a pair of tan silk pajamas, little jars of facial cream. Then she handled them absently; they were like the fascinating and mysterious objects left by a vanished civilization. She felt that each one was a symbol of something forgotten. It did not even sadden her when she knew she could not remember what the things meant. She made a bundle of the thousand-franc notes and put it at the bottom of the bag, packed everything else on top and snapped the valise shut.

That evening Belqassim dined with her, forcing her to swallow the fatty food after showing her with eloquent gestures that she was undesirably thin. She rebelled; the stuff made her feel ill. But as always it was impossible not to do his bidding. She ate it then, and she ate it the following day and the days that came after that. She grew used to it and no longer questioned it. The nights and days became confused in her mind, because sometimes Belqassim came to bed at the beginning of the afternoon and left her at nightfall, returning in the middle of the night followed by a servant bearing trays of food. Always she remained inside the windowless room, and usually in the bed itself, lying among the disordered piles of white pillows, her mind empty of everything save the memory or anticipation of Belqassim's presence. When he climbed the steps of the bed, parted the curtains, entered and reclined beside her to begin the slow ritual of removing her garments, the hours she had spent doing nothing took on their full meaning. And when he went away the delicious state of exhaustion and fulfilment persisted for a long time afterward; she lay half awake, bathing in an aura of mindless contentment, a state which she quickly grew to take for granted, and then, like a drug, to find indispensable.

One night he did not come at all. She tossed and sighed so long and so violently that the Negro woman went out and got her a hot glass of something strange and sour. She fell asleep, but in the morning her head was heavy and full of buzzing pain. During the day she ate very little. This time the servants looked at her with sympathy.

In the evening he appeared. As he came in the door and motioned the black woman out, Kit sprang up, bounded across the room and threw herself upon him hysterically. Smiling, he carried her back to the bed, methodically set about taking off her clothing and jewelry. When she lay before him, white-skinned and filmy-eyed, he bent over and began to feed her candy from between his teeth. Occasionally she would try to catch his lips at the same time that she took the sweets, but he was always too quick for her, and drew his head away. For a long time he teased her this way, until finally she uttered a long, low cry and lay quite still. His eyes shining, he threw the candy aside and covered her inert body with kisses. When she came to, the room was in darkness and he was beside her, sleeping profoundly. After this he sometimes stayed away two days at a time. Then he would tease her endlessly until she screamed and beat him with her fists. But between times she waited for these unbearable interludes with a gnawing excitement that drove every other sensation from her consciousness.

Finally there came a night when for no apparent reason the woman brought her the sour beverage and stood above her looking at her sternly while she drank it. She handed back the glass with a sinking heart. Belqassim would not be there. Nor did he come the next day. Five successive nights she was given the potion, and each time the sour taste seemed stronger. She spent her days in a feverish torpor, sitting up only to eat the food that was given her.

It seemed to her that sometimes she heard the sharp voices of women outside her door; the sound reminded her of the existence of fear, and she was haunted and unhappy for a few minutes, but when the stimulus was removed and she no longer thought she heard the voices, she forgot about it. The sixth night she suddenly decided that Belqassim never would come back. She lay dry-eyed, staring at the canopy over her head, the lines of its draperies dim in the light of the one carbide lamp by the door where the woman sat. Spinning a fantasy as she lay there, she made him come in the door, approach the bed, pull back the curtains—and was astonished to find that it was not Belqassim at all who climbed the four steps to join her, but a young man with a composite, anonymous face. Only then she realized that any creature even remotely resembling Belqassim would please her quite as much as Belqassim himself. For the first time it occurred to her that beyond the walls of the room, somewhere nearby, in the streets if not in the very house, there were plenty of such creatures. And among these men surely there were some as wonderful as Belqassim, who would be quite as capable and as desirous of giving her delight. The thought that one of his brothers might be lying only a few feet from her behind the wall at the head of her bed, filled her with a tremulous

anguish. But her intuition whispered to her to lie absolutely
still, and she turned over quietly and pretended to be asleep.

Soon a servant knocked at the door, and she knew that her
nightly glass of soporific had been handed in; a moment later
the Negro woman opened the bed curtains, and seeing that
her mistress was asleep, set the glass on the top step and went
back to her pallet by the door. Kit did not move, but her
heart was beating in an unaccustomed fashion. "It's poison,"
she told herself. They had been poisoning her slowly, which
was the reason why they had not come to punish her. Much
later, when she raised herself softly on one elbow and peered
between the curtains, she saw the glass and shuddered at the
nearness of it. The woman was snoring.

"I must get out," she thought. She was feeling strangely
wide awake. But when she climbed down from the bed she
knew she was weak. And for the first time she noticed the dry,
earthen smell of the room. From the cowhide chest nearby
she took the jewelry Belqassim had given her, as well as all he
had taken from the other three, and spread it out on the bed.
Then she lifted her little valise out of the chest and quietly
stepped over to the door. The woman still slept. "Poison!"
whispered Kit furiously as she turned the key. With great care
she managed to close the door silently behind her. But now
she was in the absolute dark, trembling with weakness, holding the bag in one hand, and lightly running the fingers of
the other along the wall beside her.

"I must send a telegram," she thought. "It's the quickest
way of reaching them. There must be a telegraph office here."
But first it was necessary to get into the street, and the street
was perhaps a long way off. Between her and the street, in the
darkness ahead of her, she might meet Belqassim; now she
never wanted to see him again. "He's your husband," she
whispered to herself, and stood still a second in horror. Then
she almost giggled: it was only a part of this ridiculous game
she had been playing. But until she sent the telegram she
would still be playing it. Her teeth began to chatter. "Can
you possibly control yourself just until we get into the street?"

The wall at her left suddenly came to an end. She took two
cautious steps forward and felt the soft edge of the floor beneath the tip of her slipper. "One of those damned stairwells

without a railing!" she said. Deliberately she set down the valise, turned around, and stepped back to the wall, following it the way she had come until she felt the door beneath her hand. She opened it soundlessly and took up the little tin lamp. The woman had not moved. She managed to shut the door without a mishap. With the light she was surprised to see how near the valise was. It was at the edge of the drop, but close to the top of the stairs; she would not have fallen very far. She went down slowly, taking care not to twist her ankle on the soft, crooked steps. Below, she was in a narrow corridor with closed doors on either side. At the end it turned to the right and led into an open court whose floor was strewn with straw. A narrow moon above gave white light; she saw the large door ahead and the sleeping forms along the wall beside it, and put her lamp out, setting it on the ground. When she advanced to the door she found that she could not budge the giant bolt that fastened it.

"You've *got* to move it," she thought, but she felt weak and ill as her fingers pushed against the cold metal of the lock. She lifted the valise and hammered once with the end of it, thinking she felt it give a little. At the same time one of the nearby figures stirred.

"*Echkoon?*" said a man's voice.

Immediately she crouched down and crawled behind a pile of loaded sacks.

"*Echkoon?*" said the voice again with annoyance. The man waited a bit for a reply, and then he went back to sleep. She thought of trying again, but she was trembling too violently, her heart was beating too hard. She leaned against the sacks and closed her eyes. And all at once someone began to beat a drum back in the house.

She jumped. "The signal," she decided. "Of course. It was beating when I came." There was no doubt now that she would get out. She rested a moment, then rose and crossed the courtyard in the direction of the sound. Now there were two drums together. She stepped through a door into darkness. At the end of a long hallway there was another moonlit court, and as she approached she saw yellow light shining from under a door. In the court she stood a while listening to the nervous rhythms coming from inside the room. The

drums had awakened the cocks in the vicinity, and they were
beginning to crow. Faintly she tapped on the door; the drums
continued, and the thin high voice of a woman started to sing
a repeated querulous refrain. She waited a long time before
finding the courage to knock again, but this time she rapped
loudly, with determination. The drumming ceased, the door
was flung open, and she stepped blinking inside the room. On
the floor among the cushions sat Belqassim's three wives, staring up at her in wide-eyed surprise. She stood perfectly rigid,
as though she had come face to face with a deadly snake. The
girl servant pushed the door shut and remained leaning
against it. Then the three threw down their drums and began
talking all at once, gesticulating, pointing upward. One of
them jumped up and approached her to feel among the folds
of her flowing white robe, apparently in search of the jewelry.
She pulled up the long sleeves, feeling for bracelets. Excitedly
the other two pointed at the valise. Kit still stood unmoving,
waiting for the nightmare to end. By dint of prodding and
pushing her, they got her to bend down and open the combination lock, whose manipulation in itself, under any other
circumstances, would have fascinated them. But now they
were suspicious and impatient. When the bag was open they
precipitated themselves upon it and pulled everything out on
to the floor. Kit stared at them. She could scarcely believe her
good luck: they were far more interested in the valise than in
her. As they carefully inspected the objects, she regained some
of her composure, presently taking heart sufficiently to tap
one of them on the shoulder and indicate that the jewelry was
upstairs. They all looked up incredulously and one of them
dispatched the servant girl to verify. But as the girl turned to
go out of the room Kit was seized with fear and tried to stop
her. She would wake the black woman. The others jumped up
angrily; there was a brief mêlée. When that had died down
and all five of them stood there panting, Kit, making a grimace of desperation, put her fingers to her lips, took a few exaggeratedly cautious steps on tiptoe, and pointed repeatedly
at the servant. Then she puffed out her cheeks and tried to
imitate a fat woman. They all understood immediately and
solemnly nodded their heads; the sense of conspiracy had
been imparted to them. When the servant had left the room

they tried to question Kit: "*Wen timshi?*" they said, their voices betraying more curiosity than anger. She could not answer; she shook her head hopelessly. It was not long before the girl returned, ostensibly announced that all the jewelry was on the bed—not only theirs but a lot more besides. Their expressions were mystified but joyous. As Kit knelt to pack her things into the bag, one of them crouched beside her and spoke with her in a voice that certainly was no longer inimical. She had no idea what the girl was saying; her mind was fixed on the image of the bolted door. "I've got to get out. I've got to get out," she told herself over and over. The pile of banknotes lay with her pajamas. No one paid them any attention.

When everything had been put back, she took up a lipstick and a small hand mirror, and turning toward a light, ostentatiously made up. There were cries of admiration. She passed the objects to one of them and invited her to do the same. When all three had brilliant red lips and were looking enraptured at themselves and at each other, she showed them that she would leave the lipstick as a gift for them, but that in return they must let her out into the street. Their faces reflected eagerness and consternation: they were eager to have her out of the house but fearful of Belqassim. During the consultation that followed, Kit sat beside her valise on the floor. She watched them, not feeling that their discussion had anything to do with her. The decision was being made far beyond them, far beyond this unlikely little room where they stood chattering. She ceased looking at them and stared impassively in front of her, convinced that because of the drums she would get out. Now she was merely waiting for the moment. After a long time they sent the servant girl away; she returned accompanied by a little black man so old that his back bent far forward as he shuffled along. In his shaking hand he held a huge key. He was muttering protestations, but it was clear that he had already been persuaded. Kit sprang up and took her bag. Each of the wives came to her as she stood there, and implanted a solemn kiss in the middle of her forehead. She stepped to the door where the old man stood, and together they crossed the courtyard. As they went along he said a few words to her, but she could not answer. He took her to another part of the house and opened a small door. She stood alone in the silence of the street.

XXVIII

The blinding sea was there below, and it glistened in the silver morning light. She lay on the narrow shelf of rock, face down, head hanging over, watching the slow waves moving inward from far out there where the curving horizon rose toward the sky. Her fingernails grated on the rock; she was certain she would fall unless she hung on with every muscle. But how long could she stay there like that, suspended between sky and sea? The ledge had been growing constantly narrower; now it cut across her chest and hindered her breathing. Or was she slowly edging forward, raising herself ever so slightly on her elbows now and then to push her body a fraction of an inch nearer the edge? She was leaning out far enough now to see the sheer cliffs beneath at the sides, split into towering prisms that sprouted fat gray cacti. Directly below her, the waves broke soundlessly against the wall of rock. Night had been here in the wet air, but now it had retreated beneath the surface of the water. At the moment her balance was perfect; stiff as a plank she lay poised on the brink. She fixed her eye on one distant advancing wave. By the time it arrived at the rock her head would have begun to descend, the balance would be broken. But the wave did not move.

"Wake up! Wake up!" she screamed.

She let go.

Her eyes were already open. Dawn was breaking. The rock she leaned against hurt her back. She sighed, and shifted her position a bit. Among the rocks out there beyond the town it was very quiet at this time of the day. She looked into the sky, saw space growing ever clearer. The first slight sounds moving through that space seemed no more than variations on the basic silence of which they were made. The nearby rock forms and the more distant city walls came up slowly from the realm of the invisible, but still only as emanations of the shadowy depths beneath. The pure sky, the bushes beside her, the pebbles at her feet, all had been drawn up from the well of absolute night. And in the same fashion the strange languor in the center of her consciousness, those vaporous ideas which kept appearing as though independently of her will, were mere tentative fragments of her own presence, looming against the nothingness of a sleep not yet cold—a sleep still powerful enough to return and take her in its arms. But she remained awake, the nascent light invading her eyes, and still no corresponding aliveness awoke within her; she had no feeling of being anywhere, of being anyone.

When she was hungry, she rose, picked up her bag, and walked among the rocks along a path of sorts, probably made by goats, which ran parallel to the walls of the town. The sun had risen; already she felt its heat on the back of her neck. She raised the hood of her haïk. In the distance were the sounds of the town: voices crying out and dogs barking. Presently she passed beneath one of the flat-arched gates and was again in the city. No one noticed her. The market was full of black women in white robes. She went up to one of the women and took a jar of buttermilk out of her hand. When she had drunk it, the woman stood waiting to be paid. Kit frowned and stooped to open her bag. A few other women, some carrying babies at their backs, stopped to watch. She pulled a thousand-franc note out of the pile and offered it. But the woman stared at the paper and made a gesture of refusal. Kit still held it forth. Once the other had understood that no different money was to be given her, she set up a great cry and began to call for the police. The laughing women crowded in eagerly, and some of them took the proffered note, examining it with curiosity, and finally handing it back to Kit. Their language was soft and unfamiliar. A white horse trotted past; astride it sat a tall Negro in a khaki uniform, his face decorated with deep cicatrizations like a carved wooden mask. Kit broke away from the women and raised her arms toward him, expecting him to lift her up, but he looked at her askance and rode off. Several men joined the group of onlookers, and stood somewhat apart from the women, grinning. One of them, spotting the bill in her hand, stepped nearer and began to examine her and the valise with increasing interest. Like the others, he was tall, thin and very black, and he wore a ragged burnous slung across his shoulders, but his costume included a pair of dirty white European trousers instead of the long native undergarment. Approaching her, he tapped her on the arm and said something to her in Arabic; she did not understand. Then he said: "*Toi parles français?*" She did not move; she did not know what to do. "*Oui,*" she replied at length.

"*Toi pas Arabe,*" he pronounced, scrutinizing her. He turned triumphantly to the crowd and announced that the lady was French. They all backed away a few steps, leaving him and Kit in the center. Then the woman renewed her demands for money. Still Kit remained motionless, the thousand-franc note in her hand.

The man drew some coins from his pocket and tossed them to the expostulating woman, who counted them and walked off slowly. The other people seemed disinclined to move; the sight of a French lady dressed in Arab clothes delighted them. But he was displeased, and indignantly tried to get them to go on about their business. He took Kit's arm and gently tugged at it.

"It's not good here," he said. "Come." He picked up the valise. She let him pull her along through the market, past the piles of vegetables and salt, past the noisy buyers and vendors.

As they came to a well where the women were filling their water jars, she tried to break away from him. In another minute life would be painful. The words were coming back, and inside the wrappings of the words there would be thoughts lying there. The hot sun would shrivel them; they must be kept inside in the dark.

"*Non!*" she cried, jerking her arm away.

"*Madame,*" said the man reprovingly. "Come and sit down."

Again she allowed him to lead her through the throng. At the end of the market they went under an arcade, and in the shadows there was a door. It was cool inside in the corridor. A fat woman wearing a checked dress stood at the end, her arms akimbo. Before they reached her, she cried shrilly: "Amar! What's that *saloperie* you're bringing in here? You know very well I don't allow native women in my hotel. Are you drunk? *Allez! Fous-moi le camp!*" She advanced upon them frowning.

Momentarily taken aback, the man let go of his charge. Kit wheeled about automatically and started to walk toward the door, but he turned and seized her arm again. She tried to shake him off.

"She understands French!" exclaimed the woman, surprised. "So much the better." Then she saw the valise. "What's that?" she said.

"But it's hers. She's a French lady," Amar explained, a note of indignation in his voice.

"*Pas possible*," murmured the woman. She came nearer and looked at her. Finally she said: "*Ah, pardon, madame.* But with those clothes—" She broke off, and suspicion entered her voice again. "You know, this is a decent hotel." She was undecided, but she shrugged her shoulders, adding with bad grace: "*Enfin, entrez si vous voulez.*" And she stepped aside for Kit to pass.

Kit, however, was making frantic efforts to disengage herself from the man's grasp.

"*Non, non, non! Je ne veux pas!*" she cried hysterically, clawing at his hand. Then she put her free arm around his neck and laid her head on his shoulder, sobbing.

The woman stared at her, then at Amar. Her face grew hard. "Take that creature out of here!" she said furiously. "Take her back to the bordel where you found her! *Et ne viens plus m'emmerder avec tes sales putains! Va! Salaud!*"

Outside the sun seemed more dazzling than before. The mud walls and the shining black faces went past. There was no end to the world's intense monotony.

"I'm tired," she said to Amar.

They were in a gloomy room sitting side by side on a long cushion. A Negro wearing a fez stood before them handing them each a glass of coffee.

"I want it all to stop," she said to them both, very seriously.

"*Oui, madame,*" said Amar, patting her shoulder.

She drank her coffee and lay back against the wall, looking at them through half-closed eyes. They were talking together, they talked interminably. She did not wonder what it was about. When Amar got up and went outside with the other, she waited a moment, until their voices were no longer audible, and then she too jumped up and walked through a door on the other side of the room. There was a tiny stairway. On the roof it was so hot she gasped. The confused babble from the market was almost covered by the buzzing of the flies around her. She sat down. In another moment she would begin to melt. She shut her eyes and the flies crawled quickly over her face, alighting, leaving, re-alighting with frantic intensity. She opened her eyes and saw the city out there on all sides of her. Cascades of crackling light poured over the terraced roofs.

Slowly her eyes grew accustomed to the terrible brightness. She fixed the objects beside her on the dirt floor: the bits of rags; the dried carcass of a strange gray lizard; the faded, broken matchboxes; and the piles of white chicken feathers stuck together with dark blood. There was somewhere she had to go; someone was expecting her. How could she let the people know she would be late? Because there was no question about it—she was going to arrive far behind schedule. Then she remembered that she had not sent her telegram. At that moment Amar came through the little doorway and walked toward her. She struggled to her feet. "Wait here," she said, pushing past him, and she went in because the sun made her feel ill. The man looked at the paper and then at her. "Where do you want to send it?" he repeated. She shook her head dumbly. He handed her the paper and she saw, written on it in her own hand, the words: "CANNOT GET BACK." The man was staring at her. "That's not right!" she cried, in French. "I want to add something." But the man went on staring at her—not angrily, but expectantly. He had a small moustache and blue eyes. "*Le destinataire, s'il vous plaît,*" he said again. She thrust the paper at him because she could not think of the words she needed to add, and she wanted the message to leave immediately. But already she saw that he was not going to send it. She reached out and touched his face, stroked his cheek briefly. "*Je vous en prie, monsieur,*" she said imploringly. There was a counter between them; he stepped back and she could not reach him. Then she ran out into the street and Amar, the black man, was standing there. "Quick!" she cried, not stopping. He ran after her, calling to her. Wherever she ran, he was beside her, trying to make her stop. "*Madame!*" he kept saying. But he did not understand the danger, and she could not stop to explain anything. There was no time for that. Now that she had betrayed herself, established contact with the other side, every minute counted. They would spare no effort in seeking her out, they would pry open the wall she had built and force her to look at what she had buried there. She knew by the blue-eyed man's expression that she had set in motion the mechanism which would destroy her. And now it was too late to stop it. "*Vite! Vite!*" she panted to Amar, perspiring and protesting beside her. They were in an open space by the road that led down to the river. A few nearly naked beggars squatted here and there, each one murmuring his own short sacred formula for them as they rushed by. No one else was in sight.

He finally caught up with her and took hold of her shoulder, but she redoubled her efforts. Soon, however, she slowed down, and then he seized her firmly and brought her to a stop. She sank to her knees and wiped her wet face with the back of her hand. The expression of terror was still strong in her eyes. He crouched down beside her in the dust and tried to comfort her with clumsy pats on the arm.

"Where are you going like this?" he demanded presently. "What's the matter?"

She did not answer. The hot wind blew past. In the distance on the flat road to the river, a man and two oxen passed along slowly. Amar was saying: "That was Monsieur Geoffroy. He's a good man. You should not be afraid of him. For five years he has worked at the Postes et Télégraphes."

The sound of the last word was like a needle piercing her flesh. She jumped. "No, I won't! No, no, no!" she wailed.

"And you know," Amar went on, "that money you wanted to give him is not good here. It's Algerian money. Even in Tessalit you have to have A.O.F. francs. Algerian money is contraband."

"Contraband," she repeated; the word meant absolutely nothing.

"*Défendu!*" he said laughing, and he attempted to get her up onto her feet. The sun was painful; he, too, was sweating. She would not move at present—she was exhausted. He waited a while, made her cover her head with her haïk, and lay back wrapped in his burnous. The wind increased. The sand raced along the flat black earth like white water streaming sideways.

Suddenly she said: "Take me to your house. They won't find me there."

But he refused, saying that there was no room, that his family was large. Instead he would take her to the place where they had had coffee earlier in the day.

"It's a café," she protested.

"But Atallah has many rooms. You can pay him. Even your Algerian money. He can change it. You have more?"

"Yes, yes. In my bag." She looked around. "Where is it?" she said vacantly.

"You left it at Atallah's. He'll give it to you." He grinned and spat. "Now, shall we walk a little?"

Atallah was in his café. A few turbaned merchants from the north sat in a corner talking. Amar and Atallah stood a moment conversing in the doorway. Then they led her into the living quarters behind the café. It was very dark and cool in the rooms, and particularly in the last one, where Atallah set her valise down and indicated a blanket in the corner on the floor for her to lie on. Even as he went out, letting the curtain fall across the doorway, she turned to Amar and pulled his face down to hers.

"You must save me," she said between kisses.

"Yes," he answered solemnly.

He was as comforting as Belqassim had been disturbing.

Atallah did not lift the curtain until evening, when by the light of his lamp he saw them both asleep on the blanket. He set the lamp down in the doorway and went out.

Some time later she awoke. It was silent and hot in the room. She sat up and looked at the long black body beside her, inert and shining as a statue. She laid her hands on the chest: the heart beat heavily, slowly. The limbs stirred. The eyes opened, the mouth broke into a smile.

"I have a big heart," he said to her, putting his hand over hers and holding it there on his chest.

"Yes," she said absently.

"When I feel well, I think I'm the best man in the world. When I'm sick, I hate myself. I say: you're no good at all, Amar. You're made of mud." He laughed.

There was a sudden sound in another part of the house. He felt her cringe. "Why are you afraid?" he said. "I know. Because you are rich. Because you have a bag full of money. Rich people are always afraid."

"I'm not rich," she said. She paused. "It's my head. It aches." She pulled her hand free and moved it from his chest to her forehead.

He looked at her and laughed again. "You should not think. *Ça c'est mauvais.* The head is like the sky. Always turning around and around inside. But very slowly. When you think, you make it go too fast. Then it aches."

"I love you," she said, running her finger along his lips. But she knew she could not really get to him.

"*Moi aussi,*" he replied, biting her finger lightly.

She wept, and let a few tears fall on him; he watched her with curiosity, shaking his head from time to time.

"No, no," he said. "Cry a little while, but not too long. A little while is good. Too long is bad. You should never think of what is finished." The words comforted her, although she could not remember what was finished. "Women always think of what is finished instead of what is beginning. Here we say that life is a cliff, and you must never turn around and look back when you're climbing. It makes you sick." The gentle voice went on; finally she lay down again. Still she was convinced that this was the end, that it would not be long before they found her. They would stand her up before a great mirror, saying to her: "Look!" And she would be obliged to look, and then it would be all over. The dark dream would be shattered; the light of terror would be constant; a merciless beam would be turned upon her; the pain would be unendurable and endless. She lay close against him, shuddering. Shifting his body toward her, he took her tightly in his arms. When next she opened her eyes the room was in darkness.

"You can never refuse a person money to buy light," said Amar. He struck a match and held it up.

"And you are rich," said Atallah, counting her thousand-franc notes one by one.

XXIX

"*Votre nom, madame.* Surely you remember your name."

She paid no attention; it was the only way of getting rid of them.

"*C'est inutile.* You won't get anything out of her."

"Are you certain there's no kind of identification among her clothing?"

"None, *mon capitaine.*"

"Go back to Atallah's and look some more. We know she had money and a valise."

A cracked little church bell pealed from time to time. The nun's garments made a rippling sound as she moved about the room.

"Katherine Moresby," said the sister, pronouncing the name slowly and all wrong. "*C'est bien vous, n'est-ce pas?*"

"They took everything but the passport, and we were lucky to find that."

"Open your eyes, madame."

"Drink it. It's cool. It's lemonade. It won't hurt you." A hand smoothed her forehead.

"No!" she cried. "No!"

"Try to lie still."

"The Consul at Dakar advises sending her back to Oran. I'm waiting for a reply from Algiers."

"It's morning."

"No, no, no!" she moaned, biting the pillowcase. She would never let any of it happen.

"It's taking this long to feed her only because she refuses to open her eyes."

She knew that the constant references to her closed eyes were being made only in order to trap her into protesting: "But my eyes are open." Then they would say: "Ah, your eyes are open, are they? Then—look!" and there she would be, defenseless before the awful image of herself, and the pain would begin. This way, sometimes for a brief moment she saw Amar's luminous black body near her in the light of the lamp by the door, and sometimes she saw only the soft darkness of the room, but it was an unmoving Amar and a static room; time could not arrive there from the outside to change his posture or split the enveloping silence into fragments.

"It's arranged. The Consul has agreed to pay the Transafricaine for her passage. Demouveau goes out tomorrow morning with Estienne and Fouchet."

"But she needs a guard."

There was a significant silence.

"She'll sit still, I assure you."

"Fortunately I understand French," she heard herself saying, in that language. "Thank you for being so explicit." The sound of such a sentence coming from her own lips struck her as unbelievably ridiculous, and she began to laugh. She saw no reason to stop laughing: it felt good. There was an irresistible twitching and tickling in the center of her that made her body double up, and the laughs rolled out. It took them a long time to quiet her, because the idea of their trying to stop her from doing something so natural and delightful seemed even funnier than what she had said.

When it was all over, and she was feeling comfortable and sleepy, the sister said: "Tomorrow you are going on a trip. I hope you will not make things more difficult for me by obliging me to dress you. I know you are capable of dressing yourself."

She did not reply because she did not believe in the trip. She intended to stay in the room lying next to Amar.

The sister made her sit up, and slipped a stiff dress over her head; it smelled of laundry soap. Every so often she would say: "Look at these shoes. Do you think they will fit you?" Or: "Do you like the color of your new dress?" Kit made no answer. A man had hold of her shoulder and was shaking her.

"Will you do me the favor of opening your eyes, madame?" he said sternly.

"*Vous lui faites mal,*" said the sister.

She was moving with others in a slow procession down an echoing corridor. The feeble church bell clanged and a cock crowed nearby. She felt the cool breeze on her cheek. Then she smelled gasoline. The men's voices sounded small in the immense morning air. Her heart began to race when she got into the car. Someone held her arm tightly, never letting go for an instant. The wind blew through the open windows, filling the car with the pungent odor of woodsmoke. As they jolted along, the men kept up a constant conversation, but she did not listen to it. When the car stopped there was a very brief silence in which she heard a dog barking. Then she was taken out, car doors were slammed, and she was led along stony ground. Her feet hurt: the shoes were too small. Occasionally she said in a low voice, as if to herself: "No." But the strong hand never let go of her arm. The smell of gasoline was very heavy here. "Sit down." She sat, and the hand continued to hold her.

Each minute she was coming nearer to the pain; there would be many minutes before she would actually have reached it, but that was no consolation. The approach could be long or short—the end would be the same. For an instant she struggled to break free.

"*Raoul! Ici!*" cried the man with her. Someone seized her other arm. Still she fought, sliding almost down to the ground between them. She scraped her spine on the tin molding of the packing case where they sat.

"*Elle est costaude, cette garce!*"

She gave up, and was lifted again to a sitting position, where she remained, her head thrown far backward. The sudden roar of the plane's motor behind her smashed the walls of the chamber where she lay. Before her eyes was the violent blue sky—nothing else. For an endless moment she looked into it. Like a great overpowering sound it destroyed everything in her mind, paralyzed her. Someone once had said to her that the sky hides the night behind it, shelters the person beneath from the horror that lies above. Unblinking, she fixed the solid emptiness, and the anguish began to move in her. At any moment the rip can occur, the edges fly back, and the giant maw will be revealed.

"*Allez! En marche!*"

She was in a standing position, she was turned about and led toward the quivering old Junker. When she was in the co-pilot's seat in the cockpit, tight bands were fastened across her chest and arms. It took a long time; she watched dispassionately.

The plane was slow. That evening they landed at Tessalit, spending the night in quarters at the aerodrome. She would not eat.

The following day they made Adrar by mid-afternoon; the wind was against them. They landed. She had become quite docile, and ate whatever was fed her, but the men took no chances. They kept her arms bound. The hotel proprietor's wife was annoyed at having to look after her. She had soiled her clothes.

The third day they left at dawn and made the Mediterranean before sunset.

XXX

Miss Ferry was not pleased with the errand on which she had been sent. The airport was a good way out of town and the taxi ride there was hot and bumpy. Mr. Clarke had said: "Got a little job for you tomorrow afternoon. That crackpot who was stuck down in the Soudan. Transafricaine's bringing her up. I'm trying to get her on the *American Trader* Monday. She's sick or had a collapse or something. Better take her to the Majestic." Mr. Evans at Algiers had finally reached the family in Baltimore that very morning; everything was all right. The sun was dropping behind the bastions of Santa Cruz on the mountain when the cab left town, but it would be another hour before it set.

"Damned old idiot!" she said to herself. This was not the first time she had been sent to be officially kind to a sick or stranded female compatriot. About once a year the task fell to her, and she disliked it intensely. "There's something repulsive about an American without money in his pocket," she had said to Mr. Clarke. She asked herself what possible attraction the parched interior of Africa could have for any civilized person. She herself had once passed a week-end at Bou Saâda, and had nearly fainted from the heat.

As she approached the airport the mountains were turning red in the sunset. She fumbled in her handbag for the slip of paper Mr. Clarke had given her, found it. *Mrs. Katherine Moresby.* She dropped it back into the bag. The plane had already come in; it lay alone out there in the field. She got out of the cab, told the driver to wait, and hurried through a door marked: *Salle d'Attente.* Immediately she caught sight of the woman, sitting dejectedly on a bench, with one of the Transafricaine mechanics holding her arm. She wore a formless blue and white checked dress, the sort of thing a partially Europeanized servant would wear; Aziza, her own cleaning woman, bought better looking ones in the Jewish quarter.

"She's really hit bottom," thought Miss Ferry. At the same time she noted that the woman was a great deal younger than she had expected.

Miss Ferry walked across the small room, conscious of her own clothes; she had bought them in Paris on her last vacation. She stood before the two, and smiled at the woman.

"Mrs. Moresby?" she said. The mechanic and the woman stood up together; he still held her arm. "I'm from the American Consulate here." She extended her hand. The woman smiled wanly and took it. "You must be absolutely exhausted. How many days was it? Three?"

"Yes." The woman looked at her unhappily.

"Perfectly awful," said Miss Ferry. She turned to the mechanic, offered him her hand, and thanked him in her almost unintelligible French. He let go of his charge's arm to acknowledge her greeting, seizing it again immediately afterward. Miss Ferry frowned impatiently: sometimes the French were incredibly gauche. Jauntily she took the other arm, and the three began to walk toward the door.

"*Merci,*" she said again to the man, pointedly, she hoped, and then to the woman: "What about your luggage? Are you all clear with the customs?"

"I have no luggage," said Mrs. Moresby, looking at her.

"You *haven't?*" She did not know what else to say.

"Everything's lost," said Mrs. Moresby in a low voice. They had reached the door. The mechanic opened it, let go of her arm, and stepped aside for them to go through.

"At last," thought Miss Ferry with satisfaction, and she began to hurry Mrs. Moresby toward the cab. "Oh, what a shame!" she said aloud. "It's really terrible. But you'll certainly get it back." The driver opened the door and they got in. From the curb the mechanic looked anxiously after them. "It's funny," went on Miss Ferry. "The desert's a big place, but nothing really ever gets lost there." The door slammed. "Things turn up sometimes months later. Not that that's of much help *now*, I'll admit." She looked at the black cotton stockings and the worn brown shoes that bulged. "*Au revoir et merci,*" she called to the mechanic, and the car started up.

When they were on the highway, the driver began to speed. Mrs. Moresby shook her head slowly back and forth and looked at her beseechingly. "*Pas si vite!*" shouted Miss Ferry to the driver. "You poor thing," she was about to say, but she felt this would not be right. "I certainly don't envy you what you've just been through," she said. "It's a perfectly awful trip."

"Yes." Her voice was hardly audible.

"Of course, some people don't seem to mind all this dirt and heat. By the time they go back home they're raving about the place. I've been trying to get sent to Copenhagen now for almost a year."

Miss Ferry stopped talking and looked out at a lumbering native bus as they overtook it. She suspected a faint, unpleasant odor about the woman beside her. "She's probably got every known disease," she said to herself. Observing her out of the corner of her eye for a moment, she finally said: "How long have you been down there?"

"A long time."

"Have you been under the weather for long?" The other looked at her. "They wired you were sick."

Neglecting to answer, Mrs. Moresby looked out at the darkening countryside. There were the many lights of the city ahead in the distance. That must be it, she thought. That was what had been the matter: she had been sick, probably for years. "But how can I be sitting here and not know it?" she thought.

When they were in the streets of the city, and the buildings and people and traffic moved past the windows, it all looked quite natural—she even had the feeling she knew the town. But something must still be quite wrong, or she would know definitely whether or not she had been here before.

"We're putting you in the Majestic. You'll be more comfortable there. It's none too good, of course, but it'll certainly be a lot more comfortable than anything down in *your* neck of the woods." Miss Ferry laughed at the force of her own understatement. "She's damned lucky to have all this fuss made about her," she was thinking to herself. "They don't all get put up at the Majestic."

As the cab drew up in front of the hotel, and a porter stepped out to open the door, Miss Ferry said: "Oh, by the way, a friend of yours, a Mr. Tunner, has been bombarding us with wires and letters for months. A perfect barrage from down in the desert. He's been very upset about you." She looked at the face beside her as the car door opened; at the moment it was so strange and white, so clearly a battlefield for desperate warring emotions, that she felt she must have said something wrong. "I hope you don't mind my presumption," she continued, a little less sure of herself, "but we promised this gentleman we'd notify him as soon as we contacted you, *if* we did. And I never had much doubt we would. The Sahara's a small place, really, when you come right down to it. People just don't disappear there. It's not like it is here in the city, in the Casbah. . . ." She felt increasingly uncomfortable. Mrs. Moresby seemed quite oblivious of the porter standing there, of everything. "Anyway," Miss Ferry continued impatiently, "when we knew for sure you were coming I wired this Mr. Tunner, so I shouldn't be surprised if he were right here in town by now, probably at this hotel. You might ask." She held out her hand. "I'm going to keep this cab to go home in, if you don't mind," she said. "Our office has been in touch with the hotel, so everything's all right. If you'll just come around to the Consulate in the morning—" Her hand was still out; nothing happened. Mrs. Moresby sat like a stone figure. Her face, now in the shadows cast by the passersby, now full in the light of the electric sign at the hotel entrance, had changed so utterly that Miss Ferry was appalled. She peered for a second into the wide eyes. "My God, the woman's nuts!" she said to herself. She opened the door, jumped down and ran into the hotel to the desk. It took a little while for her to make herself understood.

A few minutes later two men walked out to the waiting cab. They looked inside, glanced up and down the sidewalk; then they spoke questioningly to the driver, who shrugged his shoulders. At that moment a crowded streetcar was passing by, filled largely with native dock workers in blue overalls. Inside it the dim lights flickered, the standees swayed. Rounding the corner and clanging its bell, it started up the hill past the Café d'Eckmühl-Noiseux where the awnings flapped in the evening breeze, past the Bar Métropole with its radio that roared, past the Café de France, shining with mirrors and brass. Noisily it pushed along, cleaving a passage through the crowd that filled the street, it scraped around another corner, and began the slow ascent of the Avenue Galliéni. Below, the harbor lights came into view and were distorted in the gently moving water. Then the shabbier buildings loomed, the streets were dimmer. At the edge of the Arab quarter the car, still loaded with people, made a wide U-turn and stopped; it was the end of the line.

Bab el Hadid, Fez.

LET IT COME DOWN

Banquo: it will be rain tonight
First murderer: let it come down
(stabs Banquo)

Macbeth, Act iii   scene 3

I

International Zone

I

I T WAS NIGHT by the time the little ferry drew up alongside
the dock. As Dyar went down the gangplank a sudden
gust of wind threw warm raindrops in his face. The other passengers were few and poorly dressed; they carried their things
in cheap cardboard valises and paper bags. He watched them
standing resignedly in front of the customs house waiting for
the door to be opened. A half-dozen disreputable Arabs had
already caught sight of him from the other side of the fence
and were shouting at him. "Hotel Metropole, mister!" "Hey,
Johnny! Come on!" "You want hotel?" "Grand Hotel, hey!"
It was as if he had held up his American passport for them to
see. He paid no attention. The rain came down in earnest for
a minute or so. By the time the official had opened the door
he was uncomfortably wet.

The room inside was lighted by three oil lamps placed
along the counter, one to an inspector. They saved Dyar until
last, and all three of them went through his effects very carefully, without a gleam of friendliness or humor. When he
had repacked his grips so they would close, they marked them
with lavender chalk and reluctantly let him pass. He had to
wait in line at the window over which was printed *Policia*.
While he was standing there a tall man in a visored cap caught
his attention, calling: "Taxi!" The man was decently dressed,
and so he signaled yes with his head. Straightway the man in
the cap was embroiled in a struggle with the others as he
stepped to take the luggage. Dyar was the only prey that
evening. He turned his head away disgustedly as the shouting
figures followed the taxi-driver out the door. He felt a little
sick anyway.

And in the taxi, as the rain pelted the windshield and the
squeaking wipers rubbed painfully back and forth on the
glass, he went on feeling sick. He was really here now; there
was no turning back. Of course there never had been any

question of turning back. When he had written he would take the job and had bought his passage from New York, he had known his decision was irrevocable. A man does not change his mind about such things when he has less than five hundred dollars left. But now that he was here, straining to see the darkness beyond the wet panes, he felt for the first time the despair and loneliness he thought he had left behind. He lit a cigarette and passed the pack to the driver.

He decided to let the driver determine for him where he would stay. The man was an Arab and understood very little English, but he did know the words cheap and clean. They passed from the breakwater onto the mainland, stopped at a gate where two police inspectors stuck their heads in through the front windows, and then they drove slowly for a while along a street where there were a few dim lights. When they arrived at the hotel the driver did not offer to help him with his luggage, nor was there any porter in sight. Dyar looked again at the entrance: the façade was that of a large modern hotel, but within the main door he saw a single candle burning. He got down and began pulling out his bags. Then he glanced questioningly at the driver who was watching him empty the cab of the valises; the man was impatient to be off.

When he had set all his belongings on the sidewalk and paid the driver, he pushed the hotel door open and saw a young man with smooth black hair and a dapper moustache sitting at the small reception desk. The candle provided the only light. He asked if this were the Hotel de la Playa, and did not know whether he was glad or sorry to hear that it was. Getting his bags into the lobby by himself took a little while. Then, led by a small boy who carried a candle, he climbed the stairs to his room; the elevator was not working because there was no power.

They climbed three flights. The hotel was like an enormous concrete resonating chamber; the sound of each footstep, magnified, echoed in all directions. The building had the kind of intense and pure shabbiness attained only by cheap new constructions. Great cracks had already appeared in the walls, bits of the decorative plaster mouldings around the doorways had been chipped off, and here and there a floor tile was missing.

When they reached the room the boy went in first and touched a match to a new candle that had been stuck in the top of an empty Cointreau bottle. The shadows shot up along the walls. Dyar sniffed the close air with displeasure. The odor in the room suggested a mixture of wet plaster and unwashed feet.

"Phew! It stinks in here," he said. He looked suspiciously at the bed, turned the stained blue spread back to see the sheets.

Opposite the door there was one large window which the boy hastened to fling open. A blast of wind rushed in out of the darkness. There was the faint sound of surf. The boy said something in Spanish, and Dyar supposed he was telling him it was a good room because it gave on the beach. He did not much care which way the room faced: he had not come here on a vacation. What he wanted at the moment was a bath. The boy shut the window and hurried downstairs to get the luggage. In one corner, separated from the rest of the room by a grimy partition, was a shower with gray concrete walls and floor. He tried the tap marked *caliente* and was surprised to find the water fairly hot.

When the boy had brought the valises, piled them in the wrong places, received his tip, had difficulty in closing the door, and finally gone away leaving it ajar, Dyar moved from the window where he had been standing fingering the curtains, looking out into the blackness. He slammed the door shut, heard the key fall tinkling to the floor in the corridor. Then he threw himself on the bed and lay a while staring at the ceiling. He must call Wilcox immediately, let him know he had arrived. He turned his head and tried to see if there was a telephone on the low night table by the bed, but the table lay in the shadow of the bed's footboard, and it was too dark there to tell.

This was the danger point, he felt. At this moment it was almost as though he did not exist. He had renounced all security in favor of what everyone had assured him, and what he himself suspected, was a wild goose chase. The old thing was gone beyond recall, the new thing had not yet begun. To make it begin he had to telephone Wilcox, yet he lay still. His friends had told him he was crazy, his family had

remonstrated with him both indignantly and sadly, but for
some reason about which he himself knew very little, he had
shut his ears to them all. "I'm fed up!" he would cry, a little
hysterically. "I've stood at that damned window in the bank
for ten years now. Before the war, during the war, and after
the war. I can't take it any longer, that's all!" And when the
suggestion was made that a visit to a doctor might be
indicated, he laughed scornfully, replied: "There's nothing
wrong with me that a change won't cure. Nobody's meant
to be confined in a cage like that year after year. I'm just fed
up, that's all." "Fine, fine," said his father. "Only what do
you think you can do about it?" He had no answer to that.
During the depression, when he was twenty, he had been delighted to get a job in the Transit Department at the bank.
All his friends had considered him extremely fortunate; it was
only his father's friendship with one of the vice-presidents
which had made it possible for him to be taken on at such a
time. Just before the war he had been made a teller. In those
days when change was in the air nothing seemed permanent,
and although Dyar knew he had a heart murmur, he vaguely
imagined that in one way or another it would be got around
so that he would be given some useful wartime work. Anything would be a change and therefore welcome. But he had
been flatly rejected; he had gone on standing in his cage.
Then he had fallen prey to a demoralizing sensation of mo-
tionlessness. His own life was a dead weight, so heavy that
he would never be able to move it from where it lay. He had
grown accustomed to the feeling of intense hopelessness and
depression which had settled upon him, all the while resent-
ing it bitterly. It was not in his nature to be morose, and his
family noticed it. "Just do things as they come along," his
father would say. "Take it easy. You'll find there'll be plenty
to fill each day. Where does it get you to worry about the
future? Let it take care of itself." Continuing, he would issue
the familiar warning about heart trouble. Dyar would smile
wryly. He was quite willing to let each day take care of
itself—the future was furthest from his thoughts. The present stood in its way; it was the minutes that were inimical.
Each empty, overwhelming minute as it arrived pushed him
a little further back from life. "You don't get out enough,"

his father objected. "Give yourself a chance. Why, when I was your age I couldn't wait for the day to be finished so I could get out on the tennis court, or down to the old river fishing, or home to press my pants for a dance. You're unhealthy. Oh, I don't mean physically. That little heart business is nothing. If you live the way you should it ought never to give you any trouble. I mean your attitude. That's unhealthy. I think the whole generation's unhealthy. It's either one thing or the other. Overdrinking and passing out on the sidewalk, or else mooning around about life not being worth living. What the hell's the matter with all of you?" Dyar would smile and say times had changed. Times always change, his father would retort, but not human nature.

Dyar was not a reader; he did not even enjoy the movies. Entertainment somehow made the stationariness of existence more acute, not only when the amusement was over, but even during the course of it. After the war he made a certain effort to reconcile himself to his life. Occasionally he would go out with two or three of his friends, each one taking a girl. They would have cocktails at the apartment of one of the girls, go on to a Broadway movie, and eat afterward at some Chinese place in the neighborhood where there was dancing. Then there was the long process of taking the girls home one by one, after which they usually went into a bar and drank fairly heavily. Sometimes, not very often, they would pick up something cheap in the bar or in the street, take her to Bill Healy's room, and lay her in turn. It was an accepted pattern; there seemed to be no other to suggest in its place. Dyar kept thinking: "Any life would be better than this," but he could find no different possibility to consider. "Once you accept the fact that life isn't *fun*, you'll be much happier," his mother said to him. Although he lived with his parents, he never discussed with them the way he felt; it was they who, sensing his unhappiness, came to him and, in vaguely reproachful tones, tried to help him. He was polite with them but inwardly contemptuous. It was so clear that they could never understand the emptiness he felt, nor realize the degree to which he felt it. It was a progressive paralysis, it gained on him constantly, and it carried with it the fear that when it arrived at a certain point something terrible would happen.

He could hear the distant sound of waves breaking on the beach outside: the dull roll, a long silence, another roll. Someone came into the room over his, slammed the door, and began to move about busily from one side of the room to the other. It sounded like a woman, but a heavy one. The water was turned on and the wash basin in his room bubbled as if in sympathy. He lit a cigarette, from time to time flicking the ashes onto the floor beside the bed. After a few minutes the woman—he sure it was a woman—went out the door, slammed it, and he heard her walk down the hall into another room and close that door. A toilet flushed. Then the footsteps returned to the room above.

"I must call Wilcox," he thought. But he finished his cigarette slowly, making it last. He wondered why he felt so lazy about making the call. He had taken the great step, and he believed he had done right. All the way across on the ship to Gibraltar, he had told himself that it was the healthy thing to have done, that when he arrived he would be like another person, full of life, delivered from the sense of despair that had weighed on him for so long. And now he realized that he felt exactly the same. He tried to imagine how he would feel if, for instance, he had his whole life before him to spend as he pleased, without the necessity to earn his living. In that case he would not have to telephone Wilcox, would not be compelled to exchange one cage for another. Having made the first break, he would then make the second, and be completely free. He raised his head and looked slowly around the dim room. The rain was spattering the window. Soon he would have to go out. There was no restaurant in the hotel, and it was surely a long way to town. He felt the top of the night table; there was no telephone. Then he got up, took the candle, and made a search of the room. He stepped out into the corridor, picked his key off the floor, locked his door and went downstairs thinking: "I'd have him on the wire by now if there'd only been a phone by the bed."

The man was not at the desk. "I've got to make a call," he said to the boy who stood beside a potted palm smirking. "It's very important.—Telephone! Telephone!" he shouted, gesturing, as the other made no sign of understanding. The boy went to the desk, brought an old-fashioned telephone out from behind and set it on top. Dyar took the letter out of his pocket to look for the number of Wilcox's hotel. The boy tried to take the letter, but he copied the number on the back of the envelope and gave it to him. A fat man wearing a black raincoat came in and asked for his key. Then he stood glancing over a newspaper that lay spread out on the desk. As the boy made the call Dyar thought: "If he's gone out to dinner I'll have to go through this all over again." The boy said something into the mouthpiece and handed Dyar the receiver.

"Hello?"

"Hotel Atlantide."

"Mr. Wilcox, please." He pronounced the name very carefully. There was a silence. "Oh, God," he thought, annoyed with himself that he should care one way or the other whether Wilcox was in. There was a click.

"Yes?"

It was Wilcox. For a second he did not know what to say. "Hello?" he said.

"Hello. Yes?"

"Jack?"

"Yes. Who's this?"

"This is Nelson. Nelson Dyar."

"Dyar! Well, for God's sake! So you got here after all. Where are you? Come on over. You know how to get here? Better take a cab. You'll get lost. Where are you staying?"

Dyar told him.

"Jesus! That—" Dyar had the impression he had been about to say: that dump. But he said: "That's practically over the border. Well, come on up as soon as you can get here. You take soda or water?"

Dyar laughed. He had not known he would be so pleased to hear Wilcox's voice. "Soda," he said.

"Wait a second. Listen. I've got an idea. I'll call you back in five minutes. Don't go out. Wait for my call. Just stay put. I just want to call somebody for a second. It's great to have you here. Call you right back. O.K.?"

"Right."

He hung up and went to stand at the window. The rain that was beating against the glass had leaked through and was running down the wall. Someone had put a rag along the floor to absorb it, but now the cloth floated in a shallow pool. Two or three hundred feet up the road from the hotel there was a streetlight. Beneath it in the wind the glistening spears of a palm branch charged back and forth. He began to pace from one end of the little foyer to the other; the boy, standing by the desk with his hands behind him, watched him intently. He was a little annoyed at Wilcox for making him wait. Of course he thought he had been phoning from his room. He wondered if Wilcox were making good money with his travel agency. In his letters he had said he was, but Dyar remembered a good deal of bluff in his character. His enthusiasm need have meant nothing more than that he needed an assistant and preferred it to be someone he knew (the wages were low enough, and Dyar had paid his own passage from New York), or that he was pleased with a chance to show his importance and magnanimity; it would appeal to Wilcox to be able to make what he considered a generous gesture. Dyar thought it was more likely to be the latter case. Their friendship never had been an intimate one. Even though they had known each other since boyhood, since Wilcox's father had been the Dyars' family doctor, each had never shown more than a polite interest in the other's life. There was little in common between them—not even age, really, since Wilcox was nearly ten years older than he. During the war Wilcox had been sent to Algiers, and afterward it never had occurred to Dyar to wonder what had become of him. One day his father had come home saying: "Seems Jack Wilcox has stayed on over in North Africa. Gone into business for himself and seems to be making a go of it." Dyar had asked what kind of business it was, and had been only vaguely interested to hear that it was a tourist bureau.

He had been walking down Fifth Avenue one brilliant autumn twilight and had stopped in front of a large travel agency. The wind that moved down from Central Park had the crispness of an October evening, carrying with it the promise of winter, the season that paralyzes; to Dyar it gave a foretaste of increased unhappiness. In one side of the window was a large model ship, black and white, with shiny brass accessories. The other side represented a tropical beach in miniature, with a sea of turquoise gelatin and tiny palm trees bending up out of a beach of real sand. BOOK NOW FOR WINTER CRUISES, said the sign. The thought occurred to him that it would be a torturing business to work in such a place, to plan itineraries, make hotel reservations and book passages for all the places one would never see. He wondered how many of the men who stood inside there consulting their folders, schedules, lists and maps felt as trapped as he would have felt in their place; it would be even worse than the bank. Then he thought of Wilcox. At that moment he began to walk again, very fast. When he got home he wrote the letter and took it out to post immediately. It was a crazy idea. Nothing could come of it, except perhaps that Wilcox would think him a god-damned fool, a prospect which did not alarm him.

The reply had given him the shock of his life. Wilcox had spoken of coincidence. "There must be something in telepathy," he had written. Only then did Dyar mention the plan to his family, and the reproaches had begun.

Moving regretfully away from the desk, the fat man walked back to the lift. As he shut the door the telephone rang. The boy started for it, but Dyar got there ahead of him. The boy glared at him angrily. It was Wilcox, who said he would be at the Hotel de la Playa in twenty minutes. "I want you to meet a friend of mine," he said. "The Marquesa de Valverde. She's great. She wants you to come to dinner too." And as Dyar protested, he interrupted. "We're not dressing. God, no! None of that here. I'll pick you up."

"But Jack, listen—"

"So long."

Dyar went up to his room, nettled at not having been given the opportunity of deciding to accept or refuse the invitation. He asked himself if it would raise him in Wilcox's estimation if he showed independence and begged off. But obviously he had no intention of doing such a thing, since when he got to his room he tore off his clothes, took a quick shower, whistling all the while, opened his bags, shaved as well as he could by the light of the lone candle, and put on his best suit. When he had finished he blew out the candle and hurried downstairs to wait at the front entrance.

II

Daisy de Valverde sat at her dressing table, her face brilliant as six little spotlights threw their rays upon it from six different angles. If she made up to her satisfaction in the pitiless light of these sharp lamps, she could be at ease in any light later. But it took time and technique. The Villa Hesperides was never without electricity, even now when the town had it for only two hours every other evening. Luis had seen to that when they built the house; he had foreseen the shortage of power. It was one of the charms of the International Zone that you could get anything you wanted if you paid for it. Do anything, too, for that matter;—there were no incorruptibles. It was only a question of price.

Outside, the wind was roaring, and in the cypresses it sounded like a cataract. The boom of waves against the cliffs came up from far below. Mingled with the reflections of the lights in the room, other lights, small, distant points, showed in the black sheets of glass at the windows: Spain across the strait, Tarifa and Cape Camariñal.

She was always pleased to have Americans come to the house because she felt under no constraint with them. She could drink all she pleased and they drank along with her, whereas her English guests made a whiskey last an hour—not to mention the French, who asked for a Martini of vermouth with a dash of gin, or the Spanish with their glass of sherry. "The Americans are the nation of the future," she would announce in her hearty voice. "Here's to 'em. God bless their gadgets, great and small. God bless Frigidaire, Tampax and Coca-Cola. Yes, even Coca-Cola, darling." (It was generally conceded that Coca-Cola's advertising was ruining the picturesqueness of Morocco.) The Marqués did not share her enthusiasm for Americans, but that did not prevent her from asking them whenever she pleased; she ran the house to suit herself.

She had a Swiss butler and an Italian footman, but when Americans were invited to dinner she let old Ali serve at table because he owned a magnificent Moorish costume; although he was not very competent she thought his appearance impressed them more than the superior service the two Europeans could provide.

The difficulty was that both the butler and footman disapproved so heartily of this arrangement that unless she went into the kitchen at the last moment and repeated her orders, they always found some pretext for not allowing poor old Ali to serve, so that when she looked up from her plate expecting to see the brilliant brocades and gold sash from the palace of Sultan Moulay Hafid, she would find herself staring instead at the drab black uniform of Hugo or Mario. Their faces would be impassive; she never knew what had been going on. There was a chance that this would happen tonight, unless she went down now and made it clear that Ali must serve. She rose, slipped a heavy bracelet over her left hand, and went out through the tiny corridor which connected her room with the rest of the house. Someone had left a window open at the end of the upper hall, and several of the candles in front of the large tapestry had been blown out. She could not bear the anachronism of having electricity in the rooms where tapestries were hung. Ringing a bell, she waited until a breathless chambermaid had appeared, then she indicated the window and the candles with a stiff finger. "*Mire*," she said disapprovingly, and moved down the stairway. At that moment there was the sound of a motor outside. She hurried down the rest of the way, practically running the length of the hall to disappear into the kitchen, and when she came back out Hugo was taking her guests' raincoats. She walked toward the two men regally.

"Darling Jack. How sweet of you to come. And in this foul weather."

"How kind of you to have us. Daisy, this is Mr. Dyar. The Marquesa de Valverde."

Dyar looked at her and saw a well-preserved woman of forty with a mop of black curls, china blue eyes, and a low-cut black satin dress, to squeeze herself into which must have been somewhat painful.

"*How* nice to see you, Mr. Dyar. I think we've got a fire in the drawing room. God knows. Let's go in and see. Are you wet?" She felt of Dyar's sleeve. "No? Good. Come along. Jack, you're barman. I want the stiffest drink you can concoct."

They sat before a scorching log fire. Daisy wanted Wilcox to mix sidecars. At the first sip Dyar realized how really hungry he was; he glanced clandestinely at his watch. It was nine-forty. Observing Daisy, he thought she was the most fatuous woman he had ever met. But he was impressed by the house. Hugo entered. "Now for dinner," thought Dyar. It was a telephone call for Madame la Marquise. "Pour me another, sweet, and let me take it with me as consolation," she said to Wilcox.

When she had gone Wilcox turned to Dyar.

"She's one grand girl," he said, shaking his head.

"Yes," Dyar replied, without conviction, adding: "Isn't she a little on the beat-up side for you?"

Wilcox looked indignant, lowered his voice. "What are you talking about, boy? She's got a husband in the house. I said she's grand fun to be with. What the hell did you think I meant, anyway?" Mario's arrival to add a log to the fire stopped whatever might have followed. "Listen to that wind," said Wilcox, sitting back with his drink.

Dyar knew he was annoyed with him; he wondered why. "He's getting mighty touchy in his old age," he said to himself, looking around the vast room. Mario went out. Wilcox leaned forward again, and still in a low voice, said: "Daisy and Luis are practically my best friends here." There were voices in the hall. Daisy entered with a neat dark man who looked as though he had stomach ulcers. "Luis!" cried Wilcox, jumping up. Dyar was presented, and the four sat down, Daisy next to Dyar. "This can't last long," he thought. "It's nearly ten." His stomach felt completely concave.

They had another round of drinks. Wilcox and the Marqués began to discuss the transactions of a local banker who had got himself into difficulties and had left suddenly for Lisbon, not to return. Dyar listened for a moment.

"I'm sorry, I didn't hear," he said to Daisy; she was speaking to him.

"I said: how do you like our little International Zone?"

"Well, I haven't seen anything of it yet. However—" he looked around the room with appreciation—"from here it looks fine." He smiled self-consciously.

Her voice assumed a faintly maternal note. "Of course. You just came today, didn't you? My dear, you've got so much ahead of you! So much ahead of you! You can't know. But you'll love it, that I promise you. It's a madhouse, of course. A complete, utter madhouse. I only hope to God it remains one."

"You like it a lot?" He was beginning to feel the drinks.

"Adore it," she said, leaning toward him. "Absolutely worship the place."

He set his empty glass carefully on the table beside the shaker.

From the doorway Hugo announced dinner.

"Jack, one more drop all around." She held forth her glass and received what was left. "You've given it all to me, you monster. I didn't want it all." She stood up, and carrying her glass with her, led the men into the dining room, where Mario stood uncorking a bottle of champagne.

"I'm going to be drunk," thought Dyar, suddenly terrified that through some lapse in his table etiquette he would draw attention to himself.

Slowly they advanced into a meal which promised to be endless.

Built into the wall opposite him, a green rectangle in the dark paneling, was an aquarium; its hidden lights illumined rocks, shells and complex marine plants. Dyar found himself watching it as he ate. Daisy talked without cease. At one point, when she had stopped, he said: "I don't see any fish in there."

"Cuttle-fish," explained the Marqués. "We keep only cuttle-fish." And as Dyar seemed not to understand, "You know—small octopi. You see? There is one there on the left, hanging to the rock." He pointed; now Dyar saw the pale fleshy streamers which were its tentacles.

"They're rather sweeter than goldfish," said Daisy, but in such a way that Dyar suspected she loathed them. He had never met anyone like her; she gave the impression of remaining uninvolved in whatever she said or did. It was as if she were playing an intricate game whose rules she had devised herself.

During salad there was a commotion somewhere back in the house: muffled female voices and hurrying footsteps. Daisy set down her fork and looked around the table at the three men.

"God! I know what that is. I'm sure of it. This storm has brought in the ants." She turned to Dyar. "Every year they come in by the millions, the tiniest ones. When you first see them on the wall you'd swear it was an enormous crack. When you go nearer it looks more like a rope. Positively seething. They all stick together. Millions. It's terrifying." She rose. "Do forgive me; I must go and see what's happening."

Dyar said: "Is there anything I can do?" and got a fleeting glance of disapproval from Wilcox.

She smiled. "No, darling. Eat your salad."

Daisy was gone nearly ten minutes. When she returned she was laughing. "Ah, the joys of living in Morocco!" she said blithely. "The ants again?" asked the Marqués. "Oh, yes! This time it's the maids' sewing room. Last year it was the pantry. That was *much* worse. And they had to shovel the corpses out." She resumed eating her salad and her face grew serious. "Luis, I'm afraid poor old Tambang isn't long for this world. I looked in on him. It seemed to me he was worse."

The Marqués nodded his head. "Give him more penicillin."

Daisy turned to Dyar. "It's an old Siamese I'm trying to save. He's awfully ill. We'll go and see him after dinner. Luis refuses to go near him. He hates cats. I'm sure you don't hate cats, do you, Mr. Dyar?"

"Oh, I like all kinds of animals." He turned his head and saw the octopus. It had not moved, but a second one had appeared and was swaying loosely along the floor of the tank. It looked like something floating in a jar of formaldehyde—a stomach, perhaps, or a pancreas. The sight of it made him feel vaguely ill, or else it was the mixture of sidecars and champagne.

"Then you won't mind helping me with him, will you?" pursued Daisy.

"Be delighted."

"You don't know what you're letting yourself in for," said Wilcox, laughing unpleasantly.

"Nonsense!" Daisy exclaimed. "He'll wear enormous thick gloves. Even Tambang can't claw through those."

"The hell he *can't!* And he's got teeth too, hasn't he?"

"Just for this," said the Marqués, "we must make *Jack* go and be the attendant."

"No," Daisy said firmly. "Mr. Dyar is coming with me. Does anyone want fruit? I suggest we go in and have coffee immediately. We'll have our brandy afterward when we come down." She rose from the table.

"You'll need it," said Wilcox.

From the drawing room now they could hear the storm blowing louder than before. Daisy gulped her coffee standing up, lit a cigarette, and went toward the door.

"Tell Mario to keep the fire blazing, Luis, or it'll begin to smoke. It's already begun, in fact. Shall we go up, Mr. Dyar?"

She went ahead of him up the stairs. As she passed each candelabrum the highlights of her satin flashed.

From a small cloakroom at the head of the stairs she took two pairs of thick gardening gloves and gave one to Dyar.

"We don't really need these," she said, "but it's better to be protected."

The walls of the little room were lined with old French prints of tropical birds. On an antique bed with a torn canopy over it lay a large Siamese cat. An enamel pan containing lumps of raw liver had been pushed against its head, but it looked wearily in the other direction. The room smelled like a zoo. "God, what a fug!" Daisy exclaimed. "But we can't open the window." The storm raged outside. From time to time the house trembled. A branch beat repeatedly against the window like a person asking to be let in. The cat paid no attention while Daisy filed off the ends of ampoules, filled the syringe, and felt along its haunches for the right spot.

"He's got to have four different injections," she said, "but I can give the first two together. Now, stand above, and be ready to push down on his neck, but don't push unless you have to. Scratch him under the chin."

The old cat's fur was matted, its eyes were huge and empty. Once as the needle flashed above his head Dyar thought he saw an expression of alertness, even of fear, cross its face, but he scratched harder, with both hands, under the ears and along the jowls. Even when the needle went in tentatively, and then further in, it did not move.

"Now we have only two more," said Daisy. Dyar watched the sureness of her gestures. No veterinarian could have been more deft. He said as much. She snorted. "The only good vets are amateurs. I wouldn't let a professional touch an animal of mine." The odor of ether was very strong. "Is that ether?" Dyar asked; he was feeling alarmingly ill. "Yes, for sterilizing." She had filled the syringe again. "Now, hold him." The wind roared; it seemed as though the branch would crack the windowpane. "This may burn. He may feel it." Dyar looked up at the window; he could see his own head reflected vaguely against the night beyond. He thought he might throw up if he had to watch the needle go into the fur again. Only when Daisy stepped away from the bed did he dare lower his gaze. The cat's eyes were half shut. He bent down: it was purring.

"Poor old beast," said Daisy. "Now for the last. This will be easy. Tambang, sweet boy, what is it?"

"He's purring," said Dyar, hoping she would not look at his face. His lips felt icy, and he knew he must be very pale.

"You see how right I was to bring you? He likes you. Jack would have antagonized him in some way."

She did look at him, and he thought her eyes stayed an instant too long. But she said nothing.

"Don't tell me he's going to faint," she thought. "The wretched man is completely out of contact with life." But he was making a great effort.

"The cat doesn't seem to feel anything," he said.

"No, I'm afraid he won't live."

"But he's purring."

"Will you hold him, please? This is the last."

He wanted to talk, to take his mind off his dizziness, away from what was going on just below his face on the bed. He could think of nothing to say, so he kept silent. The cat stirred slightly. Daisy straightened up, and at the same moment there was a splitting sound and a heavy crash somewhere outside in the darkness. They looked at each other. Daisy set the syringe on the table.

"I know what that was. One of our eucalyptus. God, what a night!" she said admiringly.

They shut the door and went downstairs. In the drawing room there was no one. "I daresay they've gone out to look. Let's go into the library. The fireplace draws better in there. This one's smoking."

The library was small and pleasant; the fire crackled. She pushed a wall button and they sat down on the divan. She looked at him, musing.

"Jack told me you were coming, but somehow I never thought you'd actually arrive."

"Why not?" He felt a little better now.

"Oh, you know. Such things have a way of not coming off. Frightfully good idea that misses fire. And then, of course, I can't see really why Jack needs anyone there in that little office."

"You mean it's not doing well?" He tried to keep his voice even.

She laid a hand on his arm and laughed. As though she were imparting a rather shameful secret, she said in a low voice: "My dear, if you think he makes even his luncheon money there, you're gravely mistaken."

She was studying him too carefully, trying to see the effect of her words. He would refuse to react. He felt hot all over, but did not speak. Hugo entered carrying a tray of bottles and glasses. They both took brandy, and he set the tray down on a table at Dyar's elbow and went out.

She was still looking at him.

"Oh, it's not going well," he said. He would not say what he was sure she was waiting for him to say: How does he keep going?

"Not at all. It never has."

"I'm sorry to hear that," said Dyar.

"There's no need to be. If it had gone well I daresay he wouldn't have sent for you. He'd have had just about all he could manage by himself. As it is, I expect he needs you far more."

Dyar made a puzzled face. "I don't follow *that*."

Daisy looked pleased. "Tangier. Tangier," she said. "You'll follow soon enough, my pet."

They heard voices in the hall.

"You'll be wanting a good many books to read, I should think," she said. "Do feel free to borrow anything here that interests you. Of course there's a circulating library run by the American Legation that's far better than the English library. But they take ages to get the new books."

"I don't read much," said Dyar.

"But my dear lamb, whatever are you going to *do* all day? You'll be bored to distraction."

"Oh, well. Jack—"

"I doubt it," she said. "I think you'll be alone from morning to night, every day."

The voices were no longer audible. "They've gone into the kitchen," she said. He pulled out a pack of cigarettes, held it up to her.

"No, thank you. I have some. But seriously, I can't think what you'll do all day, you know." She felt in her bag and withdrew a small gold case.

"I'll probably have work to do," he replied, getting a match to the end of her cigarette before she could lift her lighter.

She laughed shortly, blew out the flame, and seized his hand, the match still between his fingers. "Let me see that hand," she said, puffing on her cigarette. Dyar smiled and held his palm out stiffly for her to examine. "Relax it," she said, drawing the hand nearer to her face.

"Work!" she scoffed. "I see no sign of it here, my dear Mr. Dyar."

He was incensed. "Well, it's a liar, then. Work is all I've ever done."

"Oh, standing in a bank, perhaps, but that's so light it wouldn't show." She looked carefully, pushing the flesh of the hand with her fingers. "No. I see no sign of work. No sign of anything, to be quite honest. I've never seen such an empty hand. It's terrifying." She looked up at him.

Again he laughed. "You're stumped, are you?"

"Not at all. I've lived in America long enough to have seen a good many American hands. All I can say is that this is the worst."

He pretended great indignation, withdrawing his hand forcibly. "What do you mean, worst?" he cried.

She looked at him with infinite concern in her eyes. "I mean," she said, "that you have an empty life. No pattern. And nothing in you to give you any purpose. Most people can't help following some kind of design. They do it automatically because it's in their nature. It's that that saves them, pulls them up short. They can't help themselves. But you're safe from being saved."

"A unique specimen. Is that it?"

"In a way." She searched his face questioningly for a moment. "How odd," she murmured presently. This empty quality in him pleased her. It was rather as if he were naked,— not defenseless, exactly—merely unclothed, ready to react, and she found it attractive; men should be like that. But it struck her as strange that she should think so.

"How odd what?" he inquired. "That I should be unique?" He could see that she believed all she was saying, and since it was flattering to have the attention being paid him, he was ready to argue with her, if necessary, just to prolong it.

"Yes."

"I've never been able to believe all this astrology and palmistry business," he said. "It doesn't hold water."

She did not answer, and so he continued. "Let's leave hands for a minute and get down to personalities." The brandy was warming him; he felt far from ill now. "You mean you think each individual man's life is different and has its own pattern, as you call it?"

"Yes, of course."

"But that's impossible!" he cried. "It stands to reason. Just look around you. There never was any mass production to compare with the one that turns out human beings—all the same model, year after year, century after century, all alike, always the same person." He felt a little exalted at the sound of his own voice. "You might say there's only one person in the world, and we're all it."

She was silent for a moment; then she said: "Rubbish." What he was saying made her vaguely angry. She wondered if it were because she resented his daring to express his ideas at all, but she did not think it was that.

"Look, my pet," she said in a conciliatory tone, "just what do you want in life?"

"That's a hard question," he said slowly. She had taken the wind out of his sails. "I suppose I want to feel I'm getting something out of it."

She was impatient. "That doesn't mean anything."

"I want to feel I'm alive, I guess. That's about all."

"Great God in heaven. Give me some more brandy."

They let the subject drop, turning to the storm and the climate in general. He was thinking that he should have answered anything that came to mind: money, happiness, health, rather than trying to say what he really meant. As an accompaniment to these thoughts there recurred the image of his room back at the Hotel de la Playa, with its spotted bedspread, its washstand that gurgled.

"He has nothing, he wants nothing, he is nothing," thought Daisy. She felt she ought to be sorry for him, but somehow he did not evoke pity in her—rather, a slight rancor which neutralized her other emotions. Finally she stood up. "We must see what has happened to Luis and Jack."

They found them in the drawing room talking.

"Which eucalyptus was it?" said Daisy. "I know it was one of them."

The Marqués frowned. "The great one by the gate. It's not the whole tree. Only one branch, but a big one, the one over-hanging the road. The road is blocked."

"Why do they always manage to fall into the road?" demanded Daisy.

"I don't know," said Wilcox. "But it screws me up fine. How am I going to get out of here?"

She laughed merrily. "You and Mr. Dyar," she said, with very clear enunciation, "will spend the night, and in the morning you'll call for a taxi. It's that simple."

"Out of the question," said Wilcox irritably.

"I assure you no taxi will come now, in this weather. That goes without saying. And it's eight kilometers to walk."

He had no answer to this.

"There are plenty of rooms for just such emergencies. Now, stop fretting and make me a whiskey and soda." She turned to Dyar and beamed.

When she had been served, Wilcox said shortly: "What about it, Dyar? Same for you?" Dyar looked quickly at him, saw that he seemed annoyed. "Please." Wilcox handed him his drink without turning to face him. "That's easy," Dyar thought. "He's afraid I'm getting on too well with her."

They talked about the house. "You must come back some-time during the daylight and see the rose garden," said Daisy. "We have the most divine rose garden."

"But what you've really got to see is that glass bedroom," said Wilcox, leaning back in his chair and yawning toward the ceiling. "Have you seen that?"

The Marqués laughed uncomfortably.

"No, he hasn't," Daisy said. She rose, took Dyar's arm. "Come along and see it. It's a perfect opportunity. Jack and Luis will discuss the week's bankruptcies."

The bedroom reminded Dyar of a vast round greenhouse. He scuffed at the zebra skins scattered about on the shining black marble floor. The bed was very wide and low, its heavy white satin spread had been partially pulled back and the sheets were turned down. The place was a gesture of defiance against the elements that clamored outside the glass walls; he felt distinctly uncomfortable. "Anybody could see in, I should think," he ventured.

"If they can see all the way from Spain." She stood staring down toward the invisible waves that broke on the rocks be-low. "This is my favorite room in the world," she declared. "I've never been able to abide being away from the sea. I'm like a sailor, really. I take it for granted that salt water is the earth's natural covering. I must be able to see it. Always." She breathed deeply.

"What's *this* act all about?" he thought.

"It's a wonderful room," he said.

"There are orange trees down in the garden. I call the place Hesperides because it's here to this mountain that Hercules is supposed to have come to steal the golden apples."

"Is that right?" He tried to sound interested and impressed. Since he had started on the whiskey he had been sleepy. He had the impression that Wilcox and the Marqués would be coming upstairs any minute; when they came he felt that Daisy and he ought not to be found standing here in her bed-room in this tentative, absurd attitude. He saw her stifle a yawn; she had no desire to be showing him the room anyway. It was merely to irk Wilcox, a game they were in together. It occurred to him then that it might be fun to play around a little with her, to see which way the wind was blowing. But he was not sure how to begin; she was a little overwhelming. Something like: That's a big bed for one small person. She would probably reply: But Luis and I sleep here, my dear. Whatever he said or did she would probably laugh.

"I know what you're thinking," she said. He started a bit. "You're sleepy, poor man. You'd like to go to bed."

"Oh," he said. "Well—"

A youngish woman hurried into the room, calling: "*On peut entrer?*" Her clothes were very wet, her face glistened with rain. She and Daisy began a lively conversation in French, scraps of which were thrown to Dyar now and then. She was Daisy's secretary, she was just returning from a dance, the taxi had been obliged to stop below the fallen tree, but the driver had been kind enough to walk with her to the house and was downstairs now having a cognac, she was soaked through, and did anyone want the cab?

"Do we!" cried Dyar, with rather more animation than was altogether civil. Immediately he felt apologetic and began to stammer his thanks and excuses.

"Rush downstairs, darling. Don't stop to say good night. Hurry! I'll call you tomorrow at the office. I have something to talk to you about."

He said good night, ran down the stairs, meeting the Marqués on the way.

"Jack is waiting for you outside. Good night, old boy," said the Marqués, continuing to climb. When he reached the top of the stairs, Daisy was blowing out the candles along the wall. "*Estamos salvados,*" she said, without looking up. "*Qué gentuza más aburrida,*" sighed the Marqués.

She continued methodically, holding her hand carefully behind each flame as she blew on it. She had the feeling her evening had somehow gone all wrong, but at what point it had begun to do that she could not tell.

The malevolent wind struck out at them as they fought their way to the taxi. They crawled under one end of the great branch that lay diagonally across the road. The driver had some difficulty turning the car; at one point he backed into a wall and cursed. When they were on their way, going slowly down the dark mountain road, Wilcox said: "Well, did you see the bedroom?"

"Yes."

"You've seen everything. You can go back to New York. Tangier holds no secrets for you now."

Dyar laughed uneasily. After a pause he said: "What's up tomorrow? Do I come around to the agency?"

Wilcox was lighting a cigarette. "You might drop in sometime during the late afternoon, yes."

His heart sank. Then he was angry. "He knows damned well I want to start work. Playing cat and mouse." He said nothing.

When they arrived in the town, Wilcox called: "Atlantide." The cab turned right, climbed a crooked street, and stopped before a large doorway. "Here's fifty pesetas," said Wilcox, pressing some notes into his hand. "My share."

"Fine," said Dyar. "Thanks."

"Good night."

"Good night."

The driver looked expectantly back. "Just wait a minute," said Dyar, gesturing. He could still see Wilcox in the lobby. When he had gone out of sight, Dyar paid the man, got out, and started to walk downhill, the rain at his back. The street was deserted. He felt pleasantly drunk, and not at all sleepy. As he walked along he muttered: "Late afternoon. Drop in, do. Charmed, I'm sure. Lovely weather." He came to a square where a line of cabs waited. Even in the storm, at this hour, the men spied him. "Hey, come! Taxi, Johnny?" He disregarded them and cut into a narrow passageway. It was like walking down the bed of a swiftly running brook; the water came almost to the tops of his shoes, sometimes above. He bent down and rolled up his trousers, continued to walk. His thoughts took another course. Soon he was chuckling to himself, and once he said aloud: "Golden apples, my ass!"

III

Thami was furious with his wife: She had a nose bleed and was letting it drip all over the patio. He had told her to get a wet rag and try to stanch it with that, but she was frightened and seemed not to hear him; she merely kept walking back and forth in the patio with her head bent over. There was an oil lamp flickering just inside the door, and from where he lay on his mattress he could see her hennaed feet with their heavy anklets shuffle by every so often in front of him. Rain fell intermittently, but she did not seem to notice it.

That was the worst part of being married, unless one had money—a man could never be alone in his own house; there was always female flesh in front of him, and when he had had enough of it he did not want to be continually reminded of it. "*Yah latif!*" he yelled. "At least shut the door!" In the next room the baby started to cry. Thami waited a moment to see what Kinza was going to do. She neither closed the door nor went to comfort her son. "Go and see what he wants!" he roared. Then he groaned: "*Al-lah!*" and put a cushion over his abdomen, locking his hands on top of it, in the hope of having an after-dinner nap. If it were not for his son, he reflected, he would send her back where she belonged to her family in the Rif. That might pave the way, at least, to his being taken back by his brothers and permitted to live with them again.

He had never considered it just of Abdelmalek and Hassan to have taken it upon themselves to put him out of the house. Being younger than they, he had of course to accept their dictum. But certainly he had not accepted it with good grace. It was typical of him to consider that they had acted out of sheer spite, and he behaved accordingly. He committed the unpardonable offense of speaking against them to others, dwelling upon their miserliness and their lecherousness; this trait had gradually estranged him from practically all his childhood friends. Everyone knew he drank and had done so since the age of fifteen, and although that was generally considered in the upper-class Moslem world of Tangier sufficient grounds for his having been asked to leave the Beidaoui residence, still, in itself it would not have turned his friends against him. The trouble was that Thami had a genius for doing the wrong thing; it was as if he took a perverse and bitter delight in cutting himself off from all he had ever known, in making himself utterly miserable. His senseless marriage with an illiterate mountain girl—surely he had done that only in a spirit of revenge against his brothers. He must certainly have been mocking them when he rented the squalid little house in

Emsallah, where only laborers and servants lived. Not only did he take alcohol, but he had recently begun to do it publicly, on the terraces of the cafés in the Zoco Chico. His brothers had even heard, although how much truth lay in the report they did not know, that he had been seen going on numerous trips by train to Casablanca, an activity which usually meant only one thing: smuggling of one sort or another.

Thami's friends now were of recent cultivation, and the relationships between him and them not particularly profound ones. Two were professors at the Lycée Français, ardent nationalists who never missed an opportunity during a conversation to excoriate the French, and threw about terms like "imperialist domination," "Pan-Islamic culture" and "autonomy." Their violence and resentment against the abuses of an unjust authority struck a sympathetic chord in him; he felt like one of them without really understanding what they were talking about. It was they who had given him the idea of making the frequent trips to the French Zone and (—for it was perfectly true: he had been engaging in petty smuggling—) carrying through with him fountain pens and wrist watches to sell there at a good profit. Every franc out of which the French customs could be cheated, they argued, was another nail in the French economic coffin; in the end the followers of Lyautey would be forced to abandon Morocco. There were also the extra thousands of francs which it was agreeable to have in his wallet at the end of such a journey.

Another friend was a functionary in the Municipalité. He too approved of smuggling, but on moral grounds, because it was important to insist on the oneness of Morocco, to refuse to accept the three zones into which the Europeans had arbitrarily divided it. The important point with regard to Europeans, he claimed, was to sow chaos within their institutions and confuse them with seemingly irrational behavior. As to the Moslems, they must be made conscious of their shame and suffering. He frequently visited his family in Rabat, always carrying with him a large bunch of bananas, which were a good deal cheaper in Tangier. When the train arrived at Souk el Arba the customs officers would pounce on the fruit, whereupon he would begin to shout in as loud a voice as possible that he was taking the bananas to his sick child. The officers, taking note of the growing interest in the scene on the part of the other native passengers, would lower their voices and try to keep the altercation as private and friendly as they could. He, speaking excellent French, would be polite in his language but noisy in his protest, and if it looked at any point as though the inspectors might be going to placate him and let the bananas by, he would slip into his speech some tiny expression of defiant insult, imperceptible to the other passengers but certain to throw the Frenchmen into a fury. They would demand that he give up the bananas then and there. At this point he would appear to be making a sudden decision; he would pick up the bunch by the stem and break the fruit off one by one, calling to the fourth-class passengers, mostly simple Berbers, to come and eat, saying sadly that since his sick son was not to have the bananas he wanted to give them to his countrymen. Thus forty or fifty white-robed men would be crouching along the platform munching on bananas, shaking their heads with pity for the father of the sick boy, and turning their wide accusing eyes toward the Frenchmen. The only trouble was that the number of customs inspectors was rather limited. They all had fallen into the trap again and again, but now they remembered the functionary only too well, and the last time he had gone through they had steadfastly refused to notice the bananas at all. When Thami heard this he said: "So you went through to Rabat with them?" "Yes," said the other a little dejectedly. "That's wonderful," said Thami with enthusiasm. The functionary looked at him. "Of course!" Thami cried. "You broke the law. They knew it. They didn't dare do anything. You've won." "I suppose that's true," said the other after a moment, but he was not sure Thami understood what it was all about.

Thami opened his eyes. It was five minutes later, although he thought it was an hour or more. She had taken the lamp; the room was in darkness. The patio door was open, and through it he could hear the splatter of rain on the tiles. Then he realized that the baby was still crying, wearily, pitifully. "*Inaal din*—" he said savagely under his breath. He jumped up in the dark, slid his feet into his slippers, and stumbled out into the wet.

The lamp was in the next room. Kinza had picked the baby up and was holding him clumsily while she prepared to nurse him. The blood still ran down her face and was dripping slowly, regularly, from the end of her chin. It had fallen in several places on the baby's clothing. Thami stepped nearer. As he did so, he saw a drop of blood fall square in the infant's face, just above his lips. A cautious tongue crept out and licked it in. Thami was beside himself. "*Hachouma!*" he cried, seizing the baby and holding it out of her reach so that it began to scream in earnest. He laid it carefully on the floor, got an old handkerchief, stood in the doorway for a moment with his hand out in the rain, and when the cloth was soaked, he threw it to her. She had let blood drip over everything: the matting, the cushions, the floor, the brass tray on the tea table, and even, he noted with a shiver of disgust, into one of the tea glasses. He picked up the tiny glass and threw it outside, heard it smash and tinkle. Now he wanted to get out of the house. At each moment it seemed to be raining harder. So much the worse, he thought. He would go anyway. He pulled his raincoat down from the nail where it hung, put on his shoes, and without saying a word, went out the door into the street. Only when he had shut it behind him did he notice that there was a violent wind to accompany the downpour.

It was late. From time to time he met a man hurrying along, face hidden under the hood of his djellaba, head bent over, eyes on the ground. The streets of Emsallah were unpaved; the muddy water ran against him all the way to the boulevard. Here a solitary cautious car moved by under the rain's onslaught, sounding its horn repeatedly.

He passed along the Place de France under the low overhanging branches of the liveoaks in front of the French Consulate. Neither the Café de Paris nor the Brasserie de France was open. The city was deserted, the Boulevard Pasteur reduced to two converging rows of dim lights leading off into the night. It was typical of Europeans, he thought, to lose courage and give up all their plans the minute there was a chance of getting themselves wet. They were more prudent than passionate; their fears were stronger than their desires. Most of them *had* no real desire, apart from that to make money, which after all is merely a habit. But once they had the money they seemed never to use it for a specific object or purpose. That was what he found difficult to understand. He knew exactly what he wanted, always, and so did his country-men. Most of them only wanted three rams to slaughter at Aïd el Kebir and new clothing for the family at Mouloud and Aïd es Seghir. It was not much, but it was definite, and they bent all their efforts to getting it. Still, he could not think of the mass of Moroccans without contempt. He had no pa-tience with their ignorance and backwardness; if he damned the Europeans with one breath, he was bound to damn the Moroccans with the next. No one escaped but him, and that was because he hated himself most of all. But fortunately he was unaware of that. His own dream was to have a small speedboat; it was an absolute necessity for the man who hoped to be really successful in smuggling.

Right now he wanted to get to the Café Tingis in the Zoco Chico and have a coffee with cognac in it. He turned into the Siaghines and strode rapidly downhill between the money changers' stalls, past the Spanish church and the Galeries La-fayette. Ahead was the little square, the bright lights of the gasoline lamps in the cafés pouring into it from all four sides. It could be any hour of the day or night—the cafés would be open and crowded with men, the dull murmuring monotone of whose talking filled the entire zoco. But tonight the square was swept by the roaring wind. He climbed the steps to the deserted terrace and pushed inside, taking a seat by the win-dow. The Tingis dominated the square; from it one could look down upon all the other cafés. Someone had left an al-most full pack of Chesterfields on the table. He clapped his hands for the waiter, took off his raincoat. He was not very dry underneath it: a good deal of water had run down his neck, and below his knees he was soaked through.

The waiter arrived. Thami gave his order. Pointing at the cigarettes he said: "Yours?" The waiter looked vaguely around the café, his forehead wrinkled with confusion, and replied that he thought the table was occupied. At that moment a man came out of the washroom and walked toward Thami, who automatically started to rise in order to sit somewhere else. As the man reached the table he made several gestures indicating that Thami remain there. "That's okay, that's okay," he was saying. "Stay where you are."

Thami had learned English as a boy when his father, who often had English people of rank staying at the house, had insisted he study it. Now he spoke it fairly well, if with a rather strong accent. He thanked the man, and accepted a cigarette. Then he said: "Are you English?" It was curious that the man should be in this part of the town at this hour, particularly with the weather the way it was.

"No. I'm American."

Appraisingly Thami looked at him and asked if he were from a boat: he was a little afraid the American was going to ask to be directed to a bordel, and he glanced about nervously to see if anyone he knew was in the café. One rumor he could not have circulating was that he had become a guide; in Tangier there was nothing lower.

The man laughed apologetically, saying: "Yeah, I guess you could say I'm from a boat. I just got off one, but if you mean do I work on one, no."

Thami was relieved. "You stay in a hotel?" he asked. The other said he did, looking a little bit on his guard, so that Thami did not ask him which hotel it was, as he had intended to do.

"How big is Tangier?" the man asked Thami. He did not know. "Are there many tourists now?" That he knew. "It's very bad. No one comes any more since the war."

"Let's have a drink," the American said suddenly. "Hey, there!" He leaned backward, looking over his shoulder for the waiter. "You'll have one, won't you?" Thami assented.

He looked at Thami for the first time with a certain warmth. "No use sitting here like two bumps on a log. What'll it be?" The waiter approached. Thami still had not decided what kind of man this was, what he could afford. "And you?" he asked.

"White Horse."

"Good," said Thami, having no idea what this might be. "For me, too."

The two men looked at each other. It was the moment when they were ready to feel sympathy for one another, but the traditional formula of distrust made it necessary that a reason be found first.

"When have you come to Tangier?" asked Thami.

"Tonight."

"Tonight, for the first time?"

"That's right."

Thami shook his head. "What a wonderful thing to be an American!" he said impetuously.

"Yes," said Dyar automatically, never having given much thought to what it would be like not to be an American. It seemed somehow the natural thing to be.

The whiskey came; they drank it, Thami making a face. Dyar ordered another set-up, for which Thami halfheartedly offered to pay, quickly slipping his money back into his pocket at Dyar's first "no."

"What a place, what a place," said Dyar, shaking his head. Two men with black beards had just come in, their heads wrapped in large turkish towels; like all the others they were completely engrossed in unceasing and noisy conversation. "They sit here talking all night like this? What are they talking about? What is there to talk about so long?"

"What are people talking about in America?" said Thami, smiling at him.

"In a bar, usually politics. If they talk. Mostly they just drink."

"Here, everything: business, girls, politics, neighbors. Or what we are talking about now."

Dyar drained his glass. "And what are we talking about?" he demanded. "I'm damned if I know."

"About them." Thami laughed and made a wide gesture.

"You mean they're talking about us?"

"Some, perhaps."

"Have fun, chums," Dyar called loudly, turning his head toward the others. He looked down at his glass, had difficulty in getting it into clear focus. For a second he forgot where he was, saw only the empty glass, the same little glass that was always waiting to be refilled. His toe muscles were flexing, and that meant he was drunk. "Which is the nearest subway?" he thought. Then he stretched his legs out in front of him voluptuously and laughed. "Jesus!" he cried. "I'm glad to be here!" he looked around the dingy bar, heard the meaningless chatter, and felt a wave of doubt break over him, but he held firm. "God knows where this is, but I'd rather be here than there!" he insisted. The sound of the words being spoken aloud made him feel more sure; leaning back, he looked up at the shadows moving on the high yellow ceiling. He did not see the badly dressed youth with the sly expression who came in the door and began to walk directly toward the table. "And I mean it, too," he said, suddenly sitting upright and glaring at Thami, who looked startled.

The first Dyar knew of his presence was when Thami grudgingly responded to his greeting in Arabic. He glanced up, saw the young man looking down at him in a vaguely predatory fashion, and immediately took a dislike to him.

"Hello, mister." The youth grinned, widely enough to show which of his teeth were of gold and which were not.

"Hello," replied Dyar apathetically.

Thami said something in Arabic; he sounded truculent. The youth paid no attention, but seized a chair and drew it up to the table, keeping his eyes fixed on Dyar.

"Spickin anglish you like wan bleddy good soulima yah mister?" he said.

Thami looked around the bar uncomfortably, relaxing somewhat when he saw no one watching the table at the moment.

"Now," said Dyar, "just start all over again and take your time. What was that?"

The youth glared at him, spat. "You no spickin anglish?"

"Not that kind, buddy."

"He wants you to go and see a film," explained Thami. "But don't go."

"What? At this hour?" cried Dyar. "He's nuts."

"They show them late because they are forbidden by the police," said Thami, looking as though the whole idea were highly distasteful to him.

"Why? What kind of movies are they?" Dyar was beginning to be interested.

"Very bad. You know." Since Thami had the Arab's utter incomprehension of the meaning of pornography, he imagined that the police had placed the ban on obscene films because these infringed upon Christian doctrine at certain specific points, in which case any Christian might be expected to show interest, if only to disapprove. He found it not at all surprising that Dyar should want to know about them, although he himself was as totally indifferent as he would have expected Dyar to be had they treated of the question as to whether the pilgrim at Mecca should run around the Kaâba clockwise or counter-clockwise. At the same time, their being prohibited made them disreputable, and he was against having anything to do with them.

"They are very expensive and you see nothing," he said.

The young man did not understand Thami's words, but he knew the drift of his argument, and he was displeased. He spat more vehemently and carefully avoided turning his head in his direction.

"Well, you must see something, at least," objected Dyar with logic. "Let's get this straight," he said to the youth. "How much?" He got no reply. The youth looked confused; he was trying to decide how far above the usual tariff he could safely go. "*Ch'hal?*" pursued Thami. "How much? The man says how much. Tell him."

"*Miehtsain.*"

"*Achrine duro,*" said Thami sternly, as if he were correcting him. They argued a while. Presently Thami announced triumphantly: "You can go for one hundred pesetas." Then he glanced about the bar and his face darkened. "But it's no good. I advise you, don't go. It's very late. Why don't you go to bed? I will walk with you to your hotel."

Dyar looked at him and laughed lightly. "Listen, my friend. You don't have to come anywhere. Nobody said you had to come. Don't worry about me." Thami studied his face a second to see if he were angry, decided he was not, and said: "Oh, no!" There was no question of leaving the American to wander off into Benider with the pimp. Even though he would have liked more than anything at the moment to go home and sleep, and despite the fact that the last thing he wanted was to be seen in the street at this hour with a foreigner and this particular young man, he felt responsible for Dyar and determined not to let him out of his sight until he had got him to his hotel door. "Oh, no!" he said. "I'll go with you."

"Suit yourself."

They rose, and the youth followed them out onto the terrace. Dyar's clothes were still wet and he winced when the wind's blast struck him. He asked if it were far; Thami conferred with the other and said that it was a two-minute walk. The rain had lessened. They crossed the zoco, took a few turnings through streets that were like corridors in an old hotel, and stopped in the dimness before a high grilled door. Thami peered uneasily up and down the deserted alley as the youth hammered with the knocker, but there was no one to see them.

"*I'm going to quit singin', I'm worried in my shoes—*" sang Dyar, not very loud. But Thami gripped his arm, terrified. "No, no!" he whispered. "The police!" The song had echoed in the quiet interior of the street.

"Jesus Christ! So we're going to see a dirty movie. So what?" But he did not sing again.

They waited. Eventually there were faint sounds within. A muffled voice spoke on the other side of the door, and the youth answered. When the grille opened there was nothing at all to see but the blackness inside. Then a figure stepped from behind the door, and at the same time there came an odor which was a combination of eau de cologne, toothpaste and perspiration. The figure turned a flashlight in their faces, ordered the young man with them, in broken Spanish, to fetch a lamp, and shut the grille behind them. For a moment they all stood without moving in complete darkness. Thami coughed nervously; the sharp sound reverberated from wall to wall. When the young man appeared carrying the lamp the figure in white retired silently into a side room, and the three started up a flight of stairs. At the top, in a doorway, stood a fat man with a grayish complexion; he wore pyjamas and held a hand that was heavy with rings in front of his mouth to cover his yawns. The air up here was stiff with the smell of stale incense; the dead smoke clogged the hall.

The fat man addressed them in Spanish. Between words he wheezed. When he discovered that Dyar spoke only English he stopped, bowed, and said: "Good night, sir. Come these way, please." In a small room there were a few straight-backed chairs facing a blank wall where a canvas screen hung crookedly. On each side of the screen was a high potted palm.

"Sit, please," he said, and stood above them breathing heavily. To Dyar he said: "We have one off the men with ladies, one from prists-nuns, and one boys altogether, sir. Very beautiful. All not wearing the clothing. You love, sir. You can looking all three these with one combination price, yes. Sir wishing three, sir?"

"No. Let's see the nuns."

"Yes, sir. Spanish gentleman liking nuns. Taking always the nuns. Very beautiful. Excuse."

He went out, and presently was heard talking in an adjoining room. Dyar lit a cigarette; Thami yawned widely. "You ought to have gone to bed," said Dyar.

"Oh, no! I will go with you to your hotel."

Dyar exploded. "God damn it, I'm not going to my hotel! Can't you get that through your head? It's not so hard to understand. When I get through here I'll go somewhere else, have another drink, maybe a little fun, I don't know. I don't know what I'll be doing. But I won't be going to the hotel. See?"

"It doesn't matter," said Thami calmly.

They were quiet for a moment, before Dyar pursued in a conciliatory tone: "You see, I've been on a ship for a week. I'm not sleepy. But you're sleepy. Why don't you go on home and call it a night?"

Thami was resolute. "Oh, no! I can't do that. It would be very bad. I will take you to your hotel. Whenever you go." He sat as low as the chair permitted and closed his eyes, letting his head fall slowly forward. The projector and film were brought and installed by another man in pyjamas, equally fat but with a full, old-fashioned moustache. By the time the whirring of the machine had started and the screen was lighted up, Thami's immobility and silence had passed over into the impetuously regular breathing of the sleeper.

IV

There had been a minor volcanic eruption in the Canaries. For several days the Spanish had been talking about it; the event had been given great prominence in the newspaper *España*, and many of them, having relatives there, had been receiving reassuring telegrams. On the disturbance everyone blamed the sultry weather, the breathless air and the grayish yellow light which had hung above the city for the past two days.

Eunice Goode had her own maid whom she paid by the day—a slovenly Spanish girl who came in at noon and did extra work the hotel servants could not be expected to do, such as keeping her clothes pressed and in order, running errands, and cleaning the bathroom daily. The girl had been full of news of the volcano that morning and had chattered on about it, much to her annoyance, for she had decided she was in a working mood. "*Silencio!*" she had finally cried; she had a thin, high voice which was quite incongruous with her robust appearance. The girl stared at her and then giggled. "I'm working," Eunice explained, looking as preoccupied as she could. The girl giggled again.

"Anyway," she went on, "this bad weather is simply the little winter arriving." "They say it's the volcano," the girl insisted. There was the little winter first, thus termed only because it was shorter, and then the big winter, the long rainy season which came two months or so afterward. They both made dim days, wet feet and boredom; those who could escaped southward, but Eunice disliked movement of any kind. Now that she was in contact with what she called the inner reality, she scarcely minded whether the sun shone or not.

The girl was in the bathroom scrubbing the floor; she sang shrilly as she pushed the wet rag back and forth on the tiles. "Jesus!" moaned Eunice after a moment. "Conchita," she called. "*Mande,*" said the girl. "I want you to go and buy a lot of flowers in the market. Immediately." She gave her a hundred pesetas and sent her out in order to have solitude for a half-hour. She did not go out much herself these days; she spent most of her time lying in her bed. It was wide and the room was spacious. From her fortress of pillows she could see the activity of the small boats in the inner port, and she found it just enough of a diversion to follow with her eyes when she looked up from her writing. She began her day with gin, continuing with it until she went to sleep at night. When she had first come to Tangier she had drunk less and gone out more. Daytimes she had sunbathed on her balcony; evenings she had gone from bar to bar, mixing her drinks and having eventually to be accompanied to the entrance of her hotel by some disreputable individual who usually tried to take whatever small amount of money was left in the handbag she wore slung over her shoulder. But she never went out carrying more than she minded losing. The sunbathing had been stopped by the hotel management, because one day a Spanish lady had looked (with some difficulty) over the concrete partition that separated her balcony from the adjoining one, and had seen her massive pink body stretched out in a deckchair with nothing to cover it. There had been an unpleasant scene with the manager, who would have put her out if she had not been the most important single source of revenue for the hotel: she had all her meals served in bed and her door was always unlocked so the waiters could get in with drinks and bowls of ice. "It's just as well," she said to herself. "Sun is anti-thought. Lawrence was right." And now she found that lying in bed she drank more evenly; when night came she no longer had the urge to rush through the streets, to try to be everywhere at once for fear she would miss what was going to happen. The reason for this of course was that by evening she was too drunk to move very much, but it was a pleasant drunkenness, and it did not stop her from filling the pages of her notebooks with words—sometimes even with ideas.

Volcanoes angered her. The talk about this one put her in mind of a scene from her own childhood. She had been on a boat with her parents, going from Alexandria to Genoa. Early one morning her father had knocked on the door of the cabin where she and her mother slept, calling excitedly for them to go immediately on deck. More asleep than awake they arrived there to find him pointing wildly at Stromboli. The mountain was vomiting flames and lava poured down its flanks, already crimson with the rising sun. Her mother had stared an instant, and then in a voice made hoarse by fury she had cried out one word: "Dis—*gust*ing!" turned on her heel and taken Eunice below. In retrospect now, although she still could see her father's crestfallen face, she shared her mother's indignation.

She lay back, closed her eyes, and thought a bit. Presently she opened them and wrote: "There is something in the silly human mind that responds beautifully to the idea of rarity—

especially rarity of conditions capable of producing a given phenomenon. The less likely a thing is to happen, the more wonderful it seems when it does, no matter how useless or even harmful it may be. The fact of its having happened despite the odds makes it a precious event. It had no right to occur, yet it did, and one can only blindly admire the chain of circumstances that caused the impossible to come to pass."

On reading over the paragraph she noted with a certain satisfaction that although it had been meant with reference to the volcano, it also had a distinct bearing upon her personal life at that moment. She was still a little awed by what seemed to her the incredible sequence of coincidences which had made it suddenly possible for her to be happy. A strange thing had happened to her about a fortnight back. She had awakened one bright morning and made a decision to take daily exercise of some kind. (She was constantly making decisions of one sort or another, each of which she was confident was going to revolutionize her life.) The exercise would be mentally stimulating and would help her to reduce. Accordingly she had donned an old pair of slacks which were too small around the waist to be fastened, and set out for the top of the Casbah. She went through the big gate and, using her cane, climbed down the steep path to the long dirty beach below where only Arabs bathed.

From there she had followed the coastline to the west, along the foot of the Casbah's lower buildings, past the stretch where all the sewers emptied and the stink was like a solid object in the air, to a further rocky beach which was more or less deserted. And here an old Arab fisherman had stopped her, holding forth a small piece of paper, and asked her with great seriousness in his halting Spanish to read him what was written on it.

It said: "Will the finder kindly communicate with C. J. Burnett, Esq., 52, Ashurst Road, North Finchley, London, England. April 12, 1949." She translated the request, indicating the address, and could not restrain herself from asking him where he had got the paper.

"Bottle in water," he replied, pointing to the small waves that broke near their feet. Then he asked her what he should do. "Write the man, if you like," she said, about to go on.

Yes, mused the old man, stroking his beard, he must write him, of course. But how, since he couldn't write? "A friend," she said. He looked at her searchingly and in a hesitant voice asked her if she would do it. She laughed. "I'm going for a walk," she said, pointing up the beach away from the town. "Perhaps when I come back." And she started walking again, leaving the old man standing there, holding his bit of paper, staring after her.

She had forgotten the incident by the time she arrived back at the same spot, but there was the fisherman sitting on a rock in his rags, looking anxiously toward her as she approached. "Now you write it?" he said. "But I have no paper," she objected. This was the beginning of a long episode in which he followed her at a distance of a few paces, all the way back along the shore, up the side hill and through the Casbah from one bacal to another in quest of an envelope and a sheet of paper.

When they had finally found a shopkeeper able to provide them with the two objects, she tried to pay for them, but the old man proudly laid his own coins on the counter and handed hers back to her. By then she thought the whole incident rather fun; it would make an amusing story to tell her friends. But she also felt in need of an immediate drink, and so she refused his invitation to go into a neighboring Arab café for tea, explaining that she must sit in a European café in order to write the letter for him properly. "Do you know one near here?" she asked him; she hoped they would not need to resort to one of the cafés in the Zoco Chico, to reach which they would have to go down steep streets and innumerable steps. He led her along several extremely narrow alleys where the shade was a blessing after the midday sun, to a small dingy place called *Bar Lucifer*. An extremely fat woman sat behind the counter reading a French movie magazine. Eunice ordered a gin and the old man had a gaseosa. She wrote the letter quickly, in the first person, saying she had found the bottle off Ras el Ihud, near Tangier, and was writing as requested, signing herself Abdelkader ben Saïd ben Mokhtar and giving his address. The fisherman thanked her profusely and went off to post the letter, first having insisted on paying for his gaseosa; she however stayed on and had several more gins.

The fat woman began to take an interest in her. Apparently she was not used to having women come into the bar, and this large foreigner who wore trousers and drank like a man aroused her curiosity. In French she asked Eunice a few questions about herself. Not being of a confiding nature, Eunice answered by improvising falsehoods, as she always did in similar circumstances. Then she countered with her own queries. The woman was only too eager to reply: she was Greek, her name was Madame Papaconstante, she had been eleven years in Tangier, the bar was a recent acquisition and had a few rooms in the back which were at the disposal of clients who required them. Presently Eunice thanked her and paid, promising to return that evening. She considered the place a discovery, because she was sure none of her friends knew about it.

At night the Bar Lucifer was quite a different matter. There were two bright gasoline lamps burning, so that the posters announcing bulls in San Roque and Melilla were visible, the little radio was going, and three Spaniards in overalls sat at the bar drinking beer. Madame Papaconstante, heavily made up and wearing an orange chiffon dress, walked to welcome her, her gold teeth glowing as she smiled. Behind the bar stood two Spanish girls with cheap permanent waves. Pretending to be following the men's conversation, they simpered when the men laughed.

"Are they your daughters?" asked Eunice. Madame Papaconstante said with some force that they were not. Then she explained that they served at the bar and acted as hostesses in the private rooms. A third girl stuck her head through the beaded curtain in the doorway that led into the back; she was very young and extraordinarily pretty. She stared at Eunice for a moment in some surprise before she came out and walked across to the entrance door.

"Who's that?" said Eunice.

A *fille indigène*, said Madame Papaconstante—an Arab girl who worked for her. "Very intelligent. She speaks English," she added. The girl turned and smiled at them, an unexpected smile, warming as a sudden ray of strong sunlight on a cloudy day.

"She's a delightful creature," said Eunice. She stepped to the bar and ordered a gin. Madame Papaconstante followed with difficulty and stood at the end beaming, her fleshy hands spread out flat on the bar so that her numerous rings flashed.

"Won't you have something?" suggested Eunice.

Madame Papaconstante looked astonished. It was an unusual evening in the Bar Lucifer when someone offered her a drink. "*Je prendrais bien un machaquito,*" she said, closing her eyes slowly and opening them again. They took their drinks to a small rickety table against the wall and sat down. The Arab girl stood in the doorway looking out into the dark, occasionally exchanging a word with a passerby.

"*Hadija, ven acá,*" called Madame Papaconstante. The girl turned and walked lightly to their table, smiling. Madame Papaconstante took her hand and told her to speak some English to the lady.

"You spickin English?" said the girl.

"Yes, of course. Would you like a drink?"

"I spickin. What you drink?"

"Gin." Eunice held up her glass, already nearly empty. The girl made a grimace of disgust.

"Ah no good. I like wan Coca-Cola."

"Of course." She caught the eye of one of the girls at the bar, and shouted to her: "*Una Coca-Cola, un machaquito y un gin!*" Hadija went to the bar to fetch the drinks.

"She's exquisite," said Eunice quickly to Madame Papaconstante. "Where did you find her?"

"Oh, for many years she has been playing in the street here with the other children. It's a poor family."

When she returned to the table with the glasses Eunice suggested she sit with them, but she pretended not to hear, and backed against the wall to remain there looking calmly down at them. There was a desultory conversation for twenty minutes or a half hour, during which Eunice ordered several more gins. She was beginning to feel very well; she turned to Madame Papaconstante. "Would you think me rude if I sat with her alone for a bit? I should like to talk with her."

"*Ça va,*" said Madame Papaconstante. It was unusual, but she saw no reason to object.

"She is absolutely ravishing," added Eunice, flinging her cigarette across the room so that it landed in the alley. She rose, put her arm around the girl, and said to her in English:

"Have another Coca-Cola and bring it inside, into one of the rooms." She gestured. "Let's sit in there where it's private."

This suggestion, however, outraged Madame Papaconstante. "*Ah, non!*" she cried vehemently. "Those rooms are for gentlemen."

Eunice was unruffled. Since to her mind her aims were always irreproachable, she rarely hesitated before trying to attain them. "Come along, then," she said to the girl. "We'll go to my hotel." She let go of Hadija and stepped to the bar, fumbling in her handbag for money. While she was paying, Madame Papaconstante got slowly to her feet, wheezing painfully.

"She works here, *vous savez!*" she shouted. "She is not free to come and go." As an afterthought she added: "She owes me money."

Eunice turned and placed several banknotes in her hand, closing the fingers over them gently. The girls behind the bar watched, their eyes shining.

"*Au revoir, madame,*" she said with warmth. An expression of great earnestness spread over her face as she went on: "I can never thank you enough. It has been a charming evening. I shall stop by tomorrow and see you. I have a little gift I should like to bring you."

Madame Papaconstante's large mouth was open, the words which had intended to come out remained inside. She let her gaze drop for a second to her hand, saw the corners of two of the bills, and slowly closed her mouth. "Ah," she said.

"You must forgive me for having taken up so much of your time," Eunice continued. "I know you are busy. But you have been very kind. Thank you."

By now Madame Papaconstante had regained control of herself. "Not at all," she said. "It was a real pleasure for me."

During this dialogue Hadija had remained unmoving by the door, her eyes darting back and forth from Eunice's face to that of her *patronne*, in an attempt to follow the meaning of their words. Now, having decided that Eunice had won in the encounter, she smiled tentatively at her.

"Good night," said Eunice again to Madame Papaconstante. She waved brightly at the girls behind the bar. The men looked around for the first time, then resumed their talk.

Eunice took Hadija's arm and they went out into the dark street. Madame Papaconstante came to the door, leaned out, saying softly: "If she does not behave herself you will tell me tomorrow."

"Oh, she will, I'm certain," said Eunice, squeezing the girl's arm. "*Merci mille fois, madame. Bonne nuit.*"

"What he sigh you?" demanded Hadija.

"She said you were a very nice girl."

"Sure. Very fine." She slipped ahead, since there was not room for them to walk abreast.

"Don't go too fast," said Eunice, panting from her attempt to keep up with her. When they came out on to the crest of the hill at Amrah, she said: "Wait, Hadija," and leaned against the wall. It was a moment she wanted to savor. She was suddenly conscious of the world outside herself—not as merely a thing that was there and belonged to other people, but as something in which she almost felt she could share. For the first time she smelled the warm odor of fulfillment on the evening air, heard the nervous beating of drums on the terraces with something besides indifference. She let her eyes range down over the city and saw clearly in the moonlight the minaret on the summit of the Charf with its little black cypress trees around it. She pounded her cane on the pavement with pleasure, several times. "I insist too hard on living my own life," she thought. The rest of the world was there for her to take at any moment she wished it, but she always rejected it in favor of her own familiar little cosmos. Only sometimes as she came out of sleep did she feel she was really *in* life, but that was merely because she had not had time to collect her thoughts, to become herself once more.

"What a beautiful night," she said dreamily. "Come and stand here a minute." Hadija obeyed reluctantly. Eunice grasped her arm again. "Listen to the drums."

"*Drbouka.* Women make."

"Aha." She smiled mysteriously, following with her eye the faint line of the mountains, range beyond range, blue in the night's clarity. She did not hope Hadija would be able to share her sensations; she asked only that the girl act as a catalyst for her, making it possible for her to experience them in their pure state. As a mainspring for her behavior there was

always the aching regret for a vanished innocence, a nostalgia
for the early years of life. Whenever a possibility of happiness
presented itself, through it she sought to reach again that
infinitely distant and tender place, her lost childhood. And in
Hadija's simple laughter she divined a prospect of return.

The feeling had persisted through the night. She exulted to
find she had been correct. At daybreak, while Hadija was still
asleep beside her, she sat up and wrote in her notebook: "A
quiet moment in the early morning. The pigeons have just
begun to murmur outside the window. There is no wind.
Sexuality is primarily a matter of imagination, I am sure.
People who live in the warmer climates have very little of it,
and so society there can allow a wide moral latitude in the
customs. Here are the healthiest personalities. In temperate
regions it is quite a different matter. The imagination's fertile
activity must be curtailed by a strict code of sexual behavior
which results in crime and depravity. Look at the great cities
of the world. Almost all of them are in the temperate zone."
She let her eyes rest a moment on the harbor below. The still
water was like blue glass. Moving cautiously so as not to wake
Hadija, she poured herself a small amount of gin from the
nearly empty bottle on the night table, and lit a cigarette.
"But of course all cities are points of infection, like decayed
teeth. The hypersensitivity of urban culture (its only virtue) is
largely a reaction to pain. Tangier has no urban culture, no
pain. I believe it never will have. The nerve will never be
exposed."

She still felt an itch of regret at not having been allowed to
go into a back room of the Bar Lucifer with Hadija. That
would have given her a certain satisfaction; in her eyes it
would have been a pure act. Perhaps another time, when she
and Madame Papaconstante had come to know each other
better, it would be possible.

Not until Hadija awoke did she telephone down for
breakfast. It gave her great pleasure to see the girl, wearing
a pair of her pyjamas, sitting up crosslegged in the bed dain-
tily eating buttered toast with a knife and fork, to show that
she knew how to manage those Western accessories. She
sent her home a little before noon, so she would not be
there when the Spanish maid arrived. In the afternoon she

called by the Bar Lucifer with a small bottle of perfume for Madame Papaconstante. Since then almost every other night she had brought Hadija back with her to the hotel. She had never seen the old fisherman again—she could hardly expect to see him unless she returned to the beach, and she was not likely to do that. She had forgotten about getting exercise; her life was too much occupied at the moment with Hadija for her to be making resolutions and decisions for improving it. She taxed her imaginative powers devising ways of amusing her, finding places to take her, choosing gifts that would please her. Faintly she was conscious through all this that it was she herself who was enjoying these things, that Hadija merely accompanied her and accepted the presents with something akin to apathy. But that made no difference to her.

When she was happy she invariably invented a reason for not being able to remain so. And now, to follow out her pattern, she allowed an idea to occur to her which counteracted all her happiness. She had made an arrangement with Madame Papaconstante whereby it was agreed that on the nights when Hadija did not go with her to the Metropole she was to remain at home with her parents. Madame Papaconstante had assured her that the girl did not even put in appearance at the bar those evenings, and up until now Eunice had not thought to question the truth of her statements. But today, when Conchita returned from the market with her arms full of flowers, notwithstanding the fact that Hadija had left the room only three hours before and did not expect to return until tomorrow night, Eunice suddenly decided she wanted her back again that same evening. She would get her some very special gift in the Rue du Statut, and they would have a little extra celebration, surrounded by the lilies and poinsettias. She would go to the Bar Lucifer and have Madame Papaconstante send someone to fetch her.

It was at this moment that the terrible possibility struck her: what if she found Hadija in the bar? If she did, it could only mean that she had been there all along, that the parent story was a lie, that she lived in one of the rooms behind the bar, perhaps. (She was working up to the climax.) Then the place was a true bordel, in which case—it had to be faced—

there was a likelihood that Hadija was entertaining the male customers in bed on those other nights.

The idea stirred her to action: she threw her notebook on to the floor and jumped out of bed with a violence that shook the room and startled Conchita. When she had dressed she wanted to start out immediately for the Bar Lucifer, but she reflected on the uselessness of such a procedure. She must wait until night and catch Hadija *in flagrante delictu*. By now there was no room in her mind for doubt. She was convinced that Madame Papaconstante had been deceiving her. Assailed by memories of former occasions when she had been trusting and complacent only to discover that her happiness had rested wholly on falsehoods, she was all too ready this time to seek out the deception and confront it.

As the afternoon advanced toward evening she grew more restless, pacing back and forth from one side of the room to the other, again and again going out onto the balcony and looking toward the harbor without seeing it. She even forgot to walk up to the Rue du Statut for Hadija's present. A black cloud gathered above the harbor and twilight passed swiftly into night. Gusts of rain-laden wind blew across the balcony into the room. She shut the door and decided, since she was dressed, to go downstairs for dinner rather than have it in bed. The orchestra and the other diners would help to keep her mind occupied. She could not hope to find Hadija at the bar before half-past nine.

When she got downstairs it was too early for dinner. There was no electricity tonight; candles burned in the corridors and oil lamps in the public rooms. She went into the bar and was engaged in conversation by an elderly retired captain from the British Army, who insisted on buying her drinks. This annoyed her considerably because she did not feel free to order as many as she wanted. The old gentleman drank slowly and reminisced at length about the Far East. "Oh God oh *God* oh God," she said to herself. "Will he ever shut up and will it ever be eight-thirty?"

As usual the meal was execrable. However, eating in the dining room she at least found the food hot, whereas by the time it reached her bed it generally had ceased being even warm. Between orchestral numbers she could hear the wind roaring outside, and the rain streamed down the long French windows of the dining room. "I shall get soaked," she thought, but the prospect was in no way a deterrent. On the contrary, the storm rather added to the drama in which she was convinced she was about to participate. She would plod through the wet streets, find Hadija, there would be an awful scene, perhaps a chase through the gale up into a forsaken corner of the Casbah or to some solitary rock far out above the strait. And then would come the reconciliation in the windy darkness, the admissions and the promises, and eventually the smiles. But this time she would bring her back to the Metropole for good.

After she had finished eating she went up to her room, changed into slacks, and slipped into a raincoat. Her hands were trembling with excitement. The air in her room was weighted down with the thick sweetness of the lilies. The candle flames waved back and forth as she moved about in haste, and the shadows of the flowers crouched, leapt to the ceiling, returned. From a drawer in one of her trunks she took a large flashlight. She stepped out, closing the door behind her. The candles went on burning.

v

It looked like a bright spring day. The sun shone on the laurel that lined the garden path where Sister Inez strolled, clutching her prayer book. Until she arrived at the fountain her long black skirts hid the fact that she was barefoot. It was the sort of garden whose air one would expect to be heavy with the sweet smell of jasmine, and although they did not appear, one could imagine birds twittering and rustling their wings with nervous delight in the shadow of the bushes. Sister Inez stretched forth one shining foot and touched the water in the basin; the sky glimmered whitely. From the bushes Father José watched, his eyes bright as he followed the two little feet moving one behind the other through the clear water. Suddenly Sister Inez undid her cowl, which was fastened with a snap-hook under her chin: her black tresses fell over her shoulders. With a second brusque gesture she unhooked her garments all the way down (it was remarkably easy), opened them wide, and turned to reveal a plump young white body. A moment later she had tossed her apparel upon a marble bench and was standing there quite naked, still holding her little black book and her rosary. Father José's eyes opened much wider and his gaze turned heavenwards: he was praying for the strength to resist temptation. In fact, the words PIDI-ENDO EL AMPARO DIVINO appeared in print across the sky, and remained there, shaking slightly, for several seconds. What followed was not a surprise to Dyar, since he had not expected the divine aid to be forthcoming, nor was he startled when a moment later three other healthy young nuns made their entrances from as many different directions to join the busy couple in the fountain, thus making the pas de deux into an ensemble number.

Subsequently the scene of activities was shifted to an altar in a nearby church. Dyar, sensing that the frenzy of this episode announced the imminent end of the film, nudged Thami and offered him a cigarette which, after awakening with a jolt, he accepted automatically and allowed to be lighted. By the time he was really conscious, the images had come to an abrupt finish and the screen was a blinding square of light. Dyar paid the first fat man, who stood in the hallway still yawning, and they went downstairs. "If two gentlemen wishing room one hour—" the fat man began, calling after them. Thami shouted something up at him in Spanish; the young man let them out into the empty street where the wind blew.

When Eunice Goode stepped into the little bar she was disappointed to see that Hadija was not in sight. She walked up to the counter, looking fixedly at the girl who stood behind it, and noted with pleasure the uneasiness her sudden appearance was causing in the latter's behavior. The girl made an absurd attempt to smile, and slowly backed against the wall, not averting her gaze from Eunice Goode's face. And, indeed, the rich foreign lady's mien was rather formidable: her plump cheeks were suffused with red, she was panting, and under her heavy brows her cold eyes moved with a fierce gleam.

"Where is everyone?" she demanded abruptly.

The girl began to stammer in Spanish that she did not know, that she thought they were out that way. Then she made for the end of the bar and tried to slip around it to get to the door that led back to the other rooms. Eunice Goode pushed her with her cane. "Give me a gin," she said. Reluctantly the girl returned to where the bottles were and poured out a drink. There were no customers.

She emptied the glass at one gulp, and leaving the girl staring after her in dismay, walked through the beaded curtain, feeling ahead of her with the tip of her cane, for the hallway was dark.

"Madame!" cried the girl loudly from behind her. "Madame!"

On the right a door opened. Madame Papaconstante, in an embroidered Chinese kimono, stepped into the hall. When she saw Eunice Goode she gave an involuntary start. Recovering, she smiled feebly and walked toward her uttering a series of voluble salutations which, as she was delivering them, did not prevent the visitor from noticing that her hostess was not only blocking the way to further progress down the hall, but was actually pushing her firmly back toward the bar. And standing in the bar she talked on.

"What weather! What rain! I was caught in it at dinner time. All my clothes soaking! You see." She glanced downward at her attire. "I had to change. My dress is drying before the heater. Maria will iron it for me. Come and have a drink with me. I did not expect you tonight. *C'est un plaisir inattendu.* Ah, yes, madame." She frowned furiously at the girl. "Sit down here," said Madame Papaconstante, "and I shall serve you myself. Now, what are we having tonight?"

When she saw Eunice finally seated at the little table she heaved a sigh of relief and rubbed her enormous flabby arms nervously, so that her bracelets clinked together. Eunice watched her discomfiture with grim enjoyment.

"Listen to the rain," said Madame Papaconstante, tilting her head toward the street. Still Eunice did not answer. "The fool," she was thinking. "The poor old god-damned fool."

"What are *you* having?" she said suddenly, with such violence that Madame Papaconstante looked into her eyes terrified, not quite sure she had not said something else. "Oh, me!" she laughed. "I shall take a *machaquito* as always."

"Sit down," said Eunice. The girl brought the drinks, and Madame Papaconstante, after casting a brief worried glance toward the street, sank onto a chair opposite Eunice Goode.

They had two drinks apiece while they talked vaguely about the weather. A beggar crawled through the door, moving forward by lifting himself on his hands, leaned against the wall, and with expressive gestures indicated his footless lower limbs, twisted like the stumps of a mangrove root. He was drenched with rain.

"Make him go away!" cried Eunice. "I can't bear to see deformed people. Give him something and get rid of him. I hate the sight of suffering." Since Madame Papaconstante did not move, she felt in her handbag and tossed a note to the man, who thrust his body forward with a reptilian movement and seized it. She knew perfectly well that one did not give such large sums to beggars, but the Bar Lucifer was a place where the feeling of power that money gave her was augmented to an extent which made the getting rid of it an act of irresistible voluptuousness. Madame Papaconstante shuddered inwardly as she watched the price of ten drinks being snatched up by the clawlike hand. Vaguely she recognized Eunice's gesture as one of hostility toward her; she cast a resentful glance at the strange woman sprawled out opposite her, thinking that God had made an error in allowing a person like that to have so much money.

Up to her arrival Eunice had fully intended to ask in a straightforward fashion whether or not Hadija was there, but now such a course seemed inadvisable. If she were in the establishment, eventually she would have to come out through the front room, since the back of the building lay against the lower part of the Casbah ramparts and thus had no other exit.

Without turning her head, Madame Papaconstante called casually in Spanish to the girl behind the bar. "Lolita! Do you mind bringing me my jersey? It's in the pink room on the big chair." And to Eunice in French: "With this rain and wind I feel cold."

"It's a signal," thought Eunice as the girl went beneath the looped-up beaded curtain. "She wants to warn Hadija so she won't come out or talk loud." "Do you have many rooms?" she said.

"Four." Madame Papaconstante shivered slightly. "Pink, blue, green and yellow."

"I adore yellow," said Eunice unexpectedly. "They say it's the color of madness, but that doesn't prevent me. It's so brilliant and full of sunshine as a color. *Vous ne trouvez pas?*"

"I like all colors," Madame Papaconstante said vaguely, looking toward the street with apprehension.

The girl returned without the sweater. "It's not there," she announced. Madame Papaconstante looked at her meaningfully, but the girl's face was blank. She returned to her position behind the bar. Two Spaniards in overalls ducked in from the street and ordered beer; evidently they had come from somewhere nearby, as their clothes were only slightly sprinkled with raindrops. Madame Papaconstante rose. "I'm going to look for it myself," she announced. "One moment. *Je reviens à l'instant.*" As she waddled down the hallway, running her hand along the wall, she murmured aloud: "*Qué mujer! Qué mujer!*"

More customers entered. When she came out, wearing over the kimono a huge purple sweater which had been stretched into utter formlessness, she looked a little happier. Without speaking to Eunice she went to the bar and joked with the men. It was going to be a fairly good night for business, after all. Perhaps if she ignored the foreign lady she would go away. The men, none of whom happened to have seen Eunice before, asked her in undertones who the strange woman was, what she was doing, sitting there alone in the bar. The question embarrassed Madame Papaconstante. "A tourist," she said nonchalantly. "Here?" they exclaimed, astonished. "She's a little crazy," she said, by way of explanation. But she was unhappy about Eunice's presence; she wished she would go away. Naively she decided to try and get her drunk, and not wishing to be re-engaged in conversation with her, sent the drink, a double straight gin, over to her table by Lolita.

"*Ahí tiene,*" said Lolita, setting the glass down. Eunice leered at her, and lifting it, drained it in two swallows. Madame Papaconstante's ingenuousness amused her greatly.

A few minutes later Lolita appeared at the table with another drink. "I didn't order this," said Eunice, just to see what would happen.

"A gift from Madame."

"*Ah, de veras!*" said Eunice. "Wait!" she cried sharply as the girl started away. "Tell Madame Papaconstante I want to speak to her."

Presently Madame Papaconstante was leaning over her table. "You wanted to see me, madame?"

"Yes," said Eunice, making an ostensible effort to focus her eyes on the fleshy countenance. "I'm not feeling well. I think I've had too much to drink." Madame Papaconstante showed solicitude, but not very convincingly. "I think," Eunice went on, "that you'll have to take me to a room and let me lie down."

Madame Papaconstante started. "Oh, impossible, Madame! It's not allowed for ladies to be in the rooms."

"And what about the girls?"

"*Ah, oui, mais ça c'est naturel!* They are my employees, madame."

"As you like," said Eunice carelessly, and she began to sing, softly at first, but with rapidly increasing stridency. Madame Papaconstante returned to the bar with misgivings.

Eunice Goode sang on, always louder. She sang: "I Have To Pass Your House to Get to My House" and "Get Out of Town". By the time she got to "I Have Always Been a Kind of Woman Hater" and "The Last Round-Up" the sound that came from her ample lungs was nothing short of a prolonged shriek.

Noticing Madame Papaconstante's expression of increasing apprehension, she said to herself with satisfaction: "I'll fix the old bitch, once and for all." She struggled to her feet, managing as she did so to upset not only her chair, but the table as well. Pieces of glass flew toward the feet of the men who stood at one end of the bar.

"*Aaah, madame, quand-même!*" cried Madame Papaconstante in consternation. "Please! You are making a scandal. One does not make scandals in my bar. This is a respectable establishment. I can't have the police coming to complain."

Eunice moved crookedly toward the bar, and smiling apologetically, leaned her arm on Madame Papaconstante's cushion-like shoulder. "*Je suis navrée,*" she began hesitantly. "*Je ne me sens pas bien. Ça ne va pas du tout.* You must forgive me. I don't know. Perhaps a good large glass of gin——"

Madame Papaconstante looked around helplessly. The others had not understood. Then she thought: perhaps now she will leave, and went behind the bar to pour it out herself. Eunice turned to the man beside her and with great dignity explained that she was not at all drunk, that she merely felt a little sick. The man did not reply.

At the first sip of her drink she raised her head, looked at Madame Papaconstante with startled eyes, and put her hand to her forehead.

"Quick! I'm ill! Where's the toilet?"

The men moved a little away from her. Madame Papaconstante seized her arm and pulled her through the doorway down the hall. At the far end she opened a door and pushed her into a foul-smelling closet, totally dark. Eunice groaned. "I shall bring a light," said Madame Papaconstante, hurrying away. Eunice lit a match, flushed the toilet, made some more groaning sounds, and peered out into the corridor. It was empty. She stepped out swiftly and went into the next room, which was also dark. She lit another match, saw a couch against the wall. She lay down and waited. A minute or two later there were voices in the hallway. Presently someone opened the door. She lay still, breathing slowly, deeply. A flashlight was turned into her face. Hands touched her, tugged at her. She did not move.

"*No hay remedio,*" said one of the girls.

A few more halfhearted attempts were made to rouse her, and then the group withdrew and closed the door.

As he climbed behind Thami through the streets that were half stairways, Dyar felt his enthusiasm for their project rapidly diminishing. The wet wind circled down upon them from above, smelling of the sea. Occasionally it splashed them with rain, but mostly it merely blew. By the time they had turned into the little street that ran level, he was thinking of his room back at the Hotel de la Playa almost with longing. "Here," said Thami.

They walked into the bar. The first thing Dyar saw was Hadija standing in the back doorway. She was wearing a simple flannel dress that Eunice had bought her on the Boulevard Pasteur, and it fitted her. She had also learned not to make up so heavily, and even to do her hair up into a knot at the back of her neck, rather than let it stand out wildly in hopeless imitation of the American film stars. She looked intently at Dyar, who felt a slight shiver run down his spine.

"By God, look at that!" he murmured to Thami.

"You like her?"

"I could use a little of it, all right."

A Spaniard had placed a portable radio on the bar; two of the girls bent over listening to faint guitar music behind a heavy curtain of static. Three men were having a serious drunken discussion at a table in the corner. Madame Papaconstante sat at the end of the bar, smoking listlessly. "*Muy buenas,*" she said to them, beaming widely, mistaking them in her sleepiness for Spaniards.

Thami replied quietly without looking at her. Dyar went to the bar and ordered drinks, keeping his eye on Hadija, who when she saw his attention, looked beyond him to the street. Hearing English being spoken, Madame Papaconstante rose and approached the two, swaying a little more than usual.

"Hello, boys," she said, patting her hair with one hand while she pulled her sweater down over her abdomen with the other. Apart from figures and a few insulting epithets, these words were her entire English vocabulary.

"Hello," Dyar answered without enthusiasm. Then he went over to the door and holding up his glass, said to Hadija: "Care for a drink?" But Hadija had learned several things during her short acquaintance with Eunice Goode, perhaps the most important of which was that the more difficult everything was made, the more money would be forthcoming when payment came due. If she had been the daughter of the English Consul and had been accosted by a Spanish fisherman in the middle of the Place de France she could not have stared more coldly. She moved across the room and stood near the door facing the street.

Dyar made a wry grimace. "My mistake," he called after her ruefully; his chagrin, however, was nothing compared to Madame Papaconstante's indignation with Hadija. Her hands on her hips, she walked over to her and began to deliver a low-pitched but furious scolding.

"She works here, doesn't she?" he said to Thami. Thami nodded.

"Watch," Dyar went on, "the old madam's giving her hell for being so snotty with the customers." Thami did not understand entirely, but he smiled. They saw Hadija's expression grow more sullen. Presently she ambled over to the bar and stood sulking near Dyar. He decided to try again.

"No hard feelings?"

She looked up at him insolently. "Hello, Jack," she said, and turned her face away.

"What's the matter? Don't you like strange men?"

"Wan Coca-Cola." She did not look at him again.

"You don't have to drink with me if you don't want to, you know," he said, trying to make his voice sound sympathetic. "If you're tired, or something——"

"How you feel?" she said. Madame Papaconstante was watching her from the end of the bar.

She lifted her glass of Coca-Cola. "Down the hotch," she said, and took a sip. She smiled faintly at him. He stood closer to her, so he could just feel her body alongside his. Then he turned slightly toward her, and moved in a bit more. She did not stir.

"You always as crazy as this?" he asked her.

"I not crazy," she said evenly.

They talked a while. Slowly he backed her against the bar; when he put his arm around her he thought she might push him away, but she did nothing. From her vantage-point Madame Papaconstante judged that the right moment for intervention had arrived; she lumbered down from her stool and went over to them. Thami was chatting with the Spaniard who owned the radio; when he saw Madame Papaconstante trying to talk to Dyar he turned toward them and became interpreter.

"You want to go back with her?" he asked him.

Dyar said he did.

"Tell him fifty pesetas for the room," said Madame Papaconstante hurriedly. The Spaniards were listening. They usually paid twenty-five. "And he gives the girl what he likes, afterward."

Hadija was looking at the floor.

*

The room smelled of mildew. Eunice had been asleep, but now she was awake, and she noticed the smell. Certain rooms in the cellar of her grandmother's house had smelled like that. She remembered the coolness and mystery of the enormous cellar on a quiet summer afternoon, the trunks, the shelves of empty mason jars and the stacks of old magazines. Her grandmother had been an orderly person. Each publication had been piled separately: *Judge*, *The Smart Set*, *The Red Book*, *Everybody's*, *Hearst's International*—— She sat up in the dark, tense, without knowing why. Then she did know why. She had heard Hadija's voice outside the door. Now it said: "This room O.K."; she heard a man grunt a reply. The door into the adjacent room was opened, and then closed.

She stood up and began to walk back and forth in front of the couch, three steps one way and three steps the other. "I can't bear it," she thought. "I'll kill her. I'll kill her." But it was just the sound of the words in her head; no violent images came to accompany the refrain. Crouching on the floor with her neck twisted at a painful angle, she managed to place her ear flush against the wall. And she listened. At first she heard nothing, and she thought the wall must be too thick to let the sound through. But then she heard a loud sigh. They were not saying anything, and she realized that when something was said, she would hear every word.

A long time went by before this happened. Then Hadija said: "No." Immediately the man complained: "What's the matter with you?" In his voice Eunice recognized a fellow American; it was even worse than she had expected. There were sounds of movement on the couch, and again Hadija said very firmly: "No."

"But, Baby—" the man pleaded.

After more shifting about, "No," said the man halfheartedly, as if in faint protest. Eunice's neck ached; she strained harder, pushing against the wall with all her strength. For a while she heard nothing. Then there was a long, shuddering groan of pleasure from the man. "As if he were dying," thought Eunice, gritting her teeth. Now she told herself: "I'll kill *him*," and this time she had a satisfactorily bloody vision, although her imaginary attack upon the man fell somewhat short of murder.

Suddenly she had drawn her head back and was pounding on the wall with her fist. And she was calling out to Hadija in Spanish: "Go on! *Haz lo que quieres! Sigue!* Have a good time!" Her own knocking had startled her, and the sound of her voice astonished her even more; she would never have known it was hers. But now she had spoken; she caught her breath and listened. There was silence in the next room for a moment. The man said lazily: "What's all that?" Hadija answered by whispering. "Quick! Give money!" She sounded agitated. "One other time I fix you up good. No like tonight. No here. Here no good. Listen, boy—" And here apparently she whispered directly into his ear, as if she knew from experience just how thin the walls were and how easily the sound carried. The man, who seemed to be in a state of profound lassitude, began nevertheless to grunt: "Huh? When? Where's that?" between the lengthy inaudible explanations.

"Okay?" said Hadija finally. "You come?"

"But Sunday, right? Not Friday—" The last word was partially muffled, she supposed by Hadija's hand.

Painfully Eunice got to her feet. She sighed deeply and sat down on the edge of the couch in the dark. Everything she had suspected was perfectly true: Hadija had been working regularly at the Bar Lucifer; probably she had often come to her fresh from the embrace of a Spanish laborer or shop-keeper. The arrangement with Madame Papaconstante was clearly a farce. Everyone had been lying to her. Yet instead of resentment she felt only a dimly satisfying pain—perhaps because she had found it all out at first-hand and through her own efforts. It was an old story to her and she did not mind. All she wanted now was to be alone with Hadija. She would not even discuss the evening with her. "The poor girl," she thought. "I don't give her enough to live on. She's forced to come here." She began to consider places where she might take her to get her away from the harmful environment, places where they could be alone, unmolested by prying servants and disapproving or amused acquaintances. Sospel, perhaps, or Caparica; somewhere away from Arabs and Spaniards, where she would have the pleasure of feeling that Hadija was wholly dependent upon her.

"But, Baby, that's all I've got," the man was protesting. They talked normally now; she could hear them from where she sat.

"No, no," said Hadija firmly. "More. Give."

"You don't care *how* much you take from a guy, do you? I'm telling you, I haven't *got* any more. Look."

"We go spick you friend in bar. He got."

"No. You got enough now. That's damn good money for what you did."

"Next time I fix—"

"I know! I know!"

They argued. It astonished Eunice to hear an American refusing to part with an extra fifty pesetas under such circumstances. Typically, she decided he must be an extremely vicious man, one who got his true pleasure from just such scenes, to whom it gave a thrill of evil delight to withhold her due from a helpless girl. But it amused her to observe the vigor with which Hadija pursued the discussion. She bet herself drinks for the house that the girl would get the extra money. And after a good deal of pointless talk he agreed to borrow the sum from the friend in the bar. As they opened the door and went out Hadija said: "You good man. I like." Eunice bit her lip and stood up. More than anything else, that remark made her feel that she was right in suspecting this man of being a particular danger. And now she realized that it was not the possibility of professional relationships on Hadija's part that distressed her most. It was precisely the fear that things might not remain on that footing. "But I'm an idiot," she told herself. "Why this man? the very first one I happen to have caught her with?" The important thing was that it be the last; she must take her away. And Madame Papaconstante must not know of it until they were out of the International Zone.

A quarter of an hour later she went out into the hallway; it was gray with the feeble light of dawn which came through the curtain of beads from the bar. There she heard Madame Papaconstante and Hadija arguing bitterly. "You let me go into the very next room!" Hadija was shouting. "You knew she was in there! You wanted her to hear!"

"It's not my fault she woke up!" cried Madame Papaconstante furiously. "Who do you think you are, yelling at me in my own bar!"

Eunice waited, hoping Madame Papaconstante would go further, say something more drastic, but she remained cautious, obviously not wishing to provoke the girl too deeply:— she brought money into the establishment.

Eunice walked quietly down the passageway and stepped into the bar, blinking a little. Her cane was lying across one of the tables. The two ceased speaking and looked at her. She picked up the cane, turned to face them. "Drinks for the house," she remembered. "Three double gins," she said to Madame Papaconstante, who went without a word behind the bar and poured them out.

"Take it," she said to Hadija, holding one of the glasses toward her. With her eyes on Eunice, she obeyed.

"Drink it."

Hadija did, choking afterward.

Madame Papaconstante hesitated and drank hers, still without speaking.

Eunice placed five hundred pesetas on the bar, and said: "*Bonne nuit, madame.*" To Hadija she said: "*Ven.*"

Madame Papaconstante stood looking after them as they walked slowly up the street. A large brown rat crept from a doorway opposite and began to make its way along the gutter in the other direction, stopping to sample bits of refuse as it went. The rain fell evenly and quietly.

V I

Wilcox sat on the edge of his bed in his bathrobe. Mr. Ashcombe-Danvers was concentrating his attention upon opening a new tin of Gold Flakes; a faint hiss came out as he punctured the top. Rapidly he cut around the edge and removed the light tin disc, which he dropped on the floor beside his table.

"Have one?" he said to Wilcox, holding up the tin to him. The odor of the fresh tobacco was irresistible. Wilcox took a cigarette. Mr. Ashcombe-Danvers did likewise. When both had lights, Mr. Ashcombe-Danvers went on with what he had been saying.

"My dear boy, I don't want to seem to be asking the impossible, and I think if you try to look at it from my point of view you'll see soon enough that actually I'm only asking the inevitable. I expect you knew that sooner or later I should require to move sterling here."

Wilcox looked uncomfortable. He ran his finger along the edge of the ash tray. "Well, yes. I'm not surprised," he said. Before the other could speak again he went on. "But if you'll excuse my saying so, I can't help feeling you've chosen a rather crude method of getting it here."

Mr. Ashcombe-Danvers smiled. "Yes. If you like, it's crude. I don't think that militates against its success in any way."

"I wonder," said Wilcox.

"Why should it?"

"Well, it's too large a sum to bring in that way."

"Nonsense!" Mr. Ashcombe-Danvers cried. "Don't be bound by tradition, my boy. That's simply superstitious of you. If one can do it that way with a small amount, one can do it in exactly the same way with a larger one. Can't you see how safe it is? There's nothing whatever in writing, is there? The number of agents is reduced to a minimum—all I need to be sure of is old Ramlal, his son and you."

"And all I need to be sure of is that nobody knows it when I go to Ramlal and take out nine thousand pounds in cash. That includes our British currency snoopers as well as the Larbi crowd. And I'd say it's impossible. They're bound to know. Somebody's bound to find out."

"Nonsense," said Mr. Ashcombe-Danvers again. "If you're afraid for your own skin," he smiled ingratiatingly, fearing that he might be treading on delicate ground, "and you've every right to be, of course, why—send someone else to fetch it. You must have someone around you can trust for a half hour."

"Not a soul," said Wilcox. He had just thought of Dyar. "Let's have some lunch. We can have it right here in the room. They have some good roast beef downstairs, or had yesterday." He reached for the telephone.

"Afraid I can't." Mr. Ashcombe-Danvers was half expecting Wilcox to raise his percentage, and he did not want to do anything which might help put him sufficiently at his ease to make him broach the subject.

"Sure?" said Wilcox. "No, I can't," repeated Mr. Ashcombe-Danvers.

Wilcox took up the telephone. "A whiskey?" He lifted the receiver.

"Oh, I think not, thank you."

"Of course you will," said Wilcox. "Give me the bar."

Mr. Ashcombe-Danvers rose and stood looking out the window. The wet town below looked freshly built; the harbor and the sky beyond it were a uniform gray. It was raining indifferently. Wilcox was saying: "Manolo? Haig and Haig Pinch, two Perriers and ice for Two Forty Six." He hung up, and in the same breath went on: "I can do it, but I'll need another two percent."

"Oh, come," said Mr. Ashcombe-Danvers patiently. "I've been waiting for you to put it up. But I must say I didn't expect a two percent increase. That's a bit thick. Ramlal ten, and now you want seven."

"A bit thick? I don't think so," said Wilcox. "And I don't think you'll think so when you have your nine thousand safely in the Crédit Foncier. It's all very well for you to keep telling me how easy it is. You'll be safe in Paris—"

"My dear boy, you probably will think I'm exaggerating when I say I can think of six persons at this moment who I know would be delighted to do it for three percent."

Wilcox laughed. "Perfectly true. I can think of plenty who'd do it for one percent, too, if it comes to that. But you won't use them." To himself he was saying that Dyar was the ideal one to use in this connection: he was quite unknown in the town, his innocence of the nature of the transaction was a great advantage, and he could be given the errand as a casual part of his daily work and thus would not have to be paid any commission at all; the entire seven percent could be kept intact. "You'll have to meet the man I have in mind, of course, and take him around to young Ramlal yourself. He's an American."

"Aha!" said Mr. Ashcombe-Danvers, impressed.

Wilcox saw that he would have his way about the percentage. "Commission figures between ourselves, you understand," he went on.

"Obviously," said Mr. Ashcombe-Danvers in a flat voice, staring at him coldly. He supposed Wilcox intended to keep five and give the man two, which was just what Wilcox intended him to think.

"You can come around to my office this afternoon and size him up, if you like."

"My dear boy, don't be absurd. I'm perfectly confident in anyone you suggest. But I still think seven percent is a bit steep."

"Well, you come and talk with him," said Wilcox blandly, feeling certain his client had no desire to discuss the matter with anyone, "and if you don't like his looks we'll try and think up someone else. But I'm afraid the seven will have to stand."

There was a knock at the door, and a waiter came in with the drinks.

Dyar awoke feeling that he had not really slept at all. He had a confused memory of the morning's having been divided into many episodes of varying sorts of noise. There had been the gurgling of the plumbing as the early risers bathed and he tried to drop off to sleep, the train that shunted back and forth on the siding between his window and the beach, the chattering of the scrubwomen in the corridor, the Frenchman in the next room who had sung "*La Vie en Rose*" over and over while he shaved, showered and dressed. And through it all, like an arhythmical percussive accompaniment there had been the constant metallic slamming of doors throughout the hotel, each one of which shook the flimsy edifice and resounded through it like a small blast.

He looked at his watch: it was twenty-five past twelve. He groaned; his heart seemed to have moved into his neck and to be beating there. He felt breathless, tense and exhausted. In retrospect the night before seemed a week long. Going to bed by daylight always made him sleep badly. And he was bothered by two things, two ideas that he felt lodged in the pit of his stomach like unwanted food. He had spent twenty dollars during the evening, which meant that he now had $460 left, and he had borrowed a hundred pesetas from an Arab, which meant that he had to see the Arab again.

"God-damned idiot!" he said as he got out of bed to look in his bags for the aspirin. He took three, had a quick shower, and lay down again to relax. A chambermaid, having heard the shower running, knocked on the door to see when she could make up the room. "Who is it?" he yelled, and not understanding her reply, did not get up to let her in. Presently he opened his eyes again and discovered that it was twenty minutes past two. Still not feeling too well, he dressed and went down into the lobby. The boy at the desk handed him a slip that read: *Llamar a la Sra. Debalberde 28-01.* He looked at it apathetically, thinking it must be for someone else. Stepping outside, he began to walk along the street without paying attention to where he was going. It was good to be in the air. The rain dripped out of the low sky in a desultory fashion, as if it were falling from invisible eaves overhead.

Suddenly he realized he was extremely hungry. He raised his head and looked around, decided there would be no restaurant in the vicinity. A half-mile or so ahead of him, sprawling over a hill that jutted into the harbor, was the native town. At his right the small waves broke quietly along the deserted beach. He turned to his left up one of the many steep streets that led over the hill. Like the others it was lined with large new apartment houses, some of which were still under construction but inhabited, nonetheless. Near the top of the hill he came to a modest-looking hotel with the word *Restaurant* printed over the doorway. In the dining room, where a radio roared, several people were eating. The tables were small. He sat down and looked at the typewritten card at his place. It was headed *Menu à 30 p.* He counted his money and grinned a little to see that he still had thirty-five pesetas. As he ate his hors d'oeuvre he found his hunger growing rapidly; he began to feel much better. During the *merlans frits* he pulled out the piece of paper the boy at the desk had given him and studied it absently. The name conveyed nothing to him; suddenly he saw that it was a message from Daisy de Valverde. "Radio Internacional," boomed the imbecilic girl's voice. A harp glissando followed. He had no particular desire to see his hostess of last night, or to see anyone, for that matter. At the moment he felt like being alone, having an opportunity to accustom himself to the strangeness of the town. But for fear she might be waiting for his call he went out into the lobby and asked the desk clerk to make the call for him. "*Veinteyochocerouno,*" he heard him shout several times, and he wondered if he would ever be able even to make a telephone call by himself. After the man handed the instrument to him he had to wait a long time for her to come to the phone.

"Dear Mr. Dyar! How kind of you to ring me! Did you get back safely last night? What vile weather! You're seeing the place at its very worst. But keep a stiff upper lip. One of these days the sun will be out and dry up all this fearful damp. I can't wait. Jack is very naughty. He hasn't telephoned me. Are you there? If you see him, tell him I'm rather put out with him. Oh, I wanted to tell you, Tambang is better. He drank a little milk. Isn't that wonderful news? So you see, our little excursion to his room did some good." (He tried to dismiss the memory of the airless room, the needles and the smell of ether.) "Mr. Dyar, I want very much to see you." For the first time she paused to let him speak. He said: "Today?" and heard her laugh. "Yes, of course today. Naturally. I'm insatiable, yes?" As he stammered protests she continued. "But I don't want to go to Jack's office for a particular reason I shall have to tell you when I see you. I was thinking, we might meet at the Faro Bar on the Place de France. It's just around the corner from the tourist bureau. Darling old snobbish Jack wouldn't be caught dead in the place, so we shall be running no risk of seeing him. You can't miss it. Just ask anyone." She spelled out the name for him. "It's sweet of you to come. Shall we say about seven? Jack closes that establishment of his at half past six. I have so much to talk to you about. And one enormous favor to ask you, which you don't *have* to grant if you don't want." She laughed. "The Faro at seven." And as he was trying to decide quickly how to word his bread-and-butter phrase for last night's hospitality, he realized that she had hung up. He felt the blood rush to his face; he should have got the sentence in somehow at the beginning of the call. The man at the desk asked him for one peseta fifty. He went back to his table annoyed with himself, and wondering what she thought of him.

The check was for thirty-three pesetas, including the service. He had fifty céntimos left, which he certainly could not leave as a tip. He left nothing, and walked out whistling innocently in the face of the waiter's accusing stare. But after he had gone a short way he stopped under the awning of a

tobacco shop and took out his two little folders of American
Express checks. There was a book of fifties and one of twenties. On the ship he had counted the checks every few days; it
made him feel a little less poor to see them and reckon their
aggregate. He would have to stop into a bank now and get
some money, but the examination of his fortune was to be
done in the privacy of the street. Whatever one wants to do in
a bank, there are always too many people there watching.
There would be six left in the first book (he counted them
and snapped the cover shut), which meant eight in the other.
He shuffled them almost carelessly, and then immediately
went through them again, to be certain. His expression
became intense; he now counted them with caution, pushing
his thumb against the edge of each sheet to separate a possible two. He still found only seven. Now he looked at the
serial numbers: it was undeniable that he had only seven
twenty-dollar checks—not eight. $440. His face assumed an
expression of consternation as he continued to recount the
checks uselessly, automatically, as though it were still an instant before he had made the discovery, as though it were still
possible for something different to happen. In his mind he
was trying to recall the time and place of the cashing of each
check. And now he remembered: he had needed an extra
twenty dollars on board the ship, for tips. The remembering,
however, did not make the new figure emotionaly acceptable;
he put his checks away profoundly troubled, and began to
walk along looking down at the pavement.

There were many banks, and each one he came to was
closed. "Too late," he thought, grimly. "Of course."

He went on, found Wilcox's office easily. It was upstairs
over a large tearoom, and the entire building smelled appetiz-
ingly of pastries and coffee. Wilcox was there, and made him
feel a little better by saying with a wide gesture: "Well, here's
your cage." He had half expected him to make some sort of
drastic announcement like: "Listen, old man, I guess it's up
to me to make a confession. I'm not going to be able to use
you here. You can see for yourself why it's out of the question." And then he might have offered to pay his fare back to
New York, or perhaps not even that. Certainly Dyar would
not have been extremely astonished; such behavior would

have been in keeping with his own feeling about the whole undertaking. He was prepared for just such a bitter blow. But Wilcox said: "Sit down. Take the load off your feet. Nobody's been in yet today, so there's no reason to think they'll come in now." Dyar sat down in the chair facing Wilcox at his desk, and looked around. The two rooms were uncomfortably small. In the antechamber, which had no window, there were a couch and a low table, piled with travel booklets. The office room had a window which gave on a narrow court; besides the desk and the two chairs there was a green filing cabinet. The room's inhospitable bareness was tempered by the colored maps covering the walls, drawing the eye inevitably to their irregular contours.

They talked for an hour or so. When Dyar remarked: "You don't seem to be doing a rushing business, do you?" Wilcox snorted disgustedly, but Dyar was unable to interpret his reaction as one of sincere discontent. The Marquesa was obviously correct: there was a slight mystery about his set-up. "I've got to change some money," he said presently. Wilcox might just possibly suggest an advance.

"What have you got?" asked Wilcox.

"Express checks."

"I'll cash whatever you want. I can give you a better rate than most of the banks, and a good deal better one than the money stalls."

Dyar gave him a fifty-dollar check. When he had his wallet stuffed with hundred-peseta notes and felt a little less depressed about his finances, he said: "When do I start work?"

"You've started," Wilcox replied. "You're working now. There's a guy coming in here this afternoon, a customer of mine. He travels a lot, and always books through me. He'll take you down to meet young Ramlal. You'd have to meet him anyway, sooner or later. The Ramlals are great friends of mine. I do a hell of a lot of business with them." This monologue made no sense to Dyar; moreover he had the impression that Wilcox was on the defensive while delivering it, as if he expected to be challenged. Soon enough, he thought, he would know what it was all about. "I see," he said. Wilcox shot him a glance which he did not at all like: it was hard and unfriendly and suspicious. Then he went on. "I've got to be at somebody's house for drinks around five, so I hope to God he comes soon. You can go down with him and come right back. I'll wait till you get here. At six-thirty just go out and shut the door behind you. I'll have a set of keys for you tomorrow." The telephone rang. There ensued a long conversation in which Wilcox's part consisted mainly of the word "yes" uttered at irregular intervals. The door opened and a tall, slightly stooped gentleman wearing heavy tweeds and a rain-coat stepped into the antechamber. Wilcox cut his telephone conversation short, stood up, and said: "This is Mr. Dyar. This is Mr. Ashcombe-Danvers. I sold him a ticket to Cairo the day after I opened this office, and he's been coming back ever since. A satisfied client. Or at least I like to think so."

Mr. Ashcombe-Danvers looked impatient. "Ah, yes. Quite." He put his hands behind his back and spun around to exam-ine a large map of the world that hung above the filing cabi-net. "I expect we'd better be going," he said.

Wilcox looked at Dyar significantly. He had meant to tell him a little more about Mr. Ashcombe-Danvers, above all to advise him not to ask any questions. But perhaps it was just as well that he had said nothing.

Dyar slipped into his raincoat as they descended the stairs. "We may as well walk," said Mr. Ashcombe-Danvers. "It's stopped raining for the present, and the shop's not very far." They went down the hill and came out into the wide square which had been empty last night save for the taxis; now it was a small city of natives engaged in noisy commerce. "Chaos," said Mr. Ashcombe-Danvers, a note of satisfaction in his voice. As they went under the bare trees in the center of the square the water dripped down upon their heads. The women huddled in rows along the pavement, wrapped in candy-striped woolen blankets, holding forth great bunches of drenched white lilies and calling out hoarsely for them to buy. The day was coming to a close; the sky was growing duller.

"Shrewd people, these mountain Berbers," remarked Mr. Ashcombe-Danvers. "But no match for the Indians."

"The Indians?" Dyar looked confused.

"Oh, not your redskins. Our Indians. Moslems, most of them, from India. Tangier's full of them. Hadn't you no-ticed? Young Ramlal, that we're on our way to see, he's one. Most shrewd. And his father, old Ramlal, in Gib. Amazing business acumen. Quite amazing. He's a bandit, of course, but an honest bandit. Never takes a shilling above what's been agreed upon. He doesn't need to, of course. His commission's enormous. He knows he has you and he piles it on because he knows he's worth it." Dyar listened politely; they were going between two rows of money changers. The men sat behind their small desks directly in the street. A few of them, spotting the two foreigners speaking English, began to call out to them. "Yes! Come on! Yes! Change money!"

"The devil of it is," Mr. Ashcombe-Danvers was saying, "the authorities are onto it. They know damned well Gib's one of the most important leakage points."

Dyar said tentatively: "Leakage?"

"Sterling leakage. They know there's probably twenty thousand pounds slipping out every day. And they're catching up with some of the chaps. It's only a question of time before they'll be able to put a stop to it altogether. Time is of the essence. Naturally it makes a man a bit nervous." He laughed apologetically. "It's a chance one must take. I like Morocco and my wife likes it. We're building a little villa here and we must have some capital, risk or no risk."

"Oh, sure," said Dyar. He was beginning to understand.

Ramlal's window was piled with cheap wrist watches, fountain pens and toys. The shop was tiny and dark; it smelled of patchouli. Once Dyar's eyes had got used to the lack of light inside, he realized that all the stock was in the window. The shop was completely empty. A swarthy young man sat at a bare desk smoking. As they entered he rose and bowed obsequiously.

"Good evening, Ramlal," said Mr. Ashcombe-Danvers in the tone of a doctor making his rounds through a ward of incurables.

"About to get under way?" Ramlal spoke surprisingly good English.

"Yes. Tomorrow. This is Mr. Dyar, my secretary." Dyar held out his hand to Ramlal, looking at Mr. Ashcombe-Danvers. "What the hell goes on?" he said to himself. He acknowledged the introduction.

"He'll arrange everything," went on Mr. Ashcombe-Danvers. "You'll give him the packet." Ramlal was looking carefully at Dyar all the while. Showing his very white teeth he smiled and said: "Yes, sir."

"Got him?" said Mr. Ashcombe-Danvers.

"Yes, indeed, sir."

"Well, we must be going. Your father's well, I hope?"

"Oh, yes, sir. Very well, thank you."

"Not too many worries, I hope?"

Ramlal smiled even more widely. "Oh, no, sir."

"That's good," grunted Mr. Ashcombe-Danvers. "Well, look after yourself, Ramlal. See you when I get back." Ramlal and Dyar shook hands again and they went out.

"Now if you'll come along with me to the Café España I'll present you to Benzekri."

Dyar looked at his watch. "I'm afraid I've got to get back to the office." It was twilight, and raining lightly. The narrow street was packed with people wearing djellabas, raincoats, turkish towels, overalls, blankets and rags.

"Nonsense," said Mr. Ashcombe-Danvers sharply. "You've got to meet Benzekri. Come along. It's essential."

"Well, since I'm your secretary," Dyar smiled.

"In this matter you are." Mr. Ashcombe-Danvers walked as close to Dyar as he could, speaking directly into his ear. "Benzekri is with the Crédit Foncier here. I'll show you the entrance as we go by it in a moment." They had come out into the Zoco Chico, filled with the drone of a thousand male voices. This evening there was electricity and the cafés were resplendent.

Working their way among the clusters of men standing engaged in conversation, they crossed slowly to the lower end of the square. "There's the entrance," said Mr. Ashcombe-Danvers, pointing at a high portal of iron grillework that stood at the top of a few steps in a niche. "That's the Crédit Foncier and that's where you'll take the packet. You'll just ask for Mr. Benzekri and go upstairs to his office. And here's the Café España."

Mr. Benzekri was there, sitting alone at one end of the terrace. He had a head like an egg—quite bald—and a face like a worried hawk. He did not smile when he shook hands with Dyar; the lines in his forehead merely deepened. "You will have a beer?" he inquired. His accent was thick.

"We'll sit for a moment. I'll not take anything," said Mr. Ashcombe-Danvers. They sat down. "None for me, either," Dyar said. He was not feeling too well, and he wanted a whiskey.

"Mr. Dyar will be bringing you a little present one of these days," said Mr. Ashcombe-Danvers. "He understands that he's to give it to no one but you."

Mr. Benzekri nodded gravely, staring down into his glass of beer. Then he lifted his head and looked sadly at Dyar for a moment. "Good," he said, as if there the matter ended.

"I know you are in a hurry," said Mr. Ashcombe-Danvers to Dyar. "So if you'd like to go on about your affairs go along. And many thanks. I shall be back in a few weeks."

Dyar said good evening. He had to fight his way across the Zoco Chico and up the narrow street; everyone was moving against him. "My new station in life: messenger-boy," he thought with a wry inner smile. He did not particularly like Mr. Ashcombe-Danvers: he had behaved exactly as though he had been paying him for his services. Not that he had expected payment, but still, the principal reason a man does not want to be paid for such things is to avoid being put into the position of an inferior. And he was in it anyway.

Wilcox was impatient when he got back to the office. "Took you long enough," he said.

"I know. He made me go on with him and meet some other guy from the bank."

"Benzekri."

"Yes."

"You didn't have to meet him. Ashcombe-Danvers is a fussy old buzzard. Be sure the window's shut, the door's locked and the lights are off. Stick around until six-thirty." Wilcox put on his coat. "Come by the Atlantide in the morning about nine and I'll give you the address where they're making the keys. If anyone calls tell 'em I had to go out and to call back tomorrow. See you."

VII

The door closed. Dyar sat looking around the room. He stood up and studied the maps a while, searched in the waiting room for magazines, and finding none, went and sat down again at the desk. A wild impatience kept him from feeling really alone in the room, an impatience merely to be out of it. "This isn't it," he told himself mechanically; he was not really sitting alone in the room because he did not believe he would ever work there. He was unable to visualize himself sitting day after day in this unventilated little box pretending to look after a non-existent business. In New York he had imagined something so different that now he had quite forgotten how he had thought it would be. He asked himself whether, knowing ahead of time what it would be like, he would have wanted to come, and he decided he would have, anyway, in spite of the profound apathy the idea of the job induced in him. Besides, the job was too chimerical and absurd to last. When it stopped, he would be free. He snorted, faintly. Free, with probably a hundred dollars between him and starvation. It was not a pleasant thought: it made him feel tense all over. He listened. Above the noise made by the automobile horns outside was the soft sound of rain falling.

He looked in the top drawer for a sheet of stationery, found it, and began to type a letter. The paper was headed EUROPE-AFRICA TOURIST SERVICE. "Dear Mother: Just a note. Arrived safely last night." He felt like adding: it seems like a month, but she would misunderstand, would think he was not happy. "The trip over was fine. We had fairly smooth weather all the way and I was not sick at all in spite of all you said. The Italians were not too bad." His parents had come to see him off, and had been upset to discover that he was to share a cabin with two Italians. "As you can see, I am writing this from the office. Jack Wilcox has gone for the day and I am in charge." He pondered a moment, wondering if the expression "in charge" looked silly, and decided to leave it. "I hope you're not going to worry about me, because there is no reason to. The climate is not tropical at all. In fact, it is quite chilly. The town seems to be clean, although not very modern." He ceased typing and gazed at a map of Africa in front of him, thinking of the crazy climb up through the dark alleys with the Arab, on the way to the bar. Then he saw Hadija's face, and frowned. He could not allow himself to think of her while he was writing his mother; there was a terrible disloyalty in that. But the memory, along with others more vivid, persisted. He leaned back in his chair and smoked a cigarette, wondering whether or not he would be able to find the bar by himself, in case he wanted to go back. Even if he were able, he felt it would be a bad idea. He had a date to meet Hadija in the Parque Espinel Sunday morning and it would be best to leave it at that; she might resent his trying to see her before then. He abandoned the attempt to write his letter, removed the paper from the machine, folded it and put it into his pocket to be continued the next day. The telephone rang. An Englishwoman was not interested in whether Mr. Wilcox was in or out, wanted a reservation made, single with bath, at the Hotel Balima in Rabat for the fourteenth through the seventeenth. She also wanted a round-trip plane passage, but she dared say that could be had later. The room however must be reserved immediately and she was counting on it. When she had hung up he wrote it all down and began studying a sheaf of papers marked *Hotels—French Zone*. At six-ten the telephone rang again. It was Wilcox. "Checking up on me," Dyar thought with resentment as he heard his voice. He wanted to know if anyone had stopped in. "No," said Dyar. "Well, that's all I wanted." He sounded relieved. Dyar told him about the Englishwoman. "I'll take care of that tomorrow. You might as well close up now. It's ten after six." He hesitated. "In fact, I wish you would. As soon as you can. Just be sure the catch is on the door."

"Right."

"Good night."

"What gives? What gives?" he murmured aloud as he slipped into his raincoat. He turned off the lights and stepped out into the corridor, shut the door and tried it vigorously.

At the pastry shop downstairs he stopped to inquire the way to the Faro Bar. When the proprietress saw him approaching the counter she greeted him pleasantly. "*Guten Abend,*" she said, and was a bit taken aback when he spoke to her in

English. She understood, however, and directed him in detail, adding that it was only one minute's walk.

He found it easily. It was a very small bar, crowded with people most of whom seemed to know each other; there was a certain amount of calling from table to table. Since there was not room at the bar itself, even for those who were already there, and all the tables were occupied, he sat down on a bench in the window and waited for a table to be vacated. Two Spanish girls, self-conscious in their Paris models, and wearing long earrings which removed all trace of chic from their clothes, came in and sat next to him in the bench. At the table in front of him was a French couple drinking Bacardis. To his left sat two somewhat severe-looking middle-aged English ladies, and on his right, a little further away, was a table full of American men who kept rising and going back to the bar to talk with those installed there. In a far corner a small, bespectacled woman was seated at a tiny piano, singing in German. No one was listening to her. He rather liked the place; it seemed to him definitely high-class without being stuffy, and he wondered why the Marquesa had said that Wilcox would refuse to be caught dead in it.

"*Y pensábamos irnos a Sevilla para la Semana Santa . . .*" "*Ay, qué hermoso!*"

"Jesus, Harry, you sure put that one down quick!"

"*Alors, tu ne te décides pas? Mais tu es marrante, toi!*"

"I expect she's most frightfully unhappy to be returning to London at this time of year."

The woman at the piano sang: "*Wunderschön muss deine Liebe sein.*"

"*Y por fin nos quedamos aquí.*" "*Ay, que lástima!*"

"*Ne t'en fais pas pour moi.*"

"Hey there, waiter! Make it the same, all the way around."

He waited, ordered a whiskey, drank it, and waited. The woman sang several old Dietrich songs. No one heard them. It was quarter past seven; he wished she would come. The Americans were getting drunk. Someone yelled: "Look out, you dumb bastard!" and a glass crashed on the tile floor. The English ladies got up, paid, and left. He decided they had timed their exit to show their disapproval. The two Spanish girls saw the empty table and gathering their things, made for it, but by the time they got there Dyar was already sitting in one of the chairs. "I'm waiting for a lady," he explained, without adding that he had arrived at the bar before they had, in any case. They did not bother to look at him, reserving all their energy for the registering of intense disgust. Presently another glass was broken. The woman in the corner played "God Bless America," doubtless with satirical intent. One of the Americans heard it and began to sing along with the music in a very loud voice. Dyar looked up: the Marquesa de Valverde was standing by the table in faded blue slacks and a chamois jacket.

"Don't get up," she commanded, as he hastily rose. "*Ça va?*" she called to someone at another table. He looked at her: she seemed less formidable than she had the preceding night. He thought it was because she was not made up, but he was mistaken. Her outdoor make-up was even more painstaking than the one she used for the evening. It merely did not show. Now she was all warmth and charm.

"I can't tell you how kind I think you are," she said when she had a whiskey-soda in her hand. "So few men have any true kindness left these days. I remember my father—what a magnificent man he was! I wish you could have known him—he used to say that the concept of nobility was fast disappearing from the face of the earth. I didn't know what he meant then, of course, but I do now, and, God, how heartily I agree with him! And nobility and kindness go together. You may not be noble—who knows?—but you certainly can't deny that it was damned kind of you to go out of your way to meet me when I had told you beforehand that I expected a favor of you."

He kept looking at her. She was too old, that was all. Every now and then, in the midst of the constantly changing series of expressions assumed by the volatile features, there was a dead instant when he saw the still, fixed disappointment of age beneath. It chilled him. He thought of the consistency of Hadija's flesh and skin, telling himself that to do so was scarcely just; the girl was not more than sixteen. Still, there were the facts. He considered the compensations of character and worldly refinement, but did they really count for much? He was inclined to think not, in such cases. "Nothing doing there," he thought. Or perhaps yes, if he had a lot of liquor in him. But why bother? He wondered why the idea had ever come to him, at all. There was no reason to think it had occurred to her, for that matter, save that he was sure it had.

The favor proved to be absurdly simple, he thought. He was merely to fill out a certain form in her name; he would find plenty of such forms in the office. This he was to send, along with a letter written on paper with the agency's letter-head, to the receptionist at the Mamounia Hotel in Marrakech, saying that a Mme. Werth's reservation for the twentieth of January had been canceled and that the room was to be reserved instead for the Marquise de Valverde. He was then to send her the duplicate of the filled-out form.

"Can you remember all that?" she said, leaning over the table toward him. "I think you're quite the most angelic man I know." He was making notes on a tiny pad. "During the season the Mamounia is just a little harder to get into than Heaven."

When he had it all written down he drained his glass and leaned over toward her, so that their foreheads were only a few inches apart. "I'll be delighted to do this for you—" he hesitated and felt himself growing red in the face. "I don't know what to call you. You know—the title. It's not *Mrs.* de Valverde. But I don't know—"

"If you're wise you'll call me Daisy."

He felt she was amusing herself at his expense. "Well, fine," he said. "What I was going to say is, I'm only too glad to do this for you. But wouldn't Jack be the man to do it? I'm just an ignoramus in the office so far."

She put her hand on his arm. "Oh, my God! Don't breathe a word of it to Jack, you silly boy! Why do you think I came to you in the first place? Oh, good God, no! He's not to know about it, naturally. I thought you understood that."

Dyar was disturbed. He said very slowly: "Oh, hell," emphasizing the second word. "I don't know about that."

"Jack's such an old maid about such things. It's fantastic, the way he runs that office. No, no. I'll give you the check for the deposit and you simply send it along with the letter and the form." She felt in her bag and brought forth a folded check. "It's all made out to the hotel. They'll understand that that's because the agency has already made its commission at the time the original reservation was made for Mme. Werth. Don't you see?"

What she was saying seemed logical, but none of it made any sense to him. If it had to be kept secret from Wilcox, then there was more to it than she admitted. She saw him running it over in his mind. "As I told you today," she said "you're not to feel under the least pressure about it. It's terribly unimportant, really, and I'm a beast even to have mentioned it to you. If someone else gets the reservation I can easily go to Agadir for my fortnight's rest. Please don't feel that I'm relying on your gallantry to do it for me."

Brusquely he cut her short. "I'll do it the first thing tomorrow morning and get it off my mind." He was suddenly extremely tired. He felt a million miles away. She went on talking; it was inevitable. But eventually he caught the waiter's eye and paid the bill.

"I have a car down the street," she said. "Where would you like to go?" He thanked her and said he was going to stop into the nearest restaurant for dinner. When she had finally gone, he walked blindly along the street for a while, swearing under his breath now and then. After his dinner he managed to find his way to the Hotel de la Playa. Even with the electricity on, the place was dim and shadowy. He went to bed and fell asleep listening to the waves breaking on the beach.

In the morning there was a watery sky; a tin-colored gleam lay on the harbor. Dyar had awakened at eight-thirty and was rushing through his toilet, hoping not to arrive too late at the Atlantide. Daisy de Valverde's request still puzzled him; it was illogical. It occurred to him that perhaps it was merely part of some complicated scheme of hers:—a scheme for encouraging an imagined personal interest in her. Or maybe she thought she was flattering his vanity in appealing to him instead of to Wilcox. But even so, the mechanics of the procedure troubled him. He resolved not to think about it, merely to get it done as quickly as possible.

Wilcox looked perturbed, took no notice of his lateness. "Have some coffee?" he asked, and indicated his breakfast tray. There was no extra cup. "I'll have it in a few minutes, thanks, across the street." Wilcox did not press him, but got back into bed and lit a cigarette.

"I have an idea the best thing right now would be for you to learn a little something," he said meditatively. "You're not of much use to me in the office as you are." Dyar stiffened, waited, not breathing. "I've got a lot of reading matter here that it would help a lot for you to know pretty much by heart. Take it on home and study it for a while—a week or so, let's say—and then come back and I'll give you a little test on it." He saw Dyar's face, read the question. "*With* salary. Don't worry—you're working. I told you that yesterday. As of yesterday." Dyar relaxed a little, but not enough. "The whole thing smells," he thought, and he wanted to say: "Can't anyone in this town tell the truth?" Instead, he decided to be a little bit devious himself for a change, thinking that otherwise he would not be able to get Daisy de Valverde's hotel reservation.

"I'd like to go over to the office for a few minutes and finish typing a letter I was writing last night. Shall I go and get those keys you're having made for me?"

He thought Wilcox looked uncomfortable. "To tell the truth, I don't think there'll be time," he replied. "I'm going over there now, and I'll be pretty busy there all day. For several days, in fact. A lot of unexpected work that's come up. It's another good reason for you to take this time off now and study up on the stuff. It fits in perfectly with my schedule. Those keys like as not wouldn't be ready anyway. They never have things when they promise them here."

Dyar took the pile of papers and booklets Wilcox handed him, started to go out, and standing in the open doorway said: "What day shall I get in touch with you?" (He hoped that somehow the words would have ironic overtones; he also hoped Wilcox would say: "Ring me up every day and I'll let you know how things are going.")

"You'll be staying on at the Playa?"

"As far as I know."

"I'll call you, then. That's the best way."

There was nothing to answer. "I see. So long," he said, and shut the door.

Because he did not trust Wilcox, he felt he had been wronged by him. Feeling that, he had a natural and overwhelming desire to confide his trouble to someone. Accordingly, when he had eaten his breakfast and read a three-day-old copy of the Paris *Herald*, he decided to telephone Daisy de Valverde, believing that the true reason he was calling her was to tell her it would not be possible for him to do the little favor for her, after all. The annoyance he now felt with Wilcox made him genuinely sorry not to be able to help her in that particular fashion. He rang the Villa Hesperides: she was having breakfast. He told her the situation, and stressed Wilcox's peculiar behavior. She was silent a moment.

"My dear, the man's a raving maniac!" she finally cried. "I *must* talk to you about this. When are you free?"

"Anytime, it looks like."

"Sunday afternoon?"

"What time?" he said, thinking of the picnic with Hadija.

"Oh, sixish."

"Sure." The picnic would be over long before that.

"Perfect. I'll take you to a little party I know you'll enjoy. It's at the Beidaouis'. They're Arabs, and I'm devoted to them."

"A party?" Dyar sounded unsure.

"Oh, not a party, really. A gathering of a few old friends at the Beidaoui Palace."

"Wouldn't I be a little in the way?"

"Nonsense. They love new faces. Stop being anti-social, Mr. Dyar. It just won't do in Tangier. My poor poached egg is getting cold."

It was agreed that she would call for him at his hotel at six on Sunday. Again he apologized for his powerlessness to help her.

"Couldn't care less," she said. "Good-bye, my dear. Until Sunday."

And as Sunday approached and the weather remained undecided, he was increasingly apprehensive. It would probably rain. If it did, they could not have a picnic and there would be no use in his going to the Parque Espinel to meet Hadija. Yet he knew he would go anyway, on the chance that she might be waiting for him. Even if the weather were clear, he must be prepared for her not being there. He began to train inwardly for that eventuality and to repeat to himself that it was of no importance to him whether she appeared or not. She was not a real person; it could not matter what a toy did. But there was no inner argument he could provide that would remove the tense expectancy he felt when he thought of Sunday morning. He spent the days learning the facts in the material Wilcox had given him, and when he got up on Sunday morning it was not raining.

VIII

Where the little side street ended they came out at the top of a high cliff. It was a windy day and the sky was full of fast-moving clouds. Occasionally the sun came through, a patch of its light spreading along the dark water of the strait below. Halfway down, where the gradient was less steep and brilliant green grass covered the slope, a flock of black goats wandered. The odor of iodine and seaweed in the air made Dyar hungry.

"This is the life," he said.

"What you sigh?" inquired Hadija.

"I like this."

"Oh, yes!" She smiled.

A long series of notches had been hewn in a diagonal line across the upper rock, forming a stairway. Slowly they descended the steps, he first, holding the picnic basket carefully, feeling a little dizzy, and wondering if she minded the steepness and height. "Probably not," he thought presently. "These people can take anything." The idea irritated him. As they got lower the sound of the waves grew louder.

On the way down, there was an unexpected grotto to their right, partially covered by a small growth of cane. A boy crouched there, the dark skin of his body showing through his rags. Hadija pointed.

"He got goats. The *guarda*."

"He's pretty young." The boy looked about six years old.

Hadija did not think so. "All like that," she said without interest.

Here and there in the strait, at varying distances from the shore, a seemingly static ship pointed eastward or westward. Dyar stopped a moment to count them: he could discern seven.

"All freighters," he said, gesturing, but it was half to himself that he spoke.

"What?" Hadija had stopped behind him; she was scanning the beach below, doubtless for natives who might recognize her. She did not want to be seen.

"Boats!" he cried; it seemed hopeless to elaborate. He moved his hand back and forth.

"America," said Hadija.

There were a few Moors fishing from the rocks. They paid no attention to the picnickers. It was high tide. Getting around certain of the points was not easy, since there was often very little space between cliffs and the waves. At one spot they both got wet. Dyar was a little annoyed, because there was no sun to dry them, but Hadija thought it an amusing diversion.

Rounding a sharp corner of rock they came suddenly on a small stretch of sand where a dozen or more boys were running about stark naked. They were of an age when one would have expected them to want to cover their nudity at the arrival of a girl, but that seemed to be the last thing in their minds. As Dyar and Hadija approached, they set up a joyous cry, some assuming indecent postures as they called out, the others entering into group activities of an unmistakably erotic nature. Dyar was horrified and incensed. "Like monkeys," he thought, and automatically looked down for a stone to fling into their midst. He felt his face growing hot. Hadija took no notice of the antics. He wondered just what indignities they were shouting at her, but he did not dare ask. It was possible that she considered this frantic exhibitionism typical of male behavior, but it hurt him to see a delicate creature like her being obliged to witness such things, and he would not believe that she could accept them with equanimity. For a second he wondered if by any chance she were so preoccupied with her thoughts that she had not noticed the boys. He stole a sidelong glance at her and was gratified at first to see that she was looking out across the strait, but then he caught the fixity of her stare.

"Son bitch," she muttered.

"The hell with them," he said, turning to smile at her. "Don't look at them."

They came to a long beach, completely deserted. Ahead of them rose a low mountain covered with cypress and eucalyptus;

large villas sat comfortably among the trees toward the summit. The wind blew harder here. Dyar took her hand, from time to time lifted it to his lips and kissed the fingers lightly.

They rounded another rocky point. The wet wind blew with added force. A shore of boulders stretched before them into the distance. Dyar turned to her.

"Hey, where is this cave?"

"You tired now?"

"Do you know where it is or do you just think you know?"

She laughed gaily and pointed ahead to the farthest cliff jutting into the sea.

"Go past there." And she indicated a left turn with her hand.

"Oh, for God's sake! That'll take us an hour. You realize that?"

"One hour. Maybe. Too much?" She looked up at him mockingly.

"*I* don't care," he said with bad grace. But he was annoyed.

They walked for several minutes without speaking, devoting all their attention to choosing the easiest way of getting past each boulder. When they climbed down to a tiny cove where there was a spring among the rocks, he decided to kiss her. It took a long time; her response was warm but calm. Finally he drew away and looked at her. She was smiling. It was impossible to tell what she felt.

"By God, I'll get a rise out of you yet!" he said, and he pulled her to him violently. She tried to answer, but the sound of her voice came out into his mouth and died there. When he released her, the same smile was there. It was a bit disconcerting. He dug in his pockets and pulled out a pack of cigarettes which she took from him, tapping the bottom so that one cigarette appeared. She held up the pack to his mouth and let him take the end of the cigarette between his lips.

"Service," he said. "But now I've got to light it myself. Let's sit down a minute."

"O.K." She chose the nearest rock and he sat beside her, his left arm around her waist. They looked out across the strait.

He was glad she had chosen the shore of the strait here for their picnic, rather than the beach along the bay, although actually there would have been more assurance of privacy on the beach than here, where one never knew what would appear around the next point or who might be hiding among the rocks. But he liked the idea of being able to see Europe across the way while knowing he was in Africa.

He pointed to the big sand-colored crest directly opposite. "Spain."

She nodded, drew her finger across her throat significantly. "Bad. They kill you."

"What do you know about it?" he said banteringly.

"I know." She shook her head up and down several times. "I got friends come here never go back. No fackin good place."

"Hadija! I don't like to hear that kind of talk from girls."

"Huh?"

"Don't say that again when I'm around, you hear?"

She looked innocent and crestfallen. "What's the matter you?"

He tossed his cigarette away and got up. "Skip it. Come on, or we'll never get there." He picked up the basket. Conversation was by no means easy with Hadija. There were many things he would have liked to tell her: that a group of American boys would never have behaved like the young Arabs they had passed a while ago. (But would she have believed him, her experience with Americans having been limited to the sailors who occasionally staggered into the Bar Lucifer, their faces smeared with lipstick and their hastily donned trousers held up by one button? He wondered.) He would have liked to tell her in his own way how lovely he thought she was, and why he thought so, and to make her understand how much more he wanted from her than she was used to having men want.

They came out onto a broad, flat shelf of land where on the side toward the cliffs there had at one time been a quarry. The surface was covered with dried thistle plants and a narrow path led straight across it. He still walked ahead of her, into the wind, feeling it push against him all the way from his face to his feet, like a great invisible, amorous body. The path, after it had traversed the field of thistles, rose and wound among the rocks. Suddenly they rounded a corner and looked out on the mountainous coastline to the west. Below them great blocks of stone rose sheer from the water.

"Be careful," said Dyar. "You go ahead here so I can keep an eye on you."

Ahead to the left he could see the cave, high in the vertical wall of rock. Birds flew in and out of smaller crevices above it; the roar of the waves covered all sound.

He was surprised to see that the cave was not dirty. Someone had made a fire in the center, and an empty tin can lay nearby. Toward the back of the cave in a corner there was a pallet of eucalyptus branches, probably arranged by some Berber fisherman months ago. Near the entrance there was one crumpled sheet of an old French newspaper. That was all. He set the basket down. Now, after all this, he felt shy.

"Well, here we are," he said with false heartiness, turning to Hadija.

She smiled as usual and carefully walked to the corner where the leaves covered the stone floor.

"Good here," she said, motioning to Dyar. She sat down, her legs akimbo, leaning against the wall of the cave. He had been about to light a cigarette to hide his confusion. Instead, he reached her in three strides, threw himself full length on the crackling leaves and twigs, and reached up to pull her face down to his. She cried out in surprise, lost her balance. Shrieking with laughter, she fell across him heavily. Even as she was still laughing she was deftly unbuttoning his shirt, unfastening the buckle of his belt. He rolled over and held her in a long embrace, expecting to feel her body hold itself rigid for a moment, and then slowly soften in the pleasure of surrender. But things did not happen like that. There was no surrender because there was no resistance. She accepted his embrace, returning his pressure with one arm while the other went on loosening his garments, attempting to slip them off. He pulled away, sat up.

"I'll fix that," he said, a little grimly, and straightway pulled off the remainder of his clothing.

"There. How's that?" His voice sounded unnatural; he was thinking: if she's going to act like a whore I'll damned well treat her like one.

"Now, you too," he said. And using both hands he began to pull her dress off over her head. She uttered a cry and struggled to a sitting position.

"No! No!"

He looked at her. It was disconcerting to be sitting there naked in front of this wild-eyed Arab girl pretending to defend her honor.

"What's the matter?" he demanded.

Her face softened; she leaned forward and kissed him on the lips.

"You lie down," she said smiling. "Leave dress alone."

As he obeyed, perplexed, she added: "You one bad boy, but I fix you up good." And indeed, in another minute she made it clear that she was by no means attempting to protect her virtue; she merely had no intention of removing her dress. At the same time she appeared to find it perfectly natural that Dyar should be unclothed; furthermore she took obvious pleasure in running her hands over his body, patting and pinching his flesh. Yet he had the conviction that notwithstanding her occasional murmurs of endearment, for her it was all a game. She was unattainable even in the profoundest intimacy. "Still, here it is. I've got her," he thought. "What more did I expect?" Outside the cave beneath the cliffs, the sea pounded against the rocks; the air, even up here, was full of fine salt mist.

"The Garden of Hesperides. The golden apple," he thought, running his tongue over her smooth, fine teeth. Soon it was as if he were floating slightly above the water, out there in the strait, the wind caressing his face. The sound of the waves receded further and further. They slept.

Dyar's first thought on waking was that twilight had come. He raised himself a bit and surveyed Hadija: she was sleeping quietly, one hand under her cheek and the other resting on his arm. Like this she looked incredibly young—not more than twelve. Overcome with a great tenderness, he reached out, smoothed her forehead, and let his hand run softly over her hair. She opened her eyes. The bland, sweet smile appeared; was it an expression of friendship or a meaningless grimace? Reaching around among the branches and leaves, he assembled his clothing, leapt up and went outside the cave to dress. The sky was more heavily covered, the sun had completely disappeared, the light was muffled. A gull balanced itself in the wind before him, turning its head from time to time to look at the rocks below. Hadija called to him. When he went in she had moved to the center of the cave where she sat taking the parcels of food out of the basket.

"No radio?" she said. "Little radio?"

"No."

"One American lady I know she got one little radio. Little. Take it in beach. Take it in room. Take it on café in Zoco Chico. You hear music every time."

"I hate 'em. I wouldn't like it here. I like the waves better. Hear 'em?" He pointed outside and listened a moment. She listened, too, and appeared to be considering the sound she heard. Presently she nodded her head and said: "Good music."

"Couldn't be better," he answered, pleased that she understood so well.

"That's the beautiful. Come from God." She pointed casually upward. He was a little embarrassed, as he always was when a serious reference to God was made. Now he was not sure whether she had really understood him or not.

"Well, let's eat." He bit into a sandwich.

"*Bismil 'lah*," said Hadija, doing likewise.

"What's that mean? Good appetite?"

"It mean we eat for God."

"Oh."

"*You* say."

She repeated it several times and made him say it until he had pronounced it to her satisfaction. Then they ate.

After lunch he went out and climbed among the rocks for a few minutes. It pleased him to see that there was not a soul in sight in either direction along the shore; he had half expected the gang of youths to follow them and perhaps continue their antics below on the rocks. But there was no one. When he returned to the cave he sat down outside it and called to Hadija.

"Come on out and sit here. It's too dark inside."

She obeyed. In a moment they were lying locked in each other's arms. When she complained of the cold rock beneath her, he got his jacket from inside the cave, put it under her, and lay down again.

"D'you know what I want?" he said, looking at the tiny black knob his head made against the sky in her eyes.

"You want?"

"Yes. D'you know what I want? I want to live with you. All the time. So we can be like this every night, every morning. You know? You understand?"

"Oh, yes."

"I'll get you a little room, a good room. You live in it and I'll come and see you every day. Would you like that?"

"I come every day?"

"No!" He moved one arm out from under her and gestured, pointing. "*I* pay for the room. *You* live in it. *I* come and see *you* every night. Yes?"

She smiled. "All right." It was as if he had said: "What do you say to starting back in about an hour?" As this occurred to him, he did say: "Want to start back pretty soon?"

"O.K."

His heart sank a little. He was right: it was the same voice, the same smile. He sighed. Still, she had agreed.

"But you promise?"

"What?"

"You'll live in the room?"

"Oh, yes." She took his head between her hands and kissed him on each cheek. "You come today?"

"Come where? The room?" He was about to begin again, to explain that he had not yet rented the room for her.

"No. No my room. Miss Goode. You come I take you. She very good friend. She got room Hotel Metropole."

"No. I don't want to go there. What would I want to do that for? You go if you want."

"She tell me you bring you drink whiskey."

Dyar laughed. "I don't think she said that, Hadija."

"Sure she say that."

"She's never heard of me and I've never heard of her. Who is she, anyway?"

"She got one little radio. I said you before. You know. Miss Goode. She got room Hotel Metropole. You come. I take you."

"You're crazy!"

Hadija tried to sit up. She looked very much upset. "I crazy? *You* crazy! You think I'm lie?" She pushed him in the chest with all her might, struggling to rise.

He was a little alarmed. To placate her he said: "I'll come! I'll come! Don't get so excited, for God's sake! What's the matter with you? If you want me to stop by and see her, I'll stop by and see her, I don't care."

"*I* no care. She tell me you bring you drink whiskey. You like whiskey?"

"Yes, yes. Sure. Now you lie back down there. I've got something to tell you."

"What?" she asked ingenuously, settling back, her great eyes wide.

"This." He kissed her. "I love you." His open lips touched hers all the way around as he said the words.

Hadija did not seem surprised to hear it. "Again?" she said, smiling.

"Huh?"

"You love me again now? This time quick one, yes? This time take few minutes. No take pants off. Then we go Hotel Metropole."

I X

On Saturday Hadija had told Eunice Goode that she would be out all the next day with a friend. After a certain amount of questioning Eunice had got an admission from her that it was the American gentleman and that they were going on a picnic. She did not think it wise to express any objections. For one thing Hadija had already made it clear that she did not by any means consider this sojourn at the Hotel Metropole a permanent arrangement, and that she would leave any time she felt like it. (What she hoped to be given eventually was an apartment of her own on the Boulevard.) And then, Eunice realized that in such a situation she was incapable herself of offering a quiet argument; she would straightway be precipitated into a violent scene. With her sometimes painfully acute objective sense she knew she would be the loser in any such quarrel: she was supremely conscious of being a comic figure.

She knew which of her attributes operated against her, and they were several. Her voice, while pleasant and easily modulated when used with low dynamics, became a thin screech as soon as it was called upon to be more than mildly expressive. Her torso bulged in rather the same fashion as that of a portly old gentleman, her arms and legs were gigantic, and her hypersensitive skin was always irritated and purplish, so that her face often looked as though she had just finished climbing to the summit of a mountain. She told herself she did not mind being a comic character; she accepted the fact and used it to insulate herself from the too-near, ever-threatening world. Dressed in a manner which accentuated the deficiencies of her body, wherever she went she was a thing rather than a person; she was determined to enjoy to the full the benefits of that exemption.

From the first she had been an object of interest in the streets of Tangier; now, appearing regularly in public with Hadija, whom a great number of the lower-class native inhabitants knew and the rest swiftly learned about, she became a full-fledged legendary figure in the Zoco Chico. The Arabs in the cafés there were delighted: it was a new variation on human behavior.

In these four days Hadija had forced her to lead a much more active life than was her wont, dragging her to all the bars and night clubs the girl had always wanted to see. Eunice had met several people she knew at these places. To them she had presented Hadija as Miss Kumari from Nicosia. She thought it unlikely that they would come across anyone who spoke modern Greek, and even if they did, she planned to explain that the dialect of Cyprus was altogether a different language.

Notwithstanding her outward coolness, Eunice was greatly disturbed when Hadija announced her projected outing. She lay back against the pillows watching the harbor as usual, saying to herself very firmly that action must be taken. It could not be against Hadija, so it must be against the American. (Since she loathed travel, and Mme. Papaconstante had so far given no sign that she was going to try and get Hadija back, she had renounced the idea of spiriting the girl away to Europe.) Going on from there, it was clear that one

had to know what one was fighting. She thought of
dwelling on the idea that the man had no money, but then
she decided that there was no line of reasoning which would
carry any weight with Hadija, and she had best keep still.
And for all she knew, perhaps he did have money, although
she had reconsidered the overheard conversation at the Bar
Lucifer and decided that the man's reluctance to part with
his money had not been due to viciousness. And he had had
to borrow the extra sum from his friend. It seemed reasonable to think that he was not too well off. She hoped that
was the case; it could be strongly in her favor. Poverty in
other people generally was.

"I know your friend," she said casually.

"You know?" Hadija was surprised.

"Oh, yes. I've met him."

"Where?" asked Hadija skeptically.

"Oh, various places. At the Taylors' on the Marshan, at the
Sphinx Club once, and I think at the Estradas' house on the
mountain. He's very nice."

Hadija was noncommittal. "O.K."

"If you want, you can ask him back here when you've
finished your picnic."

"He no like come here."

"Oh, I don't know," said Eunice meditatively. "He might
easily. I imagine he'd like a drink. Americans do, you know. I
thought you might like to invite him, that's all."

Hadija thought about it. The idea appealed to her because
she considered the Hotel Metropole magnificent and luxurious, and she was tempted to let him see in what style she was
living. She had set out for the Parque Espinel with that
intention, but on the walk back with him it occurred to her
(for the first time) that since the American seemed to be fully
as possessive about her as Eunice Goode, he might not relish
the discovery that he was sharing her with someone else. So
she hastened to explain that Miss Goode was ill most of the
time and that she often visited her. The possessiveness he
manifested toward her had already prompted her to make the
attempt to get him to buy her a certain wrist watch she
greatly admired. Eunice had definitely refused to get it for her
because it was a man's watch—an oversize gold chronograph

with calendar and phases of the moon thrown in. Eunice was eminently careful to see that the girl looked respectable and properly feminine. Hadija mentioned the watch twice on the way to the Metropole; the American merely smiled and said: "We'll see. Keep your shirt on, will you?" She did not completely understand, but at least he had not said no.

When Dyar came into the room Eunice Goode looked at him and said to herself that even as a girl she would not have found him attractive. She had liked imposing men, such as her father had been. This one was not at all distinguished in appearance. He did not look like an actor or a statesman or an artist, nor yet like a workman, a businessman or an athlete. For some reason she thought he looked rather like a wire-haired terrier—alert, eager, suggestible. The sort of male, she reflected with a stab of anger, who can lead girls around by the nose, without even being domineering, the sort whose maleness is unnoticeable and yet so thick it becomes cloying as honey, the sort that makes no effort and is thereby doubly dangerous. Except that being accustomed to an ambiance of feminine adulation makes them as vulnerable, as easily crushed, as spoiled children are. You let them think that you too are taken in by their charm, you entice them further and further out on that rotten limb. Then you jerk out the support and let them fall.

Yet in her mad inner scramble to be exceptionally gracious, Eunice got off to rather a poor start. She had been away from most people for so long that she forgot there are many who actually listen to the words spoken, and for whom even mere polite conversation is a means of conveying specific ideas. She had planned the opening sentences with the purpose of keeping Hadija from discovering that this was her first meeting with the American gentleman. Wearing an old yellow satin négligé trimmed with mink (which Hadija had never seen before and which she immediately determined to have for herself), and being well covered by the bedclothes, she looked like any other stout lady sitting up in bed.

"This is a belated but welcome meeting!" she cried.

"How do you do, Miss Goode." Dyar stood in the doorway. Hadija pulled him gently forward and shut the door. He stepped to the bed and took the proffered hand.

"I knew your mother in Taormina," said Eunice. "She was a delightful woman. Hadija, would you call downstairs and ask for a large bowl of ice and half a dozen bottles of Perrier? The whiskey's in the bathroom on the shelf. There are cigarettes in that big box there. Draw that chair a little nearer."

Dyar looked puzzled. "Where?"

"What?" she said pleasantly.

"Where did you say you knew my mother?" It had not yet occurred to him that Eunice Goode did not know his name.

"In Taormina," she said, looking at him blandly. "Or was it Juan-les-Pins?"

"It couldn't have been," Dyar said, sitting down. "My mother's never been in Europe at all."

"Really?" She meant it to sound casual, but it sounded acid. To her, such stubborn insistence on exactitude was sheer boorishness. But there was no time for showing him she disapproved of his behavior, even if she had wanted to. Hadija was telephoning. Quickly she said: "Wasn't your mother Mrs. Hambleton Mills? I thought that was what Hadija said."

"What?" cried Dyar, making a face indicating that he was all at sea. "Somebody's *all* mixed up. My name is Dyar. D, Y, A, R. It doesn't sound much like Mills to me." Then he laughed good-naturedly, and she joined in, just enough, she thought, to show that she bore him no ill-will for his rudeness.

"Well, now we have that settled," she said. She had his name; Hadija believed they had known each other before. She pressed on, to get as many essentials as possible while Hadija was still chattering in Spanish to the barman.

"Passing through on a winter holiday, or are you staying a while?"

"Holiday? Nothing like it. I'm staying a while. I'm working here."

She had expected that. "Oh, really? Where?"

He told her. "I can't quite place it," she said, shutting her eyes as if she were trying.

Hadija put the receiver on the hook and brought a bottle of whiskey from the bathroom. Suddenly Dyar became conscious of the fact that preparations were being made for the serving of drinks. He half rose from his chair, and sat down again on its edge.

"Look, I can't stay. I didn't realize—I'm sorry—"

"Can't stay?" echoed Eunice, faintly dismayed.

"I have an appointment at my hotel. I've got to get back. Hadija told me you were sick so I just thought I'd stop by. She said you wanted me to come."

"So I did. But I don't call this a visit."

The waiter had come in, set the tray on the table, and gone out.

"I know." He was not sure which would be less impolite, —to accept one drink and then go, or to leave without taking anything.

"One quick drink," Eunice urged him. He accepted it.

Hadija had ordered a Coca-Cola. She was rather pleased to see her two protectors in the same room talking together. She wondered if it were dangerous. After all, Eunice knew about the man and did not seem to mind. It was possible that he would not care too much if he knew about Eunice. But she would certainly prefer him not to know. She became conscious of their words.

"Where you go?" she interrupted.

"Home," he said, without looking at her.

"Where you live?"

Eunice smiled to herself: Hadija was doing her work for her. But then she clicked her tongue with annoyance. The girl had bungled it; he had been put off.

"Too far," he had answered drily.

"Why you go there?" Hadija pursued.

Now he turned to face her. "Curiosity killed a cat," he said with mock sternness. "I'm going to a party, Nosey." He laughed. To Eunice he said: "What a girl, what a girl! But she's nice in spite of it."

"I don't know about that," Eunice replied, as if giving the matter thought. "I don't think so, at all, as a matter of fact. I'll talk to you about it some time. Did you say a party?" She remembered that the Beidaouis were at home on Sunday evenings. "Not at the Beidaoui Palace?" she hazarded.

He looked surprised. "That's right!" he exclaimed. "Do you know them?"

She had never met any of the Beidaoui brothers; however, they had been pointed out to her on various occasions. "I know them very well," she said. "They're *the* people of Tangier." She had heard that their father had held a high official position of some sort. "The old Beidaoui who died a few years ago was the Grand Vizier to Sultan Moulay Hafid. It was he who entertained the Kaiser when he came here in 1906."

"Is that right?" said Dyar, making his voice polite.

Presently he stood up and said good-bye. He hoped she would be better.

"Oh, it's a chronic condition," she said cheerfully. "It comes and goes. I never think about it. But as my grandmother in Pittsburgh used to say: 'It'll be a lot worse before it's any better.'"

He was a little surprised to hear that she was American: he had not thought of her as having any nationality at all. And now he was worried about how to make another rendezvous with Hadija in the somewhat forbidding presence of Miss Goode. However, it had to be done if he was to see her again; he would never be able to get to the Bar Lucifer, where he supposed she was still to be found.

"How about another picnic next Sunday?" he said to her. He might be free all during the week, and then again Wilcox might telephone him tomorrow. Sunday was the only safe day.

"Sure," said Hadija.

"Same place? Same time?"

"O.K."

As soon as he had gone, Eunice sat up straight in the bed. "Hand me the telephone book," she said.

"What you sigh?"

"The telephone book!"

She skimmed through it, found the name. *Jouvenon, Pierre, ing.* Ingénieur, engineer. It sounded much more impressive in French, being connected with such words as genius, ingenuity. Engineer always made her think of a man in overalls standing in a locomotive. She gave the number and said peremptorily to Hadija: "Get dressed quickly. Put on the new black frock we bought yesterday. I'll fix your hair when I'm dressed." She turned to the telephone. "*Allô, allô? Qui est à l'appareil?*" It was a Spanish maid: Eunice shrugged with impatience. "*Quisiera hablar con la Señora Jouvenon. Sí! La señora!*" While she waited she put her hand over the mouthpiece and turned again to Hadija. "Remember. Not a word of anything but English." Hadija had gone into the bathroom and was splashing water in the basin.

"I know," she called. "No spickin Arab. No spickin Espanish. I know." They both took it as a matter of course that if Eunice went out, she went with her. At the back of her mind Eunice vaguely imagined that she was training the girl for Paris, where eventually she would take her to live, so that their successful ménage would excite the envy of all her friends.

"*Ah, chère Madame Jouvenon!*" she cried, and went on to tell the person at the other end of the wire that she hoped she was unoccupied for the next few hours, as she had something she wanted to discuss with her. Madame Jouvenon did not seem at all surprised by the announcement or by the fact that the proposed discussion would take several hours. "*Vous êtes tr-rès aimable,*" she said, purring the "r" as no Frenchwoman would have done. It was agreed that they should meet in a half hour at La Sevillana, the small tearoom at the top of the Siaghines.

Eunice hung up, got out of bed, and hurriedly put on an old, loosely-draped tea-gown. Then she turned her attention to clothing Hadija, applying her make-up for her, and arranging her hair. She was like a mother preparing her only daughter for her first dance. And indeed, as they walked carefully side by side through the narrow alleys which were a short cut to La Sevillana, sometimes briefly holding hands when the way was wide enough, they looked very much like doting mother and fond daughter, and were taken for such by the Jewish women watching the close of day from their doorways and balconies.

Madame Jouvenon was already seated in La Sevillana eating a meringue. She was a bright-eyed little woman whose hair, having gone prematurely white, she had unwisely allowed to be dyed a bright silvery blue. To complete the monochromatic color scheme she had let Mlle. Sylvie dye her brows and lashes a much darker and more intense shade of blue. The final effect was not without impact.

Evidently Madame Jouvenon had only just arrived in the tearoom, as heads were still discreetly turning to get a better view of her. Characteristically, Hadija immediately decided that this lady was suffering from some strange disease, and she shook her hand with some squeamishness.

"We have very little time," Eunice began in French, hoping that Madame Jouvenon would not order more pastry. "The little one here doesn't speak French. Only Greek and some English. No pastry. Two coffees. Do you know the Beidaouis?"

Madame Jouvenon did not. Eunice was only momentarily chagrined.

"It doesn't matter," she continued. "I know them intimately, and you're my guest. I want to take you there now because there's someone I think you should meet. It's possible that he could be very useful to you."

Madame Jouvenon put down her fork. As Eunice continued talking, now in lower tones, the little woman's shining eyes became fixed and intense. Her entire expression altered; her face grew clever and alert. Presently, without finishing her meringue, she reached for her handbag in a businesslike manner and laid some coins on the table. "*Tr-rès bien,*" she said tersely. "*On va par-rtir.*"

2

Fresh Meat and Roses

x

THE Beidaouis' Sunday evenings were unique in that any member of one of the various European colonies could attend without thereby losing face, probably because the fact that the hosts were Moslems automatically created among the guests a feeling of solidarity which they welcomed without being conscious of its origin. The wife of the French minister could chat with the lowest American lady tourist and no one would see anything extraordinary about it. This certainly did not mean that if the tourist caught sight of Mme. D'Arcourt the next day and had the effrontery to recognize her, she in turn would be recognized. Still, it was pleasant and democratic while it lasted, which was generally until about nine. Very few Moslems were invited, but there were always three or four men of importance in the Arab world: perhaps the leader of the Nationalist Party in the Spanish Zone, or the editor of the Arabic daily in Casablanca, or a wealthy manufacturer from Algier, or the advisor to the Jalifa of Tetuan. In reality the gatherings were held in order to entertain these few Moslem guests, to whom the unaccountable behavior of Europeans never ceased to be a fascinating spectacle. Most of the Europeans, of course, thought the Moslem gentlemen were invited to add local color, and praised the Beidaoui brothers for their cleverness in knowing so well just what sort of Arab could mix properly with foreigners. These same people, who prided themselves upon the degree of intimacy to which they had managed to attain in their relationships with the Beidaoui, were nevertheless quite unaware that the two brothers were married, and led intense family lives with their women and children in a part of the house where no European had ever entered. The Beidaoui would certainly not have hidden the fact had they been asked, but no one had ever thought to question them about such things. It was taken for granted that they were two debonair bachelors who loved to surround themselves with Europeans.

That morning, on one of his frequent walks along the waterfront, where he was wont to go when he had a hangover or his home life had grown too oppressive for his taste, Thami had met with an extraordinary piece of good luck. He had wandered out onto the breakwater of the inner port, where the fishermen came to unload, and was watching them shake out the black nets, stiff with salt. A small, old-fashioned motor-boat drew alongside the dock. The man in it, whom Thami recognized vaguely, threw a rope to a boy standing nearby. As the boatsman, who wore a turban marking him as a member of the Jilala cult, climbed up the steps to the pier, he greeted Thami briefly. Thami replied, asking if he had been fishing. The man looked at him a little more closely, as if to see exactly who it was he had spoken to so carelessly. Then he smiled sadly, and said that he never had used his little boat for fishing, and that he hoped the poor old craft would be spared such a fate until the day it fell to pieces. Thami laughed; he understood perfectly that the man meant it was a fast enough boat to be used for smuggling. He moved along the dock and looked down into the motor-boat. It must have been forty years old; the seats ran lengthwise and were covered with decaying canvas cushions. There was an ancient two-cylinder Fay and Bowen engine in the center. The man noticed his scrutiny, and inquired if he were interested in buying the boat. "No," said Thami contemptuously, but he continued to look. The other remarked that he hated to sell it but had to, because his father in Azemmour was ill, and he was going back there to live. Thami listened with an outward show of patience, waiting for a figure to be mentioned. He had no intention of betraying his interest by suggesting one himself. Eventually, as he tossed his cigarette into the water and made as if to go, he heard the figure: ten thousand pesetas. "I don't think you'll get more than five," he replied, turning to move off. "Five!" cried the man indignantly. "Look at it," said Thami, pointing down at it. "Who's going to give more?" He started to walk slowly away, kicking pieces of broken concrete into the water as he went. The man called after him. "Eight thousand!" He turned around, smiling, and explained that he

was not interested himself, but that if the Jilali really wanted
to sell the boat, he should put a sensible price on it, one that
Thami could quote to his friends in case one of them might
know a possible buyer. They argued a while, and Thami finally
went away with six thousand as an asking price. He felt rather
pleased with himself, because although it was by no means the
beautiful speed boat he coveted, it was at least a tangible and
immediate possibility whose realization would not involve
either an import license or any very serious tampering with
his heritage. He had thought of asking the American, whom
he liked, and who he felt had a certain sympathy for him, to
purchase the boat in his name. It would have been a way
around the license. But he thought he did not know him well
enough, and beyond a doubt it would have been a foolish
move: he would have had to rely solely on the American's
honesty for proof of ownership. As to the price, it was negligible, even at six thousand, and he was positive he could get
it down to five. There was even a faint possibility, although he
doubted it, really, that he could get Abdelmalek to lend him
the sum. In any case, among his bits of property there was a
two-room house without lights or water at the bottom of a
ravine behind the Marshan, which ought to bring just about
five thousand pesetas in a quick sale.

The end of the afternoon was splendid: the clouds had
been blown away by a sudden wind from the Atlantic. The air
smelled clean, the sky had become intense and luminous. As
Dyar waited in front of the door of his hotel, a long procession of Berbers on donkeys passed along the avenue on their
way from the mountains to the market. The men's faces were
brown and weather-burned, the women were surprisingly
light of skin, with salient, round red cheeks. Dispassionately
he watched them jog past, not realizing how slowly they
moved until he became aware of the large American convertible at the end of the line, whose horn was being blown frantically by the impatient driver. "What's the hurry?" he
thought. The little waves on the beach were coming in
quietly, the hills were changing color slowly with the dying of
the light behind the city, a few Arabs strolled deliberately
along the walk under the wind-stirred branches of the palms.
It was a pleasant hour whose natural rhythm was that of

leisure; the insistent blowing of the trumpet-like horn made no sense in that ensemble. Nor did the Berbers on their donkeys give any sign of hearing it. They passed peacefully along, the little beasts taking their measured steps and nodding their heads. When the last one had come opposite Dyar, the car swung toward the curb and stopped. It was the Marquesa de Valverde. "Mr. Dyar!" she called. As he shook her hand she said: "I'd have been here earlier, darling; but I've been bringing up the rear of this parade for the past ten minutes. Don't ever buy a car here. It's the most nerve-racking spot in this world to drive in. God!"

"I'll bet," he said; he went around to the other side and got in beside her.

They drove up through the modern town at a great rate, past new apartment houses of glaring white concrete, past empty lots crammed to bursting with huts built of decayed signboards, packing cases, reed latticework and old blankets, past new cinema palaces and night clubs whose sickly fluorescent signs already glowed with light that was at once too bright and too dim. They skirted the new market, which smelled tonight of fresh meat and roses. To the south stretched the sandy waste land and the green scrub of the foothills. The cypresses along the road were bent by years of wind. "This Sunday traffic is dreadful. Ghastly," said Daisy, looking straight ahead. Dyar laughed shortly; he was thinking of the miles of strangled parkways outside New York. "You don't know what traffic is," he said. But his mind was not on what was being said, nor yet on the gardens and walls of the villas going past. Although he was not given to analyzing his states of mind, since he never had been conscious of possessing any sort of apparatus with which to do so, recently he had felt, like a faint tickling in an inaccessible region of his being, an undefined need to let his mind dwell on himself. There were no formulated thoughts, he did not even daydream, nor did he push matters so far as to ask himself questions like: "What am I doing here?" or "What do I want?" At the same time he was vaguely aware of having arrived at the edge of a new period in his existence, an unexplored territory of himself through which he was going to have to pass. But his perception of the thing was limited to knowing that lately he had been wont to sit quietly alone in his room saying to himself that he was here. The fact kept repeating itself to him: "Here I am." There was nothing to be deduced from it; the saying of it seemed to be connected with a feeling almost of anaesthesia somewhere within him. He was not moved by the phenomenon; even to himself he felt supremely anonymous, and it is difficult to care very much what is happening inside a person one does not know. At the same time, that which went on outside was remote and had no relationship to him; it might almost as well not have been going on at all. Yet he was not indifferent—indifference is a matter of the emotions, whereas this numbness affected a deeper part of him.

They turned into a somewhat narrower, curving street. On the left was a windowless white wall at least twenty feet high which went on ahead, flush with the street, as far as the eye could follow. "That's it," said Daisy, indicating the wall. "The palace?" said Dyar, a little disappointed. "The Beidaoui Palace," she answered, aware of the crestfallen note in his voice. "It's a strange old place," she added, deciding to let him have the further surprise of discovering the decayed sumptuousness of the interior for himself. "It sure looks it," he said with feeling. "How do you get in?"

"The gate's a bit further up," replied Daisy, and without transition she looked directly at him as she said: "You've missed out on a good many things, haven't you?" His first thought was that she was pitying him for his lack of social advantages; his pride was hurt. "I don't think so," he said quickly. Then with a certain heat he demanded: "What sort of things? What do you mean?"

She brought the car to a stop at the curb behind a string of others already parked there. As she took out the keys and put them into her purse she said: "Things like friendship and love. I've lived in America a good deal. My mother was from Boston, you know, so I'm part American. I know what it's like. Oh, God, only too well!"

They got out. "I guess there's as much friendship there as anywhere else," he said. He was annoyed, and he hoped his voice did not show it. "*Or* love."

"Love!" she cried derisively.

An elderly Arab swung the grilled gate. They went into a dark room where several other bearded men were stretched out on mats in a niche that ran the length of the wall. These greeted Daisy solemnly, without moving. The old Arab opened a door, and they stepped out into a vast dim garden in which the only things Dyar could identify with certainty were the very black, tall cypresses, their points sharp against the evening sky, and the very white marble fountains in which water splashed with an uneven sound. They went along the gravel walk in silence between the sweet and acid floral smells. There were thin strains of music ahead. "I expect they're dancing to the gramophone," said Daisy. "This way." She led him up a walk toward the right, to a wide flight of marble stairs. "Evenings they entertain in the European wing. And in European style. Except that they themselves don't touch liquor, of course." Above the music of the tango came the chatter of voices. As they arrived at the top of the stairway a grave-faced man in a white silk gown stepped forward to welcome them.

"Dear Abdelmalek!" Daisy cried delightedly, seizing his two hands. "*What* a lovely party! This is Mr. Dyar of New York." He shook Dyar's hand warmly. "It is very kind of the Marquesa to bring you to my home," he said. Daisy was already greeting other friends; M. Beidaoui, still grasping Dyar's hand, led him to a nearby corner where he presented him to his brother Hassan, a tall chocolate-colored gentleman also clothed in white robes. They spoke a minute about America, and Dyar was handed a whiskey-soda by a servant. As his hosts turned away to give their attention to a new arrival, he began to look about him. The room was large, comfortable and dark, being lighted only by candles that rested in massive candelabra placed here and there on the floor. It was irregularly shaped, and the music and dancing were going on in a part hidden from his vision. Along the walls nearby were wide, low divans occupied exclusively by women, all of whom looked over forty, he noted, and certain of whom were surely at least seventy. Apart from the Beidaoui brothers there were only two other Arabs in view. One was talking to Daisy by an open window and the other was joking with a fat Frenchman in a corner. In spite of the Beidaouis,

whom he rather liked, he felt smothered and out of place, and
he wished he had not come.

As Dyar was about to move off and see who was taking part
in the dancing, Hassan tapped him on the arm. "This is
Madame Werth," he said. "You speak French?" The dark-
eyed woman in black to whom he was being presented
smiled. "No," said Dyar, confused. "It does not matter," she
said. "I speak a little English." "You speak very well," said
Dyar, offering her a cigarette. He had the feeling that someone had spoken to him about her, but he could not remember who, or what it was that had been said. They conversed a
while, standing there with their drinks, in the same spot
where they had been introduced, and the idea persisted that
he knew something about her which he was unable to call to
mind. He had no desire to be stuck with her all evening, but
for the moment he saw no way out. And she had just told him
that she was in mourning for her husband; she looked rather
forlorn, and he felt sorry for her. Suddenly he saw Eunice
Goode's flushed face appear in the doorway. "How do you
do?" she said to Hassan Beidaoui. Behind her was Hadija,
looking very smart indeed. "How do you do?" said Hadija,
with the identical inflection of Eunice Goode. A third woman
entered with them, small and grim-faced, who scarcely
acknowledged the greeting extended to her, but immediately
began to inspect the guests with care, one by one, as if taking
a rapid inventory of the qualities and importance of each.
There was not enough light for the color of her hair to be
noticeable, so, since no one seemed to know her, no one paid
her any attention for the moment. Dyar was too much astonished at seeing Hadija to continue his conversation; he stood
staring at her. Eunice Goode held her by the hand and was
talking very fast to Hassan.

"You'll be interested to know that one of my dearest friends
was Crown Prince Rupprecht. We were often at Karlsbad together. I believe he knew your father." As the rush of words
went on, Hassan's face showed increasing lack of comprehension; he moved backward a step after each few sentences, saying: "Yes, yes," but she followed along, pulling Hadija with
her, until she had backed him against the wall and Dyar could
no longer hear what she was saying. Somewhat embarrassed,

he again became conscious of Madame Werth's presence beside him.

"—and I hope you will come to make a visit to me when I am returning from Marrakech," she was saying.

"Thank you, I'd like very much to." It was then that he recalled where he had heard her name. The canceled reservation at the hotel there which he had been going to give to Daisy had originally been Madame Werth's.

"Do you know Marrakech?" she asked him. He said he did not. "Ah, you must go. In the winter it is beautiful. You must have a room at the Mamounia, but the room must have a view on the mountains, the snow, you know, and a terrace above the garden. I would love to go tomorrow, but the Mamounia is always full now and my reservation is not before the twenty of the month."

Dyar looked at her very hard. She noticed the difference in his expression, and was slightly startled.

"You're going to the Hotel Mamounia in Marrakech on the twentieth?" he said. Then, seeing the suggestion of bewilderment on her face he looked down at her drink. "Yours is nearly finished," he remarked. "Let me get you another." She was pleased; he excused himself and went across the room with a glass in each hand.

It all made perfectly good sense. Now at last he understood Daisy's request of him and the secrecy with which she had surrounded it. Madame Werth would simply have been told that there had been a most regrettable misunderstanding, and Wilcox's office would have been blamed, but the Marquise de Valverde would already have been installed in the room and there would have been no dislodging her. As he realized how close he had come to doing her the favor he felt a rush of fury against her. "The bitch!" he said between his teeth. The little revelation was unpleasant, and it somehow extended itself to the whole room and everyone in it.

He saw Daisy out of the corner of his eye as he passed the divan where she sat; she was talking to a pale young man with spectacles and a girl with a wild head of red hair. As he was on his way back she caught sight of him and called out: "Mr. Dyar! When you've made your delivery I want you to come over here." He held the glasses up higher and grinned. "Just a second," he said. He was wondering if Madame Werth would be capable of the same sort of throat-slitting behavior as Daisy, and decided against the likelihood of it. She looked too helpless, which was doubtless precisely why Daisy had singled her out as a likely prospective victim.

Back, standing again beside Madame Werth, he said as she sipped her new drink: "Do you know the Marquesa de Valverde?"

Madame Werth seemed enthusiastic. "Ah, what a delightful woman! Such vivacity! And very kind. I have seen her pick out from the street young dogs, poor thin ones with bones, and take them to her home and care for them. The entire world is her charity."

Dyar laughed abruptly; it must have sounded derisive, for Madame Werth said accusingly: "You think kindness does not matter?"

"Sure it matters. It's very important." At the moment he felt expansive and a little reckless; it would be pleasurable to sit beside Daisy and worry her. She could not see whom he was talking to from where she sat, and he wanted to watch her reaction when he told her. Presently a Swiss gentleman joined them and began speaking with Madame Werth in French. Dyar slipped away, finishing his drink quickly and getting another before he went over to the divan where Daisy was.

"Two compatriots of yours," she said, moving over so he could squeeze in beside her. "Mr. Dyar. Mrs. Holland, Mr. Richard Holland." The two acknowledged the introduction briefly, with what seemed more diffidence than coldness.

"We were talking about New York," said Daisy. "Mr. and Mrs. Holland are from New York, and they say they feel quite as much at home here as they do there. I told them that was scarcely surprising, since Tangier is more New York than New York. Don't you agree?"

Dyar looked at her closely; then he looked at Mrs. Holland, who met his gaze for a startled instant and began to inspect her shoes. Mr. Holland was staring at him with great seriousness, like a doctor about to arrive at a diagnosis, he thought. "I don't think I see what you mean," said Dyar. "Tangier like New York? How come?"

"In spirit," said Mr. Holland with impatience. "Not in appearance, naturally. Are you from New York? I thought Madame de Valverde said you were." Dyar nodded. "Then you must see how alike the two places are. The life revolves wholly about the making of money. Practically everyone is dishonest. In New York you have Wall Street, here you have the Bourse. Not like the bourses in other places, but the soul of the city, its *raison d'être*. In New York you have the slick financiers, here the money changers. In New York you have your racketeers. Here you have your smugglers. And you have every nationality and no civic pride. And each man's waiting to suck the blood of the next. It's not really such a far-fetched comparison, is it?"

"I don't know," said Dyar. At first he had thought he agreed, but then the substance of Holland's argument had seemed to slip away from him. He took a long swallow of whiskey. The phonograph was playing "*Mamá Inez.*" "I guess there are plenty of untrustworthy people here, all right," he said.

"Untrustworthy!" cried Mr. Holland. "The place is a model of corruption!"

"But darling," Daisy interrupted. "Tangier's a one-horse town that happens to have its own government. And you know damned well that all government lives on corruption. I don't care what sort—socialist, totalitarian, democratic—it's all the same. Naturally in a little place like this you come in contact with the government constantly. God knows, it's inevitable. And so you're always conscious of the corruption. It's that simple."

Dyar turned to her. "I was just talking with Madame Werth over there." Daisy looked at him calmly for a moment. It was impossible to tell what she was thinking. Then she laughed. "I being the sort of person I am, and you being the sort of person you are, I think we can skip over *that*. Tell me, Mrs. Holland, have you read *The Thousand and One Nights*?"

"The Mardrus translation," said Mrs. Holland without looking up.

"*All* of it?"

"Well, not quite. But most."

"And do you adore it?"

"Well, I admire it terribly. But Dick's the one who loves it. It's a little direct for me, but then I suppose the culture had no nuances either."

Dyar had finished his drink and was again thinking of getting in to where the dancing was going on. He sat still, hoping the conversation might somehow present him with a possibility of withdrawing gracefully. Daisy was addressing Mr. Holland. "Have you ever noticed how completely illogical the end of each one of those thousand and one nights actually is? I'm curious to know."

"Illogical?" said Mr. Holland. "I don't think so."

"Oh, my dear! Really! Doesn't it say, at the end of each night: 'And Schahrazade, perceiving the dawn, discreetly became silent'?"

"Yes."

"And then doesn't it say: 'And the King and Schahrazade went to bed and remained locked in one another's arms until morning'?"

"Yes."

"Isn't that rather a short time? Especially for Arabs?"

Mrs. Holland directed an oblique upward glance at Daisy, and returned to the contemplation of her feet.

"I think you misunderstand the time-sequence," said Mr. Holland, sitting up straight with a sudden spasmodic movement, as if he were getting prepared for a discussion. Dyar got quickly to his feet. He had decided he did not like Mr. Holland, who he imagined found people agreeable to the extent that they were interested in hearing him expound his theories. Also he was a little disappointed to find that Daisy had met his challenge with such bland complacency. "She didn't bat an eyelash," he thought. It had been no fun at all to confront her with the accusation. Or perhaps she had not even recognized his remark as such. The idea occurred to him as he reached the part of the room where the phonograph was, but he rejected it. Her reply could have meant only that she admitted she had been found out, and did not care. She was even more brazen than he had imagined. For no particular reason, knowing this depressed him, put him back into the gray mood of despair he had felt the night of his arrival on the boat, enveloped him in the old uneasiness.

A few couples were moving discreetly about the small floor-space, doing more talking than dancing. As Dyar stood watching the fat Frenchman swaying back and forth on his feet, trying to lead an elderly English woman in a turban who had taken a little too much to drink, Abdelmalek Beidaoui came up to him bringing with him a tall Portuguese girl, cadaver-thin and with a cast in one eye. It was obvious that she wanted to dance, and she accepted with eagerness. Although she kept her hips against his as they danced, she leant sharply backward from the waist and peered at him fixedly while she told him bits of gossip about the people in the other part of the room. In speaking she kept her lips drawn back so that her gums were fully visible. "Jesus, I've got to get out of here," Dyar thought. But they went on, record after record. At the close of a samba, he said to her, panting somewhat exaggeratedly: "Tired?" "No, no!" she cried. "You are marvelous dancer."

Here and there candles had begun to go out; the room was chilly, and a damp wind came through the open door from the garden. It was that moment of the evening when everyone had arrived and no one had yet thought of going home; one could have said that the party was in full swing, save that there was a peculiar deadness about the gathering which made it difficult to believe that a party was actually in progress. Later, in retrospect, one might be able to say that it had taken place, but now, while it still had not finished, it was somehow not true.

The Portuguese girl was telling him about Estoril, and how Monte Carlo even at its zenith never had been so glamorous. If at that moment someone had not taken hold of his arm and yanked on it violently he would probably have said something rather rude. As it was, he let go of the girl abruptly and turned to face Eunice Goode, who was by then well primed with martinis. She was looking at the frowning Portuguese girl with a polite leer. "I'm afraid you've lost your dancing partner," she said, steadying herself by putting one hand against the wall. "He's coming with me into the other room."

Under ordinary circumstances Dyar would have told her she was mistaken, but right now the idea of sitting down with a drink, even with Eunice Goode along, seemed the preferable, the less strenuous of two equally uninteresting prospects. He excused himself lamely, letting her lead him away across the room into a small, dim library whose walls were lined to the ceiling with graying encyclopaedias, reference books and English novels. Drawn up around a fireplace with no fire in it were three straight-backed chairs, in one of which sat Mme. Jouvenon, staring ahead of her into the cold ashes. She did not turn around when she heard them come into the room.

"Here we are," said Eunice brightly, and she introduced the two, sitting down so that Dyar occupied the chair between them.

XI

For a few minutes Eunice valiantly made conversation; she asked questions of them both and answered for both. The replies were doubtless not the ones that either Mme. Jouvenon or Dyar would have given, but in their respective states of confusion and apathy they said: "Ah, yes" and "That's right" when she took it upon herself to explain to each how the other felt. Dyar was bored, somewhat drunk, and faintly alarmed by Mme. Jouvenon's expression of fierce preoccupation, while she, desperately desirous of gaining his interest, was casting about frantically in her mind for a proper approach. With each minute that passed, the absurd situation in the cold little library became more untenable. Dyar shifted about on his chair and tried to see behind him through the doorway into the other room; he hoped to catch sight of Hadija. Someone put on a doleful Egyptian record. The groaning baritone voice filled the air.

"You have been to Cairo?" said Mme. Jouvenon suddenly.

"No." It did not seem enough to answer, but he had no further inspiration.

"You are inter-r-rested in the Middle East, also?"

"Madame Jouvenon has spent most of her life in Constantinople and Bagdad and Damascus, and other fascinating places," said Eunice.

"Not Bagdad," corrected Mme. Jouvenon sternly. "Bokhara."

"That must be interesting," said Dyar.

The Egyptian record was interrupted in mid-lament, and a French music-hall song replaced it. Then there was the sound of one of the heavy candelabra being overturned, accompanied by little cries of consternation. Taking advantage of the moment, which he felt might not present itself again even if he waited all night, Dyar sprang to his feet and rushed to the door. Directly behind him came Mme. Jouvenon, picking at his sleeve. She had decided to be bold. If, as Eunice Goode claimed, the young man was short of funds, it was likely he would accept an invitation to a meal, and so she promptly extended one for the following day, making it clear that he was to be her guest. "That's a splendid idea," said Eunice hurriedly. "I'm sure you two will have a great deal to give each other. Mr. Dyar has been in the consular service for years, and you probably have dozens of mutual friends." He did not even bother to correct her: she was too far gone, he thought. He had just had a glimpse of Hadija dancing with one of the Beidaoui brothers, and he turned to Mme. Jouvenon to decline her kind invitation. But he was not quick enough.

"At two tomorrow. At the Empire. You know where this is. The food is r-rather good. I will have the table at end, by where the bar is. This will give me gr-reat pleasure. We cannot speak here." And so it was settled, and he escaped to the table of drinks and got another.

"You rather bungled that," Eunice Goode murmured.

Mme. Jouvenon looked at her. "You mean he will not come?"

"*I* shouldn't if I were he. Your behavior. . . ." She stopped on catching sight of Hadija engaged in a rumba with Hassan Beidaoui; they smiled fatuously as they wriggled about. "The little idiot," she thought. The sight was all too reminiscent of the Bar Lucifer. "She's surely speaking Arabic with him." Uneasily she walked toward the dance floor, and presently was gratified to hear Hadija cry: "Oh, yes!" to something Hassan had said.

Without being invited this time, Dyar went and sat down beside Daisy. The room seemed immense, and much darker. He was feeling quite drunk; he slid down into a recumbent position and stretched his legs out straight in front of him, his head thrown back so that he was staring up at the dim white ceiling far above. Richard Holland sat in a chair facing Daisy, holding forth, with his wife nestling on the floor at his feet, her head on his knee. The old English lady with the turban was at the other end of the divan, smoking a cigarette in a very long, thin holder. Eunice Goode wandered over to the group, followed by Mme. Jouvenon, and stood behind Holland's chair drinking a glass of straight gin. She looked down at the back of his head, and said in a soft but unmistakably belligerent voice: "I don't know who you are, but I think that's all sheer balls."

He squirmed around and looked up at her; deciding she was drunk he ignored her, and went on talking. Presently Mme. Jouvenon whispered to Eunice that she must go, and the two went toward the door where Abdelmalek stood, his robes blowing in the breeze.

"Who is that extraordinary woman with Miss Goode?" asked the English lady. "I don't recall ever having seen her before." No one answered. "Don't any of you know?" she pursued fretfully.

"Yes," said Daisy at length. She hesitated a moment, and then, her voice taking on a vaguely mysterious tone: "I know who she is."

But Mme. Jouvenon had left quickly, and Eunice was already back, dragging a chair with her, which she installed as close as possible to Richard Holland's, and in which she proceeded to sit suddenly and heavily.

From time to time Dyar closed his eyes, only to open them again quickly when he felt the room sliding forward from under him. Looking at the multitude of shadows on the ceiling he did not think he felt the alcohol too much. But it became a chore to keep his eyes open for very long at a stretch. He heard the voices arguing around him; they seemed excited, and yet they were talking about nothing. They were loud, and yet they seemed far away. As he fixed one particular part of a monumental shadow stretching away into the darker regions of the ceiling, he had the feeling suddenly that he was seated there surrounded by dead people—or perhaps figures in a film that had been made a long time before. They were speaking, and he heard their voices, but the actual uttering of the words had been done many years ago. He must not let himself be fooled into believing that he could communicate with them. No one would hear him if he should try to speak. He felt the cold rim of his glass on his leg where he held it; it had wet through his trousers. With a spasmodic movement he sat up and took a long drink. If only there had been someone to whom he could have said: "Let's get out of here." But they all sat there in another world, talking feverishly about nothing, approving and protesting, each one delighted with the sound his own ideas made when they were turned into words. The alcohol was like an ever-thickening curtain being drawn down across his mind, isolating it from everything else in the room. It blocked out even his own body, which, like the faces around him, the candle flames and the dance music, became also increasingly remote and disconnected. "God damn it!" he cried suddenly. Daisy, intent on what Richard Holland was saying, distractedly reached out and took his hand, holding it tightly so he could not withdraw it without an effort. He let it lie in hers; the contact helped him a little to focus his attention upon the conversation.

"Oh no!" said Holland. "The species is not at all intent on destroying itself. That's nonsense. It's intent on being something which happens inevitably to entail its destruction, that's all."

A man came through the door from the garden and walked quickly across the room to where Abdelmalek stood talking with several of his guests. Dyar was not alert enough to see his face as he moved through the patches of light in the center of the room, but he thought the figure looked familiar.

"Give me a sip," said Holland, reaching down and taking his wife's glass out of her hand. "There's nothing wrong in the world except that man has persuaded himself he's a rational being, when really he's a moral one. And morality must have a religious basis, not a rational one. Otherwise it's just play-acting."

The old English lady lit another cigarette, throwing the match on the floor to join the wide pile of ashes she had scattered there. "That's all very well," she said with a touch of petulance in her cracked voice, "but nowadays religion and rationality are not mutually exclusive. We're not living in the Dark Ages."

Holland laughed insolently; his eyes were malignant. "Do you want to see it get dark?" he shouted. "Stick around a few years." And he laughed again. No one said anything. He handed the glass back to Mrs. Holland. "I don't think anyone will disagree if I say that religion all over the world is just about dead."

"*I* certainly shall," said the English lady with asperity. "But no matter."

"I'm sorry, but in most parts of the world today, professing a religion is purely a matter of politics, and has practically nothing to do with faith. The Hindus are busy letting themselves be seen riding in Cadillacs instead of smearing themselves with sandalwood paste and bowing in front of Ganpati. The Moslems would rather miss evening prayer than the new Disney movie. The Buddhists think it's more important to take over in the name of Stalin and Progress than to meditate on the four basic sorrows. And we don't even have to mention Christianity or Judaism. At least, I hope not. But there's absolutely nothing that can be done about it. You can't *decide* to be irrational. Man is rational now, and rational man is lost."

"I suppose," said the English lady acidly, "that you're going to tell us we can no longer choose between good and evil? It seems to me that would come next on your agenda."

"God, the man's pretentious," Daisy was thinking. As she grew increasingly bored and restive, she toyed with Dyar's fingers. And to himself Dyar said: "I don't want to listen to all this crap." He never had been one to believe that discussion of abstractions could lead to anything but more discussion. Yet he did listen, perhaps because in his profound egotism he felt that in some fashion Holland was talking about him.

"Oh, that!" said Holland, pretending to sound infinitely patient. "Good and evil are like white and black on a piece of paper. To distinguish them you need at least a glimmer of light, otherwise you can't even see the paper. And that's the way it is now. It's gotten too dark to tell." He snickered. "Don't talk to *me* about the Dark Ages. Right now no one could presume to know where the white ends and the black begins. We know they're both there, that's all."

"Well, I must say I'm glad to hear we know that much, at least," said the English lady testily. "I was on the point of concluding that there was absolutely no hope." She laughed mockingly.

Holland yawned. "Oh, it'll work itself out, all right. Until then, it would be better not to be here. But if anyone's left afterward, they'll fix it all up irrationally and the world will be happy again."

Daisy was examining Dyar's palm, but the light was too dim. She dropped the hand and began to arrange her hair, preparatory to getting up. "*Enfin*, none of it sounds very hopeful," she remarked, smiling.

"It *isn't* very hopeful," Holland said pityingly; he enjoyed his role as diagnostician of civilization's maladies, and he always arrived at a negative prognosis. He would happily have continued all night with an appreciative audience.

"Excuse me. I've got to have another drink," said Dyar, lunging up onto his feet. He took a few steps forward, turned partially around and smiled at Daisy, so as not to seem rude, and saw Mrs. Holland rise from her uncomfortable position on the floor to occupy the place on the divan which he had just vacated. Then he went on, found himself through the door, standing on the balcony in the damp night wind. There seemed to be no reason for not going down the wide stairs, and so he went softly down and walked along the path in the dark until he came to a wall. There was a bench; he sat down in the quiet and stared ahead of him at the nearby silhouettes of moving branches and vines. No music, no voices, not even the fountains could be heard here. But there were other closer sounds: the leaves of plants rubbed together, stalks and pods hardened by the winter rattled and shook, and high in a palmyra tree not far away the dry slapping of an enormous fanshaped branch (it covered and uncovered a certain group of stars as it waved back and forth) was like the distant slamming of an old screen door. It was difficult to believe a tree in the wind could make that hard, vaguely mechanical noise.

For a while he sat quite still in the dark, with nothing in his mind save an awareness of the natural sounds around him; he did not even realize that he was welcoming these sounds as they washed through him, that he was allowing them to

cleanse him of the sense of bitter futility which had filled him
for the past two hours. The cold wind eddied around the
shrubbery at the base of the wall; he hugged himself but did
not move. Shortly he would have to rise and go back into the
light, up the steps into the room whose chaos was only the
more clearly perceived for the polite gestures of the people
who filled it. For the moment he stayed sitting in the cold.
"Here I am," he told himself once again, but this time the
melody, so familiar that its meaning was gone, was faintly
transformed by the ghost of a new harmony beneath it,
scarcely perceptible and at the same time, merely because it
was there at all, suggestive of a direction to be taken which
made those three unspoken words more than a senseless reiteration. He might have been saying to himself: "Here I am
and something is going to happen." The infinitesimal promise
of a possible change stirred him to physical movement: he unwrapped his arms from around himself and lit a cigarette.

XII

Back in the room Eunice Goode, on her way to being a little
more drunk than usual (the presence of many people around
her often led her to such excesses), was in a state of nerves. A
recently arrived guest, a young man whom she did not know,
and who in spite of his European attire was obviously an
Arab, had come up to Hadija as she and Eunice stood
together by the phonograph, and greeted her familiarly in
Arabic. Fortunately Hadija had had the presence of mind to
answer: "What you sigh?" before turning her back on him,
but that had not ended the incident. A moment later, while
Eunice was across the room having her glass replenished, the
two had somehow begun to dance. When she returned and
saw them she had wanted terribly to step in and separate
them, but of course there was no way she could do such a
thing without having an excuse of some sort. "I shall make a
fearful scene if I start," she said to herself, and so she hovered
about the edge of the dance floor, now and then catching
hold of a piece of furniture for support. At least, as long as
she remained close to Hadija the girl would not be so likely
to speak Arabic. That was the principal danger.

Hadija was in misery. She had not wanted to dance (indeed, she considered that her days of enforced civility to strange men, and above all Moslem men, had come to a triumphant close), but he had literally grabbed her. The young man, who was squeezing her against him with such force that she had difficulty in breathing, refused to speak anything but Arabic with her, even though she kept her face set in an intransigent mask of hauteur and incomprehension. "Everyone knows you're a Tanjaouia," he was saying. But she fought down the fear that his words engendered. Only her two protectors, Eunice and the American gentleman, knew. Several times she tried to push him away and stop dancing, but he only held her with increased firmness, and she realized unhappily that any more vehement efforts on her part would attract the attention of the other dancers, of whom there were now only two couples. Occasionally she said in a loud voice: "O.K." or "Oh, yes!" so as to reassure Eunice, whom she saw watching her desperately.

"*Ch'andek?* What's the matter with you? What are you trying to do?" the young man was saying indignantly. "Are you ashamed of being a Moslem? It's very bad, what you are doing. You think I don't remember you from the Bar Lucifer? Ha! *Hamqat, entina! Hamqat!*" His breath smelled strongly of the brandy he had been drinking all day.

Hadija was violently indignant. "*Ana hamqat?*" she began, and realized too late that she had given herself away. The young man laughed delightedly, and tried to get her to go on, but she froze into absolute silence. Finally she cried out in Arabic: "You're hurting me!" and breaking from his embrace hurried to Eunice's side, where she stood rubbing her shoulder. "Wan fackin bastard," she said under her breath to Eunice, who had witnessed her linguistic indiscretion and realized that as far as the young man was concerned the game was up.

"Shut up!" She seized Hadija's arm and pulled her off into an empty corner.

"I want wan Coca-Cola," objected Hadija. "Very hot. That lousy guy dance no good."

"Who is he, anyway?"

"Wan Moorish man live in Tangier."

"I know, but who? What's he doing in the Beidaoui Palace?"

"He plenty drunk."

Eunice mused a moment, letting go of Hadija's arm. With as much dignity as she could summon, she strode across the room toward Hassan Beidaoui, who, seeing her coming, turned around and managed to be talking animatedly with Mme. Werth by the time she reached him. The maneuver proved quite worthless, of course, since Eunice's piercing "I say" began while she was still ten feet away. She tapped Hassan's arm and he faced her patiently, prepared to listen to another series of incomprehensible reminiscences about Crown Prince Rupprecht.

"I say!" She indicated Hadija's recent dancing partner. "I say, isn't that the eldest son of the Pacha of Fez? I'm positive I remember him from Paris."

"No," said Hassan quietly. "That is my brother Thami. Would you like to meet him?" (This suggestion was prompted less by a feeling of amiability toward Eunice Goode than by one of spite toward Thami, whose unexpected appearance both Hassan and Abdelmalek considered an outrage. They had suggested he leave, but being a little drunk he had only laughed. If anyone present could precipitate his departure, thought Hassan, it was this outlandish American woman.) "Will you come?" He held out his arm. Eunice reflected quickly, and said she would be delighted.

She was not surprised to find Thami exactly the sort of Arab she most disliked and habitually inveighed against: outwardly Europeanized but inwardly conscious that the desired metamorphosis would remain forever unaccomplished, and therefore defiant, on the offensive to conceal his defeat, irresponsible and insolent. For his part, Thami behaved in a particularly obnoxious fashion. He was in a foul humor, having met with no success either in attempting to get the money for the boat from his brothers, or in persuading them to agree to the sale of his house in the Marshan. And again, this hideous woman was his idea of the typical tourist who admired his race only insofar as its members were picturesque.

"You want us all to be snake-charmers and scorpion-eaters," he raged, at one point in their conversation, which he had inevitably maneuvered in such a direction as to permit him to make his favorite accusations.

"Naturally," Eunice replied in her most provoking manner. "It would be far preferable to being a nation of tenth-rate pseudo-civilized rug-sellers." She smiled poisonously, and then belched in his face.

At that moment Dyar came in. The candlelight seemed bright to him and he blinked his eyes. Seeing Thami in the center of the room, he looked surprised for an instant, and then went up to him and greeted him warmly. Without seeming to see Eunice, he took him by the arm and led him aside. "I want to settle my little debt with you, from the other night."

"Oh, that's all right," said Thami, looking at him expectantly. And as the money changed hands, Thami said: "She's here. You have seen her?"

"Yeah, sure."

"You brought her?"

"No. Miss Goode over there." Dyar jerked his chin in her direction, and Thami fell to thinking.

From where she stood Eunice watched them, saw Dyar slip some notes into Thami's hand, and guessed correctly that Thami had been the friend who had lent him the money to pay Hadija at the Bar Lucifer. It was the realization of her worst fears, and in her present unbalanced state she built it up into a towering nightmare. The two men held her entire future happiness in their hands. If anyone had observed her face closely at that moment, he would unhesitatingly have declared her mad, and he would probably have moved quickly away from her. It had suddenly flashed upon her, the realization of how supremely happy she had been at the Beidaouis' this evening—at least, it seemed so to her now. Hadija belonged completely to her, she had been accepted, was even having a small success at the moment as Miss Kumari, chatting in monosyllables with Dr. Waterman in a corner. But Miss Kumari's feet were planted at the edge of a precipice, and it required the merest push from either of the two men there (she clenched her fists) to topple her over the brink. The American was the more dangerous, however, and she already had set in motion the apparatus that was destined to get rid of him. "It can't fail," she thought desperately. But of course it could fail. There was no particular reason to believe that he would keep the appointment so clumsily arranged by Mme. Jouvenon for tomorrow, nor were there any grounds for confidence in her ability to make matters go as they were supposed to go. She opened her mouth wide and after some difficulty belched again. The room was going away from her; she felt it draining off into darkness. Making a tremendous effort, she prevented herself from tipping sideways toward the floor, and took a few steps forward, perhaps with the intention of speaking to Dyar. But the effort was too much. Her final remaining energy was used in reaching a nearby empty chair; she slid into it and lost consciousness.

Daisy had joined Dyar, without, however, paying any notice to Thami, who unobtrusively walked away. "Good God!" she cried, seeing Eunice's collapse. "That's a lovely sight. I don't intend to be delegated to carry it home, though, which is exactly what will happen unless I leave." She paused, and seemed to be changing her mind. "No! Her little Greek friend can just call for a taxi and the servants can dump her in. I'm damned if I'll play chauffeur to Uncle Goode, and I'm damned if I'll go home to keep from doing it, either. Hassan—aren't they both sweet? don't you love them?—" Dyar assented. "—He's offered to show us the great room, and that doesn't happen every day. I've seen it only once, and I'm longing to see it again. So there's going to be no victim here, making a Red Cross ambulance out of the car, and going up that fiendish narrow street to the Metropole. God!" She paused, then went on. "They're not ready to take us yet. They want to wait till a few more people have left. But I must talk to you before you disappear again. I saw you run out, darling. You've got to stop acting like a pariah. Come over here and sit down. I've got two things to say to you, and both are important, and not very pleasant."

"What do you mean?"

"Just let me do the talking, and listen." They sat down on the same divan where they had been sitting a half hour ago. The fresh air had made him feel better, and he had decided not to take any more whiskey. She laid her hand on his arm; the diamonds of her bracelets shone in the candlelight. "I'm practically certain Jack Wilcox is about to get himself into trouble. It seems *most* suspicious, the fact that he's keeping you out of his office. The moment you told me that, I knew something peculiar was going on. He's always been an ass in his business dealings, and he's no less of one now. By ass I mean stupidly careless. God, the idiots and scoundrels he's taken into his confidence! You know, everyone here's got some little pecadillo he's hoping to hide. You know, *ça va sans dire*. Everyone has to make a living, and here no one asks questions. But Jack practically *advertises* his business indiscretions. He can't make a move now without the entire scum of the Zone knowing about it. Which would be all right if there were any protection, which obviously there can't be in such cases. You just have to take your chances."

Dyar was listening, but at the same time he was uneasily watching the other end of the room where he had observed Hadija and Thami engaged in what appeared to be an intense and very private conversation. "*What* are you talking about?" he demanded rudely, turning suddenly to stare at her.

Daisy misinterpreted his question. "My dear, certainly no one but an imbecile would think of trying to enlist the help of the Police in such matters. I love Jack; I think he's a dear. But I certainly think you should be warned. *Don't* get involved in any of his easy-money schemes. They crack up. There are plenty of ways of making a living here, and quite as easy, without risking getting stabbed or shot."

Now Dyar looked at her squarely and laughed.

"I know I'm drunk," she said. "But I also know what I'm saying. I can see you're going to laugh even more at the other thing I've got to tell you." Dyar cast a troubled glance behind him at Hadija and Thami.

Daisy's voice was suddenly slightly harsh. "Oh, stop breaking your neck. He's not going to run off with your girlfriend."

Dyar turned his head back swiftly and faced her, his mouth open a little with astonishment. "What?"

She laughed. "Why are you so surprised? I told you everyone knows everything here. What do you think I have a good pair of Zeiss field-glasses in my bedroom for, darling? You didn't know I had such a thing? Well, I have, and they were in use today. There's a short stretch of shore-line visible from one corner of the room. But that's not what I was going to tell you," she went on, as Dyar, trying to picture to himself just what incidents of his outing she might have seen, felt his face growing hot. "I'd like to sock her in that smug face," he thought, but she caught the unspoken phrase. "You're angry with me, darling, aren't you?" He said nothing. "I don't blame you. It was a low thing to do, but I'm making amends for it now by giving you some *very* valuable advice." She began to speak more slowly and impressively. "Madame Jouvenon, that frightful little woman you went off into the other room with, is a Russian agent. A spy, if you like the word better." She sat back and squinted at him, as if to measure the effect of that piece of news.

It seemed to have brought him around to a better humor, for he chuckled, took her hand and smoothed the fingers slowly; she made no effort to withdraw it. "At least," she continued, "I've heard it from two distinct sources, neither of which I have any reason to doubt. Of course, it's a perfectly honorable way of making a living, and we all have our agents around, and I daresay she's not even a particularly efficient one, but there you are. So those are my two little warnings for tonight, my dear young man, and you can take them or leave them, whichever you like." She pulled her hand away to smooth her hair. "I shouldn't have told you, really. God knows how much of a chatterbox you are. But if you quote me I shall deny ever having said a word."

"I'll *bet* you would. And the same goes for the room in Marrakech. Right?"

She took the tip of one of his fingers between her thumb and forefinger, squeezed it hard, and looked at him seriously a moment before she said: "I suppose you think that was immoral."

The company was thinning; people were leaving now in groups. Abdelmalek and Hassan Beidaoui stood one on each side of the door, bowing and smiling. There were not more than ten guests left, including the Hollands, who had found an old swing record in the pile, and were now doing some very serious jitterbugging, alone on the floor. One of the two Arab gentlemen stood watching them, an expression of satisfaction on his face, as though at last he were seeing what he had come here to see.

Thami and Hadija still conversed, but the important points in their talk had all been touched upon, with the result that Thami now suspected that the money for his boat might conceivably be donated by Eunice Goode. Many members of the lower stratum of society in Tangier naturally knew perfectly well who Hadija was, but there was next to no contact between that world of cast-off clothing, five-peseta cognac and cafés whose patrons sat on mats smoking kif and playing ronda, and this other more innocent world up here in which it was only one step from wanting a thing to having it. Nevertheless, he knew both worlds; he was the point of contact. It was a privileged position and he felt it could be put to serious use. Nothing of all this had been said to Hadija; encouraged by him she had told all the important facts. No Arab is foolish enough to let another Arab know that both are stalking the same prey—after all, there is only a limited amount of flesh on any given carcass. And while the tentative maximum set by Thami was only whatever the price of the boat should finally turn out to be, still, he knew that Hadija would consider as her rightful property every peseta that went to him. Like most girls with her training, basically Hadija thought only in terms of goods delivered and payment received; it did not occur to her that often the largest sums go to those who agree to do nothing more than stay out of the way. This is not to say that she was unaware of the position of power enjoyed by Thami in the present situation. "You won't say a word?" she whispered anxiously.

"We're friends. More than friends," he assured her, looking steadily into her eyes. "Like brother and sister. And Muslimin, both of us. How could I betray my sister?"

She was satisfied. But he continued. "And tonight, what are you doing?" She knew what that meant. If it had to be, there was nothing to do about it, and tonight was the most likely time, with Eunice in her present state. Hadija glanced across at the massive body sprawled on the chair.

"Call a taxi," went on Thami. "Get the servants to put her in. Take her home and see that she's in bed. Meet me outside the Wedad pastry shop in the dark part there at the foot of the steps to the garden. I'll be there before you, so you won't have to wait."

"*Ouakha*," she agreed. She was going to get nothing for it, yet it had to be done. To remain Miss Kumari she must go back and be the Hadija of the pink room behind the Bar Lucifer. She looked at him with undissimulated hatred. He saw it and laughed; it made her more desirable.

"Little sister," he murmured, his lips so close to the lobe of her ear that they brushed it softly in forming the word.

She got up. Save for Eunice they were alone in the room. The remaining guests had gone out, were being taken through the blue court, the jasmine court, the marble pavilion, to the vast, partially ruined ballroom where several sultans had dined. But Hadija was too much perturbed to notice that she had not been invited to make the tour along with the others.

"You call a taxi. The telephone is in there." He indicated the little library. "I'll take care of her." He went out to the entrance lodge and got two of the guards to come in and carry Eunice to the gate, where they laid her on a mat along one of the niches until the cab arrived. He sat in front with the driver and went along as far as Bou Arakía, where he got out and after saying a word through the open window to Hadija, walked off into the dark in the direction of the Zoco de Fuera.

The European guests were not taken back into the European wing; Abdelmalek and Hassan led them directly to the gate on the street, bade them a gracious good-bye, and stepped behind the high portals which were closed and noisily bolted. It was a little like the expulsion from Eden, thought Daisy, and she turned and grinned at the Hollands.

"May I drive you to your hotel?" she offered.

They protested that it was nearby, but Daisy snorted with impatience. She knew she was going to take them home, and she wanted to start. "Get in," she said gruffly. "It's a mile at least to the Pension Acacias."

The final good nights were called as the other guests drove off.

"But it's out of your way," objected Richard Holland.

"Stuff and nonsense! Get in! How do you know where I'm going? I've got to meet Luis more or less in that neighborhood."

"Sh! What's that?" Mrs. Holland held up a silencing finger. From somewhere in the dark on the other side of the street came a faint chorus of high, piercing mews.

"Oh, God! It's a family of abandoned kittens," moaned Daisy. "The Moors are always doing it. When they're born they simply throw them out in a parcel into the street like garbage."

"The poor things!" cried Mrs. Holland, starting across the pavement toward the sound.

"Come back here!" shouted her husband. "Where do you think you're going?"

She hesitated. Daisy had got into the car, and sat at the wheel.

"I'm afraid it's hopeless, darling," she said to Mrs. Holland.

"Come *on*!" Holland called. Reluctantly she returned and got in. When she was beside him in the back seat he said: "What did you think you were going to do?"

She sounded vague. "I don't know. I thought we might take them somewhere and give them some milk." The car started up, skirting the wall for a moment and then turning through a park of high eucalyptus trees.

Dyar, sitting in front with Daisy, and infinitely thankful to be out of the Beidaoui residence, felt pleasantly relaxed. He had been listening to the little scene with detached interest, rather as if it were part of a radio program, and he expected now to hear an objection from Holland based on grounds of practicality. Instead he heard him say: "Why in hell try to keep them alive? They're going to die anyway, sooner or later."

Dyar turned his head sideways and shouted against the trees going by: "So are you, Holland. But in the meantime you eat, don't you?"

There was no reply. In the back, unprotected from the wet sea wind, the Hollands were shivering.

XIII

The next morning was cloudy and dark; the inescapable wind was blowing, a gale from the east. Out in the harbor the few freighters moored there rocked crazily above the whitecaps, and the violent waves rolled across the wide beach in a chaos of noise and foam. Dyar got up early and showered. As he dressed he stood in the window, looking out at the agitated bay and the gray hills beyond it, and he realized with a slight shock that not once since he had arrived had he gone to inquire for his mail. It was hard to believe, but the idea simply had not occurred to him. In his mind the break with the past had been that complete and definitive.

At the desk downstairs he inquired the way to the American Legation, and set out along the waterfront on foot, stopping, after ten minutes or so of battling against the wind, at a small café for breakfast. As he sat down at the teetering little table he noticed that his garments were sticky and wet with the salt spray in the air.

He found the Legation without difficulty; it was just inside the native town, through an archway cut in the old ramparts. In the waiting room he was asked by an earnest young man with glasses to sign the visitors' register, whereupon he was handed one letter. It was from his mother. He wandered a while in the twisting streets, pushing through crowds of small screaming children, and looking vaguely for a place where he could sit down and read his letter. From a maze of inner streets he came out upon the principal thoroughfare for pedestrians, and followed it downhill. Presently he arrived at a large flat terrace edged with concrete seats, overlooking the docks. He sat down, oblivious of the Arabs who looked at him with their eternal insolent curiosity, and, already in that peculiarly unreal state of mind which can be induced in the traveler by the advent of a letter from home, tore open the envelope and pulled out the small, closely written sheets.

Dear Nelson:

I have neglected you shamefully. Since Tuesday for one reason or another I have put off writing, and here it is Saturday. Somehow after you left I didn't have much "gumption" for a few days! Just sat around and read and sewed, and did what light housework I could without tiring myself too much. Also had one of my rip-roaring sick-headaches which knocked me out for 24 hours. However, I am fine now, and have been for several days. Let me tell you it was a terrible moment when they pulled up that gangplank! Do hope you had no unpleasant experiences with your cabin mates on the way over. They didn't look too good to me. Your father and I both thought you were in for something, from the looks of them.

We are planning on driving down to Wilmington for Aunt Ida's birthday. Your father is quite busy these days and comes home tired, so I guess one trip will be enough for this winter. Don't want him to get sick again.

Tho't you might be interested in the enclosed clipping. That Williams girl certainly didn't lose any time finding a new fiancé, did she? Well, it seems as though practically all your old friends were married and settled down now.

We were over at the Mott's (Dr.) last evening after an early movie. He is in bed with a bad kidney and we have been several times to see them. Your father had a short visit upstairs with him, has two male nurses & is a very sick man. Louise, whom I don't think you have seen in twenty years, had come down unexpectedly to see how things were going. She is a very attractive young woman, two children now. She is most interested in your doings. Says she once stopped at Tangier for an afternoon on a Mediterranean Cruise when she was in college. Didn't think much of it. She was reminiscing about the good times you all used to have, and wondered if I still made the cocoanut macaroons I used to make. Says she never forgot them and the cookies. Naturally I had forgotten.

Well, I am getting this in the mail today.

Please take care of your health, just for my sake. Remember, if you lose that you lose everything. I have been reading up on Morocco in the Encyclopaedia and I must say it doesn't sound so good to me. They seem to have practically every sort of disease there. If you let yourself get run down in any way you're asking for trouble. I don't imagine the doctors over there are any too good, either, and the hospital conditions must be very primitive.

I shall be on tenterhooks until I hear from you. Please give Jack Wilcox my best. I hope he is able to make a go of his business. What with all the difficulties placed in the way of travel nowadays, both your father and I are very dubious about it. However, he must know whether he is making money or not. I don't see how he can.

May and Wesley Godfrey were in the other evening, told
them all about your venture. They said to wish you good luck,
as you'd probably need it. Your father and I join with them in
the hope that everything goes off as you expect it to.

Well, here is the end of my paper so I will quit.

Love to you from
Mother

P.S. It seems it was *Algiers* that Louise Mott was in, not Tangier. Has never been in the latter. Your father told me just now
when he came home for lunch. He is disgusted with me. Says I
always get everything mixed up!

Love again.

When he had finished reading he folded the letter slowly
and put it back into the envelope. He raised his head and
looked around him. A little Arab boy, his face ravaged by a
virulent skin disease, stood near him, studying him silently—
his shoes, his raincoat, his face. A man wearing a tattered out-
moded woman's coat, high-waisted, with peaked shoulders
and puffed sleeves, walked up and stopped near the boy, also
to stare. In one hand he carried a live hen by its wings; the
hen was protesting noisily. Annoyed by its squawks, Dyar rose
and went back into the street. Reading the letter had left him
in an emotional no-man's land. The street looked insane with
its cheap bazaar architecture, its Coca-Cola signs in Arabic
script, its anarchic assortment of people in damp garments
straggling up and down. It had begun to rain slightly. He put
his hands into the pockets of his raincoat and walked ahead
looking down at the pavement, slowly climbing the hill. An
idea had been in his mind, he had intended to do something
this morning, but now since reading his mother's letter he did
not have the energy to stop and try to recall what it had been.
Nor was he certain whether or not he would keep the luncheon appointment with the unpleasant woman he had met
last night. He felt under no particular obligation to put in an
appearance; she had given him no chance to accept or refuse,
had merely ordered him to be at the Empire at two o'clock.
He would either go or not go when the time came. He did
not really believe Daisy's fantastic story about her being a

Russian agent—as a matter of fact, he rather hoped she would turn out to be something of the sort, something a little more serious than the rest of the disparate characters he had met here so far, and a spy for the Soviet Government would certainly be that.

Under the trees of the Zoco de Fuera the chestnut vendors' fires made a fog of heavy, rich smoke. From time to time a rough gust of wind reached down and scooped the top layer out into the air above the trees, where it dissolved. He looked suspiciously at the objects offered for sale, spread out in patterns and mounds on the stone slabs of the market. There were little truncated bamboo tubes filled with kohl, an infinite variety of roots, resins and powders; rams' horns and porcupine skins, heavy with quills, and an impressive assortment of claws, bones, beaks and feathers. As the rain fell with more determination, those women whose wares were not protected by umbrellas began to gather them up preparatory to moving off toward more sheltered places. He still felt coreless—he was no one, and he was standing here in the middle of no country. The place was counterfeit, a waiting room between connections, a transition from one way of being to another, which for the moment was neither way, no way. The Arabs loped by in their rehabilitated European footgear which made it impossible for them to walk in a natural fashion, jostled him, stared at him, and tried to speak with him, but he paid them no attention. The new municipal buses moved into the square, unloaded, loaded, moved out, on their way to the edges of the city. A little way beyond the edges of the city was the border of the International Zone, and beyond that were the mountains. He said to himself that he was like a prisoner who had broken through the first bar of his cell, but was still inside. And freedom was not on sale for $390.

He decided it would do no harm to stop in and see Wilcox. A week or so, he had said, and this was the seventh day. He approached the entrance of the building with a rapidly increasing sensation of dread, although a moment ago he had not been conscious of any at all. Suddenly he found himself inside the pastry shop, sitting down at a table, ordering coffee. Then he asked himself what was worrying him. It was not so much that he realized Wilcox would be annoyed to see him come around without waiting to be telephoned, but that he knew the time had come to bring up the subject of money. And he knew that Wilcox knew it, would be expecting it, and so he was worried. He lit a cigarette to accompany his coffee; the hot liquid reinforced the savor of the smoke. When he had finished the coffee he slapped his knee and rose with determination. "We've got to have a showdown," he thought. But the Europe-Africa Tourist Service might as well have been a dentist's office for the reluctance with which he climbed the stairs and drew near its door.

He knocked. "*Sí!*" cried Wilcox. He turned the knob; the door was locked. "*Quién?*" Wilcox called, with an edge of vexation or nervousness to his voice. Dyar hesitated, and was about to say: "Jack?" when the door was flung open.

As Dyar looked into Wilcox's face, he saw the expression in his eyes change swiftly to one of annoyance. But the first emotion he had caught there had been one of unalloyed fear. Involuntarily Wilcox made a loud clicking sound of exasperation. Then he stepped back a little.

"Come in."

They remained standing in the ante-room, one on each side of the low table.

"What can I do for you?"

"I've got all that stuff you gave me down pat, pretty much. I thought I'd drop around and say hello."

"Yeah." Wilcox paused. "I thought we said I'd call you. I thought you understood that."

"I did, but you didn't call."

"Any objection to waiting a few days? I've still got a lot of stuff here I've got to clear up. There's no room for you here now."

Dyar laughed; Wilcox broke in on his laughter, his voice a bit higher in pitch. "I don't *want* you here. Can't you get that through your head? I've got special reasons for that."

Dyar took a deep breath. "I've got special reasons for coming here. I need some cash."

Wilcox narrowed his eyes. "What happened to all those express checks you had last week? Damn it, I told you you were working for me. Do I have to sign a contract? I owe you a week's wages, right? Well, I'd planned to pay you by the month, but if you want, I can make it twice a month. I know you're short. It's a nuisance to me, but I can do it that way if you like."

"But Jesus Christ, I need it now."

"Yeah, but I can't give it to you now. I haven't got it."

"What do you mean, you haven't got it? It's not that much." Dyar leered a bit as he said this.

"Listen, Nelson," began Wilcox, his face taking on a long-suffering look—("Fake," thought Dyar)—"I'm telling you the truth. I haven't got it to give you. I've got a back bill at the Atlantide that would sink a ship. Whatever comes in goes to them now. If it didn't I'd be in the street. You can see for yourself how much business I'm doing in here."

There were footsteps in the corridor. Wilcox stepped to the door and tried it; it was locked, but a vestige of alarm flickered again across his face. Dyar said nothing.

"Look," he went on, "I don't want you to get the idea that I'm stalling or anything. You're working for me. It may just be a crazy idea of mine, but I think things are going to open up very soon, and I want you to be broken in and ready for the big day when it comes."

"I didn't say you were stalling. I just said I needed money. But if you haven't got one week's pay now, how the hell do you expect to have twice as much next week?"

"That's a chance we both have to take."

"Both!" He looked derisively at Wilcox.

"Unless you're a bigger God-damned fool than I think you are you've still got a few express checks left that'll last you at least till next week."

"That's got nothing to do with it. I'm trying to save those for an emergency."

"Well, this is your emergency."

"That's what you think." Dyar moved toward the door, opened it and stepped out into the corridor.

"Come here," said Wilcox, following him quickly. He stood in the doorway and held out a five-hundred peseta note. "You've got me all wrong. Jesus! They don't make 'em stubborner! You really think I'm trying to gyp you, don't you?" He glanced nervously up and down the corridor.

"I don't think anything," Dyar said. He was trying to decide whether or not to take the money; his first impulse had been to refuse it, but then that seemed like a gesture of childish petulance. He reached for it, and said: "Thanks." Immediately afterward he was furious with himself. This anger was not assuaged by Wilcox's next words.

"And now, for God's sake, keep out of here until I call you, will you? *Please!*" The last word was more a shout of relief than of entreaty.

Again he cast a worried glance along the hall, and stepping inside the office, shut the door.

Slowly Dyar went down the stairs, still raging against himself for his blundering behavior. The money had been handed him as though he were a blackmailer come to exact more than the usual figure. Now it would be more difficult than ever to put the affair on a normal business basis.

As he stepped out into the street he realized that the rain was pouring down now. The sidewalks were empty; everyone had taken shelter under awnings, in doorways and arcades. Only an occasional Arab splashed along, seemingly oblivious of the storm. The pastry shop was crowded with people peering out into the street, most of them standing near the door so that if they were approached by a waitress they could move outside. He pushed through their ranks, sat down again and ordered another coffee. It was only then that he began to consider the aspect of Wilcox's behavior which was not concerned with him—the much more interesting fact that he seemed to be expecting an imminent unwelcome arrival. "Daisy's probably right," he thought. Jack had incurred the displeasure of some local hooligan and was awaiting reprisal. Either that or he was trying to avoid a creditor or two. Yet neither supposition quite explained his reluctance to have Dyar visit the office.

"No money!" he thought savagely. "Then why does he stay at the Atlantide?" But he knew the answer. Even if it were true that Wilcox was broke, which seemed unlikely, he would have felt obliged, and would have managed, to go on staying at the best hotel, because the town had agreed with his decision that he was one of the big shots, one of those who automatically get the best whether or not they can pay for it. But why? Every day in Tangier several new companies were formed, most of them with the intention of evading the laws of one country or another, and every day approximately the same number failed. And the reasons for their failure or success had very little to do with the business acumen of those connected with them. If you were really a winner you found ways of intercepting your competitors' correspondence, even his telegrams; you persuaded the employees at the French Post Office to let you have the first look at letters you were interested in seeing, which was how you got your mailing lists; you hired Arabs to break into other companies' offices and steal their stationery and examples of their directors' signatures for you; and when you sent your forged replies regretting your inability to supply the merchandise you prudently went all the way to Tetuan in the Spanish Zone to post them—only no customs official at the frontier got them away from you because somehow you were not stripped naked like the others, and the seams of your clothing were not ripped open. Not that you paid bribes in order to escape being molested—but everyone knew a winner on sight; he was the respected citizen of the International Zone. If one was not a winner one was a victim, and there seemed to be no way to change that. No pretense was of any avail. It was not a question of looking or acting like a winner—that could always be managed, although no one was taken in by it—it was a matter of conviction, of feeling like one, of knowing you belonged to the caste, of recognizing and being sure of your genius. For a long time he reflected confusedly upon these things; then he paid, got up, and went out into the rain, which now fell less heavily.

"I knew you would come," said Mme. Jouvenon. This was her way of saying that she had not been at all sure of it.

Dyar was more truthful. "*I* didn't," he said with a wry smile. And as he said it, he wondered why indeed he had come. Partly out of courtesy, perhaps, although he would not have wanted to admit that. He had found himself outside the restaurant three times during the late morning, but it had been too early for the rendezvous. However, he had seen the bright displays of hors d'oeuvre through the window, and probably it was they more than anything else that had induced him finally to keep the appointment. It was the sort of place he never would have thought of eating in alone.

Mme. Jouvenon was much calmer today—even rather pleasant, he thought—and certainly she was nobody's fool. She held the reins of the conversation firmly, but directed it with gentleness so that there was no feeling of strain. When they had reached the salad course, with all the naturalness in the world she began to discuss the subject that interested her, and he found it difficult to see anything offensive in what she said or in the way she said it. He understood, she supposed, that most people in Tangier had to live as best they could, doing one thing and another, and precisely because there were so many governments represented in the Administration, there was a great need for a practical system of checking and counter-checking between each power and the others. This ought to have been worked out beforehand officially, but it had not been, and the old formula of private tallying had still to be adhered to. He nodded gravely, smiling to himself, wondering just how long it would take her to make her offer, and under what guise it would come.

He was aware, she said, that practically every Englishman in the Zone, even with a title, was constrained by his government to furnish whatever information he could gather, and that far from being a shameful pursuit, on the contrary this was considered to be a completely honorable activity.

"More than most others you could find here, I guess," Dyar laughed.

She did not know about the English, she said, but many people she knew managed to make the thing lucrative by supplying data to two or more offices simultaneously. At the moment her government (she did not specify which it was) had no representation on the Board of Administrators, which made adequate reports an even greater necessity. Inasmuch as it was common knowledge that the unseen power behind the Administration was the United States, it was particularly with regard to American activities that her government wished to be documented. The difficulty was that the American milieu in Tangier was peculiarly hermetic, not inclined to mix with the other diplomatic groups. And then of course Americans were especially unsusceptible to financial offers, simply because it was difficult to put the price high enough to make it worth the trouble to most of them.

"—But she makes the proposition to me," he thought grimly, "because I'm not a big shot."

And the proposition came out. She was empowered to offer him five hundred dollars a month, beginning with a month's advance immediately, in return for small bits of information which he might glean from conversations with his American friends, plus one or two specific facts about the Voice of America's set-up at Sidi Kacem,—things which Dyar need not even understand himself, she hastened to assure him, since her husband was a very good electrical engineer and would have no difficulty in interpreting them.

"But I don't know anything or anybody in Tangier!"

They would even provide introductions—indirectly, of course—to the necessary people, she explained. As an American he had entrée to certain places (such as the Voice of America, for instance) from which other nationals were excluded.

"R-r-really we ask very little," she smiled. "You must not have r-r-romantic idea this is spying. There is nothing to spy in Tangier. Tangier has no interest for anyone. Diplomatic, perhaps, yes. Military, no."

"How many months would you want me for?"

"Ah! How are we to know how good you are to us?" She looked archly across the table at him. "Maybe infor-r-rmation you give us is not accur-r-rate. We should not continue with you."

"Or if I couldn't get any dope for you at all?"

"Oh, I am not wor-r-ried about that."

From her handbag she pulled a folded check and handed it to him. It was a check on the Banco Salvador Hassan e Hijos, and was already carefully made out to the order of Nelson Dyar, and signed in a neat handwriting by Nadia Jouvenon. It shocked him to see his name spelled correctly there on that slip of paper, the work of this intense little woman with blue

hair; it was ridiculous that she should have known his name,
but he was not really surprised, nor did he dare ask her how
she had discovered it.

They ordered coffee. "Tomorrow evening you will take
dinner at our home," she said. "My husband will be delighted
to meet you."

A waiter came and asked for Mme. Jouvenon, saying she
was wanted on the telephone. She excused herself and went
through a small door behind the bar. Dyar sat alone, toying
with his coffee spoon, smothered by an oppressive feeling of
unreality. He had put the check into his pocket, nevertheless
at the moment he had a strong impulse to pull it out and set
a match to it in the ash tray in front of him, so that when she
reappeared it would no longer exist. They would go out into
the street and he would be free of her. Distractedly he took a
sip of coffee and glanced around the room. At the next table
sat four people chattering in Spanish: a young couple, an
older woman who was obviously the mother of the girl, and a
small boy who slouched low in his chair pouting, refusing to
eat. The girl, heavily made-up and decked with what seemed
like several pounds of costume jewelry, kept glancing surreptitiously in his direction, always looking rapidly at her mother
and husband first to be sure they were occupied. This must
have been going on since the family group had sat down, but
now was the first he had noticed it. He watched her, not taking his gaze from her face; there was no doubt about it—she
was giving him the eye. He tried to see what the husband
looked like, but he was facing the other way. He was fat; that
was all he could tell.

When Mme. Jouvenon returned to the table she seemed
out of sorts about something. She called for the check, and
occupied herself with pulling on her kid gloves, which were
skin-tight.

The call had been from Eunice Goode, who, although she
had not mentioned this fact to Mme. Jouvenon, had waked
up early, and finding Hadija missing, had immediately suspected she was with Dyar. Thus she had first wanted to know
if Dyar had kept the appointment, to which Mme. Jouvenon
had replied shortly that he had, and made as if to draw the
conversation to a close. But Eunice had not been satisfied; she

wanted further to know if they had come to terms. Mme. Jouvenon had remarked that she appreciated her interest, but that she did not feel under any obligation to tender Mademoiselle Goode a report on the results of the luncheon interview. Eunice's voice had risen dangerously. "*Ecoutez, madame!* I advise you to tell me!" she had squealed. "*Je dois absolument savoir!*" Mme. Jouvenon had informed her that she did not intend to be intimidated by anyone, but then it had occurred to her that since after all it was Eunice who had supplied the introduction to Mr. Dyar, it might be just as well to retain her goodwill, at least for a little while. So she had laughed lamely and told her that yes, an understanding had been reached. "But has he accepted money?" insisted Eunice. "*Mais enfin!*" cried the exasperated Mme. Jouvenon. "You are incredible! Yes! He has taken money! Yes! Yes! I shall see you in a few days. *Oui! C'est ça! Au revoir!*" And she had added a few words in Russian under her breath as she had put the receiver back on the hook.

The Spanish family straggled to its feet, making a great scraping of chairs on the tile floor. As she fumbled for her coat and furpiece the young wife managed to throw a final desperate glance in Dyar's direction. "She's not only nympho but nuts," he said to himself, annoyed because he would not have minded being with her for an hour in a hotel room, and it was so manifestly impossible. He watched them as they went out the door, the girl pushing her small son impatiently ahead of her. "Typical Spanish nouveaux-riches," said Mme. Jouvenon disgustedly. "The sort Fr-r-ranco has put to r-r-run the nation."

They stood in the doorway being spattered by the blowing rain.

"Well, thank you for a very good lunch," Dyar said. He wished he were never going to have to see her again.

"You see that high building there?" She pointed to the end of the short street in front of them. He saw a large white modern apartment house. "Next door to that on the r-r-right, a small building, gr-r-ray, four floors high. This is my home. Top floor, number for-r-rty five. We wait for you tomorrow night, eight. Now I r-r-run, not to get wet too much. Good-bye."

They shook hands and she hurried across the street. He watched her for a moment as she walked quickly between the row of unfinished buildings and the line of small transplanted palm trees that never would grow larger. Then he sighed, and turned down the hill to the Boulevard; it led down to the Hotel de la Playa. There was practically no one in the rainy streets, and the shops were closed because it was not yet four. But on the way he passed the Banco Salvador Hassan e Hijos. It was open. He went in. In the vestibule a bearded Arab sitting on a leather pouf saluted him as he passed. The place was new, shining with marble and chromium. It was also very empty and looked quite unused. One young man stood behind a counter writing. Dyar walked over to him and handed him the check, saying: "I want to open an account." The young man glanced at the check and without looking at him handed him a fountain pen.

"Sign, please," he said. Dyar endorsed it and said he would like to withdraw a hundred dollars in cash.

"Sit down, please," said the young man. He pushed a button and a second later an enormous fluorescent lighting fixture in the center of the ceiling flickered on. It took about five minutes to make out the necessary papers. Then the young man called him over to the counter, handed him a checkbook and five thousand two hundred pesetas, and showed him a white card with his balance written on it. Dyar read it aloud, his voice echoing in the large, bare room. "Three hundred and ninety nine dollars and seventy five cents. What's the twenty five cents taken off for?"

"Checkbook," said the young man imperturbably, still not looking at him.

"Thanks." He went to the door and asked the Arab to get him a taxi. Sitting inside it, watching the empty wet streets go past, he thought he felt a little better, but he was not sure. At least he was out of the rain.

When he got to the hotel he asked at the desk to have a drink sent up to his room, but was told that the barman did not come in until six in the evening. He went up to the damp room and stood a while at the window, fingering the dirty curtain, staring out at the cold deserted beach so wet that it mirrored the sky. He took out the money and looked at it; it seemed like a lot, and five thousand two hundred pesetas could certainly buy a good deal more than a hundred dollars. Still, it did not give him the pleasure he wanted from it. The feeling of unreality was too strong in him, all around him. Sharp as a toothache, definite as the smell of ammonia, yet impalpable, unlocatable, a great smear across the lens of his consciousness. And the blurred perceptions that resulted from it produced a sensation of vertigo. He sat down in the armchair and lit a cigarette. The taste of it sickened him; he threw it into the corner and watched the smoke rise slowly along the wall until it came opposite the windowpane, when it rushed inward with the draught.

He was not thinking, but words came into his mind; they all formed questions: "What am I doing here? Where am I getting? What's it all about? Why am I doing this? What good is it? What's going to happen?" The last question stopped him, and he began unthinkingly to light another cigarette, laying it a moment later, however, unlighted on the arm of the chair. "What's going to happen?" Something was surely going to happen. It was impossible for everything just to continue as it was. All this was too unlikely, it was weighted down with the senseless, indefinable weight of things in a dream, the kind of dream where each simple object, each motion, even the light in the sky, is heavy with silent meaning. There had to be a break; some air had to come in. But things don't happen, he told himself. You have to make them happen. That was where he was stuck. It was not in him to make things happen; it never had been. Yet when he got to this point he realized that for the moment at any rate it was the bottom; from there the way went imperceptibly up. A tiny, distant pin-prick of hope was there. He had to probe to find where it came from. Triumphantly he dragged it out and examined it: it was simply that he had a blind, completely unreasonable conviction that when the moment came if nothing happened, some part of him would take it upon itself to make something happen. It seemed quite senseless when he thought about it; it merely faded, grew weaker, and so to save it he put it away again into the dark. He could not believe it, but he liked to have it there. He rose and began to walk restlessly about the room. Presently he threw himself on the bed, and lying still, tried to sleep. A minute later he struggled out of his shoes and trousers and pulled the bedspread up over him. But his thoughts turned to Hadija with her perfect little face and her pliant body like a young cat's.

"It was only yesterday," he thought incredulously. "God, not till Sunday?" Six days to wait. There was only one way to find her, and even that might not be possible. He would go to see the fat woman, Miss Goode, at the Metropole, and see if she knew her address. After a while he grew more calm. Waves, Hadija, seagulls. When he awoke it was dark.

XIV

It was an obsession of Eunice Goode's that there was very little time left in the world, that whatever one wanted to do, one had better get it done quickly or it would be too late. Her conception of that segment of eternity which was hers to know was expressed somewhat bafflingly in a phrase she had written in her notebook shortly after arriving in Tangier: "Between the crackling that rends the air and the actual flash of lightning that strikes you, there is a split second which seems endless, and during which you are conscious that the end has come. That split second is now." Yet the fact that her mind was constantly recalled to this fixed idea (as a bit of wood floating in the basin of a waterfall returns again and again to be plunged beneath the surface by the falling water), rather than inciting her to any sort of action, ordinarily served only to paralyze her faculties. Perhaps some of the trouble was due merely to her size; like most bulky things she was set in motion with difficulty. But when she began to move, she gathered impetus. Her association with Hadija had started her off in a certain direction, which was complete ownership of the girl, and until she had the illusion of having achieved that, she would push ahead without looking right or left.

When she had finished telephoning Mme. Jouvenon, she scribbled a note to Hadija: *Espérame aquí. Vuelvo antes de las cinco,* and left it hanging crookedly from the edge of the center table, weighted down by a bowl of chrysanthemums. Hadija could get Lola the chambermaid to read it to her.

Eunice had not wept when she had awakened and found herself alone in the room. The thing was too serious, she felt, for that sort of self-indulgent behavior. It was horrible enough to find herself alone in the bed, with no sign that Hadija had been in the room at all during the night, but the real suffering had begun only when she went ahead to form her conjectures, one after the other, as to what might have happened. Even though Dyar had appeared at the Empire to lunch with Mme. Jouvenon, it was still perfectly possible that the girl had spent the night with him. She almost hoped that was the case; it would mean that the danger was all at one point—a point she felt she had at least partially under control. "The big idiot's in love with her," she said to herself, and it was some little solace to think that Hadija was unlikely to fall in love with him. But one could never count on how a girl was going to react to a man. Men had an extra and mysterious magnetism which all too often worked. She slammed her clothing around in a rage as she dressed. She had taken no breakfast—only a few small glasses of gin. Now she went to the high armoire and took down from the shelf half a dry spongecake that had been up there several days. She ate it all, fiercely crumpled the paper that had been around it, and threw the wad across the room, aiming at the wastebasket. It went in; her fleshy lips moved ever so slightly in the shadow of a grim little smile of passing satisfaction.

It was hard to know how to dress this afternoon. She felt well wearing only two kinds of uniform: slacks and shirt, or evening dress, both of which were out of the question. Finally she decided on a black suit with a cape that looked vaguely military under a good deal of gold frogging. Hoping to look as bourgeoise and proper as possible, she pulled out a choker of gold beads which she fastened around her neck. She even bothered to find a pair of stockings, and eventually squeezed into some shoes with almost two inches of heel. Looking in the mirror with extreme distaste, she powdered her face clumsily, not being able to avoid sprinkling the stuff liberally over the front of her suit, and applied a minimum of neutral-toned lipstick. The sight of her face thus disguised sickened her; she turned away from the mirror and began to brush the powder off the black flannel cape. The whole business was a ghastly bore, and she loathed going out alone into the wet streets and through the center of town. But there was no sense in doing a thing halfway. One had to see it through. She liked to remind herself that she came of pioneer stock; her grandmother had had an expression she had always loved to hear her use: "Marching orders have come," which to her meant that if a thing had to be done, it was better to do it without question, without thinking whether one liked the idea or not. Fortunately her life was such that it was very seldom anything really did have to be done, so that when such an occasion arose she played her part to the full and got the most out of it.

Eunice left the American Legation about four o'clock. They had been most civil, she reflected. (She was always expecting to intercept looks of derision.) They had listened to her, made a few notes, and thanked her gravely. She on her side thought she had done rather well: she had not told them too much,—just enough to whet their interest. "Of course, I'm passing on this information to you for what it may be worth," she had said modestly. "I have no idea how much truth there is in it. But I have a distinct feeling that you'll find it worth your while to follow it up." (When she had gone Mr. Doan, the Vice-Consul, had heaved an exaggerated sigh, remarked in a flat voice: "Oh, Death, where is thy sting?" and his secretary had smirked at him appreciatively.)

At the Metropole desk the manager handed Eunice an envelope which she opened on her way upstairs. It was a very short note written in French on the hotel stationery, suggesting that she meet the sender alone in the reading-room of the hotel at seven o'clock that evening. It added the hope that she would agree to receive the most distinguished sentiments of the signer, whose name when she saw it gave her an agreeable start. "Thami Beidaoui," she read aloud, with satisfaction. At the moment she recalled only the two brothers who lived in the palace; the entrance of the third brother had been effected too late in her evening to make any lasting impression on her. Indeed, at the moment she did not so much as suspect his existence. If she had not been so completely preoccupied with worry about Hadija she would have been delighted with the message.

When she opened the door of her room the first thing she noticed was that the note she had left was gone and the bowl of chrysanthemums had been moved back to the center of the table. Then she heard splashing in the bathtub, and the familiar wabbling vocal line of the chant that habitually accompanied Hadija's ablutions. "Thank God," she breathed. That stage of the ordeal was over, at least. There remained the extraction of the admission of guilt, and the scene. Because there was going to be a scene, of course—Eunice would see to that. Only it was rather difficult to make a scene *with* Hadija; she was inclined to sit back like a spectator and watch it, rather than participate in it.

Eunice sat down to wait, to calm herself, and to try to prepare a method of operations. But when Hadija emerged in a small cloud of steam, clad in the satin and mink négligé, it was she who led the attack. Shrilling in Spanish, she accused Eunice of thinking only of herself, of taking her to the Beidaoui Palace and embarrassing her in front of a score of people by passing out, leaving her not only to extricate herself from the unbelievably humiliating situation, but to see to the removal of Eunice's prostrate body as best she could. Eunice did not attempt to reply. It was all perfectly true, only she had not thought of it until now. However, to admit such a thing would be adding grist to Hadija's mill. She was curious to know how Hadija had managed to get her out of the place and back to the hotel, but she did not ask her.

"What a disgrace for us!" cried Hadija. "What shame you have brought on us! How can we face the Beidaoui señores after this?"

In spite of the balm brought to her soul by this use of the plural pronoun, Eunice was suddenly visited by the terrible thought that perhaps the note she had just received had something to do with her behavior at the Beidaoui Palace; one of the brothers was coming to inform her discreetly that the hospitality of his home would henceforth not be extended to her and her friend Miss Kumari.

In a very thin voice she finally said: "Where did you spend the night?"

"I am lucky enough to have a few friends left," said Hadija. "I went and slept with a friend. I would not have anything to do with that mess." She called it *ese lio* with supreme disgust. So it had not been she who had seen to getting her back to the hotel. But Eunice was too upset to go into that; she was having a vision of herself in the act of misbehaving in some spectacular manner—breaking the furniture, throwing up in the middle of the dance floor, insulting the guests with obscenities. . . .

"But what did I *do*?" she cried piteously.

"*Bastante!*" said the other, glancing at her significantly.

The conversation dragged on through the waning light, until Hadija, feeling that she now definitely had the upper hand, lit the candles on the mantel and went to stand in front of the mirror where she remained a while, admiring herself in the négligée.

"I look beautiful in this?" she hazarded.

"Yes, yes," Eunice answered wearily, adding: "Hand me that bottle and the little glass beside it."

But before Hadija complied she was determined to pursue further the subject which preoccupied her. "Then I keep it?"

"Hadija! I couldn't care less what you do with it. Why do you bother asking me? You know what I told you about my things."

Hadija did, indeed, but she had wanted to hear it repeated with reference to this particular garment, just in case of a possible misunderstanding later.

"Aha!" She pulled it tighter around her, and still watching her reflection over her shoulder, took Eunice the bottle of Gordon's Dry and the tumbler.

"I very happy," Hadija confided, going into English because it was the language of their intimacy.

"Yes, I daresay," said Eunice drily. She decided to remain as she was, to receive M. Beidaoui. Seven o'clock was early; there was no need to dress more formally.

In order to obviate any possibility of Hadija's seeing him at the Metropole, Thami had made her promise to meet him at seven o'clock in the lobby of the Cine Mauretania, which was a good half-hour's walk from the hotel. She had demurred at first, but he still held the whip hand.

"She will want to come too," she complained. "She won't let me come alone."

"It's very important," he warned her. "If you try hard you'll find a way."

Now she had to break the news to Eunice, and she dreaded it. But strangely enough, when she announced that she was going out for a walk before dinner and would return about eight, Eunice merely looked surprised for an instant and said: "I'll expect you at eight, then. Don't be late." Eunice's acquiescence at this point had a twofold origin: she felt chastened by the idea of her behavior the preceding night, and she already had been vaguely wondering how she could keep Hadija away from the impending interview with M. Beidaoui. It seemed unwise to give him an opportunity to scrutinize her too closely.

Hidden among the kif-smokers, tea-drinkers and card-players in a small Arab café opposite the Metropole's entrance, Thami watched Hadija step out the door and pass along the street in the direction of the Zoco Chico. A quarter of an hour later Eunice's telephone rang. A M. Beidaoui wished to see Mlle. Goode; he would wait in the reading room.

"*Je déscends tout de suite,*" said Eunice nervously. She gulped one more small glass of gin and with misgiving went down to meet M. Beidaoui.

When she went into the dim room with its bastard Moorish decorations she saw no one but a young Spaniard sitting in a far corner smoking a cigarette. She was about to turn and go out to the desk, when he rose and came toward her, saying in English: "Good evening."

Before anything else crossed her mind she had a fleeting but unsavory intuition that she knew the young man and that she did not want to speak with him. However, here he was, taking her hand, saying: "How are you?" And because she was looking increasingly confused, he said: "I am Thami Beidaoui. You know—"

Without actually remembering him, she knew in a flash, not only that this was the ne'er-do-well brother of the Beidaouis, but that she had had an unpleasant scene with him at the cocktail party. There were certain details in the face that seemed familiar: the strange eyebrows that slanted wildly upward, and the amused, mocking expression of the eyes beneath. Obviously, now that she saw him closely, she realized that no Spaniard could have a face like that. But it was not the grave figure clothed in white robes that she had expected to find. She was relieved, perplexed and apprehensive. "How do you do?" she said coldly. "Sit down."

Thami was not one to beat about the bush; besides, he took it for granted that it was only the dim light which had prevented her from recognizing him at once, that by now she remembered all the details of their exchange of insults, and had even more or less guessed the reason for his visit.

"You had a good time at my brothers' house yesterday?"

"Yes. It was very pleasant," she said haughtily, wondering what horrors of misbehavior he was remembering at the moment.

"My brothers like Miss Kumari, your friend. They think she's a very nice girl."

She looked at him. "Yes, she is."

"Yes. They think so." She heard the slight emphasis on the word *think*, but did not realize it was purposeful. He continued. "At the party Madame Vanderdonk ask me: Who is that girl?" (Mme. Vanderdonk was the wife of the Dutch Minister.) "She says she looks like a Moorish girl." (Eunice's heart turned over.) "I told her that's because she's Greek."

"Cypriot," corrected Eunice tonelessly. He stared an instant, not understanding. Then he lit a cigarette and went on. "I know who this girl is, and you know, too. But my brothers don't know. They think she's a nice girl. They want to invite both of you to dinner next week, an Arab style dinner with the British Minister, and Dr. Waterman and Madame de Saint Sauveur and a lot of many people, but I think that's a bad idea."

"Did you tell them so?" asked Eunice, holding her breath.

"Of course not!" he said indignantly. (Still safe! She thought; she was ready to go anywhere from here, at whatever cost, whatever hazard.) "That would be not nice to you. I wouldn't do that." Now his voice was full of soft reproof.

"I'm sure you wouldn't," she said. She felt so much better that she gave him a wry smile.

He had gone down to the port that afternoon and had managed to get the price of the boat down to five thousand seven hundred pesetas. When it came time to pay, he still hoped to be able to knock off the extra seven hundred, simply by refusing to give them.

There were roars of laughter from the next room, which was the bar.

"Will you be at the dinner party?" said Eunice, not because she was particularly interested to know.

"I'm going away, I think," he said. "I want to go to Ceuta in my boat, do a little business."

"Business? You have a boat?"

"No. I want to buy one. Tomorrow. It costs too much money. I want to get out." He made the hideous grimace of disgust typical of the low-class Arab; he certainly had not learned that at the Beidaoui Palace. "Tangier's no good. But the boat costs a lot of money."

There was a silence.

"How much?" said Eunice.

He told her.

A little over a hundred dollars, she calculated. It was surely worth it, even if he did not leave Tangier, the likelihood of which she strongly doubted. "I should like to help you," she said.

"That's very kind. I didn't mean that." He was grinning.

"I know, but I'd like to help. I can give you a check." She wanted to finish the business and get rid of him.

In the bar someone began to play popular tunes on the piano, execrably. Several British sailors drinking in there looked into the reading room with undisguised curiosity, one after the other, like children.

"I'll write you a check. Excuse me. I'll be right back." She rose and went out the door into the foyer. With this native monster under control, and the American idiot out of the way, she told herself, life might begin to be bearable. She brought the checkbook downstairs with her, and made out the check in his presence, asking him how he spelled his name.

"Suppose we make it out for six thousand," she said. It was just as well to be generous.

"That's very kind. Thank you," said Thami.

"Not at all. I hope you have a good trip." She got up and walked toward the bar. Before she got to the door she paused and called to him: "Don't get drowned."

"Good night, Miss Goode," he said respectfully, her very personal irony having gone wide of the mark.

She went into the bar and ordered a gin fizz: the whole episode had been most distasteful. "What foul people they are!" she said to herself, finding it more satisfying to damn the tribe than the mere individual. The sailors moved a little away from her on each side when she ordered her drink.

Across the street Thami was back in the café, where he intended to stay in hiding until he saw Hadija return from her fruitless mission to the Cine Mauretania; he wanted to be sure and not meet her by accident in the street. With the eagerness of a small boy he looked forward to morning, when he could go to the bank, get the money, and rush to the waterfront to begin haggling once more for the boat. Watching the Metropole's entrance, he suddenly caught sight of the American, Dyar, about to go into the hotel. There was one Nesrani he liked. He had no reason for liking him, but he did. With a joviality born of the flush of victory, he rose and rushed out into the narrow street, calling: "Hey! Hey!"

Dyar turned and saw him without enthusiasm. "Hi," he said. They shook hands, but he did not let himself be enticed into the café by the other's blandishments. "I have to go," he explained.

"You want to see Miss Goode?" Thami guessed. Dyar was annoyed. "Yes," he said shortly. Thami was not the one to whom he would confide his business: the picture of him and Hadija talking so intensely and at such length at the party was too fresh in his memory. He had decided then that Thami was trying to make her.

"You'll be a long time in the hotel?"

"No, just a few minutes."

"I'll wait for you. When you come out you come in that café. You'll see me."

"Okay," said Dyar reluctantly. On the way he had bought a bracelet for Hadija; he swung the box on one finger by the little loop the saleswoman had tied in the string. "I'll look for you."

It was an absurd-looking old hotel, a gaudy vestige of the days when England had been the important power in Tangier. Still, he had to admit it was a lot more comfortable and pleasant than the new ones like his own Hotel de la Playa. At the desk they told him they thought he would find Miss Goode in the bar. That was good luck: he would not have to see her alone in her room. They could have one drink and he would be on his way. As he went into the crowded bar one of the sailors was pounding out "Oh Susannah." The room was full of sailors, but there was Eunice Goode in the midst of them, monumentally alone, sitting on a high stool staring straight in front of her.

"Good evening," he said.

It was as though he had slapped her in the face. She drew her head back and stared at him. First the Moor and now this one. She was horrified; in her imagination he was already out of the way, gone. And here he was, back from the dead, not even aware that he was a ghost.

"Oh," she said finally. "Hello."

"Drunk again," he thought.

"What are you doing here?" she asked him. She got down from the stool and stood leaning on the bar.

"I just thought I'd drop in and say hello."

"Oh? . . . Well, what are you drinking? Whiskey?"

"What are *you* drinking? Have one with me, please."

"Certainly not! Barman! One whiskey-soda!" She rapped imperiously on the top of the bar. "I'm just on my way up-stairs," she explained. "I'm just having this one drink." She felt that she would jump out of her skin if she had to stay and talk with him another minute.

Dyar was a bit nettled. "Well, wait'll I've had my drink, can't you? I wanted to ask you something." The barman gave him his drink.

"What was that?" she said levelly. She was positive it had something to do with Hadija, and she looked at him waiting, mentally daring him to let it be that.

"Do you know where I can find Hadija, how I can get in touch with her? I know she comes by here every now and then to see you. Do you have her address, or anything?"

It was too much. Her face became redder than usual, and she stood perfectly still, scarcely moving her lips as she spoke.

"I do not! I don't know where she lives and I care less! Why don't you look for her in the whorehouse where you met her? Why do you come sneaking to me, trying to find her? Do you think I'm her madam? Well, I'm not! *I'm* not renting her out by the hour!"

Dyar could not believe his ears. "Now, wait a minute," he said, feeling himself growing hot all over. "You don't have to talk that way about her. All you have to say is no, you don't know her address. That's all I asked you. I didn't ask you anything else. I'm not interested in what you have to say about her. For my money she's a damned nice girl."

Eunice snorted. "For your money, indeed! Very apt! That little bitch would sleep with a stallion if you made it worth her while. And I daresay she has, for that matter. A special act for tourists. They love it." She was beginning to enjoy herself as she saw the fury spreading in his face. "I don't mind naïveté," she went on, "but when it's carried to the point— Aren't you finishing your drink?" He had turned away.

"Shove it up," he said, and walked out.

Considering the number of people in the street, he thought it might be possible for him to get by the café without being seen by Thami, but it was a vain hope. He heard him calling as he came opposite the entrance. Resignedly he stepped inside and sat down cross-legged on the mat beside Thami, who had had a few pipes of kif with friends, and felt very well. They talked a bit, Dyar refusing the pipe when it was passed him. Thami kept his eyes on the street, watching for Hadija. When presently he espied her walking quickly and angrily along in the drizzle, he called Dyar's attention to a large chromolithograph on the wall beside them.

"Do you know what that is?" he demanded. Dyar looked, saw a design representing a city of minarets, domes and balustrades. "No," he said.

"That's Mecca."

He saw the others watching him, awaiting his comment. "Very nice."

From the corner of his eye Thami saw Hadija disappear into the Metropole. "Let's go," he said. "Fine," agreed Dyar. They went out into the damp, and wandered up toward the Zoco Chico. In spite of the weather the streets were filled with Arabs, standing in groups talking, or strolling aimlessly up and down.

"Do you want to go see some beautiful girls?" said Thami suddenly.

"Will you quit trying to sell this town to me?" demanded Dyar. "I don't want to go and see anything. I'm all fixed up with one beautiful girl, and that's enough." He did not add that he would give a good deal to be able to find her.

"What's in that?" Thami indicated the parcel containing the bracelet.

"A new razor."

"What kind?"

"Hollywood," said Dyar, improvising.

Thami approved. "Very nice razor." But his mind was on other things.

"You like that girl? Only that one? Hadija?"

"That's right."

"You want only that one? I know another very nice one."

"Well, you keep her, chum."

"But what's the difference, that one and another?"

"All right," said Dyar. "So you don't see. But I do. I tell you I'm satisfied."

The trouble was that Thami, still tingling with memories of the preceding night, did see. He became momentarily pensive. To him it made perfect sense that he, a Moslem, should want Hadija to himself. It was his right. He wanted every girl he could get, all to himself. But it made no sense that a Nesrani, a Christian, should pick and choose. A Christian was satisfied with anything—a Christian saw no difference between one girl and another, as long as they were both attractive—he took what was left over by the Moslems, without knowing it, and without a thought for whether she was all his or not. That was the way Christians were. But not this one, who obviously not only wanted Hadija to himself, but was not even interested in finding anyone else.

Dyar broke in on his reflections, saying: "D'you think she might be at that place we saw her in that night?" He thought he might as well admit that he would like to see her.

"Of course not—" began Thami, stopping when it occurred to him that if Dyar did not know she was living with Eunice Goode, he was not going to be the one to tell him. "It's too early," he said.

"So much the better," Dyar thought. "Well, let's go up there anyway and have a drink."

Thami was delighted. "Fine!"

This time Dyar was determined to keep track of the turns and steps, so that he could find his way up alone after dinner. Through a short crowded lane, to the left up a steep little street lined with grocery stalls, out into the triangular plaza with the big green and white arch opposite, continue up, turn right down the dark level street, first turn left again into the very narrow alley which becomes a tunnel and goes up steeply, out at top, turn right again, follow straight through paying no attention to juts and twists because there are no streets leading off, downhill to large plaza with fat hydrant in center and cafés all the way around (only they might be closed later, and with their fronts boarded up they look like any other shops), cross plaza, take alley with no streetlight overhead, at end turn left into pitch black street. . . . He began to be confused. There were too many details to remember, and now they were climbing an endless flight of stone steps in the dark.

At the Bar Lucifer Mme. Papaconstante leaned her weight on the bar, picking her teeth voluptuously. "Hello, boys," she said. She had had her hair hennaed. The place reeked of fresh paint. It was an off night. Of course it was very early. They had two drinks and Dyar paid, saying he wanted to go to his hotel. Thami had been talking about his brothers' stinginess, how they would not let him have any money— even his own. "But tomorrow I'll buy that boat!" he ended triumphantly. Dyar did not ask him where he had got the money. He was mildly surprised to hear that the other had been born and brought up in the Beidaoui Palace; he did not know whether he thought more or less of him now that he knew his origins. As they left, Thami reached across the bar and seizing Mme. Papaconstante's brilliant head, kissed her violently on each flaming cheek. "*Ay, hombre!*" she cried, laughing delightedly, pretending to rearrange her undisturbed coiffure.

In the street Dyar attempted to piece together the broken thread of the itinerary, but it seemed they were going back down by another route, as he recognized no landmark whatever until they were suddenly within sight of the smoke-filled Zoco de Fuera.

"You know, Dare—" (Dyar corrected him) "—some night I'll take you to my home and give you a real Moorish dinner. Couscous, bastila, everything. How's that?"

"That would be fine, Thami."

"Don't forget," Thami cautioned him, as if they had already arranged the occasion.

"I won't."

Just by the main gateway leading into the square, Thami stopped and indicated a native café, rather larger and more pretentious than most, inside which a very loud radio was roaring.

"I'm going here," he said. "Any time you want to see me you can always find me inside here. In a few days we'll go for a ride in my boat. So long."

Dyar stood alone in the bustling square. From the far end, through the trees, came the sound of drums, beating out a complicated, limping Berber rhythm from up in the mountains. He found a small Italian restaurant in a street off the Zoco, and had an indifferent meal. In spite of his impatience to get back into the streets and look for the Bar Lucifer, he relaxed over a caffè espresso and had two cigarettes before rising to leave. There was no point in getting there too early.

He wandered vaguely downhill until he came to a street he thought might lead in the right direction. Girls walked by slowly in clusters, hanging together as if for protection, staring at him but pretending not to. It was easy to tell the Jewish girls from the Spanish, although the two looked and dressed alike: the former loped, straggled, hobbled, practically fell along the street, as if they had no control, and without a semblance of grace. And the Arab women pushed by like great white bundles of laundry, an eye peering out near the top. Ahead of him, under a streetlight, a crowd of men and boys was gathering around two angry youths, each of whom held the other at arm's length by the lapels. The pose was as formal as a bit of frozen choreography. They glared, uttered insults, growled, and made menacing gestures with their free left hands. He watched a while; no blow was struck. Suddenly one jerked away. The other shot out of sight, and while the brief general conversation that followed was still in progress, returned from nowhere with a policeman—the classical procedure. The officer of the law separated the crowd and stepped in front of Dyar, tapping arms and shoulders very gently with his white billy. Dyar studied him:—he wore an American GI uniform and a metal helmet painted white. In a white leather holster he carried a revolver wrapped carefully in tissue paper, like a Christmas present. As if he were a farmer urging his plow-horses, he murmured to the crowd softly: "Eh. Eh. Eh. Eh." And the crowd slowly dispersed, the two antagonists already having lost themselves in its midst.

Slowly he moved ahead in what seemed to him the right direction. All he needed was one landmark and he would be set. Sweet temple-incense poured out of the Hindu silk shops, a whole Berber family crouched in the shadow of a small mountain of oranges, mechanically calling out the price of a kilo. And then all at once the dark streets began, and the few stalls that remained open were tiny and lighted by carbide lamps or candles. At one point he stopped a man in European clothes and said: "Bar Lucifer?" It was a long chance, and he did not really expect a useful answer. The man grunted and pointed back the way Dyar had just come. He thanked him and continued. It was rather fun, being lost like this; it gave him a strange sensation of security,—the feeling that at this particular instant no one in the world could possibly find him. Not his family, not Wilcox, not Daisy de Valverde, not Thami, not Eunice Goode, not Mme. Jouvenon, and not, he reflected finally, the American Legation. The thought of these last two somewhat lowered his spirits. At the moment he was further from being free than he had been yesterday at this time. The idea horrified him; it was unacceptable. Yesterday at this time he had been leaving the Beidaoui Palace in a good humor. There had been the episode of the kittens, which now that he considered it, seemed to have had something to do with that good humor. It was crazy, but it was true. As he walked on, noticing less and less where he was, he pursued his memory of yesterday evening further, like a film being run backwards. When he got to the cold garden with the stone bench where he had sat in the wind, he knew he had found the setting. It had happened while he sat there. What Holland had said had started him off, feeling rather than thinking, but Holland had not said enough, had not followed through. "Here I am and something's going to happen." No connection. He said to Holland: "You're going to die too, but in the meantime you eat." No connection whatever, and yet it was all connected. It was all part of the same thing.

The fine rain came down, cold and smelling fresh. Then it became heavier and more determined. He had his raincoat. If it rained too hard he would get soaked anyway, but it made no difference. For quite a while now the streets had been almost empty. "The slums," he thought. "Poor people go to bed early." The places through which he was passing were like the tortuous corridors in dreams. It was impossible to think of them as streets, or even as alleys. There were spaces here and there among the buildings, that was all, and some of them opened into other spaces and some did not. If he found the right series of connections he could get from one place to the next, but only by going through the buildings themselves. And the buildings seemed to have come into existence like plants, chaotic, facing no way, topheavy, one growing out of the other. Sometimes he heard footsteps echoing when someone passed through one of the vault-like tunnels, and often the sound died away without the person's ever coming into view. There were the mounds of garbage and refuse everywhere, the cats whose raging cries racked the air, and that ever-present acid smell of urine: the walls and pavements were encrusted with a brine of urine. He stood still a moment. From the distance, through the falling rain, floated the sound of chimes. It was the clock in the belfry of the Catholic Church in the Siaghines striking the quarter of the hour. Ahead there was the faint roar of the sea breaking against the cliffs below the ramparts. And as he stood there, again he found himself asking the same questions he had asked earlier in the day: "What am I doing here? What's going to happen?" He was not even trying to find the Bar Lucifer; he had given that up. He was trying to lose himself. Which meant, he realized, that his great problem right now was to escape from his cage, to discover the way out of the fly-trap, to strike the chord inside himself which would liberate those qualities capable of transforming him from a victim into a winner.

"It's a bad business," he whispered to himself. If he was so far gone that when he came out to find Hadija, instead of making every effort to locate the place, he allowed himself to stumble along for an hour or so in the dark through stinking hallways like the one where he stood at the moment, then it was time he took himself in hand. And just how? It was a comforting idea, to say you were going to take yourself in hand. It assumed the possibility of forcing a change. But between the saying and the doing there was an abyss into which all the knowledge, strength and courage you had could not keep you from plunging. For instance, tomorrow night at this time he would be still more tightly fettered, sitting in the Jouvenons' flat after dinner, having some petty little plan of action prepared for him. At each moment his situation struck him as more absurd and untenable. He had no desire to do that kind of work, and he had no interest in helping Mme. Jouvenon or her cause.

However, it was nice to have the money; it was comfortable to be able to take a cab when it was raining and he was tired and wanted to get home; it was pleasant to go into a restaurant and look at the left hand side of the menu first; it was fun to enter a shop and buy a present for Hadija. (The box with the bracelet in it bulged in his raincoat pocket.) You had to make a choice. But the choice was already made, and he felt that it was not he who had made it. Because of that, it was hard for him to believe that he was morally involved. Of course, he could fail to put in an appearance tomorrow night, but that would do no good. They would find him, demand explanations, threaten him probably. He could even return the money by cashing express checks, depositing the hundred dollars back into the account and writing a check to Mme. Jouvenon for five hundred. It was still not too late for that. Or probably it was—all she had to do was to refuse. Her check had been cashed; that remained a fact, part of the bank's records.

It suddenly seemed to him that he could to some extent neutralize the harm he had done himself by reporting his action to the American Legation. He laughed softly. Then he would be in trouble, and also there would be no more money. He knew that was the action of a victim. It was typical: a victim always gave himself up if he had dared to dream of changing his status. Yet at the moment the prospect was attractive.

Right now he wanted to get out of this rubbish-heap and home to bed. By going toward the sound of the sea, he suspected, he could arrive at some sort of definite thoroughfare which would follow along inside the ramparts. That would lead him down to the port. The thing turned out to be more complicated than he had thought, but he did manage eventually to get down into the wider streets. Here there were men walking; they were always eager to point the way out of the Arab quarter, even in the pouring rain, and often even without being asked. Their fundamental hostility to non-Moslems showed itself clearly in this respect. "This way out," the children would call, in whatever language they knew. It was a refrain. Or if you were pushing your way in, "You can't get through that way," they would say.

He came out into the principal street opposite the great mosque. A little beyond, atop the ramparts, perched the Castle Club (Open All Night . . Best Wines and Liquors Served . . Famous Attractions . . Ernesto's Hawaiian Swing Band) through whose open windows spilled the sound of a high tenor wailing into a microphone.

From here on, the way was straight, and open to the sea wind. Twenty minutes later he was cursing in front of the entrance to the Hotel de la Playa, ringing the bell and pounding on the plate glass of the locked door in an attempt to waken the Arab who was asleep in a deck chair on the other side. When the man finally let him in he looked at him reproachfully, saying: "*Sí, sí, sí.*" In his mailbox with the key was a note. He went to his room, stripped off his wet clothes, and stepped into the corner to take a hot shower. There was no hot water. He rubbed himself down with the turkish towel and got into his bathrobe. Sitting on the bed, he opened the note. *Where the hell are you?* it said. *Will be by at nine tomorrow morning. Jack.*

He laid the piece of paper on the night table and got into bed, leaving the window closed. He could tell by the sound that it was raining too hard to have it open.

3

The Age of Monsters

IN THE NIGHT the wind veered and the weather changed, bringing a luminous sky and a bright moon. In his bed at the Atlantide, Wilcox blamed his insomnia on indigestion. His dreams were turbulent and broken; he had to step out of a doorway into the street that was thronged with people who pretended to be paying him no attention, but he knew that among the passers-by were hidden the men who were waiting for him. They would seize him from behind and push him into a dark alley, and there would be no one to help him. Each time he awoke he found himself lying on his back, breathing with difficulty, his heart pounding irregularly. Finally he turned on the light and smoked. As he sat partially up in bed, looking around the room which seemed too fully lighted, he reassured himself, arguing that no one had seen Dyar in his office, and that thus no one would be able to know when he left Ramlal's shop that he was carrying the money. To look at the situation clearly, he forced himself to admit that the Larbi gang did have ways of finding things out. Ever since he had discovered that the dreaded El Kebir was back from his short term in jail at Port Lyautey (he had caught sight of him in the street the very afternoon he had left Dyar alone in the office), the fear that one of them might somehow learn of Dyar's connection with him had been uppermost in his mind. But this time he had been really circumspect; he did not think they knew anything. Only, it must be done immediately. With each hour that passed, they were more likely to get wind of the project. He wondered if it had been wise to go to the Hotel de la Playa and leave the note, if it might not have been better simply to keep telephoning all night until he had found Dyar in. He wondered if by any chance the British had had their suspicions aroused. He began to wonder all sorts of things, feeling at every moment less and less like sleeping. "That damned zabaglione," he thought. "Too rich." And he got up to take a soda-mint. While he was at the medicine cabinet he shook a gardenal tablet out of its tube as well, but then he reflected that it might make him oversleep, and he did not trust the desk downstairs to call him. They occasionally missed up, and it was imperative that he rise at eight. He got back into bed and began to read the editorial page of the Paris *Herald*.

It was about this time when Daisy de Valverde awoke feeling unaccountably nervous. Luis had gone to Casablanca for a few days on business, and although the house was full of servants she never slept well when she was alone. She listened, wondering if it had been a sudden noise which had brought her back from sleep: she heard only the endless sound of the sea against the rocks, so far below that it was like a shell being held to the ear. She opened her eyes. The room was bathed in brilliant moonlight. It came in from the west, but on all sides she could see the glow of the clear night sky out over the water. Slipping out of bed, she went and tried the door into the corridor, just to be positive it was locked. It was, and she got back into bed and pulled an extra blanket up over her, torturing herself with the fantasy that it might have been unlocked, so that it would have opened just a bit when she tried it, and she would have seen, standing just outside, a great ragged Moor with a beard, looking at her evilly through slits of eyes. She would have slammed the door, only to find that he had put one huge foot through the opening. She would have pushed against it with all her might, but. . . . .

"Shall I never grow up?" she thought. Did one never reach a stage when one had complete control of oneself, so that one could think what one wanted to think, feel the way one wanted to feel?

Thami had gone home late. The considerable number of pipes of kif he had shared with his friends in the café throughout the evening had made him a little careless, so that he had made a good deal of noise in the process of getting his clothes off. The baby had awakened and begun to wail, and the kif, instead of projecting him through a brief region of visions into sleep, had made him wakeful and short of breath. During the small hours he heard each call to prayer from the minaret of the nearby Emsallah mosque, as well as the half-hourly

chants of reassurance that all was well with the faithful; each
time the arrowlike voice came out through the still air there
was a sporadic outburst of cockcrows roundabout. Finally the
fowls refused to go back to sleep, and their racket became
continuous, up there on the roofs of the houses. Instinctively,
when he had lain down, Thami had put Eunice's check under
his pillow. At dawn he slept for an hour. When he opened
his eyes, his wife was shuffling about barefoot and the baby
was screaming again. He looked at his watch and called out:
"Coffee!" He wanted to be at the bank before it opened.

    Dyar slept fitfully for a while, his mind weighted down with
half-thoughts. About four he sat up, feeling very wide-awake,
and noticed the brightness outside. The air in the room was
close. He went to the window, opened it, and leaned out,
studying the moonlit details on the hills across the harbor: a
row of black cypresses, a house which was a tiny cube of luminous white halfway between the narrow beach and the sky,
in the middle of the soft brown waste of the hillside. It was all
painted with meticulous care. He went back to his bed and
got between the warm covers. "This is no good," he said to
himself, thinking that if he were going to feel like this he
would rather remain a victim always. At least he would feel
like himself, whereas at the moment he was all too conscious
of the pressure of that alien presence, clamoring to be
released. "It's no good. It's no good." Miserable, he turned
over. Soon the fresh air coming in the window put him to
sleep. When he opened his eyes again the room was pulsing
with sunlight. The sun was out there, huge and clear in the
morning sky, and its light was augmented by the water,
thrown against the ceiling, where it moved like fire. He
jumped up, stood in the window, stretched, scratched, yawned
and smiled. If you got up early enough, he reflected, you
could get on board the day and ride it easily, otherwise it got
ahead of you and you had to push it along in front of you as
you went. But however you did it, you and the day came out
together into the dark, over and over again. He began to do a
few setting-up exercises there in front of the open window.
For years he had gone along not being noticed, not noticing
himself, accompanying the days mechanically, exaggerating
the exertion and boredom of the day to give him sleep for the

night, and using the sleep to provide the energy to go through the following day. He did not usually bother to say to himself: "There's nothing more to it than this; what makes it all worth going through?" because he felt there was no way of answering the question. But at the moment it seemed to him he had found a simple reply: the satisfaction of being able to get through it. If you looked at it one way, that satisfaction was nothing, but if you looked at it another way, it was everything. At least, that was the way he felt this morning; it was unusual enough so that he marveled at the solution.

The air's clarity and the sun's strength made him whistle in the shower, made him note, while he was shaving, that he was very hungry. Wilcox came at five minutes of nine, pounded heavily on the door and sat down panting in the chair by the window.

"Well, today's the big day," he said, trying to look both casual and jovial. "Hated to get you up so early. But it's better to get these things done as fast as possible."

"What things?" said Dyar into his towel as he dried his face.

"Ashcombe-Danvers's money is here. You're taking it from Ramlal's to the Crédit Foncier. Remember?"

"Oh." An extra and unwelcome complication for the day. He did not sound pleased, and Wilcox noticed it.

"What's the matter? Business breaking into your social life?"

"No, no. Nothing's the matter," Dyar said, combing his hair in front of the mirror. "I'm just wondering why you picked me to be messenger boy."

"What d'you mean?" Wilcox sat up straight. "It's been understood for ten days that you were going to take the job off my hands. You've been raising hell to start work. The first definite thing I give you to do, and you wonder why I give it to you! I asked you to do it because it'll be a lot of help to me, that's why!"

"All right, all right, all right. I haven't raised any objection, have I?"

Wilcox looked calmer. "But Jesus, you've got a screwy attitude about the whole thing."

"You think so?" Dyar stood in the sunlight looking down at him, still combing his hair. "It could be the whole thing's a little screwy."

Wilcox was about to speak. Then, thinking better of it, he decided to let Dyar continue. But something in his face must have warned Dyar, for instead of going ahead and bringing in the British currency restrictions as he had intended, just to let Wilcox see that by "screwy" he meant "illegal" (since Wilcox seemed to think he was wholly ignorant of even that detail), said only: "Well, it ought not to take long, at any rate."

"Five minutes," said Wilcox, rising. "Have you had coffee?" Dyar shook his head. "Let's get going, then."

"God, what sun!" Dyar cried as they stepped out of the hotel. It was the first clear morning he had seen, it made a new world around him, it was like emerging into daylight after an endless night. "Smell that air," he said, stopping to stand with one hand on the trunk of a palm tree, facing the beach, sniffing audibly.

"For Christ's sake, let's get going!" Wilcox cried, making a point of continuing to walk ahead as fast as he could. He was letting his impatience run away with him. Dyar caught up with him, glanced at him curiously; he had not known Wilcox was so nervous. And in his insistence upon taking great strides, Wilcox stepped into some dog offal and slipped, coming down full length on the pavement. Picking himself up, even before he was on his feet, he snarled at Dyar. "Go on, laugh, God damn you! Laugh!" But Dyar merey looked concerned. There was no way of laughing in such a situation. (The sudden sight of a human being deprived of its dignity did not strike him as basically any more ludicrous and absurd than the constant effort required for the maintenance of that dignity, or than the state itself of being human in what seemed an undeniably non-human world.) But this morning, to be agreeable, he smiled as he helped dust off Wilcox's topcoat. "Did it get on me?" demanded Wilcox.

"Nope."

"Well, come on, God damn it."

They stopped for coffee at the place where Dyar had taken breakfast the previous day, but Wilcox would not sit down.

"We haven't got time."

"We? Where are you going?"

"Back to the Atlantide as soon as I know you're really on your way to Ramlal's, and not down onto the beach to sun-bathe."

"I'm on my way. Don't worry about me."

They walked to the door. "I'll leave you, then," Wilcox said. "You got everything straight?"

"Don't *worry* about me!"

"Come up to the hotel when you're finished. We can have some breakfast then."

"Fine."

Wilcox walked up the hill feeling exhausted. When he got to the Metropole he undressed and went back to bed. He would have time for a short nap before Dyar's arrival.

Following the Avenida de España along the beach toward the old part of town, Dyar toyed with the idea of going to the American Legation and laying the whole story of Madame Jouvenon before them. But who would "they" be? Some sleek-jowled individual out of the *Social Register* who would scarcely listen to him at first, and then would begin to stare at him with inimical eyes, put a series of questions to him in a cold voice, making notes of the replies. He imagined going into the spotless office, receiving the cordial handshake, being offered the chair in front of the desk.

"Good morning. What can I do for you?"

The long hesitation. "Well, it's sort of hard. I don't quite know how to tell you. I think I've gotten into some trouble."

The consul or vice-consul would look at him searchingly. "You *think*?" A pause. "Perhaps you'd better begin by telling me your name." Whereupon he would give him not only his name, but the whole stupid story of what had happened yesterday noon at the Empire. The man would look interested, clear his throat, put his hand out on the desk, say: "First of all, let's have the check."

"I haven't got it. I deposited it in the bank."

"That was bright!" (Angrily.) "Just about ten times as much work for us."

"Well, I needed money."

The man's voice would get unpleasant. "Oh, you needed money, did you? You opened an account and drew on it, is that it?"

"That's right."

Then what would he say? "So now you've got cold feet and want to be sure you won't get in trouble."

Dyar imagined his own face growing hot with embarrassment, saying: "Well, the fact that I came here to tell you about it ought to prove that I want to do the right thing."

The other would say: "Mr. Dyar, you make me laugh."

Where would it get him, an interview like that? Beyond making him an object of suspicion for the rest of the time he was in the International Zone, just what would going to the Legation accomplish?

As he started up the ramp that led to the taxi stand at the foot of the Castle Club he passed a doorway where a dog and a cat, both full-grown, lay in the sun, lazily playing together. He stopped and watched for a moment, along with several passers-by, all of whom wore the same half unbelieving, pleased smile. It was as if without their knowing it the spectacle served as proof that enmity was not inescapably the law which governed existence, that a cessation of hostilities was at least thinkable. He passed along up the street in the hot morning sun, through the Zoco Chico to Ramlal's shop. The door was locked. He went back to the Zoco, into the Café Central, and telephoned Wilcox, standing at the bar beside the coffee machine, being buffeted by all the waiters.

"Not open yet!" cried Wilcox, and he paused. "Well," he said finally, "hang around until he is. That's all you can do." He paused again. "But for God's sake don't hang around in front of the store! Just walk past every fifteen or twenty minutes and take a quick look."

"Right. Right." Dyar hung up, paid the fat barman for the call, and walked out into the square. It was twenty minutes of ten. If Ramlal was not open now, why would he be any more likely to be open at ten-thirty, or eleven? "The hell with that," he thought, starting to amble once more in the direction of the shop.

It was still closed. For him that settled it. He would go down to the beach for a while and lie in the sun. It was Wilcox who had put the idea into his head. All he had to do was to get back up here a little before half-past twelve, which was when the Crédit Foncier closed. First he stopped and had coffee and several slices of toast with butter and strawberry jam.

The beach was flat, wide and white, and it curved in a perfect semicircle to the cape ahead. He walked along the strip of hard sand that the receding tide had uncovered; it was a wet and flattering mirror for the sky, intensifying its brightness. When he had left behind the half-mile or so of boarded-up bathing cabins and bars, he took off his shoes and socks and rolled up his trousers. Until now the beach had been completely empty, but ahead two figures and a donkey were approaching. When they drew near he saw that it was two very old Berber women dressed as if it were zero weather, in red and white striped wool. They paid him no attention. Out here where no hill followed the shore line there was a small sharp wind to chill whatever surface was not in the sun. Before him now he saw several tiny fishing boats beached side by side. He came up to them. They had been abandoned long ago: the wood was rotten and the hulls were filled with sand. There was no sign of a human being in any direction. The two women and the donkey had left the beach, gone inland over the dunes, and disappeared. He undressed and got into a boat that was half buried. The sand filled the bow and sloped toward the center of the boat, making a perfect couch that faced the sun.

Outside the wind blew by; in here there was nothing but the beating of the hot sun on the skin. He lay a while, intensely conscious of the welcome heat, in a state of self-induced voluptuousness. When he looked at the sun, his eyes closed almost tight, he saw webs of crystalline fire crawling across the narrow space between the slitted lids, and his eyelashes made the furry beams of light stretch out, recede, stretch out. It was a long time since he had lain naked in the sun. He remembered that if you stayed long enough the rays drew every thought out of your head. That was what he wanted, to be baked dry and hard, to feel the vaporous worries evaporating one by one, to know finally that all the damp little doubts and hesitations that covered the floor of his being were curling up and expiring in the great furnace-blast of the sun. Presently he forgot about all that, his muscles relaxed, and he dozed lightly, waking now and then to lift his head above the worm-eaten gunwale and glance up and down the beach. There was no one. Eventually he ceased doing even that. At one point he turned over and lay face down on the hard-packed sand, feeling the sun's burning sheet settle over his back. The soft, regular cymbal-crash of the waves was like the distant breathing of the morning; the sound sifted down through the myriad compartments of the air and reached his ears long afterward. When he turned back and looked straight at the sky it seemed farther away than he had ever seen it. Yet he felt very close to himself, perhaps because in order to feel alive a man must first cease to think of himself as being *on his way*. There must be a full stop, all objectives forgotten. A voice says "Wait," but he usually will not listen, because if he waits he may be late. Then, too, if he really waits, he may find that when he starts to move again it will be in a different direction, and that also is a frightening thought. Because life is not a movement toward or away from anything; not even from the past to the future, or from youth to old age, or from birth to death. The whole of life does not equal the sum of its parts. It equals any one of the parts; there is no sum. The full-grown man is no more deeply involved in life than the new-born child; his only advantage is that it can occasionally be given him to become conscious of the substance of that life, and unless he is a fool he will not look for reasons or explanations. Life needs no clarifying, no justification. From whatever direction the approach is made, the result is the same: life for life's sake, the transcending fact of the living individual. In the meantime you eat. And so he, lying in the sun and feeling close to himself, knew that he was there and rejoiced in the knowledge. He could pretend, if he needed, to be an American named Nelson Dyar, with four thousand pesetas in the pocket of the jacket that lay across the seat in the stern of the boat, but he would know that it was a remote and unimportant part of the entire truth. First of all he was a man lying on the sand that covered the floor of a ruined boat, a man whose left hand reached to within an inch of its sun-heated hull, whose body displaced a given quantity of the warm morning air. Everything he had ever thought or done had been thought or done not by him, but by a *member* of a great mass of beings who acted as they did only because they were on their way from birth to death. He was no longer a member: having committed himself, he could expect no help from anyone. If a man was not on his way anywhere, if life was something else, entirely different, if life was a question of being for a long continuous instant that was all one, then the best thing for him to do was to sit back and be, and whatever happened, he still was. Whatever a man thought, said or did, the fact of his being there remained unchanged. And death? He felt that some day, if he thought far enough, he would discover that death changed nothing, either.

The pleasant bath of vague ideas in which his mind had been soaking no longer sufficed to keep him completely dormant. Making an effort, he raised his head a little and turned his wrist to see the time. It was ten minutes past twelve. He sprang up, dressed quickly save for his socks and shoes, and started back along the still-deserted beach. Even though he walked so fast that he was painfully out of breath, by the time he reached the first buildings it was quarter of one. The Crédit Foncier would be closed; he would have to do the job after lunch. He came opposite the Hotel de la Playa, crossed the beach, climbed the steps to the street and went in barefooted. The boy at the desk handed him a message. "Jack has been phoning; he's going nuts," he thought, as he looked at the slip. But it said: "*Sr. Doan, 25-16. Inmediatamente.*" Still assuming that this was probably Wilcox trying frantically to reach him, perhaps from the office or home of someone else, he gave the boy the number and stood drumming with his fingers on the desk until the communication was made.

He took the telephone, heard a man's voice say: "American Legation." Quietly he hung up, and without explaining anything to the boy went and sat down in a corner where he put on his socks and shoes. After he had tied the second lace carefully he sat back and shut his eyes. Under the fingers of each hand he felt the smooth beveled wood of a chair-arm. A truck went by slowly, backfiring. The lobby smelled faintly of chloride of lime. For the first few minutes he felt neither calm nor perturbation; he was paralyzed. Then when he opened his eyes he thought, almost triumphantly: "So this is what it's like." And immediately afterward he was conscious for the second time that day of being extremely hungry. He had no plan of action; he wanted to eat, he wanted to get the Ramlal business over with and let Wilcox know it was finished. After that, depending on how he felt, he might call Mr. Doan at the Legation and see what he wanted. (It consoled him to think there was no certainty that the call had to do with the Jouvenon nonsense; as a matter of fact, at moments he was almost certain it could not be that at all.) But as to the dinner at Mme. Jouvenon's apartment. . . .

He jumped up and shouted for the boy, who was hidden by the desk. "Taxi!" he cried, pointing at the telephone. He went to the door and stood looking up the avenue, trying to reassure himself by considering that if they had been going to handle the thing roughly they would not have begun by telephoning. But then he remembered something Daisy had said to him—that the Zone was so small it was generally possible for the police to put their finger on anyone in a few hours. The Legation could afford to sit back and be polite, at least until they saw how he intended to play it.

The taxi came coasting down the side street from the town above, drew up before the entrance. He hurried to get in, and leaning forward from the back seat directed it along the Avenida de España to the foot of the Arab town.

The day moved by; the city lay basking in the hot bright air. About noon, up on the mountain in the rose garden of the Villa Hesperides Daisy de Valverde did a bit of weeding. Then when the exertion became too much for her she had a rubber mattress put by the pool and lay on it in her bathing suit. There were far too few days like this in Tangier during the winter. When Luis came back from Casablanca she would talk with him again seriously about Egypt. Each year since the war they had spent part of the winter in Cairo, Luxor or Wadi Halfa, but this year for one reason and another they had not summoned the energy to set forth. Then she had tried at the last minute to get a room at the Mamounia in Marrakech, and finding it impossible, had hit on the idea of appropriating Mme. Werth's reservation, arguing that in any case that lady, always in poor health, was likely to be unable to avail herself of it when the time came. That little plan had of course been frustrated by Jack Wilcox's infuriating behavior.

"He's really rather sweet," she said to herself, thinking not of Wilcox, but of Dyar. Soon she rose, walked into the house and rang for Mario. "Get me the Hotel de la Playa on the telephone," she said.

Wilcox had gone to the Atlantide, undressed, and got into bed. There, in spite of his anxiety about the Ashcombe-Danvers sterling transfer, he had fallen into a deep slumber, exhausted finally by the wakeful night behind him. He awoke at twenty-five minutes past one (just as Dyar was entering Ramlal's shop), saw the time, and in a fury called downstairs to see what had happened. When anything went wrong, it was usually the fault of one of the employees at the desk.

"Have I had any calls?" he demanded. The young man did not know; he had just come on at one o'clock.

"Well, look in my box!" shouted Wilcox. The young man was rattled. He began to read him the messages for the person in the room on the floor beneath. "Oh, good Jesus Christ Almighty!" Wilcox yelled, and he dressed and went down to the desk to see for himself. His box was empty. There was nothing he could do, so he gave the youth at the desk a tongue-lashing and went into the bar to sit gloomily over a whiskey and grunt briefly now and then in answer to the barman's sporadic chatter, thinking how possible it was for Dyar to have come, announced himself at the desk, and been told that Mr. Wilcox was out.

XVI

Perspiring a little after his rapid climb up from the port, Dyar stepped from the street's yellow glare into the darkness of the shop. Young Ramlal was reading a newspaper; he sat dangling his legs from a high table which was the only piece of furniture in the tiny room. When he glanced up, no expression of recognition appeared on the features of his smooth face, but he jumped down and said: "Good morning. I expected you to come earlier."

"Well, I came by twice, but you were closed."

"Ah, *too* early. Will you have a cigarette?"

"Thanks."

Tossing his lighter onto the table, the Indian continued: "I have been waiting for you. You see, I could not leave the package here, and I did not want to carry it with me when I go to eat lunch. If you had not come I'd have waited. So you see I am glad to see you." He smiled.

"Oh," said Dyar. "I'm sorry to have kept you waiting."

"Not at all, not at all." Ramlal, happy to have extracted an apology, took a key from his trousers pocket and opened a drawer in the table. From this he lifted a large cardboard box marked *Consul. Twenty Tins of Fifty. A Blend of the Finest Matured Virginian Grown Tobaccos.* "I would not advise counting it here," he said. "But here it is." He opened the box and Dyar saw the stacks of thin white paper. Then swiftly he closed it, as if more than this rapid exposure to air and light risked spoiling its delicate contents. Keeping one thin dark hand protectingly spread over the carton, Ramlal went on: "They were counted of course by my father in Gibraltar, and by me again last night. Therefore I assure you there are one thousand eight hundred five-pound notes in the box. If you wish to make a count now, it is quite all right. But—" He waved expressively at the throng passing in the street a few feet away, and smiled. "One never knows, you know."

"Oh, hell. That doesn't matter." Dyar tried to look friendly. "I'll take your word for it. If there's any mistake we know where to find you, I guess."

The other, looking faintly offended as he heard the last sentence, turned away and brought out a large sheet of shiny blue and white wrapping paper with the words "Galeries Lafayette" printed across it at regular intervals. With professional dexterity he made a smart package and tied it up with a length of immaculate white string.

"There we are," he said, stepping back and bowing slightly. "And when you write Mr. Ashcombe-Danvers please don't neglect to give him my father's greetings and my respects."

Dyar thanked him and went out into the street holding his parcel tightly. Half done, anyway, he thought. By the time he had eaten something the Crédit Foncier would be open. He strolled up through the Zoco de Fuera to the Italian restaurant where he had eaten the previous night. The bundles of big soiled white notes had not looked like money at all; the

color of money was green, and real bills were small and convenient. It was no new sensation for him to have in his hands
a large sum of banknotes which did not belong to him, so
that the idea of his responsibility did not cause him undue
nervousness. At the restaurant he laid the package on the
floor near his feet and glanced down at it occasionally during
the meal. Today of all days, he thought, he would have liked
to be free, to rent a little convertible, perhaps, and drive out
into the country with Hadija, or even better, to hop on a
train and just keep going down into Africa, to the end of the
line. (And from there? Africa was a big place and would
offer its own suggestions.) He would even have settled for
another pilgrimage to the beach, and this time he would have
gone into the water and had a little exercise. Instead of
which the best part of the afternoon would be occupied by
the visits the Crédit Foncier and the Hotel Atlantide, and
Wilcox would find fault and yell at him, once he knew the
money was safe in the bank. He decided to tell him he had
gone by Ramlal's and found it closed three times, instead of
twice.

A few minutes after two he got up, took his parcel, and
paid the check to the stout *patronne* who stood behind the
bar by the door. As he stepped into the brilliant sunlight he
pitied himself a little for his obligations on such an afternoon.
When he got to the Crédit Foncier the doors were open, and
he went into the shabby gloom of its public room. Behind the
iron grillework of the wickets the accountants were visible,
seated on high stools at their chaotic desks. He started up the
chipped marble staircase; an Arab in uniform called him back.
"Mr. Benzekri," he said. The Arab let him continue, but
looked after him suspiciously.

The buff walls of the little office were disfigured by rusty
stains that spread monstrously from the ceiling to the floor.
Mr. Benzekri sat in a huge black chair, looking even sadder
than when they had met at the Café España. He nodded his
head very slowly up and down as he unwrapped the box, as if
he were saying: "Ah, yes. More of this dirty paper to count
and take care of." But when he saw the carefully tied bundles
inside, he looked up at Dyar sharply.

"Five-pound notes? We cannot accept these."

"What?" The loudness of his own voice surprised Dyar. "Can't accept them?" He saw himself embarking on an endless series of trips between an irascible Wilcox and a smiling Ramlal. However, Mr. Benzekri was very calm.

"Five-pound notes are illegal here, as you know." Dyar was about to interrupt, to protest his ignorance, but Mr. Benzekri, already wrapping the blue and white paper around the box, went on: "Chocron will change this for you. He will give you pesetas, and we will buy them for pounds. Mr. Ashcombe-Danvers of course wants pounds for his accounts. He will lose twice on the exchange, but I am sorry. These notes are illegal in Tangier."

Dyar was still confused. "But what makes you think this man—" he hesitated.

"Chocron?"

"—What makes you think *he's* going to buy illegal tender?"

A faint, brief smile touched Mr. Benzekri's melancholy lips. "He will take it," he said quietly. And he sat back, staring ahead of him as if Dyar had already gone out. But then, as Dyar gathered up the neatly tied parcel once again, he said: "Wait," bent forward and scribbled some words on a pad, tearing off the sheet and handing it to him. "Give this to Chocron. Come back before four. We close at four. The address is at the top of the paper." "A lot of good that's going to do me," Dyar thought. He thanked Mr. Benzekri and went downstairs, out into the Zoco Chico where the striped awning over the terrasse of the Café Central was being let down to shield the customers from the hot afternoon sun. There he approached a native policeman who stood grandly in the center of the plaza and inquired of him how to get to the Calle Sinagoga. It was nearby: up the main street and to the left, by what he could gather from the man's gestures. All hope of getting to the beach was gone. The next sunny day like this might come in another two weeks; there was no telling. Silently he cursed Ramlal, Wilcox, Ashcombe-Danvers.

Chocron's office was at the top of a flight of stairs, in a cluttered little room that jutted out over the narrow street below, and the gray-bearded Chocron, who looked distinguished in the long black tunic and skullcap worn by the older Jews of the community, beamed when he read Benzekri's note. His English, however, was virtually non-existent. "Show," he said, pointing to the box, which Dyar opened. "Sit," suggested Chocron, and he removed the packets from the box and began to count the bills rapidly, moistening his finger on the tip of his tongue from time to time. "This one and Benzekri are probably crooks," Dyar thought uneasily. Still, the value of the pound in pesetas was posted on blackboards every few feet along the street; the rate could not go too far astray. Or perhaps it could, if the pounds were illegal. Even if the notes themselves had been valid, their very presence here was due to an infringement of the law; there was no possibility of recourse to any authority, whatever rates Chocron and Benzekri took it into their heads to charge. Below in the street the long cries of a candy-vendor passing slowly by sounded like religious chanting. Mr. Chocron's expert fingers continued to manipulate the corners of the notes. Occasionally he held one up to the light that came through the window and squinted at it. When he had finished with a bundle he tied it up again meticulously, never looking toward Dyar. Finally he placed all the bundles back in the box and taking the slip of paper Mr. Benzekri had sent him, turned it over and wrote on the other side: 138 pesetas. He pushed the paper toward Dyar and stared at him. This was a little higher than the street quotation, which varied between 133 and 136 to the pound. Still suspicious, making grimaces and gestures, Dyar said: "What do you do with money like this?" It seemed that Chocron understood more English than he spoke. "Palestina," he answered laconically, pointing out the window. Dyar began to multiply 138 by 9,000, just to amuse himself. Then he wrote the figures 1 4 2, and passed the paper back to the other, to see what the reaction would be. Chocron became voluble in Spanish, and it was easy to see that he had no intention of going that high. Somewhere along the flow of words Dyar heard the name of Benzekri; that, and the idea that one hundred forty two was too many pesetas to pay for a pound, was all he grasped of the monologue. However, he was warming to the game. If he sat quietly, he thought, Chocron would raise his offer. It took a while. Chocron pulled a notebook out of a drawer and began to do a series of involved arithmetical exercises. At one point he produced a small silver case and inhaled a bit of snuff through each nostril. Deliberately he put it away and continued his work. Dyar tapped his right toe against the red tile floor in a march rhythm, waiting. You could change the price of anything here, Wilcox had insisted, if you knew how, and the prime virtues in the affair were patience and an appearance of indifference. (He remembered Wilcox's anecdote of the country Arab in the post office who had tried for five minutes to get a seventy-five-céntimo stamp for sixty céntimos and finally had turned away insulted when the clerk refused to bargain with him.) In this case the indifference was more than feigned; he had no interest in saving Ashcombe-Danvers a few thousand pesetas. It was a game, nothing more. He tried to imagine how he would feel at the moment if the money were his own. Probably he would not have had the courage to attempt bargaining at all. There was a difference between playing with money that was not real and money that was. But at this point nothing was real. The little room crowded with old furniture, the bearded man in black opposite him, making figures mechanically in the notebook, the golden light of the waning afternoon, the intimate street sounds outside the window,—all these things were suffused with an inexplicable quality of tentativeness which robbed them of the familiar feeling of reassurance contained in the idea of reality. Above all he was aware of the absurdity of his own situation. There was no doubt now in his mind that the call from the American Legation had to do with a proposed questioning on the matter of Mme. Jouvenon. If he disregarded both the call and the dinner engagement, by tomorrow they would be pulling on him from both sides.

With each day as it passed Dyar had been feeling a little further from the world; it was inevitable that at some point he should make a voluntary effort to put himself back in the middle of it again. To be able to believe fully in the reality of the circumstances in which a man finds himself, he must feel that they bear some relation, however distant, to other situations he has known. If he cannot find this connection, he is cut off from the outside. But since his inner sense of orientation depends for its accuracy on the proper functioning, at least in his eyes, of the outside world, he will make any readjustment, consciously or otherwise, to restore the sense of balance. He is an instrument that strives to adapt itself to the new exterior; he must get those unfamiliar contours more or less into focus once again. And now the outside was very far away—so far that the leg of Chocron's desk could have been something seen through a telescope from an observatory. He had the feeling that if he made a terrible effort he could bring about a change: either the leg of the desk would disappear, or, if it stayed, he would be able to understand what its presence meant. He held his breath. Through the dizziness that resulted he heard Chocron's voice saying something that made no sense. "*Cientocuarenta. Mire.*" He was holding up a piece of paper for him to look at. With the sense of lifting a tremendous weight, Dyar raised his eyes and saw figures written on it, conscious at the same time that inside himself a vast and irresistible upheaval was taking place. "Huh?" he said. Chocron had written "140."

"All right."

"One minute," said Chocron; he rose, took the box of money, and went into another room, closing the door behind him.

Dyar did not move. He stared out the window at the wall of the building opposite. The quake was quieting down; the principal strata had shifted positions, and their new places seemed more comfortable. It was as if something which had been in his line of vision had now been removed, something that had been an obstacle to discovering how to change the external scene. But he distrusted this whole series of private experiences that had forced themselves upon him since he had come here. He was used to long stretches of intolerable boredom punctuated by small crises of disgust; these violent disturbances inside himself seemed no part of his life. They were much more a part of this senseless place he was in. Still, if that were the way the place was going to affect him, he had better get used to the effects and learn how to deal with them.

When Chocron returned he carried the box with him, but this time the bills in it were smaller, brownish-green, violet, and there were fewer of them. He set the box on the desk and still standing, wrote in his notebook for Dyar to see: 1260 @ 1000p. "Count," he said.

It took him a long time, even though most of the bills were new and crisp.

Well, this is fine, he thought, when he had finished. Twenty-five thousand two hundred bucks or thereabouts and no one to stop you. You just walk out. He looked up at Chocron's face, curiously, for a second. No one but Wilcox. It was true. And Wilcox alone—not Wilcox with the police. By God, what a situation, he thought. It's almost worth playing, just for the hell of it.

He did not pay much attention to Chocron's handshake and to the steep stairs that led down into the street. Walking along slowly, being jostled by water carriers and elderly Jewish women in fringed shawls, he kept his eyes on the pavement, not thinking. But he felt the glossy paper around the box, and knew that Chocron had wrapped it carefully, that it was once again a parcel from the Galeries Lafayette. He went beneath a high arch where Arabs hawked bananas and thick glassware; to the left he recognized Thami's café.

When he looked inside the door the radio was not playing. It was dark in the café, and he had the impression that the place was practically empty.

"*Quiere algo?*" said the qaouaji.

"No, no." The air was aromatic with kif smoke. A hand grasped his arm, squeezed it gently. He turned.

"Hello," said Thami.

"Hi!" It was almost like seeing an old friend; he did not know why, except that he had been alone all during a day that had seemed endless. "I didn't think you'd be here."

"I told you I'm always here."

"What d'you have a home for?"

Thami made a face and spat. "To sleep when I have no other place."

"And a wife? What d'you have a wife for?"

"Same thing. Sit down. Take a glass of good tea."

"I can't. I have to go." He looked at his watch: it was quarter of four. "I have to go fast." The walk down to the Crédit Foncier was only a three-minute one, but he wanted to be sure and get there before they shut that iron grille.

"Are you going up or down?"

"To the Zoco Chico."

"I'll walk with you."

"Okay." He did not want Thami along, but there was no way out of it, and anyway, he thought they might have a drink afterward.

As they walked, Thami looked disparagingly down at his own trousers, which were very much out of press and smeared with grease.

"My old clothes," he remarked, pointing. "Very old. For working on my boat."

"Oh, you bought that boat?"

"Of course I bought it. I told you I was going to." He grinned. "Now I have it. Mister Thami Beidaoui, *propietario* of one old boat. One very old boat, but it goes fast."

"Goes fast?" Dyar repeated, not paying attention.

"I don't know how fast, but faster than the fishing boats down there. You know, it's an old boat. It can't go like a new one."

"No. Of course."

They passed Ramlal's shop. It was closed. Ramlal had added six batteries for portable radios to the array of fountain pens, celluloid toys and wrist watches. They passed El Gran Paris, its show windows a chaos of raincoats. It was always difficult to navigate the Zoco Chico with its groups of stationary talkers like rocks in the sea, around which the crowd surged in all directions. Arrived at what Dyar thought was the entrance to the Crédit Foncier, at the top of some steps between two cafés, he saw that even the way into the outer courtyard was barred by high gates which were closed.

"This isn't it," he said, looking uneasily up and down the plaza.

"What do you want?" Thami asked, perhaps slightly annoyed that Dyar had not already told him exactly where he was going and on what errand. Dyar did not reply; his heart sank, because he knew now that this was the Crédit Foncier and that it was closed. He ran up the steps and shook the gate, pounded on it, wondering if the sound could be heard through the vast babble of voices that floated in from the zoco.

Thami slowly climbed the steps, frowning. "Why do you want to get in? You want to go to the bank?"

"It's not even five of four yet. It shouldn't be closed."

Thami smiled pityingly. "Ha! You think this is America, people looking at their watches all the time until they see if it is exactly four o'clock, or exactly ten o'clock? Today they might stay open until twenty minutes past four, tomorrow they might lock the door at ten minutes before four. The way they feel. You know. Sometimes you have a lot of work. Sometimes not much."

"God damn it, I've got to get in there!" Dyar pounded on the gate some more, and called out: "Hey!"

Thami was used to this urgency on the part of foreigners. He smiled. "You can get in tomorrow morning."

"Tomorrow morning hell. I *have* to get in now."

Thami yawned and stretched. "Well, I would like to help you, but I can't do anything."

Pounding and calling out seemed fairly useless. Dyar continued to do both, until a very thin Arab with a broom in his hand appeared from a corner of the courtyard, and stood looking between the bars.

"*Ili firmi!*" he said indignantly.

"Mr. Benzekri! I've got to see him!"

"*Ili firmi, m'sio.*" And to Thami: "*Qoullou rhadda f's sbah.*" But Thami did not deign to notice the sweeper; he went back down the steps into the zoco and shouted up to Dyar: "Come on!" Seeing that the latter remained at the gate trying to argue with the man, he sat down in a chair nearby on the sidewalk to wait until he had finished. Presently Dyar came down to join him, muttering under his breath.

"The son of a bitch wouldn't even go and call Mr. Benzekri for me."

Thami laughed. "Sit down. Have a drink. Be my guest." A waiter had approached. Dyar threw himself into a chair. "Give me a White Horse. No water," he said.

Thami ordered. Then he looked at Dyar and laughed again. He reached over and slapped Dyar's knee. "Don't be so serious. No one is going to die because you can't get in the bank today instead of tomorrow. You can go tomorrow."

"Yes," said Dyar. Even as he said it he was thinking: Legally the money belongs to whoever has it. And I've got it.

"You need money?" said Thami suddenly. "How much? I'll give you some money. How much?"

"No thanks, Thami. I appreciate it. You're a good guy. Just let me think. I just want to think a minute."

Thami was silent until the whiskey was brought. Then he began to talk again, about an Englishman he had once known. The Englishman had invited him to go to Xauen with him, but for some reason there had been difficulties at the frontier. Never very perceptive, he did not notice that Dyar was still sunk inside himself, formulating, rejecting possibilities.

"*A votre santé, monsieur,*" said Thami, raising his glass expectantly.

"Yeah," said Dyar. "Yeah." And looking up suddenly: "Right. *Prosit.*" He drained his glass. He was thinking: if only Ramlal had gotten the money yesterday morning instead of last night I'd be in the clear. No Legation wondering when I'm going to phone. No Madame Jouvenon. Damn Madame Jouvenon. He did not realize how illogical his reasoning was at this point, how inextricably bound up with his present decision was his involvement with that lady.

"Let's get out of here." He rose to his feet. The suddenness of the remark and the tone in which it was said made Thami look up at him wonderingly.

In the street, going down toward the port, he began to speak confidentially, holding his mouth close to Thami's ear. "Can you run that boat?"

"Well—"

"You can't run it. All right. Do you know anyone who can? How about the guy you bought it from? He can run it, can't he? Where is he now?"

"Where is he now?"

"Yes. Right now."

"He lives in Dradeb."

"Where's that?"

"You know," said Thami obligingly. "You go from the Zoco de Fuera into Bou Arakía. You go past the Moorish cemetery and you come to Cuatro Caminos—"

"Can we go there in a taxi?"

"Taxi? We don't need a taxi. We can walk. The taxi charges fifteen pesetas."

"We can get there in a taxi, though?"

Thami, looking increasingly surprised, said that they could.

"Come on!" Dyar rushed ahead, toward the cab-stand at the foot of the ramparts. Laughing and protesting, Thami followed. At last the American was behaving like an American. They got to the foot of the hill. Dyar looked at his watch. Ten after four. I'm glad I thought of *that*, he said to himself. "Hotel de la Playa," he told the driver. If Wilcox just happened to be at the hotel waiting for him, he could still have an alibi. Chocron had kept him so long that the Crédit Foncier was closed when he got there, so he had come back immediately to lock up the money until tomorrow. Wilcox could either take it with him, or leave it, as he liked. But if he returned to the hotel any later than this and happened to find Wilcox, there would be no way of explaining the time that had elapsed between four and whatever time he got there. "If you just do each thing as it comes along and keep calm you can get away with this. Get rattled and you're screwed for good," he told himself.

The sun had gone behind the high buildings on the hill, but it still shone on the freighters at anchor in the harbor; all their white paint was turning faintly orange in its light. Beyond them on its cliff stood the whitewashed tower of the lighthouse at Malabata.

At the hotel he had Thami wait in the cab. With his parcel he jumped out and went into the lobby. There was no sign of Wilcox. That was all right, but the more dangerous moment would be when he came back downstairs. Even then he could still say he had thought of locking it in one of his valises, then had decided to give it to the management to put into the hotel safe. The boy gave him his key and a telephone message, which he put into his pocket without reading. He ran upstairs. The air in his room was dead, colder by several degrees than the air outdoors. He laid his brief case on the bed, quickly put into it his razor, shaving cream, blades, toothbrush, toothpaste, comb and four handkerchiefs. Then he unwrapped the box and laid the bundles of bills in among the toilet articles. There was still room for a pair of shorts. The door was locked; if Wilcox rapped on it at this moment he would have time to take out the money and throw the brief case into the closet. He felt in his pocket to see if his passport, wallet and express checks were all there. He stuffed a woolen scarf and a pair of gloves into the pocket of his overcoat and slung it over his arm, closed the brief case, spun its Sesamee lock to triple zero, and looked once more around the room. Then, with a caution which he felt was absurd even as he used it, he unlocked the door and opened it. The corridor was empty. Through the window at the end he saw the distant dunes behind the beach; their shadows reached out along the flat sand toward the harbor. A radio upstairs was playing Flamenco music, but there was no sound in the halls or stairway.

"Let's go," he whispered, and he went quietly downstairs. Wilcox was not in the lobby. The taxi outside had not moved. He handed his key to the boy and walked out. "Good bye, Playa," he said under his breath.

"Now give that address to the driver."

"The Jilali?" Thami was mystified, but knowing something was in the air he had every intention of playing along until he satisfied his curiosity, both as to what Dyar was doing and as to whether there might be some money in it for him. He leaned forward and began to give the man complicated instructions.

"Come on! Let's get started!" Dyar cried, glancing anxiously down the Avenida de España. "You can do that on the way."

The cab backed and turned up the road that went over the hill. Now the setting sun shone directly into their faces; Dyar put on a pair of dark glasses, turned to Thami. "What did you pay for your boat?"

Thami gulped and floundered, saying: "Who, me?" which is what any Arab would have said under similar circumstances; then, remembering that such an answer was calculated to infuriate any American, he quickly told him the only price he could think of, which was the true one.

"How's this?" said Dyar. "You rent the boat to me tonight for twenty-five hundred pesetas, and I'll give you another twenty-five hundred to come along and see that I get where I want to go. You'll have your boat and your five thousand."

The emotions engendered in Thami by the unfamiliar situation caused him further to abandon his European habits of thought. Good luck, like bad luck, comes directly from Allah to the recipient; the intermediary is of little importance save as a lever to help assure the extraction of the maximum blessing. "I have no money for *gasolina*," objected Thami.

By the time they got to the crowded main street of the suburb that was Dradeb, they had reached an agreement on all the main points of finance; the Jilali remained an uncertain factor, but Thami was optimistic. "I'll tell him seven hundred fifty and then we can go up to one thousand if we have to," he said, figuring on a fifty percent split (which might not be so easy to get, he reflected, considering that with his five thousand pesetas the Jilali was not immediately in need of money.)

The cab drew up to the curb and stopped in front of a grocery store. Thami leaped out, disappeared down one of the twilit alleys, was back to make inquiries at the shop, and hurried ahead up the main street. The driver got out and walked in the other direction.

Left alone in the taxi, oblivious of the inquisitive stares of passers-by, Dyar relaxed voluptuously, savoring the first small delights of triumph. It was already a very pleasant thing to have Thami rushing around out there, intent on helping him.

Then he remembered the message the boy at the hotel had given him. He took it out of his pocket and snapped on the overhead light. "*Llame Vd. Al 28-01*," it said, and he knew that was Daisy de Valverde's number. The brief case in his hand, he got out and stepped into the grocery store. By now it was fairly dark in the street, and there was only one candle in here to add to the failing blue daylight that still came through the door. A placid Soussi sat behind the counter, his eyes almost closed. Dyar saw the telephone on a crate behind the broken Coca-Cola cooler. It was a dial phone: he was thankful for that. He had to strike a match to see the numbers.

Surprisingly, Daisy herself answered. "You villain," she said. "You just got my message? I called hours ago. *Can* you come to dinner? All very informal, all very *private*, I might even add. Luis is in Casa. I'm in bed. Not really ill. Only sciatica. Just you and I, and I should love it if you could come. About seven? So we can talk? It'll be wonderful to see you, darling."

He laid the money for the call on the counter; the Soussi nodded his head once. When he got to the taxi, the driver was back at the wheel, opening a pack of cigarettes. He got in, slammed the door, and sat waiting. It seemed a perfect solution to the problem of dinner; it would keep him completely out of the streets, out of the town.

Presently he saw Thami coming along toward the cab. He had someone with him. He came up, opened the door and leaned in. "I found him," he announced, pleased with the financial arrangements he had just completed, on the way from the Jilali's house.

"Fine. Now we go to your house," said Dyar. "Stick him in front and let's go."

The Jilali's name was Zaki; he was a man of thirty-five (which meant that he looked fifty), unkempt in his attire and very much in need of a shave, so that to Dyar his appearance suggested an extra in a pirate film.

"Does he understand any English?" he asked Thami.

"That man? Ha! He doesn't even understand Spanish!" Thami sounded triumphant. "*Verdad, amigo?*" he called to the one in front.

"*Chnou?*" said the Jilali, not turning around.

The street where Thami lived became increasingly bumpy and full of puddles whose depth it was impossible to judge; the driver suddenly stopped the car and announced that he would proceed no further. There ensued an argument which promised to be lengthy. Dyar got out and surveyed the street with distaste. The houses were ramshackle, some with second stories still in construction, and their front doors gave directly on to the muddy lane, no room having been left for a future laying of sidewalks. Impatiently he called to Thami. "Have him wait here, then. Hurry up!" The driver however, after locking the car, insisted on accompanying them. "He says we owe him sixty-five pesetas already," confided Thami. Dyar grunted.

Thami entered first, to get his wife out of the way, while the others waited outside in the dark.

"You stay here," Dyar said to the driver, who appeared satisfied once he had seen which house they were going to enter.

Soon Thami came to the door and motioned them in, leading the way through the unlit patio into a narrow room
where a radio was playing. The mattress along the wall was
covered with cheap green and yellow brocade; above it hung
a group of large gilt-framed photographs of men wearing
gandouras and fezzes. Three alarm clocks, all ticking, sat atop
a hanging cupboard at the end of the room, but each one
showed a different hour. Ranging along a lower shelf beneath
them was a succession of dusty but unused paper cups which
had been placed with care so as to alternate with as many
small red figurines of plaster, representing Santa Claus; below
and to both sides, the wall was papered with several dozen
colored brochures, all identical, each bearing the photograph
of an enormous toothbrush with a brilliant blue plastic handle. "DENTOLINE, LA BROSSE A DENTS PAR EXCELLENCE,"
they said, over and over. The radio on the floor in the corner
was turned up to its full volume; Om Kalsoum sang a tortured lament, and behind her voice an orchestra sputtered
and wailed.

"Sit down!" shouted Thami to Dyar. He knelt and reduced
the force of the music a little. As Dyar stepped over to the
mattress, the electric light bulb which swung at the end of a
long cord from the center of the ceiling struck him on the
forehead. "Sorry," he said, as the light waved crazily back and
forth. The Jilali had removed his shoes at the door and was
already seated at one end of the mattress, his legs tucked
under him, swaying a bit from side to side with the music.

Dyar called across to Thami: "Hey! Cut off the funeral!
Would you mind? We've got a lot to talk about, and not
much time."

Out of the silence that followed came the sound of the
baby screaming in the next room. Dyar began to talk.

XVII

What did it mean, reflected Daisy, to be what your friends
called a forceful woman? Although they intended to mean it as
such, they did not manage to make it a flattering epithet; she
knew that. It was adverse criticism. If you said a woman was
forceful, you meant that she got what she wanted in too direct

a manner, that she was not enough of a woman, that she was unsubtle, pushing. It was almost as much of an insult as to say that a man had a weak character. Yet her closest friends were in the habit of using the word openly to describe her; "even to my face," she thought, with mingled resentment and satisfaction. It was as if, in accepting the contemporary fallacy that women should have the same aims and capacities as men, they assumed that any quality which was a virtue in a man was equally desirable in a woman. But when she heard the word "forceful" being used in connection with herself, even though she knew it was perfectly true and not intended as derogation, she immediately felt like some rather ungraceful predatory animal, and the sensation did not please her. There were very concrete disadvantages attached to being classified that way: in any situation where it would be natural to expect an expression of concern for her well-being on the part of the males in the group, it was always the other women about whom they fretted. The general opinion, often uttered aloud, was that Daisy could take care of herself. And how many other husbands went off and left their wives for five or six days, alone in the house with the servants? It was not that she minded being alone—on the contrary, it was rather a rest for her, since she never entertained when Luis was away. But the fact that he took it so much as a matter of course that she would not mind—for some reason this nettled her, although she could not have found a logical explanation for her annoyance. "I suppose one can't have one's cake and eat it too," she would say to herself at least once during each of his absences. If you had spent your childhood astride a horse, riding with your four brothers around the fifty thousand acres of an estancia, it was natural that you should become the sort of woman she had become, and you could hardly expect men to feel protective toward you. As a matter of fact, it was often quite the reverse: she sometimes found her male friends looking to her for moral support, and she always gave it unhesitatingly even though she was aware as she did so that at each moment she was moving farther from the privileged position modern woman is expected to occupy vis-à-vis her male acquaintances.

The majority of Daisy's friends were men: men liked her and she prided herself on knowing how to handle them. Yet her first two husbands had died, the one leaving her with a child and the other with a considerable fortune. The little girl she had more or less abandoned to the care of her father's family in Buenos Aires; the fortune however she had kept. At loose ends in London, and for want of anything better to do, she had decided to set out in leisurely fashion around the world. The trip took three years; she ended up in the south of France during the autumn of 1938, where she took a small house at Saint Paul du Var, intensely conscious of her solitude and with the feeling that somehow her life had not yet begun.

It was at the Palm Beach in Cannes that she had first met Luis, a thin and dramatically dark Spaniard who wore an opera cape and handled it as arrogantly as a matador his muleta, who was rude to everyone without being actually offensive, who used incredibly obscene language and yet managed to remain very much a gentleman. He was the owner of several vast estates in Andalucía which he had very little hope of recovering, even assuming that Franco were able to put an end to the Republican resistance. "They are all eediot!" he would bellow to the entire casino. "All thee Spaniard can eat sheet!" Little by little Daisy found herself thinking with admiration of this strange man who bragged that he had never read a book and was unable to write more than his own signature. He managed horses as well as the most seasoned gaucho, was as good a marksman as she, and had not a trace of sentimentality or condescension in his character. He was as dry, hard and impersonal as a rock, and she once told him that he reminded her of certain Andalucían landscapes. She was scarcely prepared, however, for his reaction, which came immediately and with astonishing force. Turning to her with the violence of one who has just been insulted, he shouted: "That is a declaration of love!" seized her in his arms, and began to make love to her with such brutality that she cried out and struck him in the face. The incident had taken place in the bar of the Carlton, in front of several people, and after a few moments of shame and fury in the ladies' room, to which she had retired when he had released her, she had come out and apologized to him for her behavior, expecting him, naturally enough, to do likewise. But he had laughed, paid the barman, and walked out.

Afterward, each time they met (since meetings were unavoidable in Cannes) he inquired if she still admired the Andalucían landscape as much as ever. It would have been a violation of her code to do anything but admit that she did. Her answers gave him immense satisfaction. "Aaah!" he would cry delightedly, "*Ya ves?*" for they had fallen into the habit of speaking Spanish together. He had a small villa at Le Cannet, packed with furniture and paintings he had succeeded in getting out of Spain, and she used to drive down sometimes in the late afternoon and visit him. Since it was well known that he sold a picture from time to time in order to go on living, she did not hesitate, when one day she saw a Goya she particularly admired, to ask him its price. The Marqués de Valverde went into a rare fury. "Andalucía is not for sale!" he yelled. "Don't be absurd," said Daisy. "I'll give you a good price for it. You need the money." But her host continued to rail, saying that he would rather put his foot through the Goya than let her have it, whatever sum she might be prepared to give him for it. Understanding that all this vehemence, although perfectly sincere, was merely a part of the abnormally developed pride which governs the behavior of the Spanish peasant or aristocrat, Daisy made an audacious suggestion. "I like that picture," she said, "and if you won't sell it to me you must give it to me." The Marqués had smiled with delight. "Anything in my house is yours for the asking," he had replied. Their friendship had begun at that moment. The man was magnificent, she decided, and it was not surprising that from being inseparable friends they soon turned to being passionate lovers. Daisy was slightly over thirty, her face radiant with a healthy, strident kind of beauty that perfectly suited her statuesque figure. It was inevitable that a man like Luis should fall in love with her, that having done so he should perceive much more in her character than he had suspected, and thus determine to marry her, in order to own her completely. It was also inevitable that once having added her to his list of possessions he should cease to be in love with her, but Daisy knew this beforehand and did not care, because she also knew that she would never cease to admire him, whatever he might do, and she was sure she would be able to keep him, which for her, an eminently practical woman, was after all the main consideration.

And so to Daisy there was nothing surprising about Luis's first infidelities. After a very small wedding in the church at Saint Paul du Var they had closed their respective houses and shipped Luis' more valuable belongings to Rio, on the advice of Daisy's banker. "Jewish bankers always know when there's going to be a war," said Daisy. "You can trust them implicitly." They went off to Brazil, the war came, and they stayed there until it was over. Luis had begun with a nightclub dancer, had continued with chambermaids, and eventually had moved on to one of Daisy's own friends, a certain Senhora da Cunha, and Daisy never had said a word to show that she knew. Luis was perceptive enough to realize that she could not help being aware of his indiscretions, but whether she minded or not, he was bound to continue them, and they both knew this, so that the matter remained forever unmentioned, as if by mutual agreement. For a while, when they had first come to Tangier at the end of the war, there had been no one. Daisy knew this was merely a quiet interval; soon enough it would end. When his business trips to Casablanca had begun, she understood. Even now she had no idea who it was, nor, she kept telling herself, did she care too much. Still, somehow she always found herself making an effort to find out who the woman was, and if possible to meet her, because she felt each time that the knowledge gave her the key to yet another chamber of Luis' mysterious personality. The more she could learn about his mistress, the more she would know about him. Having been brought up in a world of Latins, Daisy believed that promiscuity was as proper for men as it was improper for women. She would have thought it shocking for her even to consider the idea of having a lover. For a decent woman there was no possibility of anyone but her husband, and since she was so firmly decided on this score, she allowed herself to follow a pattern of behavior which to women of less resolute character often seemed highly questionable. Her reputation among the feminine members of the English colony was not all that it might have been, precisely because she knew where she stood and could allow herself liberties that would have proven disastrous in the

case of most of the others. Knowing herself, she had respect
for herself; knowing the others, she had none for them, and
thus it was of little importance to her what they whispered
about her. What, she wondered, could they think but the very
worst, if they heard that she had invited this young American
to the Villa Hesperides during Luis' absence? And now as she
lay in her bed and methodically searched to unearth her
motives, she felt a tiny chill of apprehension. Was she completely safe from herself with regard to this young man? *He*
was harmless enough; (she smiled as she remembered his
ingenuousness, his apparent innocence of the world, and the
impression she had of his utter helplessness in the face of it.)
But even the most innocuous element by itself could prove to
be dangerous in its meeting with a different element. She
thought about it, and felt small doubts rising. "Or am I really
hoping that something will happen, and is this just my way of
punishing myself?" It was hard to say. She reached for the bell
button that lay on the table among a welter of perfume bottles and medicines, and pushed it. A maid knocked at the
door. "Have Hugo come up," she told her.

"Ah, Hugo," she said when he appeared. "If the telephone
rings this evening while Mr. Dyar is here, I've gone out to
dinner and you don't know where, or what time I'll be back."
After he had closed the door she got out of bed, wincing a
little, more in anticipation of pain than because she felt it, and
walked across the room to the window. It was a little before
six and almost dark, the water down there was black and
choppy, and the fading colorless sky made it look cold. Spain
had disappeared, there were only the rocks and the sea, and
soon there would be less than that: only the roar of the waves
in the darkness. She pulled the curtains across all the windows
carefully and turned on an electric heater by her dressing
table. The little spotlights came on. She seated herself in front
of the mirror and set to work on her face. It would be quicker
than usual tonight because she knew exactly what light she
would be in all during the evening. As she worked she found
herself wondering exactly what this rather strange Mr. Dyar
thought of her. "An aging nymphomaniac, most likely," she
suggested, determining to be as realistic and ruthless with
herself as she could. But then she asked herself why she was

being so violent; it could only be in order to kill whatever hope might be lurking within—hope that somehow he might find her attractive. "But that's nonsense," she objected. "What do I want of a callow, dull man like that? He's a definite bore." However, she could not convince herself. He did not bore her; he was like an unanswered riddle, a painting seen in semi-darkness, its subject only guessed at, which could prove to be of something quite different once one looked at it in the light. When she reminded herself that he could not possibly turn out to be anything worthwhile or interesting, even if she did manage to understand him, the fact that he was mysterious remained, and that, for her, was the important thing about him. But why should she find any mystery in a person like that? Again she experienced a feeling of misgiving, a pleasurable little shudder of fear. "I can manage him," she said to the half-finished face in the blinding mirror, "but can I manage *you*?"

The distant, multiple sounds of domestic activity came through the thick walls of the house, a series of muted, scarcely audible thuds rather than as noises actually distinguishable from one another; she, nevertheless, had learned through the years to interpret them. The pantry door swinging to, Mario's evening tour of the lower floor, closing the shutters and drawing the curtains, Inez climbing the staircase, Paco going out to the kennels with the dogs' dinner, she knew without question when each was happening, as the usher in a theatre knows from the dialogue exactly how the stage looks at any given moment, without needing to glance at it. Above these muffled sounds now emerged another, heard through the window: an automobile coming up the main road, turning into the driveway, stopping somewhere between the gate and the front door. Unconsciously she waited to hear it continue, to hear the car doors slam shut, the faint buzz of the bell in the kitchen, and the business of Hugo's getting to the front entrance. But nothing happened. The silence outside went on for so long that she began to doubt she had really heard any car come into the driveway; it must have continued up the mountain.

When she had finished she turned off the spots, slipped into a new black and white négligée that Balenciaga had made

for her in Madrid, rearranged the pillows, and got back into
bed, thinking that perhaps it had been a very bad idea, after
all, to invite Mr. Dyar alone for dinner. He might easily be
made shy by the absence of other guests, and particularly by
the fact that Luis was not there. "If he's tongue-tied, what in
God's name shall I talk to him about?" she thought. With
drinks enough he might be more at ease, but there was the
worse danger of his having too many. Spurred on by her nervousness to speculations of disaster, she began to wish she had
not acted so quickly on her impulse to invite him. But he
would arrive at any moment now. She shut her eyes and tried
to relax in the way a Yogi at Benares had taught her to do. It
was only partially successful; nevertheless, the effort made
time pass.

Suddenly there was a knock at the door. Hugo entered,
announcing Mr. Dyar.

XVIII

Daisy struggled to a sitting position, a little resentful at having been caught unawares. Dyar held a brief case in his hand;
he looked more wide-awake than she remembered him. She
wondered in passing why Hugo had not taken the brief case
from him along with his coat, and even more fleetingly she
wondered why she had not heard the taxi arrive, but he was
advancing toward the bed, and Hugo was going out and closing the door.

"Hi!" he said, shaking her hand vigorously. "I hope you're
sicker than you look, because you look fine." He bent over
and pushed the brief case under the table beside the bed.

"I'm not really sick at all. It's just a twinge of sciatica that
comes now and then. Nothing at all, darling. But I'm such a
God-damned crybaby and I loathe pain so, that I simply pam-
per myself. And here I am. Sit down." She indicated the foot
of the bed.

He obeyed, and she looked at him attentively. It seemed to
her that his eyes were unusually bright, that his whole face
shone with an unaccustomed physical glow. At the same time
he struck her as being nervous and preoccupied. None of
these things tallied with what she remembered about him; he

had been restless at the Beidaoui party, but it was a restless-
ness that came from boredom or apathy, whereas at the
moment he looked uneasy, intense, almost apprehensive.
They talked a bit; his remarks were not the sort she would
have expected from him; neither more intelligent nor more
stupid, they nevertheless seemed to come from a different
person. "But then, how do I know what he's like? I scarcely
know him at all," she reflected.

"It feels good to get inside where it's warm," he said. "It's
chilly out."

"I take it your taxi wasn't heated. Unless the car was delivered last week the heater would be broken by now. The Arabs
have an absolute genius for smashing things. If you want to get
rid of anything, just let an Arab touch it, and it'll fall to pieces
as he hands it back to you. They're fantastic! *What* destructive
people! God! Drinks will be along any minute. Tell me about
yourself in the meantime." She pushed herself further back
into the mound of pillows behind her and peered out at him
with the expression of one about to be told a long story.

Dyar glanced at her sharply. "About myself," he said, looking away again. "Nothing much to tell. More of the same. I
think you know most of it." Now that everything was arranged, with Thami waiting in the mimosa scrub below the
garden, and the Jilali dispatched to fetch the boat and bring
it to the beach at Oued el Ihud at the foot of the cliffs, he was
eager to be off, anxious lest some unforeseen event occur
which could be a snag in his plans. The arrival of Wilcox, for
instance, to pay an unexpected after-dinner call—that was one
idea whose infinite possibilities of calamity paralyzed him; he
forced himself to think of something else.

"Have you seen our silly Jack since night before last?"
asked Daisy suddenly, as if she were inside Dyar's mind. He
felt such acute alarm that he made a great effort to turn his
head slowly and look at her with a carefully feigned expression
of preoccupation turning to casual interest. "I'm worried
about him," she was saying. "And I was certainly not reassured by your little description of his behavior."

But he thought: "Night before last? Why night before last?
What happened then?" In his mind the party at the Beidaoui
Palace had been weeks ago; it did not occur to him that she

was referring to that. "No, I haven't seen him," he said, forgetting even that he had had breakfast with him that very morning. Hugo entered, wheeling a table covered with bottles and glasses. "I've learned one thing in my life, if nothing else," Daisy said. "And that is, that it's utterly useless to give anyone advice. Otherwise I'd ask Luis to talk with him. He might be able to worm something out of him. Because I have a distinct feeling he's up to something, and whatever it is, he won't get away with it. I'll wager you ten pounds he doesn't. Ten pounds! Why have you brought just these few pieces of ice? Bring a whole bowl of it," she called after Hugo as he closed the door behind him.

"I don't know," Dyar said. "Don't know what?" he thought, suppressing a tickling desire to laugh aloud. "Jack's pretty careful. He's nobody's fool, you know. I can't see him getting into any serious trouble, somehow." He felt that he must put a stop to this conversation or it would bring him bad luck. The mere fact that he was in a position for the moment to be offhand about the subject, even though his nonchalance was being forced upon him, seemed to indicate likely disaster. "Pride before a fall," he thought. It was a moment for humility, a moment to touch wood. The expression *get away with it* bothered him. "I don't know," he said again.

"Ten pounds!" Daisy reiterated, handing him a whiskey-soda. He sipped it slowly, telling himself that above all things he must not get drunk. At the end of ten minutes or so she noticed that he was not drinking.

"Something's wrong with your drink!" she exclaimed. "What have I done? Give it to me. What does it need?" She reached out for the glass.

"No, no, no!"' he objected, hanging on to it. "It's fine. I just don't feel like drinking, somehow. I don't know why."

"Aha!" she cried, as though she had made a great discovery. "I see! Your system's hyperacid, darling. It's just the moment for a little majoun. I don't feel much like whiskey myself tonight." She made a place for her glass among the bottles and tubes on the night-table, opened the drawer and took out a small silver box which she handed him.

"Have a piece," she said. "Just don't tell anyone about it. All the little people in Tangier'd be scandalized, all but the

Arabs, of course. They eat it all the time. It's the only thing allowed the poor darlings, with alcohol forbidden. But a European, a Nazarene? Shocking! Unforgivable! Depths of depravity! Tangier, sink-hole of iniquity, as your American journalists say. 'Your correspondent has it on reliable authority that certain members of the English colony begin their evening meal with a dish of majoun, otherwise known as hashish.' Good God!"

He was looking with interest at the six cubes of greenish black candy which exactly filled the box. "What is it?" he said.

"Majoun, darling. Majoun." She reached out, took a square and bit it in half. "Have a piece. It's not very good, but it's the best in Tangier. My sweet old Ali gets it for me." She rang the bell.

The candy was gritty, its flavor a combination of figs, ginger, cinnamon and licorice; there was also a pungent herbal taste which he could not identify. "What's it supposed to do?" he asked with curiosity.

She put the box back onto its shelf. "The servants would be horrified. Isn't it ghastly, living in fear of one's own domestics? But I've never known a place like Tangier for wagging tongues. God! The place is incredible." She paused and looked at him. "What does it do?" she said. "It's miraculous. It's what we've all been waiting for all these years. If you've never had it, you can't possibly understand. But I call it the key to a forbidden way of thought." She leaned down and patted his arm. "I'm not going mystical on you, darling, although I easily could if I let myself go. *J'ai de quoi,* God knows. There's nothing mystical about majoun. It's all very down to earth and real." A maid knocked. Daisy spoke to her briefly in Spanish. "I've ordered tea," she explained, as the girl wheeled the table of drinks away.

"Tea!"

She laughed merrily. "It's absolutely essential."

To Dyar, who had pulled his left cuff up so he could glance surreptitiously now and then at his watch, the time was creeping by with incredible slowness. Daisy talked about black magic, about exhibitions of hatta-yoga she had seen in Travancore, about the impossibility of understanding Islamic legal procedure in Morocco unless one took for granted the everyday use of spells and incantations. At length the tea came, and they each had three cups. Dyar listened apathetically; it all sounded to him like decoration, like the Pekineses, incense-burners and Spanish shawls with which certain idle women filled their apartments, back in New York. He let her talk for a while. Then he said: "But what's the story about that candy? What is it? Some kind of dope, isn't it? I think you were cheated. I don't feel anything."

She smiled. "Yes, I know. Everyone says that. But it's very subtle. One must know which direction to look in for the effect. If you expect to feel drunk, you're looking the wrong way, it takes twice as long, and you miss half the pleasure."

"But what *is* the pleasure? Do *you* feel anything, right now?"

She closed her eyes and remained silent a moment, a slightly beatific expression coming to rest on her upturned face. "Yes," she answered at length. "Definitely."

"You do?" The incredulity in his voice made her open her eyes and look at him an instant reproachfully. "You don't believe me? I'm not just imagining things. But I've had it before and I know exactly what to expect. Darling, you're not comfortable there on the edge of the bed. Draw up that big chair and relax."

When he was sprawled in the chair facing the bed, he said to her: "Well, then, suppose you try and tell me what it feels like. I might as well get some benefit out of the stuff, even if it comes second-hand."

"Oh, at the moment it's nothing very exciting. Just a slight buzzing in my ears and an accelerated pulse."

"Sounds like fun," he scoffed. For a few minutes he had forgotten that this evening he was waiting above all for time to pass. Now he turned his arm a bit, to see the face of his watch; it was eight-twenty. He had set the meeting with Thami for no definite hour, not knowing exactly when he would be able to get away, but he had assured him it would not be after midnight. The understanding was that the Jilali would go back to town to the port, and would bring the boat to a small beach just west of Oued el Ihud, also not later than twelve o'clock. In the meantime Thami was to sit and wait, a little below the far end of the garden, so that when Dyar left the house he could lead him down across the face of the mountain, directly to the beach. Thami had insisted he would not be bored by waiting so long: he had his supper and his kif pipe with him.

"Yes," Daisy was saying. "If I let too much time go by, I shan't be able to tell you anything at all. One becomes fantastically inarticulate at a certain point. Not always, but it can happen. One thinks one's making sense, and so one is, I daresay, but in a completely different world of thought."

It seemed to him that the wind outside was rising a little, or else a window had opened a minute ago to let the sound in. He turned his head; the drawn curtains did not move. "What are you looking at?" she asked. He did not answer. At the same time he had a senseless desire to turn his head in the other direction and look at the other wall, because he thought he had seen a slight movement on that side of the room. Instead, he pulled out a pack of cigarettes and offered her one.

"No thanks, darling. I couldn't. You have a house. You see?"

"What?" He stared at her.

"I'm explaining, darling, or at least trying to. You have a house. In the middle of some modest grounds, where you're used to walking about." She waited, apparently to be certain he was following her argument. Since he said nothing, she went on. "You can always see the house. At least, from most parts of the property, but in any case, you know it's there. It's the center of your domain. Call it your objective idea about yourself."

He toyed with the pack of cigarettes, extracted one and lighted it, frowning.

"Say it's the idea of yourself by which you measure what's real. You have to keep it straight in your mind, keep it in working order. Like a compass."

He was making an effort to go along with the sense of what she was saying, but all he could follow was the words. "Like a compass," he repeated, as if he thought that might help.

"And so. You know every path, every plant, every stone on the grounds. But one day while you're out walking you suddenly catch sight of what looks like a path in a spot

where you've never noticed, nor even suspected one before." Slowly her voice was taking on dramatic fervor. "The
entrance is perhaps half hidden by a bush. You go over and
look, and find there actually is a path there. You pull the
bush aside, take a few steps down the path, and see ahead
of you a grove of trees you never before knew existed.
You're dumfounded! You go through the grove touching
the tree trunks to be sure they're really there, because you
can't believe it. . . ."

This time he jerked his head quickly to the left, to catch
whatever was over there by the windows, staring at the blank
expanse of unmoving white curtain with disbelief. "Just
relax," he said to himself, as he turned back to see if she had
noticed him; she seemed not to have. "Relax, and be careful.
Be careful." Why he was adding the second admonition he
did not know, save that he was conscious of an overwhelming
sense of uneasiness, as if a gigantic hostile figure towered
above him, leaning over his shoulder, and he believed the
only way to combat the feeling was to remain quite calm so
that he could control his movements.

". . . . Then through the trees you see that the path leads
up a hill. 'But there *is* no hill!' you exclaim, probably aloud by
this time, you're so excited and muddled. So you hurry on,
climb the hill, which is rather high, and when you get to the
top you see the countryside, perfectly familiar on all sides.
You can identify every detail. And there's your house below,
just where it should be. Nothing is wrong. It's not a dream
and you've not gone mad. If you hadn't seen the house, of
course, you'd know you'd gone mad. But it's there. Everything is all right." She sighed deeply, as if in relief. "It's just
upsetting to find that grove of trees and that strange hill in
the middle of your land. Because it can't be there, and yet it
is. You're forced to accept it. But it's how you think once
you've accepted it that makes what I call the forbidden way of
thought. Forbidden, of course, by your own mind, until the
moment you accept the fact of the hill. That's majoun for
you. You find absolutely new places inside yourself, places you
feel simply couldn't be a part of you, and yet there they are.
Does what I said mean anything at all to you, or have I been
ranting like a maniac?"

"Oh, no. Not at all." All his effort was going to giving a sincere ring to the words. An intense silence followed, which he felt he was also making, as he had uttered the words, only it went on for an endless length of time, like telegraph wires across miles of waste land. A pole, a pole, a pole, a pole, the wires strung between, the flat horizon lying beyond the eyes' reach. Then someone said: "Not at all" again, and it was he who had said it.

"What the hell is this?" he asked himself in a sudden rage. He had promised himself not to get drunk; it was the most important thing to remember while he was at the Villa Hesperides this evening. "I'm not drunk," he thought triumphantly, and he found himself on his feet, stretching. "It's stuffy in here," he remarked, wondering if she would think he was being rude.

She laughed. "Come, now, darling. Admit you're feeling the majoun at last."

"Why? Because I say it's stuffy? Nope. I'm damned if I feel anything." He was not being obstinate; already he had forgotten the little side-trip his mind had made a moment ago. Now that he was standing up the air in the room did not seem close. He walked over to a window, pulled the heavy curtain aside, and peered out into the dark.

"You don't mind being alone here at night?" he said.

"Sometimes," she answered vaguely, wondering if his question would be followed by others. "Stop thinking like that," she told herself with annoyance.

He still stood by the window. "You're pretty high up here."

"About six hundred feet."

"Have you ever been down to the bottom?"

"Over those rocks? God, no! Do you think I'm a chamois?"

He began to walk around the room slowly, his hands behind him, stepping from one zebra skin to the next as if they were rocks in a stream. There was no doubt that he felt strange, but it was not any way he had expected to feel, and so he laid it to his own perturbation. The evening was going to be agonizingly long. "I'd like to be saying good night right now," he thought. Everything he took the trouble to look at carefully seemed to be bristling with an intense but undecipherable meaning: Daisy's face with its halo of white pillows, the light pouring over the array of bottles on the table, the glistening black floor and the irregular black and white stripes on the skins at his feet, the darker and more distant parts of the room by the windows where the motionless curtains almost touched the floor. Each thing was uttering a wordless but vital message which was a key, a symbol, but which there was no hope of seizing or understanding. And inside himself, now that he became conscious of it, in his chest more than anywhere else, there was a tremendous trembling pressure, as though he were about to explode. He breathed in various ways to see if he could change it, and then he realized that his heart was beating too fast. "Ah, hell," he said aloud, because he was suddenly frightened.

"Come and sit down, darling. What's the matter with you? You're as restless as a cat. Are you hungry? Or has the majoun got you?"

"No," he said shortly. "Nothing's got me." He thought that sounded absurd. "If I go and sit down," he thought, "I'll get up again, and she'll know something's the matter." He felt he must make every effort to prevent Daisy from knowing what was going on inside him. The objects in the room, its walls and furniture, the air around his head, the idea that he was in the room, that he was going to eat dinner, that the cliffs and the sea were below, all these things were playing a huge, inaudible music that was rising each second toward a climax which he knew would be unbearable when it was reached. "It's going to get worse."

He swallowed with difficulty. "Something's got to happen in a minute. Something's got to happen." He reached the chair and stood behind it, his hands on the back. Daisy looked at him distraughtly. She was thinking: "Why have I never dared tell Luis about majoun?" She knew he would disapprove, if only because it was a native concoction. But that was not why she had kept silent. She had never told *anyone* about it; the taking of it was a supremely private ritual. The experience was such a personal one that she had never wanted to share it with another. And here she was, undergoing it with someone she scarcely knew. All at once she wanted to tell him, so that he might know he was the first to be invited into this inner chamber of her life. She took a deep breath, and instead, said petulantly: "For God's sake, sit down. You look like a Calvinist rector telling his flock about Hell."

He laughed and sat in the chair. Under the table in the shadow he saw his brief case. The tremulous feeling inside him suddenly expressed a great elation; it was still the same sensation, but it had changed color. The relief made him laugh again.

"Really!" exclaimed Daisy. "You may as well admit you're feeling the majoun. Because I know damned well you are. At least admit it to yourself. You'll have more fun with it. You've been fighting it for the past ten minutes. That's not the way to treat it. Just sit back and let it take its course. It's in you, and you can't get rid of it, so you may as well enjoy it."

"How about you?" He would not admit it.

"I told you long ago I was feeling it. At the moment I'm about to take off on a non-stop flight to Arcturus."

"You are, are you?" His voice was unfriendly. "Personally, I think the stuff is a fake. I'm not saying it has no effect at all, but I don't call feeling jumpy and having my heart beat twice too fast, I don't call that a kick, myself."

She laughed commiseratingly. "You should have drunk your whiskey, darling. You'd have felt more at home with it. *Mais enfin . . .*" She sat up and rang the bell. "I expect the kitchen is in a turmoil because we're taking so long with our tea."

XIX

All during the dinner Daisy talked unceasingly; often Dyar found himself replying in monosyllables, not because he was uninterested, although occasionally he had very little idea what she was saying, but because half the time he was off somewhere else in a world of his own. He did not know what he was thinking about, but his brain was swarming with beginnings of thoughts fastened on to beginnings of other thoughts. To receive so many took all his attention; even had they not been incommunicable he would have had no desire to impart them to Daisy. It was as if his mind withdrew to a remote, dark corner of his being. Then it would come out into the light again, and he would find himself actually believing

that he sat having dinner at a small table in a quiet room while
a woman lay in bed nearby eating the same food from a tray.

"You're awfully untalkative," Daisy said presently. "I'd
never have given the majoun to you if I'd known it was going
to make a statue out of you."

Her words made him uncomfortable. "Oh," he said. And
what seemed to him a long time later: "I'm all right."

"Yes, I daresay you are. But you make a God-damned
unsatisfactory dinner partner."

Now he became fully present, began to stammer apologies
more florid than the occasion warranted. "I couldn't feel
worse," he said finally, "if I'd kicked you. I don't know what
was the matter with me. It must be that stuff that did something crazy to me."

"It's all my fault. Don't give it another thought, poor
darling."

He would not have it that way. "No, no, no," he said.
"There's no excuse." And in an excess of contrition he rose
and sat down heavily on the bed beside her. The tray tipped
perilously.

"Be careful, darling!" she exclaimed. "I shall have peas and
wine all over me in another moment." But he had already
seized her hand and was covering it with quick kisses. He was
floating in the air, impelled by a hot, dry wind which enveloped him, voluptuously caressed him. For the space of two
long breaths she was silent, and he heard his own breathing,
and confused it with the sound of the wind that was blowing
him along, above the vast, bare, sunlit valley. The skin of
her arm was smooth, the flesh was soft. He pulled her further
toward him, over the balancing tray.

"Be careful!" she cried again in alarm, as the tray tilted in
his direction. "No, no!"

The wine glass went over first; the icy stain on his thigh
made him jump convulsively. Then, very slowly it seemed to
him, plates slid and tumbled toward him as the tray overturned and buried the lower part of his body in a confusion
of china, glassware and warm food. "Oh!" she cried. But he
held her more tightly with one arm, sweeping the tray and
some of the dishes onto the floor with the other. And he
scrambled up to be completely near her, so that there were

only a few thicknesses of wet cloth, a fork and a spoon or two between them, and presently, after a short struggle with pieces of clinging clothing, nothing but a few creamed mushrooms.

"For God's sake, no! Not like this!" she was on the point of shouting, but as if she sensed how tenuous was the impulse that moved him, she thought: "At this very moment you're hoping desperately that nothing will happen to stop this. So you did want it to happen. Why wouldn't you admit it? Why can't you be frank? You wanted it; let it happen, even this way. Even this way." And so she said nothing, reaching out and turning off the light beside the bed. A word, she told herself, could have broken the thread by which he hung suspended from the sky; he would have fallen with a crash into the room, a furiously embarrassed young man with no excuse for his behavior, no escape from his predicament, no balm for his injured pride. "He's very sweet. And a little mad. So compact. Not at all like Luis. But could I really love any man I don't respect? I don't respect him at all. How can one respect an impersonal thing? He's scarcely human. He's not conscious of me as me. As another natural force, perhaps, yes. But that's not enough. I could never love him. But he's sweet. God knows, he's sweet."

The soft endless earth spread out beneath him, glowing with sunlight, untouched by time, uninhabited, belonging wholly to him. How far below it lay, he could not have said, gliding soundlessly through the pure luminous air that admitted no possibility of distance or dimension. Yet he could touch its smooth resilient contours, smell its odor of sun, and even taste the salt left in its pores by the sea in some unremembered age. And this flight—he had always known it was to be made, and that he would make it. This was a corner of existence he had known was there, but until now had not been able to reach; at present, having discovered it, he also knew he would be able to find his way back another time. Something was being completed; there would be less room for fear. The thought filled him with an ineffable happiness. "Ah, God," he murmured aloud, not knowing that he did so.

Beyond the windows the rising wind blew through the cypresses, bringing with it occasionally the deeper sound of the sea below. Regularly the drawn white curtains on one side of the room glowed white as the lighthouse's beam flashed across it. Daisy coughed.

"You're a slut," she said to herself. "How could you ever have allowed this to happen? But it's ghastly! The door's not locked. One of the servants may knock at any minute. Just collect yourself and do something. Do something!"

She coughed again.

"Darling, this is dreadful," she said softly, smiling in the dark, trying to keep her voice free of reproach. He did not answer; he might have been dead. "Darling," she said again hesitantly. Still he gave no sign of having heard her. For a moment she drifted back into her thoughts. If one could only let go, even for a few seconds, if only one could cease caring about everything, but really everything, what a wonderful thing it would be. But that would probably be death. Life means caring, is one long struggle to keep from going to pieces. If you let yourself have a really good time, your health goes to pieces, and if your health goes, your looks go. The awful part is that in the end, no matter what you have done, no matter how careful you may have been, everything falls apart anyway. The disintegration merely comes sooner, or later, depending on you. Going to pieces is inevitable, and you haven't even any pieces to show when you're finished. "Why should that be a depressing thought?" she wondered. "It's the most obvious and fundamental one there is. *Mann muss nur sterben*. But that means something quite different. That means we are supposed to have free will. . . ."

Far in the distance, out over the Atlantic, she heard the faint hum of a plane as the dark mountain and the Villa Hesperides were included briefly within the radius of its sound. Northward to Lisbon, southward to Casablanca. In another hour Luis might be hearing that same motor as it circled above the airport.

"Darling, *please!*" She struggled a little to free herself from his embrace. Since he still held her, she squirmed violently and managed to sit up, bathed in sweat, wine and grease. The air of the room suddenly seemed bitter cold. She ran her hand tentatively over her stomach and drew it back, disgusted. Quickly she jumped out of bed, locked the door into the corridor, drew her peignoir around her, and disappeared into the bathroom without turning on any light.

She stayed in the shower rather longer than was necessary, hoping that by the time she came out he would have got up, dressed, and perhaps cleared away some of the mess around the bed. Then she could ring, say: "I've had a little accident," and have coffee served. When she opened the bathroom door the room was still in darkness. She went over to the night table and switched on the light. He lay asleep, partially covered by the sheet.

"But this is the *end*!" she told herself. And with an edge of annoyance in her voice: "Darling, I'm sorry. You absolutely *must* get dressed immediately." He did not stir; she seized his shoulder and shook it with impatience. "Come along! Up with you! This little orgy has gone on long enough. . . ."

He heard her words with perfect clarity, and he understood what they meant, but they were like a design painted on a wall, utterly without relation to him. He lay still. The most important thing in the world was to prolong the moment of soothing emptiness in the midst of which he was living.

Taking hold of the sheet, she jerked it back over the foot of the bed. Then she bent over and shouted in his ear: "You're stark naked!" Immediately he sat upright, fumbling ineffectively around his feet for the missing cover. She turned and went back into the bathroom, calling over her shoulder: "Get dressed immediately, darling." Looking into the mirror, arranging her hair, she said to herself: "Well, are you pleased or displeased with the episode?" and she found herself unable to answer, dwelling rather on the miraculous fact that Hugo had not walked in on them; the possibility of his having done so seemed now more dreadful each minute. "I must have been quite out of my senses." She closed her eyes for an instant and shuddered.

Dyar had pulled on his clothing mechanically, without being fully conscious of what he was doing. However, by the time he came to putting on his tie, his mind was functioning. He too stood before a mirror, smiling a little triumphantly as he made the staccato gestures with the strip of silk. He combed his hair and knelt by the bed, where he began to scrape up bits of food from the floor and put them on the tray. Daisy came out of the bathroom. "You're an angel!" she cried. "I was just going to ask if you'd mind trying to make a little order out of this chaos." She lay down on a chaise longue in the center of the room and pulled a fur coverlet around her, and she was about to say: "I'm sorry there was no opportunity for you to have a shower, too," when she thought: "Above all, I must not embarrass him." She decided to make no reference to what had occurred. "Be a darling and ring the bell, will you, and we'll have coffee. I'm exhausted."

But apparently he was in no way ill at ease; he did as she suggested, and then went to sit cross-legged on the floor at her side. "I've got to get going," he said to himself, and he was not even preoccupied with the idea of how he would broach the subject of his departure; after the coffee he would simply get up, say good-bye, and leave. It had been an adventure, but Daisy had had very little to do with it, beyond being the detonating factor; almost all of it had taken place inside him. Still, since the fact remained that he had had his way with her, he was bound to behave in a manner which was a little more intimate, a shade on the side of condescension.

"You warm enough?" He touched her arm.

"No. It's glacial in this room. Glacial. God! I can't think why I didn't have a fireplace installed when they were building the house."

Hugo knocked on the door. For ten minutes or so the room was full of activity: Inez and another girl changing the sheets, Mario cleaning up the food from the floor, Paco removing grease spots from the rug beside the bed, Hugo serving coffee. Daisy sat studying Dyar's face as she sipped her coffee, noting with a certain slight resentment that, far from being embarrassed, on the contrary he showed signs of feeling more at ease with her than earlier in the evening. "But what do I expect?" she thought, whereupon she had to admit to herself that she would have liked him to be a little more impressed by what had passed between them. He had come through untouched; she had the uneasy impression that even his passion had been objectless, automatic.

"What goes on in your head?" he said when the servants had all gone out and the room had fallen back into its quiet.

Even that annoyed her. She considered the question insolent. It assumed an intimacy which ought to have existed between them, but which for some reason did not. "But *why* not?" she wondered, looking closely at his satisfied, serious expression. The answer came up ready-made and absurd from her subconscious; it sounded like doggerel. "It doesn't exist because he doesn't exist." This was ridiculous, certainly, but it struck a chord somewhere in the vicinity of the truth. "Unreal. What does it mean for a person to be unreal? And why should I feel he is unreal?" Then she laughed and said: "My God! Of course! You want to feel you're alive!"

He set his cup and saucer on the floor, saying: "Huh?"

"Isn't that what you said to me the first night you came here, when I asked what you wanted most in life?"

"Did I?"

"You most assuredly did. You said those very words. And of course, you know, you're so right. Because you're *not* really alive, in some strange way. You're dead." With the last two words, it seemed to her she heard her voice turning a shade bitter.

He glanced at her swiftly; she thought he looked hurt.

"Why am I trying to bait the poor man?" she thought. "He's done no harm." It was reasonless, idiotic, yet the desire was there, very strong.

"Why dead?" His voice was even; she imagined its inflection was hostile.

"Oh, not dead!" she said impatiently. "Just not alive. Not really. But we're all like that, these days, I suppose. Not quite so blatantly as you, perhaps, but still. . . ."

"Ah." He was thinking: "I've got to get out of here. I've got to get going."

"We're all monsters," said Daisy with enthusiasm. "It's the *Age* of Monsters. Why is the story of the woman and the wolves so terrible? You know the story, where she has a sled full of children, crossing the tundra, and the wolves are following her, and she tosses out one child after another to placate the beasts. Everyone thought it ghastly a hundred years ago. But today it's much more terrible. Much. Because then it was remote and unlikely, and now it's entered into the realm of the possible. It's a terrible story not because the woman is a monster. Not at all. But because what she did to save herself is exactly what we'd all do. It's terrible because it's so desperately true. I'd do it, you'd do it, everyone we know would do it. Isn't that so?"

Across the shining stretches of floor, at the bottom of a well of yellow light, he saw his brief case waiting. The sight of it lying there reinforced his urge to be gone. But it was imperative that the leavetaking be casual. If he mentioned it vaguely now, the suggestion would be easier to act upon in another five minutes. By then it would be eleven-thirty.

"Well," he began, breathing in deeply and stretching, as if to rise.

"Do you know anyone who wouldn't?" He suddenly realized that she was serious about whatever it was she was saying. There was something wrong with her; she ought to have been lying there contentedly, perhaps holding his hand or ruffling his hair and saying a quiet word now and then. Instead she was tense and restless, talking anxiously about wolves and monsters, seeking either to put something into his mind or to take something out of it; he did not know which.

"*Do* you?" she insisted, the words a despairing challenge. It was as if, had he been able to answer "Yes," the sound of the word might have given her a little peace. He might have said: "Yes, I do know someone," or even: "Yes, such a person exists," and she would perhaps have been comforted. The world, that faraway place, would have become inhabitable and possible once again. But he said nothing. Now she took his hand, turned her face down to him coquettishly.

"Speaking of monsters, now that I recall your first evening here, I remember. God! You're the greatest monster of all. Of course! With that great emptiness in your hand. But my God! Don't you remember? Don't you remember what I told you?"

"Not very much of it," he said, annoyed to see his chance of escape being pulled further away from him. "I don't take much stock in that sort of stuff, you know."

"Stock, indeed!" she snorted. "Everyone knows it's perfectly true and quite scientific. But in any case, whether you take stock or not—what an expression!—just remember, you can do what you want. If you know what you want!" she added, a little harshly. "You have an empty hand, and vacuums have a tendency to fill up. Be careful what goes into your life."

"I'll be careful," he said, standing up. "I'm afraid I've got to be going. It's getting late."

"It's not late, darling," she said, but she made no effort to persuade him to stay on. "Call a cab." She pointed to the telephone. "It's 24-80."

He had not thought of that complication. "I'll walk," he said. "I need the exercise."

"Nonsense! It's five miles. You can't."

"Sure I can," he said smiling.

"You'll get lost. You're mad." She was thinking: "He probably wants to save the money. Shall I tell him to have it put on our bill?" She decided against it. "Do as you like," she said, shrugging.

As he took up his brief case, she said: "I shall see you down to the door," and despite his protestations she walked ahead of him down the stairs into the hall where a few candles still burned. The house was very still.

"The servants are all in bed, I guess," he said.

"Certainly not! I haven't dismissed Hugo yet." She opened the door. The wind blew in, rippling her peignoir.

"You'd better go up to bed. You'll catch cold."

He took the hand she held forth. "It was a wonderful evening," he declared.

"Luis will be back in a few days. You must come to dinner then. I'll call you, darling."

"Right." He backed away a few steps along the gravel walk.

"Turn to your left there by that clump of bamboo. The gate's open."

"Good night."

"Good night."

Stepping behind the bamboo thicket, he waited to hear her close the door. Instead, he heard her say: "Ah, Hugo. There you are! You may lock the gate after Mr. Dyar."

"Got to do something about *that*," he thought, walking quickly to the right, around the side of the house to the terrace where the swimming pool reflected the stars in its black water. It was a chance to take, because she would probably have been watching, to see him go out through the gate. But she might think he already had slipped out when she was not looking; otherwise it would be very bad. The idea of just how bad it could be struck him with full force as he hesitated there by the pool, and as he hurried ahead down the steps into the lower garden he understood that he had committed an important tactical error. "But I'd have been locked out of the garden, God damn it," he thought. "There was nothing else I could do."

He had now come out from behind the shadow of the house into the open moonlight. Ahead of him something which had looked like part of the vegetation along the path slowly rose and walked toward him. "Let's go," said Thami.

"Shut up," Dyar whispered furiously. At the moment they were in full view of the house.

And as she strained to identify the second person, even to the point of opening one of the doors and silently stepping out onto the terrace to peer down through the deforming moonlight, the two men hurried along the path that led to the top of the cliff, and soon were hidden from her sight.

4

Another Kind of Silence

D YAR lay on his back across the rear seat of the boat, his hands beneath his head, looking up at the stars, vaguely wishing that at some time or another he had learned a little about astronomy. The rowboat they had brought along to get aboard and ashore in scudded on top of the dark waves a few feet behind him, tied to a frayed towing rope that was too short. He had started out by arguing about the rope, back at Oued el Ihud when they were bobbing around out there a hundred feet or so from the cliffs, trying to attach the two craft together, but then he had decided to save his words for other, more important, things. And in any case, now that the Jilali was away from the land, he paid no attention to what was said to him, feeling, no doubt, that he was master of the immediate situation, and could afford to disregard suggestions made by two such obvious landlubbers as Thami and the crazy Christian gentleman with him. The moment of greatest danger from the police had been passed when the Jilali was rounding the breakwater, before the others had ever got into the boat. Now they were a good mile and a half from shore; there was little likelihood of their being seen.

From time to time the launch passed through choppy waters where the warmer Mediterranean current disagreed with the waves moving in from the Atlantic. Small whitecaps broke and hissed in the dark alongside, and the boat, heaving upward, would remain poised an instant, shuddering as its propeller left the water, and then plunging ahead like a happy dolphin. To the right, cut out by a razor blade, the black mountains of Africa loomed against the bright sky behind them. "This lousy motor's going to give us trouble yet," thought Dyar: the smell of gasoline was too strong. An hour ago the main thing had been to get aboard; now it was to get ashore. When he felt the land of the Spanish Zone under his feet he supposed he would know what the next step was to be; there was no point in planning unless you knew what the possibilities were. He relaxed his body as much as he could without risking being pitched to the floor. "Smoke?" called Thami.

"I told you no!" Dyar yelled, sitting up in fury, gesturing. "No cigarettes, no matches in the boat. What's the matter with you?"

"He wants one," Thami explained, even as the Jilali, who was steering, struck a match and tried to shelter the flame from the wind. The attempt was unsuccessful, and Thami managed to dissuade him from lighting another. "Tell him he's a God-damned fool," called Dyar, hoping thus to enlist Thami on his side, but Thami said nothing, remaining hunched up on the floor near the motor.

There was no question of sleeping; he was much too alert for that, but as he lay there in a state of enforced inactivity, thinking of nothing at all, he found himself entering a region of his memory which, now that he saw it again, he thought had been lost forever. It began with a song, brought back to him, perhaps, by the motion of the boat, and it was the only song that had ever made him feel really happy. "Go. To sleep. My little pickaninny. Mammy's goin' to slap you if you don't. Hushabye. Rockabye. Mammy's little baby. Mammy's little Alabama coon." Those could not have been the words, but they were the words he remembered now. He was covered by a patchwork quilt which was being tucked in securely on both sides—with his fingers he could feel the cross-stitching where the pieces were joined—and his head was lying on the eiderdown pillow his grandmother had made for him, the softest pillow he had ever felt. And like the sky, his mother was spread above him; not her face, for he did not want to see her eyes at such moments because she was only a person like anyone else, and he kept his eyes shut so that she could become something much more powerful. If he opened his eyes, there were her eyes looking at him, and that terrified him. With his eyes closed there was nothing but his bed and her presence. Her voice was above, and she was all around; that way there was no possible danger in the world.

"How the hell did I think of that?" he wondered, looking behind him as he sat up, to see if the lights of Tangier had yet been hidden by Cape Malabata. They were still there, but the black ragged rocks were cutting across them slowly, covering them with the darkness of the deserted coast. Atop the cliff the lighthouse flashed again and again, automatically, becoming presently a thing he no longer noticed. He rubbed his fingers together with annoyance: somehow they had got resin on them, and it would not come off.

And as the small boat passed more certainly into a region of shadowed safety, farther from lights and the possibility of discovery, he found himself thinking of the water as a place of solitude. The boat seemed to be making less noise now. His mind turned to wondering what kind of man it was who sat near him on the floor, saying nothing. He had talked with Thami, sat and drunk with him, but during all the moments they had been in one another's company it never had occurred to him to ask himself what thoughts went on behind those inexpressive features. He looked at Thami: his arms were folded around his tightly drawn-up knees, and his head, thrown back, rested against the gunwale. He seemed to be looking upward at the sky, but Dyar felt certain that his eyes were closed. He might even be asleep. "Why not?" he thought, a little bitterly. "He's got nothing to lose. He's risking nothing." Easy money for Thami—probably the easiest he ever would make with the little boat. "He doesn't give a damn whether I get there or not. Of course he can sleep. I ought to have come alone." So he fumed silently, without understanding that the only reason why he resented this hypothetical sleep was that he would have no one to talk to, would feel more solitary out there under the winter sky.

The Jilali, standing in the bow, began to sing, a ridiculous song which to Dyar's ears sounded like a prolonged and strident moaning. The noise it made had no relation to anything—not to the night, the boat, not to Dyar's mood. Suddenly he had a sickeningly lucid glimpse of the whole unlikely situation, and he chuckled nervously. To be tossing about in a ramshackle old launch at three in the morning in the Strait of Gibraltar with a couple of idiotic barbarians, on his way God only knew where, with a brief case crammed with money—it made no sense. That is to say, he could not find a way of believing it. And since he could not believe it, he did not really have any part in

it; thus he could not be very deeply concerned in any outcome
the situation might present. It was the same old sensation of
not being involved, of being left out, of being beside reality
rather than in it. He stood up, and almost fell forward onto the
floor. "Shut up!" he roared; the Jilali stopped singing and
called something in a questioning voice. Then he resumed his
song. But as Dyar sat down again he realized that the dangerous moment had passed: the vision of the senselessness of his
predicament had faded, and he could not recall exactly why it
had seemed absurd. "*I* wanted to do this," he told himself. It
had been his choice. He was responsible for the fact that at the
moment he was where he was and could not be elsewhere.
There was even a savage pleasure to be had in reflecting that he
could do nothing else but go on and see what would happen,
and that this impossibility of finding any other solution was a
direct result of his own decision. He sniffed the wet air, and
said to himself that at last he was living, that whatever the reason for his doubt a moment ago, the spasm which had shaken
him had been only an instant's return of his old state of mind,
when he had been anonymous, a victim. He told himself,
although not in so many words, that his new and veritable
condition was one which permitted him to believe easily in the
reality of the things his senses perceived—to take part in their
existences, that is, since belief is participation. And he expected
now to lead the procession of his life, as the locomotive heads
the train, no longer to be a helpless incidental somewhere in
the middle of the line of events, drawn one way and another,
without the possibility or even the need of knowing the direction in which he was heading.

These certainties he pondered explain the fact that an hour
or so later, when he could no longer bear the idea that Thami
had not once shifted his position, Dyar lurched to his feet,
stepped over, and kicked him lightly in the ribs. Thami
groaned and murmured something in Arabic.

"What's the idea? You can sleep later."

Thami groaned again, said: "What you want?" but the
words were covered by the steady stream of explosions made
by the motor. Dyar leaned down, and yelled. "It's going to be
light soon, for God's sake! Sit up and keep an eye open.
Where the hell are we?"

Thami pointed lazily toward the Jilali. "He knows. Don't worry." But he rose and went to sit in the bow, and Dyar squatted down between the motor and the gunwale, more or less where Thami had been sitting. It was warmer here, out of the wind, but the smell of the gasoline was too strong. He felt a sharp emptiness in his stomach; he could not tell whether it was hunger or nausea, because it wavered between the two sensations. After a few minutes he rose and walked uncertainly to join Thami. The Jilali motioned to them both to go and sit in the stern. When Dyar objected, because the air was fresh here by the wheel, Thami said: "Too heavy. It won't go fast this way," and they stumbled aft to sit side by side back there on the wet canvas cushions. Long ago the moon had fallen behind a bank of towering, thick clouds in the west. Above were the stars, and ahead the sky presently assumed a colorless aspect, the water beneath melting smokelike, rising to merge momentarily with the pallid air. The Jilali's turbaned head took on shape, became sharp and black against the beginning eastern light.

"You sure you know where we're going?" Dyar said finally.

Thami laughed. "Yes. I'm sure."

"I may be wanting to stay up there quite a while, you know."

Thami did not speak for a moment. "You can stay all your life if you want," he said sombrely, making it clear that he did not relish the idea of staying at all.

"What about you? How do you feel about it?"

"Me? Feel about what?"

"Staying."

"I have to go to Tangier with him." Thami indicated the Jilali.

Dyar turned to face him furiously. "The hell you do. You're going to stay with me. How the hell d'you think I'm going to eat up there all by myself?"

It was not yet light enough to see the contours of Thami's face, but Dyar had the feeling he was genuinely surprised. "Stay with you?" he repeated slowly. "But how long? Stay up there?" Then, with more assurance: "I can't do that. I have to work. I'll lose money. You're paying me for the boat and to go with you and show you the house, that's all."

"He knows I've got money here," Dyar thought savagely. "Damn his soul."

"You don't think I'm giving you enough?" He heard his own voice tremble.

Thami was stubborn. "You said only the boat. If I don't work I lose money." Then he added brightly: "Why you think I bought this boat? Not to make money? If I stay with you at Agla I make nothing. He takes the boat to Tangier, everything is in Tangier. My boat, my house, my family. I sit in Agla and talk to you. It's very good, but I make no money."

Dyar thought: "Why doesn't he ask me why I want to stay up there? Because he knows. Plain, ordinary blackmail. A war of nerves. I'm God damned if I give in to him." But even as he formed the words in his mind, he knew that what Thami was saying had logic.

"So what d'you expect me to do?" he said slowly, proceeding with caution. "Pay you so much a day to stay up there?"

Thami shrugged his shoulders. "It's no use to stay at Agla anyway. It's no good there. What do you want to do there? It's cold and with mud all over. I have to go back."

"So I have to make you an offer," he thought grimly. "Why don't you ask me how much I've got here in the brief case?" Aloud he said: "Well, you can stay a few days at least. I'll see you don't lose anything by it." Thami seemed satisfied. But Dyar was ill at ease. It was impossible to tell how much he knew, even how much he was interested in knowing, or to form any idea of what he thought about the whole enterprise. If he would only ask an explicit question, the way he phrased it might help determine how much he knew, and the reply could be formed accordingly. Since he said nothing, he remained a mystery. At one point, when they had been silent for some minutes, Dyar said to him suddenly: "What are you thinking about?" and in the white light of dawn his smooth face looked childishly innocent as he answered: "Me? Thinking? Why should I think? I'm happy. I don't need to think." All the same, to Dyar the reply seemed devious and false, and he said to himself: "The bastard's planning something or other."

With the arrival of daylight, the air and water had become calmer. On the Spanish side of the strait they saw a large freighter moving slowly westward, statuelike, imperturbable. The progress of the launch was so noisy and agitated in its motion that it seemed to Dyar the freighter must be gliding

forward in absolute silence. He looked in all directions uneasily, scanning the African coast with particular attention.
The mountains tumbled precipitately down into the froth-
edged sea, but in a few spots he thought he could see a small
stretch of sand in a cove.

"What's this Spanish Zone like?" he asked presently.

Thami yawned. "Like every place. Like America."

Dyar was impatient. "What d'you mean, like America? Do
the houses have electric lights? Do they have telephones?"

"Some."

"They do?" said Dyar incredulously. In Tangier he had
heard vaguely that the Spanish Zone was a primitive place,
and he pictured it as a wilderness whose few inhabitants lived
in caves and talked in grunts or sign language. "But in the
country," he pursued. "They don't have telephones out there,
do they?"

Thami looked at him, as if mildly surprised at his insistence
upon continuing so childish a conversation. "Sure they do.
What do you think? How they going to run the government
without telephones? You think it's like the Senegal?" The
Senegal was Thami's idea of a really uncivilized country.

"You're full of crap," said Dyar shortly. He would not
believe it. Nevertheless he examined the nearby coastline more
anxiously, telling himself even as he did so that he was foolish
to worry. The telephoning might begin during the day; it
certainly had not already begun. Who was there to give the
alarm? Wilcox could not—at least, not through the police. As
for the American Legation, it would be likely to wait several
days before instigating a search for him, if it did anything at
all. Once it was thought he had left the International Zone,
the Legation would in all probability shelve the entire Jouvenon affair, to await a possible return, even assuming that was
why they had telephoned him. Then who was there to worry
about? Obviously only Wilcox, but a Wilcox hampered by his
inability to enlist official aid. Relieved in his mind for a moment, he stole a glance at Thami, who was looking at him
fixedly like a man watching a film, as if he had been following
the whole panorama of thoughts as they filed past in Dyar's
mind. "I can't even think in front of him," he told himself. He
was the one to look out for, not Wilcox or anybody Wilcox

might hire. Dyar looked back at him defiantly. "*You're* the one," he made his eyes say, like a challenge. "I'm onto you," he thought they were saying. "I just want you to know it." But Thami returned his gaze blandly, blinked like a cat, looked up at the gray sky, and said with satisfaction: "No rain today."

He was wrong; within less than half an hour a wind came whipping around the corner of the coast out of the Mediterranean, past the rocky flanks of Djebel Musa, bringing with it a fine cold rain.

Dyar put on his overcoat, holding the brief case in his lap so that it was shielded from the rain. Thami huddled in the bow beside the Jilali, who covered his head with the hood of his djellaba. The launch began to make a wide curve over the waves, soon turning back almost in the direction from which it had come. They were on the windward side of a long rocky point which stretched into the sea from the base of a mountain. The sheer cliffs rose upward and were lost in the low-hanging cloudbank. There was no sign of other craft, but it was impossible to see very far through the curtain of rain. Dyar sat up straight. The motor's sound seemed louder than ever; anyone within two miles could surely hear it. He wished there were some way of turning it off and rowing in to shore. Thami and the Jilali were talking with animation at the wheel. The rain came down harder, and now and then the wind shook the air, petulantly. Dyar sat for a while looking downward at his coat, watching rivulets form in valleys of gabardine. Soon the boat rested on water that was smoother. He supposed they had entered an inlet of some sort, but when he raised his head, still only the rocks on the right were visible. Now that these were nearer and he could see the dark water washing and swirling around them, he was disagreeably conscious of their great size and sharpness. "The quicker we get past, the better," he thought, glad he had not called to the Jilali and made a scene about shutting off the motor. As he glanced backward he had the impression that at any moment another boat would emerge from the grayness there and silently overtake them. What might happen as a result did not preoccupy him; it was merely the idea of being followed and caught while in flight which was disturbing. He sat there, straining to see farther than it was possible to see, and he felt that the motor's monotonous racket was the one thin rope which might haul him to safety. But at any instant it could break, and there would be only the soft sound of the waves touching the boat. When he felt a cold drop of water moving down his neck he was not sure whether it was rain or sweat. "What's all the excitement about?" he asked himself in disgust.

The Jilali stepped swiftly to the motor and turned it off; it died with a choked sneeze, as if it could never be started again. He returned to the wheel, which Thami held. The launch still slid forward. Dyar stood up. "Are we there?" Neither one answered. Then the Jilali moved again to the center of the boat and began desperately to force downward the heavy black disc which was the flywheel. With each tug there was another sneeze, but the motor did not start. Raging inwardly, Dyar sat down again. For a full five minutes the Jilali continued his efforts, as the boat drifted indolently toward the rocks. In the end the motor responded, the Jilali cut it down to half speed, and they moved slowly ahead through the rain.

XXI

There was a small sloping beach in the cove, ringed by great half-destroyed rocks. The walls of the mountain started directly behind, rose and disappeared in the rainfilled sky. They leaped from the rowboat and stood a moment on the deserted strip of sand without speaking. The launch danced nearby on the deep water.

"Let's go," Dyar said. This also was a dangerous moment. "Tell him you'll write him when you want him to come and get you."

Thami and the Jilali entered into a long conversation which soon degenerated from discussion into argument. As Dyar stood waiting he saw that the two were reaching no understanding, and he became impatient. "Get him out of here, will you?" he cried. "Have you got his address?"

"Just a minute," Thami said, and he resumed the altercation. But remembering what he considered Dyar's outstanding eccentricity—his peculiar inability to wait while things took their natural course—he turned presently and said: "He wants money," which, while it was true, was by no means the principal topic of the conversation. Thami was loath to see his boat, already paid for, go back to Tangier in the hands of its former owner, and he was feverishly trying to devise some protective measure whereby he could be reasonably sure that both the Jilali and the boat would not disappear.

"How much?" said Dyar, reaching under his overcoat into his pocket, holding his brief case between his knees meanwhile. His collar was soaked; the rain ran down his back.

Thami had arranged a price of four hundred pesetas with the Jilali for his services; he had intended to tell Dyar it was eight hundred, and pay the Jilali out of that. Now, feeling that things were turning against him from all sides, he exclaimed: "He wants too much! In Dradeb he said seven fifty. Now he says a thousand." Then, as Dyar pulled a note from his pocket, he realized he had made a grievous error. "Don't give it to him!" he cried in entreaty, stretching out a hand as if to cover the sight of the bill. "He's a thief! Don't give it to him!"

Dyar pushed him aside roughly. "Just keep out of this," he said. He handed the thousand-peseta note to the expectant Jilali. "D'you think I want to stand around here all day?" Turning to the Jilali, who stood holding the note in his hand, looking confused, he demanded: "Are you satisfied?"

Thami, determined not to let any opportunity slip by, immediately translated this last sentence into Arabic as a request for change. The Jilali shook his head slowly, announced that he had none, and held the bill out for Dyar to take back. "He says it's not enough," said Thami. But Dyar did not react as he had hoped. "He knows God-damned well it's enough," he muttered, turning away. "Have you got his address?" Thami stood unmoving, tortured by indecision. And he did the wrong thing. He reached out and tried to snatch the note from the Jilali's hand. The latter, having decided that the Christian gentleman was being exceptionally generous, behaved in a natural fashion, spinning around to make a running dash for the boat, pushing it afloat as he jumped in. Thami hopped with rage at the water's edge as the other rowed himself out of reach laughing.

"My boat!" he screamed, turning an imploring face to Dyar. "You see what a robber he is! He's taking my boat!"

Dyar looked at him with antipathy. "I've got to put up with this for how many days?" he thought. "The guy's not even a half-wit." The Jilali kept rowing away, toward the launch. Now he shouted various reassurances and waved. Thami shook his fist and yelled back threats and curses in a sobbing voice, watching the departing Jilali get aboard the launch, tie the rowboat to the stern, and finally manage to start the motor. Then, inconsolable, he turned to Dyar. "He's gone. My boat's gone. Everything."

"Shut up," Dyar said, not looking at him. He felt physically disgusted, and he wanted to get away from the beach as quickly as possible, particularly now that the motor's noise had started up again.

Listlessly Thami led the way along the beach to its western end, where they walked among the tall rocks that stood upright. Skirting the base of the mountain, they followed an almost invisible path upward across a great bank of red mud dotted with occasional boulders. It was a climb that became increasingly steeper. The rain fell more intensely, in larger drops. There were no trees, no bushes, not even any small plants. Now cliffs rose on both sides, and the path turned into a gully with a stream of rust-colored water running against them. At one point Dyar slipped and fell on his back into the mud. It made a sucking sound as Thami helped him up out of it; he did not thank him. They were both panting, and in too disagreeable a humor to speak. But neither one expected the other to say anything, in any case. It was a question of watching where you put each foot as you climbed, nothing more. The walls of rock on either side were like blinders, keeping the eye from straying, and ahead there were more stones, more mud, and more pools and trickles of red-brown water. With the advance of the morning the sky grew darker. Dyar looked occasionally at his watch. "At half-past nine I'm going to sit down, no matter where we are," he thought. When the moment came, however, he waited a while until he found a comfortable boulder before seating himself and lighting a cigarette which, in spite of his precautions, the rain managed to extinguish after a few puffs. Thami pretended not to have noticed him, and continued to plod ahead. Dyar let him walk on, did not call to him to wait. He had only a half-pack of cigarettes, and he had forgotten to buy any. "No more cigarettes, for how long?" The landscape did not surprise him; it was exactly what he had expected, but for some reason he had failed to imagine that it might be raining, seeing it always in his mind's eye as windswept, desolate and baking in a brilliant sunlight.

Those of his garments which had not already been wet by the rain were soaked with sweat, for the steady climbing was arduous and he was hot. But he would not take off his overcoat, because under his arm, covered by the coat, was the brief case, and he determined to keep it there, as much out of the rain as possible.

He kept thinking that Thami, when he had got to a distance he considered dignified, would stop and wait for him, but he had mistaken the cause of his companion's depression, imagining that it was largely pique connected with his defeat at the hands of the Jilali, whereas it was a genuine belief that all was lost, that for the time being his soul lay in darkness, without the blessing of Allah. This meant that everything having to do with the trip was doomed beforehand to turn out badly for him. He was not angry with Dyar, whom he considered a mere envoy of ill-luck; his emotion was the more general one of despondency.

Thami did not stop; he went on his way until a slight change in the direction of the gully took him out of Dyar's view. "The son of a bitch!" Dyar cried, jumping up suddenly and starting to run up the canyon, still holding his sodden cigarette in his hand. When he came to the place where the passage turned, Thami was still far ahead, trudging along mechanically, his head down. "He wants me to yell to him to wait," Dyar thought. "I'll see him in Hell first."

It was another half-hour before he arrived within speaking distance of Thami's back, but he did not speak, being content to walk at the other's pace behind him. As far as he could tell, Thami had never noticed his short disappearance. Thami climbed and that was all.

And so they continued. By midday they were inland, no longer within reach of the sea's sound or smell. Still Dyar felt that had it not been for the miles of rainy air behind them the sea would be somewhere there spread out below them, visible even now. The sky continued gray and thick, the rain went on falling, the wind still came from the east, and they kept climbing slowly, through a vast world of rocks, water and mud.

A ham sandwich, Dyar found himself thinking. He could have bought all he wanted the day before while he waited to get into Ramlal's. Instead he had gone and lain on the beach. The sunbaked hour or so seemed impossibly distant now, a fleeting vista from a dream, or the memory of a time when he had been another person. It was only when he considered that he could not conceivably have bought food then for this excursion since he had not in any way suspected he was going to make it, that he understood how truly remote yesterday was, how greatly the world had changed since he had gone into Chocron's stuffy little office and begun to watch the counting of the money.

Looming suddenly out of the rain, coming toward them down the ravine, a figure appeared. It was a small gray donkey moving along slowly, his panniers empty, drops of rain hanging to the fuzz along his legs and ears. Thami stood aside to let the animal pass, his face showing no expression of surprise. "We must be getting near," said Dyar. He had meant to keep quiet, let Thami break the silence between them, but he spoke without thinking.

"A little more," said Thami impassively. An old man dressed in a tattered woolen garment came into view around a bend, carrying a stick and making occasional guttural sounds at the donkey ahead. "A little more," Dyar thought, beginning to feel light-headed. "How much more?" he demanded. But Thami, with the imprecise notions of his kind about space and time, could not say. The question meant nothing to him. "Not much," he replied.

The way became noticeably steeper; it required all their attention and effort to continue, to keep from sliding back on loose stones. The wind had increased, and was blowing what looked like an endless thick coil of cloud from the crags above downward into their path. Presently they were in its midst. The world was darker. "This isn't funny," Dyar found himself thinking, and then he laughed because it was absurd that a mere sudden change in lighting should affect his mood so deeply. "Lack of food," he said to himself. He bumped against Thami purposely now and then as he climbed. If they should get too far apart they would not be able to see each other. "I hope you've got something to eat up in this cabin of yours," he said.

"Don't worry." Thami's voice was a little unpleasant. "You'll eat tonight. I'll get you food. I'll bring it to you. Don't worry."

"You mean there's no food in the house? Where the hell are you going to get it?"

"They got nothing to eat at the house because no one is living there since a long time. But not very far is the house of my wife's family. I'll get you whatever you want there. They won't talk about it. They're good people."

"He thinks he's going to keep me cooped up," Dyar said to himself. "He's got another think coming." Then as he climbed in silence: "But why? Why does he want to keep me hidden?" And so the question was reduced once more to its basic form: "What does he know?" He resolved to ask him tonight, point-blank, when they were sitting quietly face to face and he could observe whatever changes might come into Thami's expression: "What did you mean when you said your wife's family wouldn't talk about it?"

As the gradient increased, their climb became an exhausting scramble to keep from sliding backward. The heavy fog was like wind-driven smoke; every few seconds they were revealed briefly to each other, and even a sidewall of rock beyond might appear. Then with a swoop the substance of the air changed, became white and visible, and wrapped itself around their faces and bodies, blotting out everything. They went on and on. It was afternoon; to Dyar it seemed to have been afternoon forever. All at once, a little above him Thami grunted with satisfaction, emitted a long: "Aaah!" He had sat down. Dyar struggled ahead for a moment and saw him. He had pulled out his kif pipe and was filling it from the long leather mottoui that was unrolled across his knees. "Now it's easy," he said, moving a little along the rock to make room for Dyar. "Now we go down. The town is there." He pointed straight downward. "The house is there." He pointed slightly downward, but to the left. Dyar seated himself, accepting the pipe. Between puffs he sniffed the air, which had come alive, smelled now faintly like pine trees and farmyards. When he had finished the pipe he handed it back. The kif was strong; he felt pleasantly dizzy. Thami refilled the pipe, looking down at it lovingly. The stem was covered with tiny colored designs of fish, water-jars, birds and swords. "I bought this sebsi three years ago. In Marrakech," he said.

They sat alone in the whiteness. Dyar waited for him to smoke; the kif was burned in three long vigorous puffs. Thami blew the ball of glowing ash from the little bowl, wound the leather thongs around the mottoui, and gravely put the objects into his pocket.

They got up and went on. The way was level for only an instant, almost immediately becoming a steep descent. They had been sitting at the top of the pass. After the long hours of breathing in air that smelled only of rain, it was pleasantly disturbing to be able to distinguish signs of vegetable and animal life in the mist that came up from the invisible valley below. Now their progress was quicker; they hurried with drunken movements from one boulder to another, sometimes landing against them with more force than was comfortable. It had stopped raining; Dyar had pulled the brief case out from under his coat and was carrying it in his left hand, using his free right arm for balance and as a bumper when it was feasible.

Soon they were below the cloud level, and in the sad fading light Dyar stood a moment looking at the gray panorama of mountains, clouds and shadowy depths. Almost simultaneously too, they were out of reach of the wind. The only sound that came up from down there was the soft unvaried one made by a stream following its course over many rocks. Nor could he distinguish any signs of human habitation. "Where's the house?" he said gruffly. That was the most important detail.

"Come on," Thami replied. They continued the downward plunge, and presently they came to a fork in the trail. "This way," said Thami, choosing the path that led along the side of the mountain, a sheer drop on its right, and on the left above, a succession of cliffs and steep ravines filled with the debris of landslides.

Then Thami stood still, one eyebrow arched, his hand to his ear. He seized Dyar's wrist, pulled him back a few paces to a huge slab of rock slightly off the path, pushed him to a squatting position behind it, and bent down himself, peering around every few seconds. "Look," he said. Half a hundred brown and gray goats came along the path, their hooves making a cluttered sound among the stones. The first ones stopped near the rock, their amber eyes questioning. Then the pressure of those following behind pushed them ahead, and they went on past in disorder, the occasional stones they dislodged bouncing from rock to rock with a curious metallic ring. A youth with a staff, wearing a single woolen cape slung over his shoulders, followed the flock. When he had passed, Thami whispered: "If he sees you, my friend, it would be very bad. Everybody in Agla would know tomorrow."

"What difference would that make?" Dyar demanded, not so much because he believed it did not matter, as because he was curious to know exactly what his situation was up here.

"The Spaniards. They would come to the house."

"Well, let 'em come. What difference would it make?" He was determined to see the thing through, and it was a good opportunity. "I haven't done anything. Why should they take the trouble to come looking for me?" He watched Thami's face closely.

"Maybe they wouldn't hurt you when you show them you got an American passport." Thami spoke aloud now. "Me, I'd be in the jail right away. You have to have a visa to get here, my friend. And then they'd say: How did you get in? Don't you worry. They'd know you were coming in by a boat. And then they'd say: Where is the boat? And whose boat? And worst: Why did you come by a boat? Why didn't you come by the *frontera* like everybody else? Then they talk on the telephone to Tangier and try to know why from the police there. . . ." He paused, looking questioningly at Dyar, who said: "So what?" still studying Thami's eyes intently.

"So what?" said Thami weakly, smiling. "How do I know so what? I know you said you will give me five thousand pesetas to take you here, and so I do it because I know Americans keep their word. And so you want to get here very much. How do I know why?" He smiled again, a smile he doubtless felt to be disarming, but which to Dyar's way of thinking was the very essence of Oriental deviousness and cunning.

Dyar grunted, got up, thinking: "From now on I'm going to watch every move you make." As Thami rose to his feet

he was still explaining about the Spanish police and their insistence upon getting all possible information about foreigners who visited the Protectorate. His words included a
warning never to stand outside the house in the daytime, and
never—it went without saying—to set foot inside the village
at any hour of the day or night. As they went along he embroidered on the probable consequences to Dyar of allowing
himself to be seen by anyone at all, in the end making everything sound so absurdly dangerous that a wave of fear swept
over his listener—not fear that what Thami said might be
true, for he did not believe all these variations on catastrophe
for an instant, but a fear born of having asked himself only
once: "Why is he saying all this? Why is he so excited about
nobody's seeing me?" For him the answer was to be found,
of course, at the limits of Thami's infamy. It was merely a
question of knowing how far the man was prepared to go, or
rather, since he was an Arab, how far he would be able to
go. And the answer at this point was, thought Dyar: he will
go as far as I let him go. So I give him no chance. Vigilance
was easy enough; the difficulty lay in disguising it. The other
must not suspect that he suspected. Thami was already playing the idiot; he too would be guileless, he would encourage
Thami to think himself the cleverer, so that his actions might
be less cautious, his decisions less hidden. One excellent protective measure, it seemed to him, would be to go to the village and then tell Thami about it. That would let him know
that he was not afraid of being seen, thus depriving Thami of
one advantage he seemed to feel he had over him. "And
then he'd think twice before pulling anything too rough if
he realized people knew I had been up here with him," he
reasoned.

"Well," he said reluctantly, "I'm going to have a fine time
up here. I can see that. You down in the town all the time and
me sitting on my ass up here on the side of a mountain."

"What you mean, all the time? How many days do you
want to stay? I have to go to Tangier. My boat. That Jilali's
no good. I know him. He's going to sell it to somebody else.
You don't care. It's not your boat—"

"Don't start in again," said Dyar. But Thami launched into
a lengthy monologue which ended where it had been meant

to end, on the subject of how many pesetas a day Dyar was willing to pay him for his presence at Agla.

"Maybe I want him here and maybe I don't," he thought. It would depend on what he found and learned in the town. Plans had to be made carefully, and they might easily include the necessity of having Thami take him somewhere else. "But the quicker I can get rid of him the better." That much was certain.

Was this haggling, genuine enough in appearance, merely a part of Thami's game, intended to dull whatever suspicion he might have, replacing it with a sense of security which would make him careless? He did not know; he thought so. In any case, he must seem to take it very seriously.

"D'you think I'm made of money?" he said with simulated ill-humor, but in such a tone that Thami might feel that the money eventually would be forthcoming. The other did not answer.

There was an olive grove covering the steep side hill that had to be gone through, a rushing stream to cross, and a slight rise to climb before one reached the house. It was built out on a flat shelf of rock whose base curved downward to rest against the mountainside astonishingly far below.

"There's the house," said Thami.

It's a fort, thought Dyar, seeing the little structure crouching there atop its crazy pillar. Its thick earthen walls once had been partially whitewashed, and its steep roof, thatched in terraces, looked like a flounced petticoat of straw. The path led up, around, and out onto the promontory where the ground was bare save for a few overgrown bushes. There were no windows, but there was a patchwork door with a home-made lock, to fit which Thami now pulled from his pocket a heavy key as long as his hand.

"This is the jumping-off place all right," said Dyar, stepping to the edge and peering down. Below, the valley had prepared itself for night. He had the feeling that no light could pierce the profound gloom in which the lower mountainside was buried, no sound change the distant, impassive murmur of water, which, although scarcely audible, somehow managed to fill the entire air. After struggling a moment with the lock Thami succeeded in getting the door open. As Dyar walked toward the house he noticed the deep troughs dug in the earth by the rain that had run from the overhanging eaves; it still dripped here and there, an intimate sound in the middle of the encompassing solitude—almost with an overtone of welcome, as if the mere existence of the house offered a possibility of relief from the vast melancholy grayness of the dying afternoon.

At least, he thought, as he stepped inside into the dark room that smelled like a hayloft, this will give me a chance to catch my breath. It might be only for a day or two, but it provided a place to lie down.

Thami opened a door on the other side of the room and the daylight came in from a tiny patio filled with broken crates and refuse. "There's another room there," he said with an air of satisfaction. "And a kitchen, too."

Surprisingly, the earth floor was dry. There was no furniture, but a clean straw mat covered almost half the floor space. Dyar threw himself down and lay with his head propped against the wall. "Don't say kitchen to me unless you've got something in it. When are we going to eat? That's all I want to know."

Thami laughed. "You want to sleep? I'm going now to the house of my wife's family and get candles and food. You sleep."

"The hell with the candles, chum. You get that food."

Thami looked slightly scandalized. "Oh, no," he said with great seriousness and an air of faint reproof. "You can't eat without candles. That's no good."

"Bring whatever you like." He could feel himself falling asleep even as he said it. "Just bring food too." He slipped his fingers through the handle of the brief case and laid it over his chest. Thami stepped out, closed the door and locked it behind him. There was the sound of his footsteps, and then only the occasional falling of a drop of water from the roof outside. Then there was nothing.

XXII

Even when he was fully conscious of the fact that Thami had returned and was moving about the room making a certain amount of noise, that a candle had been lighted and was shining into his face, his awakening seemed incomplete. He rose

from the mat, said: "Hi!" and stretched, but the heaviness of
sleep weighed him down. He did not even remember that he
was hungry; although the emptiness was there in him, more
marked than before he had slept, it seemed to have transformed itself into a simple inability to think or feel. He took
a few steps out into the center of the room, grunting and
yawning violently, and immediately wanted to lie down again.
With the sensation of being half-dead, he staggered back and
forth across the floor, stumbling over a large blanket which
Thami had ostensibly brought from the other house, and
from which he was extracting food and dishes. Then he went
back to the mat and sat down. Triumphantly Thami held up
a battered teapot. "I got everything," he announced. "Even
mint to put in the tea. You want to sleep again? Go on. Go to
sleep." There was a crackle and sputter from the patio as the
charcoal in the brazier took fire. Dyar still said nothing; it
would have cost him too great an effort.

As he watched Thami busying himself with the preparations
he was conscious of an element of absurdity in the situation. If
it had been Hadija preparing his dinner, perhaps he would have
found it more natural. Now he thought he should offer to
help. But he said to himself: "I'm paying the bastard," did not
stir, and followed Thami's comings and goings, feeling nothing but his consuming emptiness inside, which, now that at last
he was slowly waking, made itself felt unequivocally as hunger.

"God, let's eat!" he exclaimed presently.

Thami laughed. "Wait. Wait," he said. "You have to wait a
long time still." He pulled out his kif pipe, filled and lit it,
handed it to Dyar, who drew on it deeply, filling his lungs
with the burning smoke, as if he might thereby acquire at
least a little of the nourishment he so intensely wanted at the
moment. At the end of the second pipeful his ears rang, he
felt dizzy, and an extraordinary idea had taken possession of
him: the certainty that somewhere, subtly blended with the
food Thami was going to hand him, poison would be hidden.
He saw himself awakening in the dark of the night, an ever-
increasing pain spreading through his body, he saw Thami
lighting a match, and then a candle, his face and lips expressing sympathy and consternation, he saw himself crawling to
the door and opening it, being confronted with the utter

impossibility of reaching help, but going out anyway, to get away from the house. The detailed clarity of the visions, their momentary cogency, electrified him; he felt a great need to confide them immediately. Instead, he handed the pipe back to Thami, his gestures a little uncertain, and shutting his eyes, leaned back against the wall, from which position he was roused only when Thami kicked the sole of his shoe several times, saying: "You want to eat?"

He did eat, and in great quantity—not only of the vermicelli soup and the sliced tomatoes and onions, but also of the chopped meat and egg swimming in boiling bright green olive oil, which, in imitation of Thami, he sopped up with ends of bread. Then they each drank two glasses of sweet mint tea.

"Well, that's that," he finally said, settling back. "Thami, I take my hat off to you."

"Your hat?" Thami did not understand.

"The hat I don't own." He was feeling expansive at the moment. Thami, looking politely confused, offered him his pipe which he had just lighted, but Dyar refused. "I'm going to turn in," he said. If possible he wanted to package the present feeling of being at ease, and carry it with him to sleep, so that it might stay with him all night. A pipe of kif and he could easily be stuck with nightmares.

Surreptitiously he glanced at his brief case lying on the mat in the corner near him. In spite of the fact that he had carried it inside his coat whenever it rained, thus drawing at least some attention to it, he thought this could be accounted for in Thami's mind by its newness; he would understand his not wanting to spot the light-colored cowhide and the shining nickel lock and buckles. Thus now he decided to pay no attention to the case, to leave it nonchalantly nearby once he had tossed his toothbrush back into it, near enough on the floor so that if he stretched his arm out he could reach it. Putting it under his head or holding it in his hand would certainly arouse Thami's curiosity, he argued. Once the light was out, he could reach over and pull it closer to his mat.

Thami took out an old djellaba from the blanket in which he had brought the food, put it on, and handed the blanket to Dyar. Then he dragged a half-unraveled mat from the room across the patio and spread it along the opposite wall, where he lay continuing to smoke his pipe. Several times Dyar drifted into sleep, but because he knew the other was there wide awake, with the candle burning, the alarm he had set inside himself brought him back, and he opened his eyes wide and suddenly, and saw the dim ceiling of reeds and the myriad gently fluttering cobwebs above. Finally he turned his head and looked over at the other side of the room. Thami had laid his pipe on the floor and ostensibly was asleep. The candle had burned down very low; in another five minutes it would be gone. He watched the flame for what seemed to him a half-hour. On the roof there were occasional spatters of rain, and when a squall of wind went past, the door rattled slightly, but in a peremptory fashion, as if someone were trying hurriedly to get in. Even so, he did not witness the candle's end; when he opened his eyes again it was profoundly dark, and he had the impression that it had been so for a long time. He lay still, displeased with the sudden realization that he was not at all sleepy. The indistinct call of water came up from below, from a place impossibly faraway. In the fitful wind the door tapped discreetly, then shook with loud impatience. Silently he cursed it, resolving to make it secure for tomorrow night. Quite awake, he nevertheless let himself dream a little, finding himself walking (or driving a car—he could not tell which) along a narrow mountain road with a sheer drop on the right. The earth was so far below that there was nothing to see but sky when he glanced over the precipice. The road grew narrower. "I've got to go on," he thought. Of course, but it was not enough simply to go on. The road could go on, time could go on, but he was neither time nor the road. He was an extra element between the two, his precarious existence mattering only to him, known only to him, but more important than everything else. The problem was to keep himself there, to seize firmly with his consciousness the entire structure of the reality around him, and engineer his progress accordingly. The structure and the consciousness were there, and so was the knowledge of what he must do. But the effort required to leap across the gap from knowing to doing, that he could not make. "Take hold. Take hold," he told himself, feeling his muscles twitch even as he lay there in his revery. Then the door roused him a little, and he smiled in the dark at his own nonsense. He had already gone over the mountain road, he said to himself, insisting on taking his fantasy literally; that was past, and now he was here in the cottage. This was the total reality of the moment, and it was all he needed to consider. He stretched out his arm in the dark toward the center of the room, and met Thami's hand lying warm and relaxed, directly on top of the brief case.

If he had felt the hairy joints of a tarantula under his fingers he could scarcely have drawn back more precipitately, or opened his eyes wider against the darkness. "I've caught him at it," he thought with a certain desperate satisfaction, feeling his whole body become tense as if of its own accord it were preparing for a struggle of which he had not yet thought. Then he considered how the hand had felt. Thami had rolled over in his sleep, and his hand had fallen there, that was all. But Dyar was not sure. It was a long way to roll, and it seemed a little too fortuitous that the brief case should happen to be exactly under the spot where his hand had dropped. The question now was whether to do something about it or not. He lay still a while in the dark, conscious of the strong smell of mildewed straw in the room, and decided that unless he took the initative and changed the situation he would get no more sleep; he must move the brief case out from under Thami's hand. He coughed, pretended to sniffle a bit, squirmed around for a moment as if he were searching for a handkerchief, reached out and pulled the brief case by the handle. Partially sitting up, he lit a match to set the combination of the lock, and before the flame went out he glanced over toward the middle of the room. Thami was lying on his mat, but at some point he had pulled it out, away from the wall; his hand still lay facing upward, the fingers curled in the touching helplessness of sleep. Dyar snuffed the match out, took a handkerchief from the case, and blew his nose with energy. Then he felt inside the brief case: the notes were there. One by one he removed the packets and stuffed them inside his undershirt. Without his overcoat he might look a little plumper around the waist, but he doubted Thami could be that observant. He lay back and listened to the caprices of the wind, playing on the door, hating each sound not so much because it kept him from sleeping as because in his mind the loose door was equivalent to an open door. A little piece of wood, a hammer and one nail could arrange every-thing: the barrier between himself and the world outside would be much more real. He slept badly.

When it first grew light, Thami got up and built a charcoal fire in the brazier. "I'm going to my wife's family's house," he said as Dyar surveyed him blinking, from his mat. There was tea and there was a little bread left, but that was all. As he drank the hot green tea which Thami had brought to his mat, he no-ticed that the other had pushed his own mat back to the oppo-site wall where it had been at the beginning of the night. "Well, that's that," he thought. "No explanation offered. Nothing."

"I'll come back later," Thami said, gathering up the blan-ket from Dyar's feet. "I got to take this to carry things. You stay in the house. Don't go out. Remember."

"Yes, yes," said Dyar, annoyed at being left alone, at not having slept well, at having the blanket removed in case he wanted to try to sleep now, and most of all at the situation of complete dependence upon Thami in which he found himself at the moment.

When Thami had gone out, the feeling of solitude which re-placed his presence in the house, contrary to his expectations, proved to be an agreeable one. First Dyar got up and looked at the door. As he thought, a small chip of wood nailed to the jamb would do the trick. When the door was shut you would simply pull the piece of wood down tight like a bolt. Then he set out on an exploratory tour of the cottage, to search for a hammer and a nail. The terrain was quickly exhausted, because the place was empty. There was nothing, not even the tradi-tional half candle, empty sardine tin and ancient newspapers left by tramps in abandoned houses in America. Here every-thing had to be bought, he reminded himself; nothing was discarded, which meant that nothing was left around. An old tin can, a broken cup, an empty pill bottle, these things were put on sale. He remembered walking through the Joteya in Tangier and seeing the thousands of things on display, hope-lessly useless articles, but for which the people must have man-aged to find a use. His only interesting discovery was made in the corner between Thami's mat and the door leading into the patio, where behind a pile of straw matting partially consumed by dry-rot he found a small fireplace, a vestige of the days when the house had been someone's home. "We'll damned well have a fire tonight," he thought. He went back to the entrance door, opened it, and stood bathing in the fresh air and the sensation of freedom that lay in the vast space before him. Then he realized that the sky was clear and blue. The sun had not risen high enough behind the mountains to touch the valley, but the day danced with light. Immediately an extraordinary happiness took possession of him. As if some part of him already had suspected the arrival of the idea which was presently to occur to him, and which was to make the day such a long one to live through, he said to himself: "Thank God" when he saw the blueness above. And far below, on a ridge here, in a ravine there, a minute figure moved, clothed in garments the color of the pinkish earth itself. It even seemed to him that in the tremendous stillness he could hear now and then the faint frail sound of a human voice, calling from one distant point to another, but it was like the crying of tiny insects, and the confused backdrop of falling water blurred the thin lines of sound, making him wonder a second later if his ears had not played him false.

He sat down on the doorstep. It was nonsense, this being dependent on an idiot, and an idiot who had given every sign, moreover, of being untrustworthy. For instance, he had said he was going to his relatives' house. But what was to prevent him from going instead to the town and arranging with a group of cutthroats down there to come up after dark? Or even in the daytime, for that matter? What Thami did not quite dare do himself, he could get others to do for him; then he would act his part, looking terrified, indignant, letting them hit him once or twice and tie him up. . . . The scenes Dyar invented here were absurdly reminiscent of all the Western films he had seen as a child. He was conscious of distorting probability, and yet, goaded by an overwhelming desire to make something definite out of what was now equivocal (to assume complete control himself, in other words), he allowed his imagination full play in forming its exaggerated versions of what the day might bring forth. "Why did I let him out of my sight?" he thought, but he knew quite well it had been inevitable. His sojourn up here was predicated on Thami's making frequent trips, if not to the village, at least to the family's abode. "Like a rat in a trap," he told himself, looking longingly out at the furthest peaks, which the sun was now flooding with its early light. But now he knew it would not be like that, because he was going to get out of the trap. It was a morning whose very air, on being breathed, gave life, and there was the path, its stones still clean and shadowless because they lay in the greater shadow of the cliffs above. He had only to rise and begin to walk. There was no problem, unless he asked himself "Where?" and he took care not to allow this question to cross his mind; he wanted to believe he must not hesitate. Yet to make sure that he would act, and not think, he got up and went inside to where he knew Thami had left his two little leather cases—one containing the sections of the dismantled kif-pipe, and the other with the kif itself in it. He picked them both up and put them in his pocket. Since he had decided to leave the house, it now seemed a hostile place, one to get out of quickly. And so, seizing his brief case, taking a final disapproving sniff of the moldy air in the room, he stepped outside into the open.

Once before, two days ago, he had become intoxicated upon emerging into a world of sun and air. This morning the air was even stranger. When he felt it in his lungs he had the impression that flying would be easy, merely a matter of technique. Two days ago he had been moved to feel the trunks of the palms outside the Hotel de la Playa, to raise his head doglike into the breeze that came across the harbor, to rejoice at the fact of being alive on a fine morning. But then, he remembered, he had still been in his cage of cause and effect, the cage to which others held the keys. Wilcox had been there, hurrying him on, standing between him and the sun in the sky. Now at this moment there was no one. It was possible he was still in the cage—that he could not know—but at least no one else had the keys. If there were any keys, he himself had them. It was a question of starting to walk and continuing to walk. Slowly the contours of the valleys beneath shifted as he went along. He paid no attention to the path, save to note that it was no longer the one by which he had come yesterday. He met no one, nothing. After an hour or so he sat down and had two pipes of kif. The sun still had not climbed high enough to strike this side of the mountain, but there were eminences not far below which already caught its rays. The bottoms of the valleys down there were green snakes of vegetation; they lay warming themselves in the bright morning sun, their heads pointing downward toward the outer country, their tails curling back into the deep-cut recesses of rock.

He continued with less energy, because the smoke had cut his wind somewhat, and his heartbeat had accelerated a little. In compensation, however, he felt a steadily increasing sense of well-being. Soon he no longer noticed his shortness of breath. Walking became a marvelously contrived series of harmonious movements, the execution of whose every detail was in perfect concordance with the vast, beautiful machine of which the air and the mountainside were parts. By the time the sun had reached a point in the sky where he could see it, he was not conscious of taking steps at all; the landscape merely unrolled silently before his eyes. The triumphant thought kept occurring to him that once again he had escaped becoming a victim. And presently, without his knowing how he had got there, he found himself in a new kind of countryside. At some point he had wandered over a small crest and begun going imperceptibly downward, to be now on this upland, sloping plain, so different from the region he had left. Long ago he had ceased paying attention to where he was going. The sun was high overhead; it was so warm that he took off his coat. Then he folded it and sat down on it. His watch said half-past twelve. "I'm hungry," he let himself think, but only once. Determinedly he pulled out the sections of the pipe, fitted them together, and buried the little terra cotta bowl in the mass of fragrant, moist kif that filled the mottoui. And he drew violently on the pipe, holding the smoke inside him until his head spun and his eyes found themselves unable to move from the contemplation of a small crooked bush that grew in front of him. "With this you don't need food," he said. Soon enough he had forgotten his hunger; there were only the multiple details of the bright landscape around him. He studied them attentively; it was as though each hill, stone, gully and tree held a particular secret for him to discover. Even more—the configuration of the land seemed to be the expression of a hidden dramatic situation whose enigma it was imperative that he understand. It was like a photograph of a scene from some play in which the attitudes and countenances of the players, while normal enough at first glance, struck one as equivocal a moment later. And the longer he considered the mysterious ensemble, the more undecipherable the meaning of the whole became. He continued to smoke and stare. "I've got to get this straight," he thought. If he could catch the significance of what he saw before him at the moment, he would have understood a great deal more than what was denoted by these few bushes and stones. His head was clear; all the same, he felt peculiarly uneasy. It was the old fear of not being sure he was really there. He seized a stone and from where he sat threw it as far as he was able. "All right," he told himself, "you're here or you're not here. It doesn't matter a good God damn. Forget about it. It doesn't matter. Keep going from there. Where do you get?" He rose suddenly, took up his coat and began to walk. Perhaps the answer lay in continuing to move. Certainly the natural objects around him went on acting out their silent pantomime, posing their ominous riddle; he was aware of that as he went along. But, he reflected, if he felt strange and unreal at this instant he had good reason to: he was full of kif. "High as a kite," he chuckled. That was a consolation, and if it were not enough, there was the further possibility that he was right, that it was completely unimportant whether you were here or not. But unimportant to whom? He began to whistle as he walked, became engrossed in the sounds he made, ceased his game of mental solitaire.

Little by little the uncertain trail led downward across regions of rough pastureland and stony heaths. It was with astonishment that he saw on a hillside a group of cows grazing. During the morning he had grown used to thinking of himself as the only living creature under this particular sky. If he were coming to a village, so much the worse; he would continue anyway. His hunger, which long ago had reached mammoth proportions, no longer expressed itself as such, but rather as a sensation of general nervous voraciousness which he felt could be relieved only by more kif. And so he sat down and smoked some more, feeling his throat turn a little more inevitably to the iron it was on its way to becoming. If the cows had surprised him, the sight now of a dozen or more natives working in a remote field did not. Only their minuteness amazed him; the landscape was so much larger than it looked. He sat on a rock and stared upward. The sky seemed to have reached a paroxysm of brilliancy. He had never known it was possible to take such profound delight in sheer brightness. The pleasure consisted simply in letting his gaze wander over the pure depths of the heavens, which he did until the extreme light forced him to look away.

Here the terrain was a chorus of naked red-gray valleys descending gently from the high horizon. The clumps of spiny palmetto, green nearby, became black in the distance. But it was hard to tell how far away anything was in this deceptive landscape. What looked nearby was far off; the tiny dots which were the cattle in the foreground proved that—and if his eye followed the earth's contours to the farthest point, the formation of the land there was so crude and on such a grand scale that it seemed only a stone's throw away.

He let his head drop, and feeling the sun's heat on the back of his neck, watched a small black beetle moving laboriously on its way among the pebbles. An ant, hurrying in the opposite direction, came up against it; apparently the meeting was an undesirable one, for the ant changed its course and dashed distractedly off with even greater haste. "To see infinity in a grain of sand." The line came to him across the empty years, from a classroom. Outside was the winter dusk, dirty snow lay in the empty lots; beyond, the traffic moved. And in the stifling room, overheated to bursting, everyone was waiting for the bell to ring, precisely to escape from the premonition of infinity that hung so ominously there in the air. The feeling he associated with the word *infinity* was one of physical horror. If only existence could be cut down to the pinpoint of here and now, with no echoes reverberating from the past, no tinglings of expectation from time not yet arrived! He stared harder at the ground, losing his focus so that all he saw was a bright blur. But then, would not the moment, the flick of the eyelid, like the grain of sand, still be imponderably weighted down with the same paralyzing element? Everything was part of the same thing. There was no part of him which had not come out of the earth, nothing which would not go back into it. He was an animated extension of the sunbaked earth itself.

But this was not quite true. He raised his head, fumbled, lit another pipe. There was one difference, he told himself as he blew the smoke out in a long white column that straightway broke and dissolved. It was a small difference, self-evident and absurd, and yet because it was the one difference that came to him then, it was also the only suggestion of meaning he could find in being alive. The earth did not know it was there; it merely was. Therefore living meant first of all knowing one was alive, and life without that certainty was equal to no life at all. Which was surely why he kept asking himself: am I really here? It was only natural to want such reassurance, to need it desperately. The touchstone of any life was to be able at all times to answer unhesitatingly: "Yes." There must never be an iota of doubt. A life must have all the qualities of the earth from which it springs, plus the consciousness of having them. This he saw with perfect clarity in a wordless exposition—a series of ideas which unrolled inside his mind with the effortlessness of music, the precision of geometry. In some remote inner chamber of himself he was staring through the wrong end of a telescope at his life, seeing it there in intimate detail, far away but with awful clarity, and as he looked, it seemed to him that now each circumstance was being seen in its final perspective. Always before, he had believed that, although childhood had been left far behind, there would still somehow, some day, come the opportunity to finish it in the midst of its own anguished delights. He had awakened one day to find childhood gone—it had come to an end when he was not looking, and its elements remained undefinable, its design nebulous, its harmonies all unresolved. Yet he had felt still connected to every part of it by ten thousand invisible threads; he thought he had the power to recall it and change it merely by touching these hidden filaments of memory.

The sun's light filtered through his closed eyelids, making a blind world of burning orange warmth; with it came a corresponding ray of understanding which, like a spotlight thrown suddenly from an unexpected direction, bathed the familiar panorama in a transforming glow of finality. The years he had spent in the bank, standing in the teller's cage, had been real, after all; he could not call them an accident or a stop-gap. They had gone by and they were finished, and now he saw them as an unalterable part of the pattern. Now all the distant indecisions, the postponements and unsolved questions were beyond his reach. It was too late to touch or change anything. It always had been too late, only until now he had not known it. His life had not been the trial life he had vaguely felt it to be—it had been the only one possible, the only conceivable one.

And so everything turned out to have been already complete, its form decided and irrevocable. A feeling of profound contentment spread through him. The succession of ideas evaporated, leaving him with only the glow of well-being attendant upon their passage. He looked among the pebbles for the beetle; it had disappeared along the path. But now he heard voices, nearby. A group of turbaned Berbers came past, and looking at him without surprise went on, still conversing. Their appearance served to bring him back from the interior place where he had been. He took the pipe to pieces, put it away. Feeling drunk and light-headed, he rose and followed behind them at a discreet distance. The path they presently chose led over a hill and down—down across a wilderness of cactus, through shady olive groves (the decayed trunks were often no more than wide gnarled shells), over cascades of smooth rocks, through meadows dotted with oleander bushes, becoming finally a narrow lane bordered on either side by high holly. Here it twisted so frequently that he lost sight of the men several times, and eventually they disappeared completely. Almost at the moment he realized they were gone, he came unexpectedly out onto a belvedere strewn with boulders, directly above the rooftops, terraces and minarets of the town.

XXIII

Sometimes on Friday mornings, Hadj Mohammed Beidaoui would send one of his older sons to fetch the last-born, Thami, where he was playing in the garden, and the little boy would be carried in, squirming to prevent his brother from covering his cheeks with noisy kisses all the way. Then he would be placed on his father's knee, his face would momentarily be buried in the hard white beard, and he would hold his breath until his father's face was raised again, and the old man began to pinch his infant cheeks and smooth his hair. He remembered clearly his father's ivory-colored skin, and how beautiful and majestic the smooth ancient face had seemed to him framed in its white silk djellaba. When he thought of it now, perhaps he was referring in memory to one particular morning, a day radiant as only a day of spring in childhood can be, when his father, after sprinkling him with orange flower water until he was quite wet and almost sick from the sweet smell, had taken him by the hand and led him through the streets and parks of sunlight and flowers to the mosque of the Marshan, through the streets openly, where everyone they met, the men who kissed the hem of Hadj Mohammed's sleeve, and those who did not, could see that Thami was his son. And Abdelftah and Abdelmalek and Hassan and Abdallah had all been left home! That was the most important part. The conscious campaign to seek to gain more than his share of his father's favor dated from that morning; he had waged it unceasingly from then until the old man's death. Then, of course, it was all over. The others were older than he, and by that time disliked him, and he returned their antipathy. He began to bribe the servants to let him out of the house, and this got several of them into trouble with Abdelftah, master of the household then, who was short-tempered and flew into a rage each time he learned that Thami had escaped into the street. But it was the street with its forbidden delights that tempted the boy more than anything else, once the world had ceased being a place where the greatest good was to climb into his father's lap and listen to the flow of legends and proverbs and songs and poems that he wished would never come to an end. There was one song he still recalled in its entirety. It went: *Ya ouled al harrata, Al mallem Bouzekri. . . .* His father had told him all the boys of Fez ran through the streets singing it when rain was needed. And there was one proverb which he associated intimately with the memory of his father's face and with the sensation of being held by him, surrounded by the mountains of brocade-covered cushions, with the great lanterns and high looped draperies above, and no matter how often his father acceded to his pleas to repeat it, always it was fresh with a mysterious, magical truth when he heard it.

"Tell about the day."

"The day?" Old Hadj Mohammed would repeat, looking deliberately, cunningly vague, and pulling at his lower lip while he rolled his eyes upward with a vacant expression. "The day? What day?"

"The day," Thami would insist.

"Aaah!" And the old man would begin, and begin at the same time the dovening motion which accompanied the utterance of any words that were not extemporaneous. "The morning is a little boy." He made his eyes large and round. "Noon is a man." He sat up very straight and looked fierce. "Twilight is an old man." He relaxed and looked into Thami's face with tenderness. "What do I do?" Thami knew, but he remained silent, waiting breathless, spellbound for the moment when he would take part in the ritual, his eyes unwaveringly fixed on the ivory face.

"I smile at the first. I admire the second. I venerate the last." And as he finished saying the words, Thami would seize the frail white hand, bend his head forward, and with passion press his lips against the back of the fingers. Then, renewed love in his eyes, the old man would sit back and look at his son. Abdallah once had spied on this game (of the brothers he was the nearest Thami's age, being only a year older), and later when he got him alone, he had subjected Thami to a series of tortures which the boy had borne silently, scarcely offering resistance. It seemed to him a small enough price to pay for his father's favor. "And if you tell Father I'll tell Abdelftah," Abdallah had warned him. Abdelftah would devise something infinitely worse—of that they were both certain—but Thami had laughed scornfully through his tears. He had no intention of telling; to bring to his father's attention the fact that the others could be jealous of his participation in this sacred game would have meant to risk losing his privilege of playing it.

Later it was the streets, the hidden cafés at Sidi Bouknadel that closed their doors leaving the boys inside sitting on mats playing ronda and smoking kif and drinking cognac until morning; it was the beach where they played football and, pooling their money, would rent a caseta for the season, which they used for drinking competitions and the holding of small private orgies whose etiquette demanded that the younger boys be at the entire disposal of the older ones. And

above all it was the bordels. By the time Thami was eighteen
he had had all the girls in all the establishments, and a good
many more off the street. He took to staying away from home
for several days at a time, and when he returned it would be
in a state of dishevelment which infuriated his brothers. After
his sixth arrest for drunkenness Abdelmalek, who was now the
head of the family, Abdelftah having moved to Casablanca,
gave orders to the guards of the house to refuse him entrance
unless he was in a state of complete sobriety and properly
dressed. This meant, more than anything else, that he would
no longer receive his daily spending money. "This will change
him," he said confidently to Hassan. "You'll see the difference
very soon." But Thami was more headstrong and resourceful
than they had suspected. He found ways of living—what ways
they never knew—without needing to return home, without
having to forego the independence so necessary to him. And
since then he never had gone back, save now and then for a
moment of conversation with his brothers at the entrance
door, usually to ask a favor which they seldom granted. There
was nothing basically anti-social about Thami; hostility was
alien to him. He merely had expended almost all his capacities
for respect and devotion upon his father, so that he could not
give the traditional amount of either to his brothers. Also he
would not agree to pretend. He did not respect them, and he
had had too much contact with European culture to believe
he was committing a sin in refusing to feign a respect which
custom demanded but which he did not feel.

It was at the annual moussem of Moulay Abdeslam, where
serious men go for the good of their souls, that Thami had
met Kinza, among the tents and donkeys and fanatical pilgrims. The situation was one with which Moslem tradition is
totally unprepared to deal. Young men and women cannot
know each other, and if by some disgraceful chance they happen to have managed to see each other alone for a minute, the
idea is so shameful that everyone forgets it immediately. But to
follow it up, to see the girl again, to suggest marrying her—it
would be hard to conceive of more outrageous conduct.
Thami did all these things. He went back to Agla at the same
time as she did, got to know the family, who were naturally
much impressed with his city ways and his erudition, and

wrote to Abdelmalek saying that he was about to be married and thought it time he received his inheritance. His brother's reply was a telegram bidding him return to Tangier at once to discuss the matter. It was then that the two had their serious falling-out, since Abdelmalek refused outright to let him touch his money or his property. "I'll go to the Qadi," threatened Thami. Abdelmalek merely laughed. "Go," he said, "if you think there is anything about you he doesn't already know." In the end, after lengthy discussions with Hassan, who thought marriage, even with a shamefully low peasant girl, might possibly be a means of changing Thami's ways, Abdelmalek gave him a few thousand pesetas. He fetched the whole family from Agla and they had a wedding in Emsallah, the humblest quarter of Tangier, all of which nevertheless seemed magnificent to Kinza and her tribe. In due time all but the bride returned to the farmhouse on the mountain above Agla, where they lived working their fields, gathering the fruit from their trees and sending the children to tend the goats on the heights above.

To them Thami was a glamorous, important figure, and they had been overjoyed to see him come knocking at the door the previous evening. They were not so pleased, however, to learn that he had a Nazarene with him, up in the other house, and although he had managed last night to slide over it by talking of other things and then leaving suddenly, he could see that his father-in-law had not finished expressing his views on the subject.

At the house they told him that the men were down in the orchard. He followed the high cactus fence until he came to a gate made of sheet tin. When he knocked, the sound was very loud, and it was with a certain amount of mild apprehension that he waited for someone to come. One of the sons let him in. An artificial stream ran through the orchard, part of the system which irrigated the entire valley with the spring water that came out of the rocks above the town. Kinza's father was watering the rose-bushes. He hurried back and forth, his baggy trousers hitched above his knees, stooping by the edge of the channel to fill an ancient oil can that spouted water from all corners, running with it each time, to arrive before it was empty. When he saw Thami he ceased his labors, and together they sat down in the shade of a huge fig tree.

Almost immediately he brought up the subject of the Nazarene. Having him in the house would make trouble, he predicted. No one had ever heard of a Spaniard living in the same house with a Moslem, and besides, what was the purpose, what was the reason for such a thing? "Why doesn't he stay at the fonda at Agla like all the others?" he demanded. Thami tried to explain. "He's not a Spaniard," he began, but already he foresaw the difficulties he was going to meet, trying to make the other understand. "He's an American." "Melikan?" cried Kinza's father. "And where is Melika? Where? In Spain! Ah! You see?" The oldest son timidly suggested that perhaps the Nazarene was a Frenchman. Frenchmen were not Spaniards, he said. "Not Spaniards?" cried his father. "And where do you think France is, if it's not in Spain? Call him Melikan, call him French, call him English, call him whatever you like. He's still a Spaniard, he's still a Nazarene, and it's bad to have him in the house." "You're right," said Thami, deciding that acquiescence was the easiest way out of the conversation, because his only argument at that point would have been to tell them that Dyar was paying him for the privilege of staying in the house, and that was a detail he did not want them to know. The old man was mollified; then, "Why doesn't he stay at the fonda, anyway? Tell me that," he said suspiciously. Thami shrugged his shoulders, said he did not know. "Ah! You see?" the old man cried in triumph. "He has a reason, and it's a bad reason. And only bad things can happen when Nazarenes and Moslems come together."

There was a halfwit son who sat with them; he nodded his head endlessly, overcome by the wisdom of his father's utterances. The other sons looked at Thami, slightly embarrassed at hearing these ideas, which they supposed he must consider ridiculously old-fashioned. Then they talked of other things, and presently the old man returned to watering his flowers. Thami and the sons retired to a secluded part of the orchard where they could not be seen by him, and smoked, Thami feeling that under the circumstances he could not very well insult the family by returning to the house on the mountain solely to take food to the Christian. They passed the day eating, sleeping and playing cards, and it was twilight when he took his leave, not having dared to suggest that they give him food again, nor even finding the courage to ask for the use of the blanket. But he could not go back up to the house without food, for Dyar would be ravenous by now, and this meant that he must go into Agla and buy supplies for dinner. "*Yah latif, yah latif,*" he said under his breath as he followed the path that led downward to the village.

There was little doubt in Dyar's mind, as he stumbled along the cobbled road that led through the town gate, that the place was Agla. He had merely come down by a very wide detour, by going around to the back of the mountain, and then returning to the steep side once again. Thus there was a real possibility of his running into Thami, who, it now occurred to him, would be convinced he had run away in order to avoid having to pay him what he owed him. Or no, he thought, not at all. If Thami were after everything, such a detail would naturally be of no importance. In that case the meeting would bring matters to a head very quickly. The men he had chosen to help him would be nearby; by some casual gesture as they walked along the street together, he and Thami, in full view of the populace, the signal would be given. Or they might even be with him. The only hope would be to defend the brief case as though his whole life were locked inside. Then, when they got it open and found it empty, he might possibly be far enough away to escape.

The tiny streets and houses were smothered with whitewash, which glowed as if all during the day it had been absorbing the sunlight and now, at dusk, were slowly giving it off into the fading air. It all looked, he thought, as though it had been made by a pastry-cook, but probably that was only because at the moment he did not need much imagination for things to look edible. With infallible intuition he chose the streets that led to the center of town, and there he saw a small native restaurant where the cooking was being done in the entrance. The cook lifted the covers of the various copper cauldrons for him; he looked down into them and ordered soup, chickpeas stewed with pieces of lamb, and skewered liver. There was a small dim room behind the kitchen with two tables in it, and beyond that a raised niche covered with matting where several rustics squatted with enormous loaves

of bread which they tore into pieces and put into the soup.
For Dyar the assuaging of his appetite was a voluptuous act;
it went on and on. What he had ordered at first proved to be
completely inadequate. Thami had told him that the desire
for food after smoking kif was like no other appetite. He
sighed apprehensively. Thami and his kif. How would he feel
when he realized his prisoner had escaped, taking with him
even Thami's own pipe and mottoui? He wondered if perhaps
that might not be considered a supreme injury, an unforgivable act. He had no idea; he knew nothing about this country, save that all its inhabitants behaved like maniacs. Maybe it
was not Thami himself of whose reactions he was afraid, he
reflected—it might be only that Thami was part of the place
and therefore had everything in the place behind him, so to
speak. Thami in New York—he almost laughed at the image
the idea evoked—he was the sort no one would even take the
trouble to look at in the street when he asked for a dime.
Here it was another matter. He was a spokesman for the
place; like Antaeus, whatever strength he had came out of the
earth, and his feet were planted squarely upon it. "So you're
afraid of him," he remarked to himself in disgust. He looked
through the bright kitchen out into the black street beyond.
"Afraid he might walk in that door." He sat perfectly still,
somehow expecting the idea to conjure up the reality. Instead, an oversized Berber appeared in the doorway, his
djellaba slung loosely over one shoulder, and ordered a glass
of tea. While he waited the five minutes it always took to prepare the tea, (because the water, while hot, was never boiling,
and the mint leaves had to be stripped one by one from the
stalk) he stood staring at Dyar in a manner which the other at
first found disconcerting, then disturbing, and finally, because
he had begun to ask himself the possible reason for this insolent scrutiny, downright frightening. "Why does he block the
door like that?" he thought, his heart beginning to beat too
fast in a sudden wave of desperate conjecture. For the moment there was only one answer: one of Thami's henchmen
had arrived to keep watch, to prevent his escape. They were
probably posted in every café and eating-place in the town.
For the first time it occurred to him that they might do their
work on him in Thami's absence, with Thami conveniently

seated in some respectable home, laughing, drinking tea, strumming on an oud. And this possibility seemed in a way worse, perhaps because he had never been able to see Thami in the role of a brutal torturer, the tacit understanding with his own imagination having been that things would somehow be done with comparative gentleness, painlessly. He looked up once again at the Neanderthal head, the deep furrows in the slanting forehead and the brows that formed a single ragged line across the face, and knew that for such a man there were no halfway measures. Yet he could not see any baseness in the face, nor even any particular cunning—merely a primal, ancient blindness, the ineffable, unfocused melancholy of the great apes as they stare between the cage bars.

"I don't want any of this," he told himself. You didn't try to outwit such beings; you simply got out if you could. He rose and walked over to the stove. "How much?" he said in English. The man understood, held up his two hands, the fingers outspread, then raised one lone forefinger. Turning his back on the giant in the doorway, so as to hide as well as possible the fistful of bills he pulled out of his pocket, he handed the cook a hundred-peseta note. The man looked startled, indicated he had no change. Dyar searched further, found twenty-five pesetas. Dubiously the cook accepted it, and pushing aside the Berber in the entrance, went out into the street to get change. "But good God," Dyar thought, seeing the prospect of a whole new horizon of difficulties spreading itself before him. No change for a hundred pesetas. Then a thousand pesetas would be just ten times as hard to get rid of. He moved his shoulder a little, to feel the twelve hundred and sixty thousand-peseta notes against his skin, around his middle. He stood there, conscious of the huge Berber's gaze, but not for an instant returning it, until the cook came back and handed him fourteen pesetas. When he went out into the street he turned to the right, where there seemed to be the greater number of passers-by, and walked quickly away, looking back only once just before he forced himself through the middle of an ambling group, and being not at all surprised to see the Berber step out of the restaurant and start slowly in the same direction. But Dyar was going rapidly; the next time he turned around to look, he was satisfied that he had lost him.

The whitewashed cobbled street was full of strollers in djellabas moving in both directions; the groups saluted each other constantly as they passed. Dyar threaded his way among them as unostentatiously as he could for a man in a hurry. Sometimes the street would turn into a long, wide flight of stairs with a shop no bigger than a stall on each step, and he would run lightly all the way down, gauging his distances with care to be sure of not plunging into a group of walkers, not daring to look up to see what effect his passage was having on the populace. When he came out into an open space lined on one side with new one-story European buildings he stopped short, not certain whether to continue or go back. There was a café over there with tables and chairs set out along a narrow strip of sidewalk, and at the tables sat Spaniards, some of whom wore the white uniforms of officers in the Moroccan army. His instinct told him to stay in the shade, to go back into the Arab town. The question was: where would he be safer? There was no doubt that the greater danger was the possibility of being stopped and questioned by the Spanish. Yet the fear he felt was not of them, but of what could happen back in the streets he had just come from. And now as he stood there clutching his brief case, the people pushing past him on both sides, his mind still muzzy from the kif, he saw with terror that he was hopelessly confused. He had imagined the town would be something else, that somewhere there would be a place he could go into and ask for information; he had counted on the town to help him as a troubled man counts on a friend to give him advice, knowing beforehand that he will follow whatever advice he gets, because the important thing is to do *something*, to move in any direction, out of his impasse. Once he had been to Agla, he had thought, he would know more about his situation. But he had not understood until now how heavily he was counting on it, partly perhaps because all day he had been thinking only of escaping from Thami. However, at this moment he was conscious that the props that had held up his future were in the act of crumbling: he never had had any plan of action, he could not imagine now what he had ever intended to "find out" here in the town, what sort of people he had thought he would be able to see in order to get his information, or even what kind of information he had meant to get. For an instant he looked upward into the sky. The stars were there; they did not tell him what to do. He had turned, he had started to walk, back through the town's entrance gate into the crooked street, but his legs were trembling, and he was only indistinctly aware of what went on around him. This time, since a part of the mechanism that held his being together seemed to have given way, he somehow got turned off the principal street which led steeply upward, and let his legs lead him along a smaller flat one that had fewer lights and people in it, and no shops at all.

XXIV

Sometimes there was the dribbling of fountains into their basins, sometimes only the sound of the fast-running spring water under the stones, behind the walls. Occasionally a single large night-bird dipped toward the ground near a lamp, its crazy shadow running swiftly over the white walls; each time, Dyar started with nervousness, cursing himself silently for not being able to dislodge the fear in him. He walked slowly now, overtaking no one. Ahead, when the way was straight enough, he sometimes caught sight of two men in dark robes, walking hand in hand. They were singing a song with a short vigorous refrain which kept recurring at brief intervals; in between was a lazy variation on the refrain which followed like a weak, uncertain answer to the other. This in itself Dyar surely would not have noticed, had it not been for the fact that each time the meandering section began, just for the first few notes, he had the distinct impression that the sound came from somewhere behind him. By the time he had stopped to listen (his interest aroused not by the music, but by his own fear) the two ahead had always started in again. Finally, in order to be sure, he stood quite still for the space of several choruses, while little by little the voices of the two ahead grew fainter. There was no longer any doubt in his mind; a querulous falsetto voice was singing the same song, coming along behind him. He could hear it more plainly now, like a mocking shadow of the music that went on ahead. But from the strategic spaces that were left in the design of the melody and rhythm by the two men for the single voice in the rear to fill in, he knew immediately that they were conscious of the other's participation in the song. He stepped back into a recess between the houses, where there was a small square tank with water pouring into it, and waited for the owner of the single voice to go by. From in here he could hear nothing but the hollow falling of the water into the cistern beside him, and he strained, listening, to see if the other, on noticing his disappearance, would stop singing, change the sound of his voice, or in some other manner send a signal to those who went ahead. If only he had a good-sized flashlight, he thought, or a monkey-wrench, he could hit him on the back of the head as he went past, drag him into the dark here, and go back quickly in the other direction. But when the lone vocalist appeared, he turned out to be accompanied by a friend. Both were youths in their teens, and they stumbled along with the air of not having a thought in their heads, beyond that of not losing the thread of the song that floated back through the street to them. He waited until they had gone past, counted to twenty, and peered around the corner of the house: they were still going along with the same careless, unsteady gait. When they had disappeared he turned and went back, still by no means convinced that when they noticed his absence ahead of them, they would not hurry to confer with the other couple and set out with them to look for him.

Because fear is without any true relationship to reality each time he left a lighted patch of street and entered the dark, he now expected the singers and their friends to be somewhere there waiting, having taken a short cut and got there before him. An iron arm would reach out of an invisible doorway and yank him inside before he knew what was happening, a terrific blow from behind would fell him, and he would come to in some deserted alley, lying in a pile of garbage, his money gone, his passport gone, his watch and clothes gone, with no one to help him either here or in Tangier or anywhere else. No one to cover his nakedness or to provide him with even tomorrow morning's meal. From the jail where they would lodge him they would telephone the American Legation, and he would soon see Tangier again, a thousand times more a victim than ever.

Going by each side street and passageway he opened his eyes wider and stared, as if that might help him to see through the darkness. Back on the main street, climbing the long stairs, where the light from the stalls spilled across the steps, he felt a little better, even though his legs were hollow and seemed not to want to go where he tried to direct them. There was some comfort in being back among people; all he had to do here was walk along with his head down and not look up into their faces. When he had got almost back up to the place where he had eaten, he heard drums beating out a peculiar, breathless rhythm. Here the street made several abrupt turns, becoming a series of passageways that led through the buildings. He glanced up at the second-story window overlooking the entrance to one of these tunnels, and saw, through the iron grillework, the back of a row of turbaned heads. At the same instant a peremptory voice in the street behind him called out, "*Hola, señor! Oiga!*" He turned his head quickly and saw, fifty feet back, a native in what looked like a policeman's uniform and helmet, and there was no doubt that the man was trying to attract his attention. He plunged ahead into the darkness, made the first turn with the street, and seeing a partially open door on his right, pushed against it.

The light came from above. A steep stairway led up. The drums were there, and also a faint, wheezing music. He stood behind the door at the foot of the stairs, not having pushed it any further shut than it had been. He waited; nothing happened. Then a man appeared at the top of the stairs, was about to come down, saw him, motioned to another, who presently also came into view. Together they beckoned to him. "*Tlah. Tlah. Agi,*" they said. Because their faces were unmistakably friendly, he slowly started to mount the steps.

It was a small, very crowded café with benches along the walls. The dim light came from a bulb hung above a high copper samovar which stood on a shelf in a corner. All the men wore white turbans, and they looked up with interest as Dyar entered, making room for him at the end of a bench by the drummers, who sat in a circle on the floor at the far end of the room. Over here it was very dark indeed, and he had the impression that something inexplicable was taking place on the floor almost at his feet. The men were looking downward through the smoke at a formless mass that quaked, jerked, shuddered and heaved, and although the room shook with the pounding of the drums, it was as if another kind of silence were there in the air, an imperious silence that stretched from the eyes of the men watching to the object moving at their feet. As his own eyes grew accustomed to the confused light, Dyar saw that it was a man, his hands locked firmly together behind him as if they were chained there. Until this moment he had been writhing and twisting on the floor, but now slowly he was rising to his knees, turning his head desperately from side to side, an expression of agony on his tortured face. Even when, five minutes later, he had finally got to his feet, he did not alter the position of his hands, and always the spasms that forced his body this way and that, in perfect rhythm with the increasing hysteria of the drums and the low cracked voice of the flute, seemed to come from some secret center far inside him. Dyar watched impassively. He was completely hidden by the ranks of the men who stood near him looking at the spectacle, and more of whom kept crowding up; from the door he was invisible, and the consciousness of that gave him momentary relief. Someone passed him a glass of tea from the other end of the long table. As he held it under his nose, the sharp fumes of hot spearmint cleared his head, and he became aware of another odor in the air, a spicy resinous smell which he traced to a brazier behind one of the drummers; a heavy smudge of sweet smoke rose constantly. The man had begun to cry out, softly at first, and then savagely; his cries were answered by rhythmical calls of "*Al-lah!*" from the drummers. Dyar stole a glance around at the faces of the spectators. The expression he saw was the same on all sides: utter absorption in the dance, almost adoration of the man performing it. A lighted kif pipe was thrust in front of him. He took it and smoked it without looking to see who had offered it to him. His heart, which had been beating violently when he came in, had ceased its pounding; he felt calmer now.

After a day passed largely in the contemplation of that far-off and unlikely place which was the interior of himself, he did not find it difficult now to reject flatly the reality of what he was seeing. He merely sat and watched, content in the conviction that the thing he was looking at was not taking place in the world that really existed. It was too far beyond the pale of the possible. The kif pipe was refilled several times for him, and the smoke, rising to his head, helped him to sit there and watch a thing he did not believe.

According to Dyar's eyes, the man now at last moved his hands, reached inside his garments and pulled out a large knife, which he flourished with wide gestures. It gleamed feebly in the faint light. Without glancing behind him, one of the drummers threw a handful of something over his shoulder and resumed beating, coming in on the complex rhythm perfectly: the smoke rose in thicker clouds from the censer. The chanted strophes were now antiphonal, with "*Al-lah!*" being thrown back and forth like a red-hot stone from one side of the circle to the other. At the same time it was as if the sound had become two high walls between which the dancer whirled and leapt, striking against their invisible surfaces with his head in a vain effort to escape beyond them.

The man held up his bare arm. The blade glinted, struck at it on a down beat of the drum pattern. And again. And again and again, until the arm and hand were shining and black. Then the other arm was slashed, the tempo increasing as the drummers' bodies bent further forward toward the center of the circle. In the sudden flare of a match nearby, Dyar saw the glistening black of the arms and hands change briefly to red, as if the man had dipped his arms in bright red paint; he saw, too, the ecstatic face as an arm was raised to the mouth and the swift tongue began to lick the blood in rhythm. With the shortening of the phrases, the music had become an enormous panting. It had kept every detail of syncopation intact, even at its present great rate of speed, thus succeeding in destroying the listeners' sense of time, forcing their minds to accept the arbitrary one it imposed in its place. With this hypnotic device it had gained complete domination. But as to the dancer, it was hard to say whether they were commanding him or he them. He bent over, and with a great sweep of his arm began a thorough hacking of his legs; the music's volume swelled in accompaniment.

Dyar was there, scarcely breathing. It could not be said that he watched now, because in his mind he had moved forward from looking on to a kind of participation. With each gesture the man made at this point, he felt a sympathetic desire to cry out in triumph. The mutilation was being done for him, to him; it was his own blood that spattered onto the drums and made the floor slippery. In a world which had not yet been muddied by the discovery of thought, there was this certainty, as solid as a boulder, as real as the beating of his heart, that the man was dancing to purify all who watched. When the dancer threw himself to the floor with a despairing cry, Dyar knew that in reality it was a cry of victory, that spirit had triumphed; the expressions of satisfaction on the faces around him confirmed this. The musicians hesitated momentarily, but at a signal from the men who bent solicitously over the dancer's twitching body they resumed playing the same piece, slowly as at the beginning. Dyar sat perfectly still, thinking of nothing, savoring the unaccustomed sensations which had been freed within him. Conversation had started up; since no one passed him a pipe, he took out Thami's and smoked it. Soon the dancer rose from where he lay on the floor, stood up a little unsteadily, and going to each musician in turn, took each head between his hands from which the blood still dripped, and planted a solemn kiss on the forehead. Then he pushed his way through the crowd, paid for his tea, and went out.

Dyar stayed on a few minutes, and after drinking what remained of his tea, which had long ago grown cold, gave the qaouaji the peseta it cost, and slowly went down the steps. Inside the door he hesitated; it seemed to him he was making a grave decision in venturing out into the street again. But whatever awaited him out there had to be faced, he told himself, and it might as well be now as a few minutes or hours later. He opened the door. The covered street was deserted and black, but beyond the furthest arch, where it led into the open, the walls and paving stones glowed as the moonlight poured over them. He walked out into a wide plaza dominated by a high minaret, feeling only acute surprise to find that none of his fear was left. It had all been liberated by the past hour in the café; how, he would never understand, nor did he care. But now, whatever circumstance presented itself, he would find a way to deal with it. The confidence of his mood was augmented by the several pipes of kif he presently smoked sitting on the ledge of the fountain in the center of the plaza.

A hundred feet away, in a café overlooking the same plaza, Thami was lamenting having left his pipe and mottoui behind in the house. He had to accept the qaouaji's generosity, and it was embarrassing to him. With the number of parcels he had, he was understandably loath to set off up the mountain, and besides, he had just eaten heavily. He had wanted very much to buy a bottle of good Terry cognac to drink that night, but his money had proved insufficient for such a luxury. Instead, he had got a large mass of majoun, at the same time making a firm resolution to demand his five thousand pesetas as soon as he got back up to the house. The extra money he had been promised could wait, but not that initial sum. Dyar would be in no mood to give it to him, he knew, but after all, he had the upper hand: he would simply threaten to leave tomorrow. That would bring him around.

Dyar sat, watching the strong moonlight flood the white surface of the plaza, letting his mind grow lucid and hard like the objects and their shadows around him. (At noon the kif had had a diffusing effect, softening and melting his thought, spreading it within him, but now it had tightened him; he felt alert and fully in touch with the world.) Since the situation was worse than he had imagined, because of the patent impossibility of his getting change for the notes anywhere in Agla, the only thing to do was to spend a little money improving that situation. It would mean taking Thami into his confidence, but it was simple, and if he could instill into him the idea that once a man has agreed to be an accomplice he is as guilty as his companion, he thought the risk would not be too great. The fact that he had already dismissed as childish and neurotic the fear which had driven him out of the house and along the mountainside all day, did not strike him as suspect or worthy of any particular scrutiny. The important thing, he thought, was to get over the border into French Morocco, which was many times larger than the Spanish Zone, where he would be less conspicuous (because, while he might be taken for French, he could never pass for a Spaniard), and where the police were less on the lookout for strangers. But before that they would have to have change for the banknotes. Feeling the need to walk as he made his plans, he rose and went across to the dark side of the plaza, where small trees lined the walk. Without paying attention to where he was going, he turned off into a side street.

Every day for the next week he would send Thami down here to Agla for provisions, and each time he would give him a thousand peseta note with which to purchase them. He was confident Thami could get change. That way at the end of the week they would at least have enough to start south. He would also give Thami five hundred pesetas a day until they were across the border, with a promised bonus of an extra five thousand when they were in French territory, and a hundred on each thousand-peseta note Thami could change into francs for him once they were there. Assuming he were able to get it all changed, this project would cost him over two thousand dollars, but that was a small price to pay for being in the clear.

From ahead came the noise of voices raised in angry dispute. Although the plaza out there was empty, the town was by no means entirely asleep. Turning a bend in the street he came out upon a small square darkened by a trellis of vines overhead. A group of excited men had gathered around two small boys who apparently had been fighting; they had started by being onlookers, and then, inevitably, had entered into the altercation with all the passion of the original participants. The rectangles of yellow light that lay on the pavement came from the shops that were open; in contrast the mottles of moonlight in dark corners were blue. He did not stop to watch the argument: walking along the white street in the moon's precise light was conducive to the unfolding of plans. The commotion was such that no one noticed him as he passed through the shady square. The shops, which seemed to belong primarily to tailors and carpenters, were empty at the moment, having been deserted at the first indication of a diversion in the street. The way twisted a little; there was one more stall open here, and beyond, only the moonlight. It was a carpenter's shop, and the man had been working in the doorway, building a high wooden chest shaped like a steamer trunk. The hammer lay where he had left it. Dyar saw it without seeing it; then he looked at it hard, looked involuntarily for the nails. They too were there, a bit long, but straight and new, lying on a little square stool nearby. Only when he had passed the shouting group again and had got so far beyond that he could no longer hear the hoarse cries, the hammer and one big nail in his coat pocket, did he realize that for all his great clarity of mind sitting by the fountain smoking his kif, he had been unbelievably stupid. What were the hammer and nail for? To fix the door. What door? The door to the cottage, the rattling door that kept him from sleeping. And where was the cottage, how was he going to get there?

He stood still, more appalled by the revelation of this incredible lapse in his mental processes than by the fact itself that he could not get to the house, that he had nowhere to sleep. This kif is treacherous stuff, he thought, starting ahead slowly.

Back in the deserted plaza he seated himself once again on the edge of the fountain and pulled out the pipe. Treacherous or not, like alcohol it at least made the present moment bearable. As he smoked he saw a figure emerge from the shadows on the dark side of the plaza and come sauntering over in his direction. When it was still fairly far away, but near enough for him to see it was a man carrying a large basket, it said: "*Salam.*" Dyar grunted.

"*Andek es sebsi?*"

He looked up unbelieving. It was impossible. The stuff was treacherous, so he did not move, but waited.

The man came nearer, exclaimed. Then Dyar jumped up. "You son of a bitch!" he cried, laughing with pleasure, clapping Thami's shoulder several times.

Thami was delighted, too. Dyar had eaten, was in a good humor. The return to the house with its attendant furious reproaches no longer had to be dreaded. He could broach the subject of the money. And there was his own kif-pipe, whose absence he had been so lately regretting, right in Dyar's hand. But he was nervous about being here in the plaza.

"You're going to have trouble here," he said. "It's very bad. I told you not to come. If one moqaddem sees you, '*Oiga, señor,* come on to the comisaría, we look at your papers, my friend.' Let's go."

The moonlight was very bright when they had left the town behind and were among the olive trees. Halfway up the mountain, among the ragged rocks, they sat down, and Thami took out the majoun.

"You know what this is?" he asked.

"Sure I know. I've had it before."

"This won't make you drunk for an hour yet. Or more. When we got to the house I'll make tea. Then you'll see how drunk."

"I know. I've had it before, I said."

Thami looked at him with disbelief, and divided the cake into two unequal pieces, handing the larger to Dyar.

"It's soft," Dyar remarked in some surprise. "The kind I had was hard."

"Same thing," Thami said with indifference. "This is better." Dyar was inclined to agree with him, as regarded the flavor. They sat, quietly eating, each one conscious in his own fashion that as he swallowed the magical substance he was irrevocably delivering himself over to unseen forces which would take charge of his life for the hours to come.

They did not speak, but sat hearing the water moving downward in the gulf of moonlight and shadows that lay open at their feet.

XXV

"Home again!" Dyar said jovially as he went inside the house, greeted by the close mildewed smell he had said good-bye to so long ago. "Let's make that fire before we blow our respective tops." He tossed the brief case into a corner, glad to be rid of it.

Thami shut the door, locked it, and stared at him, not understanding. "You're already hashish," he said. "I know when I look at you. What are you talking about?"

"The fire. The fire. Get some wood. Quick!"

"Plenty of wood," said Thami imperturbably, pointing to the patio with its crates. Dyar stepped out and began to throw them wildly into the center of the room. "Break 'em up!" he shouted. "Smash 'em! It's going to be God-damned cold in here without any blanket. We've got to keep the fire going as long as we can."

Thami obeyed, wondering at the surprising transformation a little majoun could work in a Christian. He had never before seen Dyar in good spirits. When he had an enormous pile of slats, he pushed it to one side and spread the two mats, one on top of the other, in front of the fireplace. Then he went out into the kitchen and busied himself building a charcoal fire in the earthen brazier, in order to prepare the tea.

"Ah!" he heard Dyar cry in triumph from the patio. "Just what we wanted!" He had unearthed several small logs in one corner, which he carried in and dumped beside the fireplace. He joined Thami in the kitchen. "Give me a match," he said. "My candle's gone out." Thami was squatting over the brazier, and he looked up smiling. "How do you feel now?" he asked.

"I feel great. Why? How do you feel?"

Thami handed him his box of matches. "I feel good," he answered. He was not sure how to begin. Perhaps it would be better to wait until they were lying in front of the fire. But by then Dyar's mood might have changed. "I wanted to buy a big bottle of cognac tonight, you know." He paused.

"Well, why didn't you? I could do with a drink right now."

Thami rubbed his forefinger against his thumb, back and forth, expressively.

"Oh," said Dyar soberly. "I see." He went back into the other room, stuffed some paper into the fireplace, put some crate wood on top, and lighted it. Then he walked over to the darkest corner of the room and keeping his eye on the door into the patio, pulled out five notes from the inside of his shirt. "This'll show him I'm playing straight with him," he said to himself. He returned to the kitchen and handed the money to Thami, saying: "Here."

"Thank you," Thami said. He stood up and patted him on the back lightly, three pats.

"When you come in I'll talk to you about the rest of it." He went out into the patio and stood looking up at the huge globe of the full moon; never had he seen it so near or so strong. A night bird screamed briefly in the air overhead—a peculiar, chilly sound, not quite like anything he had heard before. He stood, hearing the sound again and again in his head, a long string of interior echoes that traced an invisible ladder across the black sky. The crackling of the fire inside roused him. He went in and threw on a log. He crouched down, looking into the fire, following the forms of the flames with his eyes. The fireplace drew well; no smoke came out into the room.

They were putting their feet carefully on the square gray flagstones that led through the grass across the garden, having to step off them at one point onto the soaked turf to avoid the hose with a sprinkler attachment. It went around and around, unevenly. Mrs. Shields had pulled down all the shades in the big room, because the sun shone in and faded the drapes, she said. Once the windows were shut, the thunderstorm could come whenever it liked; it had been threatening all afternoon. Across the river it looked very dark. It was probably raining there already, but the rolling of the thunder was more distant. Far up the valley toward the gap it groaned. There was wild country up there, and the people did not have the same friendliness they had here where the land was good. Mrs. Shields had let the hose spot her dress. It was a shame, he thought, looking closely at the paisley design.

He did not want to be in the house when they left. Turning to the empty rooms where the air still moved with the currents set up by their last-minute hurryings, feeling the seat of a chair in which one of them had sat, because of that a little warmer than the others, but the warmth still palpable after they had gone, seeing the cord of a window-shade still swinging almost imperceptibly—he could not bear any of those things. It was better to stay in the garden, say good-bye to them there, and wait to go in until the house was completely dead. And the storm would either break or it would growl around the countryside until evening. The grapes are getting ripe, she said as they passed under the arbor. And the sailboats will be making for the harbor. He stood against a cherry tree and watched the ants running up and down across the rough brown bark of the trunk, very near his face. That summer was in a lost region, and all roads to it had been cut.

Thami came in, carrying the burning brazier. He set it down in the middle of the room, went and got the teapot and the glasses. While he waited for the water to boil, blowing from time to time on the glowing coals, Dyar told him of his plans. But when he came to the point of mentioning the sum he had, he found he could not do it. Thami listened, shook his head skeptically when Dyar had finished. "Pesetas are no good in the French Zone," he said. "You can't change them. You'd have to take them to the Jews if you did that."

"Well, we'll take 'em to the Jews, then. Why not?"

Thami looked at him pityingly. "The Jews?" he cried. "They won't give you *anything* for them. They'll give you five francs for one peseta. Maybe six." Dyar knew the current rate was a little over eight. He sighed. "I don't know. We'll have to wait and see." But secretly he was determined to do it that way, even if he got only five.

Thami poured the boiling tea into the glasses. "No mint this time," he said.

"It doesn't matter. It's the heat that does it."

"Yes." He blew out the candle and they sat by the light of the flames. Dyar settled back, leaning against the wall, but immediately Thami objected. "You'll get sick," he explained. "That wall is very wet. Last night I moved my bed, it was so wet there."

"Ah." Dyar sat up, drew his legs under him, and continued to drink his tea. Was the hand on the brief case explained away for all time? Why not, he asked himself. Believing or doubting is a matter of wanting to believe or doubt; at the moment he felt like believing because it suited his mood.

"So, are you with me?" he said.

"What?"

"We stay a week, and you go every day and change a thousand pesetas?"

"Whatever you say," said Thami, reaching for his glass to pour him more tea.

The room was getting taut and watchful around him; Dyar remembered the sensation from the night at the Villa Hesperides. But it was not the same this time because he himself felt very different. The bird outside cried again. Thami looked surprised. "I don't know how you call that bird in English. We call it *youca*."

Dyar shut his eyes. A terrible motor had started to throb at the back of his head. It was not painful; it frightened him. With his eyes shut he had the impression that he was lying on his back, that if he opened them he would see the ceiling. It was not necessary to open them—he could see it anyway, because his lids had become transparent. It was a gigantic screen against which images were beginning to be projected—tiny swarms of colored glass beads arranged themselves obligingly into patterns, swimming together and apart, forming mosaics that dissolved as soon as they were made. Feathers, snow-crystals, lace and church windows crowded consecutively onto the screen, and the projecting light grew increasingly powerful. Soon the edges of the screen would begin to burn, and the fire would be on each side of his head. "God, this is going to blind me," he said suddenly; he opened his eyes and realized he had said nothing.

"Do you know what they look like?" Thami asked.

"What what look like?"

"*Youcas.*"

"I don't know what anything looks like. I don't know what you're talking about!"

Thami looked slightly aggrieved. "You're hashish, my friend. Hashish *bezef*!"

Each time Thami spoke to him, he raised his head and shook it slightly, opened his eyes, and made a senseless reply. Thami began to sing in a small, faraway voice. It was a sound you could walk on, a soft carpet that stretched before him across the flat blinding desert. *Ijbed selkha men rasou.* . . . . But he came up against the stone walls of an empty house beside a mountain. The fire was raging behind it, burning wildly and silently, the door was open and it was dark inside. Cobwebs hung to the walls, soldiers had been there, and there were women's silk underclothes strewn about the empty rooms. He knew that a certain day, at a certain moment, the house would crumble and nothing would be left but dust and rubble, indistinguishable from the talus of gravel that lay below the cliffs. It would be absolutely silent, the falling of the house, like a film that goes on running after the sound apparatus has broken. *Bache idaoui sebbatou.* . . . The carpet had caught on fire, too. Someone would blame him.

"I'm God damned if I'll pay for it," he said. Regular hours, always superiors to give you orders, no security, no freedom, no freedom, no freedom.

Thami said: "*Hak.* Take your tea."

Dyar reached forward and swam against the current toward the outstretched glass shining with reflected firelight. "I've got it. *Muchas gracias, amigo.*" He paused, seemed to be listening, then with exaggerated care he set the glass down on the mat beside him. "I put it there because it's hot, see?" (But Thami was not paying attention; already he was back in his own pleasure pavilion overlooking his miles of verdant gardens, and the water ran clear in blue enamel channels. *Chta! Chta! Sebbatou aând al qadi!*)

"Thami, I'm in another world. Do you understand? Can you hear me?"

Thami, his eyes shut, his body weaving slowly back and forth as he sang, did not answer. The perspective from his tower grew vaster, the water bubbled up out of the earth on all sides. He had ordered it all to be, many years ago. (The night is a woman clothed in a robe of burning stars. . . . .) *Ya, Leïla, Lia* . . .

"I can see you sitting there," Dyar insisted, "but I'm in another world." He began to laugh softly with delight.

"I don't know," he said reflectively. "Sometimes I think the other way around. I think. . . ." He spoke more slowly. "We . . . . would be better . . . . . . I think . . . . . if you can get through . . . . if you can get through . . . . Why can't anyone get through?" His voice became so loud and sharp here that Thami opened his eyes and stopped singing.

"*Chkoun entina?*" he said. "My friend, I'm hashish as much as you."

"You get here, you float away again, you come to that *crazy* place! Oh, my *God!*" He was talking very fast, and he went into a little spasm of laughter, then checked himself. "*I've* got nothing to laugh about. It's not funny." With a whoop he rolled over onto the floor and abandoned himself to a long fit of merriment. Thami listened without moving.

After a long time the laughter stopped as suddenly as it had begun; he lay quite still. The other's little voice crept out again: "*Ijbed selkha men rasou* . . ." and went on and on. From time to time the fire stirred, as an ember shifted its position. Every small sound was razor-sharp, but inside there was a solid silence. He was trying not to breathe, he wanted to be absolutely motionless, because he felt that the air which fitted so perfectly around him was a gelatinous substance which had been moulded to match with infinite exactitude every contour of his person. If he moved ever so slightly he would feel it pushing against him, and that would be unbearable. The monstrous swelling and deflating of himself which each breath occasioned was a real peril. But that wave broke, receded, and he was left stranded for a moment in a landscape of liquid glassy light, greengold and shimmering. Burnished, rich and oily, then swift like flaming water. Look at it! Look at it! Drink it with your eyes. It's the only water you'll ever see. Another wave would roll up soon; they were coming more often.

Ya Leïla, lia. . . . For a moment he was quite in his senses. He lay there comfortably and listened to the long, melancholy melodic line of the song, thinking: "How long ago was it that I was laughing?" Perhaps the whole night had gone by, and the effect had already worn off.

"Thami?" he said. Then he realized it had been almost impossible to get the word out, because his mouth was of cardboard. He gasped a little, and thought of moving. (I must remember to tell myself to move my left hand so I can raise myself onto my elbow. It must move back further before I can begin to pull my knees up. But I don't want to move my knees. Only my hand. So I can raise myself onto my elbow. If I move my knees I can sit up. . . .)

He was sitting up.

(I'm sitting up.) *Is this what I wanted? Why did I want to sit up?*

He waited.

(I didn't. I only wanted to raise myself onto my elbow.) *Why?* (I wanted to lie facing the other way. It's going to be more comfortable that way.)

He was lying down.

(. . . . . from the gulf of the infinite, Allah looks across with an eye of gold. . . . .) *Alef leïlat ou leïla, ya leïla, lia!*

Before the wind had arrived, he heard it coming, stirring stealthily around the sharp pinnacles of rock up there, rolling down through the ravines, whispering as it moved along the surface of the cliffs, coming to wrap itself around the house. He lay a year, dead, listening to it coming.

There was an explosion in the room. Thami had thrown another log onto the fire. "That gave me designs. Red, purple," said Dyar without speaking, sitting up again. The room was a red grotto, a theatre, a vast stable with a balcony that hung in the shadows. Up there was a city of little rooms, a city inside a pocket of darkness, but there were windows in the walls you could not see, and beyond these the sun shone down on an outer city built of ice.

"My God, Thami, water!" he cried thickly. Thami was standing above him.

"Good-bye," said Thami. Heavily he sat down and rolled over onto his side, sang no more.

"Water," he tried to say again in a very soft voice, and tremblingly he made a supreme effort to get to his feet. "My God, I've got to have water," he whispered to himself; it was easier to whisper. Because he was looking down at his feet from ten thousand feet up, he had to take exquisite care in walking, but he stepped over Thami and got out into the patio to the pail. Sighing with the effort of kneeling down, he put his face into the fire of the cold water and drew it into his throat.

When it was finished he rose, threw his head up, and looked at the moon. The wind had come, but it had been here before. Now it was necessary to get back into the room, to get all the way across the room to the door. But he must not breathe so heavily. To open the door and go out. Out there the wind would be cold, but he must go anyway.

The expedition through the magic room was hazardous. There was a fragile silence there which must not be shattered. The fire, shedding its redness on Thami's masklike face, must not know he was stealing past. At each step he lifted his feet far off the floor into the air, like someone walking through a field of high wet grass. He saw the door ahead of him, but suddenly between him and it a tortuous corridor made of pure time interposed itself. It was going to take endless hours to get down to the end. And a host of invisible people was lined up along its walls, but on the other side of the walls, mutely waiting for him to go by—an impassive chorus, silent and without pity. "Waiting for me," he thought. The sides of his mind, indistinguishable from the walls of the corridor, were lined with messages in Arabic script. All the time, directly before his eyes was the knobless door sending out its ominous message. It was not sure, it could not be trusted. If it opened when he did not want it to open, by itself, all the horror of existence could crowd in upon him. He stretched his hand out and touched the large cold key. The key explained the heaviness in his overcoat pocket. He put his left hand into the pocket and felt the hammer, and the head and point of the nail. That was work to be done, but later, when he came in. He turned the key, pulled open the door, felt the bewildered wind touch his face. "Keep away from the cliff," he whispered as he stepped outside. Around him stretched the night's formless smile. The moon was far out over the empty regions now. Relieving himself against the wall of the house, he heard the wind up here trying to cover the long single note of the water down in the valley. Inside, by the fire, time was slowly dissolving, falling to pieces. But even at the end of the night there would still be an ember of time left, of a subtle, bitter flavor, soft to the touch, glowing from its recess of ashes, before it paled and died, and the heart of the ancient night stopped beating.

He turned toward the door, his steps short and halting like those of an old man. It was going to require a tremendous effort to get back to the mat, but because the only thing he could conceive of at this instant was to sink down on it and lie out flat by the fire, he felt certain he could make the effort. As he shut the door behind him he murmured to it: "You know I'm here, don't you?" The idea was hateful to him, but there was something he could do about it. What that thing was he could not recall, yet he knew the situation was not hopeless; he could remedy it later.

Thami had not stirred. As he looked down from his remote height at the relaxed body, a familiar uneasiness stole over him, only he could connect it with no cause. Partly he knew that what he saw before him was Thami, Thami's head, trunk, arms and legs. Partly he knew it was an unidentifiable object lying there, immeasurably heavy with its own meaninglessness, a vast imponderable weight that nothing could lighten. As he stood lost in static contemplation of the thing, the wind pushed the door feebly, making a faint rattling. But *could* nothing lighten it? If the air were let in, the weight might escape of its own accord, into the shadows of the room and the darkness of the night. He looked slowly behind him. The door was silent, staring, baleful. "You know I'm here, all right," he thought, "but you won't know long." He had willed the hammer and nail into existence, and they were there in his pocket. Thinking of their heaviness, he felt his body lean to one side. He had to shift the position of his foot to retain his balance, to keep from being pulled down by their weight. The rattle came again, a series of slight knockings, knowing and insinuating. But now, did they come from the mat below him? "If it opens," he thought, looking at the solid, inert mass in front of him in the fire's dying light, his eyes staring, gathering fear from within him. "If it opens." There was that thing he had to do, he must do it, and he knew what it was but he could not think what it was.

A mass of words had begun to ferment inside him, and now they bubbled forth. "Many Mabel damn. Molly Daddy lamb. Lolly dibble up-man. Dolly little Dan," he whispered, and then he giggled. The hammer was in his right hand, the nail in his left. He bent over, swayed, and fell heavily to his knees on the mat, beside the outstretched door. It did not move. The mountain wind rushed through his head, his head that was a single seashell full of grottoes; its infinitely smooth pink walls, delicate, paper-thin, caught the light of the embers as he moved along the galleries. "Melly diddle din," he said, quite loud, putting the point of the nail as far into Thami's ear as he could. He raised his right arm and hit the head of the nail with all his might. The object relaxed imperceptibly, as if someone had said to it: "It's all right." He laid the hammer down, and felt of the nail-head, level with the soft lobe of the ear. It had two little ridges on it; he rubbed his thumbnail across the imperfections in the steel. The nail was as firmly embedded as if it had been driven into a cocoanut. "Merry Mabel dune." The children were going to make a noise when they came out at recess-time. The fire rattled, the same insistent music that could not be stilled, the same skyrockets that would not hurry to explode. And the floor had fallen over onto him. His hand was bent under him, he could feel it, he wanted to move. "I must remember that I exist," he told himself; that was clear, like a great rock rising out of the sea around it. "I must remember that I am alive."

He did not know whether he was lying still or whether his hands and feet were shaking painfully with the effort of making himself believe he was there and wanted to move his hand. He knew his skin was more tender than the skin of an overripe plum; no matter how softly he touched it, it would break and smear him with the stickiness beneath. Someone had shut the bureau drawer he was lying in and gone away, forgotten him. The great languor. The great slowness. The night had sections filled with repose, and there were places in time to be visited, faces to forget, words to understand, silences to be studied.

The fire was out; the inhuman night had come into the room. Once again he wanted water. "I've come back," he thought; his mouth, gullet, stomach ached with dryness. "Thami has stayed behind. I'm the only survivor. That's the way I wanted it." That warm, humid, dangerous breeding-place for ideas had been destroyed. "Thank God he hasn't come back with me," he told himself. "I never wanted him to know I was alive." He slipped away again; the water was too distant.

A maniacal light had fallen into the room and was hopping about. He sat up and frowned. The ear in the head beside him. The little steel disc with the irregular grooves in it. He had known it would be there. He sighed, crept on his hands and knees around the ends of the drawn-up legs, arrived in the cold, blinding patio, and immersed his face in the pail. He was not real, but he knew he was alive. When he lifted his head, he let it fall all the way back against the wall, and he stayed there a long time, the mountains' morning light press-ing brutally into his eyelids.

Later he rose, went into the room, dragged Thami by his legs through the patio into the kitchen and shut the door. Overpowered by weakness, he lay down on the mat, and still trembling fell into a bottomless sleep. As the day advanced the wind increased, the blue sky grew white, then gray. The door rattled unceasingly, but he heard nothing.

XXVI

The pounding on the door had been going on for a long time before, becoming aware of it, he began to scramble up the slippery sides of the basin of sleep where he found himself, in a frantic attempt to escape into consciousness. When finally he opened his eyes and was back in the room, a strange languor remained, like a great, soft cushion beneath him; he did not want to move. Still the fist went on hitting the door insistently, stopping now and then so that when it began again it was louder after the silence that had come in between.

There were cushions under him and cushions on top of him; he would not move. But he called out: "Who is it?" several times, each time managing to put a little more force into his unruly voice. The knocking ceased. Soon he felt a faint curiosity to know who it was out there. He sat up, then got up and went to the door, saying again, his mouth close to the wood: "Who is it?" Outside there was only the sound of the casual dripping of water from the eaves onto the bare earth. "So it's been raining again," he thought with unreasoning anger. "Who is it?" he said, louder, at the same time being startled as he put his hand to his face and felt the three-day beard there.

He unlocked the door, opened it and looked out. It was a dark day, and as he had expected, there was no one in sight. Nor was he still any more than vaguely interested in knowing who had been knocking. It was not indifference; he knew it concerned him vitally—he knew that he should care very much who had stood outside the door a moment ago. But now there was not enough of him left to feel strongly about anything; everything had been spent last night. Today was like an old, worn-out film being run off—dim, jerky, flickering, full of cuts, and with a plot he could not seize. It was hard to pay attention to it.

As he turned to go back in, for he felt like sleeping again, a voice called: "Hola!" from the direction of the stream. And although he was having difficulty focusing (the valley was a murky gray jumble), he saw a man who a second before had been standing still looking back at the house turn and start walking up toward it. Dyar did not move; he watched; on the top of his head now and then he felt the cold drops that fell singly, unhurriedly, from the sky.

The man was a Berber in country clothes. As he drew near the house he began to walk more slowly and to look back down the path. Soon he stopped altogether, and stood, obviously waiting for someone behind him. From between the rocks two figures presently emerged and climbed up across the stream, around the curve in the path. Dyar, remaining in the doorway, observing this unannounced arrival, feeling sure that it meant something of great importance to him, was unable to summon the energy necessary for conjecture; he watched. When the two figures had reached the spot where the lone one stood, they stopped and conferred with him; he waved his arm toward the house, and then sat down, while they continued along the path. But now Dyar had begun to stare, for one man was wearing a uniform with jodpurs and boots, while the other, who seemed to need assistance in climbing, was in a raincoat and a brilliant purple turban. When the two had got about halfway between the seated Berber and the house, he realized with a shock that the second person was a woman in slacks. And an instant later his mouth opened slightly because he had recognized Daisy. Under his breath he said: "Good God!"

As she came nearer and saw him staring at her she waved, but said nothing. Dyar, behaving like a small child, stood watching her approach, did not even acknowledge her greeting.

"Oh!" she exclaimed, gasping a little as she came on to the level piece of ground where the house stood. She walked toward the door and put her hand out. He took it, still looking at her, unbelieving. "Hello," he said.

"Look. Will you please not think I'm a busybody. How are you?" She let go of his hand and directed a piercing glance at his face; unthinkingly he put his hand to his chin. "All right?" Without waiting for an answer she turned to the man in the chauffeur's uniform. "*Me puedes esperar ahí abajo.*" She pointed to the native waiting below. The man made a listless salute and walked away.

"Oh!" said Daisy again, looking about for a place to sit, and seeing nothing but the wet earth. "I must sit down. Do you think we could go in where it's dry?"

"Oh, sure." Dyar came to life. "I'm just surprised to see you. Go on in." She crossed the room and sat down on the mat in front of the dead fireplace. "What are you doing here?" he said, his voice expressionless.

She had her knees together out to one side, and she had folded her hands over them. "Obviously, I've come to see you." She looked up at him. "But you want to know *why*, of course. If you'll be patient while I catch my breath, I'll tell you." She paused, and sighed. "I'll lay my case before you and you can do as you like." Now she reached up and seized his arm. "Darling" (the sound of her voice had changed, grown more intense), "you must go back. Sit down. No, here, beside me. You've got to go back to Tangier. That's why I'm here. To help you get back in."

She felt his body stiffen as he turned his head quickly to look at her. "Don't talk," she said. "Let me say my little piece. It's late, and it's going to rain, and we must leave Agla while there's still daylight. There are twenty-seven kilometers of trail before one gets to the *carretera*. You don't know anything about the roads because you didn't come that way."

"How do you know how I came?"

"You *do* think I'm an utter fool, don't you?" She offered him a cigarette from her case and they smoked a moment in silence. "I saw the little business in the garden the other night, and I thought I recognized that drunken brother of the Beidaoui's. And I had no reason to doubt his wife's word. According to her he brought you here. So that's that. But all that's of no importance."

He was thinking: "How can I find out how much she knows?" The best idea seemed to be simply to ask her; thus he cut her short, saying: "What have they told you?"

"Who?" she said drily. "Jack Wilcox and Ronny Ashcombe-Danvers?"

He did not reply.

"If you mean them," she pursued, "they told me everything, naturally. You're all bloody fools, all three of you, but you're the biggest bloody fool. What in *God's* name did you think you were doing? Of course, I don't know what Jack was thinking of in the first place to let you fetch Ronny's money, and he's so secretive I couldn't make anything out of his silly tale. It wasn't until I met Ronny yesterday at the airport that I got any sort of story that hung together at all. Ronny's an old friend of mine, you know, and I can tell you he's more than displeased about the whole thing, as well he may be."

"Yes," he said, completely at a loss for anything else to say.

"I've argued with him until I'm hoarse, trying to persuade him to let me come up here. Of course he was all for coming himself with a band of ruffians from the port and taking his chances on getting the money back by force. Because obviously he can't do it by legal means. But I think now he understands how childish that idea is. I made him see how much better it would be if I could get you to come back of your own accord."

Dyar thought: So Ashcombe-Danvers is an old friend of hers. He's promised her a percentage of everything she can get back for him. And he remembered Mme. Werth's reservation at the hotel in Marrakech; Daisy might as well have been saying to him: "Do come back and be a victim again for my sake."

"It's out of the question," he said shortly.

"Oh, is it?" she cried, her eyes blazing. "Because little Mr. Dyar says it is, I suppose?"

He flushed. "You're God-damned right."

She leaned toward him. "Why do you think I came up here, you bloody, bloody fool, you conceited idiot? God!"

"I don't know. I'm wondering, myself," he said, tossing his cigarette into the fireplace.

"I came," she paused. "Because I'm the biggest fool of all, because through some ghastly defect in my character, I—because I've somehow—let myself become fond of you. God knows why! *God* knows why! Do you think I'd come all the way here *only* to help Ronny get his money back? ("Yes, you would," he thought.) "He's better equipped for a manhunt than I am, with his gang of cutthroats from the Marsa." ("She doesn't believe any of that. She thinks she can do the job better," he told himself.) "I'm here because Ronny's a friend of mine, yes, and because I should like to help him get back what belongs to him, what you've stolen from him." (Her voice trembled a little on the word *stolen*.) "Yes, of course. All of that. And I'm here also because what will help him happens to be the only thing that'll help you."

"Do my soul good. I know. Walk in and make a clean breast of it."

"Your soul!" she snapped. "Bugger your soul! I said help you. You're in a mess. You know damned well what a mess you're in. And you're not going to get out of it without some help. I want very much to see you through this. And if I must be quite frank, I don't think anyone else can or will."

"Oh, I know," he said. "I don't expect anybody to take up a collection for me. Nobody can help me. Fine. So how can you?"

"Don't you think Luis knows a few people in Tangier? It's a question of getting you and the money across the frontier. In any case, I've borrowed a diplomatic car. With the CD plates one goes right through, usually. Even if we don't it's all seen to. You run no risk."

"No risk!" he repeated, with a brief laugh. "And in Tangier?"

"Ronny? What can he do? I assure you he'll be so delighted to see his money, he'll—"

He cut her short. "Not that," he said. "I'm not worried about that. I'm just thinking."

She looked puzzled an instant. "You don't mean the check you accepted from that hideous little Russian woman?"

"Oh, Jesus," he groaned. "Is there anything you don't know?"

"In the way of Tangier gossip, no, darling. But everyone knows about that. She's been ordered to leave the International Zone. Day before yesterday. She's probably already gone. The only useful thing Uncle Goode's done since she arrived in Tangier. I don't know what the official American attitude would be toward your sort of stupid behavior. But that's a chance you'll have to take. I think we've talked about enough, don't you?"

"I guess we have," he said. It was a solution, he thought, but it was not the right one, because it would undo everything he had done. It had to be his way, he said to himself. He knew what the other way was like.

"Do you think we could have some tea before we leave?" Daisy inquired suddenly. "It would help." ("She doesn't understand," he thought.)

"I'm not going," he said.

"Oh, darling, don't be difficult." He had never seen her eyes so large and serious. "It's late. You know God-damned well you're going. There's nothing else you can do. The trouble is you just can't make up your mind to face Jack and Ronny. But you've *got* to face them, that's all."

"I tell you I'm not going."

"Rot! Rubbish! Now come! Don't disgust me with your fear. There's nothing more revolting than a man who's afraid."

He laughed unpleasantly.

"Come along, now," she said in a comfortable voice, as though each sentence she had uttered until then had succeeded in persuading him a little. "Make some good hot tea and we'll each have a cup. Then we'll go back. It's that simple." As a new idea occurred to her, she looked around the room for the first time. "Where's the Beidaoui boy? Not that I can take him; he'll have to get back by himself, but I daresay that offers no particular problem."

Because what had been going on for the past half-hour had been in a world so absolutely alien to the one he had been living in (where the mountain wind blew and rattled the door), that world of up here, like something of his own invention, had receded, become unlikely, momentarily effaced itself. He caught his breath, said nothing. At the same time he glanced swiftly over her shoulder toward the kitchen door, and felt his heart make a painful movement in his chest. For an instant his eyes opened very wide. Then he looked into her face, frowning and not letting his eyelids resume their natural position too quickly. "I don't know," he said, hoping that his expression could be interpreted as one of no more than normal concern. With the wind, the door had swung outward a little, and a helpless hand showed through the opening. "I haven't seen him all day. He was gone when I woke up."

Now his heart was pounding violently, and the inside of his head pushed against his skull as if it would break through the fragile wall. He tried to play the old game with himself. "It's not true. He's not lying there." It would not work. He knew positively, even without looking again; games were finished. He sat in the room, he was the center of a situation of whose every detail he was aware; the very presence of the hand gave him his unshakable certainty, his conviction that his existence, along with everything in it, was real, solid, undeniable. Later he would be able to look straight at this knowledge without the unbearable, bursting anguish, but now, at the beginning, sitting beside Daisy in the room where the knowledge had been born, it was too much. He jumped to his feet.

"Tea?" he cried crazily. "Yeah, sure. Of course." He stepped to the front door and looked out: the chauffeur and the guide were still sitting down there in the gathering gloom, on opposite sides of the path. "I don't know where he is," he said. "He's been gone all day." It was still raining a little, but in a moment it would fall harder. A dense cloud was drifting down from the invisible peaks above. In the wet gray twilight everything was colorless. He heard a sound behind him, turned and stood frozen as he watched Daisy rise slowly, deliberately, walk into the patio, her eyes fixed on the bottom of the kitchen door. She pulled it all the way open, and bent down, her back to him. He was not sure, but he thought he heard, a second later, a slight, almost inaudible cry. And she stayed crouching there a long time. Little by little the dead, flat sound of the falling rain spread, increased. He started to walk across the room toward the patio, thinking: "This is the moment to show her I'm not afraid. Not afraid of what she thinks." Because of the rain splattering from the eaves into the patio, she did not hear him coming until he was almost in the doorway. She looked up swiftly; there were tears in her eyes, and the sight of them was a sharp pain inside him.

He stood still.

"Did—?" She did not try to say anything more. He knew the reason: she had looked at his face and did not need to finish her question. She stood only a second now in front of him, yet even in that flash many things must have crossed her mind, because as he stared into her eyes he was conscious of the instantaneous raising of a great barrier that had not been there a moment before, and now suddenly was there, impenetrable and merciless. Quickly she walked in front of him into the room and across to the door. Only when she had stepped outside into the rain did she turn and say in a smothered voice: "I shall tell Ronny I couldn't find you." Then she moved out of his vision; where she had paused there was only the rectangle of grayness.

He stood there in the patio a moment, the cold rain wetting him. (A place in the world, a definite status, a precise relationship with the rest of men. Even if it had to be one of open hostility, it was his, created by him.) Suddenly he pushed the kitchen door shut and went into the room. He was tired, he wanted to sit down, but there was only the mat, and so he remained standing in the middle of the room. Soon it would be dark; stuck onto the floor was the little piece of candle the other had blown out last night when the fire was going. He did not know whether there was another candle in the kitchen, nor would he look to see. More to have something to do than because he wanted light, he knelt down to set the stub burning, felt in his pocket, in all his pockets, for a match. Finding none, he stood up again and walked to the door. Out in the murk there was no valley, there were no mountains. The rain fell heavily and the wind had begun to blow again. He sat down in the doorway and began to wait. It was not yet completely dark.

—Amrah, Tangier

THE SPIDER'S HOUSE

The likeness of those who choose other patrons than Allah is as the likeness of the spider when she taketh unto herself a house, and lo! the frailest of all houses is the spider's house, if they but knew.

THE KORAN

FOR MY FATHER

PROLOGUE

I T WAS just about midnight when Stenham left Si Jaffar's door. "I don't need anyone to come with me," he had said, smiling falsely to belie the sound of his voice, for he was afraid he had seemed annoyed or been abrupt, and Si Jaffar, after all, was only exercising his rights as a host in sending this person along with him.

"Really, I don't need anybody." For he wanted to go back alone, even with all the lights in the city off. The evening had been endless, and he felt like running the risk of taking the wrong turnings and getting temporarily lost; if he were accompanied, the long walk would be almost like a continuation of sitting in Si Jaffar's salon.

But in any case, it was too late now. All the male members of the household had come to the door, even stood out in the wet alley, insisting that the man go with him. Their adieux were always lengthy and elaborate, as if he were leaving for the other side of the world rather than the opposite end of the Medina, and he consciously liked that, because it was a part of what he thought life in a medieval city should be like. However, it was unprecedented for them to force upon him the presence of a protector, and he felt there was no justification for it.

The man strode ahead of him in the darkness. Where'd they get him from? he thought, seeing again the tall bearded Berber in tattered mountain garb as he had looked when he had first caught sight of him in the dim light of Si Jaffar's patio. Then he recalled the fluttering and whispering that had gone on at one end of the room about an hour and a half earlier. Whenever these family discussions arose in Stenham's presence, Si Jaffar made a great effort to divert his attention from them by embarking on a story. The story usually began promisingly enough, Si Jaffar smiling, beaming through his two pairs of spectacles, but with his attention clearly fixed on the sound of voices in the corner. Slowly, as the whispered conversation over there subsided, his words would come more haltingly, and his eyes would dart from side to side as his smile became paralyzed and meaningless. The tale would never be completed. Suddenly, "Ahah!" he would cry triumphantly, apropos of nothing at all. Then he would clap his hands for snuff, or orange-flower water, or chips of sandalwood to throw onto the brazier, look still more pleased, and perhaps whack Stenham's knee playfully. A similar comedy had been played this evening about half past ten. As he thought it over now, Stenham decided that the occasion for it had been the family's sudden decision to provide him with someone to accompany him back to the hotel. Now he remembered that after the discussion Abdeltif, the eldest son, had disappeared for at least half an hour; that must have been when the guide had been fetched.

The man had been crouching in the dark patio entrance just inside the door when they had gone out. It was embarrassing, because he knew Si Jaffar was not a well-to-do man, and while a little service like this was not abnormally expensive, still, it had to be paid for; Si Jaffar had made that clear. "Don't give this man anything," he had said in French. "I have already seen to that."

"But I don't need him," Stenham had protested. "I know the way. Think of all the times I've gone back alone." Si Jaffar's four sons, his cousin and his son-in-law had all murmured: "No, no, no," together, and the old man had patted his arm affectionately. "It's better," he said, with one of his curiously formal little bows. There was no use in objecting. The man would stay with him until he had delivered him over to the watchman at the hotel, and then he would disappear into the night, go back to whatever dark corner he had come from, and Stenham would not see him again.

The streets were completely without passers-by. It would have been quite possible to go most of the way along somewhat more frequented thoroughfares, he reflected, but obviously his companion preferred the empty ones. He took out his little dynamo flashlight and began to squeeze it, turning the dim ray downward to the ground at the man's feet. The insect-like whirring it made caused him to turn around, a look of surprise on his face.

"Light," said Stenham.

The man grunted. "Too much noise," he objected.

He smiled and let the light die down. How these people love games, he thought. This one's playing cops and robbers now; they're always either stalking or being stalked. "The Oriental passion for complications, the involved line, Arabesques," Moss had assured him, but he was not sure it was that. It could just as easily be a deep sense of guilt. He had suggested this, but Moss had scoffed.

The muddy streets led down, down. There was not a foot of level ground. He had to move forward stiff-ankled, with the weight all on the balls of his feet. The city was asleep. There was profound silence, broken only by the scuffing sound he made as he walked. The man, barefooted, advanced noiselessly. From time to time, when the way led not through inner passages but into the open, a solitary drop of rain fell heavily out of the sky, as if a great invisible piece of wet cloth were hanging only a few feet above the earth. Everything was invisible, the mud of the street, the walls, the sky. Stenham squeezed the flashlight suddenly, and had a rapidly fading view of the man moving ahead of him in his brown *djellaba*, and of his giant shadow thrown against the beams that formed the ceiling of the street. The man grunted again in protest.

Stenham smiled: unaccountable behavior on the part of Moslems amused him, and he always forgave it, because, as he said, no non-Moslem knows enough about the Moslem mind to dare find fault with it. "They're far, far away from us," he would say. "We haven't an inkling of the things that motivate them." There was a certain amount of hypocrisy in this attitude of his; the truth was that he hoped principally to convince *others* of the existence of this almost unbridgeable gulf. The mere fact that he could then even begin to hint at the beliefs and purposes that lay on the far side made him feel more sure in his own attempts at analyzing them and gave him a small sense of superiority to which he felt he was entitled, in return for having withstood the rigors of Morocco for so many years. This pretending to know something that others could not know, it was a little indulgence he allowed himself, a bonus for seniority. Secretly he was convinced that the

Moroccans were much like any other people, that the differences were largely those of ritual and gesture, that even the
fine curtain of magic through which they observed life was
not a complex thing, and did not give their perceptions any
profundity. It delighted him that this anonymous, barefoot
Berber should want to guide him through the darkest, least
frequented tunnels of the city; the reason for the man's desire
for secrecy did not matter. These were a feline, nocturnal
people. It was no accident that Fez was a city without dogs.
"I wonder if Moss has noticed that," he thought.

Now and then he had the distinct impression that they
were traversing a street or an open space that he knew perfectly well, but if that were so, the angle at which they had
met it was unexpected, so that the familiar walls (if indeed
they *were* familiar walls) were dwarfed or distorted in the
one swiftly fading beam of light that he played on them. He
began to suspect that the power plant had suffered a major
collapse: the electricity was almost certainly still cut off, because it would be practically impossible to go so far without
coming upon at least one street light. However, he was used
to moving around the city in the darkness. He knew a good
many ways across it in each direction, and he could have
found his way blindfolded along several of these routes.
Indeed, wandering through the Medina at night was very
much like being blindfolded; one let one's ears and nose do
most of the work. He knew just how each section of a familiar way sounded when he walked it alone at night. There
were two things to listen for: his feet and the sound of the
water behind the walls. The footsteps had an infinite variety
of sound, depending on the hardness of the earth, the width
of the passageway, the height and configuration of the walls.
On the Lemtiyine walk there was one place between the
tannery and a small mosque where the echo was astounding:
taut, metallic reverberations that shuddered between the
walls like musical pistol shots. There were places where his
footfalls were almost silent, places where the sound was
strong, single and compact, died straightway, or where, as
he advanced along the deserted galleries, each succeeding
step produced a sound of an imperceptibly higher pitch, so
that his passage was like a finely graded ascending scale,

until all at once a jutting wall or a sudden tunnel dispersed the pattern and began another section in the long nocturne which in turn would slowly disclose its own design. And the water was the same, following its countless courses behind the partitions of earth and stone. Seldom visible but nearly always present, it rushed beneath the sloping alleyways, here gurgled, here merely dripped, here beyond the wall of a garden splashed or dribbled in the form of a fountain, here fell with a high hollow noise into an invisible cistern, here all at once was unabashedly a branch of the river roaring over the rocks (so that sometimes the cold vapor rising was carried over the wall by the wind and wet his face), here by the bakery had been dammed and was almost still, a place where the rats swam.

The two simultaneous sound-tracks of footsteps and water he had experienced so often that it seemed to him he must know each portion by heart. But now it was all different, and he realized that what he knew was only one line, one certain sequence whose parts became unrecognizable once they were presented out of their accustomed context. He knew, for instance, that in order to be as near the main branch of the river as they were now, at some point they had had to cross the street leading from the Karouine Mosque to the Zaouia of Si Ahmed Tidjani, but it was impossible for him to know when that had been; he had recognized nothing.

Suddenly he realized where they were: in a narrow street that ran the length of a slight eminence above the river, just below the mass of walls that formed the Fondouk el Yihoudi. It was far out of their way, not on any conceivable route between Si Jaffar's house and the hotel. "Why have we come out here?" he asked with indignation. The man was unnecessarily abrupt in his reply, Stenham thought. "Walk and be quiet."

"But they always are," he reminded himself; he would never be able to take for granted their curious mixture of elaborate circumspection and brutal bluntness, and he almost laughed aloud at the memory of how the ridiculous words had sounded five seconds ago: *Rhir zid o skout.* And in another few minutes they had circumnavigated the Fondouk el Yihoudi and were going through a wet garden under banana trees; the heavy tattered leaves showered cold drops as they brushed against them. "Si Jaffar has outdone himself this time." He decided to telephone him tomorrow and make a good story of it. *Zid o skout.* It would be a hilarious slogan over the tea glasses for the next fortnight, one in which the whole family could share.

It was a freakish summer night; a chill almost like that of early spring paralyzed the air. A vast thick cloud had rolled down across the Djebel Zalagh and formed a ceiling low over the city, enclosing it in one great room whose motionless air smelled only of raw, wet earth. As they went silently back into the streets higher up the hill, an owl screamed once from somewhere above their heads.

When they had arrived at the hotel's outer gate, Stenham pushed the button that rang a bell down in the interior of the hotel in some little room near the office where the watchman stayed. For a moment he thought: It won't ring; the power's off tonight. But then he remembered that the hotel had its own electric system. It was usually a good five minutes before the light came on in the courtyard, and then another two or three before the watchman got to the gate. Tonight the light came on immediately. Stenham stepped close to the high doors and peered through the crack between them. The watchman was at the far end of the courtyard talking to someone. "*Ah, oui,*" he heard him say. A European in the court at this hour, he thought with some curiosity, trying to see more. The watchman was approaching. Like a guilty child, Stenham stepped quickly back and put his hands in his pockets, looking nonchalantly toward the side wall. Then he realized that his guide had disappeared. There was no sound of retreating footsteps; he was merely gone. The heavy bolt of the gate was drawn back and the watchman stood there in his khaki duster and white turban, the customary anxious expression on his face.

"*Bon soir, M'sio Stonamm,*" he said. Sometimes he spoke in Arabic, sometimes in French; it was impossible to know which he would choose for a given occasion. Stenham greeted him, looking across the courtyard to see who was there with him. He saw no one. The same two cars stood there: the hotel's station wagon and an old Citroën that belonged to the manager, but which he never used. "You came quickly tonight," he said.

"*Oui, M'sio Stonamm.*"

"You were outside, near the gate, perhaps?"

The watchman hesitated. "*Non, m'sio.*"

He abandoned it rather than become exasperated with the man, which he knew he would do if he went on. A lie is not a lie; it is only a formula, a substitute, a long way around, a polite manner of saying: None of your business.

He had his key in his pocket, and so he went directly up the back way to his room, a little ashamed of himself for having started to pry. But when he stood in his room in the tower, looking out over the invisible city spread below, he found that he could justify his inquisitiveness. It was not merely the watchman's patent lie which had prodded him; much more than that was the fact of its having come directly on the heels of the Berber's strange behavior: the unnecessary detour, the gruff injunctions to silence, the inexplicable disappearance before he had had a chance to hand him the thirty francs he had ready to give him. Not only that, he decided, going further back to Si Jaffar. The whole family had so solemnly insisted that he be accompanied on his way home to the hotel. That too seemed to be a part of the conspiracy. "They're all crazy tonight," he told himself with satisfaction. He refused to tie all these things together by attributing them to the tension that was in the city. Ever since that day a year ago when the French, more irresponsible than usual, had deposed the Sultan, the tension had been there, and he had known it was there. But it was a political thing, and politics exist only on paper; certainly the politics of 1954 had no true connection with the mysterious medieval city he knew and loved. It would have been too simple to make a logical relationship between what his brain knew and what his eyes saw; he found it more fun to play this little game with himself.

Each night when Stenham had locked his door, the watchman climbed up the steep stairs into the tower of the *ancien palais* and snapped off the lights in the corridors, one by one. When he had gone back down, and the final sounds of his passage had died away, there was only the profound silence of the night, disturbed, if a wind blew, by the rustle of the poplars in the garden. Tonight, when the slow footsteps approached up the staircase, instead of the familiar click of the switch on the wall outside the door, there was a slight hesitation, and then a soft knock. Stenham had taken off his tie, but he was still fully dressed. Frowning, he opened the door. The watchman smiled apologetically at him—certainly not out of compunction for the lie in the courtyard, he commented, seeing that wistful, vanquished face. In the five seasons he had spent here at the hotel Stenham had never seen this man wear another expression. If the world went on he would grow old and die, night watchman at the Mérinides Palace, no other possibility having suggested itself to him. This time he spoke in Arabic. "*Smatsi.* M'sio Moss has sent me. He wants to know if you'll go to see him."

"Now?" said Stenham incredulously.

"Now. Yes." He laughed deprecatingly, with infinite gentleness, as if he meant to imply that his understanding of the world was vast indeed.

Stenham's first thought was: I can't let Moss start this sort of thing. Temporizing, he said aloud: "Where is he?"

"In his room. Number Fourteen."

"I know the number," he said. "Are you going to his room again, to take him my message?"

"Yes. Do I tell him you'll come?"

Stenham sighed. "For a minute. Yes." This would be disregarded, of course; the man would simply tell Moss that Monsieur Stonamm was coming, and disappear. Now he bowed, said: "*Ouakha,*" and shut the door.

He stood before the mirror of the armoire, putting his necktie back on. It was the first time Moss had ever sent him a message at night, and he was curious to know what had made the Englishman decide to vary his code of strict discretion. He looked at his watch: it was twenty minutes past one. Moss would begin with florid apologies for having disturbed his work, whether he believed he had caused such an interruption or not, for Stenham encouraged his acquaintances to hold the impression that he worked evenings as well as mornings. It assured him more privacy, and besides, occasionally, if the weather were bad, he went to bed early and did manage to add an extra page to the novel that was still far from completed. Rain and wind outside the window in the darkness provided the incentive necessary to offset fatigue. Tonight, in any case, he would not have worked: it was far too late. Day in Fez began long before dawn, and it made him profoundly uneasy to think that he might not be asleep before the early call to prayer set off the great sound of cockcrow that spread slowly over the city and never abated until it was broad daylight. If he were still awake once the muezzins began their chant, there was no hope of further sleep. At this time of year they started about half past three.

He looked at the typed pages lying on the table, placed a fat porcelain ash tray on top of them, and turned to go out. Then he thought better of it, and put the entire manuscript in the drawer. He went to the door, cast a brief longing glance back at his bed, stepped out and locked the door behind him. The key had a heavy nickel tag attached to it; it felt like ice in his pocket. And there was a strong, chill draft coming up the tower's narrow stairwell. He went down as quietly as he could (not that there was anyone to disturb), felt his way through the dim lobby, and walked onto the terrace. The light from the reception hall streamed out across the wet mosaic floor. No isolated raindrops fell from the sky now; instead, a faint breeze moved in the air. In the lower garden it was very dark; a thin wrought-iron grill beside the Sultana's pool guided him to the patio where on sunny days he and Moss sometimes ate their lunch. The lanterns outside the great door of Number Fourteen had not been turned on, but slivers of light came through from the room between the closed blinds. As he knocked, a startled animal, a rat or a ferret perhaps, bolted, scurried through the plants and dead leaves behind him. The man who opened the door, standing stiffly aside to let him pass, was not someone he had ever seen before.

Moss stood in the center of the room, directly under the big chandelier, nervously smoothing his moustache, an expression of consternation in his eyes. The only feeling of which Stenham could be conscious at the moment was a devout wish that he had not knocked on the door, that he could still be standing outside in the dark where he had been five seconds ago. He disregarded the man who stood beside him. "Good evening," he called to Moss, his intonation carrying a hint of casual heartiness. But Moss remained taut.

"Will you please come in, John?" he said dryly. "I must talk to you."

BOOK ONE

The Master of Wisdom

I have understood that the world is a vast emptiness built upon emptiness. . . . And so they call me the master of wisdom. Alas! Does anyone know what wisdom is?

—SONG OF THE OWL:
THE THOUSAND AND ONE NIGHTS

CHAPTER I

THE SPRING SUN warmed the orchard. Soon it would drop behind the high canebrake that bordered the highway, for the time was mid-afternoon. Amar lay beneath an old fig tree, embedded in long grass that was still damp with dew from the night before. He was comparing his own life with what he knew of the lives of his friends, and thinking that certainly his was the least enviable. He knew this was a sin: it is not allowed to man to make judgments of this sort, and he would never have given voice to the conclusion he had reached, even if it had taken the form of words in his mind.

He saw the trees and plants around him and the sky above, and he knew they were there. And since he felt a great disappointment in the direction his short life had taken, he knew the dissatisfaction was there. The world was a beautiful place, with all its animals and birds that moved, and its flowers and fruit trees that Allah had generously provided, but in his heart he felt that they all belonged really to him, that no one else had the same right to them as he. It was always other people who made his life unhappy. As he lay there propped indolently against the tree trunk, he carefully pulled the petals from a rose he had picked a half hour earlier when he had come into the orchard. There was not much more time for him to find out what he was going to do.

If he were going to run away he must go quickly. But already he felt that Allah was not going to reveal his destiny to him. He would learn it merely by doing what it had been

543

written that he would do. Everything would continue as it
was. When the shadows lengthened he would get up and go
out onto the highway, because the twilight brought evil spirits out of the trees. Once he was on the road there would be
nowhere for him to go but home. He had to go back and be
beaten; there was no alternative. It was not fear of the pain
that kept him from going now and getting it over with. The
pain itself was nothing; it could even be enjoyable if he did
not wince or cry out, because his hostile silence was in a sense
a victory over his father. Afterward it always seemed to him
that he was stronger, better prepared for the next time. But it
left a bitter flavor in the center of his being, something that
made him feel just a little farther away and lonelier than
before. It was not through dread of the pain or fear of this
feeling of loneliness that he stayed on sitting in the orchard;
what was unbearable was the thought that he was innocent
and that he was going to be humiliated by being treated as
though he were guilty. What he dreaded encountering was his
own powerlessness in the face of injustice.

The warm breeze that moved down across the hillsides and
valleys from Djebel Zalagh found its way into the orchard between the stalks of cane, stirred the flat leaves above his head.
Its tentative caress on the back of his neck sent a fleeting
shiver through him. He put a rose petal between his teeth and
chewed it into wet fragments. Out here there was no one at
all, and no one would arrive. The guardian of the orchard had
seen him come in and had said nothing. Some of the orchards
had watchmen who chased you; the boys knew them all. This
was a "good" orchard, because the guard never spoke, save to
shout a command to his dog, to make it stop barking at the
intruders. The old man had gone down to a lower part of the
property near the river. Except for a truck that went by now
and then on the highway beyond the canebrake, this corner of
the orchard lay in complete silence. Because he did not want
to imagine what such a place would be like once the daylight
had gone, he slipped his feet into his sandals, stood up, shook
out his *djellaba*, inspected it for a while because it had belonged to his brother and he hated wearing it, and finally
flinging it over his shoulder, set out for the gap in the jungle
of canes through which he had entered.

Outside on the road the sun was warmer and the wind blew harder. He passed two small boys armed with long bamboo poles, who were hitting the branches of a mulberry tree while a larger boy scooped up the green berries and stored them in the hood of his *djellaba*. All three were too busy to notice his passage. He came to one of the hairpin bends in the road. Ahead of him on the other side of the valley was Djebel Zalagh. It had always looked to him like a king in his robes, sitting on his throne. Amar had mentioned this to several of his friends, but none of them had understood. Without even looking up at the mountain they had said: "You're dizzy," or "In your head," or "In the dark," or had merely laughed. "They think they know once and for all what the world is like, so that they don't ever have to look at it again," he had thought. And it was true: many of his friends had decided what the world looked like, what life was like, and they would never examine either of them again to find out whether they were right or wrong. This was because they had gone or were still going to school, and knew how to write and even to understand what was written, which was much more difficult. And some of them knew the Koran by heart, although naturally they did not know much of what it meant, because that is the most difficult thing of all, reserved for only a few great men in the world. And no one can understand it completely.

"In the school they teach you what the world means, and once you have learned, you will always know," Amar's father had told him.

"But suppose the world changes?" Amar had thought. "Then what would you know?" However, he was careful not to let his father guess what he was thinking. He never spoke with the old man save when he was bidden. Si Driss was severe, and liked his sons to treat him with exactly the same degree of respect he had shown to his own father fifty or sixty years before. It was best not to express an unasked-for opinion. In spite of the fact that life at home was a more serious business than it would have been had he had a more easygoing parent, Amar was proud of the respected position his father held. The richest, most important men of the quarter came to him, kissed his garments, and sat silent while he spoke. It had been written that Amar was to have a stern

father, and there was nothing to do about it but to give
thanks to Allah. Yet he knew that if ever he wanted anything
deeply enough to defy his father, the old man would see that
his son was right, and would give in to him. This he had discovered when his father had first sent him to school. He had
disliked it so much the first day that he had gone home and
announced that he would never return, and the old man had
merely sighed and called upon Allah to witness that he himself had taken the child and left him in the *aallem's* charge, so
that he could not be held accountable for what might come
afterward. The next day he had wakened the boy at dawn,
saying to him: "If you won't go to school, you must work."
And he had led him off to his uncle's blanket factory in the
Attarine, to work at the looms. This had not been nearly so
difficult as school, because he did not have to sit still; nevertheless, he did not stay, any more than he had stayed at any
one of the several dozen different places where he had
worked since. A week or two, and off he went to amuse
himself, very likely without having been paid anything. His
life at home was a constant struggle to keep from being led
off to some new work of his father's devising.

Thus it was that among all his early friends Amar was the
only one who had not learned to write and to read other people's writing, and it did not matter to him in the least. If his
family had not been Chorfa, descendents of the Prophet, his
life no doubt would have been easier. There would not have
been his father's fierce insistence on teaching him the laws of
their religion, or his constant dwelling on the necessity for strict
obedience. But the old man had determined that if his son were
to be illiterate (which in itself was no great handicap), at least
he was not going to be ignorant of the moral precepts of Islam.

As the years had passed, Amar had made new friends like
himself, boys of families so poor that there had never been
any question of their going to school. When he met his childhood friends now and talked to them, it seemed to him that
they had grown to be like old men, and he did not enjoy
being with them, whereas his new friends, who played and
fought every minute as though their lives depended upon the
outcome of their games and struggles, lived in a way that was
understandable to him.

A great thing in Amar's life was that he had a secret. It was a secret that did not even have to be kept secret, because no one could ever have guessed it. But he knew it and lived by it. The secret was that he was not like anybody else; he had powers that no one else possessed. Being certain of that was like having a treasure hidden somewhere out of the world's sight, and it meant much more than merely having the *baraka*. Many Chorfa had that. If someone were ill, or in a trance, or had been entered by some foreign spirit, even Amar often could set him right, by touching him with his hand and murmuring a prayer. And in his family the *baraka* was very strong, so powerful that in each generation one man had always made healing his profession. Neither his father nor his grandfather had ever done any work save that of attending to the constant stream of people who came to be treated by them. Thus there was nothing surprising about the fact that Amar himself should possess the gift. But it was not this he meant when he told himself that he was different from everyone else. Of course, he had always known his secret, but earlier it had not made so much difference. Now that he was fifteen and a man, it was becoming more important all the time. He had discovered that a hundred times a day things came into his head that never seemed to come into anyone else's head, but he had also learned that if he wanted to tell people about them—which he certainly did—he must do it in a way that would make them laugh, otherwise they became suspicious of him. Still, if one day in his enthusiasm he forgot and cried: "Look at Djebel Zalagh! The Sultan has a cloud on his shoulder!" and his friends answered: "You're crazy!" he did not mind. The next time he would try to remember to include their world, to say it in reference to some particular thing in which they were interested. Then they would laugh and he would be happy.

Today there were no clouds on any part of Djebel Zalagh. Each tiny olive tree along its crest stood out against the great, uniformly blue sky; and the myriad ravines that furrowed its bare slopes were beginning to fill with the hard shadows of late afternoon. A threadlike road wound along the side of one of the round hills at its feet; tiny white figures were moving very slowly up the road. He stood and watched them awhile: country people returning to their villages. For a moment he

wished passionately that he could be someone else, one of
them, with a simple, anonymous life. Then he began to spin
a fantasy. If he were a *djibli*, from the country, with his cleverness—for he knew he was clever—he would soon amass
more money than anyone in his *kabila*. He would buy more
and more land, have increasing numbers of people working
on it, and when the French tried to buy the land from him,
no matter how much they offered, he would refuse to sell to
them. Then the peasants would have great respect for him; his
name would begin to be known further and further afield,
men would come to him as to a *qoadi* for help and advice,
which he would give generously. One day a Frenchman
would arrive with an offer to make him a *caïd*; he saw himself
laughing good-naturedly, easily, saying: "But I am already
more than a *caïd* to my people. Why should I change?" The
Frenchman, not understanding, would make all kinds of supplementary, underhanded offers: percentages of the taxes,
girls of his choosing from distant tribes, an orange grove here,
a farm there, the deed to an apartment house in Dar el Beida,
and money in great quantities, but he would merely go on
laughing pleasantly, saying that he wanted nothing more than
what he already had: the respect of his own people. The
Frenchman would be mystified (for when had any Moroccan
ever made such a statement?) and would go away with fear in
his heart, and the news of Amar's strength would travel fast,
until even as far as Rhafsai and Taounate everyone would have
heard of the young *djibli* who could not be bought by the
French. And one day his chance would come. The Sultan
would send for him secretly, to advise him on matters per-
taining to the region he knew so well. He would be simple
and respectful in his manner, but not humble, and the Sultan
would find this very strange, and be a bit resentful at first,
until Amar, without saying it in so many words, would let him
see that his refusal to prostrate himself was a result only of his
realization that sultans, however great, were merely men, all
too mortal and all too fallible. The monarch would be
impressed by Amar's wisdom in having such an attitude, and
by his courage in showing it, and would invite him to stay on
with him. Little by little, with a whispered word here and
there, he would come to be more valuable to the Sultan than

El Mokhri himself. And there would arrive a time of crisis, when the Sultan would not be able to make a decision. Amar would be ready. With no hesitation he would step in and take control. At this point certain difficulties might arise. He would solve them the way every great man solves his problems: by staking everything on his own force. He saw himself sadly issuing the order for the Sultan's execution; it must be done for the people. And after all, the Sultan was nothing but an Alaouite from the Tafilalet—to use plain language, a usurper. Everyone knew that. There were scores of men in Morocco with far more right to rule, including anyone in Amar's own family, for they were Drissiyine, descendants of the first dynasty, the only rightful one in the land.

Slowly the distant figures moved up the hillside. They would probably keep going all night, and arrive home only sometime after dawn. He knew well enough how the country people lived; he had spent long months on his father's farm at Kherib Jerad, before they had had to sell it, and each year they had gone to collect the family's share of the crops. In his case the amused disdain that the city dweller feels for the peasant was tempered with respect. While a townsman was announcing his intentions at great length, a peasant would simply go ahead, without saying a word, and do what he had to do.

Still standing there, looking out over the great expanse of bare sunlit land, his eyes following the little figures that crawled up the face of the slope, he considered the extent of his misfortune. If only his older brother had not happened to turn his head at a given, precise moment three nights earlier in an alley of Moulay Abdallah, Amar could now have been swimming in the river, or playing soccer outside Bab Fteuh, or merely sitting quietly on the roof making tunes on his flute, without the weight of dread inside him. But Mustapha had turned his head, seen him there in that forbidden place among the painted women. And the next day he had approached him, demanding twenty rial. Amar had no money—and no means of obtaining any. He promised Mustapha that he would pay him little by little, as he got hold of small amounts, but Mustapha, being bright as well as merciless, had a plan and was not interested in the future. He did not intend to inform upon Amar; that went without saying. Their father would have been angrier with the informer than with the betrayed. That morning Mustapha had said to Amar: "Have you got the money?" and when Amar had shaken his head: "I'll be at Hamadi's café at sunset. Bring it or look out for your father when you go home."

He did not have the money; he would not go to the café and listen to further threats. He would go straight home and receive the beating so that it would become a thing of the past, rather than of the future. Behind him he heard the warning bell of a bicycle, and he turned to recognize a boy he knew. The boy stopped and he got on, sitting sidewise in front of the rider. Around the curves they coasted, one way and the other, with the sun-filled valley and Djebel Zalagh first on the left, then on the right.

"How are the brakes?" Amar asked. He was thinking that it might be pleasanter to be catapulted into a ditch or down the hillside than to be delivered safely to the gate of his quarter. Whatever he was going to be punished for might be forgiven when he got out of the hospital.

"The brakes are good," the boy replied. "What's the matter? Are you afraid?"

Amar laughed scornfully. They crossed the bridge and the ground became level. The boy began to pedal. As they approached the uphill stretch from the river valley to the Taza road intersection, the work got to be too arduous. Amar jumped off, said good-bye, and took a cross-cut through a grove of pomegranate trees. He had never owned a bicycle; it was not an object the son of an impoverished *fqih* could ever hope to have. Money came only to those who bought and sold. The boys whose fathers owned shops could own bicycles; Amar could only rent one now and then, because the people whom his father treated with his holy words and incantations generally had only coppers to spare, and when an occasional rich man consulted him and attempted to give him a larger sum in payment, Si Driss was adamant in his refusal.

"When your money comes from Allah," his father would tell him, "you do not buy machines and other Nazarene follies. You buy bread, and you give thanks to Him for being able to do that." And Amar would answer: "*Hamdoul'lah.*"

At a café just inside Bab Fteuh he stopped and watched a card game for a few minutes. Then he walked miserably home. His mother, who let him in, looked meaningfully at him, and he saw his father standing in the courtyard by the well. There was no sign of Mustapha.

CHAPTER 2

"Come upstairs," said his father, leading the way up the narrow flight of broken steps. He went into the smaller of the two rooms and switched on the light. "Sit on the mattress," he commanded, pointing at a corner of the room. Amar obeyed. Everything within him was trembling; he could not have told whether it was with eagerness or terror, any more than he could have known whether it was a consuming hatred or an overpowering love that he felt for the elderly man who towered above him, his eyes fiery with anger. Slowly his father unwound his long turban, revealing his shaven skull, and while he did this he spoke.

"This time you have committed an unpardonable sin," he said, fixing Amar with his terrible eyes. The pointed white beard looked strange with no turban above to balance it. "Only Hell lies before a boy like you. All the money in the house, that was to buy bread for your father and your family. Take off your *djellaba*." Amar removed the garment, and the old man snatched it from him, looking inside the hood as he did so. "Take off your *serrouelle*." Amar unfastened his belt and stepped out of his trousers, holding one hand in front of him to cover his nakedness. His father felt through the pockets, found them empty save for the broken penknife Amar always carried with him.

"Gone! All of it!" shouted the old man.

Amar said nothing.

"Where is it? Where is it?" The voice rose higher at each syllable. Amar merely looked into his father's eyes, his mouth open. There were a hundred things to say; there was nothing to say. He felt as if he had been turned to stone.

With astonishing force the old man pushed him down onto the mattress, and ripping the belt from the trousers, began to flail him with the buckle end. To protect his face, Amar threw himself over upon his belly, his hands cupped across the back of his head. The hard blows came down upon his knuckles, his shoulders, his back, his buttocks, his legs.

"I hope I kill you!" his father screamed. "You'd be better dead!"

I hope he does, Amar thought. He felt the lashes from a great distance. It was as if a voice were saying to him: "This is pain," and he were agreeing, but he was not convinced. The old man said no more, putting all his energy into the blows. Behind the swish of the belt in the air and the sound of the buckle hitting his flesh Amar heard a cat on the terrace above, calling: "Rao . . . rao . . . rao . . . ," the cries of children, and a radio somewhere playing an old record of Farid al Atrache. He could smell the *tajine* his mother was cooking down in the courtyard: cinnamon and onions. The blows kept coming. All at once he felt he must breathe; he had not yet drawn breath since he had been thrown upon the mattress. He sighed deeply and found himself vomiting. He raised his head, tried to move, and the pain forced him back down. Still the rhythmical beating continued, whether with less intensity or more he could not tell. His face slid about in the mess beneath it; behind his eyelids he had a vision. He was running down the Boulevard Poëymirau in the Ville Nouvelle with a sword in his hand. As he passed each shop the plate glass of the show window shattered of its own accord. The French women screamed; the men stood paralyzed. Here and there he struck at a man, severing his head, and a fountain of bright blood shot up out of the truncated neck. A hot wave of fierce delight surged through him. Suddenly he realized that all the women were naked. With dexterous upward thrusts of his blade he opened their bodies; with downward thrusts he removed their breasts. Not one must be left intact.

The beating had stopped. His father had gone out of the room. The radio was still playing the same piece, and he heard his parents talking below. He lay completely still. For a moment he thought perhaps he was really dead. Then he heard his mother enter the room. "*Ouildi, ouildi,*" she said, and her two hands began to touch him softly, rubbing oil over his skin. He had not cried out once during the beating, but now he found himself sobbing fiercely. To be able to stop, he imagined his father above his mother, looking on. The ruse worked, and he lay there quietly, submitting to the strong, gentle hands.

He was sick the next day, and the following. As he lay in his little room on the roof, his mother came many times with oil and rubbed his bruises. He was dizzy with fever and miserable with pain, and he had no desire for food, other than the soup and hot tea she brought him from time to time. The third day he sat up and played his *lirah*, the reed flute he had made. That day his mother let Diki bou Bnara, his pet rooster, out of his crate, and the magnificent bird wandered in and out of the room, strutting about, scratching and listening to Amar's songs in his praise. But the third day at sunset, when Diki bou Bnara had been chased back into his cage and the muezzins had finished calling the *maghreb*, Amar heard his father's footsteps approaching as they mounted the stairway to the roof. He quickly turned over to face the wall, pretending to be asleep. Then his father was in the room, speaking.

"*Ya ouildi! Ya Amar!*"

Amar did not move, but his heart beat fast and his breathing was difficult. The mattress moved as his father sat down by Amar's feet.

"Amar!"

Amar stirred, rubbed his eyes.

"I want to talk with you. But first I want to be sure that you have no hatred. I am very unhappy with what you have done. Your mother and your brother and your sister have not had enough food these last days. That is nothing. That's not why I want to talk with you. You must listen. Have you any hatred in your heart for me?"

Amar sat up. "No, Father," he said quietly.

The old man was silent for a moment. Diki bou Bnara suddenly crowed.

"I want to make you understand. *Bel haq, fel louwil.* . . . First, you have to know that *I* understand. Perhaps you think that because I am old I know nothing about the world, how the world has changed."

Amar murmured a protest, but his father continued.

"I know you think that. All boys do. And now the world has changed more than ever before. Everything is new. Everything is bad. We're suffering more than we've ever suffered. And it is written that we must suffer still more. All that is nothing. Like the wind. You think I have never been to Dar Debibagh, never seen how the French have their life. But what if I tell you I have, many times? What if I say I have seen their cafés and their shops, and walked in their streets, ridden in their buses, the same as you?"

Amar was astonished. He had taken it for granted that since the arrival of the French soldiers many years ago, his father had never gone outside the walls of the Medina, save to the country or to the Mellah to buy ingredients for his medicines which only certain Jews sold. Ever since he could remember, the schedule of his father's life had been the same, had consisted of the five trips a day he made to the mosque, together with the hours he spent in conversation at the shops of friends en route to and from the mosque. Outside of that there was nothing, save the administering of his services when they were required. It was surprising to hear him say he had been to the French town. Amar doubted it: if he had been there, why had he never mentioned it until now?

"I want you to know that I have been there many times. I have seen their Christian filth and shame. It can never be for us. I swear they're worse than Jews. No, I swear by Allah they're lower than the godless Jews of the Mellah! And so if I speak against them it's not because of what men like Si Kaddour and that carrion Abdeltif and the other Wattanine have told me. What they say may be the truth, but their reason for saying it is a lie, because it is *politique*. You know what *politique* is? It is the French word for a lie. *Kdoub! Politique!* When you hear the French say: our *politique*, you know they mean: our lies. And when you hear the Moslems, the Friends of Independence, say: our *politique*, you know they mean: *our* lies. All lies are sins. And so, which displeases Allah more, a lie told by a Nazarene, who doesn't know the true faith from the false, or a lie told by a Moslem, who does?"

Now Amar thought he saw where his father's words were leading. He was warning him against associating with certain of his friends, with whom he sometimes played soccer or went to the cinema, and who were known to be members of the Istiqlal. His father was afraid Amar would be put in prison like Abdallah Tazi and his cousin, who had shouted: "*A bas les Français!*" in the Café de la Renaissance one night. How wrong he was, Amar thought with a tinge of bitterness. There was not even the remotest chance of such a thing. That possibility had been ruled out for him from the beginning because he spoke no French and could neither read nor write. He knew nothing, not even how to sign his own name in Arabic. Maybe he'll stop talking now and go downstairs, he thought.

"Do you understand what I'm saying to you?"

"I understand," Amar replied, twisting the sheet between his toes. He felt better; he would have liked to go out and walk a bit, but he knew that if he got up he would no longer feel like going out. Through the iron grillwork of the window he could see the flat rooftops of a distant corner of the city, with a square of darkening sky above.

"It is worse for a Moslem to lie," resumed his father. "And who among all the Moslems commits the greatest sin if he lies or steals? A Cherif. And thanks to Allah you are a Cherif. . . ."

"*Hamdoul'lah,*" murmured Amar, obediently but with feeling. "Thanks to Allah."

"Not only *Hamdoul'lah, Hamdoul'lah!* No! You must become a man and *be* a Cherif. The Cherif lives for his people. I would rather see you dead than growing to be like the carrion you talk with in the street. Dead! Do you understand?" The old man's voice rose. "There will be no more Moslems unless every young Cherif obeys the laws of Allah."

He went on in this vein. Amar understood and silently agreed, but at the same time he could not keep himself from thinking: "He doesn't know what the world is like today." The thought that his own conception of the world was so different from his father's was like a protecting wall around his entire being. When his father went out into the street he had only the mosque, the Koran, the other old men in his mind. It was the immutable world of law, the written word, unchanging beneficence, but it was in some way wrinkled and dried up. Whereas when Amar stepped out the door there was the whole vast earth waiting, the live, mysterious earth, that belonged to him in a way it could belong to no one else, and where anything at all might happen. The smell of the morning breeze moving in across the walls from the olive groves, the sound of the river falling over the rocks as it rushed in its canyons through the heart of the city, the moving shadows of the trees on the white dust beneath, when he sat at midday in their shelter—such things had a particular message for him that they could not have for anyone else, least of all his father. The world where the old man lived, he imagined, must look something like a picture in one of those newspapers that were smuggled in from Egypt: gray, smudged, meaningless save as an accompaniment to the written text.

He listened to his father's words with growing impatience. There were repeated references to his duties as a descendant of the Prophet. To whom could the people turn in times of difficulty, if not to the Chorfa? Every Cherif was a leader. It was true, but he knew there was something wrong with the picture. The Chorfa were the leaders, but they could lead their followers only to defeat, and this was something he could never say to anyone. As if the old man had sensed the emotion, if not the precise idea that was in his son's mind, he stopped talking for a moment, and then began to speak again in a much lower voice, sadly. "I have committed a very great sin," he said. "Allah will be the judge. I should have beaten you day and night, dragged you to school by your hair, until you knew how to write. Now you will never learn. It's too late. You will never know anything. And this is my fault."

Amar was shocked; his father had never spoken in such a manner. "No," he said tentatively. "My fault."

In the dimness Amar saw his father's arms reach out toward him. A hand was placed on each temple, and the old man bent forward and touched his lips lightly to the boy's forehead. Then he sat back, shook his head back and forth several times in silence, rose, and went out of the room without saying any more.

A few minutes later Mustapha appeared frowning in the doorway, obviously having been sent by his father to inquire after Amar's health. The first instant, upon seeing him, Amar had been about to say something bitter; then a strange calm took possession of him, and he found himself saying in the most benign accents: "*Ah, khai, chkhbarek?* It's several days since I've seen you. How is everything?"

Mustapha seemed bewildered; inexpressively he murmured a perfunctory phrase of greeting, turned and went downstairs. Amar lay back smiling; for the first time he felt that he had the upper hand in a situation where he had never dared hope to have it. Mustapha was his older brother; he had been born first, and twenty-six sheep had been sacrificed that day, two of them paid for by his father, whereas when Amar had come into the world Si Driss had bought only one. It was true that there had been another sheep, donated by a friend, but for Amar that one did not count. It was also a fact that Mustapha had been born up in the hills in Kherib Jerad, and the other twenty-four sheep had been brought as gifts by peasants over-joyed to see a Cherif born among them, while Amar had been born in the heart of the city, and only the family had rejoiced, but that did not ever occur to him when he began sifting over his wrongs. The important thing now was that Mustapha was puzzled; he had not expected his father to send him upstairs to inquire after Amar, and he had not imagined that Amar could possibly be in good spirits. Amar knew his brother. Mustapha would go on being troubled by this small mystery until he had solved it. And that Amar had no intention of allowing him to do. Indeed, he himself could not have told what was in his heart regarding Mustapha, save that on some remote, as yet invisible horizon he divined the certitude of victory for himself, and a total defeat for his brother.

And now there came to his mind an incident which his mother had recounted to him many times. Long ago, when her father had been on his deathbed in this room where Amar now lay, and the whole family was gathered there to say good-bye to him, the old man had commanded Mustapha to approach the bed, so that he might bestow his blessing on the first-born. But Mustapha had been a headstrong, sulky child; whining, he had hidden beneath his mother's skirts, and no amount of cajoling could induce him to go near the bed. It was a shameful moment, miraculously saved by Amar, who for some unaccountable reason had suddenly toddled across the room and kissed his grandfather's hand. Immediately the old man had bestowed his blessing on Amar instead of Mustapha;

not content with that, he had gone on to prophesy that the baby would grow up to be a much better man than his brother. A few minutes later he had drawn his last breath. The story had always greatly impressed Amar, but since he was fairly certain that neither of his parents had ever told it to Mustapha, it had not been fully satisfactory as a consolation for the twenty-six sheep. But now he thought of it again, and it began to assume an importance he had not perceived before. What were twenty-six sheep, or, indeed, a hundred sheep, compared to the magic power of a blessing sent direct to him by Allah through the heart and lips of his grandfather? In the darkness he murmured a short prayer for the departed, and an even shorter one of thanks for his own good fortune.

That night in the bowl of soup his mother brought him there were almonds as well as chickpeas. He longed to know whether the whole family was having them too, or whether they had been bought especially for him and for him alone, but he did not dare ask. He could imagine his mother running downstairs in a fit of laughter, crying: "Now Master Amar imagines that we went out and bought the almonds just for him and that nobody else is having any!" There would be even louder laughter from his sister and Mustapha.

"What good soup," he remarked.

CHAPTER 3

The next morning he felt perfectly well. He got up very early and went out onto the roof to look over the wall at the city spread out around him. Fog lay in the valley. A few of the higher minarets pushed up from the sea of grayness below like green fingers pointing skyward, and the hills on both sides were visible, with their raw earth and their rows of tiny olive trees. But the bowl where the center of the city lay was still brimming with the nocturnal, unmoving fog. He stood awhile looking, letting the fresh early air bathe his face and chest, and he said a few holy words as he turned his head in the direction of Bab Fteuh. Beyond the gate was the waste land by the cemetery where he played soccer, and then the village of reed huts where there were many goats, and then the wheatfields leading gently down toward the river, and then the mud villages under the high clay cliffs. And if you went farther there was a sort of canyon-land all made of clay, where in the spring after the rains the water rushed through, often carrying with it drowned sheep and even cows.

In this region there were no plants at all—only the clay with its deep crevasses and crazy turrets made by the rain. Beyond this were great mountains where the Berbers lived, and then desert, and other lands whose names only a few people could tell you, and then, of course, behind everything, in the center of the world, shining in an eternal unearthly light, there was Mecca. How many hours he had spent examining the bright chromolithographs that lined the walls of the barber shops! Some were of historic battles waged by Moslems against demons; some showed magnificent flying horses with women's heads and breasts—it was on these animals that important people used to travel before they discarded them for airplanes—some were of Adam and Eve, the first Moslems in the world, or of Jerusalem, the great holy city where Christians and Jews were still murdering Moslems every day and putting their flesh in tins to be shipped abroad and sold as food; but there was always a picture, more beautiful than any, of Mecca, with its sharp crags above and its tiers of high houses topped with terraces and studded with balconies, its arcades and lamps and giant pigeons, and finally, in the center, the great rock draped with black cloth, which was of such beauty that many men fainted, or even died, on beholding it. Often at night he had stood in this very spot, his hands on the wall, straining his eyes as he peered into the star-filled darkness of the sky, trying to imagine that he saw at least a faint glimmer of the light which streamed up forever into the heavens from the sacred shrine.

Usually from the terrace he could hear the shrill voices and the drums from the market at Sidi Ali bou Ralem. Today, what with the fog, only the sounds from the immediate neighborhood were audible. He went back into his room, lay down on his bed, resting his feet against the wall above his head, and began to play his flute: no particular tune—merely an indeterminate, neutral succession of notes with an occasional long wait—the music for the particular way he felt on this cool,

misty morning. When this had gone on for a while, he suddenly jumped up and dressed himself in the only European
outfit he owned: a pair of old military trousers and a heavy
woolen sweater, along with a pair of sandals he had bought in
the Mellah—these last he slipped under his arm, as they were
to be put on only when he got into the middle of town, away
from the danger of enemy attacks in the streets of his own
quarter. It was easier to fight, and to walk, for that matter,
barefoot, unencumbered by the weight of shoes. A friend had
given him a leather wrist strap which he wore on gala occasions, pretending it had a watch with it. He looked at it for a
moment, decided against it, combed his hair carefully, glancing into a pocket mirror which was hung on the wall, and
tiptoed down the two flights of stairs into the courtyard.
When his mother saw him she called out: "Come and eat
breakfast! You think you're going out without eating first?"

He was extremely hungry, but without knowing why, he had
wanted to get out of the house immediately, before he had to
speak to anyone, and change the way he felt. However, it was
too late now. He sat down and ate the boiled oats with cinnamon bark and goat's milk that his little sister brought him. She
squatted in the doorway, looking slyly at him now and then
out of the corner of her eye. There were streaks of henna on
her temples and forehead, and her hands were brick red with
the dye. She was old enough to be given in marriage; already
two offers had come in, but old Si Driss would not hear of it,
partly because he wanted to see her around the house a bit
longer (it seemed only last year that she had been born), and
partly because neither of the offers had been substantial
enough to consider seriously. Amar's mother was in complete
agreement with her husband; the longer she could forestall the
marriage the happier she would be. It was no pleasure to have
sons because they were never home; they bolted their food and
disappeared, and when they grew older one could not even
know whether they would return to sleep or not. But a daughter, since she was not allowed to stir from the house alone,
even to fetch a kilo of sugar from the shop next door, could
always be counted on to be there when one needed her. In any
case, each year that passed gave Halima more charms: her eyes
seemed to grow larger and her hair thicker and glossier.

When he had eaten, Amar got up and went out into the courtyard. There he petted his two pigeons for a while, watching his mother in the hope that she would go upstairs, so that his departure would be unnoticed by her. Finally he decided to go out anyway.

"It may rain," she called as he reached the door.

"It's not going to rain," he said. "*B'slemah.*" He knew she wanted to say more—anything at all, so long as the conversation kept him there. It was always this way when he came to go out. He smiled over his shoulder and shut the door behind him. There were three turnings in the alley before it got to the street. At the second he came face to face with his father. As Amar was stooping to kiss his hand, the old man pulled it quickly away.

"How did you awaken, my boy?" he said. They exchanged greetings, and Si Driss looked penetratingly at his son. "I want to talk to you," he said.

"*Naam, sidi.*"

"Where are you going?"

Amar had no destination in his head. "Just for a walk."

"This is not a world just to go for a walk in. You're a man, you know, not a boy any longer. Think this over, and be home for lunch, because this afternoon you're going with me to see Abderrahman Rabati."

Amar inclined his head and walked on. But the joy of being in the street in the morning was gone. Rabati was a big, loud-mouthed man who often got work for the boys of the quarter with the French in the Ville Nouvelle, and Amar had heard countless stories of how difficult the work was, how the French were constantly in a bad humor and found pretexts for not paying when the end of the week came, and as if that were not bad enough, how Rabati himself habitually extracted small tributes from the boys in return for having found them their jobs. Besides, Amar knew no French beyond "*bon jour, m'sieu,*" "*entrez,*" and "*fermez la porte,*" expressions taught him by a well-meaning friend, and it was common knowledge that the boys who did not understand French were treated even worse, made the butt of jokes not only by the French but by the boys who were fortunate enough to know the language.

He turned into the principal street of the quarter, nodded

to the mint-seller, and looked unhappily around him, not even sure any longer that he wanted to take a walk. His father's words had spread a film of poison over the morning landscape. There was only one way out, and that was to find himself some sort of work immediately, so that when he went home for lunch he would be able to say: "Father, I'm working."

He turned left and went up the dusty hill past the great carved façade of the old mosque, and, further on, the concrete box that had been the scene of so many afternoons of childhood pleasure, the cinema, plastered with shiny photographs of men with guns. Then he turned left again through a narrow street jammed with waiting donkeys and men pushing wheelbarrows, whose downhill course shortly burrowed beneath the houses. Presently he came out into a vast open place dotted here and there with circular towers. It was like a burning village: greasy black smoke poured from the turrets of baked earth. Boys in rags ran back and forth carrying armfuls of green branches which they stuffed into the doors of the ovens. The smoke billowed and hovered in the air close to the ground, not seeming willing to venture upward toward the gray sky. In a further corner, built against the high ramparts of the city, was a section where the ovens had been constructed on two levels. There was a stairway onto the enormous flat mud roof, and he climbed up to survey the scene. Near by in the doorway of a small shed crouched a bearded man. Amar turned and spoke to him.

"Any work for me?"

The man stared at him for a moment without showing any interest. Then he said: "Who are you?"

"The son of Driss the *fqih*," he replied.

The man stared harder. "What's the use of lying?" he demanded. "*You're* the son of Driss the *fqih*? *You*?" He turned away and spat.

Amar was taken aback. He looked down at his bare feet, wriggled his toes, and reflected that he should have put his shoes on before climbing up here.

"What's the matter with me?" he said finally, with a certain belligerency. "And what difference does it make, my name? I only asked you if you had any work."

"Can you make clay?" the man said.

"I can learn how to do anything in a quarter of an hour."

The man laughed, stroked his beard, and slowly got to his feet. "Come," he said, and he led him to the entrance of another small shed further along the roof. Inside in the dimness was a boy squatting on the floor beside a large tank of water, rubbing his hands together. "Go in," the man said. They stood looking down at the boy, who did not glance up. "You rub as hard as you can," he told Amar, "and if you find even the smallest pebble you take it out, and then you keep rubbing until each handful is like silk."

"I see," said Amar. It seemed like the easiest sort of work. He waited until they got back outside, and then he asked: "How much?"

"Ten rial a day."

It was the normal wage.

"With lunch," added Amar, as though it went without saying.

The man opened his eyes wide. "Are you crazy?" he cried. (Amar merely looked at him fixedly.) "If you want to work, step inside here and start. I don't need any help. I'm only doing you a favor."

Any work that Amar did, even of the simplest kind, such as carrying water at the tannery or holding the long threads with which the tailors made the frogging on the fronts of the *djellabas*, fascinated him while he was doing it; it was sheer pleasure for him to be completely occupied—the sort of delight he could not know when there was room in his mind for him to remember that he was himself. He set to work mixing water with the clay, rubbing, smoothing, washing, removing particles. At the end of the morning the man came inside, looked, and raised his eyebrows. He stooped over, examined the quality of the mixture carefully, dipping the tips of his fingers into it and squeezing them together.

"Good," he said. "Go home to lunch."

Amar glanced up. "I'm not hungry yet."

"Come with me."

They went to the end of the long roof, down the stairs, and across a stretch of bare ground to where great bundles of branches had been piled. Here another stairway had been cut into the earth. The astringent smell of wet clay was tempered with a sweeter, musky odor which came from several fig trees down below, beside a channel of the river where the water flowed by very quickly and without a sound. In the cliff at the bottom of the steps was a door. The man removed the padlock and they went in.

"Let's see if you can run the *mamil*."

Amar let himself down into the opening in the floor, made himself comfortable on the seat which was on a level with the man's shoes, and began to turn the large wooden wheel with his foot. It took a certain strength and dexterity, but none that he had not already used while playing soccer.

"Do you understand how it works?" the man asked, pointing to a smaller wheel that spun near Amar's left hand. He piled some clay on the turning disc, squatted down. With manipulating and sprinkling of water the shapeless mass soon took the form of a plate.

"Just keep turning the wheel," he said, apparently expecting Amar to tire and stop. "I'll take care of this part." But it was clear to Amar that the apparatus was arranged so that one man could do everything by himself, using his hands and feet at the same time. After a bit the bearded man stood up. "You'd better go home for lunch now," he said.

"I want to make a jar," said Amar.

The man laughed. "It takes a long time to learn how to do that."

"I can do it now."

The other, saying nothing, removed the plate he had been making, and stood back, his arms folded, an expression of amusement on his face. "*Zid.* Go on, make a jar," he said. "I want to see you."

The clay and the water were at his right hand, the revolving wheel at his left. There was no light in the room save that which came through the door, so that he had necessarily missed the finer points of the man's work; nevertheless, he did exactly as he had seen him do, not forgetting to maintain a continuous sideward pushing with the flat of his bare foot on the big wheel. Slowly he modeled a small urn, taking great care to make its shape one that pleased him. The man was astonished. "You've worked a *mamil* plenty of times before," he finally said. "Why didn't you say so? I'm always ready to pay ten rials and lunch to a good workman, somebody who knows something."

"The blessing of Allah be upon you, master," said Amar. "I'm very hungry." Even though he would not be home for lunch, his father would be pacified by the good news he would give him at dinner time.

CHAPTER 4

A certain rich merchant, El Yazami by name, who lived in the quarter and had once sent his sister to Si Driss for treatment, was leaving for Rissani that afternoon. Already his servants had carried seven enormous coffers to the bus station outside Bab el Guissa, where they were being weighed and hoisted to the top of the vehicle, and there were many more crates and amorphous bundles of all sizes constantly being carried from the house to the terminus. El Yazami was making his annual pilgrimage to the shrine of his patron saint in the Tafilalet, from which he always returned many thousands of rial the richer, given the fact that like any good Fassi he was in the habit of combining business with devotion, and knew just what articles could be transported to the south and sold there with the maximum of profit. And it occurred to him as he stood looking up at the workers loading his merchandise on the top of the big blue bus that about five hundred medium-sized water jars would be a remunerative addition to his cargo. Allowing twenty percent for breakage, he calculated, the gain could still be about one hundred fifty percent, which would be worth while. And so, accompanied by one of his sons, he set out for Bab Fteuh to make a quick purchase. When he came within sight of the village of mud ovens and smoke, he sent his son to examine the wares on one side of the road while he went to investigate the other side. So large a quantity was not always available at such short notice. The first person his son ran into was Amar, up from his damp workroom under the fig trees for a breath of air and furtive cigarette. Amar knew the boy by sight, although they had never been friends. After greetings had been exchanged, the young Yazami told him what he was looking for.

"We can supply them all for you," said Amar immediately.

"We need them now," said El Yazami.

"Of course." He had no idea whether such a large number could be furnished or not, but it was important that he be the one to communicate the order to his employer, who would surely reward him.

The man with the beard was incredulous. "Five hundred?" he cried. "Who wants them?" He knew he could get the jars from his colleagues; what interested him was to know whether this was a serious offer or some fantasy of Amar's.

"Over there." Amar indicated the young Yazami, who was idly chinning himself on the underside of a ladder. The potter was not impressed. The youth did not look like someone who was going to buy even one water jar.

"*Son of sin*," began the man under his breath. Amar had run over to the boy, taken him by the arm.

"Fifty rial for you tomorrow if you buy them here," he whispered.

"I don't know . . . my father . . ." He pointed in the direction of the elder Yazami, who was inspecting jars on the far side of the thoroughfare.

"Bring him over here fast, and come by for your fifty rial tomorrow." There was no guarantee that the potter would give him anything if he put the sale through, but he had decided simply to leave if he did not. The world was too big, too full of magnificent opportunities, to waste time with unappreciative masters.

The boy went across the road to the other side and talked awhile with his father. Amar could see him pointing in his direction. The potter returned to his crouching position outside the shed. "Go back to work," he called. Amar stood, hesitating. Then, risking everything, he ran across the road, and presently returned with El Yazami and his son. The potter stood up; as the three approached, he heard the portly gentleman saying to Amar: "I remember you as a boy no bigger than a grasshopper. Don't forget to greet Si Driss for me. May Allah preserve him."

The purchase was made quickly, and Amar was dispatched to round up a group of boys who could carry the baskets of jars to Bab el Guissa. When the last load had departed, the potter went down the steps into the dark little room where Amar sat.

"*Zduq*," he said, looking at him with bewilderment, "you really are the son of Si Driss the *fqih*."

Amar stared at him in mild mock surprise. "Yes. I told you that."

The man fingered his beard meditatively. "I didn't believe you. Forgive me."

Amar laughed. "Allah forgives," he said lightly. Without looking up he went on working, pretending to be completely absorbed in his gestures, and wondering if the potter were going to offer him his reward now. Since the man said no more on the subject, but began to talk about a load of clay that was due, he decided that it would be necessary to take action. Hoisting himself out of the hole in the floor, he seized the man's arm and kissed the sleeve of his *djellaba*. The man pulled back.

"No, no," he objected. "A Cherif—"

"An apprentice to a master potter," Amar reminded him.

"No, no—"

"I am only a *metallem*. But I can make a prophecy. From this day on, your life will prosper. My gift tells me that. Allah in His infinite wisdom has granted me the knowledge." The potter moved backward a step, looking at him with wide eyes. "And I'd tell you even if at this moment you were raising your hand to strike me." The potter made a gesture of puzzled protest. "Allah is all-powerful, and knows what is in my heart. Therefore how can I withhold it from you? He knows that this moment my father is lying ill at home without the money to buy a keg of buttermilk which would make him well. He knows that you have a generous heart, and that is why He sent the rich man here this afternoon to buy from you, to make it possible for you to use your heart."

The man was looking at him now with mingled wonder and suspicion. Amar saw this, and decided to come to the point.

"With five days' pay in advance I would leave here this evening the happiest man in the world."

"Yes," the potter said, "and have I got my own policeman to go and find you tomorrow and drag you here? How do I know you'll ever come back? I'd probably find you down in Dar Debbagh carrying hides to the river, trying the same trick on them there."

Amar was convinced the man would give him the money; without further words he turned away and climbed back down to his sunken seat to resume his work. When he had the wheel going, he looked up and said: "Forgive me, *sidi.*"

The man stood perfectly still. Finally he said, almost plaintively: "How do I know you'll come back tomorrow?"

"*Ya, sidi,*" Amar said. "Since the world began has any man ever been able to know what would happen tomorrow? The world of men is today. I'm asking you to open your heart today. Tomorrow belongs to Allah, and *incha'Allah*"—he said the words with great feeling—"I shall come back tomorrow and every day after that. *Incha'Allah!*"

The man reached into his *choukra* and pulled out the money.

"Here is your father's buttermilk," he said. "May he get well quickly."

The waste land at the foot of the cemetery opposite Bab Fteuh was not on his way home, nevertheless Amar contrived to pass by it when he had finished his day's work, on the slim chance that the younger Yazami might possibly be among the two dozen or more boys practicing there with a football. He did not find him, but he found a student who claimed to know where he was, and in his company began a quest which led through the damp streets of El Mokhfia and across the river to a small café he had never seen before. El Yazami was here, seated among a group of boys his age, playing checkers. When he saw Amar his face fell: the only reason Amar could have for seeking him out so soon was to tell him the money was not to be forthcoming. After urging Amar to have a Coca-Cola, which he politely refused—for, this being an expensive café with tables and chairs instead of mats, he did not want in any way to get involved—El Yazami took his arm and propelled him outside, where they stood in the dark under a high plane tree and talked.

Amar's principal interest was in keeping the other away from his place of work, where the boy's presence would immediately arouse the suspicions of the potter. He wondered how he could have been so foolish as to have made that meeting-place.

"It would be better if you didn't come tomorrow," he said. Then he added: "He only gave me twenty-five rial." In the darkness he handed over the coins; the other went to the doorway to count them by the dim light that came from within. It was an agreeable surprise because he had expected nothing.

"I still owe you twenty-five," Amar was saying, "and you'll get them as soon as I do. But try and bring in some more business, yes? You'll get the rest sooner." This seemed sensible enough to El Yazami, and he agreed to do what he could. They parted, each one reasonably pleased with the outcome of the meeting.

Surprisingly enough, during the days that followed, El Yazami did make efforts to find customers for Amar's employer, and these were not in vain. Indeed, they were so successful that one evening at the end of the week the potter came down into Amar's little workroom. He stood a moment looking at the boy before he spoke. When he did begin to speak, it was with satisfaction and a slight awe in his voice. "*Sidi*," he said. (Amar smiled inwardly: he had never addressed him thus before.) "Since you have been here with me Allah has favored me with more success than I had ever thought was possible."

"*Hamdoul'lah*," said Amar.

"Do you like your work?"

"Yes, master."

"I hope you'll stay with me," the man said. It cost him an effort to go on, but he managed it. After all, he told himself, it was surely Allah who had made him take the boy on; he had not believed he was a Cherif and had the *baraka*, and he could not remember now what had prompted him to be friendly to him. If Allah were involved it would be safer to be generous. "Suppose I double your wages."

"If it is Allah's will," said Amar, "I should be very happy."

The man pulled a small ring from his pocket and held it forth to Amar. "Put this on your finger," he said. "A little gift. No one can ever say that Saïd is not grateful for favors shown him by Allah."

"Thank you very much," said Amar, slipping the ring on to various fingers to try the size and appearance. "There's one thing I'd like to know. When does the new wage go into effect? Beginning today or beginning the first day I came to work for you?"

The man stared at him, was about to say something harsh, but decided not to, and instead shrugged his shoulders.

"It can begin at the beginning if you like," he said; in spite of the fact that he did not particularly like Amar, he was determined to keep him on with him if possible. It was not only the divine favor of which the boy seemed to be a symbol, but also the fact of the sales. Although the two could be considered facets of the same thing, he preferred to try to think of them separately: it was more acceptable to Allah.

"If it's not worth it to you . . ." Amar began.

"Of course it is. Of course it is," he protested.

"The day you have no money, I'll work for you without pay, twice as hard, so that Allah may favor us with money again."

The potter thanked him for his generosity and turned to go out.

"Six days at twenty rial," Amar was thinking. "He gave me fifty. He still owes me seventy. And twenty-five still for Yazami . . . *bel haq*, not yet . . . Why doesn't he just pay, instead of talking so much?" And he determined to get the money that night.

"Master!" he cried, to stop the man from going through the door. The potter looked at him, surprised. Now Amar had to go on. It was an unheard-of thing, but he was going to ask his employer to sit with him in a café. And the words he heard himself saying probably astonished him more than they did the older man.

"All right," said the potter. When the day was finished they went together to a café near Bab Sidi bou Jida, where there was a small garden in the back, through which one of the myriad channels of the river had been directed. Weeping willows and young plum trees edged the stream, and one small light bulb hung from a trellis overhead, almost buried in grape leaves. The mat where they seated themselves was only a few centimeters from the swift surface of the water.

Amar ordered the tea with dignity; he was bursting with a pride and a delight which he took pains to conceal. It occurred to him that he would be still happier if he did not have ahead of him the problem of finding the right chink in

the conversation where he could gain a foothold for reasonably requesting the money, and he was momentarily tempted
to let it go for this time, and relax in the pleasure of the
occasion. But then he reminded himself that the only reason
for the invitation was to get his wages, and sighing, he steeled
himself to go through with the business at hand.

The potter told him about his two sons, his altercation with
a neighbor which had amounted almost to a feud, and finally
about his great dream, which was to make the *hadj*, the pilgrimage to Mecca. Amar became enthusiastic; his eyes shone.

"To go there by Allah's grace, and then die happy in your
heart," Amar whispered, a beatific smile on his lips. He leaned
back, closed his eyes. "*Al-lah!*"

"Not this year," said the potter meaningfully.

"Perhaps next year there will be enough money. *Incha'-
Allah.*"

The man snorted. Then he leaned forward, putting his
lips close to Amar's ear. "It's all right here. There's no one
listening."

Amar did not understand, but he smiled and looked around
the dim little garden. How peaceful it was, with the light
evening breeze stirring the small leaves of the grapevine that
clustered around the electric bulb, making the shadows move
and change on the yellow mat below. For a moment he
pushed aside the thought of money. From time to time the
dark water beside them rippled audibly, as if a tiny fish had
come to the surface for an instant and then darted beneath. It
was in peaceful moments such as this, his father had said, that
men were given to know just a little of what paradise was like,
so that they might yearn for it with all their soul, and strive
during their time on earth to be worthy of going there. He
felt utterly comfortable and happy; soon the hot mint tea
would be carried out to them, and he had asked for a sprig of
verbena to be put in each glass. And when he had the money
he would begin looking for real European shoes, and sell his
Jewish sandals. . . .

"No, not this year," the man resumed, a wicked light
suddenly in his eyes. "May their race rot in Hell."

Amar looked at him in surprise. If anyone said that, he
could mean only the French, but he was not aware that the

man had made any previous allusion to them. As he turned the subject over in his mind, he was conscious that the potter was staring at him with a nascent suspicion.

"Don't you know about Ibn Saud?" he asked suddenly. "Have you never heard of him?"

"Of course," said Amar, stung by the tone of the other's voice. "The Sultan of the Hejaz."

"*Huwa hada*," said the man, "but I can see you don't know anything about what's going on in the world. You should wake up, boy. There are great things happening. Ibn Saud is a man with a head. This year not a single *hadji* from Morocco has got into Mecca. They all got as far as Djedda and had to turn back."

"Poor things," said Amar, commiserating immediately.

"Poor things?" the man cried. "Poor donkeys! They should have stayed home. Is this a year to go off to Mecca, when that filthy carrion of a dog they gave us is still sitting there on the Sultan's throne? No, I swear if I had power I'd shut the doors of every mosque in the country until we get our Sultan back. And if that doesn't bring him, you know what will."

Amar did indeed know. The man meant *jihad*, the wholesale slaughter by every Moslem of all available unbelievers. He sat silent, a little stunned by the man's violence. By no means was he unaware of the fact that the French had put a false monarch on the throne of his country; he assumed that everyone in the world knew that. He resented the indignity the same as anyone else, but he did so without giving the matter any thought. In his experience the substitution of Ben Arafa for Sidi Mohammed had not altered anything; the reason was that he had not come in contact with anyone who had strong political convictions. His father had fulminated against unbelievers and their evil work in Morocco ever since he could remember, and this new bit of malevolence on their part—to kidnap the Sultan and hold him prisoner on an island in the sea, replacing him with a doddering old man who might as well be deaf, dumb and blind—was merely the most recent in a long list of hostile acts on their part.

But now he saw for the first time that there were men who gave it much more than a passing glance, for whom it was more than a concept, a string of words about a distant happening; he saw the symbolic indignity turn into a personal affront, disapproval transformed into rage. The man sat there glaring at him, a vague shadow, that of a grape leaf, played across his wrinkled forehead. An owl suddenly uttered an absurd, melancholy sound in the canebrake across the stream, and Amar was made conscious in an instant of a presence in the air, something which had been there all the time, but which he had never isolated and identified. The thing was in him, he was a part of it, as was the man opposite him, and it was a part of them; it whispered to them that time was short, that the world they lived in was approaching its end, and beyond was unfathomable darkness. It was the premonition of inevitable defeat and annihilation, and it had always been there with them and in them, as intangible and as real as the night around them. Amar pulled two loose cigarettes out of his pocket and handed one to the potter. "Ah, the Moslems, the Moslems!" he sighed. "Who knows what's going to happen to them?"

"Who knows?" said the man, lighting the cigarette. When the *qaouaji* brought their tea they drank it without speaking, slowly. The breeze blew harder, bringing with it the chill odors of the higher air on the mountains. It was not until after they had separated in the street that Amar realized he had forgotten to ask the man for his money. He shrugged his shoulders and went home to dinner.

CHAPTER 5

The young spring grew, wheeled along toward summer, bringing drier nights, a higher sun and longer days. And along with the numberless infinitesimal natural things that announced the slow seasonal change, there was another thing, quite as impalpable and just as perceptible. Perhaps if Amar had not been made aware of it by the potter, he could have continued for a while not suspecting its presence, but now he wondered how it had been possible for him to go on as long as he had without noticing it. One might have said that it hung in the air with the particles of dust, and settled with them into the pores of the walls, so completely was it a part of the light and atmosphere of the great town lying sprawled there between its hills. But it expressed itself in the startled look over the shoulder that followed the tap on the back, in the silence that fell over a café when an unfamiliar figure appeared and sat down, in the anguished glances that darted from one pair of eyes to another when the family, squatting around the evening *tajine*, ceased chewing at the sound of a knock on the door. People went out less; at night the twisting lanes of the Medina were empty, and Friday afternoons, when there should have been many thousands of people, all in their best clothing, in the Djenane es Sebir—the men walking hand in hand or in noisy groups among the fountains and across the bridges between the islands, the women sitting in tiers on the steps or on the benches in their own reserved bamboo grove—there were only a few unkempt kif-smokers who sat staring vacantly in front of them while urchins scuffed up the dust as they kicked around an improvised football made of rags and string.

It was strange to see the city slowly withering, like some doomed plant. Each day it seemed that the process could go no further, that the point of extreme withdrawal from normal life had been reached, that an opening-up would now begin; but each new day people realized with a kind of awe that no such point was in sight.

They wanted their own Sultan back—that went without saying—and in general they had faith in the political party that had pledged to bring about his return. Also, a certain amount of intrigue and secrecy had never frightened them; the people of Fez were well known to be the most devious and clever Moslems in Morocco. But scheming in their own traditional fashion was one thing, and being caught between the diabolical French colonial secret police and the pitiless Istiqlal was another. They were not used to living in an *ambiance* of suspicion and fear quite so intense as the state of affairs their politicians were now asking them to accept as an everyday condition.

Slowly life was assuming a monstrous texture. Nothing was necessarily what it seemed; everything had become suspect— particularly that which was pleasant. If a man smiled, beware of him because he was surely a *chkam*, an informer for the French. If he plucked on an *oud* as he walked through the street he was being disrespectful to the memory of the exiled

Sultan. If he smoked a cigarette in public he was contributing to French revenue, and he risked a beating or a knifing later in some dark alley. The thousands of students from the Medersa Karouine and the College of Moulay Idriss went so far as to declare an unlimited period of national mourning, and took to walking morosely by themselves, muttering a few inaudible syllables to each other when they met.

For Amar it was difficult to accept this sudden transition. Why should there be no more drums beaten, no flutes played, in the market at Sidi Ali bou Ralem, through which he liked to pass on his way home from work? He knew it was necessary to drive the French out, but he had always imagined that this would be done gloriously, with thousands of men on horseback flashing their swords and calling upon Allah to aid them in their holy mission as they rode down the Boulevard Moulay Youssef toward the Ville Nouvelle. And the Sultan would get an army from the Germans or the Americans and return victorious to his throne in Rabat. It was hard to see any connection between the splendid war of liberation and all this whispering and frowning. For a long time he debated with himself whether to discuss his doubts with the potter. He was earning good wages now and was on excellent terms with his master. Since the night several weeks ago when they had gone to the café, he had attempted no further consolidation of intimate friendship, because he was not sure that he really liked Saïd. It seemed to him partly the man's fault that everything was going wrong in the town, and he could not help feeling that had he never known him, somehow his own life would be different now.

He decided finally to take the risk of speaking with him, but at the same time to make sure that his real question was masked with another.

One afternoon he and Saïd had locked themselves into the upper shed to have a cigarette together. (No one smoked any more save in the strictest secrecy, because the Istiqlal's decision to destroy the French government's tobacco monopoly provided not only for the burning of the warehouses and all shops that sold tobacco, but also for the enforcement by violence of the party's anti-smoking campaign. The commonest punishment for being caught smoking was to have your cheek slashed with a razor.) Being shut into this small space with his master, and sharing with him the delightful sensation of danger which their forbidden activity occasioned, gave Amar the impetus to speak. He turned to the older man and said nonchalantly: "What do you think of the story that the Istiqlal may sell out to the French?"

The potter almost choked on his smoke. "What?" he cried.

Amar invented swiftly. "I heard that the Resident, the *civil* they have there now, offered the big ones a hundred million francs to forget the whole thing. But I don't think they'll take it, do you?"

"What?" the man roared, again. Amar felt a thrill of excitement as he watched his reaction. It was as if until this moment he had never seen him save asleep, and now were seeing him awake for the first time.

"Who told you that?" he yelled. The intensity of his expression was so great that Amar, a little alarmed, decided to make the report easily discreditable.

"A boy I know."

"But who?" the man insisted.

"Ah, a crazy *derri*, a kid who goes to the College of Moulay Idriss. Moto, we call him. I don't even know his real name."

"Have you repeated this story to anyone else?" The potter was glaring at him with a frightening fixity. Amar felt uncomfortable.

"No," he said.

"It's lucky for you. That's a story invented by the French. Your friend was paid by them to spread it. He'll probably be killed soon."

Amar was incredulous; it showed on his face. The man tossed his cigarette away and put his two hands on the boy's shoulders. "You don't know anything," he declared. "You're only a *derri* yourself. But be careful and don't spread stories, about the Istiqlal, about the French, about politics at all, any kind of story, or you'll get us both thrown in the river. And when you go into the river you're already taken care of. *Fhemti?*" He made a quick horizontal movement with his forefinger across his throat, then returned his hand to Amar's shoulder and shook him slightly.

"What do you think's going on here, a game? Don't you know it's a war? Why do you think they killed Hamidou, that fat one, the *mokhazni*, last week? Do you think it was for fun? And the thirty-one others here in Fez, this month alone? Or did you never hear about them? All just a game? It's a war, boy, remember that. A war! And if you haven't got the sense to have faith in the Istiqlal, at least keep your mouth shut and don't repeat the lies you hear from *chkama*." He stopped a moment and looked at Amar incredulously. "I thought you were brighter than that. Where have you been all this time?"

Amar, used to a much more gentle and respectful attitude on the part of his employer, went back to his workroom feeling injured and resentful. He sensed that the potter would like to change him, to see him become otherwise than the way he was; his rancor was largely a continuation of what he had felt that night when they had sat in the café together, save that now there was an added grievance. The man had awakened his sense of guilt. Where, indeed, had he been all this time? Right there with everyone else, only he had been so intent on his own little childhood pleasures that he had let it all go by without paying any attention. He knew that bombings by the Istiqlal had been a daily occurrence in Casablanca for the past six months, but Casablanca was far away. He had also heard all about the riots and assassinations in Marrakech, but these things might almost as well have been happening in Tunis or Egypt, as far as their ability to awaken his interest was concerned. When the first bodies of Moslem policemen and *mokhaznia* had been found in his own city he had seen no connection whatever with the events in other places.

Fez was Fez, but it was also synonymous with Morocco to him and his friends, and they used the words interchangeably. Since crimes were always committed for personal reasons, each new murder had automatically been attributed in his mind to a new enemy with a new grudge. But now he saw how overwhelmingly right the potter was. Every man whose body had been found at dawn lying in an alley or at the foot of the ramparts, or floating in the river below the Recif bridge, beyond a doubt either had been working for the French or had inadvertently done something to anger the Istiqlal. Then that meant the Istiqlal was powerful, which did not at all coincide with his conception of it, nor with the picture the organization painted of itself: a purely defensive group of self-less martyrs who were willing to brave the brutality of the French in order to bring hope to their suffering countrymen.

This was a discrepancy, but he felt it was only a small part of a much greater and more mysterious discrepancy whose nature he could not for the moment discover. Had it been Frenchmen they were killing he would have understood and approved unquestioningly, but the idea of Moslems murdering Moslems—he found it difficult to accept. And there was no one he could talk with about it; his father would never say more than he had already said, that all politics was a lie and all men who engaged in it *jiffa*, carrion. But the French worked ceaselessly with their politics against the Moslems; was it not essential that the Moslems have their own defensive organization? He knew his father would say no, that everything is in the hands of Allah and must remain there, and ultimately he knew that this was true; but in the meantime, how could any young man merely sit back and wait for divine justice to take its course? It was asking the impossible.

Now since this new problem had begun to ferment in his head he no longer experienced the same pleasure when he worked. For him to have felt the accustomed happiness, the work would have had to continue to occupy his consciousness entirely, and that was no longer possible. He felt that he was merely waiting, making the hours pass forcibly by filling them with useless gestures. It was his first indication of what it is like to be truly aware of the passage of time; such awareness can exist only if something is going on in the mind which is not completely a reflection of what is going on immediately outside. Also, for the first time in his life he found himself lying awake at night, staring up into the darkness, turning the problem over and over in his head without ever arriving at any further understanding. Sometimes he would be still awake at three, when his father always rose, dressed, and went to the mosque, first to wash and then to pray, and only after he had heard him go out and the house was quiet once more would he fall suddenly asleep.

One such night, when his father had closed the door into the street and turned the key twice in the lock, he got up and stole out onto the terrace. Mustapha stood there in the gloom, leaning against the parapet, looking out over the silent town. Amar grunted to him; he was annoyed to see him there in what he considered his own private nocturnal vantage point. Mustapha grunted back.

"*Ah, khai, 'ch andek?*" said Amar. "Can't you sleep, either?"

Mustapha admitted that he could not. He sounded miserable.

It was not thinkable that he could confide in Mustapha; nevertheless there was an absurd note of hope in Amar's voice as he said: "Why not?"

Mustapha spat over the edge into the alley below, listening for the sound of its hitting before he answered. "My *mottoui's* empty. I didn't have any money to buy kif."

"Kif?" Amar had smoked on many occasions with friends, but a pipe of kif meant less to him than a cigarette.

"I always have a few pipes before I go to sleep."

This was something recent, Amar knew. On various occasions when they had had to share the same room there had been no kif, and Mustapha had slept perfectly well.

"*Ouallah?* Can't you sleep without it? Do you have to smoke it first?"

Now Mustapha's initial burst of confidence was over, and he was himself once more. "What are you doing out here, anyway?" he growled. "Go in to bed."

Reluctantly Amar obeyed; he had one more thing to think about as he fell asleep.

BOOK TWO

Sins Are Finished

You tell me you are going to Fez.
Now, if you say you are going to Fez,
That means you are not going.
But I happen to know that you are going to Fez.
Why have you lied to me, you who are my friend?
                                    —MOROCCAN SAYING

CHAPTER 6

RAMADAN, the month of interminable days without food, drink or cigarettes, had come and gone. The nights—which in other years had always been sheer pleasure, with the Medina brightly lighted, the shops kept open until early morning, the streets filled with men and boys sauntering happily back and forth through the town until it should be time to eat again—were dismal and joyless. It is true that the *rhaitas* sounded from the minarets as heretofore, the drums were beaten and the rams' horns blown to call sleepy people to the final meal, the same as always, but they caused no pleasure to those who heard them. The whole feeling of Ramadan, the pride that results from successful application of discipline, the victory of the spirit over the flesh, seemed to be missing; people observed the fast automatically, passively, without bothering to make the customary jokes about the clothing that was now too big, or the remarks about the number of days left before the feast that marked the end of the ordeal. It was even whispered around that many of the Istiqlal were not even observing Ramadan, that they could be seen any noon, brazenly eating in the restaurants of the Ville Nouvelle, but this was generally believed to be French propaganda. Then the rumor had begun to circulate that there would be no Aïd-es-Seghir, no festival when the fast was finished. This grew in volume until it had acquired sufficient stature to be able to be considered an established fact. And indeed, when the day arrived, instead of finding the streets full of men in new clothes—since that day out of all days in the year everyone was supposed to wear as many new garments as he could afford—early strollers discovered that hundreds of respectable citizens were already out, clad in their shabbiest *djellabas* and suits; and many who had not placed credence in the rumors had to hurry home through back streets to change, before they dared appear in public. A few new outfits had been ruined by deft razor slashes, but there had been no fights. And with this inglorious exit the month of Ramadan had made way for the month of Choual.

Now the heat had come in earnest. Amar rose at daybreak, worked until mid-morning, when he stretched out on a mat he had spread along the floor of his cave, and slept through the unbearable hours of the day until late afternoon; after eating he resumed his work and continued until dark. Then he would wander listlessly homeward through the breathless streets, sometimes stopping to listen for the sound of distant cries coming from another quarter of the town, the noise made by a mob, something to announce that the tension was taking a physical form. Everyone had this strange compulsion, to stand still a moment in the street and listen, because everyone was convinced that the tautness could not go on indefinitely. Some day something had to happen—that much was certain. What form the release might take could only be guessed at. And lying out on the roof at night under the stars—for it was too hot to sleep in the room on the mattress—he would strain his ears, trying to imagine he could hear, perhaps in the direction of Ed Douh or the Talâa, the faint sound of many voices calling. But it was always silence that was there, broken now and then by a sleepy rooster crowing on some distant housetop, or a cat wailing in the street below, or a truck far out on the Taza road, backfiring as it coasted down the hill toward the river.

There came an early morning, when even as he stepped out of his room onto the roof he knew that he was not going to work that day. The idea of doing something else, anything else, filled him with a great excitement. It seemed years that he had been going every day to the village of mud huts, greeting the potter, getting the key to the cave from him, climbing down the steps and going into the damp room where the *mamil* was, letting himself down onto the seat in the floor, and beginning to turn the wheel. Each day was like the day before; nothing changed, and the forms of the jars and vessels he made no longer interested him. None of it meant anything—not even the money, half of which he gave regularly to his father and some of which he saved, carrying it with him in a knotted handkerchief wherever he went. Each day he would untie the handkerchief and count the contents again, perhaps adding a little to them, and wondering what he could buy with what he now had. There was not yet enough to buy a pair of real shoes, but that was because he had had other expenses.

He was hungry, but the house was still. His father, back from the mosque, had returned to bed, and the family slept. Quickly he dressed and went downstairs. The pigeons were making their soft noises on the shelf by the well. In the street the air smelled like the beginning of the world. Most of the stalls were closed, and the few that had opened still harbored the dark air of night in their recesses. He bought a large disk of bread, six bananas, and a paper of dates, and went on his way along the Recif. Here the fish shops were all open and the powerful medicinal odor of fresh fish was like a knife in the air. Little by little the streets were filling, as people came out their doors. When he got to the newer houses of El Mokhfia there were trees here and there behind the walls where birds sang. He went out of the city through Bab Djedid and across the bridge. The dusty road led between two high walls of cane that leaned in all directions. When he reached the main road he stood a moment trying to decide which way to go. It was then that a soft voice called: "Amar!" from very near by. He turned his head and recognized Mohammed Lalami, a boy somewhat taller than he, and perhaps a year or two older. He was emerging from the thicket on the bank of the river, his hair dripping with water. They exchanged greetings.

"How's the water?" Amar asked.

"No good. Too low. You can't swim. It's all right if you just want to rub off the dirt." He kept shaking his head vigorously, like a dog, and sleeking his hair back, to get the water out of it.

"Why don't we go to Aïn Malqa and swim?" said Amar. Although they had been friendly in the past, it was several months since he had seen Mohammed, and he was curious to talk with him and see what was in his head.

"Ayayay!" said Mohammed. "And how do we get there?"

"We can get bicycles in the Ville Nouvelle."

"Hah! They're giving them away now?"

"*Ana n'khalleslik*," Amar said promptly. "It's on me. I've got some money."

Mohammed, showing mock embarrassment, accepted by not refusing, and they started out. When the city bus came by, on its way from Bab Fteuh to the Ville Nouvelle, they boarded it and stood on the back platform bracing themselves against the curves, and joking with a one-legged man in a military jacket who claimed to be a veteran of the war.

"What war?" Amar demanded, belligerently, because he was with Mohammed.

"The *war*," said the man. "Didn't you ever hear of the war?"

"I've heard of a lot of wars. The war of the Germans, the war of the Spanish and the *rojos*, the war of Indochine, the war of Abd-el-Krim."

"I don't know anything about all that," the man said impatiently. "I was in the war."

Mohammed laughed. "I think he means the war of Moulay Abdallah. He got into the wrong bordel and somebody caught him with the wrong girl. Is that all he cut off, just your leg? You're lucky, that's all I can tell you." The man joined the two boys in their laughter.

In the Ville Nouvelle the Frenchman who rented bicycles inspected their *cartes d'identité* with prolonged care before he let them ride off.

"The son of a whore," muttered Mohammed as they pedaled down the Avenue de France under the plane trees, "he didn't want to let us have them. The Frenchman who came in while we were waiting, you noticed he let him take the bicycle and didn't even ask to see his card."

"He was a friend of his," said Amar. It would have been a good opportunity to start a conversation about what was on his mind, but he did not feel like it yet; it was too early and he felt too happy.

Once they had left the town and there was no more shade, they realized how painfully hot the sun was. But it only made them more eager to get to Aïn Malqa. They were on the plain now; the fields of cracked earth and parched stubble rolled slowly by. There was a narrow channel on each side of the long straight road, filled with water that ran toward them. Twice they stopped and drank, bathing their faces in the cold water and letting it run down their chests. "A piece of bread?" asked Amar; he was dizzy with hunger. But Mohammed had already breakfasted and did not want anything, so he decided to wait until they got to where they were going.

About a kilometer before Aïn Malqa the road led into a eucalyptus grove and began to curve round and round, going downward toward the lake. Mohammed coasted ahead, and Amar, looking at the back of his neck and legs, found himself wondering whether he would be able to hold his own, should he ever get into a fight with him. As he was watching, he saw that Mohammed had gone a bit to the side of the road and was expecting him to come abreast of him, but he pressed a little more on the handbrake to remain behind. He decided that although Mohammed was taller, he himself was stronger and lither, and could probably even come out the winner. He had once seen a film about judo, and he liked to imagine that when the moment came he would know how to use some of its tricks successfully against his adversary. You moved your wrist suddenly, and the man fell powerless at your feet. Now he released the brake, allowing the bicycle to spurt ahead and catch up with the other. "It's cooler here," he said.

It was as if they were making a slow descent down one side of a gigantic funnel. The sloping ground beneath the trees was brown with a deep mass of the dried long leaves from other years; the light, a constantly shifting mixture of filtered sun and shade, had become gray. The grove was completely silent, save for the sound of the wheels on the fine gravel.

When they arrived at the bottom, they got down and walked, for the ground was soft. Through the willows ahead they could see the still surface of the tiny lake.

"Ah," said Mohammed with satisfaction. "This is paradise."

There was no one in sight. He propped his bicycle against a tree and before Amar had even arrived at the spot, he had stripped off his shirt and *serrouelle*. He had no underwear.

"You're going to swim like that?" said Amar, surprised. Since he had been working with the potter he had bought himself two pairs of cotton shorts, one of which he was now wearing under his trousers.

Mohammed was hopping up and down, first on one foot and then on the other, in his eagerness to get into the water. He laughed. "Just like this," he said.

"But suppose someone comes? Suppose women come, or some French?"

Mohammed was not concerned. "You can come and get my trousers for me."

It did not seem like a very practical arrangement to Amar, but there was nothing else to do; if Mohammed were going to swim at all he would have to swim naked. Together they ran out into the sheet of icy water, splashing ahead until it was up to their shoulders. Then they swam back and forth violently, exaggerating each gesture because of the cold. When they had used up their first spurt of energy they climbed onto a small concrete dam that had been built at one end of the lake, and rested in the sun on the dry part of the construction that was above the spillway. Here they told jokes and chuckled until the sun became so hot on their bodies that the dark world beneath the surface of the water again began to seem a desirable place to be. However, it appeared to have been tacitly agreed that they would wrestle to keep from being the first one to go in. They soon stopped, because they had both realized simultaneously that the drop from the dam's far side down onto the dry rocks below was a good deal too high to risk in case one of them slipped. Standing up, they caught their breath, and as if at a signal, dove into the water. By this time Amar had only one thing in his mind, and that was his breakfast. In the middle of a series of gasps, bubbles and flying water-drops he announced the fact to Mohammed; the shoreward trip became a race.

Amar arrived at the muddy bank first, loped under the willows to where his bicycle was, and unstrapped the parcel tied to the back of it. They took the food to a rock up the shore a bit and sat there in the sun eating. It was while they were sitting here that they became aware of the presence, among the rocks on the opposite shore, of another boy, who was carefully washing his clothes and spreading them on the rocks to dry. Shading his eyes with his hand, Mohammed watched for a while. "*Djibli*," he announced presently. It was of no interest to Amar whether the boy was from the mountains or the city, and he continued to munch on his dates and bread, looking out over the water, around at the small cactus-studded hills that ringed the lake basin, and occasionally up at the sky, where at one point a hawk came sailing into the range of his vision, plunged, glided, and moved off behind the high curved horizon.

"Where are you working now?" asked Mohammed. Amar told him. "How much?" Amar cut the true figure in half. "How is it? Good *maallem*?" Amar shrugged. The shrug and the grimace that went with it meant: Is anything good now? and the other understood and agreed. Mohammed, Amar knew, worked on and off in one or another of his father's shops. He settled back; his position on the rock was comfortable, and all he wanted was to recline there for a few minutes in the sun and enjoy the feeling of having eaten. But Mohammed was fidgety and kept shifting around and talking; Amar found himself wishing that he had come alone.

"Another big fire near Ras el Ma last night," said Mohammed. "Eighteen hectares."

"When the summer's over, there won't be any wheat left in Morocco," Amar remarked.

"Hope not."

"What'll we do for bread next winter?"

"There won't be any," said Mohammed flatly.

"And what'll we eat?"

"Leave that to the French. They'll send wheat from France."

Amar was not so sure. "Maybe," he said.

"Better if they don't. The trouble will start sooner if people are hungry."

It was easy for Mohammed to talk that way, because he was reasonably certain that he himself would not ever be in need of food. His father was a merchant, and probably had enough flour and oil and chickpeas stored in the house to last for two years if the need should arise. The middle-class and wealthy Fassi always had enormous private provisions to draw on in the event of emergency. To be able to weather a siege was part of the city's tradition; there had been several such situations even since the French occupation.

"Is that what the Istiqlal says?" Amar asked.

"What?" Mohammed was staring across at the country boy, who had finished his laundering and now was squatting naked atop a large rock, waiting for the garments to dry.

"That people should be hungry?"

"You can see that yourself, can't you? If people are living the same as always, with their bellies full of food, they'll just go on the same way. If they get hungry and unhappy enough, something happens."

"But who wants to be hungry and unhappy?" said Amar.

"Are you crazy?" Mohammed demanded. "Or don't you want to see the French get out?"

Amar had not intended to get caught this way on the wrong side of the conversation. "May the dogs burn in Hell," he said. That was one of the troubles with the Istiqlal, with all politics: you talked about people as though they were not really people, as though they were only things, numbers, animals, perhaps, but not really people.

"Have you been in the Zekak er Roumane this week?" Mohammed asked.

"No."

"When you go through, look up at the roofs. Some of the houses there have tons of rocks. *Ayayay!* You can see them. They have them piled so they look like walls, but they're all loose, ready to throw."

Amar felt his heart beat faster. "*Ouallah?*"

"Go and look," said Mohammed.

Amar was silent a moment. Then he said: "Something big's going to happen, right?"

"*B'd draa.* It's got to," Mohammed said casually.

Suddenly Amar remembered something he had been told about the Lalami family. Mohammed's father, having discovered that Mohammed's elder brother was a member of the Istiqlal, had put him out of the house, and the brother had gone off to Casablanca and been caught by the police. He was now in prison, awaiting trial along with some twenty other youths who had been apprehended at the same time for their activity in terrorist work, particularly in smuggling crates of hand grenades over the frontier from Spanish Morocco. He was something of a hero, because people said that he and another Fassi had been singled out by the French press as being particularly dastardly and brutal in certain of the murders they had committed. Then probably Mohammed knew a good deal more than he would say, and he could not even be asked whether the story about the brother were true or false; etiquette forbade it.

"What are you going to do when the day comes?" he finally said.

"What are *you* going to do?" countered Mohammed.

"*Ana?* I don't know."

Mohammed smiled pityingly. Amar looked at the shape of his mouth and felt a wave of dislike for him.

"I'll tell you what I'm going to do," Mohammed said firmly. "I'm going to do what I'm told."

Amar was impressed in spite of himself. "Then; you're a—"

Mohammed interrupted. "I'm not a member of anything. When the day comes everybody will take orders. *Majabekfina.*"

Amar tried not to think of the scene that would ensue were he to say what was on the tip of his tongue at the moment. This was: "Including rich men, like your father?" It was too much of an insult to utter, even in fun. Then for a moment, like a true Moslem, he contemplated the beauties of military discipline. There could be nothing, he reflected, to equal a government which was simply the honest enforcement, by means of the sword, of the laws of Islam. Perhaps the Istiqlal, if it were successful, could bring back that glorious era. But if the party wanted that, why had it never mentioned it in its propaganda? While the true Sultan had been in power the party had talked about the rich and the poor, and complained about not being able to print its newspaper the way it wanted to, and indirectly criticized the monarch for little things he had done and other little things he ought to have done. But ever since the French had taken the Sultan away, the party had spoken of nothing but bringing him back. If he returned, everything would be the same as it had been before, and the Istiqlal had certainly not been pleased with the state of affairs then.

"*Yah*, Mohammed," said Amar presently. "Why does the party want to see Sidi Mohammed Khamis back on the throne?"

Mohammed looked at him incredulously, and spat over the edge of the rock into the water. "*Enta m'douagh*," he said with disgust. "The Sultan will never come back, and the party doesn't want to see him back."

"But—"

"It's not the party's fault, is it, if all the people in Morocco are *hemir*, donkeys? If you can't understand that, then you'd better begin eating a different kind of hay yourself."

Mohammed's head was tilted far back, his eyes were closed; he looked very pleased with himself. Amar felt his own heart suddenly become pointed in his chest. It was fortunate, he thought, that Mohammed could not see his expression at that moment, as he looked at him, for he surely would not have liked it. Some of his anger was personal, but most of it was resentment at having been allowed a sudden unexpected glimpse of what was wrong with his native land, of what had made it possible for a few Nazarene swine to come in and rule over his countrymen. In a situation where there was everything to be gained by agreement and friendliness there could be nothing but suspicion, hostility and bickering. It was always that way; it would go on being that way. He sighed, and got to his feet.

Mohammed sat up and looked across the water. The country boy was wandering among the rocks over which he had spread his pieces of clothing, feeling them to see if they were dry. Mohammed went on looking, his eyes very narrow. Finally he glanced up at Amar.

"Let's swim across and have some fun with him," he suggested. And as Amar did not respond, he continued: "If you'll hold him for me I'll hold him for you."

The words that came out escaped from Amar's lips before he had formed them in his mind. "I'll hold your mother for you," he said viciously, without looking down at him.

Mohammed leapt to his feet. "*Kifach?*" he cried. "What was that?" His eyes were rolling; he looked like a maniac.

Now Amar looked at him, calmly, although his heart had more sharp points than ever, and he was breathing fast. "I said I'd hold your mother for you. But only if you'll hold your sister for me."

Mohammed could not believe his ears. And even when he reminded himself that Amar had said it twice, so that there could be no doubt, he still had no immediate reflex. There seemed to be no possible gesture to make: they were standing too close together, their faces and bodies almost touching. Accordingly Mohammed stepped backward, but lost his balance, and fell into the shallow water at the foot of the rocks. Amar sprang after him, conscious of being still in the air as Mohammed's back hit the surface of the water, and conscious, an instant later, of having landed more or less astride Mohammed's belly, which was only slightly submerged. Mohammed was bubbling and groaning, trying to lift his head above the water; the water was so shallow that he had hit the stones. Amar stood up; Mohammed staggered to his feet, covered with mud, and still wailing. Then with a savage cry he lunged at Amar, and the two fell together back into the water. This time it was Amar's turn to have his head pounded upon the bed of the lake. Pebbles, stiff, slippery leaves and rotten sticks were ground against his face; the world was a chaotic churning of air and water, light and darkness. He felt Mohammed's hard weight pushing him down—an elbow here, a knee there, a hand on his throat. He relaxed a second, then put all his effort into a rebound which partially dislodged Mohammed's grip. Twice he drove his fist up into Mohammed's belly as hard as he could, managing to lift his head above the water and breathe once. Drawing his leg back, he delivered a kick which reached a soft part of Mohammed's body. A second later they were both on their feet, each one conscious only of the eyes, nose and mouth of the other. Now it was merely a matter of perseverance. Amar's fist went well into the socket of Mohammed's left eye. "Son of gonorrhea!" Mohammed bellowed. Almost at the same instant Amar had the impression that he had run headlong into a wall of rocks. The pain was just below the bridge of his nose. He choked, knew it was blood running down his throat, recoiled and spat what he had collected of it into Mohammed's face, hitting him just below the nose. Then he rammed his head into Mohammed's stomach, knocking him backwards, and following through with another, better planned blow with the top of his head which sent Mohammed sprawling on the muddy ground of the shore. He leapt, sat once more astride him and pounded his face with all his might. At first Mohammed made powerful efforts to rise, then his resistence lessened, until eventually he was merely groaning. Still Amar did not stop. The blood that poured from his nose had run down his own body onto Mohammed's head and chest.

When he was positive that Mohammed was not merely playing a trick in order to lunge at him unexpectedly, he got unsteadily to his feet and gave the boy's head a terrific kick with his bare heel. He had to keep sniffing to keep the blood from coming out his nostrils; the thought came to him that he had better wash himself.

He squatted a few meters out from the shore and bathed hurriedly, constantly glancing back to be sure that Mohammed was still lying in the same position. The cold water seemed to be stanching the bleeding, and he continued to splash handfuls of it into his face, snuffing it up his nose. When he went back to dress he stopped and knelt down beside Mohammed. Seen this way, his features in repose, the downy tan skin of his face looking very soft where it showed among the smears of blood and dirt, he was not hateful. But what a difference there was between what Amar could see now of Mohammed and what Mohammed was like inside! It was a mystery. He had been going to bang his head against the ground, but now he no longer wanted to, because Mohammed was not there; it was a stranger lying naked before him. He got up and went to dress. Without looking back again, he led his bicycle out to the road, got on, and rode away. When the gradient got too steep he had to walk.

The eucalyptus grove seemed even more silent than it had a while ago. At the top, as he was about to emerge onto the long straight road across the plain, he imagined he heard a voice calling from below. It was hard to tell; what would Mohammed be calling him for? He stood still and listened.

Certainly someone was shouting in the grove, but far away.
The voice sounded hollow and distorted. And he still would
have said that it was saying his name, save that it was inconceivable under the circumstances that Mohammed should do
such a thing. Or perhaps not; perhaps he had no money and
was more frightened of facing the Frenchman in the bicycle
shop than he was ashamed of calling out to Amar. In any case,
Amar was not going to wait and see. Feeling perverse and
unhappy, he mounted the bicycle again and sped off under
the noonday sun, back toward the city.

CHAPTER 7

Like most of the boys and younger men who had been born
in Fez since the French had set up their rival Fez only a few
kilometers outside the walls, Amar had never formed the
habit of going to a mosque and praying. For all but the well-
to-do, life had become an anarchic, helter-skelter business,
with people leaving their families and going off to other cities
to work, or entering the army where they were sure to eat.
Since it is far more sinful to pray irregularly than not to pray
at all, they had merely abandoned the idea of attempting to
live like their elders, and trusted that in His all-embracing
wisdom Allah would understand and forgive. But often Amar
was not sure; perhaps the French had been sent as a test of
the Moslems' faith, like a plague or a famine, and Allah was
watching each man's heart closely, to see whether he was truly
keeping the faith. In that case, he told himself, how irate He
must be by this time, seeing into what evil ways His people
had fallen. There were moments when he felt very far from
Allah's grace, and this was one of them, as he pedaled at top
speed through the dried-up fields, with the huge sun above
his head sending down its deadly heat upon him.

He knew that Mohammed had been at fault, but only in a
way he could not help—only for being Mohammed; whereas
he himself was truly to blame for wanting Mohammed to be
something other than what it had been written that he must
be. He knew that no man could be changed by anyone but
Allah, yet he could not prevent himself from feeling resentful

that Mohammed had not turned out to be the possible friend he was looking for, in whom he could confide, who could understand him.

Djebel Zalagh was there ahead of him, behind the invisible Medina, looking not very imposing from this angle—merely a higher part of the long ridge that seemed to continue indefinitely from one side of the horizon to the other. And in the heat haze today, it had no color but gray, a dead color, like ashes. The Arab city of course could not be seen because it was built in what was really a wide crevasse below the plateau of the plain; its position made it warmer in the winter, because it was sheltered from the icy winds that swept across the plain, and cooler in summer, because the merciless rays of the sun did not strike it with quite so much force. Then, too, the river coursed in countless channels through the ravine on whose slopes the Medina was built, and that helped to cool the air. The inhabitants were fond of pointing out to one another, as well as to visitors, the insufferable climate of the Ville Nouvelle, for the French had built their city squarely in the plain, and as a consequence it was open to all the excesses of the intemperate Moroccan weather. Amar could not understand how anyone, even the French, could be so stupid as to waste so much money building so large a city when it could never be any good, since the land on which it was built was worthless in the beginning. He had been there in the winter and felt the blasts of bitterly cold wind that rushed through the wide streets; nowhere in the world, he was sure, could the air be more inhospitable and unsuited for human beings to live in. "It's poison," he would report when he returned to the Medina from a trip to the Ville Nouvelle. And in the summer, in spite of the trees they had planted along their avenues, the air was still and breathless, and at the end of each street you saw the dead plain there, baking in the terrible sunlight.

Far ahead he could see the white spots that were the new city's apartment houses; they looked like bird droppings piled in the immensity of the plain. "All that will disappear in one night," he thought, to reassure himself. It had been written that the works of the unbelievers were to be destroyed. But when? He wanted to see the flames soaring into the sky and hear the screams, he longed to walk through the ruins while they were still glowing, and feel the joy that comes from knowing that evil is punished in this world as well as in the next, that justice and truth must prevail on earth as well as hereafter.

This was the hour when no one was abroad; he had not met a soul since leaving Aïn Malqa. One would have said that the earth had been deserted by mankind and left to the insects, which screamed their song in praise of heat as he sped along—one endless shrill fierce note that rose on all sides, perpetually renewed.

His nose had started to bleed again, not so profusely as before, but dripping regularly every three or four pedals; it was beginning to feel as wide as his head, and painful. He stopped, knelt down by the channel of water beside the road, and bathed his face. The water was cold; he did not remember it as being that deliciously cold. He took a deep breath, bent far over, and submerged his head; the force of the current made the flesh of his cheeks vibrate. When he had finished his ablutions and immersions he felt refreshed and relaxed. Feeling that way made him want to rest a bit. He stood up and scanned the plain for a tree, but there was none, and so he went on. A few kilometers further ahead he caught sight of a mass of green a good distance away on his left. It looked like a small fruit orchard, and there was a lane leading across the fields toward the spot. He turned off. The lane was bumpy and hard to ride on; he managed however to make slow progress without having to get down. If he had had to walk, he would have considered that it was not worth his while to make the side trip. The orchard proved to be larger and more distant than he had thought. It lay in a slight depression; what he had seen from the road was only the tops of the trees, and as he approached they grew taller. Such a wealth of green meant the presence of underground springs. "Olives, pears, pomegranates, quinces, lemons . . ." he murmured as he entered the orchard.

At that moment he heard ahead of him the sound of an approaching motorcycle. The idea had not crossed his mind that the land might have a house on it, that the house might be inhabited, but now it did occur to him, the hypothesis made more unpleasant by his suspicion that the inhabitants were likely to be French, in which case they would either beat him, shoot him, or turn him over to the police, the last possibility being the most fearsome. It was a very bad thing to be caught on a Frenchman's farm at any time, but particularly now, when for the past few weeks hundreds of *domaines* had been raided by the Istiqlal and the crops set afire.

Quickly he leapt to the ground, and lifting the bicycle, began to run clumsily with it among the trees, looking for a place to hide. But it was a well-tended orchard, without bushes or undergrowth, and he could see that his project was absurd: he would have had to run very far in order not to be seen, if the cyclist happened to be looking his way as he passed. And the noise was already very loud, almost upon him. He turned, set the bicycle down, and walked slowly back. When the motorcycle appeared he had almost reached the lane. The rider, a small, plump man wearing goggles and a visored cap, was bouncing uncomfortably as the machine veered from one old rut to another, hitting clods of earth that were like rocks. As he came along, he was looking straight at Amar; he stopped, let the motor idle an instant, then turned it off. The sudden silence was astonishing, but then it proved not to be silence at all; there were the cicadas singing in the trees.

"*Msalkheir,*" the man said, carefully removing his cap, then his goggles, and never taking his eyes from Amar's face. "Where are you going, and where are you coming from?"

"Taking a walk," said Amar. "Looking for a tree to lie under." He had decided that the man was a Moslem (not because he spoke perfect Arabic, for some Frenchmen could do that, but because of his manner and the way in which he spoke), and that relieved his anxiety to such an extent that he found himself telling him the simple truth.

"Taking a walk with a bicycle?" The man laughed, not unpleasantly, but in a way that meant he did not believe a word Amar had said.

"Yes," Amar said. Then a drop of blood fell from his nose, and he realized that his shirt was decorated with red spatters of it.

"What's the matter?" asked the man. "What happened to your face? Did you fall off the bicycle?"

It was too late to do any lying now, Amar reflected ruefully. "No, I had a fight. With a friend," he added quickly, lest the man might suppose that his fight had been with one of the workmen or one of the guards on the property.

The man laughed again. He had a round face with large mild eyes, and he was growing bald. "A fight? And where's the friend? Lying dead somewhere in my orchard?" In the man's eyes Amar could distinguish nothing beyond an interested amusement.

"At Aïn Malqa."

Now the man frowned. "Excuse me, but I think you're crazy. Do you know which way Aïn Malqa is?"

Amar sniffed, to keep another drop of blood from coming out his nostril. "I haven't touched any of your fruit," he said aggrievedly. "If you want me to get out, tell me and I'll go."

The man's face assumed a pained expression. "*La, khoya, la,*" he said gently, as if he were soothing a skittish horse. "Where do you get such foolish ideas? Nothing of the sort." He started up his motor. "He's leaving," thought Amar hopefully. But then his heart sank as the man, one foot on the ground, made a U-turn with the machine and brought it to a halt facing back the way he had come.

Above the clamor of the motor, he shouted: "Get on your bicycle!" Amar obeyed. "Ride ahead of me!" He pointed, and Amar set off, going deeper into the orchard, the roar of the slowly moving cycle behind him.

They kept going. There seemed to be no reason for turning his head around, because the man kept at an unvarying distance behind him. Amar was miserable. It was absurd to think of trying to escape; such a thing was manifestly impossible. But he was frightened: he had never before met a Moslem like this, one whose intentions were so difficult to guess that he might as well have been a Nazarene.

The road curved suddenly to the right, and there was an old house, standing in a clearing of the orchard. A path led up to its door; it was bordered by high rose-bushes that had been left to grow wild. For the country the house was enormous, its long expanse of windowless wall being fully ten meters high. There were cracks zigzagging down from the top; plants and bushes had grown in them, but they were all dead save for a tiny gnarled fig tree whose gray trunk thrust itself through the wall like a fat snake. The roar of the motor behind him stopped, and Amar at last looked back with some nervousness. The man had jumped off his motorcycle and was letting down the standard that would keep it upright. He caught Amar's eye and smiled briefly. "Here we are," he said. "The door is open. Walk in."

Amar, however, went only as far as the doorway and stood waiting for his host, who, when he came, pushed him ahead impatiently. Inside the door was a long staircase which they climbed, coming out at the top onto a covered gallery which ran around three sides of a large square courtyard. In places the railing had rotted away, and several of the great beams overhead sagged precariously. In the air there was the humming of innumerable wasps.

"In here," said the man, and he pushed him gently through a doorway into a long room whose light came from a series of small windows placed above the roof of the gallery. At the far end, seated on the cushions that went the length of the room, were three boys, all of them older than Amar by two or three years. The man led him over to them and he shook hands with each one, noticing as he did so that they all greeted him in the European fashion, without bothering to lift their fingers to their lips after touching his hand. And for that matter, they were all dressed completely like Frenchmen, not only in the choice of the garments they wore, but in their way of wearing them. One boy had been reading a book and the other two had been talking while one of them rubbed the sleeve of a jacket with a cloth soaked in gasoline, but now they all politely ceased what they had been doing and leaned forward expectantly as Amar sat down.

The man seated himself on a high hassock facing them and held out his arm to indicate Amar as though he were a rare animal he had run to earth. "Look at this, will you?" he cried. "Here I was going to the city to meet Lahcen, who's waiting at this minute at the Renaissance, and I come across this gazelle in the orchard. Not in the lane, you understand, but coming from the mill."

"What mill?" interrupted Amar. The blood had finally managed to run down to his lip.

"Then he says," the man went on imperturbably, "he's coming from Aïn Malqa." The boy who had been reading laughed. "Oh, he has a bicycle," the man assured him. "It's completely possible. But what's happened to him? Look at him. He won't talk. He says he had a fight with a friend."

The boys needed no invitation; they were studying Amar carefully but without insolence. To avoid their scrutiny, which, however civil and unhostile, embarrassed him, Amar began to look nonchalantly around the strange room. He had never seen a room remotely like it. It was, by his standards, extremely disorderly, with no sign of the scrubbed neatness that characterized the rooms in his own house, although he could not have said that it was precisely dirty. There were great crooked piles of books and magazines everywhere on the floor, and fat leather hassocks that looked as though they had been tossed purposely here and there, with no attempt to place them in a row, the way they should have been placed. On three small coffee tables, also just put down anywhere in the middle of the room, there were huge baskets of peaches; the air was thick with their rich odor. The walls, which one would have expected to bear large gold-framed photographs of relatives—for this was obviously a rich man's house, even though it was old—were empty of any kind of picture or adornment, save for a very large map of Morocco printed in pastel colors; he had seen one like it when he peeked through a window at the Bureau du Contrôle Civil one day. And in whichever direction he looked he saw bowls of cigarette stubs and ashes, and there were ashes on the floor as well. He decided that this was a typical French room, and that the man wanted people to think he was French.

"This isn't the Tribunal," said the man, smiling at Amar. "Still, the fact is, I caught you on my property and I want to know what you were doing here. Do you blame me?"

Amar had never heard his own tongue spoken quite in this way before: the man used all the local expressions, but at the same time he interspersed his sentences with words which showed that he knew true Arabic, the language of the mosque and the *medersa*, the *imam* and the *aallem*. And the manner in which he mixed the two languages was so skillful that its result sounded almost like a new tongue, easy and sweet to the ear.

"No," said Amar. "But I told you the truth." He was uncomfortably aware that his own speech was hopelessly crude, the language of the street.

"Perhaps, but you didn't tell me enough. *Zid*. Go on. Tell us the whole story. Maybe you'd like a drink."

Amar was thirsty, and so he said: "Yes." One of the boys jumped up and stepped to the other end of the room, returning with a tall bottle and several very small glasses. Amar looked at the bottle suspiciously. The boy caught his glance, said: "Chartreuse," and poured a little out for him. Then he served the others. This was not at all what Amar wanted, but he sipped it and proceeded to recount the happenings of the day. When he got to the fight, the man stopped him. "*Essbar*," he said. "What were you fighting about?"

He wanted to say: "I don't know," for he did not know how to put into words the real reason why he had felt like proffering the insult to Mohammed. Certainly it was not the suggestion Mohammed had made; there was nothing unusual in that, nor would there have been anything extraordinary in his accepting it. It had more to do with Mohammed's smug sureness of being right—he was simply the kind of person you feel a need of hitting. But he knew he could scarcely hope to make his listeners understand that, without going into a long digression which would lead them into politics, and even if he had been mentally equipped to engage in such a discussion with them, the thing was unthinkable. He did not even know where his audience's sympathies lay; they could easily all be with the French.

"I didn't like him," said Amar. "He was the kind of *ouild* that needs a good punch now and then."

"I see," the man said seriously, turning his head and taking in the three boys with a glance which seemed to be warning them not to laugh. "So you punched him. *Zid*."

Amar was a little more relaxed now; he felt that the man believed him, and this set him enough at his ease so that he could remember all the details of the fight, which he told minutely. The man was frankly amused now—Amar could see it in his eyes—but he remained sitting solemnly listening while Amar brought the story up to the moment when he had heard a motorcycle coming through the orchard and had tried vainly to escape among the trees, only to turn back and he discovered before he had reached the lane. The man reached over and clapped him on the shoulder, laughing. "Very good, very good," he said. "I think we can take that story just as it comes. Now I've got to go to the city for a little while, but I'll be back. You stay here, and the house is yours. If you want anything, just ask for it."

He got up; Amar automatically jumped to his feet. He had heard and understood the man's invitation, but he considered it mere urbane politeness. Besides, he wanted to be off; the house and the boys and his host were somehow all unexplained, like a dream, and he was overwhelmed by uneasiness. He looked up and saw almost wistfully the patches of blue sky through the windows at the top of the wall.

"Sit down," the man said. This was certainly a command, and he obeyed. The man stepped lightly to the door and disappeared. An instant later the motorcycle roared, and then its sound slowly became fainter.

CHAPTER 8

As if it were part of a ritual, everyone sat perfectly quiet until the hum of the motor had died away completely, and it was no longer possible for them to hear anything, even by listening with great attention. Then the boy who had been reading turned to Amar and said: "Have some peaches. There are thousands of them."

Amar rubbed his hand across his face. "I'm very thirsty." He looked at his hand and saw dried blood and fresh blood, and the day suddenly seemed endless. "I ought to go," he said tentatively.

The three immediately murmured polite protests. He could see that they would prevent him from leaving, perhaps even by force if they had to. "I ought to go home," he said again. "My nose—"

The boy who had spoken got up and stood looking down

at him. "Look," he said. "You lie down here and I'll take
care of you." He went to the doorway and called: "*Yah,
Mahmoud!*" An elderly man in a slightly soiled white *gandoura* appeared presently; the boy stepped out onto the
gallery and conferred briefly with him. Then he returned,
knelt in front of Amar, and began to remove his sandals. Embarrassed, Amar pushed his hands away and took them off by
himself. "Now lie down here," the boy commanded, indicating the place where he had been sitting. The other two
watched while he helped Amar to make himself comfortable,
stuffing pillows under his head, Amar feebly protesting the
while, ashamed at having such a fuss made over him. But it felt
good to be stretched out. He was very tired. No one spoke
until the servant came in bearing a tray, which he set down on
the floor beside the cushion where Amar lay. Raising himself
on one elbow, Amar drank the glass of cold water. There were
storks on the glass, embossed in bright red outline.

"Perhaps I can come back and visit your father some other
day," he began. He was certain the man was not the father of
any one of them, but he wanted to hear what they would
reply. There was silence for a moment; it was clear that the
others were not sure what they ought to say.

"Moulay Ali will be back very soon," said the boy who had
taken charge of him; apparently he was to be spokesman. "Lie
down. I'm going to put some *filfil* on your face." Amar lay
back. "Close your eyes, tight." This was unnecessary advice,
as Amar did not intend to let any of the red pepper get into
his eyes, whatever happened. The boy gently smeared the
paste over his forehead and across the bridge of his nose.
"You ought to go to a doctor," he said, when he had finished.
"I think your nose is broken."

Mektoub, thought Amar, mentally shrugging. He had no
desire to consult a doctor; he was going to keep his money
for shoes.

The boy sat down somewhere further along on the cushion, beyond the other two, who Amar felt were merely sitting
there watching him. It was very silent in the room; now and
then there was the sound of the page of a magazine being
turned, or one of them cleared his throat. He could hear the
steady hum of the wasps on the gallery, and beyond, an occa-

sional cock crowing, out in the afternoon sunlight. He had been pressing his eyes very tightly shut, but slowly the facial muscles relaxed and he felt himself in danger of falling asleep. That could certainly not be done here in this house, with strangers looking at him; the idea of it terrified him. He decided to talk, about anything at all, so long as he remained awake. It was imperative that he open his mouth and say something. It seemed to him that he was sitting up, having a long, serious discussion with the three boys, and they were listening and agreeing with him. And somewhere, very far away, there was the booming of thunder in the sky. Suddenly someone coughed, and he realized that he was not sitting up at all; that meant that he had very nearly fallen asleep.

"Tell me," he said aloud. "Did Moulay Ali really think I had come to set fire to his place?"

Unexpectedly all three boys laughed. "You'd better ask him about that," said the one who had helped him. "How do I know what he thought? He'll be here in a minute."

"Do you all live in Fez?" It did not matter what the others thought of his foolish questions, if only he could keep from falling asleep.

"They do. I live in Meknès."

"Are you staying here now?"

"*Sa'a, sa'a,* sometimes I come and stay a few days. Moulay Ali is a great friend. I've learned more from him than from any *aallem.*" The other two murmured in agreement.

This seemed a strange statement to make. "But what does he teach you?"

"Everything," the other said, almost fervently.

"I want to sit up," said Amar. "Could you wipe off the *filfil,* please?"

"No, no. Lie still. Moulay Ali will be coming. I want him to see that I've taken care of you."

Amar had succeeded in rousing himself sufficiently so as to be no longer afraid of sleeping. Again the thunder rolled in some far-off part of the world. He lay still. Fairly soon there was the sound of the motorcycle in the distance, coming along the road, turning into the lane, arriving in the orchard among the trees, and finally, in a blast of noise, drawing to a stop before the house. In the stairway there were voices, and

Moulay Ali entered the room, accompanied by another man with an extraordinarily resonant, deep voice. "This is Lahcen," said Moulay Ali. The three boys acknowledged the introduction. "Aha! I see our friend is asleep! What's that you've smeared over his face? *Filfil?*"

"I'm not asleep," said Amar. He would have liked not to be obliged to take part in the conversation, but obviously he could not merely lie there saying nothing.

"He'd better sit up," said Moulay Ali. The boy from Meknès held Amar's head and began to scrape the dried paste from his forehead and eyebrows with a knife. When he had cleaned it all off, he bathed the places with a damp cloth. Lahcen and Moulay Ali were holding a conversation which made no sense whatever.

"This?" "Yes, nine." "I have that." "I thought you said eleven." "No! Not that. This, this!" "Oh, yes." "This one, five." "*Ouakha.*" "Now, this, I was telling you about. You see, you can't be sure." "I'm sure." "It's impossible to be sure. Take my word for it." "All right, leave it open." "Put six plus and leave it." "And what about . . . ?" "We'll get to that later. Have a peach. The best in the Saïs."

When he thought the area around his eyes was dry, Amar opened them and sat up. "Ah, there he is!" cried Moulay Ali. "*Kif enta?* Better now?"

In the center of the room a tall man with a soft gray *tarbouche* on his head was bending over, eating a peach and trying to keep it from dripping onto his clothes. Eventually he straightened, pulled out a handkerchief and wiped his mouth and hands. Then at Moulay Ali's request he stepped over and greeted Amar. The iris and pupil of his left eye were completely white, like a milky marble. Straightway Amar guessed that he was not of the same social condition as the three boys and his host. Assuredly he had not had the same education: his language was scarcely more distinguished than Amar's. So this is Lahcen, he thought, and he could not imagine why Moulay Ali had rushed into the Ville Nouvelle to fetch him.

"We'll leave our buying and selling until later," Moulay Ali remarked pointedly, "and get Mahmoud to make us some tea." He went to the door and called the servant.

Amar had been dreading the mention of tea; it meant that

he could not leave until he had drunk at least three glasses with his host. He sat back disconsolately and looked at Lahcen, who was picking his nose. The *tarbouche* on his head was the only article of Moslem clothing in the entire room, and it looked strangely out of place, both in its surroundings and on that bullet-shaped head. It was the sort of hat you would expect to see on an elderly, slightly eccentric gentleman of means, who might be taking his grandchildren out for a Friday stroll.

"Sit down," said Moulay Ali to his new guest. "Talk to our friend here." To one of the boys he said: "Chemsi, come over here. I want to show you something." Lahcen smiled at Amar and sat down.

"I hear you went swimming at Aïn Malqa today," he said. "How's the water these days? Still cold?"

"Very cold."

"Been to Sidi Harazem lately?"

"No. I work. It's too far."

"Yes. It's far." He was silent a moment. Then he said: "You work in the Ville Nouvelle?"

"No, at Bab Fteuh."

"That's my quarter."

Amar did not recall ever having seen him, but he said: "Ah."

"Have you ever been to Dar el Beida?" Lahcen asked him. Amar said he had not. "That's a place to swim. At the beach, the sea. Nothing better."

"French women by the million," Amar said.

Lahcen laughed. "By the million."

They talked on for a time about Casablanca, Amar wondering anxiously all the while how soon the daylight would begin to fade. It seemed to him that he had been shut into this room for a week. But since tea was coming, he could not even mention the fact that he wanted to leave.

"It says: *dans la région de Bou Anane*," Moulay Ali was saying. "Does that mean anything to you?"

Chemsi hesitated, and said it did not.

Moulay Ali snorted. "It does to Ahmed Slaoui."

"Oh!" exclaimed Chemsi.

Moulay Ali nodded his head slowly up and down, looking slyly at Chemsi. "Do you see what I mean?" he asked him at

length. "Use the whole article word for word, put Maroc-
Presse and the date, and then add what you know about the
région de Bou Anane."

"Poor Slaoui," said Chemsi.

"He may not be there now," Moulay Ali reminded him.

Mahmoud arrived carrying an enormous copper tray, with
a silver teapot and glasses. The two returned from the corner
where they had been talking, and Moulay Ali tossed the
folded newspaper he had been holding in his hand to the two
other boys. He sat down and began to fill the glasses. The tea
bubbled and steamed, and the odor of the mint came up.

"What's your name?" he said suddenly to Amar.

Amar told him. Moulay Ali raised his eyebrows. "Fassi?" he
asked.

"My family has always lived in Fez," Amar answered
proudly; he was aware that the boys were scrutinizing him
afresh. Perhaps they had thought he was a *berrani*, an
outsider.

"What *haouma*?" Moulay Ali was passing out the glasses of
tea.

"Keddane, below the Djemaa Andaluz."

"Yes, yes."

Amar was waiting for his host to say: "*Bismillah,*" before he
tasted his tea, but he said nothing at all. Nor did anyone else.
Usually Amar murmured his prayer under his breath, so that
it was scarcely audible, but this time, seeing that the others all
had been so remiss, he said it in a normal voice. Lahcen
turned his head to look at him.

The boy who was reading the newspaper put it down
slowly and took his glass. There was consternation on his face.
"Bubonic plague," he said. "That's a terrible disease. You
burst."

"*Eioua!*" agreed Moulay Ali, as if he were saying: "I told
you."

Lahcen took a noisy sip of tea, licked his lips, said:
"Laghzaoui—I mean, Lazraqi says Algeria's full of it now."

"It must have come across the border," began the boy.

"Rumors!" snapped Moulay Ali, looking fixedly at Chemsi.
"We don't know anything about Algeria." Chemsi nodded his
head in agreement.

They went on discussing remote towns in the south of the country, "as though they were important places," thought Amar. It was perfectly clear to him that the conversation was being made around a central point which they all saw but were taking pains that he should not see. After he had drunk his third glass of tea, he stood up. "It's very late," he said.

"Of course, you want to go," said Moulay Ali, smiling. "Very well. But don't forget us. Come back some day and we'll have a party, with music. Now you know where the house is."

Lahcen grinned. "Our friend Moulay Ali plays the flute and the violin."

"And if I'm not wrong our friend Lahcen plays the liter bottle," added Moulay Ali archly. The boys laughed. "Especially Aït Souala rosé," he added.

"But he's very good on the flute," went on Lahcen. "Play a little," he urged.

Moulay Ali shrugged. "Amar wants to go. Another day. And Chemsi'll bring his *oud* from Meknès." Chemsi protested shyly that he played badly. "What do you play?" Moulay Ali asked Amar, taking his hand without rising from the hassock.

Amar was embarrassed. "The *lirah*, a little."

"*Baz!* That's perfect! You can take my place when I get tired. Good-bye. Take care of your war scars." His face grew serious. "And don't wander into any more private roads, do you understand? Suppose I hadn't been me? Suppose I had been Monsieur Durand or Monsieur Blanchet? *Eioua!* You wouldn't be going home on your bicycle now, would he?" He turned to the boys for corroboration. They smiled. Lahcen said: "*Ay!*" with great feeling.

Amar stood there, searching in his head for something to say that would show them he was not a fool, not a child, that he was aware that all their words had an inner core of meaning which they had kept hidden from him. He decided that the best thing was to be mysterious himself, to let them think that perhaps he had understood them in spite of all their precautions, but not in such a way that they might imagine he bore any resentment toward them for playing what was, after all, no more than a rather childish game.

"Thank you for your trust in me," he said gravely to Moulay Ali.

It had its effect; he saw that in Moulay Ali's eyes, although Moulay Ali did not move a muscle. Perhaps precisely because he did not move; he seemed to freeze for a fraction of a second, eyes and all. And so did everyone else, if only for that short instant. But before the instant was over, Amar had pushed ahead, taking momentary command. He held out his hand and said: "Good-bye," and then moved on to the three boys, one by one, and finally Lahcen. And bowing again briefly to his host, he turned and walked to the door. As far as he could tell, no one said anything as he went down the stairs.

He was convinced that before he could get well away from the house someone would call him back; it seemed too good to be true that he should at last be out in the open again. Quickly he hopped on the bicycle and in a great burst of energy began pedaling along the bumpy lane. The sun was still fairly high in the sky; it was not quite so late as he had thought. The light in the orchard was golden; the shadows of the tree trunks made straight black stripes along the earth. Cicadas still whirred their song in the branches above his head, but the sound was less intense than it had been at noon. He continued to ride as hard as he was able, to get sooner onto the main road. Once out there, he felt, he could refuse to return to the house if Moulay Ali should come roaring after him on the motorcycle. He was sweating and panting by the time he reached the road, but then there were no more ruts and clods and bumps, and he relaxed into an easy, steady speed. The hundred-meter slabs sped past; he began to feel happy again. There were shadows in the back of his mind, questions that needed to be answered, matters that had to be faced, and they were imminent, all around him, but for the moment the strength of the present was great enough to keep them all there at bay, backed up against the wall of eventuality.

CHAPTER 9

The sun was rapidly retiring from its vague position in the bowl of the sky overhead, toward the definite remotenesses of the Djebel Zerhoun; the dark mass of peaks at the extremity of the plain had been brought nearer by the intense light behind them. Somewhere there in the heart of the mountains nestled the holy city of Moulay Idriss, built by his own family many centuries ago when Haroun er Rachid was still alive. He knew how it looked from the postcards he had seen—draped like a white cloth over its escarpments, and surrounded by whole forests of giant olive trees, forests that stretched in all directions through the valleys and up the slopes. He was whistling as he passed the first small farms that were scattered at the outskirts of the town. The odious little dogs that French people seemed to like so much rushed out at him as he rode by, barking furiously. He pretended they were Frenchmen, tried to run them down, and called out: "*Bon jour, monsieur!*" to them when he had gone by.

The daytime air with its hot smell had made room for the new evening air that was rolling down from the heights ahead. The difference between them was the difference there is between a boulder and a flock of birds flying, or, he thought, between being asleep and being awake. "Perhaps I've been asleep all day," he said to himself as a joke. No dream could have been more senseless than his day had been; that was certain. But because the events of the day had really taken place, he was troubled by their possible meaning in the pattern of his destiny. Why had Allah seen fit to make him meet Mohammed Lalami as he came up from his bath in the river, and why had He directed his bicycle to the hidden house of Moulay Ali in the fruit orchard? Since nothing in all existence could ever be counted as accidental, it had to mean that his life was fated to be linked with Mohammed's and Moulay Ali's, and this he did not want at all. Perhaps by saying the proper prayers he could persuade Allah to direct the path of his life in such a way that he could miss seeing them again, all of them, including Lahcen and the three boys. It was always the entrance of other people into his life that made it difficult. But then the happy thought occurred to him that it was possible Allah had given him his secret strength precisely in order to enable him to protect himself in these entanglements with other people, which were, after all, inevitable. If he could learn to trust it, use it when it was needed, was it not likely that he could win out over them? He pondered the question. Surely that was what Allah had meant by making Amar Amar, by giving him the gift of knowing what was in the hearts of other men. The problem was to make this gift strong and absolutely sure, as he had done to his body during his childhood, while the other boys were sitting in classrooms; he had done that not by imposing any conscious discipline, for he had no conception of discipline (save that he had watched athletes training, and felt sorry for them) but by a process opposed to discipline—by simply allowing his body to express itself, to take complete command, and develop itself as it wished.

He pedaled past the suburban villas with their plots of green lawn, through small streets that were short cuts to the side of town where he was going. The last open space before the beginning of the city proper was the botanical garden. Part of the land was a nursery enclosed by a fence of barbed wire; the rest was an uncultivated wilderness veined with well-trodden paths. If you wandered quietly in here at twilight you sometimes came upon surprising scenes, for it was the only place near the town where the French boys and girls could find any degree of privacy. On several occasions Amar had discovered couples lying tightly embraced in the bushes, oblivious of his passage, or merely indifferent to it. What puzzled him was why they did not do their kissing and love-making in the brothels. The girls obviously worked as prostitutes, otherwise they would not be out walking with the boys. Why then did they leave the brothels and carry on their work in the open air, like animals? Was it that all the rooms were full at the moment, or that they were doing this without the knowledge of the *batrona*, so that they could keep all the money themselves and not give her any? Or were they merely evil, vicious creatures that had lost all shame, whose hearts Allah in His wrath had changed to the hearts of dogs? This was perhaps the facet of Nazarene life which shocked him most profoundly, but still, it amused him to walk silently along the paths until he came upon a couple, and then to cough loudly as he passed near them.

When he arrived opposite the entrance to the garden, he turned in and bumped along the path for a while, until it became so rough that he had to get down and walk. As he jumped off the bicycle there was an ear-splitting clap of thunder overhead; he felt the sound in the earth under his feet. Fearfully he looked up and saw that a great, black curtain had been stealing across the sky from the south, following him as he rode; and a huge cloud that looked like a fist was thrusting itself outward from the blackness behind it into the clear sky above.

There was no point in going back to the road: the rain would be arriving any second. Its smell was already in the air. He looked up again. The strange fat cloud was billowing like smoke. Ahead there were several greenhouses, and if no Frenchman were around one of these would be his shelter. Any Moslem who might be working on the grounds would surely let him go in; it was unthinkable to refuse a person protection from a storm. He tried to go faster, but with the bicycle it was impossible. At last he got to the opening in the wire fence. Beside it there was a sign written in both Arabic and French characters; this, he supposed, was a warning to people that it was forbidden to enter. But which was worse, he asked himself, an angry man or the wrathful spirits in the air at the moment? There was no doubt as to the answer. One could go mad just from being brushed against by a storm demon, and the air was swarming with them. When the first drops fell he leaned the bicycle against a tree and ran swiftly ahead to the door of the nearest greenhouse. It was not locked. He stepped inside: the sweet vegetable odor was very strong in the heavy air, and the fading light that came through the dusty panes of glass seemed old, as though it had been in here for many years. He closed the door and stood against it looking out. Some distance down the path he could see the rear wheel of the bicycle sticking out from behind a bush. He watched it fixedly. It would be a terrible thing for him if anyone should make off with the bicycle, but when the rain began to pour down so heavily that he could no longer see anything but a rapidly darkening blur beyond the streaming windowpanes, he knew that no matter what happened he would not go out there now.

The inside of the greenhouse had grown almost as dark as night. It seemed to him that he felt the damp hot breath of the silent plants at the back of his neck, and he could not bring himself to turn his head, or even to move his eyes in one direction or the other. The thunder crashed and the rain fell against the thousand panes of glass over his head. Soon the water was running through and splattering on the floor somewhere back there in the dark. He pressed his forehead against the cold glass and waited. Perhaps there had been someone in the greenhouse when he came in, hidden behind the plants—a Frenchman with a pistol. Even now he might have it pointed at him, at any moment he might speak, and when Amar turned around or opened the door to escape he would shoot. The great ambition of every Frenchman in Morocco was to kill as many Moslems as possible. But a moment later it occurred to him that it was likely that Allah was protecting him today with His blessing. First there had been his victory over Mohammed, then his adventure with Moulay Ali, which had begun ominously but terminated well, and now his steps had been directed into the park so that he might find shelter from the rain. If he had continued to ride, he would have been caught in the storm. Why should he now lack faith in Allah's willingness to continue to hold him in His favor at least until the end of the day? "*Hamdoul'lah,*" he whispered.

And an instant later the rain's wide voice was still; it merely ceased falling, all at once, and there was nothing but the diminishing sound of its dripping from the trees.

Without looking around even now, he opened the door and ran down the path. It was almost completely dark, but he could distinguish the wheel of the bicycle ahead. He led the vehicle quickly to the outer part of the garden, and continued to the road. Then he hopped on, wet seat and all, and went triumphantly toward the town.

It was a pleasure to ride along the smooth-surfaced streets in the evening. The lights in the shops were doubly bright with their reflections shining from the wet pavements; the sidewalks were crowded with French people and Jews, most of them adolescents, who joked with each other as they met and passed. It was the hour when everyone who was able came out and walked up and down the Boulevard Poeymirau, covering only the few blocks between the Avenue de France and the Café de la Renaissance. At last it was cooler in the street than inside the houses and apartments.

Amar knew he had run up an enormous bill for the rental of his bicycle, for he had added the hours in his head, but still he was loath to give it up; only the fear that the shop might close, so that he would have to pay an extra twelve hours for the night, forced him now to the side street where the Frenchman stood smoking outside the door of his shop. He got down and led the bicycle across the sidewalk. The man looked at him suspiciously, took it from him and without saying anything began to inspect it with great care. Not being able to find any broken or missing parts, he wheeled it inside, and with a piece of chalk on a blackboard calculated the sum that Amar owed him. It was even more than he had expected. In his chagrin at hearing the figure, he forgot how he had arrived at his own estimate, so that he could not discover where the discrepancy lay. It was clear to him that the man was cheating him, but it was worth paying the difference to avoid an argument which could have got him nowhere but the *commissariat de police*. He was curious to know whether Mohammed had come back with the other bicycle, and, if he had, how he had paid for it, but even had he known how to speak the man's language, he would have thought it wiser to be silent. He untied his handkerchief, counted out the money and gave it to the man; the latter was watching him with an infuriating sneer which was only partly covered by the cloud of smoke that rose from the cigarette hanging at the corner of his mouth. It was only after he had left the shop and was walking along under the trees that he noticed how fast his heart was beating, and from that fact realized how badly he had wanted to hit the Frenchman. He smiled to himself; he had escaped from that trap, at least. The Ville Nouvelle was a succession of such traps. If you kept out of one you were likely to fall into another. It was not for nothing that the biggest and most imposing building on the Boulevard Poeymirau was the police station, or that outside it there was always a long line of jeeps and radio patrol cars that stretched around the block. That was why it was best not to come here at all. If you minded your own business in the Medina you were reasonably safe, but here, no matter what you did, you could suddenly be informed that it was forbidden, which meant that you disappeared for a month or two, and worked on the roads or in a quarry somewhere during that time. And if this had happened to you once, it was that much easier for it to happen a second time; your dossier always worked against you.

The nearest bus stop was on the corner opposite the police station. As he waited in line he observed with interest the abnormal activity in front of the main entrance. There was a great amount of coming and going of men both in and out of uniform. What was missing, however, was the usual contingent of Arab youths who were generally to be seen outside the door; these were petty (that is, non-political) informers and errand-runners, procurers of black-market cigarettes and other commodities for the police. He wondered what had happened to them.

When his bus finally came, he stood on its back platform. The next stop was at the corner of the Avenue de France and the Boulevard du Quatrième Tirailleurs. From here you could see some of the lights of the Medina down in the valley. He watched the people crowding onto the bus: a Berber in a saffron-colored turban who acted as though he had never seen a bus before, a very fat Jewish woman with two small girls, all of them speaking Spanish rather than Arabic (the more presumptuous dwellers of the Mellah conversed in this archaic tongue; it was frowned upon, considered almost seditious, by the Moslems), an Arab woman wearing a *haik*, in whom Amar thought he discerned a prostitute from the *quartier réservé*, and several French policemen, two of whom had to hang to the railing outside because there was no possible way for them to squeeze themselves further. He expected the vehicle to continue straight ahead to the Taza road and go down the hill; instead it swung to the left and followed the Boulevard Moulay Youssef. "*Ah, khaï*, where does this bus go?" he asked of a workman covered with whitewash who was standing pressed against him. "The Mellah," said the man. "But the last one went to the Mellah," Amar protested. "This one should be going to Bab Fteuh." The man turned his head one way and then the other. Amar saw his face briefly in the light of a passing street lamp; he would have said it bore an expression of fright. "*Skout*," the workman said in a low voice. "There aren't any buses going to Bab Fteuh. Don't talk."

CHAPTER 10

Amar hesitated. If what the man said were true, then it was useless to get out and walk back to the corner to wait for the right one. It would be quicker to go on to the Place du Commerce outside the Mellah and catch a bus going to Bou Jeloud than to walk all the way to Bab Fteuh, and besides, the Taza road was outside the walls in the darkness of the country. It was not at all the kind of walk that he relished making: there were far too many trees and streams along the way, places where evil spirits, *djenoun* and *affarit* abounded, not to speak of Moslem bandits and French police. It was better to continue this way, even though he had to walk the length of the Medina afterward.

Before the bus roared into the Place du Commerce he realized that something quite extraordinary was going on there. At first it was hard to tell just what: there was a great amount of light, but it was light which was constantly changing and moving, so that the trees and the buildings appeared to be in a state of flux. And the noise was unidentifiable: giant raspings that seemed to be being dropped down into the square from the balconies—mass upon mass of meaningless, buzzing sounds that reverberated between the walls. As the bus moved through the open space that swarmed with people, the sound shifted, and he could hear that there were other focal points of wild racket; each loudspeaker was giving forth different noises, and the mechanisms were such that the noises had long ago ceased to bear any resemblance to what they originally had been intended to sound like. In front of the Ciné Apollon a samba might easily have been pieces of scrap iron falling from a great height onto a metal floor. In the corner between the public latrines and the subcommissariat of police, the voice of a young man describing a set of china that could be won in a lottery sounded like an express train crossing a trestle. The young man may have been conscious of this, for now and then he limited his message to the simple, rapid reiteration of the one word *tombola*. A candy stand whose machine was playing an Egyptian selection might have been a range for machine-gun practice, and a soft-drink bar whose concessionaire had chosen a pile of Salim Hilali records was making a series of sounds that would not have been unusual coming from a particularly brutal abattoir. For this was a *fechta*, a traveling fair, each of whose booths boasted a separate gramophone and loudspeaker, and some were lucky enough to be furnished with microphone as well. The fair had come from Algeria, where its equipment had been bought second-hand, the purchaser rightly assuming that the uncritical audience of Morocco and the border towns of the Algerian desert, where it was destined to travel, would not hold it against him if paint were chipped and metal rusted and paneling patched. The important thing was to make it as loud and as bright as possible. Both these things had been done; where the lights were concerned, the impresario had managed even more than brightness. He had arranged it so that all the bulbs massed on the façades of the booths and strung through the branches of the trees continually flashed on and off, slowly, regularly, in great groups that worked independently of each other; the studied purpose of this was to induce first vertigo, and then euphoria.

Amar got out of the bus, surrendered his ticket to the inspector, and stood still for a moment, letting the chaos soak in. Then, already a little exalted, he moved toward a stand where some youths were pounding a platform with an enormous mallet. At each crash a vertical red bar shot up to what was assumed to be a height corresponding to the force of the blow, and a stout man with black teeth unenthusiastically pushed the bar back down to zero, crying either: "*Magnifique!*" or "*Allez, messieurs! Voyons, on est des enfants?*"

Amar wandered on to where a great crowd was gathered around two legionnaires shooting at a long procession of white cardboard ducks that moved jerkily in front of a panorama of palm trees and minarets. This place stood in the crossfire of two equally powerful loudspeakers. He moved ahead to the lottery: holding the microphone, the young man was bellowing: ". . . *bolatombolatombolatombola . . .*" Among the spectators, he recognized a boy from his quarter. They grinned at each other; it was all they could do under the circumstances. Further along, standing on a platform, an apelike man with a two-day beard, wearing a red satin dress and long dangling earrings, his hands folded behind his head, was making the rudimentary motions of a *danse du ventre*. Seated on his right, gazing out with empty eyes over the heads of the crowd toward the invisible mountains at the east, was a girl wearing a kepi and a Spahi uniform, listlessly beating a snare drum. On his left stood a middle-aged woman, flashing an entire mouthful of gold teeth at the public as she smiled, crying into her microphone in a voice of iron: "*Entrez, messieurs-dames! Le spectacle va commencer!*"

The friend also had drifted here, and now stood next to Amar. "*Hada el bourdel,*" he shouted to him; Amar nodded sagely. The platform had been erected at the entrance of what he supposed must be a very expensive traveling brothel, and presently he was much astonished to see several Jewish women among those buying entrance tickets.

Now he moved ahead, to a kind of shed in front of which three mechanical dolls jiggled on a high pedestal. They were as large as children and wore real clothes. To Amar there was something indefinably obscene in the idea of putting good wool, cotton and leather on these dead, jittering objects; it outraged his sense of decorum. He stood watching their spasmodic movements, feeling a mixture of repugnance and indignation. One figure was playing a violin and opening and shutting a very wide mouth. A second banged together a pair of tin cymbals soundlessly, its senseless head turning from side to side atop its elongated neck. The third swayed back and forth from the hips as it pushed and pulled on a miniature accordion. The shifting light made their hesitant movements more plausible, at the same time removing them wholly from the world of reality and making them somehow believable inhabitants of another world that was all too possible, a pitiless world whose silence would be this crackling inferno of noise, and whose noon and midnight would shine with the same shadowless glare. "*Le Musée des Marionettes!*" cried an Arab boy at the door. "*Dix francs, messieurs! Dix francs, mesdames! Juj d'rial! Juj d'rial! Juj d'rial!*"

After a prolonged inner debate on the seemliness of his being observed entering such a place, since almost all the people who were going in and coming out were country folk and Berbers, he decided that not too much opprobrium would attach to his buying a ticket and going in. The museum consisted of a U-shaped corridor with a row of glass exhibit-cases along the inner wall. It was brightly lighted, and crowded with Moslem women in various stages of mirthful hysteria. Why they found the exhibits funny to such a degree he could only guess; to him they were only mildly amusing. All of them were crudely caricatured scenes of life among Moslems: a schoolmaster, ruler in hand, presiding over a class of small boys, a fellah plowing, a drunk being ordered out of a bar. (This last he considered a gross insult to his people.) The scenes which delighted the women so much that they could scarcely move away from them were those showing Moslem females. One was a domestic drama, in which the wife sat with a mirror in one hand and a whip in the other; her husband was on his knees scrubbing the floor. Back and forth twitched the woman's head: she would raise the mirror and gaze into it, and then she would turn to the man and deliver a blow with the whip. At that instant without fail there would be a renewed scream of laughter from the white bundles clustered in front of the glass. The other scene was the interior of a bus, where a man sat next to a woman in a *djellaba*. Here she would lower one side of her veil, disclosing a hideous face, and replace it just as the man's head swung around toward her. It was a less complicated game than the other, but being highly improper it evoked equal merriment on the part of the feminine spectators. Amar stood for a while watching, and thought: "This is the way the Nazarenes corrupt our women, by teaching them how whores behave." He wanted to say it aloud, but the prospect of having so many women turn and stare at him intimidated him, and he strode out into the street with as intense an expression of disgust on his face as he could muster.

". . . *latombolatombo* . . ." cried the young man of the lottery. Now he held an alarm clock in his hand, now a great, fat doll dressed in pink satin, whose eyes, Amar noted with interest, opened and shut when she was bent forward or backward. "Like a cow's eyes," he thought, and he wondered what made them work, even as he was conscious of hating the idea that he should be interested at all in such childish nonsense. They would forbid things like this, he was certain, when the Moslems took power. By what right did the French assume that such absurdities would amuse the Moroccans? The fact that they *were* amused by them was beside the point; they would have to change. He could imagine the French coming here from the Ville Nouvelle, not to look at the exhibits, but to be entertained by watching the Moslems look at them. Is it my fault, Mohammed Lalami had said, if the people of Morocco are donkeys? There he was right.

He found himself being pushed from behind toward the long counter where the prizes were displayed. There were sets of shining aluminum cooking utensils, tablecloths and mantillas draped over the counter, umbrellas hanging by their crooks, fountain pens arranged by the score in designs on sheets of painted cardboard, table lamps with red bulbs in them, flashing on and off, along with all the other lights, and even a small radio, which the young man now and then announced would be given as a special prize to anyone who picked the winning number three times in succession. This detail was lost on Amar, who was thinking that it would be a wonderful thing for a man to have his own radio right in the room with him. So far he had seen them only in cafés. "For thirty francs," the young man was crying, "you can have this magnificent apparatus." That much Amar did understand, and at the risk of being laughed at by the onlookers (for one never knew quite what was happening in the world of the Nazarenes) he worked his way ahead to the edge of the counter and held out thirty francs. Of course, it was wrong; he saw that immediately in the expression on the young man's face. "Only one number at a time!" he shouted to the crowd, as though they all had made the same mistake. "Only ten francs!" He took one coin from Amar's hand. "*Messieurs-dames!* This time it will be Monte Carlo! Players will choose their own numbers! Only five players! One more?" Someone at the far end of the counter raised his hand; a girl working at that end took his coin. "*Les numéros?*" The players called their choices.

The only number Amar was certain of pronouncing correctly was *dix*. He said the word clearly; the young man seemed satisfied, turned and spun the disk that was affixed to the wall, moving the microphone so that it picked up the clicking sound made by the metal flange as it hit the large pins that marked the numbers. The clicking slowed down, the wheel stopped, and Amar saw with more terror than satisfaction that the indicator was without a doubt directly over a thin yellow slice of the disk which bore the number ten. "*Numéro dix!*" shouted the young man without emotion. The girl at the other end reached out nonchalantly and took up a strange-looking object which she tossed to the announcer. The Christians and Jews, and doubtless some of the Moslems watching, recognized it as a rag doll which was meant to be a comic representation of a French sailor. It had a pot-belly and a hideous painted face, but its uniform and headgear had been made with an eye to detail. The young man held it up so everyone could admire it; then he handed it to Amar.

For Amar this was a minor crisis: he did not want to accept the thing, but he knew it was the only possible procedure. If he refused it, there would be roars of laughter from the onlookers, the loudest and most derisive of whom would be the Moslems. He reached up, seized the doll by its neck, and without paying any attention to the young man's question as to whether or not he wanted to take another number, burrowed through the crowd until he reached its outer edges. He stood still for a moment in a comparatively deserted space outside the entrance to the school. The problem was to find a sheet of paper in which to wrap his prize; he could not very well walk through the streets carrying it this way. It would be worth the money, he decided, to buy a newspaper; that would certainly be the quickest way to hide it.

There were usually two or three newsboys on the other side of the *place*, in front of the large café where the bus drivers got their quick glasses of coffee or wine. As he was making his way around the periphery of the square under the trees, all the lights and loudspeakers went off. For a second there was complete silence and darkness, as if a giant breath from above, extinguishing the light with one puff, had also blown everyone away. Then on all sides a great sound rose up—the sound a thousand or more people make when they all say: "Ahhh!" at once. Even when that sound had died down, everything was different from what it had been a minute before; it was like being in another city. Now Amar saw that it was not really dark. Through the leaves of the trees overhead the stars were very bright, and here and there at the far side of the square was a food stall lighted by the single spurting flame of a carbide lamp. When he had got across to the other side he stood still, listening through the vast babble for the high voice of a newsboy crying: *Laa Viigiiie!*, but the sound did not come. In the breeze that blew by his face he was conscious of the heavy smell of wet earth and the smoke of burning oil from ten thousand kitchens behind the walls of the nearby Mellah. Suddenly he was extremely hungry. He determined to go home now, taking the first bus that left for Bab Bou Jeloud. It would not do to arrive back home too late, in any case: they might suspect that he had not been to work.

Again he stood on the back platform, as the bus rolled through the dark Mellah. There was more light crossing Fez-Djedid, perhaps because the proprietors of the cafés and shops had had time to bring out candles, oil lamps and tin cans filled with carbide. A good many legionnaires got off at Bab Dekakène, to pass the evening in the *quartier réservé* of Moulay Abdallah.

When the bus got to Bou Jeloud, he waited until everyone had left the vehicle, and then stepped inside the dimly illumined interior. There on a seat was what he was looking for— a newspaper. Quickly he snatched it up, before the driver should see it. He was still wrapping the doll as he walked under the great arch of the gate. Emerging on the other side, he was unpleasantly startled to collide with a figure that had stepped in front of him, its arm raised to halt him. He recognized a *mokhazni* in uniform.

"What's that?" The *mokhazni* pulled the bundle out of Amar's hands and ripped the paper off. The doll fell limply forward against his arm; he held it out and fixed the beam of his flashlight on it. Then he shook it and squeezed it between his fingers systematically, all over its body. Finally with a grunt he tossed it to Amar, who, fumbling in the darkness, dropped it. "*Cirf halak*," said the *mokhazni*, as though it were Amar who had done the bothering. "Get out of here." And he returned to the shadows where he had been waiting.

"Son of a dog," Amar said between his teeth, but so softly, he knew, that his words were covered by the sound of the voices of passers-by. He had heard of other people's having similar experiences recently, but the world in which he moved was so circumscribed, even geographically, that he had never until now come in contact with the new vigilance that was being exercised. He turned left into the covered *souks* of the Talâa el Kebira, now holding the doll by its feet, and so intent upon giving a semblance of variety to the string of curses he was muttering under his breath that he was not immediately conscious of the person walking beside him. Suddenly he turned his head, and in the flickering light from one of the meat stalls saw the older brother of Mokhtar Benani, a boy he often played with on the soccer field.

"*Ah, sidi, labès? Chkhbarek?*" he said, embarrassed, hoping first that the boy had not heard his private tirade, and next that he would not look down and see the absurd thing he was carrying. At the same time, his intuition told him that there was an element of strangeness, if not in the fashion of this salutation, in its very fact. There was no possible reason for the older Benani, whose first name he did not even know, to be stopping at this moment in the Talâa el Kebira to speak with Amar. Until now they had never exchanged a word; on various occasions this boy had come to the soccer field to fetch his younger brother, there often had been an argument involved in the fetching, and Amar remembered the older brother because he had never lost his temper or raised his voice during the discussions. Now that he heard that voice again, he marveled fleetingly. It had a rich, burnished quality which made it not quite like any other voice he had ever heard, and its mellifluousness was heightened by the fact that the boy used a large complement of Egyptian words in his phrases and pronounced the "*qaf*" perfectly. This last feat Amar considered wholly remarkable in itself; like most Fassiyine he was incapable of pronouncing the letter.

Amar was neither analytical nor articulate, but he generally knew exactly why he was following a particular course of behavior. If he had been asked at this moment why he did not utter a simple "*'Lah imsik bekhir*" and go on his way, he would have replied that Benani's voice was something pleasant in the world, and that he enjoyed listening to it. On his side, Benani may have been dimly conscious of this, for he seemed disposed to talk at some length, making discreet inquiries as to Amar's health and that of his family, as well as to his work and his general state of mind. "And the world," he said, at several junctures in the conversation. Amar was quite aware that he was referring to the political situation in Morocco, but he had no intention of showing that awareness here, nor, he imagined, did the other expect him to.

"Where are you going?" Benani finally inquired, shifting his position and glancing downward at Amar's hand, which he was holding as far behind him as he could.

"Home." Amar also turned imperceptibly, trying to keep the doll behind him in the dark.

"Why don't you eat with us? I'm meeting a few *drari* in the Nejjarine, and we're going to eat somewhere."

Amar ignored the question for the moment. "And Mokhtar?" he said. "Where's Mokhtar? Will he be there?"

Benani's lip curled scornfully before he said: "No. He won't be there. He has to study. These are older *drari*."

He's trying to flatter me, Amar decided. He knows I'm Mokhtar's age. Still, he was curious to see why, and so he stood there.

"I've got to go home," he said. He knew that if his suspicion were correct, now would begin the cajoling, the pressing of the arm, the faint tugs at the sleeve and lapel.

He was quite right: all this did happen, and presently he found himself wandering slowly along the interminable dark street with him, downhill, downward, down, firm now in his conviction that Benani wanted something very definite from him.

CHAPTER II

The café was like any other large street café in the Medina: bare and uncomfortable, with tables that rocked on their unequal legs, and chairs that threatened to collapse under the weight of the sitter. The plaster on the walls had been clumsily splashed with pink and blue paint to give a marbled effect; in many places it had cracked and fallen, and the mud of the outer wall was visible.

There were six of them. They had brought bread and olives

with them, and now they sent out for skewers of lamb. At first they sat at a table near the *qaouaji's* booth, where the charcoal fire occasionally showered them with sparks. When the skewers of *qotbanne* arrived, they moved in a body to a small niche in the back which had no table and no chairs—only a width of matting on the floor and another strip around the walls. They exactly filled the niche, with two sitting along each side, and a newspaper spread out in the center.

The shameful problem of the sailor doll had been settled while Amar and Benani were still alone together. Mercifully Allah had decreed that Benani was to stop at a latrine halfway down the hill; Amar had seized that moment to fling it up into the network of rafters in the ceiling of the edifice, and it had flopped over one of them and stuck there. It was certain Benani had noticed that he had been carrying something, for Amar caught him looking surreptitiously toward the hand which he still held behind him as they emerged from the latrine. But now Benani could surmise as much as he liked; it did not matter.

The others were indeed older than Amar by a few years, all of them being seventeen or over. However, from the beginning they had been civil with him and had made an obvious effort to put him at his ease—an effort which was not entirely successful, since he could not help feeling out of place among them, yet being both flattered by and suspicious of their attention. It was Benani who sat beside him and joked with him; he seemed to have taken it upon himself to play the role of apologist for Amar that evening. If Amar made a remark with which the others appeared not to sympathize, he would either question Amar in order to get him to go on and be more explicit, or he would give them his own explanation of Amar's words. Unfortunately this seemed destined to happen again and again; although they all understood and spoke the same dialect, and used the same symbols of reference, it was as if they had come from separate countries.

The difference was principally in the invisible places toward which their respective hearts were turned. They dreamed of Cairo with its autonomous government, its army, its newspapers and its cinema, while he, facing in the same direction, dreamed just a little beyond Cairo, across the Bhar el Hamar to Mecca. They thought in terms of grievances, censorship, petitions and reforms; he, like any good Moslem who knows only the tenets of his religion, in terms of destiny and divine justice. If the word "independence" was uttered, they saw platoons of Moslem soldiers marching through streets where all the signs were written in Arabic script, they saw factories and power plants rising from the fields; he saw skies of flame, the wings of avenging angels, and total destruction. Slowly Benani became aware of this vast disparity, and secretly began to despair. However, his task for the evening was not that of trying to reconcile two points of view; it was something quite distinct from that. He knew that the others had completely lost patience with him for bringing them together with this ignoramus, this anomalous shadow from the world of yesterday; they felt that he should have taken care of him by himself. But he was convinced that it was his duty to conduct the gathering in the way he believed best.

"*Yah*, Abdelkader!" he called. "Let's have a Coca-Cola."

The *qaouaji* arrived with a bottle.

"Is it cold?" demanded Benani.

"Hah! It's cold and a half," the *qaouaji* informed him.

Benani took the bottle and offered it first to Amar. "Have a little," he urged him. As Amar tipped the bottle to his lips, Benani said to him casually: "Played any soccer recently?" Amar swallowed and said he had not. "Been swimming?" pursued Benani. "Today," Amar said, passing the bottle back to him. "A lot of people at Sidi Harazem?" Benani inquired. Amar said he had not been there. He decided to sit back and enjoy himself. The others with their sudden silence and watchful eyes had given the show away. He would offer no information except that explicitly demanded by Benani, and then he would confuse him by telling the truth. Nothing could be more upsetting, because one always judiciously mixed false statements in with the true, the game being to tell which were which. It was axiomatic that a certain percentage of what everyone said had to be disbelieved. If he made nothing but strictly true statements, Amar told himself, Benani would necessarily be at a disadvantage, for he would be bound to doubt some of them.

As he had foreseen, the casual conversation quickly turned

into a grilling as Benani lost first his poise and then, at least partly, his temper.

"Oh, so you went to Aïn Malqa. I see."

"Yes."

"Then you came back."

Amar looked surprised. "Yes."

"You were just getting back when I met you?"

"No. I was at the *fechta*."

"That doesn't start until eight," Benani said in an accusatory tone.

"I don't know. I wasn't there very long."

"You must have stayed late at Aïn Malqa."

"Not very. The sun was on top when I left."

Benani took a gulp of Coca-Cola and passed the bottle on to the boy on his right. Then he whistled for a moment, as if that little interlude might give the scene a semblance of naturalness.

"You must have stopped to sleep on the way back," he said presently.

Amar laughed. "No. I was looking for a place, but I couldn't find one. I got into somebody's orchard by mistake."

"Ay! That was dangerous. The French are shooting fast these days."

If he lied and pretended to have met no one and seen nothing, they would be convinced that he had understood more than he really had. The important thing was not to seem to have noticed anything very unusual about Moulay Ali.

"It wasn't a French orchard. It belonged to a Moslem."

"A Moslem?" echoed Benani in a tone of disbelief. "On the Aïn Malqa road?"

"You know, a Moslem with a motorcycle. Moulay Somebody. A little bald, and walks like an owl."

One of the boys laughed briefly. Benani winced with annoyance, but did not turn his head. Instead, he shut his eyes, as if he were trying to place the man.

"Moulay Somebody," repeated Amar.

Benani shook his head. "I don't know him," he said uncertainly.

"He lives in an old house."

"With his family?"

"I don't know."

"Did you go inside?"

"Oh, yes. He invited me in. . . . Look," said Amar suddenly. "If you want to know who was there and what they were doing, why don't you go and ask him?"

"Who, me?" Benani cried. "I don't know him. Why would I know him?"

"*Khlass!*" said Amar, smiling tolerantly. "You know him better than I do." And taking an even greater chance, he continued. "And you saw him tonight."

The others all sat up just a little straighter at that instant. Amar was delighted. He decided to try to clean up the disorder of the conversation.

"I can't tell you anything about your friend because I don't know him. But you don't want to know about him, anyway. You want to know about me. *Zduq*, ask me more questions."

"Don't be angry," said Benani. Amar laughed. "We're all friends. What difference does it make whose orchard you went into? He wasn't French and he didn't shoot you. That's the important thing."

It was as though Amar had said nothing; he saw that they were not going to be honest with him, and he wondered if it would give him a greater advantage to go on being honest with them, or whether he should stop and begin to play the game their way. He decided to go on a little further.

"At first I thought you spoke to me because you'd heard what I was saying in the Talâa, when I was talking to myself."

"Would that be a reason?" asked Benani.

So he did hear me, thought Amar, feeling more satisfaction at having discovered the truth about that. "It might be," he replied.

"*Enta hmuq bzef,*" Benani said disgustedly. "You're crazy." One of the boys was whispering in the ear of another. The latter, whose face was bursting with very red pimples, suddenly spoke up. "At first you thought that, you say. But what do you think now?" Benani looked angrily at him; Amar hazarded the guess that it was because he had not managed to ask him that himself. He glanced out into the café. The place was empty. The *qaouaji* had shut the door and lay asleep in front of it. He looked at the faces of the five older boys and saw no friendliness in them.

"*El hassil*," he said slowly. "I don't know what to think."

He could not go on being truthful now; it was out of the question, because what he saw with complete clarity was that not only had Moulay Ali sent Benani after him to investigate him—he had instructed him to do it in the manner of the police; that is, without divulging anything on his side and using any means he saw fit, as long as he extracted the information. Benani had played his part too crudely for there to be any room for doubt. Probably more than anything Moulay Ali wanted to know what he had heard out there in the orchard house, how much he had understood and deduced, and whether he was going to hold his tongue.

He had not told them very much, he reflected, but perhaps he should have told them nothing at all. He looked down at his hands, saw the ring the potter had given him, and remembered the potter's warning. It was quite possible that some of these very *drari* sitting here with him had stabbed or shot an *assas* or a *mokhazni*; there was no way of knowing.

They were still looking at him expectantly.

"*El hassil*," he said again. It was no use; he could not pretend innocence. "I think you want to know if my heart is with your hearts."

Benani frowned, but Amar could see that he approved of his reply.

"We're interested in your head, too," he said. "It's no good having a heart if you haven't got a head. You haven't got much of a head. That didn't matter until today. But now—" he looked at Amar fixedly—"you've got to have a head, you understand?"

He did understand perfectly. Benani was saying that since he had stumbled onto Moulay Ali he was necessarily involved; there was no way of pretending otherwise.

"I have a head, but no tongue," he said.

Benani laughed shortly. "I know, I know. They all say that. But after the first five minutes in the *commissariat* they have a tongue that would reach from Bab Mahrouk to Bab Fteuh. Until you get to the *commissariat* you need a head. It's only when you get there that you find out what sort of heart you have, and know what's more important to you, your own skin or your Sultan's faith in you."

Benani was watching him closely, probably to trace the effect of his words on Amar's countenance. This seemed scarcely the moment to recall Mohammed Lalami's words: "The Sultan will never come back, and the party doesn't want him back," but he could not help hearing them again in his mind's ear, as well as what Mohammed had said immediately afterward: "It's not the party's fault, is it, if the people of Morocco are all donkeys?" Benani was taking him for one of the donkeys, was telling him, in fact, that he had got to be one. The lie had to be at the center of any understanding he could have with these people. He nodded his head slowly, as if he were pondering the profound wisdom of Benani's statement.

"We're your friends," Benani said, leaning forward and wrapping the debris of the meal in the newspaper, "but you've got to prove that you know how to have friends."

What bad luck, Amar thought. He did not want any of them as friends. "*B'cif*," he said, "of course." He looked at them. There was the pimply one who seemed to consider himself Benani's henchman, a yellow-skinned, sickly one with thick glasses, a rather fat one who looked as though he had never walked farther than from the Kissaria to the Medersa Attarine, and a tall Negro whom he seemed to remember having seen at the municipal swimming pool in the Ville Nouvelle.

Benani sat up straight again, holding the folded paper in his hand. "*Rhaddi noud el haraj men deba chouich*," he said sententiously. "It's going to be war this time, not just games." Amar felt a thrill of excitement in spite of himself. "Do you know what's happened?" Benani went on, his eyes suddenly blazing dangerously. "Tonight five thousand partisans are sleeping outside Bab Fteuh. Did you know that?"

Now Amar's heart was beating very fast, and his eyes were wide open. "What?" he cried.

"It's no secret," said Benani grimly. He called to the *qaouaji*, who got sleepily to his feet and staggered to where they sat. "We're on our way," Benani told him. The *qaouaji* shuffled back to the door, opened it, and peered out. Then he shut it again. The four others rose, shook hands solemnly with Amar and Benani, and went to the door; the *qaouaji* let them out. Benani remained seated where he was, silently staring at the mat on the floor, and Amar, not knowing whether the audience was over or not, also merely sat, until the other, who was taking the precaution of waiting until those who had left should be completely dispersed, finally rose to his feet.

"You'd better not go outside the walls tomorrow," he said, "or you may not see your family for a long time. I'm going to walk home with you."

Amar protested politely, although he knew that Benani's decision had not been made through solicitude for his safety.

"*Yallah,*" said Benani paying no attention to him. "Let's go." He paid the *qaouaji*, said a few words to him, and they stepped into the street. The arc-lights in the Medina were so sparsely placed that they had to walk awhile before they could tell whether the electricity was still cut off. It was, but Benani had a flashlight which he used from time to time. The wind was damp and the sky was still covered over. So far they had not met a single passer-by.

"It's going to rain," said Benani.

"Yes."

"But it won't last. Not at this time of the year."

Amar thought this a useless sort of thing to say. Only Allah could know whether it would rain and for how long. He held his tongue, however, and continued to walk along beside Benani. When they got to the entrance of his alley Amar said: "Here's my *derb,*" and began to thank him and bid him good night. But apparently Benani wanted to see exactly where Amar lived. "I'll take you to your house," he said. "It's nothing."

"You'll have to come all the way back. There's no way out," Amar warned him.

"Nothing."

Even when Amar had knocked on the door, Benani did not leave. He stood against the wall where he would not be seen by whoever opened to let Amar in. It was Amar's father who called out: "*Chkoun?*" and who eventually, with a good deal of banging about and clinking of keys, swung open the door, shielding his candle from the wind with his key hand. Seeing Amar, sensing that there was someone with him, he held the candle up and out, trying to see beyond. "Where have you been?" he demanded querulously. "Who's with you?" Amar could not answer. Benani, now convinced that this house was not a false address, and, from the genuineness of the scene, that the old man was indeed Amar's father, darted off into the night, leaving Amar to cope with the situation. For once Si Driss's relief at seeing his son was greater than his anger at having waited for him.

"*Hamdoul'lah*," he said several times, as he bolted the door and padded across the courtyard to wash his hands in a pail by the well. The doves shivered and fluttered once, startled at having been wakened.

Amar's principal desire was to get upstairs quickly, before the old man's mood changed. He stooped and kissed the sleeve of his father's *gandoura*, murmured: "Good night," and started up the first steps.

"Wait," said Si Driss. Amar's heart sank.

A minute later they both went slowly up the stairs, the old man first, carrying the candle, and Amar following. When they got to the top of the second flight Si Driss was panting, and reached for the support of Amar's arm. Inside his room Amar fixed the candle to the floor, and they sat down on the mattress.

His father leaned toward him, to see him better.

"*Yah latif!* What's the matter with your face?" he cried. "It looks like a rotten peach. How did that happen? Who hit you?"

"One," said Amar quietly. He did not expect his father to press the point, and he was right. The old man merely said despairingly: "Why do you fight?" The question that Amar was expecting: "Where have you been?" did not come. Instead, after a pause, his father asked him: "Have you seen anything?"

There was to be no punishment. Amar was astonished. "No," he said uncertainly.

"Tomorrow, *incha'Allah*, we must get up very early and buy whatever we can get. Who knows when it will begin? We have nothing in the house. Si Abderrahman will sell me fifty kilos of flour. That we can be sure of. The rest is in the hands of Allah."

"Yes," said Amar. He did not know what else to say.

The old man was shaking his head back and forth. "This time it will be very bad. The French have sent the Berbers to make war on us. May Allah save us all. Who knows what will become of us? There's not one gun in the Medina; they saw to that."

Amar comforted his father with inadequate phrases, secretly amazed that Si Driss should at last be taking politics so seriously, and uncomfortable to see that the calm he had always thought adamant was now shattered.

"You must sleep a little," said his father at last. "We have work to do tomorrow."

When he had gone, Amar lay wide-eyed, staring into the empty night. A light rain had begun to fall; beyond its soft sound there was only silence.

CHAPTER 12

The next day was not the day that Si Driss had feared it would be. The Berber troops outside Bab Fteuh stayed where they were, making their temporary quarters more comfortable for themselves. Rain fell quietly in the morning, but at noon it suddenly cleared, and a curtain of rising mist over the city made the light painful. Amar and his father had gone out at dawn, leaving Mustapha at home with the womenfolk, and had brought back the flour from Si Abderrahman's house, which was near by. Then they had scoured the Medina to find sugar, chickpeas, candles and oats. Almost all the shops had been boarded up, and at those which were doing business there were clusters of agitated men trying with cajolery, threats and pleas to buy food at normal prices. The food was there, but the few shopkeepers who were courageous enough to have remained open (for roving bands of young vigilantes were reported to be wrecking the shops in the center of the city) hoped to profit quickly by their daring. Tramping through the streets were groups of glum-faced French policemen who looked straight ahead with hard eyes. No children were visible, and there was a noticeable absence of young men.

Amar arrived at work only about an hour late. The potter
was squatting on his terrace as usual, but there was no sign of
his merchandise lying about; all the water jars, bowls and
dishes had been stacked inside the shed. There was an unaccustomed silence lying over the mud village below, and the
smoke rose from only a handful of ovens.

"*Sbalkheir*," said the potter, looking up at him unhappily.
"I was afraid they'd caught you."

Amar laughed. "*Sbalkheir*," he replied. For a moment he
was not sure whether Saïd meant the French or the Istiqlal,
then his own doubt struck him as absurd; he could only have
been referring to the French. "No, I had a lot of work to do
for my father," he said, hoping that the potter would let it
rest there and not press him for details.

"It doesn't matter," said the other, fingering his beard.
"I'm going to close up anyway, until *they*—" he gestured with
his head toward Bab Fteuh—"go back where they came from.
Allah! There's a city of them out there. This is just the
beginning. There'll be more tonight, and they'll be at Bab
Guissa and all the other gates. They put them there first
because of the sheep market. Only four days to the Aïd."

Amar's face fell. If that were the case, it meant that they
would surely have no sheep to sacrifice this year at his
house, because all the money had gone to buy the staples he
and his father had just lugged home. He had not realized
the time was so short; vaguely he had hoped that somehow
between now and the festival there would be a way of
amassing enough money to buy a sheep, even if it were a
small one. The prospect of having no sheep at all was a
social disgrace of enormous proportions, and one which the
family had never yet had to face. "Four days," he said sadly.
The warm rain suddenly fell with more force, spattering
their legs with the mud from the roof. They shrank against
the wall.

"There are a lot of fools out there buying sheep anyway,"
Saïd went on. "There'll be trouble. Wait; you'll see. In my
derb this morning they beat up an old man who was leading
his sheep home. They beat up the sheep too, left them both
lying there against the wall in a heap." He grinned at the
memory. Amar was listening incredulously.

"It's the only thing to do," Saïd continued. "What right has anybody got to make a feast when the Sultan is in prison in the middle of the ocean?"

"But it's a sin not to have the Aïd el Kebir," said Amar slowly. "Which is greater, the Sultan or Islam?"

The potter glared at him. "Sin! Sin!" he cried. "Is there any sin worse than living without our Sultan? Like dogs? Like heathens, *kaffirine?* There are no sins any more, I tell you! It doesn't matter what anyone does now. Sins are finished!"

Secretly Amar agreed with him, but he would have preferred to say all that himself. Coming from Saïd, it sounded a little silly. He was too old to feel that way, Amar thought.

Saïd's rancor had been aroused; his expression was distinctly unfriendly now. He seemed to think he was having an argument with Amar.

"At any rate," he grumbled, "I don't need you around here. I've let the others go. I don't need anybody. Who's going to buy jars now?"

Amar was thinking of the money the potter owed him. It was not much, but it was something. "And afterward?" he said.

"Afterward, come back. If there is any afterward," he added with a harsh laugh.

"We'll leave the money until then, Si Saïd." Amar looked at him dreamily; it was the soft, veiled look which is meant to hide the scheming behind the eyes, but no Fassi could mistake it. The potter jumped to his feet and dug into his pocket.

"No!" he shouted, holding out some bills. "I don't do things that way. Here."

Amar took the money with bad grace. He had hoped to gain two things by letting it go until later: prestige in the eyes of Saïd, and possibly a greater sum when the time for collection came, in the event that Saïd had forgotten the exact amount.

"Very good," he said hesitatingly, pocketing the money. "I'll be around now and then, to see you."

"*Ouakha,*" replied Saïd without enthusiasm. And as Amar moved away he called after him, possibly remembering the prosperity the boy had brought to his establishment, and feeling that he had been abrupt with him. "These are bad days, Si Amar. We're all unhappy. We speak quickly."

Amar turned, stepped over to the man, and kneeling, kissed the sleeve of his *djellaba*. "Good-bye, master," he said.

The potter looked down at him distraughtly and pulled him to his feet. "Good-bye," he said.

So now he was free again, Amar reflected, as he wandered back through the wet streets. On the one hand he was happy to feel that the world was open, that once more anything might happen; at the same time, he had enjoyed the sensation of building up his power and prestige, the feeling of moving toward something which he had had while he had been working at Saïd's. Now it had all been destroyed at one blow. But no man has the right to lament the arrival of the inevitable.

A string of donkeys came plodding through the narrow street, their panniers bulging with sand. "*Balek, balek,*" chanted the man at their rear. He wore a slit sugar sack over his head as a *djellaba* to protect his face from the rain. As he passed by, Amar for some reason looked down at the ground. There, directly in front of him, lay a twenty-rial coin in the mud. Swiftly he bent over and picked it up, murmuring: "*Bismil'lah ala maketseb Allah.*" And suddenly he was reminded of a similar occasion long ago, when he had been working at the brick factory in the Taza road. That time it had been more than a hundred rial that he had come upon, lying in the street unnoticed. Since he had been on his way to work, he had taken the money directly to his master. The man had flown into a rage, and flinging the money on the ground, had struck him in the face, a blow whose unexpectedness made it only more painful. "Is that money yours?" the man had demanded. Amar had said it was not. "Then why did you pick it up? Next time when you see something in the street, leave it there and go on your way." Then the man had sent a boy to Amar's home to fetch his father. When Si Driss had arrived, the master had given him the money and advised him to beat his son, but Si Driss had taken exception to the man's counsel and gently led Amar home, telling him that the man was right about the money, but wrong in his desire that Amar be punished, and that he would find a new master elsewhere. A few days later he had installed him as a shoemaker's apprentice in the Cherratine. How many times, he wondered, had his father gone to protest the unjust treatment of his son by his employers? A great many times, certainly; Si Driss could not countenance even the smallest infraction of his conception of the Moslem code of justice, and on this account primarily Amar bore him an intense, undying love. Beyond the gates of justice lay the world of savages, *kaffirine*, wild beasts.

When he got home, his father and Mustapha were there, sitting quietly in the room off the courtyard, waiting while his mother and Halima prepared tea in the corner. His father was not surprised to hear that he was no longer working; he took the money that Amar handed him without saying anything more than: "Sit down and drink tea." (The twenty-rial piece, the gift from Allah, remained in his pocket, but he had given him all that he had collected from the potter.)

Mustapha sat there, looking even glummer than usual. He had not had any work in several weeks, and it had secretly irked him to see that Amar had stayed on at the potter's so long; now he could meet his brother's gaze with equanimity. The center of his life seemed to be elsewhere than at home— in the cafés of Moulay Abdallah most likely, Amar thought; around the house he was merely a hollow shell, grunting a reply if he were spoken to, but never coming to life.

"It's still swollen," said his mother, looking up at the bridge of Amar's nose from where she sat on the floor fanning the charcoal.

Si Driss sighed. "His nose is broken," he said gently.

"*Ay, ouildi, ouildi!*" she began, and burst into tears.

"It's nothing, woman," the old man said, looking at her sternly. But she was inconsolable, and abandoned herself to a fit of weeping. Halima continued the tea-making. When she had served the others, she handed her mother a glass and induced her to sip a little.

"Listen!" said Si Driss, raising a silencing finger. In the distance there was the sound of strenuous chanting, as if the people who were doing it were walking very quickly. "The students," he said. It was hard to tell how far away they were, because there were none of the usual neighborhood noises. "Our soldiers," the old man added with bitterness.

"May Allah preserve them!" sobbed Amar's mother.

Mustapha spoke up unexpectedly. "Every tobacco store in the Medina is smashed."

"Good," said Amar.

Mustapha glared at him. "Good in your head," he growled.

Si Driss overlooked the impropriety of this exchange of conversation in his presence, motioning to Halima to refill his glass. Amar rose and went upstairs to his room. He sat on his mattress, thinking of what a useless and unpleasant man his brother was going to be. It seemed certain that Mustapha's present ill-humor was due solely to the fact that he had not been able to get any kif in the past few days. Probably his usual source of supply had been cut off by the trouble.

Now that there was a stock of food in the house, so that although they might not eat particularly well, it was unlikely that they would go hungry even if the trouble became very bad, Amar should have been relieved and felt more or less at ease. Not at all—he had never been more nervous and restless. He wanted to go out and be everywhere in the town at once, but it was still raining a little, and in any case he had the feeling that no matter where he went the streets would be empty, and that the sounds of activity would be coming from some distant, unlocatable spot.

He tried playing his flute for a few minutes, but it made an unreasonably loud noise in the middle of this quiet morning, an absurd and sour sound that finally made him toss it up onto a shelf between the broken alarm clock and the colored picture of Ben Barek the soccer idol, in his red and blue uniform. Then he stepped out onto the roof and tried to see beyond the nearby housetops, but the fine drizzle that was falling obscured everything. However, the sky was brightening. He went back in and lay down. The air was hot and breathless. Today even the roosters of the neighborhood seemed to have agreed to observe the general silence. And with only four days to go before the Aïd, it was incredible that there should be no sign or sound of sheep on the terraces. Never before had such a strange thing happened; in other years you could hear the bleating coming from every direction during the ten or fifteen days before the feast. Some families bought their animals as much as a month ahead of time, to be able to fatten them properly for the sacrifice. This year—silence, which was why he had not realized that the day was so close. If his father had been alone downstairs, he would have taken the unusual step of going down and discussing it with him. But Mustapha was there, and it was, after all, an affair between his father and Mustapha, in which he had no part. When the old man died, it would be Mustapha who would attend to the buying and killing of the sheep, not Amar.

And now he began to wonder what the outdoor ceremony of the Aïd at Emsallah would be like, with the Berber soldiers spread out there just below. It was the most important event of the year, upon which the prosperity and well-being of the city depended. There were always at least a hundred thousand people there, swarming through the cemetery and ranged across the hillside above it, come to watch the *khtib* slit the throat of the sheep sent by the Sultan, and to see whether the runners, who operated in wonderfully organized shifts, would arrive opposite the Andaluz mosque with it while it still breathed. This was essential, for if the sheep had expired before they threw it down at the feet of the *gzara*, it was a very bad omen for the coming year. But with Bab Fteuh blocked by the soldiers, how were the runners going to get through? Allah was watching them, each one of them must exert himself to the utmost; if their teamwork were faulty in passing the sheep from one group of four to the next, if one of them fell, if the way were not completely cleared, the sheep might breathe its last while they were still on the way, and although the final group might arrive in the courtyard with each man holding one of its legs in the most perfect position, it would all be in vain, and the city would suffer the displeasure of Allah for the entire year to come, until the fault could be obliterated at the next Aïd el Kebir.

It was intolerable that the gate should be barred by the presence of all those soldiers; the French could only mean it as a provocation. "They want us to try and break through, so their Berbers will shoot," he thought with sudden fury. Just as they had taken the Sultan away on the very day of the Aïd a year ago, to make sure that there could not possibly be any good fortune or happiness, so they were going to try and prevent the Moslems from finding favor with Allah again this year. The thought, once it had occurred to him, was too awful for him to keep it to himself. He bounded up from the mattress and ran down the two flights of stairs.

The family had finished tea, but they were still sitting just as before, save that his mother had moved onto the small mattress beside Halima. Her face was pink with weeping, and she looked scarcely older than the girl. Si Driss had married her when she was thirteen; she still had the flesh and force of a young woman. Amar looked at her now as he came into the room, saw the traces of tears on her face, knew that she had shed them for him because it hurt her to think of his becoming other than the way he was (even if were only a bone in his nose that had changed its shape) and felt a terrible urge to take her in his arms, kiss her cheeks and eyes. He sat down quietly, letting his arms hang at his sides. What he had it in his mind to say retreated from him for a short moment. When the awareness came that he and his mother had in some strange manner become the two focal points of attention on the part of the others, he forced himself out of his brief stupor, turned to his father, who was watching him with an uncomprehending expression on his face, and said: "What's going to happen at Bab Fteuh?"

"Who can know? With those devils there—"

"How are they going to get the sheep through?"

His father looked surprised. "There's not going to be any sheep. Don't you know that?"

Amar stared at him wildly. "But there has to be."

"There has to be, yes, but there's not going to be. It's the end of Islam, all this. Just as it was written. By the Moslems' own will."

Amar was aghast. "The Moslems'!" he cried. "The Moslems' own will!"

"Of course. Who forbade us to buy sheep, threatened to kill us if we did? The Wattanine. The friends of Si Allal, the Istiqlal, whatever you want to call them. Who goes snooping around to be sure nobody has a sheep on his roof? The boys from the Karouine with their schoolbooks under their arm, the friends of freedom. Who beats and stabs the people trying to carry out Allah's commandments? The same boys. Why? They say the *khtib* can't accept a sheep from Arafa because he is a French Sultan. They say there must be no rejoicing until Mohammed ben Youssef comes back."

"Arafa's not our Sultan," said Amar hesitantly.

"And was Si Mohammed?" asked his father, his eyes bright with excitement. During the Sultan's quarter of a century on the throne, Si Driss had never allowed a portrait of him to be hung in the house. Now that it was a prison offense to possess such portraits, although there were countless thousands of them hidden in the Medina, he felt somehow doubly righteous. "Remember *Hakim Filala*." And he proceeded to quote the saying that had been popular among malcontents ever since the beginning of the Alaoui dynasty three centuries back. "'The reign of the Filala: it's not costly but it's not cheap. It's not noisy but it's not quiet. You have a king but you have no king. That's the reign of the Filala.' And that's the truth. Who let the carrion French into Morocco in the first place? A Filali. Don't ever forget that when you're listening to your friends tell you about the Sultan, the Sultan, the Sultan. . . ."

Amar knew all this perfectly, but to him it seemed a most inopportune moment to go over it. His father was really getting old. "But the soldiers at Bab Fteuh," he began. That at least was a hostile act which had clearly been instigated by the French.

"Use your head," said the old man. "The friends of freedom don't want the festival, and they'll stop it anyway, all by themselves. Don't you think the French know that? But the French can't afford to let *them* stop it. Then everyone would know how strong the Istiqlal is. If someone is going to do something, the French have got to be the ones to do it. They want just what the Istiqlal wants, but they want the credit. They have to make it look as though they were the ones who did it. They're all working together against us. In five years the children of Fez will be saying: 'Aïd el Kebir? What's the Aïd el Kebir?' No one will remember it. This is the end of Islam. *Bismil'lah rahman er rahim*." He sat, staring vacantly ahead of him for a moment. No one spoke. "The fault is all our own," he went on presently. "Because Satan stands next to you, you don't make him your friend. There is sin everywhere now." Si Driss shook his head sadly, but his glittering black eyes looked dangerous.

Listening, Amar could not help hearing again the potter's words of only a few short hours ago: "Sins are finished." In some hideous, perverse fashion the two statements coincided. If there were no sins, then everything was necessarily a sin, which was what his father meant by the end of Islam. He felt the imperative and desperate need for action, but there was no action which could possibly lead to victory, because this was a time of defeat. Then the important thing was to see that you did not go down to defeat alone—the Jews and the Nazarenes must go, too. The circle was closed; now he understood the Wattanine whom the French called *les terroristes* and *les assassins*. He understood why they were willing to risk dying in order to derail a train or burn a cinema or blow up a post office. It was not independence they wanted, it was a satisfaction much more immediate than that: the pleasure of seeing others undergo the humiliation of suffering and dying, and the knowledge that they had at least the small amount of power necessary to bring about that humiliation. If you could not have freedom you could still have vengeance, and that was all anyone really wanted now. Perhaps, he thought, rationalizing, trying to connect the scattered fragments of reality with his image of truth, vengeance was what Allah wished His people to have, and by inflicting punishment on unbelievers the Moslems would merely be imposing divine justice.

"*Ed dounia ouahira*," he sighed. "The world is a difficult place." He looked out into the courtyard: the drizzle had ceased entirely, and the sun was beginning to break through the mist. He decided to go out, but at the very moment he was making the decision his mother spoke.

"You mustn't go out again today. This is a bad day."

Amar turned hopefully to his father. "Let him go," the old man said. "He's not a woman. Tomorrow will be worse."

"I'm afraid," she complained. Amar smiled.

CHAPTER 13

In the street he walked along looking at the mud that oozed up around his toes at each step; the covered stretches were dry, and there the dust lay thick on the ground. Wherever there was a pile of fish heads or some donkey manure, the flies were innumerable; they rose in black swarms and settled again quickly. What good was it to have the *baraka*, he was thinking, and to be different from everyone else, if you could do nothing for your people? Something terrible was going to happen—of that he was convinced—yet it was of no help to know it. The tautness that had been going on for so long was at last going to break, the blood was ready to come out and spill on the ground. And no one wanted to prevent it; on the contrary, the people were eager to see it, even if it was to be their own blood.

Each shop-front along the way was boarded up and padlocked. The narrow alleys seemed hotter for being deserted. Occasionally a man passed, walking quickly, the rustling of his garments audible in the silence. "As though it were late at night," Amar thought. He stood still suddenly. The long empty vista of the Souk Attarine, with its pale sunlight filtered into thousands of small squares by the latticework overhead, looked like a dried river bed stretching off into the dusty distance. The strong smell of all the spices was there as always, but the small squares of sunlight that should have been moving up and down hundreds of *djellabas* and *haiks*, as their wearers wandered beneath the trellises, lay flat on the ground in still, regular patterns.

From the street of the lawyers' booths at his left came the long mechanical whine of a beggar. Again and again he heard the sound, repeating exactly the same words in exactly the same way. "Poor man," Amar said to himself. "He'll starve today." He started to walk again, more deliberately, as though he were beginning to derive a small amount of pleasure from it. The street bore to the left, became very narrow, and opened upon a tiny square lined with shops where the students of the Karouine bought their textbooks. The beggar's voice was still clearly audible. He turned back and down the alley where he knew the man would be sitting. He found him further along than he had expected, squatting with his back against the wall, a crude staff in one hand, his face with its two purplish eyeless sockets raised toward the absent multitude, chanting his endless song. He was a young man with a full, pointed black beard and very white teeth. Amar stopped walking and stood watching him for a moment. Someone had given him a fairly new *djellaba*, but beneath it, around his

legs, nameless rags emerged, and his turban was yellow with
dust. In the direction from which Amar had just come, above
the man's sharp litany, he now heard the confused sound of
voices and cries. As he debated whether to go toward them or
away from them, he realized that they were approaching
rapidly, and that mixed with the shouts were other less usual
noises, the indefinite scufflings that accompany a struggle. For
a moment he considered stepping over to the beggar, seizing
his turban, putting it on his own head so that it would cover
part of his face, and sitting down beside the man. But then it
occurred to him that the beggar, being blind, might not understand quickly enough, in which case he could still be demanding an explanation as the others came into view. Instead,
he turned and rapidly scaled the façade of the stall behind
him, using the iron bolts as rungs for his bare feet. It took a
big effort to hoist himself to the roof, because there was nothing to grasp at the top, but he made it, and silently. Up here,
and on the other formless roofs of the shops in the alley,
everything was a jumble of packing cases, broken iron bed-
steads, waste paper and rags. A gaunt cat stared at him malev-
olently from atop a roll of rotten matting a few roofs away.
Carefully he lay face downward, his head behind a battered
washtub, and peered around its crooked edge, up the alley.

Soon they came into view, surrounded by a cloud of dust.
About twenty young men were walking with comparative
swiftness in a tight group; in their midst, struggling to break
through to the outside, and being propelled ahead with the
aid of shoves and blows, were two powerfully built *mokhaznia*, their navy blue uniforms hanging from them in strips, so
that parts of their bare chests and shoulders showed through.
As they heaved themselves desperately against the living wall
that imprisoned them, strange sounds like sobs came from
their mouths, and their eyes rolled back and forth in their
heads like the eyes of madmen. Their faces and necks ran with
blood from the blows they had received. In fact, everyone was
spattered with it, the captors scarcely less than their prisoners.
The dust that was in the air around them they had raised a
few paces back, where the alley was covered; now they slid
clumsily in the mud. If one of the men began to fall, he was
kicked into an upright position by a dozen feet around him.

From the corner of his eye Amar saw the cat flatten itself to the roof and, sliding away like a serpent, disappear.

Above the chaos the beggar's voice continued its hopeful chant, louder than before. He must be crazy, Amar thought, not to realize what was going on right in front of him. But now, when they were directly below him, so that Amar could have spit into their midst, there came the sound of shouts and police whistles from the brighter end of the alley, toward Ras Cherratine. It was as if an electric shock had passed through all of them at the same instant. Everything happened with lightning speed. The two *mokhaznia* made two final, superlative lunges in opposite directions. The circle gave momentarily; several of the young men lost their balance. Amar felt the impact of their bodies against the wall below him. But at the same time the knives briefly mirrored pieces of the sky; those left standing closed in. One *mokhazni* screamed: "Ahhh!" and the other fell soundlessly. The young men stumbled over each other as they fled back the way they had come. Amar saw the faces of some of them as they panted their final curses above the two figures lying on the ground. They too looked like madmen, he thought, but he had a powerful and senseless desire to be one of them, to know what they had experienced as they had felt the blades of their knives going inside the enemy's flesh.

Now they were gone, and the beggar was still singing, like some insect in a summer field; if he had moved his right leg forward he would have kicked the head of one of the *mokhaznia*. But he did not move; his face remained tilted upward at the same angle, and his mouth continued to move, forming the holy words. The French would be there in a minute, and they would doubtless drag the poor blind man off to jail as a witness; they were capable of such incredible stupidity.

Amar had raised his head now, and was rapidly examining the topography of the rooftops. It would not be good to be caught up here, but if he jumped down into the alley it was likely that he would fail to get to either end of it before the police arrived. He scrambled to his feet, and carefully stepping over the objects whose contact would give off sound, made his way along the string of roofs until he came to the wall of a higher building. A ledge built the length of this led back from the alley and became a narrow wall dividing two courtyards. Feeling no dizziness and keeping his eyes fixed firmly on his feet, he moved along the top of the wall to its end, and hoisted himself onto another roof there. Looking backward for an instant, he saw that an old woman in the courtyard immediately below was watching his progress with interest. That was bad. "Look the other way, grandmother," he said, glancing about the clean-swept surface of the cube-like structure on which he stood. There must be a street somewhere near by.

The old woman's voice came up from below: "May Allah bless you." Or had she said: "May Allah burn you?" He was not sure which: the two Arabic words sounded so much alike. At the edge he peered down; there was another wide roof considerably lower than the one where he was at the moment. Further down at the side he saw a marble-paved court, with a small orange tree in each corner, but the angle was such that he could not tell whether or not the street lay beyond. If he jumped down onto the roof it would make a noise; he would have to continue quickly, and it was too far to climb back up to where he stood now. Even had there been no trouble in the city, for him to be caught on the roofs would have meant being taken to jail: the roofs were for the women. A man climbing from terrace to terrace could be only one of two things: a thief or an adulterer. Today of course it was worse. They would simply shoot at him. He said a short prayer, let himself hang down as far as he could, and dropped the rest of the way. If there were people inside the building, they had certainly heard the noise he made when he hit. He ran to the other end of the roof, saw the empty street below, and dropped again, landing very hard with his bare feet flat in the mud. It was a small complicated alley with a great many dead ends where there were merely doors on all sides, and he had to follow several false leads until he had found the exit passage, a little wider than the others, which, after rounding three corners, at last led out into another alley that in turn gave on a through street. Unless one knew a particular *derb* by heart, one could always be fooled. He had come out into the basket *souk*, but how strange it looked, completely boarded up and deserted! If only one among its several dozen shops had been open, it would still have been itself, but this way, only its distinctive shape, its steeply sloping floor and the hundreds of bunches of tiny green grapes that hung from its lattices above made it recognizable.

He decided that for the moment he was safe, that no one had seen him jump down, and he began to walk. When he turned the corner of the small street that led to the gate of Moulay Idriss, he realized that he would have done better to go in the other direction. A group of French police stood by the gate ahead of him. He hesitated, started to turn around.

"*Eh, toi! Viens ici!*" one of them called. Reluctantly he walked toward them. If he had gone the other way, he could have got up through Guerniz, he reflected, but he had come this way. Visions of torture flitted across his mind. They put you between vises and turned the screws until your bones cracked. They covered the floor of your cell with pails full of slippery soap and then smashed bottles on it, then they made you walk back and forth naked, and you kept falling, until you had pieces of glass sticking out of you all around, like the top of a wall. They horsewhipped you, burned you with acids, starved you, made you curse Allah, put strange poisons into you with needles, so that you went crazy and answered whatever questions they asked you. And always they laughed at you, even at the moment when they were beating you. They were laughing now, looking at him, perhaps because it was taking him so long to get to them, for he felt that he was scarcely moving at all. When he got fairly near, the one who had called to him began to speak in a loud voice, but Amar had no idea what he was saying. He stopped walking. The policeman roared: "*Viens ici!*" That he did understand. He moved ahead once again. The man stepped toward him and grabbed him roughly by the shoulder, talking angrily all the while. Unexpectedly he pushed him against the side of a stall behind him, banging his head on the long iron bolt. His movements were sudden, unforeseeable, violent. Now with one enormous red hand across Amar's throat he pinned him against the wall, while another man lazily approached and looked at him, smiling. This one also spoke to him. He stuck his hands into Amar's pockets, felt everywhere in the creases of his clothing—silently Amar gave fervent thanks to Allah for having directed him to leave his folding knife at home—and then struck him once on the cheek with the back of his hand. At this point he walked away, as if he were disgusted, either at the contact with Amar's flesh or at not having found what he had been looking for. The first man removed his hand from across Amar's neck, hit him once on the same cheek, exactly as the other had done, and gave him a violent push which sent him sprawling. Amar looked up at him, expecting to see the man's boot approaching to kick him or stamp on him, but he had turned away, and was sauntering back toward the others. "*Allez! Fous le camp!*" said one who was leaning against the side of the archway. Amar sat up in the muddy street and looked at them; something about his expression—perhaps its mere intensity—displeased one of the other men, for he called the attention of the man beside him to it, and they both came forward toward him, slowly and menacingly. Now his intuition whispered to him that the safe thing to do was to get up and run as fast as he could, that that was what they wanted to see. But he was determined not to give them that satisfaction. With exaggerated care he picked himself up, and not looking at any of them, took a few steps away from them.

Out of prudence he decided to compromise on a limp. And so, clutching at the door of a shop now and then for support, he made his slow progress down the street, sure that from one second to the next a blow would come from behind. When he finally looked back, at a point beyond the exit into the basket *souk*, the walls of the passageway had curved sufficiently to hide the men from his view. He stopped limping and went on to a public fountain, where he laboriously washed the mud from the legs of his trousers. There was not much he could do about the seat of them. The sun was strong now; he sat awhile by the fountain letting it dry the large wet patches he had made on the cloth.

Merely sitting still this way, gazing down the empty street, helped to calm the churning he felt inside his chest. He had just seen two Moslems killed, but he had not felt even a stirring of pity for them: they were in the pay of the French, for one thing, and then they had surely committed some unspeakable crime against their own people to have been singled out that way for annihilation. Although he was grateful for having been vouchsafed the spectacle of their death, he wished it might have been slower and more dramatic; they had fallen so quickly and unceremoniously that he felt a little cheated. Under his breath he began to invent a long prayer to Allah, asking Him to see to it that every Frenchman, before he was dragged down to Hell, which was a foregone conclusion in any case, might suffer, at the hands of the Moslems, the most exquisite torture ever devised by man. He prayed that Allah might help them discover new refinements in the matter of causing pain and despair, might show them the way to the imposing of hitherto undreamed-of humiliation, degradation and agony. "And drop by drop their blood will be licked by dogs, and ants and beetles will crawl in and out of their shameful parts, and each day we will cut away one more centimeter from each Frenchman's entrails. Only they must not die, *ya rabi, ya rabi*. Never let them die. At each corner of the street let us have one hung up in a little cage, so when the lepers come by they can use them as latrines. And we will make soap of them, but only for washing the sheets of the brothels. And one month before a woman is to give birth we will pull the child out and make a paste of it and mix it with the flesh of pigs and the excrement from the bellies of the Nazarenes' own dead, and feed their virgins with it."

It took energy to invent these fantasies; soon he tired of it, and with a final impassioned invocation, to make his impromptu prayer more formal, he rose and started on his way once more. By taking back streets he might be able to get all the way up to Bou Jeloud. The emptiness of the city spurred him on; he wanted to be in the midst of people. Up there, in the large cafés, there was sure to be at least someone.

CHAPTER 14

He went ahead, up the long steep hill through Guerniz with its great high houses on either side of the street. Here there was always the sweet smell of cedar wood and the gurgling of water behind the walls. A goat stood under an arch and looked out at him with its questioning yellow eyes. Through these streets and squares an occasional well-dressed man hurried, on his way to some nearby house for lunch, and

looking askance at Amar, with his battered face and muddy
European garments. Each time he caught this expression of
fastidiousness mixed with fear he smiled to himself: the ones
who wore it were not friends of freedom. It was a sure way of
telling. They had what they wanted in this world, and they
shared no desire with the students and other youths to see the
world change. At the same time it was dangerous to try to
judge people's sympathies by their appearance: there were
many wealthy men who gave their money and time to the
Istiqlal, and by no means all of the poor agreed with, or even
understood, the party's program, although the party made
constant bids for the favor of the lower classes.

But he would have staked all he possessed on his conviction
that these few men he saw now taking their quick dainty steps
along the streets of Guerniz were afraid—afraid of what might
happen as a result of the present crisis. France might lose part
of her power to protect the system under which they lived
and prospered. Then thoughtfully he asked himself how he
would feel if his father still owned the land at Kherib Jerad,
and the orchard by Bab Khokha, and the three houses in the
Keddane, if all of that, as well as the oil press and the mill,
had not long since been sold and the money spent. While he
was posing this question to his conscience and waiting for a
reply to come out, his attention was distracted by the sound
of wild cheering from the direction of the Talâa. Where there
was a crowd, that was where he wanted to be. Abandoning
his decision to use only the back streets, he cut through the
nearest alley that led off to his right, and was almost running
when he came up against the first bystanders, trying to witness things from a safe distance. He zigzagged ahead until he
reached a point where there were so many men packed into
the narrow alley that he was unable to push his way further.
He could see nothing at all, but he could hear the shouting
and singing. Occasionally the men beside him, from whom
the procession was likewise hidden, took up a chanted refrain,
and filled the small space around them with resonant sound.
Not Amar: it would have embarrassed him to open his mouth
and shout or sing along with them. It was part of his nature
to push his way to the inside and yet at the last moment to
remain on the outside. When the time came he always found

it difficult to participate; he could only grin and be thrilled by the others. His friends had long ago given up trying to instill in him a sense of teamwork on the soccer field. His principal interest there was in the brilliance of his own plays. Sometimes they would ask him if he thought he were playing alone against both teams. When they complained he would say impatiently: "*Khlass!* Was that a good pass or wasn't it? Do you want me to play or don't you? Just tell me that much and then shut up. *Khlass men d'akchi!*"

Now he stood here awhile, listening and looking at the men around him. They were ordinary people: small shop-keepers, artisans and their apprentices, all of them carried away by the excitement of the moment. The students marching in the Talâa were carrying portraits of the former Sultan; they were bound to meet the police when they got to Bou Jeloud, if not before, and there would be a fight. But that was what they wanted. They were unarmed, and they knew the French would attack. Each one secretly hoped to become a martyr; it would be almost as glorious as death on the battle-field. Amar wanted to see their faces and admire them, but being shut off from them he could feel only an abstract sympathy which was easily replaced by impatience. Soon he fought his way out of the crowd and returned the way he had come. It was possible that further up the hill he could double back to the Talâa above the head of the procession and catch it there. But each alley he chose was equally crowded, and he had to keep turning around and continuing upward on the parallel thoroughfare. When he got to Ed Douh he took a way that not everyone knew about, going down a flight of steps, across a public latrine, and out the other side, along a passage so narrow that if two people were to meet each other, one had to stand flat against the wall while the other squeezed through. The sun was very strong now, and the mud had dried almost completely. Down in here the stench was terrible; he hurried along, trying to breathe as seldom as possible until he arrived at the Talâa a little below the house of Si Ahmed Kabbaj. The cortege had not yet arrived, no police were in sight, and people were lined up along the sides of the thoroughfare or dashing excitedly from one side to the other. Amar knew where he wanted to go: it was a café one

flight up, above a grocery store, a little way inside the Bou
Jeloud gate.

The place was full, everyone was talking very loud, and
there was not a single place to sit. Disappointed, he resigned
himself to staying in the back room. If something happened
outside, he could always run through and watch from one of
the windows.

Even in the inner room there was not much choice in the
way of places to sit. He found a table in the corner furthest
from the main room; two men were already seated there playing dominoes, probably because all the cards and chess sets
were in use, but there was space on the bench for another.
When the boy came by, Amar ordered half a bread and a salad
of tomatoes and turnips.

The conversation around the café, although it never
touched on the situation of the day, was louder and more
animated than it would have been normally. A sizable group
of men stood at each window that gave on the street, merely
waiting. When Amar's food came, he murmured "*Bismil'lah*"
and ate it ravenously, sopping up the almost liquid salad with
small pieces of bread. Then he sat awhile quietly, prey to a
growing impatience; it spread from his chest upward and
downward, so that he drummed with his fingers on the bench
and the table, and jiggled his feet. The domino players looked
up from their game now and then, and stared at him, saying
nothing. Even if they had spoken he would not have minded.
The day was important and glorious; he felt that much with a
conviction which increased every moment. Whether it pre-
saged joy or misery was unimportant; it was different from all
other days, and by virtue of that fact alone, it deserved to be
lived differently.

Then suddenly he made an important decision: to leave
here and have tea at the Café Berkane, which was just outside
the walls, beyond the bus stop. Benani had warned him to
stay inside the walls today, but after all, Benani was not his
father. He called the boy, complained about the food, refused
to pay, then did pay, joked awhile with the proprietor, and left
smiling. It was excessively hot in the open square, and there
was still no sign of the demonstration. Slowly he walked up to
the big gate and passed under its main arch, out into the

world of motors and exhaust fumes. He had never seen so many policemen; they were lined up all around the outer square, against the walls, along the waiting room for the buses, in front of the Pharmacie de la Victoire, and as far up the road as he could see—many more than there had been the year the Sultan had come on a visit. This was very fine, and he was delighted that he had taken the courageous step of coming outside the Medina. They were all enemies, of course—he did not lose sight of that fact—but they looked admirably impressive in their uniforms, massed this way around the periphery of the square, and they had various models of guns with them which he had not seen before. It was decidedly worth seeing.

The Café Berkane, a fairly new establishment, had made use of a long, narrow strip of land between the ramparts of the Casbah Bou Jeloud and one of the branches of the river. The entrance to the building was reached by going across a small wooden footbridge, but there were generally tables on the outer side of the stream as well, scattered here and there under the delicate vertical fronds of the pepper trees. Today, however, the tables had not been put out, and the space usually given over to them was empty save for a few policemen who had been stationed there out of the glare, glad to be even in the thin, powdery shade that was half sunlight. Amar expected them to stop him as he approached the little bridge and perhaps search him again, or forbid him to enter, as if he were crossing a frontier, but they seemed not even to notice him.

The interior here, in contrast to the place he had just left, was almost deserted, and the few clients who occupied tables, if they spoke at all, conversed quietly, almost in whispers. This was most unusual; Amar quickly decided it was because they realized that they were outside the walls, and consequently felt less sure of themselves with regard to what this strange day might bring forth. Then, of course, there was the fact that those who sat near the windows and door had a clear and sobering view of the policemen standing out there in the sun. There were several rooms in the Café Berkane, all but one of which had windows on the front, directly over the water; if you spat or dropped a cigarette butt out, it landed in the river and was rapidly rushed downstream. The other room, a small afterthought tacked on to the back of the building, had an entirely different atmosphere: instead of facing north it faced south and east, and its view consisted of a section of the massive rampart walls and a square basin of still water—nothing more. The water in the pool was not deep—perhaps a meter—nor was it stagnant, since it was connected with the stream by a channel which went under the café. The owner had meant to plant bamboo and iris around its edge and to have water lilies floating on its surface; it had seemed such an excellent idea at the time he had built the café that he had been willing to spend the money for the cement to make the basin. Once he had opened the establishment, however, he had forgotten his original intention, and now the edges of the pool were ragged with masses of dying weeds, encouraged by the proximity of water but weighted down with the constantly descending dust from the nearby square. The small back room was the one Amar preferred, because it was the quietest, and the still water seemed to him more desirable and rare than the moving stream: in Fez rushing water was no novelty.

He knew just which table he wanted. It was behind the door, beside the window, all by itself. Often when he was not working he had come here and sat an entire afternoon, lulled by the din and music from the other rooms into a stage of vague ecstasy, while he contemplated the small sheet of water outside the window. It was that happy frame of mind into which his people could project themselves so easily—the mere absence of immediate unpleasant preoccupation could start it off, and a landscape which included the sea, a river, a fountain, or anything that occupied the eye without engaging the mind, was of use in sustaining it. It was the world behind the world, where reflection precludes the necessity for action, and the calm which all things seek in death appears briefly in the guise of contentment, the spirit at last persuaded that the still waters of perfection are reachable. The details of market life and the personal financial considerations that shoot like rockets across the dark heavens of this inner cosmos serve merely to give it scale and to emphasize its vastness, in no wise troubling its supreme tranquillity.

He passed through the first two rooms of the café, and into the small back one, where he was relieved to see that the table he wanted was unoccupied. In fact, there was no one in the room at all, which made him decide that he would stay only long enough to drink one tea, and then move to a more populous spot in another room. This was a small ceremony that he was inventing, for his feeling about the day demanded the observance of some sort of ritual. When he paid for the tea, he would change the twenty-rial piece he had found that morning in the street. It would be a most acceptable way in the eye of Allah, he thought, to use the money.

Today, without the customary hubbub, and without the usual unceasing noise of the radio (for the electricity had not yet been turned back on), the room in the rear seemed less a refuge than a small dungeon. He could hear the chugging sound of the buses' idling motors out in the square. He ordered his tea. While he was waiting, a boy came through the café carrying a huge tray of pastries, and stuck his head in the door. For some reason, perhaps because the boy looked vaguely like the friend who had ridden past that day on his bicycle and given him a ride, or perhaps because a man had just walked through the outer room whom he had often seen in cafés selling small amounts of kif clandestinely, Amar found himself thinking of the day he had determined to run away. Each time he reviewed that incident in his mind, he was conscious of a still active desire to avenge himself. At the same time he knew that he would never lift a finger against Mustapha, any more than Mustapha himself had done against him. It had to be done some other way. Allah had decreed that Mustapha should be born first. Therefore it was Mustapha's duty vis-à-vis his brother to compensate for that superiority with extra kindnesses. Mustapha had never understood that; on the contrary, he had used his position tyrannically, always to extort further offerings. Injustice could be redeemed only by successful retaliation. He stood up and peered around the doorway into the next room: the kif seller was talking in a corner by the window. The man had to be extremely careful in establishing the identity of his customers, or he could fall into the hands of an agent for the police. It was well known that the French had suppressed the sale of kif in the hope of getting the Moslems into the habit of drinking spirits; the revenue for the government would be enormous.

The fact that the religion of the Moslems expressly forbade alcohol was naturally of no interest to them: they always befriended those who broke the laws of Islam and punished those who followed them.

At this moment something strange happened: a man and a woman, both Nazarenes, came across the footbridge and went into the first room. An instant later they appeared in the second room, staring about shamelessly for a table at which to sit. For a moment they seemed to have found one that pleased them, then the woman said something and the man walked over to the doorway where Amar stood and peered inside the small room. It was when he looked out the window and saw the pool that he seemed to be deciding to install the woman in the inner room. Amar sat down quickly at his table, for fear they might choose that one to sit at. The *qaouaji* arrived with his tea. As he was leaving, the man called to him in Arabic, and ordered two teas and two *cabrhozels*. Now Amar looked closely at the man, decided he was not French, and felt the wave of hatred that had been on its way recede, leaving a residue of disappointment and indifference tinged with curiosity. When after a moment he realized that the man and the woman were both aware of his scrutiny, he turned quickly away and stared out at the pool, sipping his tea slowly. A little later he looked back at them. They were talking together in low voices and smiling at each other. The woman was obviously a prostitute of the lowest order, because her arms and shoulders were completely uncovered, and the dress she wore had been cut shockingly low in the neck. As if to confirm Amar's verdict, she presently took from her handbag a small case containing cigarettes, and put one in her mouth, waiting for the man to light it for her. Amar was astounded at her brazenness. Even the French women in the Ville Nouvelle did not go to quite such extremes in their lewd dress and behavior. And even the most disreputable prostitute would have taken the care to keep herself from being so badly burned by the sun. This woman had obviously come from working in the fields: she was completely brown from having been out in the open for a very long time. Yet here she was, wearing gold bracelets. His intuition now told him that he had made a mistake in his evaluation of her. She was probably not from the fields at all, but had had some misfortune which had obliged her to walk for many days in the sun's glare, and now she was ashamed, and wanted to hide herself from the crowd until she should be white again, which was why she had sought out the empty back room in which to sit. If this were the case, she would not be pleased to catch him staring at her. He sipped his tea assiduously and looked out the window. Soon he rose again and glanced through the doorway into the corner where the kif seller had been. The man had sat down, evidently on the invitation of a client, and was having a glass of tea. Amar walked over and spoke to him. The man nodded, handed him a little paper packet. Amar paid him, returned to his seat, and resumed his surreptitious examination of the two tourists. (Not being French, they fell perforce into that category.) What peculiar people they were, he reflected; the most foreign of all the foreigners he had seen. Their clothing was unusual, their faces were different, they laughed almost constantly, yet they did not seem to be drunk, and the most unaccountable detail to Amar was the fact that although, judging by all the small external signs by which one can judge such things, these two were interested in each other, the man never once seized even the woman's hand, never leaned toward her to touch her or smell her, nor did she, in spite of her otherwise lax conduct, once lower her eyes, find it impossible to meet his gaze. She merely sat there, as though she were unconscious of the difference in their sex. At the same time Amar divined an intensity in the air, as it were, between the two, a factor that for him weighed more heavily than their outward demeanor, which, after all, could have been entirely simulated. He had watched a good many French couples together, and while their definition of accepted public deportment included certain excesses which were unthinkable with Moslems, the two over-all patterns did not differ radically; French behavior contained no glaring disparities. But he found this couple basically incomprehensible.

When he had finished his tea, he decided to go outside and walk around the pool, but the small door had not been opened for a long time, and the bolt was rusty. This occupied him for a while, until he had succeeded in hammering it back with a stone which lay in the corner near by, perhaps kept there for that purpose. Then he opened the door, breaking all the spiderwebs, and stepped out. The sun was painfully hot in the airless space here between the café and the high city wall, and the pool was a malignant mirror magnifying its white light. He knelt down to feel the water: it also was hot. A dragonfly had skimmed too close to the surface and wet its wings; it made desperate contortions in its struggle to rise from the water. He watched it for a moment with interest, then, feeling sorry that it was about to die, he rolled his trouser-legs up as high as he could and lowered himself into the pool. It was rather deeper than he had imagined; the water came up to his thighs. The floor felt slippery and unpleasant on the soles of his feet, but he waded out, put his hand under the dragonfly and lifted it up. Then he stood there in the water looking at it and grinning, because its two enormous eyes seemed to be returning his stare. Perhaps it was thanking him. "How great are the works of Allah," he whispered. When the hot sunlight had dried its wings, it moved them a few times, and suddenly flew off into the air toward the ramparts. Amar climbed out of the pool, rolled his trouser-legs down, and wrung them out. Then he sat by the edge of the pool in the sun letting them dry. It seemed to him that in the distance, coming up over the roofs out of the dusty city, he could distinguish the clamor of human voices. But it was far away, and it sounded a little like the wind blowing through a crack in the door. If the procession came through Bab Bou Jeloud he wanted to be in the outer room to watch, and if there were a fight, a few of the French police were bound to be knocked down; that was what he wanted to see. It was always the Moslems who were pushed about, beaten and killed, even, as had happened today before his eyes, when it was Moslems who did the beating and killing. For a moment he felt a belated surge of sympathy for the two *mokhaznia* back in the alley near the lawyers' booths. Perhaps they had not known when they accepted their jobs with the French that they would be required to inform against their own people, and when they discovered it, it was already too late, they knew too much for the French to let them go free, and they were caught fast.

But in that case, he argued, it was their duty, even under pain of death, to refuse to carry out orders. How much more heroic it would have been for them to die as martyrs at the hands of the French than to be shot down shamefully like animals, their bodies cursed and spat upon by their brothers! He knew that a Moslem who died on the battlefield went directly to Paradise, without waiting for judgment, but he was not well documented on the fate of traitors. However, it seemed logical that they should be consigned straightway to the jurisdiction of Satan. He shuddered inwardly at the thought of what awaited anyone who landed in Hell. It was not the idea of the suffering that seemed fearful, but the certainty of its eternal continuation, no matter how repentant the victim might be. Suppose a man's heart changed, and he longed for Allah with all his might. The pain would lie, not in being forever roasted on a spit like a *mechoui* of lamb, or in being torn limb from limb the way the friends of freedom said the French had done to the Moslems at Oued Zem, but in the knowledge that never under any conditions could he be vouchsafed the presence of Allah. Death is nothing, he told himself, looking between his almost closed eyelids at the blinding sun reflected in the pool; the fortunate man is the one who can make of his death a glorious event that people will not forget. It occurred to him that perhaps that was why Mohammed Lalami had been so smug yesterday: he might already have known that his brother was going to be executed by the French. Some day, he thought, Mohammed would lie in wait for him and catch him unawares, and he would have a real fight on his hands. It might be a good idea, if ever he should catch sight of Mohammed, to go up to him and offer him his hand in apology. Probably Mohammed would not accept, but it might soften his heart and prepare the ground for a future reconciliation.

The sounds of shouting and singing were coming louder, and his trousers were nearly dry. He got up and went inside.

BOOK THREE

The Hour of the Swallows

*To my way of thinking, there is nothing more delightful
than to be a stranger. And so I mingle with human beings,
because they are not of my kind, and precisely in order to
be a stranger among them.*

—SONG OF THE SWALLOW:
THE THOUSAND AND ONE NIGHTS

CHAPTER 15

MORNINGS, Stenham and Moss were in the habit of sending little notes to one another via the servants. Since
his apartment gave on the garden, Moss would hand his missives to old Mokhtar, the man who swept the walks and
tended the flowers outside his door; Mokhtar would go up to
the main lobby and pass them to Abdelmjid, who had charge
of vacuum-cleaning the rugs of the public rooms. The year
before, it had been Abdelmjid himself who would climb up
into the tower and deliver the envelopes at Stenham's door,
but recently he had married Rhaissa, a jolly black girl whose
mother had been a slave in the house of a former pacha, and
since she cleaned the three rooms of the tower every day, it was
now she who came and knocked at his door when there was
a note that had been sent up from Room Fourteen for him.

The heart's desire of every modern Moroccan girl is to
have her incisors and canines capped with gold. Originally
Rhaissa's teeth had been healthy enough, but when her
mother had found a husband for her, she had naturally taken
her to have the necessary embellishments installed in her
daughter's mouth before the marriage. The work had been
done by a native specialist in the Medina, and ever since, poor
Rhaissa had suffered a great deal. Each day she insisted on
showing Stenham her inflamed gums; in her opinion the dentist had worked an evil spell on her during the treatment because her mother had demurred at paying the price he had
asked. But now, out of her own earnings, she had paid every

franc herself, and still she had pain. Stenham came to dread
her morning invasion of his quiet; he had bought her a packet
of sodium perborate, and she was using it regularly, first having emptied the powder from the pharmacist's envelope into
a special paper covered with magic symbols she had got from
a *fqih*. She thought it was doing some good, but she intended
to go back to the *fqih* soon and get another paper with a different set of symbols.

"I want to help the poor girl," he told Moss, "but I can't
go on looking into that red crocodile mouth every damned
time she comes in to make the bed."

It was one of those mornings when the city steamed quietly
under the strong sun. A haze of wood smoke and mist hung
above the flat terraces, enclosing and unifying the sounds that
rose from below, until when they reached his window they
were as monotonous and soporific as the uninterrupted humming of bees. Between ten and eleven o'clock in such weather
the city sounds always took on this strange character. He
wondered if perhaps it had to do with the direction of the
wind, since the one recognizable noise was that of a distant
sawmill somewhere over toward Bab Sidi bou Jida. A few
sluggish flies would sail into the room and go to sleep on the
tile floor in the sun. During this hour or so, Stenham would
abandon his work and, putting two chairs together face to
face in front of the windows, would stretch out voluptuously
in the hot sunlight, from time to time raising himself to scrib-
ble a few words in a notebook he kept lying beside him. He
had to be sure to lock the door first, to prevent Rhaissa from
bursting in on him and finding him naked; she had not completely mastered the difficult task of remembering to knock
before turning the door handle.

Today however she did knock, and he struggled up and
into his bathrobe, muttering: "Who the hell?" Any disturbance before lunch, other than the arrival of his breakfast tray,
infuriated him. He flung the door open and Rhaissa tendered
him the note she held in her hand. He thanked her gruffly,
saw that she was eager to discuss the state of her gums, and
shut the door in her face.

The note, from Moss, read: "What a beautiful day! Hugh
has promised to join me for lunch at the Zitoun. Bastela has

been ordered. Will you come too? May I expect you here in my room at half past twelve? My new model is a monster!!! Affly., Alain."

He lay down again in the sun, but found it impossible to go on inventing details in his description of the court of the Sultan Moulay Ismail. Soon he sprang up, shaved and dressed, and went down to Moss's room, hoping to catch him in the act of painting. But the model, an extremely gnarled old man, was just shuffling across the patio when he arrived, and Moss was cleaning his brushes. "This is most unusual," he said. "You've come early. You'll have to wait while I change. There's a new *Economist* on the table behind you; it just came this morning. Why don't you take it out into the garden with you? Or do you think you'd find it too dull after the incredible excesses of your creative imagination?"

Stenham snorted; he was tired of having to react to Moss's banter. "Excesses?" he said, picking up the magazine and stepping back out into the sunlight. "Excesses?" Down here there were sparrows twittering, and the air was strong with the scent of datura blossoms. Moss was bright; he knew fairly well where to stick the needles, but now the spots that had been tender were leathery, and Stenham, when he reacted at all, did so only out of courtesy and laziness. It made conversation easier, for Moss would simply have gone on, poking about, looking for other vulnerable points in his friend's character which so far he had not exploited.

He liked Moss because he was an enigma, and he was certain Moss enjoyed playing the magician, the mystery man with a thousand unexpected eccentricities up his sleeve. "I'm a simple businessman," Moss would declare piteously, "and I don't understand this mad jungle that seems to be the natural habitat of all you Americans." . . . "Don't take anything for granted when you talk to me. I must have everything explained. Your American ethical system is so utterly fantastic that my simple brain is quite at a loss trying to contemplate it."

But other times he would forget himself and complain: "After all, the English are really too much. One can't live in that constipated fashion forever. The world is a very lovely place. Have you ever been to Bangkok? I rather think you'd approve. Delectable people." . . . "The only thing that makes life worth living is the possibility of experiencing now and then a perfect moment. And perhaps even more than that, it's having the ability to recall such moments in their totality, to contemplate them like jewels. Do you understand?"

Stenham would bait him, saying very seriously: "No, I don't think I do. I'm afraid perfection doesn't interest me. It's always the exception; it's outside everything, outside reality. I don't see life that way."

"I know," Moss would say. "You see life from the most unattractive vantage-point you can find."

Stenham had long ago seen through the simple businessman pose; Moss had even confided on one occasion that he was writing a book, but without going further to say what kind of book it was going to be. And once from London, enclosed along with a rather pointless letter whose purpose was patently that of making the enclosure seem an afterthought, he had sent him a sheaf of short lyric poems, not very original but sufficiently well fashioned to convince Stenham that their author was by no means new to the muse. "He's as guilty as I am," Stenham liked to remind himself.

The sun down here in the garden was hot; the moist black earth exuded a sweetness, the heavy and disturbing odor of spring. Old Mokhtar came along the walk, his spent *babouches* scuffing the mosaics beneath. His turban always gave the impression of being about to come unwound. Not that it mattered how presentable he looked; ill health and overwork had drained all character from his soft, small face, and the turban, firmly or loosely wound, could do nothing for his woebegone appearance. Stenham always felt vaguely uneasy in his presence: the gentle vanquished expression he wore awoke a distant sense of guilt.

Moss moved out onto the terrace, adjusting his dark glasses, dressed as always for a stroll along Piccadilly. "I think I'm about ready to go, if you are. Shall we start?"

In the courtyard they looked to see whether Kenzie's MG were there, but it was not. Moss frowned.

"He's gone. We shall have to walk. And do let's go the short way."

"There are a dozen short ways," Stenham objected.

"The least labyrinthine, the least tiring. The quickest! Really, you are so difficult."

Stenham leading, they turned into the street to the left, making their way around the donkeys loaded with olives that were being carried to the press. "What do you mean, difficult? Why do you say that?" Stenham never could quite decide why it pleased him to lure Moss into a particular vein of querulousness; it was a game that could go on for hours, Moss playing the part of the simple, ingenuous soul, mystified and complaining, to Stenham's patient, mundane mentor, and it added pungency if Stenham occasionally made a direct accusation, such as: "Why do you insist on pretending this crazy unworldly innocence? What are you trying to discover?" It increased the savor because he said these things in such a way that they fell far short of the truth, of what he would have said had he really wanted to put an end to the game. Moss was quite aware of this, and knew that Stenham knew he was aware, and thus the game continued, growing always more ramified, more complex, more subtle, and taking up more of the time they spent together. Some day, thought Stenham, there would come a moment when it would no longer be possible to pull Moss out of it; whatever he said or did would only be in character, and the words would be uttered, the gestures made, no longer by Moss, but by this absurd creation of his that had nothing in common with the man it was meant to mask. I started him on this, he told himself, but he was there waiting to respond. And he picked the role of imbecile. And here I am, as usual, leading him, and he's pretending he doesn't know the way.

Here a public fountain dribbled in its niche; women and girls waited with their pails under its blue and green tiled vault. 1352, read the smaller tiles under the florid Arabic script that, praising the institution of monotheism, warned against substitutes for the one and only variety of it. "1352; that makes it a little over twenty years old," he thought. The constant slopping of water from the pails had made a cloaca of the street at this point; the clay had turned to viscid and slippery gray mud, and milky water bubbled up to fill each new footprint.

"Now, really, I say!" cried Moss. When he was pretending

to be outraged, his voice became sharper, his accent more exaggeratedly Oxonian. "*Where are you taking me?*"

"You've been through here half a dozen times before," Stenham shouted over his shoulder.

Eleven hundred years ago the city had been begun at the bottom of a concavity in the hills, a formation which had the contours of a slightly tilted bowl; through the centuries as it grew, a vast, eternally spreading construction of cedar wood, marble, earth and tiles, it had climbed up the sides and over the rim of the bowl. Since the center was also the lowest part, all the passageways led to it; one had to go down first, and then choose the direction in which one wanted to climb. Except the paths which followed the river's course out into the orchards, all ways led upward from the heart of the city. The long climb through the noonday heat was tiring. An hour after they had started out they were still struggling up the crowded lanes of the western hill. The mist had been totally dissipated, the sky had gone blue, hard and distant. The street widened, was suddenly filled with small boys on their way home from school. Moss and Stenham were finally able to walk abreast. Through the din of childish voices Moss said: "Will you tell me where we're coming out? I should have said there was no way of getting through the walls this far down. Don't you think we should have tried to get to Bab el Hadid?"

"D'you think so?" Stenham made his voice deliberately vague. He knew perfectly well where he was going, but the fun consisted in seeming to be wandering until the last minute, and then making a sudden virtuoso turn which would bring Moss out into a place that would be all the more startling for being completely familiar.

"I expect you've got one of your impressive conjurer's tricks up your sleeve," murmured Moss with a false air of resignation, "but I must say that this time I don't quite see how you can."

"No trick at all," Stenham assured him simply. "We're merely taking the most direct route to the Zitoun. Or, at least, I think we are. As soon as we get to the next turn I can tell you."

The next turn took them along a short dusty lane. Under an archway ahead a native policeman in a fez stood talking to a Senegalese soldier. As they stepped beneath the arch the breeze hit their faces, and there was the sound of a fast-running torrent. A panorama of hills lay before them.

"You *are* extraordinary!" said Moss delightedly. "I think you broke the doorway through the wall yourself. What's it called? Or has it a name?"

Stenham crossed the road and stood at the edge of the parapet looking over the narrow valley to the green slopes beyond. "Of course it has a name. They call it Bab Dar el Pacha."

"Oh, do shut up!" cried Moss. "You *know* there's no such gate. I've learned them all by rote, from Bab Segma to Bab Mahrouk and back again, and there's no such gate in the list."

"You'd better amend your list. Bab Dar el Pacha's a new gate they hacked in the wall twenty or thirty years ago so the Pacha could get a car up to his door."

"Vandalism," Moss remarked.

There was a short climb from here up to the hotel. Students from the College of Moulay Idriss came coasting down the hill on bicycles, going home to lunch, most of them wearing horn-rimmed spectacles, and all of them clothed in formless European suits that had never seen an iron or a sponge since the day they had been made.

Less spectacular than the tall trembling poplars that lined the road, but of more interest to the small boys who swarmed there, were the mulberry trees growing by the stream. The boys swished their long bamboo poles violently through the foliage above: the leaves sailed down and the green berries fell. Kenzie's yellow MG was parked in front of the Zitoun's entrance. It was covered with children; they were standing on the headlights and bumper, climbing over the doors and fighting on the front seat for the honor of sitting at the steering wheel. When Stenham and Moss arrived abreast of the car, the youth who stood beside it, studiously inscribing the word MOHAMMED with a ball pen on the gray canvas top, did not move. Probably he did not consider his contribution to the collection of scribblings which the car bore to be of much importance; there were so many others more showy and startling. Grinning faces, hands of Fatima, and various devices in both Roman and Arabic script had been scratched into the paint with nails and pebbles.

"Watch this," said Stenham. He went up close to the youth, who glanced at him and continued his careful work.

"*Chnou hada?* What are you doing?" he asked the boy.

The boy smiled. "Nothing," he answered simply.

Stenham pointed at the letters written on the cloth. "And that? What's that?"

"An automobile." The coldness that had come into his voice was doubtless due to the fact that he thought the Nazarene gentleman was taking him for an ignorant country boy.

"No, that word."

"Mohammed."

"Why did you write it?"

"Because it's my name."

"But why did you write it on the car?"

The youth shrugged, making it apparent that he considered this inquisition without cause or interest, and raised his hand again to complete the flourishes he was designing around the already written name. But Stenham seized the hand and pulled it away with some force. Some of the smaller children had drawn near and were watching. "Get out of here!" he yelled at them. They retreated to a safer distance.

"What's the matter with all of you?" He addressed his words to the adolescent, who still held the pen in his hand as if he were determined to finish what doubtless seemed to him a fine example of his signature. There was, of course, no answer, and so he was forced to continue. "That won't come off. Don't you know that?" Still there was no answer.

Moss came nearer, and beaming at the boy, said in his mellifluous if slightly English-sounding French: "Automobiles are very expensive. You shouldn't spoil them."

Now the boy reacted. "I haven't spoiled it at all," he said with dignity.

"But look!" exclaimed Moss, pointing to the disfigurations everywhere on the yellow paint. "See what the boys in this town have done! All that was done since this gentleman came here two weeks ago. It's going to cost him a lot of money to repair all that."

"How much?" said the youth impassively.

Moss thought quickly. "Perhaps fifty thousand francs. Or more."

The youth's face brightened. "He could sell it and buy a new one."

Stenham could not contain himself. "*Mahboul!*" he yelled. "You're an idiot! Get away from the car, you and all the rest of you! Go on! Go on!" He pushed the youth roughly out into the road, returned and lifted two of the smaller boys out of the front seat. The rest ran silently off and joined a group of berry-whackers.

The garden was a level square of ground which lay protected by the high embankment and the masses of unkempt vegetation along its side; the light wind that stirred the tops of the trees did not at the moment reach it. Tables were here and there, and canvas deck chairs to loll in. The place was deserted save for Kenzie, sitting in a far corner near the teahouse, having an animated discussion with a waiter in a white jacket, who crouched beside his chair. He had seen them come into the garden, but he affected not to be aware of their presence until they had arrived at his very feet. Then he glanced up and smiled casually, as if he had just left them only five minutes earlier. The waiter pulled up chairs for them and disappeared into the tea-house, from which now issued the scratching and clicking that in an Arab café marks the beginning of a phonograph record. "*Bilèche tabousni fi aynayah?*" complained Abd el Wahab in an enormous, dusty voice. "Why do you kiss me on my eyelids?"

"I've got a guest coming," Kenzie said suddenly.

CHAPTER 16

Kenzie had been sitting with no glass in front of him, and he appeared to have no intention of ordering anything, either for himself or for those who had just joined him. Stenham knew that Moss had observed this, and he was waiting to see what he proposed to do about it; he himself never drank, nevertheless he would have liked a glass of mint tea to wash down the dust he felt he had swallowed during the climb up through the Medina. But he was determined not to do the suggesting or the ordering: he did not intend to have the drinks charged to him. For one thing, he was living on a strict budget at the moment, hoping to make the advance on his present book last until he had completed it. And then, he felt that he, as the only American present, ought not to be expected to pay for everyone's drinks. Besides this, he had noticed on similar occasions during the past fortnight a certain sparring between Moss and Kenzie, as if each one had decided that the other should be forced to disburse a little more than his share; neither one ever seemed to have any small change on hand. Kenzie had confided to him that if he and Moss took a carriage together from Bou Jeloud to the Ville Nouvelle in the afternoon, Moss always rushed forward to pay, so that Kenzie would have to pay the return trip. "Well," Stenham had said, "why not?" "Because at six o'clock the tariff goes up," Kenzie had explained, with perfect seriousness. Now he felt that the situation might actually come to a head, if he merely sat still and waited. All that seemed destined to happen, however, was a mutual offering and refusing of cigarettes, with each man settling back to smoke one of his own brand.

"She's staying here at the Zitoun," Kenzie said presently, continuing the conversation of a moment ago.

"Curious," Moss observed, breathing out a thick cloud of smoke which he watched a second before going on. "An American staying here. You wouldn't expect it to be comfortable enough for her."

Stenham held his tongue, certain that Moss was trying to bait him.

"She's rather a good sort, and not at all stupid," Kenzie went on. "Yesterday I found her sitting all alone here in the garden reading. We got to talking, and I told her you were here"—he looked at Stenham—"and she's heard of you. I thought it might be fun if the only four English-speaking people in Fez had a grand reunion."

"Don't forget the missionaries and the Consul and his wife," advised Stenham.

"But I said people." Kenzie was an avowed enemy of the British Consul: there had been unpleasantness over the mislaying of a pile of mail. Stenham and Moss were well informed on the subject.

"I rather wish you'd told me she was going to eat with us," Moss said; he sounded aggrieved. "And the reason is"—he raised his voice—"that I'm jolly hungry and I'd have eaten more breakfast if I'd known. Where is she?"

"She'll be along in a minute," Kenzie assured him.

"Incidentally," said Stenham, "you'll find a new addition to the collection of graffiti on your car when you go out. The word 'Mohammed' nicely written in indelible ink on the hood, just behind the strut. I caught him in the act."

"I hope you gave him a good buffeting," said Kenzie.

"Well, no, as a matter of fact, I didn't."

"A good clout on the head works wonders. They don't forget it."

"Maybe," said Stenham, "but then another one comes along who hasn't had the benefit of a clout. You can't discipline the whole country."

"Still," Moss said dreamily, "that's what must be done before they can ever accomplish anything."

Stenham bridled. "What d'you want them to accomplish? You sound like a leader of the Istiqlal. Why have they got to accomplish something? Can't they just be let alone and go on as they are?"

Moss smiled. "No, my dear fellow. You know very well they can't."

Stenham looked around the garden and thought: It's too nice a place to spoil with an argument. To Moss he said pleasantly: "My question was rhetorical. You're worse than my wife. She always thought everything needed an answer."

Moss cleared his throat and signaled the waiter, who had come out of the tea-house and was pulling dead leaves from one of the vines that covered its sides.

"A bottle of Sidi Brahim rosé, and set the table, please, and bring a big bowl of ice to cool the wine in. We'll have the *bastela* first. How is it today?"

"*Magnifique, monsieur,*" said the waiter gravely.

"*Magnifique,* eh?" Moss echoed, amused.

The waiter hurried off. Stenham glanced at Kenzie, to see how he was taking Moss's petulance. Kenzie smoked blandly. A stork sailed slowly past overhead, not moving its wings, but balanced, soaring on some invisible air-current. From the loudspeaker in the tea-house came the enigmatic phrases of a Chleuh dance: rasping *rebab*, excitable *guinbri*, high childish voices making their long, throaty mountain calls above the hopping accompaniment.

Moss was really very pro-French, Stenham was thinking. Like them, he refused to consider the Moroccans' present culture, however decadent, an established fact, an existing thing. Instead, he seemed to believe that it was something accidentally left over from bygone centuries, now in a necessary state of transition, that the people needed temporary guidance in order to progress to some better condition, "So that," Stenham had bitterly remarked, "they can stop being Moroccans." For the French had basically the same idea as the Nationalists; they quarreled only over externals, and even there he was beginning to wonder if these supposed disagreements were not part of a gigantic Machiavellian act, put on under the combined auspices of the French and Moroccan Communists in governmental positions, who, knowing better than anyone that before there can be change there must be discontent, were willing to drag the country to the verge of civil war in the process of manufacturing that discontent. The methods and aims of the Istiqlal were fundamentally identical with those of Marxism-Leninism; that much had been made abundantly clear to him by reading their publications and talking with members and friends of the organization. But wasn't it possible that any movement toward autonomy in a colonial country, especially one where feudalism had remained intact, must almost inevitably take that road?

He was always hearing the complaint: "America has not helped us." That was only the first sentence of a long and fearful indictment whose final import was, to him at least, terrifying. And time passed, with hatred of France and America growing each day, being artificially inculcated in every segment of the population by the clever young cynics sent out for that purpose. Yet it was impossible for him to take sides in such a controversy, because whenever he thought it all through to some sort of conclusion, the controversy always seemed to evaporate: it was as though the two sides were working together to achieve the same sinister ends.

"Or is Moss right, and am I a hopeless reactionary?" The key question, it seemed to him, was that of whether man was to obey Nature, or attempt to command her. It had been

answered long, long ago, claimed Moss; man's very essence lay
in the fact that he had elected to command. But to Stenham
that seemed a shallow reply. To him wisdom consisted in the
conscious and joyous obedience to natural laws, yet when he
had said that to Moss, Moss had laughed pityingly. "My dear
man, wisdom is a primitive concept," he had told him. "What
we want now is knowledge." Only great disillusionment
could make a man say such a thing, Stenham believed.

For protection, to follow out his train of thought, he
closed his eyes and tilted his head upward so that he might
appear to be listening to the conversation. Perhaps thus he
could be assured of a few extra seconds alone. But it soon
became evident that his very resolve to escape for a moment
was on the contrary a sign that he had been absent and was
being drawn back. The words of Kenzie and Moss began to
penetrate to his hearing; he was on his way back to consciousness of the canvas chair, the sun in the garden, the
trembling poplars.

"Are you asleep, by any chance?" Moss inquired. Stenham
forced himself to smile indulgently before he opened his eyes.

"No, just content."

"I believe you're invited tonight to Si Jaffar's for one of
those interminable dinners, aren't you?"

"Now I'm not content. Why did you remind me?" Stenham asked.

"I didn't suppose you had forgotten it, and I mentioned it
because I intend to talk about Si Jaffar, and I want to caution
you against repeating any of what I'm going to say." Moss
now ceased looking seriously over his spectacles and smiled.
"It's a perfectly absurd tale, but I think you and Hugh would
enjoy it. Yesterday the old man and I met by chance in the
Ville Nouvelle, and I invited him to sit with me at the Ver-
sailles. He ordered one of your ghastly American drinks—one
of those outlandish medicinal mixtures called Tipsy Kola or
some such thing, and then proceeded to hug the glass as
though it were at least Armagnac. An hour later he was still
taking tiny sips, and talking, talking, of course, all the while,
in his incredible French."

"What about?" asked Kenzie.

"Oh, scandal of various sorts, juicy bits about the French,

mostly. And a little about the Moroccans. They *are* extraordinary people, these Fassiyine."

"I expect he told you some amusing things."

"Some were most amusing," Moss answered absently. "Toward the end of our interview I managed, only God knows how, to take enough control of the conversational reins to steer us into the highly delicate subject of Moulay Abdallah. I began by asking him if he knew how many prostitutes the quarter housed. His little eyes became even more pig-like than usual, and he began to wring his hands, but so violently I thought the skin would come off any minute. 'Oh *là*, Monsieur Mousse!' he wailed. 'This is a very difficult problem. It is so many years since I have paid a visit to our renowned quarter, you understand—' The old reprobate! I'm told he's there every week at least once. But I asked him if he'd say it was nearer five thousand or twenty thousand. By this time he was rubbing his hands in the other direction to ease the pain. 'Ah, Monsieur Mousse! None of my acquaintances has ever attempted to count the unfortunate girls!' This is merely to illustrate the difficulties and hazards that one can't escape if one wants to converse with the old fox."

Stenham did not feel that Moss's caricature did Si Jaffar justice, even though it was recognizable; there was a whole other side upon which it did not touch at all.

"But I'm nothing if not persevering," Moss continued. "I went ruthlessly ahead, as you can imagine, in the hope of getting to my point before some friend of his came by and ruined everything. I was finally able to get down to age groups, and mentioned little Khémou and my divine baby Haddouj, making it quite clear that anything over fifteen was not for me. At this point his smiles were dripping like treacle from his old face, and he was merely caressing his fingers rather lecherously. 'Ah, you are so right, Monsieur Mousse! It is the little ones who are the precious pearls. Among us it is said that they are like the first tender shoots of wheat that spring up to announce the return of life to the earth,' or some such balderdash. I can't possibly remember all he said, because he went on and on, absolutely delighted with the turn the conversation had taken, singing praises of budding trees, early adolescence, swollen streams, young doves learning to fly, and

keeping it all, now that I think of it, quite general and impersonal, so that actually in the end it was I who had said everything and he nothing—but nothing at all. Wherever I was
able, I dropped a hint, you know, how it was jolly difficult for
a painter to get a model, and how I realized it was out of the
question even to dream of getting one anywhere *except* from
some house in Moulay Abdallah, and how even there I knew
it was almost impossible. And each time he would nod understandingly and agree: 'Oh, yes, out of the question, naturally.'. . . 'Ah, yes, Moulay Abdallah.' . . . 'Ah, of course,
almost impossible. You are quite right.' And so eventually I
had to put it to him. I said: 'Si Jaffar, do you think you could
use your influence to get me a model?' At this the old monster merely closed his eyes like a cat. He had on both pairs of
glasses by this time, and he made a most peculiar-looking cat,
I can assure you, with his white silk hood up over his fez.
When he opened his eyes, he said: 'Monsieur Mousse, I understand your difficulties. I am able to sympathize with you. I
sympathize even very strongly, and I assure you that no matter what hardship it may cost me, you will have a model at
your door at nine o'clock tomorrow morning.' That sounded
more like what I wanted to hear, and I thought it would be
only politic to let the subject drop."

Stenham listened apathetically. For one thing, whenever the
two Englishmen talked together in his presence, he felt, unreasonably enough no doubt, that he was in some subtle fashion being left out of the conversation. And then, since it was
he who originally had brought Moss and the Moroccan family together, he did not wholly approve of Moss's efforts,
however roundabout they might be, to enlist the old gentleman as a procurer. However, a story told by Moss never
became downright boring, because its course followed a carefully plotted graph. And so he listened. Suddenly, before the
tale was anywhere nearly finished, he knew how it was going
to come out. "My new model is a monster!" Moss's note had
read. And he remembered the bent and misshapen old man
he had met in the patio. A feeling akin to admiration for Si
Jaffar awoke in him, and he began to chuckle. Moss turned
reproachful eyes upon him. "You beast!" he cried. "Don't
you spoil my story!"

"I won't. I'm sorry." He ceased laughing aloud, and merely smiled. It ended exactly as he had foreseen: the ancient gentleman was indeed the model Si Jaffar had sent.

"Priceless," said Kenzie.

"That seems to me a rather civilized way of having a good time," Stenham said. He did not want to see enmity develop between Moss and Si Jaffar: in a place where the circle of acquaintances was so small, a feud could complicate everyone's life no end. "It's a practical joke, I'll admit, but about a thousand percent more subtle than our kind, don't you think?"

"No," Moss objected, turning around in his chair to look for the waiter, "I rather fancy it's more than a mere joke. They don't go in for jokes, you know. My feeling is that it was meant decidedly as a rebuff. But there you are; you can cudgel your brains about it for the next ten years, but you'll get nowhere. The old fox will be as innocent as a newborn babe the next time I see him. What can you do? It's rather devastating, I must say."

"But what amuses me," insisted Stenham, "is the note of madness they can inject into any situation at the drop of a hat. Like the other day when I met the hotel manager in the Medina and stopped to talk for a minute. You know I never go into the office, so I never see him except in the street somewhere, and then's when I have to pass the time of day, which means a little dissertation on the weather. Which is what we were doing, when suddenly a very dignified gentleman approaches and says in French: '*Pardon, messieurs,* but I believe you were discussing amber? May I ask if you were referring to cut pieces, or to amber in its natural state?' What do you say then?"

Moss did not appear to see any connection between this story and his own experience. "What, indeed?" he said distraughtly, craning his neck again to catch sight of the waiter.

At the far end the gate opened; the day, the garden acquired sudden meaning as she skipped down the steps. All of what a moment ago had seemed a complete cosmos now retreated instantly into the background to become nothing more than the décor in front of which the principal character was to move. She was in her early or middle twenties, and she wore a white silk shirt and white slacks. The men rose as she came lightly toward them, turning this way and that among the tables and chairs.

"Ah, charming," Moss murmured, but in a very low voice.

Her form and face were such that she belonged to the happy category of women who can always be sure they are attractive under any circumstances, even the most adverse; her carriage and manner of walking made it clear that she knew this. Also, Stenham felt, she took it so much for granted that she did not attach very great importance to it. He had a brief vision of windswept sunny places as she came near. Then Kenzie said: "And this is Mr. Stenham, a compatriot of yours. Madame Veyron."

The waiter had come into the garden behind her, and stood at a respectful distance during the first moments of conversation. Again it was Moss who called him over and impatiently told him to set the table.

"If I've kept you waiting," she said, "you must blame it on this town. I suppose it's an old story to all of you, but when I get wandering around down in those *souks* I just can't leave. It's fascinating."

"It never gets to be an old story," Stenham assured her. "At least, not to those who like it. Of course, not everybody likes it."

She put her elbows on the table and leaned forward. "Now, really. How could anyone help loving it?"

Kenzie laughed. "A great many people seem to be able. It's not one of the favorite tourist spots, by any means. A bit overpowering, I should think, on first contact."

She seemed to be considering; the serious expression enhanced the straightforward beauty of her features. "Overpowering. Of course it is. But don't we all like to be overpowered, one time or another?"

"Oh, yes," agreed Moss. "For a while it's pleasant. But once one ceases to be awestruck by the complexity of the streets or the completeness of the still medieval society, unless one has discovered other virtues in a town like this, it can become most *un*overpowering—a bloody bore, as a matter of fact, I should think. So the tourists come, stay a day or two, and go on somewhere else. For which I confess I give thanks."

"Well," she said, in a suddenly very flat, American fashion

(as she spoke it came and went, Stenham noticed, that small reminder of the part of the world in which she had grown up, and which had formed her), "I've been here all of three days, and so perhaps you can believe me when I say I think, I *think*, anyway, that I've found enough unspectacular aspects around the town to qualify me as a potential Fez-lover." She folded her hands together and squeezed them, hunching her shoulders at the same time; the gesture seemed that of a small girl. "It's so *exciting*!" Then she fished in the pocket of her slacks and pulled out a pack of Casa Sport.

"Here," said Kenzie. "Have one of these."

She shook her head vehemently. "No, I like this black tobacco. It goes with the place. I'll always associate the smells here—the cedar wood, the mint, the fig trees, all the other mad, wonderful smells—with the taste of this tobacco. At home in Paris I always smoked Gauloises anyway, but these are very different, somehow. Not the same taste at all." She took two puffs and turned completely to face Kenzie. "I have a confession to make. I've ticked off that guide you got me, and found myself another who can at least walk. Your old Santa Claus couldn't keep up with me. He was always straggling miles behind, panting and rolling his eyes like a lunatic. He hated me, anyway. I *had* to get rid of him."

Kenzie's expression was one of displeasure, but he merely said: "Oh? You want to be careful."

She looked to Stenham for confirmation of this opinion. "Do you think so, Mr. Stenham? I know you know the place inside out."

He did not want to pique Kenzie by assuming the omniscient part she had assigned him. "A girl can't be too careful," he said with a grin.

"And you, Mr. Moss, what do you say?" she went on, making a game of it.

"Oh, I should think if he was an authorized guide he'd be safe enough."

"No. I mean in general. Do you think it's dangerous for me to go around alone?"

"I should say that in normal times the place was absolutely safe, but of course now— Well, they *are* dreadfully fanatical, you know."

"You're all a bunch of old fuddy-duds," she complained.

Moss and Kenzie seemed to stiffen imperceptibly, and turned their heads toward Stenham, as if to discover from his expression whether she were seriously annoyed. Her remark obviously was not one to be expected during the first few minutes of an acquaintanceship. He decided not to enlighten them, and changed the subject.

While they ate the *bastela*, over which Mme Veyron continued to enthuse (and it was very good; the pastry was flaky and the little pieces of steamed pigeon-breast were perfectly cooked), Moss held forth upon the deviousness of the native mind, as illustrated by his previous anecdote. Then the question of wine arose. Moss wanted more rosé, but of a different brand; Kenzie thought some white would be better. "You don't *drink* wine with *bastela*," objected Stenham.

"What nonsense!" Moss snapped. He clapped his hands, and this time the waiter came running. "*Une bouteille de Targui rosé*," he told him. "You'll see," he assured Mme Veyron. "It goes perfectly." To Stenham he remarked: "You have a rather unpleasant puritanical strain."

"Say puristic. I just can't see wine with Arab food."

"Really?" said Mme Veyron with the interest of one being told a fact not generally known. Moss ignored her.

"No, I say puritanical, because I mean that. I've observed you, my dear man, over a period of time, and I've come to the conclusion that you simply don't want to see anyone enjoy himself. You don't even like to see people eat well. You're happiest when the food is tasteless and insufficient. I've watched you, my boy. Whenever we happen to get a really miserable little meal your spirits soar. Disgusting trait."

"You're so wrong," Stenham said, attempting to give his voice the proper ring of sincerity. However, he was troubled. There was at least an element of truth in what Moss said, but it was not that simple; a reason came in between. It had to do with a sense of security. He could not feel at ease with gourmets and hedonists; they were a hostile species.

"Why *don't* you ever drink?" Kenzie asked him gently.

"Because it makes me sick. Can you think of a better reason?"

"I don't believe it," Moss said flatly.

Stenham was annoyed with himself; he felt it was his fault that the conversation had taken this inquisitorial turn. It seemed to him that if he had been going to answer such a question at all, he should have taken a more belligerent and irrational tack, and not exposed himself this way in front of her. It was as though he had shown them his biceps and they had said: "You need the exercise." For years people had been asking him this same question, and he considered it a private matter, one which could not possibly interest anyone but himself. "You don't drink! Not even wine? Why not?"

"Don't get me started on it," he said, raising his voice slightly. "Let's say that for me it's what we Americans call a low-grade kick. You understand that?" He was looking only at Moss.

"Oh, quite! And may I ask what you consider a high-grade kick?"

"There are plenty of those," he replied imperturbably.

His tone may have nettled Moss, for he pressed on. "Such as—?"

"You're on the carpet, Mr. Stenham," said Mme Veyron.

Stenham pushed away his plate; he had finished anyway, but he liked the dramatic gesture as an accompaniment to the words he was going to say. A sudden gust of wind from the south swept through the garden, bringing with it the smell of the damp river valley below. A corner of the tablecloth flapped up and covered the serving dishes. Kenzie lifted it and dropped it back where it belonged.

"Such as keeping these very things private. After all, one's thoughts belong to oneself. They haven't yet invented a machine to make the human mind transparent."

"We're not discussing thoughts," said Moss with exasperation. "You're more English than the English, my dear John. I find it most difficult to understand you. You have all the worst faults of the English, and from what I can see, very few of the virtues we've been led to expect from Americans. Sometimes I feel you're lying. I can't believe you really are an American at all."

Stenham looked at her. "Won't you vouch for me?"

"Of course," she said smiling, "but I'll bet you're from New England."

"What do you mean, *but*? Of course I'm a New Englander. I'm American *and* a New Englander. Like a Frenchman I met once in a jungle town in Nicaragua. He had the only hotel there. 'Are you French, monsieur?' I asked him. And he answered: '*Monsieur, Je suis même Gascon.*' I'm *even* a Gascon, and I like to keep the state of my finances private. And my politics and religion. They're all high-grade kicks as far as I'm concerned. But only if they're kept private."

"The world's not going in that direction," said Moss dryly. "You should be flexible, and prepare for what's coming." He had finished peeling an orange and now, splitting it into sections, he began to eat it. "You're preposterous," he added, but without conviction, as if he were thinking of something which might or might not be connected with the conversation.

"I know just what Mr. Stenham means," announced Mme Veyron, rising suddenly. "Excuse me a second. I'm going to my room for a minute. I'll be right back. I don't want to miss any of this."

They stood up, holding their napkins in their hands. "It's all over," said Stenham meaningfully. "You won't miss anything."

Moss shook his head slowly back and forth. "I dislike to see anyone so ill equipped for the future. The difference between us, my boy, is that I believe in the future." (That and God knows how many million dollars, thought Stenham.) "One of these days the future will be here, and you won't be ready for it."

Mme Veyron returned to the table; she had put on a little white canvas hat with a crush brim. "I'm a little afraid of this sun," she explained. "It's awfully treacherous, and I've had some horrible experiences."

"Sunburn can be pretty bad," Stenham agreed.

"No, I can take any amount of it on my skin. But I get sunstroke so easily. It wasn't so bad when I had Georges with me—my husband—but when I left him and began batting around alone, it wasn't funny. It's frightening to be all alone and have a fever and be delirious, and know there's not a living soul within a thousand miles who gives a damn whether you live or die. And I nearly did die last year in Cyprus. The doctor I called in gave me aspirins, one after the other, and when they didn't seem to have any effect he went off to consult an old woman, and I found out later she was the local witch."

"But at least you came out of it all right," Stenham said.

"It looks like it." She smiled. "Anyway, her treatment was all done over her own fire in her own hut somewhere on the edge of town. I never even laid eyes on her."

Kenzie was laughing, a little too enthusiastically, Stenham thought. "Priceless!" he exclaimed. An instant later he rose, saying to her: "Would you like to see the inside of the teahouse? It's quite attractive. Order coffee, will you, Alain?" The two moved off, she stooping every few steps to examine a flower or a leaf.

Stenham arranged his chair so that he could lie far back in it, staring into the blue afternoon sky. "*Bastela's* an indigestible dish," he said heavily. The inevitable languor that followed on the heels of such a noonday meal was announcing itself. He was not sleepy, but he felt an utter disinclination to move or think. In his mind's eye he began to see vignettes of distant parts of the town: arched stone bridges over the foaming river, herons wading in shallow places among the reeds and cane, the little villages that the very poor had recently built at the bottoms of the ancient quarries—you could stand at the top and look down vertically upon their houses made in building-block patterns; the people were not so impoverished that their terraces could not be spread with orange and magenta rugs being aired, and women sat in tiny courtyards that were pools of shade, out of the venomous sun, thumping on their drums of clay. Now he saw the entrances to the vast caves in the further quarries, hidden by the wild fig trees that had grown up; inside the huge rooms and long corridors it was cool, and the greenish light came down through deep shafts, filtered by the vegetation that choked their openings. The silence of centuries was in here; no one ever entered but an occasional outlaw who did not fear the *djenoun* that inhabited such places. It was all these strange and lonely spots outside the walls, where the city-dwellers unanimously advised him not to walk, that he loved. Yet their beauty existed for him only to the degree that he was conscious of their outsideness, or that he could conjure up the sensation of compactness which the idea of the Medina gave him. It was the knowledge that the swarming city lay below, shut in by its high ramparts, which made wandering over the hills and along the edges of the cliffs so delectable. They are there, of it, he would think, and I am here, of nothing, free.

Soon Kenzie and Mme Veyron came out of the tea-house, chatting affably. The waiter appeared with coffee (although Stenham could not have told when Moss had ordered it), and the general conversation was resumed feebly, with isolated remarks and distraught if polite rejoinders. It was dying because everyone wanted nothing better than merely to sit in silence. But of course silence was unthinkable, and so they talked.

Interesting things would be happening in the not-too-distant future, Kenzie promised. Although Casablanca was the present theatre of activity, Fez was the fountainhead of resistance to French rule, and the government was nearly ready to crack down on the rebellious elements there. But it would be extremely serious because it would mean mass arrests on a gigantic scale. The concentration camps were being enlarged at the moment, to have everything in readiness for the day. This was all being recounted for Mme Veyron's benefit, but it was not eliciting the response which it should have; from time to time she said: "Oh," or "I see," or "My God!" and that was all. And Stenham thought sadly: "He enjoys all this. He wants to see trouble." For Kenzie was making it very clear that he sided wholly with the Moroccans. Stenham, for his part, could find no such simple satisfaction. There was no possible way, he felt, of telling who was right, since logically both sides were wrong. The only people with whom he could sympathize were those who remained outside the struggle: the Berber peasants, who merely wanted to continue with the life to which they were accustomed, and whose opinion counted for nothing. They were doomed to suffer no matter who won the battle for power, since power in the last analysis meant disposal of the fruits of their labor. He could not listen to Kenzie's excited recounting of arms discoveries by the police in the homes of wealthy citizens of the Medina, or of what the followers of Si Mohammed Sefrioui were rumored to be plotting in some stinking cell of the Medersa Sahrij at that very moment, because it was all of no importance. The great medieval city had been taken by force and strategy innumerable times; it would be taken again some day, the difference being, he feared, that on that day it would cease for all time being what it was. A few bombs would transform its delicate hand-molded walls into piles of white dust; it would no longer be the enchanted labyrinth sheltered from time, where as he wandered mindlessly, what his eyes saw told him that he had at last found the way back. When this city fell, the past would be finished. The thousand-year gap would be bridged in a split second, as the first bomb thundered; from that instant until the later date when the transformed metropolis lay shining with its boulevards and garages, everything would have happened mechanically. The suffering, the defeat or victory, the years of reconstruction—none of it would have had any meaning, it would have come about all by itself, and on a certain day someone would realize for the first time that the ancient city had been dead since the moment the first bomb had gone off.

Moreover, no one would care. Perhaps one could say it was already dead in one sense, for most of those who lived in it, (and certainly the younger ones without exception) hated it, and desired nothing more than to tear it down and build something more in accordance with what they considered present-day needs. It looked too impossibly different from any city they had ever seen in the cinema, it was more exaggeratedly ancient and decrepit than the other towns of Morocco. They were ashamed of its alleys and tunnels and mud and straw, they complained of the damp, the dirt and the disease. They wanted to blast the walls that closed it in, and run wide avenues out through the olive groves that surrounded it, and along the avenues they wanted to run bus lines and build huge apartment houses. Fortunately the French, having declared the entire city a *monument historique*, had made their aims temporarily unattainable. The plans for every new construction had to be submitted to the Beaux Arts; if there was any departure from the traditional style it could not be built.

"One thing you must give the French credit for," he was fond of saying, "is that they've at least managed to preserve Fez intact."

But often he felt there was a possibility that this was true only architecturally, that the life and joy had gone out of the place a long time ago, that it was a city hopelessly sick.

Suddenly Mme Veyron stood up. "I'm sorry, gentlemen," she said, stifling a yawn. "This has been very nice, but I'm simply overcome with sleep. I've got to lie down and have a little siesta."

Kenzie was disappointed. "I'd hoped to take you to the gardens later," he said. They were strolling toward the gate.

"Why don't you give me a ring about five-thirty from your hotel? Would there still be time?"

"It would be a good deal quicker if I called by here for you then."

She assumed an expression of dubiousness, but not before Stenham had caught a flash of resentment in her eyes.

"Well," she said slowly, "you may have to wait awhile for me to get myself ready."

He would do some waiting, too, thought Stenham; she'd see to that. Then he decided to try his hand. "Why don't you all have tea tomorrow with me? We can go to some out-of-the-way little café."

They had climbed the steps and were standing in front of the entrance door. Kenzie stood to one side with the waiter, paying the check.

"I think it would be wonderful. Let's," she said.

CHAPTER 17

Stenham awoke the next morning with a slight headache. The food at Si Jaffar's had been unusually heavy, and as a result he had passed a night of fitful sleep during whose frequent moments of wakefulness he was leadenly conscious that he was suffering from indigestion. *Bastela* at noon, and then at night lamb with lemon and almonds, drowned in hot olive oil, and that glutinous bread, helped down by six glasses of mint tea that was so sweet it stung the throat. . . . The more honor they wanted to pay you, the more inedible they made the food, weighing it down with sugar and oil.

It was a day of violent clarity, throbbing with sunlight. Any part of the sky he stared at from his pillow blinded him. The doves that had their nests somewhere outside his windows gurgled beatifically, and he had the feeling that they were some sweet substance melting out there in the fierce morning sun; soon they would be nothing more than a bubbling syrup, but the sound would go on, the same as now. He yawned, stretched, and got slowly out of bed. The telephone was attached to the opposite wall. Moss found this an insufferable inconvenience. "I shouldn't like to have to stagger across the room to order breakfast," he had said when he first saw it. "Do take a comfortable room, and with a proper bath," he had urged him. "Like yours?" Stenham had said. "Yours happens to be just four times as expensive as this. Have you thought of that?" "Come, now, John. When things are as cheap as they are here, such mathematics don't mean anything," Moss had objected. "And you have dollars. I with my poor pounds have some excuse for trying to make my money stretch." This was another facet of the little game they played together. Stenham knew perfectly well that Moss had one of the largest fortunes left in England, and that moreover he owned apartment houses, cinemas and hotels in places that dotted the globe from Havana to Singapore, including several cities of Morocco, to which he made constant little trips, referring to these as "tours of inspection." But he also knew that it gave Moss intense pleasure to play poor, to pretend that the security which his several million pounds gave him was not there in the background, because, as he had exclaimed one day when he was in a confiding mood, "it's a stifling sensation, I assure you; every consideration is dictated by the existence of that *thing* there behind you. You have no freedom—none." At the time Stenham had replied rather tartly that you had whatever freedom you really desired. But he was willing to abet him in his pretense.

He took the receiver off the hook; it began to make a loud, tinny purring which continued until there was a small explosion as a man's voice said: "*Oui, monsieur.*"

"I should like to order breakfast."

"*Oui, monsieur, tout de suite.*"

The man hung up and the noise began again. Furious, Stenham jiggled the hook until the voice returned and spoke again with some asperity. "*Vous désirez, monsieur?*"

"I want breakfast," said Stenham with exaggerated clarity, "*mais ce matin j'ai envie de boire du thé. Au citron. Vous avez compris?*"

"But I have already ordered coffee for you, the same as every day," the voice objected.

"Change the order."

"I shall do my best," the voice said with dignity, "but it will be somewhat difficult, since the coffee is at this moment being prepared in the kitchen."

"I won't drink the coffee," announced Stenham severely. "I want tea." He hung up, certain that he was going to find it impossible to work this morning. Any small incident at this hour could prove a barrier. And now the blood seemed to be pounding harder in his head. After swallowing two Empirins with a glass of cold water, he unlocked the door into the corridor and lay back to relax. He knew it was absurd to think so, but a day which did not provide at least some progress to his book seemed a day completely lost. In vain he argued with himself that a man could scarcely make his writing a reason for living unless he believed in the validity of that writing. The difficulty was that he could find no other reason; the work had to be it. At the same time he was unable to attach any importance to the work itself. He *knew*, no matter what anyone said to the contrary, that it was valueless save as a personal therapy. "Life has to be got through some way or other," he would tell himself. To others he said: "Writing is harmless, and it keeps me in dinners and out of trouble."

The tea came, brought by Rhaissa, who had a new tale of woe. Her relatives from the country had arrived without warning and deposited themselves in her house, seven of them, and being, of course, wildly envious of her good fortune as a city-dweller, had set about making her life miserable. They had appropriated her clothing, some of which they had sold in the Joteya; the rest they were wearing on their persons at the moment. They had broken several of her dishes, and let the children gouge holes in her walls. And worst of all, they had either stolen or destroyed her precious sodium perborate, because in an unguarded moment she had been foolish enough to tell them of its magic properties. Her eyes blazed with indignation when she came to this part of the recital. Stenham lay back against the pillows watching her, sipping his tea, thinking that at least the two disturbances had come simultaneously, that it would have been worse had the tea difficulty been today and Rhaissa's saga tomorrow. When she had stopped he said, with the inflection of outrage he had learned from years of speaking with these people: "*Menène jaou? O allèche?* And why don't you put them out?"

She smiled sadly. Of course that could not even be considered. They were relatives. One had to put up with them. In another two weeks or so they would be gone, if Allah willed it so. Until then she would have to feed them and bear their depredations in silence.

"Don't you ever go to visit them?" he asked her.

She shook her head with contempt. Why should she? They lived in the country, far away, and you had to walk or go on a donkey after you got off the bus, and their village was several hours away from the road.

"But if you did go, wouldn't you do the same thing, just sit down and eat their food and make yourself at home?"

Rhaissa began to laugh gently. Such ingenuousness touched her sense of the ridiculous. In the first place, she explained, they hid all their food when they saw you coming. And then, you never went to visit the people who lived in the country unless there was an important marriage or a death which involved a possible inheritance, because why would anyone go to the country otherwise? It was empty, there was nothing to see. And if for some reason you did have to go, then you took all your food with you from the city.

"But that's crazy," objected Stenham. "The food all comes from the country."

"*Hachouma,*" said Rhaissa, shaking her head. (It was the classical Moroccan reply, which, along with "*Haram,*" provided an unanswerable argument that could end any discussion; Shame and Sin were the two most useful words in the common people's vocabulary.) If you were lucky enough to live in the city, you had to pay for that privilege by being an uncomplaining, if not eager prey to the greed of your rustic relations; any other course of behavior was shameful, and that was that.

"I'll give you another paper of powder tomorrow, *in-cha'Allah*," he told her.

A flood of blessings poured forth. Grinning, Rhaissa went out. Presently he heard her singing as she scrubbed the floor of the corridor.

His headache was going away. At the back of his mind there was expectation: he was looking forward to the tea later in the day with the American girl. "Madame Veyron" was the most inapposite name that fate could have provided for her. She should be called something like Susan Hopkins or Mary Williams. He found himself wondering what her name really was, and what she was really like. But if he allowed himself to dwell on such conjectures he would do nothing all day. Was it a foregone conclusion that he would not be able to work? With the prospect in mind of seeing her, it should be possible for him to discount the telephone scene and Rhaissa's interruption. He sprang out of bed and shaved. Then he sat and worked quite well until half past twelve, when he dressed and went down to the dining room for an early lunch, having decided to write letters afterward.

If there happened to be many tourists staying in the hotel, the restaurant proved to be slightly understaffed. These last few weeks, however, the news of unrest in Morocco had apparently frightened away all but the most hardy prospective visitors: there had been only a handful of transients, so that the waiters spent most of their time standing along the walls talking together in low voices. The Europeans stood by the entrance door and the Moroccans lined up near the door that led into the kitchen.

The three most desirable tables were those in front of the windows, looking over part of the hotel garden, the crenelated walls of the former palace, and the Medina beyond. Recently Stenham had been able to sit here when he pleased. Today he was annoyed to see that all three tables were occupied by groups of Americans. He sat down at a small table where the light was fairly good, and began to read. The waiters were used to his eating habits; sometimes he took two hours to complete a meal, turning page after page before he signaled to them that he was ready for the next course.

The Americans nearest him were discussing their purchases, made that morning in the *souks*. Eventually they shifted to the subject of a woman acquaintance who had been present at the bombing of a café in Marrakech; she still had pieces of shrapnel in her, they claimed, and the doctor had told her it was quite safe to leave them there. A man's voice then declared that such a procedure was dangerous, that they could work their way to the heart. Stenham tried without success to cut the sound of their talk from his consciousness and isolate himself in his book. He went on listening. When the people left the table, he managed to read a bit; this was interrupted by an unexpected tap on his shoulder. He looked up angrily into the amused face of Mme Veyron.

"That's a good way to get indigestion," she said as he got to his feet. "Reading at mealtime."

"How are you? I didn't see you come in."

"Of course not. I saw *you* come in. I was sitting over there in the corner." Today she wore a simple tailored suit of powder-blue sharkskin worsted; the severity of its lines were negated by her mannequin-like figure, whose presence the suit emphatically proclaimed.

"Won't you sit down a second with me?" he asked her.

She looked hesitant. "My friends are outside waiting. We're going to have coffee on the terrace."

"Sit down anyway," he said firmly, and she did.

"But really, I can't stay."

"Who are your friends?" he inquired, conscious of a faint envy: they had had her with them all during lunch.

"An American couple and a friend of theirs I met this morning in the *souks* down below. They're stationed at one of the air bases near Casablanca somewhere. They asked me to have lunch with them." She cast a quick glance around the dining-room. "How does it happen you're all alone? Where's Mr. Kenzie? And the other one? I forget his name."

"Oh, I never eat with them," he said, as if eager to vindicate himself for having been with the two Englishmen the day before. "Yesterday was a special occasion, unusual. I don't know where they are." He looked at her. The flesh could not have been molded more artfully around her cheekbones and the corners of her mouth. Actually it was that, he decided, and nothing else, which made her beauty. It was a face to be sculpted, not painted. The eyes were of a neutral color, grayish hazel, the hair was medium light, halfway between blonde and brunette, perfectly straight and worn quite short in a coiffure that looked too anarchic to have been planned, and too smart to be accidental. It was all in those strange, perfect, multiple curves that led the vision upward from the lips over the cheek to the temple. He knew she was aware of his appraisal and that she felt no self-consciousness or resentment. "It's nice to see you," he said after a moment.

"I really can't sit here. They want to get started back to Casablanca in a few minutes and they've been awfully nice to me."

"Why don't you join me after they've gone? I'll be sitting over at the end of the terrace at one of the tables under the big palm tree."

"Well," she said doubtfully, "they offered to drop me at my hotel on their way back. I don't know."

"Remember, you're due to see me at five, you know, anyway. You hadn't forgotten?"

"Of course I hadn't forgotten," she said indignantly.

"If you have to go home, I'll take you back in a cab, but stay and have another coffee with me after your friends leave."

"All right." She smiled very briefly, but radiantly, and walked out.

He ate the rest of his lunch at what for him was an uncommonly rapid pace; he did not really believe she might change her mind and leave with her friends, but there was, after all, the possibility of it, and the fact that she was now out of sight made it seem more real. But when he went outside he saw her there in the sun with the others, looking a little grave and nodding her head. In order not to cross the terrace where she sat, he went through the bar and down the dark corridor that led toward the main entrance hall, then out into a small shady courtyard where goldfish swam in a pool beneath a group of tall banana plants. From there he came out upon an extension of the terrace and took a table at the remote end, against the wall, and almost hidden by the huge green fan of spears made by a palm branch that waved in front of his face. When the Americans had left he intended to wait a decent interval, perhaps five minutes, and then go and join her. However, she rose almost immediately and came to his shady corner.

"They've gone," she announced. "I'm thinking of moving to this hotel. I didn't realize it was as reasonable as it is. They told me they had a double room without bath last night for twelve hundred francs. I'm only staying over at my little horror because I have to watch the pennies these days. But the difference is so little. Do you realize I have to pay seven hundred for my closet, and they don't even sweep it out? There's still a big piece of bread under the bed that was there the day I came."

"Seven hundred!" he exclaimed. "But I have a fine room for eight. You're being royally rooked." It was too good to be true, that she might move here. He decided to say no more, for fear she might sense his eagerness and change her mind.

"I'd like to talk with the manager and see what they have, at least."

"The place is pretty empty. Which brings me to a question I've been wanting to ask you. How does it happen you're wandering around Morocco alone, this year of all years?"

She looked at him fixedly, as if debating the wisdom of entering the conversational room whose door he was holding open for her. A second later she seemed to have made her decision, but he could not tell whether it had been made with full confidence in him or with certain reserves. And the fact that the question of confidence had arisen at all in his mind reopened an airless chamber of his past where suspicion had been mandatory and trust in others a matter open to hourly question.

"This year of all years," she echoed. "That's the answer. I'd always wanted passionately to see Morocco, and I had an awful premonition that I'd better come now or I'd miss it altogether."

"Why?" He thought he knew what she meant, but he wanted to be sure.

"Well, my God, look at the papers!" she cried. "It doesn't

take any great brain to see what's happening." Now he felt almost certain that she had divined his thought, and was on the defensive. "There's a little war in progress here. There won't be anything left of the place if it goes on at this rate." (But it's hard to feign innocence if you've eaten the apple, he reflected.) "And it looks to me as if it *is* going to go on, because the French aren't going to give in, and certainly the Arabs aren't, because they can't. They're fighting with their backs to the wall."

"I thought maybe you meant you expected a new world war," he lied.

"That's the least of my worries. When *that* comes, we've had it. You can't sit around mooning about Judgment Day. That's just silly. Everybody who ever lived has always had his own private Judgment Day to face anyway, and he still has. As far as that goes, nothing's changed at all."

A little Algerian waiter, who sometimes served as assistant barman, had come up to the table.

"*Vous prenez que'que chose, Monsieur Stenhamme?*" he inquired.

"Coffee?" Stenham asked her.

She shrugged her shoulders. "Yes. I might as well. I'll be hopped up all afternoon, but it doesn't matter."

"Or have a liqueur."

"Cointreau, Chartreuse, Pippermenthe, Crème de Cacao, Grand Marnier, Whiskey, Benedictine, Armagnac, Gin, Banania, Curaçao—" the waiter intoned.

"Stop him!" she cried. "He'll have Pilsner in there any minute. No, no, no! Coffee was the suggestion, and coffee it is."

"*Deux cafés.*"

She lighted a cigarette. "Before I was married, I worked in Paris for UNESCO awhile. Just a secretarial job—nothing important. But I did get around, and it did give me a new kind of interest in things. I wouldn't say I'm fascinated by politics, but at least I know they exist." (Her least intelligent remark to date, he thought; very much on the defensive.)

"And before, what did you know?"

She laughed. "Not very much, I'm afraid. Dances, dates, art school, even dramatic school." She was silent a moment.

The terrace was completely deserted now, and the only sounds were the sporadic twittering of sparrows down in the lower garden and the steady clicking of a typewriter at the reception desk across the terrace.

Stenham was dissatisfied; he felt he had bungled things. He had not got the answer he had been wanting; perhaps he had not put his question properly. Not the great question, which it was of no use to ask anyway, since the information had to be volunteered, but the first, vague, general query which might lead the way. Again, maybe it was not one question, but many. Why was she interested in Morocco? What did she want to see here? What was she doing here all alone, when most people refused to come even with large groups? Why was she not afraid, where had she been, how long was she staying? His intuition told him that an inquisition was not in order at this stage of the acquaintanceship, that if he put questions now, she would not take offense, would not so much as show by any word or gesture that she minded them, but would merely disappear without a word of warning, and then she would take good care that he never saw her again. This was certainly not the way he wanted things to happen.

"I don't know what you've seen here in Morocco," he said, "but I don't think you're likely to see anything greater than this town."

"Oh, I know. I'm sure of that. That's why I decided to stay awhile. Originally I was only going to give it a day. Can you imagine? I decided that even if I miss certain other things it'll be worth it, to see more of Fez. But I've only got a given amount of energy. I can't keep going night and day."

"There are a lot of questions I'd like to ask you," he said suddenly, in spite of himself, and a little scandalized at his own lack of control. (But perhaps this was the right way to intimacy—the neutral approach. Had not everything been completely natural so far? And what did he want, in any case, but intimacy, in the final analysis?) "The sort I can't expect to get any intelligible answers to from our English friends."

Her expression had not changed at all. "What sort of questions?" she said.

"About your—*our*—reactions to this place. Just what it means to you or to me. It's sort of important, don't you think? I mean, what do we see in it, why do we like it, what have we got in us that responds to such a city? Or perhaps you don't respond completely, the way I do."

"Oh, I love it! I love it!" she protested.

This was not the kind of answer he wanted, and he wondered fleetingly if she were, after all, only a very pretty American tourist, if he were not making a novel of a simple meeting. Later, he told himself; he could never get further than she was willing he should. The problem was not to discover who she was, but rather to assume that he knew, and make her willing to confirm the identification. She must never feel that his conversation was attempting to enfold her. Later, at some still unforeseeable moment, if he were lucky, he would be granted that necessary glimpse into her mind that would tell him what he wanted to know. Forget it all, he said to himself. Beyond the trees the day was hot and clear, waiting to be used.

"It's a shame to be sitting here," he told her.

She looked surprised. "What's the matter with here? It's delightful."

"Wouldn't you like to hire a carriage, and be driven by two clodhopping old horses all the way around the Medina? It's a beautiful drive, if you don't mind the sun."

"Oh, I love the sun," she said.

"But you have to have your head covered," he reminded her; he felt that if it were he who made the objections for her, she might be more likely to accept.

"It's not so bad if you're in motion. It's lying still on the beach that's fatal. Anyway, I have an enormous handkerchief in my handbag I could wrap around. But—"

"Ah, you wanted to look at rooms, of course. Let's do that now. Then afterward, if you still felt like going, we could call a cab."

"I thought you said a carriage."

"I know, but the nearest carriage-stand is at Bab Bou Jeloud. It would be about an hour and a half before they got here. Perhaps not quite that long," he quickly added, fearful that she might come to the correct conclusion that the complete tour would take a very long time indeed. "It's getting the message to the driver, and so on. You know how slow they are. What you have to do is go in a car to Bou Jeloud and take your carriage there."

"Well, I think it would be wonderful. But you've probably done it ten thousand times."

"Not that many. And certainly I've never done it with you."

She laughed.

"Why don't you look at the rooms now, and I'll call for the taxi. It'll be on its way while you're looking." He wanted to make the decision irrevocable.

"Fine, fine." She got up, and they went across the terrace to the desk. When he came out of the telephone booth she and the receptionist had gone upstairs, up *his* stairs, to the tower. This was where he had been almost positive the man would take her, because it was there in the old wing where the cheapest rooms were. The regular tourists inevitably preferred the spacious modern bedrooms of the other parts of the hotel. He hoped the receptionist would be tactful enough not to point at his door as they went past, and say: "Monsieur Stenham's room"; it would be like him to do something stupid like that. Then she would undoubtedly decide on another floor, or perhaps the new wing or a room down in the garden near Moss, or she might even give up the idea entirely. He walked back across the terrace and stood looking over the balustrade down into the lower garden, feeling almost jittery and not at all pleased with himself. This unpleasant condition he attributed to the sense of failure he felt with regard to the little conversation they had carried on during coffee. Whatever happens with her, he thought, will be my fault a hundred percent. Usually when he had discovered the reason for his perturbation, the understanding sufficed to mitigate it somewhat; this time it changed nothing. "Wrong explanation," he decided. He stood there, his eyes fixed now on one branch of trembling poplar leaves, keeping his mind a blank, because he heard voices coming down the stairs to the lobby, and he had renounced trying to discover the reason for his momentary depression. It was they; they stood a moment in the lobby talking. Then, smiling, she came out and joined him.

"Well, what's the verdict?" he said.

"I'm calling him tonight to let him know definitely. I've

got to do a little bookkeeping first, and see just where I am financially, before I step into high life."

"How'd you like the rooms?"

"Oh, well, of course they're charming. There's one, especially, that looks like something out of Haroun er Rachid's palace. And the views are so wonderful."

They went up the main stairs and waited at the gate for the taxi. It came, an incredibly battered old vehicle; the driver kept the motor running while he poured water into the radiator, but as they got in it stalled. "Patience is all we need," murmured Stenham. After a good deal of violent cranking and advice volunteered by a slowly collecting crowd of hotel employees and interested passers-by, the chauffeur managed to start the engine shuddering again, and they jounced out through the two arched gates onto the steep serpentine road that wound upward through the cemeteries and olive groves. At Bou Jeloud they stepped from the running-board of the cab into the creaking carriage. It took Stenham a while to arrange the price with the driver, an enormously fat man who wore a crimson cummerbund to match his fez, and even the final agreement was for more money than it should have been. However, he thought, a little recklessness often made him feel more satisfied with himself; it might do that now.

"Let's go!" he cried. "*Yallah!*"

CHAPTER 18

They moved slowly through the throngs of people who were on their way to and from the Joteya carrying mattresses, worn clothing, broken alarm clocks and hammered brass trays from the Seffarine. "This is their coliseum," Stenham told her. "This is where they really enjoy themselves. A man may have a brand-new shirt or pair of shoes and be delighted with whatever it is, but in a few days the urge will get too strong, and he'll come up here and spend a day trying to see what he can sell it for. Then he'll sell it at a loss, of course, and buy something secondhand to take its place. He's had his money's worth, though: the pleasure a whole day of haggling has given him. And he goes back home happy, with an old shirt or an old pair of shoes instead of a new one. The French have caught on; they charge them admission just to get into the market, and look at the waiting-line."

When they were finally outside the ramparts in the country, going between the dusty walls of cane, the horses established their rhythm, jangling the brass bells of their harnesses, and the carriage lurched crazily. To brace themselves, they put their feet up on the worn black leather seat facing them, their legs out straight in front of them.

"This is absolute heaven," she said happily. "Just the right speed for seeing this landscape."

At each new curve the vista changed: sand-colored hills, rows of green-gray olive trees, distant glimpses of the eroded country to the east, with its bare mesa-topped mountains hard in the afternoon sunlight, a sudden view of the vast oyster-gray Medina at their feet, formless honeycomb of cubes, terraces, courtyards, backed by the groved slopes of Djebel Zalagh. "There just isn't a straight stretch anywhere on this road. It's all curves," she said as he lighted a cigarette for her. Still the landscape went on unfolding, the countryside revealing its graceful variations on the pastoral theme. Small, hot ravines of bare yellow earth where only agaves grew, like giant stalks of asparagus, sudden very green orchards where people sat smiling in the shade (and the musky, almost feline odor of the fig trees was like an invisible cloud through which the carriage had to pass), an ancient, squat, stone bridge, cows standing in the mud, now and then a motionless stork sailing on a high air-current above the city. The road had dipped down to the river and climbed up again, it had gone near to the ramparts, past the arches of Bab Fteuh, veered off into the country, still descending through deserted terrain, as though it would never stop. When it flattened out, the pace slowed a little, and later, when it began to wind upward once more, the driver occasionally cracked his whip, calling a lengthy, falsetto: "Eeeee!" to the tired horses.

"Don't let him whip them, please," she implored, as the long leather thong descended with the sound of a firecracker for the fifth or sixth time.

Stenham knew the uselessness of arguing with an Arab about anything at all, and particularly if it had to do with the performance of his daily work, but he leaned forward, saying in a tone of authority: "*Allèche bghitsi darbou? Khallih.*" The fat man turned halfway around and said laughing: "They're lazy. They always have to be beaten."

"What does he say?" she inquired.

Taking a chance, he replied: "He says if you don't want him to whip them he'll stop, but they go faster if they hear the whip."

"But he's actually hitting them with it. It's awful."

To the driver in Arabic he said: "The lady is very unhappy to see you beat the horses, so stop it."

This did not please the fat man, who made an involved speech about letting people do their work the way they always did it; if the lady knew a great deal about horses he expected to see her driving a carriage one day soon. Stenham secretly sympathized with the man, but there was nothing to do save forbid the use of the whip—if he could manage it.

"Put it away, please. *Khabaeuh.*"

The man was now definitely in bad spirits; he went off into a muttered monologue, addressing it to the horses. The latter continued to go ahead with decreasing speed, until the carriage was moving approximately at the pace of a man walking. Stenham said nothing; he was determined that if there were to be any further suggestions for the driver, they should be made by her.

They could never have got back to the hotel by five o'clock in any case; that he had known from the beginning. And at this rate it would be dark before they completed the tour. Stones and bushes moved past in leisurely fashion. The air smelled clean and dry. He turned to her. "This is a strange situation," he said, smiling.

She looked a little startled. "What do you mean?"

"Do you realize that I don't even know your name?"

"My name? Oh, I'm sorry. It's spelled V-e-y-r-o-n."

"Oh, I know that," he said with impatience. "I mean, your own name. After all, you're not living with your husband, are you?"

"Actually, the idea of using Georges' last name only occurred to me here in Morocco. And I've found it makes everything so much easier. I don't know why I didn't do it before. My maiden name is Burroughs, and the French can't get anywhere near it, either in spelling or pronunciation."

"You have a first name, I suppose." He smiled, to offset the dryness of his remark.

She sighed. "Yes, unfortunately. It's Polly, and I loathe it. You know it's impossible to take anyone named Polly seriously. So I've always used just the last syllable."

"Polly Burroughs," he said reflectively. "Lee Burroughs. I don't know. I think I like Polly better."

"Well," she said firmly. "You're not going to call me Polly. I can tell you that right now. If you want to send me into an emotional tailspin, all you have to say is 'Hello, Polly,' and I'm gone. I can't *bear* it!"

"I promise never to do the awful thing."

They drove on with painful slowness, upward round the innumerable curves, each bend bringing new vistas of empty, sun-flooded valleys to the north and a wider expanse of the flat lands to the east where the river made its leisurely meanders. The light became more intense as the afternoon progressed. Now that he knew her first name he felt closer to her, and several times in the conversation he called her Lee, watching her to see if she minded. She appeared to take it for granted.

It was six o'clock when they came to the little café atop the cliff overlooking the city, and he told the driver to stop. The place was deserted.

"We've committed a *faux pas* of major proportions, I'm afraid," she said as they got down from the carriage. "Our English friends will never forgive us. They were expecting us at five. But it's all been so beautiful I must confess I don't care."

They sat in the late sunlight at the very edge of the precipice and ordered tea. The vast city, made more remote by its silence, lay spread out below.

"What's very hard to believe," she said presently, "is that this can be existing at the same moment, let's say, that people are standing in line at the information booth in the Grand Central Station asking about trains to New Haven. You know what I mean? It's just unthinkable, somehow."

He was delighted. "Lee, you understand this place better than anybody I've ever met. You're so right. It's a matter of

centuries, rather than thousands of miles." He was silent a
moment thinking: Even the smallest measure of time is
greater than the greatest measure of space. Or is that a lie?
Does it only seem so to us, because we can never get back
to it?

"It's very, very strange and disturbing, this place," she was
saying, as if to herself. "I don't quite see how you can stay in
it. It would be like being constantly under the influence of
some drug, to live here. I should think going out of it could
be terribly painful, when you've been here a long time. But
then of course, perhaps after a while the effect wears off.
That's probably it. It must."

A man in a turban brought the tea. Small, furry bees began
to appear and to balance themselves on the edges of the
glasses. Their movements were slow and clumsy, but they
were determined to get to the sweet liquid. Stenham proceeded to describe a series of complicated flourishes in the air
with his glass, in the hope of putting them off the scent long
enough to raise it to his lips, but when he was about to drink
he saw that one had fallen in and been scalded to death. He
fished it out with his finger and flipped it away; others had
now arrived and were crawling down the inside of the glass.

"It's sort of hopeless," she said.

"Do you want the tea?" he asked her.

"Of course I do."

"Then we'll have to go inside the café. It's the only remedy."

They carried their glasses into the tiny room and sat down.
The air smelled musty. There was no window.

"Now, aren't they funny people?" she demanded. "Wouldn't
you think that with this fantastic view outside they'd have
at least some sort of peep-hole, instead of shutting themselves into a cell this way? Or don't they even know there *is* a
view?"

"Oh, I think they know, all right. Sometimes they'll sit for
hours looking at a view. But my guess is that they still think
in terms of tents. Any building's a refuge, something to get
inside of and really *feel* inside, and that means it has to be
dark. They hate windows. It's only when they've shut themselves in that they can relax. The whole world outside is hostile and dangerous."

"They can't be that primitive," she objected.

"Will you give me one of your Casa Sports? I'm all out of mine." The taste of the black tobacco reminded him of the *souks*, and for a second he had an image of the slanting rays of sunlight that filtered through the latticework above, each ray blue with a mixture of smoke and dust-motes. Or was he being reminded of something she had said in the garden the day before?

"They're not primitive at all. But they've held on to that and made it a part of their philosophy. Nothing's ever happened to change that."

She sighed. "But has anything ever happened to change anything? I wish I knew what makes them tick. They're such a mixture, such a puzzle."

They would have to be leaving, he thought. Night came down quickly, and he wanted to get inside the ramparts before it was completely dark. But he did not intend to alarm her by saying such a thing, and in any case she had drunk only a little of her tea.

"There's one thing I've found that helps," he said. "And that is that you must always remember it's a culture of 'and then' rather than one of 'because,' like ours."

Frowning, she said: "I don't think I follow."

"What I mean is that in their minds one thing doesn't come from another thing. Nothing is a result of anything. Everything merely *is*, and no questions asked. Even the language they speak is constructed around that. Each fact is separate, and one never depends on the other. Everything's explained by the constant intervention of Allah. And whatever happens had to happen, and was decreed at the beginning of time, and there's no way even of imagining how anything could have been different from what it is."

"It's depressing," she said.

He laughed. "Then I've said it wrong. I've left out something important. Because there's nothing depressing about any of it. Except what the place has become under the Christians," he added sourly. "When I first came here it was a pure country. There was music and dancing and magic every day in the streets. Now it's finished, everything. Even the religion. In a few more years the whole country will be like all the other Moslem countries, just a huge European slum, full of poverty and hatred. What the French have made of Morocco may be depressing, yes, but what it was before, never!"

"I think that's the point of view of an outsider, a tourist who puts picturesqueness above everything else. I'm sure if you had to live down there in one of those houses you wouldn't feel the same way at all. You'd welcome the hospitals and electric lights and buses the French have brought."

This was certainly the remark of a tourist, and an ignorant tourist, too, he thought, sorry that it should have come from her.

"At least you can say you were in on the last days of Morocco," he told her. "How's your tea? Finished? I think we ought to be going."

The driver glowered at them as they climbed into the carriage. From the café the road was downgrade all the way. The horses needed no prodding to make them go along briskly. A cool breeze swept across the hillside as they came down toward Bab Mahrouk, and the day had almost faded from the sky.

Twilight is an hour which, by subtly making them conscious of the present, can bring two people together, or it can set each one digging among his own private memories. Stenham was thinking of an evening more than twenty years before, when, as a college freshman on vacation, he had driven down this same road, more or less at the same hour (and possibly even in the same carriage—who could tell?). His state had been one of unquestioning happiness. The world was beautiful and life was eternal, and it was not necessary to think further than that. Now he had changed of course, but he was convinced that the world also had changed; it seemed unthinkable that any youth of seventeen today could know the same light-heartedness, or find the same lyrical sweetness in life that he had found then. Sometimes for the space of a breath he could recapture the reality, a delicious pain that was gone almost as it appeared, and it provided him with proof that there was a part of him which still lay bathed in the clear light of those lost days.

She too had gone back into memory, but all the way to her childhood. What is there, she thought, that's missing now, and that I had when I was little? And a second later she had the answer. It was the sense of timelessness that had been there inside her and was gone forever. She had been robbed of it the day her aunt had come to her and said: "You will never see your mother and father again." The fact that there had been a plane crash had meant nothing to her, and even the knowledge that her parents were dead had been only a mysterious, awesome abstraction. Mingled with her feeling of loss she had experienced a strange sense of liberation. But now she knew that what had happened was that time had begun to move inside her. She was alone, therefore she was herself, and at last on her way. And ever since then she had been on her way, moving toward the end. There was nothing tragic or even pathetic about it, any more than there is anything tragic or pathetic about the rotation of the earth. It was merely the difference between being a child and being an adult. She had become an adult early, that was all. The long ride had shaken something loose in her spirit; she felt now rather the way she often felt at the end of a concert—a little battered, but emotionally refreshed.

Suddenly he reached out and took her hand. "How are you?" he said gently, forcing his fingers between hers. They had gone through the gate, were in an open space where a few feeble flares guttered on the counters of stalls; shadowy figures moved by very close to the carriage, almost brushing its wheels with their garments as they passed. She laughed shortly, not returning his pressure. "I'm fine," she answered. "Perhaps a little tired."

"Shall we take a cab to my hotel? How about having dinner with me?"

"It's awfully sweet of you, but I just don't feel up to it."

"Are you sure?"

"Yes, really. All I want is to lie out flat in bed and have a little something to eat, right in bed, I mean, and then sleep, sleep, sleep!"

"Perhaps it's just as well," he said, determined not to sound disappointed. "Mr. Kenzie and Mr. Moss would probably be in the dining-room, and we'd have to face them. If you go to your hotel I'm going to eat at an Arab place here near Bou Jeloud. Sure you wouldn't like to join me?"

"I'd love to," she said, carefully disengaging her hand to light a cigarette, "but I'm not going to tonight. May I take a rain check on it?"

"Any time. The place'll always be there." He was saying exactly the wrong things; surely she was going to detect the degree of his chagrin. But his effort to mask it seemed to leave no margin of energy for conversation. How difficult it is, he thought, to hide the fact that you really care about a thing, and how right people are to distrust suavity. "I'll make our excuses tomorrow when I see our friends," he went on, casting about for any subject to talk about. "I'll say you weren't feeling well—"

"You certainly won't!" she exclaimed indignantly. "If you do that I'll call Mr. Kenzie myself and tell him the truth. After all, *I* didn't know we were going to be gone all afternoon. I wasn't feeling well, indeed!"

The carriage had drawn up and come to a halt at the end of a long line of other carriages; the driver, in a good humor at last, because he was about to be paid, called out: "*Voilà, messieurs-dames!*" When Stenham handed him the money he demanded considerably more, citing the wait and the speed at which he had been required to move. After a short altercation he gave him half the supplementary sum. That appeared to be sufficient, for the fat man shouted "*Bon soir!*" in a jovial voice, and jumped down from his seat, hoisting a small boy up to guard the vehicle while he went across the square for tea.

They walked in the dark through the street that smelled stronger than any stable; the stars overhead were there in such quantity and brilliance that they looked artificial. In most places of the world the sky was not completely powdered with them—there were also dark patches. He wanted to call her attention to the fact, but something in him would not move, and he remained silent. When they came to the Café Bou Jeloud, where there were always a few old taxis waiting, he said: "Remember, you have work to do tonight."

"Work?" she inquired, not understanding.

"Or so you said. You were going to make financial calculations and call the hotel in the morning."

"Yes." Her voice had no expression. They got into a cab,

and were off, around corners and through crowds, with an incredible racket of banging metal, wheezing motor and constantly bellowing horn.

"Thank God there are no cars in the Medina," he said. "The casualty list would be something."

"I'm really awfully tired," she answered, as if he had inquired how she felt. He did not believe her.

In front of her little hotel with its single light over the door they got out, and he paid the cab. "Aren't you keeping it?" she said, surprised.

"My restaurant's a ten-minute walk through the Medina."

"Well, thanks again," she said, holding out her hand. "It's been delightful. At the moment I'm just knocked out."

"I'll call you tomorrow," he told her.

"Good night." She went through the door into the office. He stood outside in the dark a moment, and saw her pass the doorway with her key in her hand. Then he turned and went up the quiet road to Bab el Hadid.

The next morning as he lay in bed working, Abdelmjid came up from downstairs with a telegram in his hand. It read: THANKS JOING MEKNES LEE.

He stared at it and worked no more that day.

CHAPTER 19

It had been a shock, her sudden departure. On the one hand it obviated the necessity for an explanation to Moss and Kenzie of his failure to keep the rendezvous, for she had sent similar telegrams to both of them, and that permitted him to lie vaguely, saying that he had been around to her hotel and found her already gone; they put the incident down to feminine caprice and American ill-breeding. But on the other hand it set in motion a whole machinery of self-questioning and recrimination. He was completely convinced that he had somehow frightened her off. The question was: at what point had she taken alarm?

A good many times he went back over, in as much detail as his memory allowed, the sequence of their conversations, trying to force himself to recall her expression and tone of voice at each point. It was a difficult task, above all since, obviously, even though he might arrive at isolating the precise moment when he suspected that she had been put on her guard, there was no possible way of being certain that he was right, or, indeed, of knowing whether he had had anything at all to do with her bolting from Fez. Nevertheless, he continued with his attempt at recall and analysis of the afternoon and arrived at the conclusion that the whole thing had taken place at the very beginning, before they had ever left the hotel.

What brought him to this, was, of course, his very clear memory of leaning against the balustrade looking down into the garden, the feeling that everything had gone wrong, and the inability he had met with in his effort to explain to himself the sense of nervousness and frustration to which he had been prey. "I was right about her!" he would think with triumph. All the tortured little turnings of her mind that he had imagined he had observed had actually been taking place, then; her replies and remarks had been a welter of subterfuge. But a moment later he would return to doubt. A few days of this went on, and then he determined to talk to Moss about it.

"Alain," he said one day as they sat at lunch in a restaurant of the Ville Nouvelle, "what did you feel about Mme Veyron? What was your impression of her?"

"Mme Veyron?" said Moss blankly. "Oh, that rather intelligent, pretty American girl that Hugh had us to lunch with. You ask my impression? Well, I had no particular impression. She seemed pleasant enough. Why?"

"But you did have the impression that she was bright. So did I. And yet, if you think back, I'll bet you can't remember her making one intelligent remark, because she didn't."

"Well, really," Moss said, "I can't say that I remember very much at all about the conversation. Certainly it wasn't brilliant, if that's what you mean. It seems to me that it was Kenzie who did most of the talking that day. In any case, Mme Veyron made no shining contributions, there's no doubt about that. But I must say, I did have the distinct feeling she was not at all stupid."

Stenham beamed. "Exactly. The reason I'm saying all this, and you're going to laugh your head off at me, is that I've been thinking a lot about her. I think she's a Communist."

Moss did laugh, but discreetly. "I should think it was *utterly* unlikely," he said. "But do go on. How extraordinary you are, really! No, really, how extraordinary! Why on earth would you imagine such a thing about that poor girl?"

"Well, you know my history," Stenham began, feeling his heart beat faster, as it always did when he began to refer to this particular episode in his past. "I was with them night and day when I was in the Party, and you get so you can recognize them almost infallibly."

He suddenly wondered what had prompted him to talk about all this; Moss could not possibly have anything helpful to say, could throw no light on the dark sections of the subject, could not even share his interest. "As far as I know," he went on, "I haven't met a Communist in fourteen years, ever since I got out. But my sense of smell is still acute, and I'm convinced I'm right about her. And if I am, she's a lot brighter than either of us thought, because she put on a magnificent little act for herself."

"Really," complained Moss, "how can you believe a person's political convictions will change him to such an extent? Why shouldn't she be like everyone else, even if she is a Communist? I daresay I've met dozens and never been aware of the fact."

"You've got a lot to learn about them, then. That's all I can say. A real Communist, a consecrated one, is as different from us as we are from a Buddhist monk. It's a new species of man."

"Oh, balls, my dear John, balls." Moss signaled the waiter. "*La suite,*" he said. "For a normally intelligent man you have some of the *most* unconsidered opinions. And you? I suppose you were a new species of man for the term of your adherence to the Party?"

Stenham frowned. "I never was a believer. I joined just for the hell of it. When I found out what it really was, I got out fast." He stopped for a second, then corrected himself. "That's not quite true. I don't think I remember my exact motives for getting out, but I do know I stopped being interested the day we became Russia's ally, in the summer of 1940. And a month or so after that I went around and told them I was leaving. The crowning touch was that they told me I couldn't leave on my own initiative."

Moss had listened to this with obvious impatience. "It wouldn't be, by any chance, that you admire her and suspect she has the constancy of mind and purpose that you lack? It couldn't be that?" He looked at Stenham with a droll expression, reminiscent of a robin listening for a worm.

"Good God! Are you mad?" Stenham cried. He waved away the platter that Moss tendered him. "No, none of those cardboard string-beans. I'd rather go without vegetables. All I can say is, you're absolutely, completely wrong."

"It's always possible, I admit," Moss said complacently. "But my personal conclusion is that the very instability that originally made it possible for you to go to such extremes—and it is an extreme, joining an organization like that—now makes you suspect everyone of being equally capable of such fanaticism. And of course, the world isn't like that for a moment. Good heavens, John, stop seeing life as melodrama. From the moral viewpoint you're fundamentally a totalitarian; you realize that, I hope?"

Stenham smiled. "That's the last thing I am, Alain, the very last thing."

The unpleasant accusation remained in his mind, however, and on his walks he thought about it. What disturbed him, he told himself, was not the fact that he believed there was any truth in it, but that Moss should have known so well exactly which dart to throw and where the unprotected spot lay. He was not sure that Moss himself had known what he meant when he had made the indictment, but that had slight importance beside the fact of his obsession with the meaning which he himself had unconsciously chosen to read into Moss's words: the imperfections in his character which once had caused him to open his arms to the Communists were still there; he still saw the world in the same way. That in essence was what he imagined the other had meant, and if it were true, then he had made no progress whatever through all the years.

In his mind he followed his retreat from where he had been to where he was now. First he had lost faith in the Party, then in Marxism as an ideology, then slowly he had come to execrate the concept of human equality, which seemed inevitably to lead to the evil he had renounced. There could be no equality in life because the human heart demanded hierarchies. Having arrived at this point, he had found no direction in which to go save that of further withdrawal into a subjectivity which refused existence to any reality or law but its own. During these postwar years he had lived in solitude and carefully planned ignorance of what was happening in the world. Nothing had importance save the exquisitely isolated cosmos of his own consciousness. Then little by little he had had the impression that the light of meaning, the meaning of everything, was dying. Like a flame under a glass it had dwindled, flickered and gone out, and all existence, including his own hermetic structure from which he had observed existence, had become absurd and unreal.

Accepting this, he had fallen back upon the mere reflex action of living, the automatic getting through the day that had to be done if one were to retain any semblance of sanity. He had begun to be preoccupied by an indefinable anxiety which he described to himself as a desire to be "saved." But from what? One hot day when he was taking a long walk over the hills behind Fez he had been forced to admit to himself with amazement and horror that there was no better expression for what he feared than the very old one: eternal damnation. It was a shocking discovery, because it revealed the existence of a mysterious, basic cleavage somewhere in him: he had not even the rudiments of any sort of faith, nor yet the memory of a time in childhood when such faith had been present. He had been shielded from faith. Religion in his family had been an unmentionable subject, on a par with sexuality.

His parents had told him: "We know there is a force for good in the world, but no one knows what that force is." In his child's mind he had come to think of the "force" of which they spoke as luck. There was good luck and bad; that was the extent of his religious understanding. There were also millions of people in the world who still practiced some form of religion; they were to be considered with a spirit of tolerance, like the very poor. Some day, with the necessary education, they might advance into the light of rationalism. The presence of a religious person in the household had always been regarded as something of an ordeal. He had been carefully coached ahead of time. "Some people in this world have strange beliefs, like Ida with her rabbit's foot, and Mrs. Connor with her crucifix. We know those things don't mean anything, but we must have respect for everyone's beliefs and be very careful never to offend anyone."

But even at that early age he knew that his parents didn't really mean *have* respect; they meant that it was good manners to pretend to have it in the presence of the person concerned. Above all else, any reference to the doctrine of the immortality of the soul was regarded as the acme of bad taste; he had seen his parents shudder inwardly when a guest innocently touched on it in the course of the conversation. As a child of six he had known that when the physical organism ceased to function, consciousness was extinguished, and that was death, beyond which there was nothing. Until this minute the idea had been there, one of the pillars in the dark at the back of the cave of his mind, as much an axiom of practical life as the law of gravity.

Nor did he have any intention, if he could help it, of letting it change its status. His first reaction, that day, when he had identified his fear, was to sit down on a rock and stare at the ground. You've got to get hold of yourself, he thought. He could usually discover the origin of a state of anxiety; as often as not it was traceable to some precise physical cause, like insufficient sleep or indigestion. But what he had experienced in that flash had been almost like a momentary vision: he had seen consciousness as a circle, its end and beginning joined so that there was no break. Matter was conditioned by time, but not consciousness; it existed outside time. Was there then any valid basis for assuming that it was possible to know what went on inside the consciousness at the moment of death? It might easily seem forever, that instant when time ceased to function and life closed in upon itself, therefore it could prove to be inextinguishable. The immediacy of the experience had left him with a sensation of nausea; it was impossible to conceive anything more horrible than the idea that one was powerless to stop existing if one wanted, that there was no way to reach oblivion because oblivion was an abstraction, a fallacy. And so he sat, trying to shake off the nightmare feeling that had settled on him, thinking: What strange things happen in the mind of man. No matter what went on outside, the mind forged ahead, manufacturing its own adventures for itself, and who was to know where reality was, inside or out? He thought with passing envy of the people down in the city below. How wonderful life would be if they were only right, and there were a god. And in the final analysis what more commendable and useful thing had mankind accomplished during its whole existence, than the inventing of gods in whom its members could wholly believe, and believing, thereby find life more bearable?

When he had sat awhile, smoked three cigarettes, and let the intensity of his vision pale, he got up and went on his way, reflecting ruefully that if he had not originally had the senseless impulse to confide his suspicions concerning the girl to Moss, Moss might never have made the particular remark which, no matter how indirectly, was responsible for the mental agitation that had finally produced the unpleasant vision of a few minutes ago.

And then it occurred to him that if his suspicion about her were correct, then almost certainly she knew all about him. Kenzie had said: "She's heard of you." That could have been either merely the innocent reference to his books that it was meant to sound, or it could have been something else. Certainly the Party never forgot the names of those who had been of it. But nothing provided a satisfactory explanation of the manner of her departure.

That week the political situation in the region worsened considerably. A wave of arson spread over the land; everywhere the fields of wheat, gold, dry, ready to be harvested, caught fire, went up in flame and heavy blue smoke. The firefighters, French volunteers from neighboring farms, and from Fez and Meknès, were often shot at, sometimes hit. The express train on its way to Algier through the valleys of the waste land to the east of Fez was derailed and wrecked, then strafed. A bomb exploded in the post office of the Medina, just five minutes' walk from the hotel. Because a dozen Jews had been burned alive in a political manifestation at Petitjean, a monstrous little town some sixty miles back of Fez, there were riots in Fez between Jews and Moslems, and the police threw a protective cordon around the Mellah.

"If we catch a Jew alone in the street at night now, we treat him like a Moslem woman," Abdelmjid had said one morning when he came to get the breakfast tray.

"What do you mean?" Stenham had asked him; he expected a shocking revelation, a new, lurid sidelight on the socio-sexual deportment of the Moroccans.

"Why, we throw stones at him until he falls down. Then we throw more stones and kick him."

"But surely you don't do that to Moslem women," Stenham protested; he had seen examples of unparalleled brutality to women, but there had always been some motive.

"Of course we do!" Abdelmjid had replied, surprised that the Christian should not be acquainted with such a basic tenet of public behavior. "Always," he added firmly.

"But suppose you were sick," Stenham began, "and your wife, Rhaissa, had to go out and get medicine or help for you?"

"At night, alone? Never!"

"But if she did?" he insisted.

Abdelmjid, used to the Europeans' futile fondness for playing with possibilities, humored him in the elaboration of his improbable fantasy. "Then she would run the risk of being killed, and it would serve her right."

Stenham had no more to say. Sometimes the senselessness of their violence paralyzed him. They were like maniacal robots; perhaps once there had been some reason for their behavior, but the reason was long since gone, no one remembered what it had been, and no one cared.

For the past few days not a single guest had arrived at the hotel. Outside the entrance gate there were always four or five French policemen standing; Stenham imagined they looked accusingly at him as he passed. At the outer gate, hidden in among the buses, they parked their command-car, but only during the day; at night the place was empty. An army could have assembled there undetected. Kenzie had twice been called to the Prefecture and been solemnly advised to drive his MG out of the city and back to wherever he had come from. "Is that an order?" he had inquired. "If so, the British Consul will be most interested to hear about it."

"What cheek!" he had snorted when he returned to tell Moss of his experience. "My visa's in order. Just trying to scare me out, the bloody bastards."

Moss, however, was inclined to take a more serious view of it. "I think you should go about on foot and in public conveyances, like the rest of us," he counseled him. "You're so conspicuous there in your solitary splendor, riding through the mob in Fez-Djedid. I noticed it the other day when I was sitting in one of the Algerian cafés there and you passed, and I thought: What a patient race they are, really. I wonder they haven't attacked you."

"Attacked me!" Kenzie cried indignantly. "Why should they?"

"Yes, attacked you," Moss repeated imperturbably. "Any situation like this is largely a matter of the have-nots versus the haves, you know. You're only tempting Providence, I assure you."

"But the car has English plates," objected Kenzie.

Moss was shaken by laughter. "I daresay those people are aware of that! The few who've ever heard the word probably would tell you England was a town somewhere in Paris. Why don't you have an enormous Union Jack made and spread it over the hood? Then they might think you were advertising a circus."

"They haven't bothered me yet. It's the French I have to look out for."

From day to day they were following the situation by reading the papers from Casablanca and Rabat, and this gave the events a character that was official and at the same time vaguely legendary, removing them a little from reality. Sometimes they felt that they were living in the middle of an important moment of history, although they had to remind themselves and each other of it from time to time. Also, the news sources, all French, gave a firm impression that the authorities were completely in command of things, that nothing serious had happened or was going to happen. Even if one made allowances for the natural tendency of the government-controlled press to play down the gravity of the events, one still felt confidence in the ability of the French to keep the situation from getting out of hand. The closing off of the Mellah seemed somehow an unreal event, an absurd and arbitrary precaution. One could determine how people felt only by observing their faces, and to Stenham those faces looked the same as always. So that he was forced to suppress a smile when Rhaissa came bursting into his room one morning with the news that a certain *mejdoub* had been murdered in the Zekak al Hajar by the French only an hour ago, and that before the day was out very bad things would happen. She was in a state of excitement bordering on hysteria; this made it difficult for him to get any sort of clear picture of what had happened.

He knew that the only difference between a *mejdoub* and an ordinary maniac was that the *mejdoub* was a Cherif. It was impossible for a Cherif to be crazy; by virtue of his holy blood his madness was automatically transformed into the gift of prophecy. For this reason, no matter how outrageous a person's behavior in public might be, it was dangerous to attribute it to a mere derangement of the mind. Unless one knew the person and his family, one might commit the sinful mistake of imagining he was a madman when in reality he was a man directly in touch with the truth of God. Many times Stenham had observed this attitude on the part of the common people. If a man were rolling in the dust of some foul alley, half latrine, or addressing the sun in the middle of the crowd, or screaming unintelligible insults to a café-ful of card-players, the others carefully ignored him. If he offered them violence, they met it with determined gentleness, and even though Stenham was aware that their reaction was motivated by fear rather than kindness, he often had admired the restraint and patience they showed in dealing with these obstreperous creatures.

"The French shot a *mejdoub*?" he repeated incredulously. "They couldn't have. There's a mistake somewhere."

No, no, she insisted, there was no mistake. Everyone had seen it. He had been calling maledictions upon the French, crying: "*Ed dem! Ed dem!* The Moslems must have blood!" the way he always did, and two policemen on their way down to the Nejjarine had stopped and watched him for a moment. And when he had seen them, he had identified them as emissaries of Satan, and shrieked louder for Allah to exterminate their race, and suddenly the two Frenchmen had spoken a few words with each other, gone over to him and pushed him against the wall. Then he had rushed at them and struck them and scratched them, and they had reached for their pistols and shot him down, each with one bullet. And the *mejdoub* (the blessing of Allah be upon his head) had fallen down, still howling: "*Ed dem!*" and died right in front of all the people, and more police had come and taken the body away, and hit the people in the street to make them keep walking along. And it was a terrible, terrible sin, one which Allah would not find it in His heart to forgive, and one which the Moslems would be obliged, whether they wished it or not, to avenge. Today was an accursed day, *bismil'lah rahman er rahim.* "And my husband and I, who work for the Nazarenes here in the hotel, who knows what will happen to us? The Moslems are very bad. They may kill us," she finished tearfully. There was always that element of ambivalence in the mind of a Moslem when he talked to a Christian about his own people. For a while it was "we," then suddenly it shifted to "they," and as likely as not out came some sort of bitter criticism or condemnation.

"No, no, no," said Stenham. "They might kill *me*, because I'm a Nazarene, but why should they kill you? You're a good Moslem. You're just earning your living."

Rhaissa was not consoled. She could think of too many good Moslems who had been earning their living working for the Nazarenes, and who had been shot down or stabbed without a chance to defend themselves; the fact that they had been working for the police was not relevant in her mind. "*Aymah!*" she wailed. "This is a very bad day!"

When he had finally got rid of her he went to the window and listened. The day was like any other day, the same sleepy sounds rose up from the Medina: the distant droning of the sawmill, donkeys braying, here and there a snatch of Egyptian song from a radio, and the cries of children. In the garden sparrows chirped. He sat down to work, found it impossible, and silently cursed Rhaissa. Then he tried lying in the sun for a while, with the hope that it might relax him, or start the flow of thought, or whatever it was he needed. But for the past week or ten days the weather had been too hot for sun-bathing, and surely it was too hot today. The sweat ran down all the creases of his flesh, wet the cushions of the chairs. So he began to type letters at the table in the center of the room, lifting his gaze at frequent intervals to let it run unthinkingly across the panorama of hills and walls. After an hour or so, he slowly became conscious of the fact that he was spending most of his time looking out at the Medina. He incorporated the discovery in the letter, in one of those apologetic passages a person is wont to include when he feels that the missive he is engaged in writing, as a result of inattention or interruptions, is not going to be as well composed as it should be. "This is the damnedest place for trying to concentrate. It's quiet, but that seems to count for nothing. Even while I'm writing this I find myself stopping every other minute to stare out the window. It isn't to admire the view, because I don't even see it. I know it by heart. You can imagine how much worse it is when I'm trying to work. . . ."

He stopped again and reread what he had typed. It was absurd; he would have done better to try to find out *why* he kept staring out at the Medina. What did he think of that vast object out there, shining in the morning sun? He knew it was a medieval city, and he knew that he loved it, but that had nothing to do with what went on below the surface of his mind as he sat looking at it. What he really felt was that it was not there at all, because he knew that one day, sooner or later (and more likely sooner), it would not be there. And it was the same with all objects, all people. The city was, in a rough sense, a symbol; that was easy to see. It represented everything in the world that was subject to change or, more precisely, to extinction. Although this was not a comforting point of view, he did not reject it, because it coincided with one of his basic beliefs: that a man must at all costs keep some part of himself outside and beyond life. If he should ever for an instant cease doubting, accept wholly the truth of what his senses conveyed to him, he would be dislodged from the solid ground to which he clung and swept along with the current, having lost all objective sense, totally involved in existence. He was plagued by the suspicion that some day he would discover he always had been wrong; until then he would have no choice but to continue as he was. A man cannot fashion his beliefs according to his fancy.

When he had finished four letters he shaved, dressed, and went out the back way into the courtyard. There was no one there; even the tall Riffian *huissier* who watched the cars was not in sight, perhaps because there were no cars at the moment to watch. On the other side of the gate in the street, life went on as usual. The proprietor of the antique shop that operated exclusively for guests of the hotel bowed low when he saw Stenham. For the first three or four years he had persisted with tenacity in the belief that this tourist could be persuaded to buy *something*; many times he had lured him into the shop and offered him tea, cigarettes and pipes of kif, all of which Stenham had accepted with the warning that he was there solely as a friend, not as a customer. This had not hindered the man from going to the trouble of unfolding Berber rugs to spread across the floor, calling his sons and bidding them act as models to show off the ancient brocaded kaftans in front of the Nazarene gentleman, or opening the studded chests covered with purple and magenta velvet to bring out daggers and swords and powder horns and snuff boxes and chapelets and fibulae and a hundred other obsolete items in which Stenham had absolutely no interest.

Now, after all this time, the man had finished by being a little in awe of this inexplicable foreigner who had withstood so many onslaughts without once succumbing; the two were on the politest of terms. Nevertheless, Stenham did not like the man's unctuousness, and he knew him to be an unofficial informer for the French. That was almost inevitable, of course, and was not the man's fault. Any native who came in regular contact with tourists was obliged to tender reports to the police on their activities and conversation (although it was hard to understand what importance such superficial information could have for those who kept the records of the Deuxième Bureau). On several occasions the proprietor had attempted to engage Stenham in conversations that were, if carried through to their natural conclusion, obviously going to come out into the realm of politics, but Stenham, in accepted Moroccan fashion, had gently led them in other directions and left them dangling in mid-air, impaled on the hooks of *Moulana* and *Mektoub*, from which no man could decently remove them.

"I hope the health is fine this beautiful day," said the man, in French, as Stenham came near. Even his insistence on using the despised language annoyed Stenham; he liked Moroccans to speak to him in their own tongue. Then, without changing his facial expression or the debonair inflection of his voice, he added: "*Un mot, monsieur.*"

"What?" said Stenham, startled.

"Don't wander today." The man smiled vacuously. "*Ah, oui,*" he went on, as if in answer to a remark by Stenham. "*Ah, oui, il fait très beau.* The sun is a little warm, of course, but that's normal. It's the summer now. Better to stay in the hotel. And Monsieur Alain? Is he well? Give him my salutations, please. I have some very fine Roman coins now, a perfect merchandise for a great *connoisseur comme Monsieur Alain.* Tell him, please. You see, the front of my shop is closed. I am about to go inside and lock the door. *Bon jour, monsieur! Au plaisir!*"

He bowed again and stepped into his shop. Stenham stood quite still for a moment, fascinated by this unexpected performance. The entire front of the store was indeed boarded up, with heavy iron bars running diagonally in both directions across the shutters. He had not noticed it until now. And the man did, even as he watched, close the door, lock it, and noisily slide its three bolts, one after the other.

He walked on to the outer gate and stood there in the midst of hurrying porters, peering up and down the winding road. For once there were no policemen visible, and so he continued along the open space between the city walls and the cemetery where the native buses stood, looking, out of curiosity, for the command-car. It was not there. He began to suspect that there might be some truth in Rhaissa's tale, that the police had been ordered to potential trouble spots down in the city. But here the work of loading and unloading the buses and trucks was going on as always, and there was no intimation that the day had anything unusual about it. Bored and hot, he strolled back to the hotel, met the receptionist on the main terrace.

"It's hot today," he said.

The tall man glanced up at the sky. "I think we may have thunder showers later this afternoon." In his striped trousers and cutaway jacket he looked like a distinguished undertaker.

"Tell me," said Stenham, "there are no other guests in the hotel now, besides the two English gentlemen and me, are there?"

The man looked startled, hesitated. "We are expecting others this evening. Why? If you wish to change your room, there is a choice, yes."

Stenham laughed. "No. I'm delighted with my room, and also delighted to have the hotel empty. Not for your sake, of course," he added. "But it's more agreeable this way."

The receptionist smiled thinly. "A question of taste, *bien entendu*."

"All your European help sleep here in the hotel, don't they?"

Now the man permitted himself to draw his head back slightly and stare into Stenham's face. "I think I know what is in your mind, Monsieur Stenham. But allow me to reassure you. There is nothing to fear. Our native help is completely reliable." (Stenham smiled to himself: the man had come out to Morocco for the first time four months ago and was already speaking like a *colon*.) "Most of them, as you know, go home at night. The few who are stationed here have long records of loyal service, and with the exception of the watchman, all are locked into their rooms by the major domo, who keeps the keys on his person."

To Stenham this was both ludicrous and shocking. He said: "Really? I didn't know."

"Besides," pursued the other, thinking he had made his point, "there is absolutely no cause for anxiety here in Fez."

"Oh, I realize that," said Stenham. "But this has been a bad season for you, even so."

"The hotel is losing some fifty thousand francs a day, monsieur," the man announced gravely. "The season will show an enormous deficit, naturally. We keep the quantity of our food purchases down to the minimum, but I believe you will have noticed no lowering of the quality?"

"Oh, no, no," Stenham assured him. "The food is always excellent." This was not true, and they both knew it; at their best the meals were only adequate.

Suddenly Moss appeared on the stairs coming up from the lower garden. He was swinging a cane. The receptionist greeted him, excused himself, and disappeared.

They sat down at a table in the shade. The little Algerian came rushing over. Moss ordered a Saint Raphael. "I say, John, have you heard the latest? It's too fantastic."

"I've heard two or three fantastic things today so far. What's yours?"

"It all has to do with a wild man the Istiqlal had been coaching to excite the mob—one of those poor demented things in rags who go about waving their arms, you know? The police fell directly into the trap." He proceeded to tell what was substantially Rhaissa's story, but with the added element of premeditated provocation on the part of the Nationalists. "It's not very sporting of them, to sacrifice the poor old fool so cold-bloodedly, I must say. In any case, Hugh went dashing off in the car to investigate, and was promptly arrested. He telephoned a while ago, in a complete rage, because they won't let him go until he produces his passport, which means that I've got to take it in to him. It's rather curious how he manages always to botch things, isn't it? All so unnecessary."

"But why are you sitting here calmly having a drink, if he's waiting?"

"Oh, I've ordered a cab," Moss said wearily. "It'll be here in a moment. But I really can't take it too seriously, or feel too sorry for Hugh, you know, because he's an idiot. His whole attitude is that of a boy at a cricket match. And of course it's not a cricket match, is it? One doesn't sit back and cheer when people are being killed. My feeling is that unless one can be of help in some way, one stays out of it entirely, don't you think?"

Stenham agreed. Moss had finished his drink, wiped his mustache with a handkerchief; now he stood up. "Well, my boy, I'll see you anon. And do stay here in the hotel. They may arrest me too, who knows, and I'll need you to get me out. Of course the blasted Consul has gone off somewhere for the day. I think it's deliberate on his part. Be on the lookout for a telephone call."

CHAPTER 20

When he got to his room, slightly out of breath, for the day was not only hot but unaccountably sultry and oppressive, his door was open and Rhaissa was scrubbing the floor. She had taken up the rugs and hung them over the balconies in the windows. The room smelled of the creosote solution in her pail. Pillows and bedclothes were piled on the chairs; his presence in the room at the moment was clearly redundant. However, he stepped inside and said to her: "Any more news?" She looked up, startled, and motioned for him to close the door behind him, which he did. Then, standing up and rolling her eyes in a way meant to imply conspiracy, she said: "There's not going to be any feast."

"Feast? What feast?" He had quite forgotten the advent of the Aïd el Kebir.

"Why, the Feast of the Sheep, the great feast! We've had our sheep on the roof for three weeks. Now he is very fat. But they will kill anyone who makes the sacrifice."

"Who will? What are you talking about?" He was in an unpleasant humor, he realized now, but he felt that it was partly her fault. Besides that, he wanted to sit down, and there was no place.

"The Moslems. The friends of freedom. They say anyone who sacrifices his sheep is a traitor to the Sultan."

One more step toward death, he thought bitterly. Whether the rumor were true or not, the fact that they were saying such things, that such an inconceivable heresy should even occur to them, was indicative of the direction in which they were moving.

"*B'sah?*" He said harshly. "Really? And I suppose everyone is going to listen to them and obey them? Politics is more important than religion? Allal al Fassi is greater than Allah? Why don't they call him Allah el Fassi and have done with it?" The pun seemed rather good to him.

She could not follow his reasoning; she understood only enough of what he had said to be profoundly shocked. "No one is greater than Allah," she replied gravely, considering what punishment was going to be meted out by God to this ignorant Nazarene for his outrageous utterances.

"Are you going to sacrifice your sheep or not?" he demanded.

She shook her head slowly from side to side, keeping her eyes on his. "*Mamelouah,*" she said. "It's forbidden."

He was exasperated with her. "It's not forbidden!" he

shouted. "On the contrary, it's forbidden not to! Allah demands it. Has there ever been a year when there was no sacrifice?"

She continued to shake her head. "Last year," she said, "there was no feast."

"Of course there was! Didn't Abdelmjid kill a sheep last year?"

"His father killed it. We were not married until afterward, just before Mouloud."

"But he did kill it."

"Oh, yes. But it was wasted, because the Sultan was taken away that very day."

"Ah," said Stenham thoughtfully. "I see. Of course." The French had chosen the holiest day of the year to whisk the Sultan away, and it had been the false Sultan who had performed the sacrifice. Therefore there had been no sacrifice. He was silent a moment. Presently he asked her: "Why can't you sacrifice your sheep in the name of the true Sultan?"

"The Istiqlal doesn't want any feast," she said patiently. "It's a sin to make a feast when everyone is unhappy."

"You mean the people might forget they were unhappy if they had their feast, and that's what the Istiqlal doesn't want. It wants them to remember they're unhappy. Isn't that it?"

"Yes," she said, a little uncertainly.

"But can't you see?" he cried, shouting in spite of himself, aware that she couldn't see at all, never would see. "Can't you see that they're trying to take your religion away from you so they can have all the power? They want to close the mosques forever and make slaves out of all the Moslems. Slaves!"

"My mother was a slave in the Pacha's house," said Rhaissa in a matter-of-fact tone. "She used to have chicken every day, and she had four bracelets of heavy gold and a silk kaftan."

As people have a way of doing when they know they are lost, Stenham resorted to sarcasm. "And I suppose she loved being a slave," he said.

"It was written." Rhaissa shrugged.

"Yes. Of course," he said, wondering how he had happened once again to allow himself to fall into the error of engaging in an argument with one of these people, since it was manifestly impossible to keep control of any discussion, and since the discussion's inevitable failure to remain on the road of logic always gave him a depressing sense of his own futility. After all, if they were rational beings, he thought, the country would have no interest; its charm was a direct result of the people's lack of mental development. However, one could scarcely hope for them to be consciously and militantly backward. Once they had got hold of even the smallest fragment of the trappings of European culture they clung to it with an absurd desperation, but they were able to make it their own solely to the extent that the fragment was isolated from its context, and therefore meaningless. But after so many centuries in the deep-freeze of isolation, it was to be expected that, having been brought out of it, the culture should now undergo a very rapid decomposition. "It was written," she had told him, and he had agreed with her; that was the final and all-embracing truth about Morocco—about the world, for that matter. Discussion was nothing more than the clash of personalities.

"*Mektoub.*" She was standing there, still looking at him inquiringly. He did not know what she was expecting him to add, and since he had nothing to say, he smiled at her, opened the door and went back downstairs. She would never finish the room if he stayed there.

For a while he sat in a dark corner of the lobby looking at old numbers of magazines dealing with the commercial aspects of the French colonies; they were illustrated with what were to him inconceivably dull photographs of factories, warehouses, bridges and dams under construction, housing projects and native workers. It all reminded him of the old Soviet publications he had used to study. After all, he reflected, Communism was merely a more virulent form of the same disease that was everywhere in the world. The world was indivisible and homogeneous; what happened in one place happened in another, political protestations to the contrary. Or perhaps the great difference was that the West was humane; it allowed its patients to be anesthetized, whereas the East took suffering for granted, plunged ahead toward the grisly future with supreme indifference to pain.

"The trouble with you, John," Moss had declared, "is that you have no faith in the human race." He had admitted it, but his argument had been that for him it was necessary first to have faith in God. "And have you the faith?" Moss had asked him. He said he had not. Moss was triumphant. "And you never will have!" he had cried. "The two are inseparable." Stenham had qualified this as specious reasoning, typical of the lack of humility of modern man. "Don't give me that," he had said. "I don't want it. It's exactly where all the trouble has come from." It was little scenes such as this one which he dreaded most when he was with Moss, and Moss was always provoking them; they would be in the midst of one before he realized it. Moss was so sure of himself, so comfortably anchored and so untroubled by the surges of existence; his facile homilies were meaningless.

He slapped the magazines down on the table and went to eat lunch. The silence of the dining-room was disturbing. The waiters came and went on tiptoe, and their conversation with each other was carried on in whispers. For the first time he heard orders being given in the kitchen. And then from the open window came the long, slowly rising note of a muezzin calling the prayer of the *loulli*. Immediately it was joined by another, until it became a great ascending chorus of clear tenor voices. Just as there was always the first lone voice, there was also the last, after the others had finished. He listened to the way it drew out the final syllable of its *Allah akbar!* Having called to the east and south and west, the man was now facing the north, and the voice came floating over the city clear as the sound of an oboe. Then a rooster's crowing on some nearby roof covered it, and the waiter arrived with a large *vol au vent* and set it before him. All at once he was conscious of the absurdity of the moment. This entire mechanism, the kitchen with its chef, the busboys in the pantry, the hierarchy of waiters, the assortments of china, glassware and cutlery, the wagon with its rotating display of hors d'oeuvres, the trays on wheels with their aluminum ovens and flickering blue alcohol flames, all of it was for him, was functioning for him alone. It was not as though there were a possibility that someone else might come in and lift the weight of responsibility from his shoulders. No one would come, and when he finished, the whole array would be cleared away and the tables set for dinner that night, and then even he might not be there, if he decided to go and eat in the city. Suddenly, aloud, he said: "Oh, my God!" He had just remembered that he was expected at Si Jaffar's for dinner.

It would certainly be rude to call and ask whether under the circumstances he ought still to come, for although he knew the family well enough to be aware that they would never admit the existence of any political situation, he had no idea on which side their sympathies lay. On several occasions in the house he had met officers in the French army with their wives, and the atmosphere had been one of complete cordiality. Furthermore, two of Si Jaffar's sons worked as functionaries with the French administration; the chances were pretty good, he thought, that the family was pro-French. And yet, every one of them had at some time or another voiced the strongest criticism of the French. He had used to join in, but lately he had thought it wiser merely to laugh and let them do the excoriating. If they were indeed on the side of the French, his own police dossier must have grown by leaps and bounds as a result of the evenings he had spent with them, for they would have had no choice but to report everything. There was no way of collaborating halfway with the French; if you were with them you had their complete protection, at least until such time as they decided you were no longer useful, and if you were not with them you were against them. To telephone Si Jaffar and say to him: "I wondered if you still wanted me to come, in view of what is going on at the moment," would have yielded no result at all, for he would have claimed absolute ignorance. Besides, just what was going on? Stenham himself did not know. The man in the antique store had been very kind to tender him his cryptic warning (he had not thought him capable of such a disinterested gesture), but he was going to disregard it, all the same. When he had finished his lunch he would go out the gate and down into the Medina on a little inspection tour of his own.

But the long meal and the heavy heat, and perhaps the silence of the dining-room, had their effect, and when he had eaten his fruit he rose and went upstairs to stretch out on the bed for a few minutes. First he drew the curtains so that the room was protected from the afternoon's yellow glare. A few

flies buzzed in circles over the table; he directed a short blast
at them from an aerosol bomb and took off his shoes and
trousers. Then he lay down. The air was clogged with heat,
and the gloom in the room was so deep that he could not see
the painted arabesques on the beams of the high ceiling above
his head. Somewhere off in the mountains, down in the Middle Atlas, there was the triumphant rolling of thunder, muted
and gentle at this great distance. The sound came at regular
intervals, enfolding him in its softness. Nothing lay between
him and sleep.

And there he was suddenly, a century later, sitting up,
blinking at a hostile unreal room invaded by lavender emptiness. The thunder crashed again in the garden, and he swung
himself out of bed and ran to the windows. The rain was just
arriving, angry and violent, and the city glowed in an unnatural twilight. It was quarter past five. He went back to the
bed and lay down, reaching over his head for the bell. The
sound of its ringing in the maids' room on the floor below
was covered by the storm, but it had rung, for a moment later
there was a loud knocking at the door.

"*Trhol!*" he shouted.

Rhaissa's head appeared, her eyes looking very white in the
dimness. Surely she was eager to discuss the weather, but he
was still paralyzed by sleep. "Bring me my tea, please," he
told her, and she closed the door.

A moment later there was another knock. He thought he
must have dozed again, for it was always at least a quarter of
an hour before the tea arrived. "*Trhol!*" he cried, and then,
since there was no response, he said it louder. The door
opened, and a man stepped in. Stenham snapped on the light
and saw Moss, his suit irregularly splashed with water, his
cane under his arm.

"Come in, come in," he told him.

"I don't disturb you?"

"Not at all. I'm just about to have tea. I'll have her bring
an extra cup."

"No, no. I must go down and change. I'm quite wet. I
shan't even sit down. I merely wanted to report to you. It's
been an incredible day. Details later." He wiped his forehead,

blew his nose. "Hugh's in his room, so at least I accomplished my mission. I must say my opinion of the French has altered somewhat since this morning. Shall I see you at dinner?"

"Yes," Stenham said. "If the hotel's still standing, and hasn't been washed down into the river. Listen." He held up a finger: the rain roared. Moss smiled and went out.

Before Rhaissa brought the tea, the rain stopped with dramatic suddenness. It was now dark. He opened the windows, heard the water still clamoring in the drainpipes and spattering from the trees onto the terrace. But the air was quiet and chill. He stood awhile leaning out, listening and taking deep breaths.

Later, while he was drinking the tea, he again remembered his appointment at Si Jaffar's. There was no remedy for it; he would merely put on an old suit and splash through the mud to the house. By taking a series of short-cuts that he had worked out over the years, he could arrive in about a half hour. He gulped down the last of the tea, dressed quickly, put his flashlight in his hip pocket, and telephoned Moss.

It took a long time to get him, and when he answered, his voice sounded gruff. "*Oui? Qu'est-ce qu'il y a?*" he demanded.

"Have I waked you up?" Stenham began.

"No, John, but I'm dripping water all over the rug. I was in the bath."

Stenham apologized, explained why he would not be at dinner. Moss hesitated before saying: "John? I'm not sure I'd go if I were you. I don't think it's wise at this point."

"I've got to go," said Stenham flatly. "Get back into your tub and I'll see you tomorrow."

The streets were deserted. He walked at the side, keeping against the walls to avoid the brooks that ran down the middle. As he approached the river there was much more water; he was forced eventually to turn back and take a higher point at which to cross. Had he kept to his original course, he would have been in rushing water up to his knees by the time he had got to the bottom. The few men who passed were too much occupied with the business of walking to pay him any attention.

It was a difficult climb up the steep streets of the Zekak er

Roumane; the mud was as bad as the water, and he kept sliding back. Behind the wet walls of the dwellings and from the terraces above, cocks were crowing senselessly, and small bats swooped in the air around the infrequent street lights. When he came out into the Talâa he found it almost as unpopulated as the side streets: the stalls were boarded up, and it was only now and then he passed a lone man sitting silently beside a donkey or a load of charcoal or a roll of matting. Even the beggars who usually crouched by the fountain below the turn-off to Si Jaffar's alley were gone tonight. He glanced at his watch and saw that it was almost eight o'clock. If only it were eleven, he thought, and he were on his way back to the hotel, the ordeal behind him. These endless evenings at Si Jaffar's were excruciating; he dreaded them with almost the intensity most people dread an appointment with the dentist. The conversation was of necessity highly superficial, and it went without saying that nothing which was said had even a trace of sincerity; if a truth happened to be uttered, it was a matter of sheer accident. Sometimes he tried to get the family on the subject of native customs, but even here on various occasions he had discovered them in the act of lying to him, purposely misinforming him, doubtless in order to enjoy a good laugh at his expense after he had gone. All the members of the family were most amiable, however, even if their friendliness was expressed in an arbitrary and usually ceremonious manner, and he felt that it did him good to tax his patience by sitting among them and learning to chat and joke with them on their level. Had anyone asked him why he thought it beneficial to make this strenuous effort regularly, his answer would have been that theory without practice was worthless. Si Jaffar and his family were typical middle-class Moroccans who had offered him the unusual honor of throwing their home open to him. (He had even met the wife, the daughters, unveiled, the aunts and the grandmother, an ancient lady who crawled everywhere through the house on her hands and knees.) It seemed to him that he could scarcely afford to miss any opportunity of seeing them.

Moss had once said to him: "For you Moslems can do no wrong," and Stenham had laughed sourly, agreed, and reflected that if that were so, neither could they do any right.

They did what they did; he found it all touching and wholly ridiculous. The only ones he judged, and therefore hated, were those who showed an inclination to ally themselves with the course of Western thought. Those renegades who prated of education and progress, who had forsaken the concept of a static world to embrace that of a dynamic one—he would gladly have seen them all quietly executed, so that the power of Islam might continue without danger of interruption. If Si Jaffar and his sons had sold their services to the French, that still did not invalidate their purity in his eyes, so long as they continued to live the way they lived: sitting on the floor, eating with their fingers, cooking and sleeping first in one room, then in another, or in the vast patio with its fountains, or on the roof, leading the existence of nomads inside the beautiful shell which was the house. If he had felt that they were capable of discarding their utter preoccupation with the present, in order to consider the time not yet arrived, he would straightway have lost interest in them and condemned them as corrupt. To please him the Moslems had to tread a narrow path; no deviation was tolerated. In conversation with them he never lost an opportunity to revile Christianity and its concomitants. It was the greatest pleasure for him when they looked at one another with wonder and said, shaking their heads: "This one understands the world. Here is a Nazarene who sees the evil in his own people." A question which often came up at this point in such discussions was: "And have you never wanted to become a Moslem?" This embarrassed him profoundly, for it seemed to him that he was less equipped to embrace their faith than any other faith: it demanded a humility and submission that he could not conceive himself as feeling. He admired it in them, but he could never accept it for himself. Discipline for the sake of discipline, mindless and joyous obedience to arbitrary laws, that was an element of their religion which, praiseworthy though it might be, he knew was not for him. It was too late; even his ancestors of several centuries ago would have said it was too late. Who was wrong and who was right he did not know or care, but he knew he could not be a Moslem.

Still, it seemed to him that it was this very fact which made contact with them so desirable and therapeutic. Certainly it

was this which lent the obsessive character to his preoccupation with them. They embodied the mystery of man at peace
with himself, satisfied with his solution of the problem of life;
their complacence came from asking no questions, accepting
existence as it arrived to their senses fresh each morning, seeking to understand no more than that which was directly useful for the day's simple living, and trusting implicitly in the
ultimate and absolute inevitability of all things, including the
behavior of men. And this satisfaction they felt in life was to
him the mystery, the dark, precious and unforgivable stain
which blotted out comprehension of them, and touched
everything they touched, making their simplest action as fascinating as a serpent's eye. He knew that the attempt to
fathom the mystery was an endless task, because the further
one advanced into their world, the more conscious one became that it was necessary to change oneself fundamentally in
order to know them. For it was not enough to understand
them; one had to be able to think as they thought, to feel as
they felt, and without effort. It was a lifetime's work, and one
of which he was aware he would some day suddenly tire.
However, he considered it the first step in establishing an
awareness of people; when he had told Moss that, Moss had
exploded in laughter.

"Morally you're still a totalitarian." Sometimes it seemed
impossible that Moss had been serious in confronting him
with such an accusation; surely he had said it out of pure per-
verseness, knowing it was the antithesis of what was true
about him. But if that were so certain, why then did the idea
stick there, embedded like a burr in his mind? He tried to
think back, to recall whether one day he might have used an
inconsidered word which could have led Moss to misunderstand later remarks, but of course it was useless; he could
remember no such occurrence. "Maybe I am," he said to
himself once again, listening to his footsteps echo in the covered passageway. If it was "totalitarian" to estimate the worth
of an individual according to what he produced, or to evalu-
ate any segment of humanity using as a scale its culture, then
Moss was right. There was no other criterion to use in determining the right of an organism to exist (and in the end any
judgment one passed on another human being was reducible

to the consideration of that right). If, for instance, he deplored the violence that resulted in the daily bombings and shootings in the streets of Casablanca, it obviously was not because he felt pity for the victims, who, however pathetic, were still anonymous, but because he knew that each sanguinary incident, by awakening the political consciousness of the survivors, brought the moribund culture nearer to its end. Now he recalled an occasion when they had been talking about war, and he had said: "People can be replaced, but not works of art." Moss had been indignant, called him selfish and inhuman. Perhaps it was a few careless phrases such as this that Moss had stored in his memory and used as a springboard for making his accusation. He would bring up the subject again at the right moment. This was the door to Si Jaffar's house. Seizing the knocker, he banged the iron ring against the wood, twice.

The youngest son had led him into the patio where the orange trees still let fall drops of rain onto the mosaic beneath. There he stood for a minute or two, alone by the central fountain, waiting for Si Jaffar. The wrought-iron balustrade around the basin was hung with cleaning rags. Some were even looped around the lower branches of one of the trees. From somewhere in the house there came the insistent pounding of a pestle in a mortar: one of the women was grinding spices. When Si Jaffar appeared, he was wearing striped pajamas, a loosely wound turban was around his head, and he was wringing his hands and smiling his eternal smile.

"We have had a little accident, with slight damage," he said. "I hope you will forgive the inconvenience." He led him into the large reception room. Several tons of rubble lay piled up at one end: stones, earth and plaster. The wall of the house across the street was visible through the gaping hole. The family had retrieved most of the mattresses and cushions, and ranged them in the center of the room. "The rain," Si Jaffar said apologetically. "This is an old house. One is afraid the entire wall may crumble."

Stenham glanced nervously up at the ceiling. Si Jaffar noticed his movement and laughed indulgently. "No, no, Monsieur Jean! The roof is not going to fall. The house is strong."

Stenham was not reassured, but he smiled and sat down on the mattress indicated for him, against the opposite wall.

"You must forgive my informality. I am late," said his host, touching his pajama-top and his turban with a forefinger. "With all this disturbance I had not found the time to dress. But now with your permission I shall go and change. I have arranged for my cousin, Si Boufelja, to amuse you on the *oud* while you wait. One can't have one's guests sitting idle. Just a small moment, please." He went out across the patio, bent forward like an old man with his hands folded against his chest. Immediately afterward he reentered the room in company with a tall bearded man in a navy blue *djellaba*, who carried a very large lute in front of him as if it were a tray. Si Jaffar, beaming, neglected to introduce the two men, watched his cousin only long enough to see that he sat down and began to tune the strings, and then he excused himself.

The man continued to test the pitch of the strings, listening intently, never once glancing in Stenham's direction. A cat went by in the street outside, wailing raucously; it was as though the animal were in the room with them. The man disregarded the noise, soon began to play what sounded like a wandering improvisation that consisted of short breathless phrases separated from each other by long silences. Stenham listened carefully, thinking how much pleasanter his other evenings might have been if only the cousin's aid had been enlisted. One by one the other male members of the family came in, greeted him discreetly, and sat down to pay attention to the music. A good deal later Si Jaffar made his entrance, resplendent in white silk robes, with a dark red *tarbouche* stuck at a saucy angle on the top of his head. As if there were no music at all going on, he began to speak in a normal voice. This was obviously a signal for the volume of sound to be reduced, to pass to the background. The cousin now played softly, but he seemed to have lost interest: his expression of intentness relaxed, his gaze wandered from face to face, and he nodded his head absently in rhythm with his notes. When the servants brought in the dinner tables, they placed one in front of Si Jaffar and Stenham, who ate in uncrowded comfort while the six others sat surrounded by debris at the second table in the center of the room. Stenham presently made the bold suggestion that perhaps the cousin would be more comfortable at their table with them, where there was more space. Si Jaffar, smiling blandly, said: "We will all be happier this way."

"I didn't mean to be indiscreet," began Stenham.

Si Jaffar, licking his fingers one by one, did not reply. Now he clapped his hands for the servant; when the latter had come in, gone out again, Si Jaffar grinned widely, showing a whole set of gold teeth, and remarked complacently: "My cousin is very timid."

In the middle of the meal the electric light bulbs, which hung naked from the ceiling, went out. The room was absolutely dark; a husky voice from the other table muttered: "*Bismil'lah rahman er rahim*," and there was silence for an instant. Then Si Jaffar called very loudly to the servant for candles.

"In a moment the light will be back again," he assured Stenham, as the man came in, a burning candle in each hand. But they went on eating, and the power remained off.

The room was now mysterious and huge, with a theatre of shadows above, on the distant ceiling. During dessert the servant entered triumphantly with an old oil lamp which smoked abominably; everyone but Stenham greeted its arrival with murmurs of delight. Two or three times there was a flurry of conversation at the other table; on each occasion Si Jaffar tried to distract his guest's attention by beginning a pointless story. Stenham, annoyed by the clumsiness of these attempts to keep him from hearing what the members of the family were saying, pointedly turned his face toward the other table now and then while Si Jaffar talked.

After they all had finished eating, washing their hands, rinsing their mouths and drinking tea, they sat back and launched into the telling of a series of comic anecdotes. As usual, Stenham found it impossible to follow these stories; he understood the words, but he never got the point. However, he enjoyed watching the family during their telling, and hearing the loud laughter that followed each tale. The only member of the family who enjoyed the prerogative of smoking was Si Jaffar; to emphasize his privilege he chain-smoked, plying Stenham with a fresh cigarette every five minutes, occasionally while Stenham was still puffing on the previous one. The others did not have the right to light up in his presence.

"Do you understand our nonsense?" he asked Stenham.

"I understand the words, yes. But—"

"I shall explain the story Ahmed just told. The legionnaire liked the lantern, but he imagined he could buy it for a hundred rial. You know what figs are?"

"Yes."

"Well, the Filali had filled the lantern with figs, and his wife had hidden her bracelet at the bottom of the basket, so that the figs covered it up. That was why the Jew didn't see it when he put his head under the bed. You see? If he had had time before the legionnaire knocked at the door he would have taken all the figs out, but of course there was no time. That's what the Filali meant when he said: 'A young eucalyptus tree cannot be expected to give the shade of an old fig tree.' You follow this?"

"Yes," Stenham said uncertainly; he was expecting some further clue which might connect all the parts.

Si Jaffar looked pleased. "And that's the reason the Filali's wife had to dress up as a slave of the Khalifa. If she had allowed the Jew to guess her identity, he would have told the legionnaire, of course, and made his commission, which as you remember was fifty percent. I don't know whether you are acquainted with young eucalyptus trees? Their leaves are very narrow and small. So that what the Jew said to the Filali's wife was a compliment of a high order. But it was really only flattery, not sincere, you understand?"

By now Stenham understood absolutely nothing of the story, but he smiled and nodded his head. The others were still repeating the important line about the shade of the young eucalyptus tree, savoring its nuances at length, chuckling appreciatively. "I'm not certain you have understood," Si Jaffar told him after a moment. "There are too many things to explain. Some of our stories are very difficult. Even the people from Rabat and Casablanca often must have them explained, because the stories are meant only for the people of Fez. But that's what gives them their perfume. They wouldn't be amusing if everyone could follow them. Also some of them are very impolite, but we shan't tell any of those tonight, because you are here." He closed his eyes, apparently remembering one of the improper stories, and presently giggled with delight. Then he opened one eye and looked at Stenham. "I think the shocking stories are the most delicious," he said coyly.

"Tell one," urged Stenham. He was very sleepy, and he felt that if he should close his eyes for a moment like Si Jaffar, he would fall asleep directly. At his suggestion everyone laughed uproariously. Then the oldest son began to relate an involved tale about a hunchback with a sack of barley and a jackal. Before it had gone on for very long there was a lion in it, and then a French general who had lost a kilo of almonds. Whether or not the story was of the improper variety it was impossible for Stenham to guess; however, when it was finished he laughed with the others. A good deal later the cousin was called upon to play once again. This time he sang as well, in a tiny falsetto that was sometimes barely audible under the plucking of the strings. In the middle of the selection Si Jaffar seemed to become impatient: he pulled out his snuffbox and meticulously sniffed a pinch through each nostril. Then he took off his *tarbouche* and scratched his bald head, put it back on, tapped indolently with his fingertips on the snuffbox, and finally clapped his hands for the servant, bidding him bring a brazier. The cousin continued his piece imperturbably, even when the servant arrived carrying the vessel full of hot coals and set it in front of his master. Si Jaffar rubbed his hands in happy anticipation, and produced from the folds of his garments a packet containing small strips of sandalwood. With a spoon which had been brought for that purpose he poked the coals until he had uncovered the brightest ones, and placed the pieces of wood among them. Next he squatted over the brazier, so that it was completely covered by his garments, and remained that way for a minute or so, his eyes closed and an expression of beatitude on his face. When he rose, a cloud of sweet smoke billowed out from beneath his *djellaba*, and he murmured reverently: "*Al-lah! Al-lah!*" Then he sat down and picked his ears with a small silver earpick. The music continued. Stenham, comfortably ensconced in a mound of pillows, closed his eyes, and for a time did actually doze. Then he sat up straight, looking around guiltily to see who had noticed. Probably all of them, he thought, although no one was looking at him. Someone drove a squeaking wheelbarrow along the street on the other side of the open wall; the noise was so loud that the musician stopped to wait for it to pass. "Aha!" cried Si Jaffar. "That was very beautiful. Enough music for tonight, no?" He looked significantly at his cousin, who set the *oud* on the mattress and lay back against the cushions.

Stenham decided to seize this opportunity to announce his departure. Si Jaffar replied what he always replied at this point, regardless of the hour: "Already?" Then he continued: "Come and let me show you the damage. It is interesting." Now everyone got up and began to move around the room distractedly. With the lamp in one hand—its chimney was by now black with soot—one of the sons led the way across the stricken room.

They examined the wall and the composition of the rubble, discussed the relative costs of trying to repair the present wall and tearing it down to build a new one, inquired of Stenham whether American houses often caved in when it rained, and when he told them that was not the case, wanted to know in detail why it was not. Nearly an hour later they moved slowly in a group out through the patio to the antechamber by the front door, where in the dimness a ragged Berber sat waiting.

"This man will take you to your hotel," said Si Jaffar.

The man got slowly to his feet. He was tall and powerfully built; his inexpressive face could have been that of a cutthroat or a saint.

"No, no," Stenham protested. "You're very kind, but I don't need anyone."

"It's nothing," Si Jaffar said gently, with the modest gesture of a sultan who has just presented a subject with a bag of diamonds.

It was useless to offer objections; the man was going with him whether he liked it or not, and so he thanked them all together, separately, and together once more, and stepped through the doorway into the street. "*Allah imsik bekhir,*" "*B'slemah,*" "*Bon soir, monsieur,*" "*A bientôt, incha'Allah,*" they chorused, and one of the sons said shyly: "*Gude-bye, sair,*" a phrase with which he had been planning for some time to surprise Stenham, only now finding the courage to utter it.

CHAPTER 21

He was tired after his long walk back through the darkness of the Medina, and he did not feel like going downstairs again. Standing before the mirror of the armoire, putting his necktie back on, he reflected that this was the first time Moss had ever sent him a message at night. He looked at his watch: it was twenty minutes past one. From the doorway he cast a brief, longing glance at his bed; then he stepped out and locked the door behind him. The key had a heavy nickel tag attached to it; it felt like ice in his pocket.

In the lower garden it was very dark; the lanterns outside Moss's door had not been turned on, but slivers of light came through the closed blinds. A stranger opened the door in answer to his knock, stepped aside stiffly to let him pass, and closed it again after him. Moss had been standing in the center of the room, directly under the big chandelier, but now he began to pace slowly back and forth, his hands locked behind him. Stenham turned and saw a second stranger standing by the wall beside the door.

Moss did not bother to introduce the two to Stenham. He merely said: "*Enfin. Voici Monsieur Stenham.*"

The two murmured, inclining their heads ever so slightly.

"*Vous m'excusez si je parle anglais, n'est-ce pas?*" said Moss to his two guests. It was only Stenham who detected the acid tones of mockery in his politeness, and he thought: It's unlike Moss to be rude. He must have had provocation. Now he looked at the two men. One was short and plump, with round pink cheeks and large eyes; the taller one, who wore spectacles, was gaunt and yellow-skinned. Neither could have been more than twenty-five years old, and, he reflected, neither could have laughed if his life depended on it. It was obvious that for years they had insisted upon being serious, and the intensity of their effort had left its indelible mark; their common obsession showed in their faces and in the movements of their bodies. Immediately Stenham identified them as Nationalists. They were unmistakable.

"These two gentlemen have been kind enough," Moss went on, "to come and warn us that we should leave the hotel at once. It seems the situation has suddenly become very grave indeed."

"Ah," said Stenham. The two young men stood watching them with alert eyes. He felt sure they understood English perfectly. "Well, I suppose there's nothing to do but thank them. Tomorrow we can look into the matter and see what's what."

"But—at once, John! That means this minute."

"That's ridiculous," Stenham snapped. He turned to the taller Moslem, and said to him in Arabic: "Why? What's happened?"

The other looked first surprised and then pained, to hear his own tongue being spoken. With dignity he replied in French: "Things are going very badly. I can scarcely give you details, but I assure you there will be unpleasant events here in the Medina within twenty-four hours—very likely much sooner. The French will not be in a position to offer the hotel any protection whatever."

"Why should we want the protection of the French?" demanded Stenham. "And why should anyone bother us? We're not French."

The young man looked at him with the searching stare of the extremely myopic, but his expression revealed the depths of his hatred and scorn. "You are foreigners, Christians," he said. The plump young man broke in, with an attempt at affability; he had a rather strong Arab accent. "For the people in the street the enemy is the non-Moslem," he explained.

"Why?" demanded Stenham angrily. "This isn't a religious war. It's a fight purely against the French."

The near-sighted man's face had assumed a frozen expression, the mouth slightly twisted. He breathed more quickly. "A religious war is precisely what it threatens to become. *C'est malheureux, mais c'est comme ça.*"

Stenham turned to Moss; he did not want to look at the grimacing face. Then he turned back and said: "You mean, that's what you want to make it."

"Easy, John," Moss said quietly. "These gentlemen came as friends, you know, after all."

"I doubt it," Stenham muttered.

"The movement," pursued the man with glasses, "is as you say, directed above all against the French imperialists. Likewise it is against all those who assist the French. *Je vous demande pardon, monsieur,* but the arms used against the Moroccan people were largely supplied by your government. They do not consider America a nation friendly to their cause."

"Of course she is not an enemy either," said the other in a conciliatory tone. "Had you been Frenchmen we should not have given ourselves the trouble of coming here tonight. What would have happened to you would have been your own lookout. But, as you see, we are here."

"It's very kind of you," said Moss. He had begun to pace back and forth thoughtfully. A sudden flurry of rain spattered on the tiles outside the door.

"*Oui, nous vous sommes bien reconnaissants,*" Stenham said. He offered them each a cigarette; they both refused curtly. "These are English, not American," he informed them lightly. They did not bother to reply. He lighted a cigarette and stood considering them.

"*Enfin,*" said Moss, "we are all very tired, I'm sure. I think the time of our departure will have to be left for us to decide. It's impossible for us to leave tonight. Where could we go at this hour?"

"Go to the station in the Ville Nouvelle. There will be a train to Rabat at half past seven in the morning."

"Half past eight," corrected the shorter one.

The other made an impatient movement with his head, as though a fly had alighted on his face. "The station is under the protection of the French at present," he continued.

"*Non, merci!*" Stenham laughed. "There's a train blown up every other day. I'd rather walk. You take the train."

The young man with glasses lowered his head and thrust it forward aggressively. "We have not come here to amuse ourselves, monsieur. I see that it was a great waste of effort. Perhaps you would like to telephone the police and inform them of our visit." He pointed to the telephone. "*Yallah,*" he said gruffly to the other, and started toward the door. Before he reached it he stopped, turned, and said furiously: "Your frivolity and stubbornness may easily cost you your lives. *On ne badine pas avec la volonté du peuple.*"

Stenham snorted. The man continued to the door and opened it. Without offering him his hand the other bowed slightly to Moss, and followed.

"The will of the people! What people?" Stenham shouted. "You mean the leaders of your party?"

"John!" said Moss sharply.

The two young men went out, leaving the door open behind them. Moss stepped across the room, closed it and locked it.

"I must say, John, that was a most unpolitic performance on your part. There was no need to antagonize them. I'd been doing my best to keep on their good side, and I'd managed quite well until you came. They left in a jolly ugly mood, you know."

Stenham sat down, waited a moment before he spoke. "Do you think it matters what kind of a mood they're in?"

"I think common courtesy matters, yes. Always."

"Were they courteous with me, would you say?" Stenham demanded.

"Oh, my dear man, one can scarcely put oneself on their level," Moss said impatiently. "That's a feeble excuse, my boy, most feeble. After all, they're only patriots trying to help their country. One must look at the thing in that light. See their behavior in its proper perspective. No one is himself under the stress of passion, you know."

Stenham laughed shortly. "The only passion those cold fish know is hatred; I can tell you that. And they're not *patriots*, anyway. I object."

"We won't go into it," Moss said hastily. "I'm far too exhausted to argue. I was almost asleep when the office telephoned to say those two were here to see me. I hadn't a clue as to who they were, and of course I had to dress before having them down, and it was a bloody nuisance, I can tell you. Coming on the heels of my day with the police it was almost too much."

"You should be glad I got rid of them so quickly. Now you can get some sleep."

"Oh, I'm delighted with that side of it. But I do feel they have a right to their point of view. Then there's another thing." Moss's face became thoughtful. "If there *is* to be the kind of trouble they predict, it's quite obvious that we should be better off here if we were on friendly terms with them."

Stenham looked at him. "Friendly terms!" he repeated. "And the French?"

Moss laughed indulgently. "I think my connections at the Résidence in Rabat are sufficient to place me above suspicion. You know as well as I that the French are not fools, whatever else they may be. They'd understand perfectly, no matter what I did, that I'd done it purely as a matter of tactics. Don't be absurd."

"Well, I'm afraid I've got no such guarantee," Stenham said.

"You?" said Moss, and he waited a moment. "No," he said finally, "I'm afraid you haven't."

"And I don't want one, either. The French can go to Hell, and so can the Nationalists. It's as simple as that."

Moss smiled wryly. "Now that you've disposed of them all, what about us? Have you a helpful suggestion as to where we might go? Hugh, I meant to tell you, has gone to Tangier. He left directly after dinner."

"What?" Stenham cried; for some reason he felt that this was a desertion. "You mean he just suddenly packed up and left? But he was so determined not to let them scare him off. I don't get it."

Now Moss sat down on the bed, removed his glasses wearily. Without them his face took on an expression of sadness. Stenham regarded him with vague curiosity.

"My dear John," Moss said, twirling the glasses by a stem, "I think if you had seen the things we saw today you'd understand better why he no longer cared. As he himself said at dinner, up until then he'd thought of the whole show as a kind of game and it was a part of the game to stick it out, obviously. But this afternoon—" he shook his head deliberately and paused—"I must confess I had never expected to be that close to brutality and suffering. One reads about such things in the newspapers and is horrified by them, but even with the most active imagination one falls far short of the actuality. It's all the unexpected details, the expressions on the faces, the helpless little gestures, the senseless and unrelated words that come out of their mouths, things that one would never be able to invent, those are what does one in, when one is actually there."

"What did you see, for God's sake?" Stenham demanded. Without Kenzie's car available, the situation was different; he felt less easy in his mind, although he told himself it was illogical.

"We merely saw hundreds of Arabs at the police station being brought in, being beaten, knocked down, kicked in the places where it would do the most damage, and tortured. Yes, tortured," Moss repeated, raising his voice. "That's the only word for it. When one says torture, one's inclined to picture something refined and slow and diabolical, but I assure you, it can also be swift and brutal. If you'd merely seen the floor, slippery with blood, and with teeth lying here and there, I think you'd find it easier to understand why Hugh suddenly felt no desire to go on playing his game with the French. He couldn't think of it in those terms any longer."

Moss was silent for a moment, listening to the wind in the poplars. "At first they had him locked up, and it took me about two hours of ranting even to get to see him. Then we had to wait on a bench in the corridor until almost four o'clock to see some monstrous little functionary who was to give the final official word that he was to be released. That was when we saw them being dragged in. But, John, the French have lost their minds! Those people had simply been taken in off the streets! Old men who hadn't the slightest idea what was happening to them, boys of ten screaming for their mothers. The police simply clubbed them all without discrimination. They pounded them, kicked them in the face with their boots when they fell. I don't know. It's useless to think about it, and still more useless to talk about it, and I'm going to stop. But don't judge Hugh too harshly for beating a retreat. I personally think he's shown very good sense, and I can't imagine what I'm doing staying on, as a matter of fact, except that with all my paraphernalia I couldn't very well get packed in time to go with him, and in any case I don't want to go to Tangier." He put his spectacles on and stood up.

"How curious the world is," he said, as if to himself; then he turned and walked toward Stenham's chair. "There's no end to violence and bloodshed, is there? I had a peculiar presentiment today as I sat there speechless, watching it all, that it was only a prologue to a whole long period of suffering that hasn't even begun. But I hope I shan't see it."

"I hope not," said Stenham.

"Good night, John. I'm sorry to have dragged you down here at this hour, but they did ask for you, you know, and anyway, I needed a bit of moral support. Let's see what tomorrow brings forth, and plan accordingly."

"Right," said Stenham.

The garden lay in darkness, bathed by a mild, damp wind. When he got to his room he opened the table drawer and stood a moment looking down at the pages of typescript lying there; he had a sudden desire to pick them up, crumple them into a ball, and throw them out the window. Instead, he undressed, brushed his teeth, and got into bed. But he could not sleep.

CHAPTER 22

And yet, he thought, when he entered again into the world, becoming conscious of the daylight out there beyond the window, he must have slept, because the ritual he was in the act of performing at the moment was the accustomed one of awakening. In his mind he had planted firmly the idea that he was not sleeping, had not slept, would not sleep, and he became aware only now that each time he had reminded himself: "I am still awake," he had actually had to come back from sleep to do it. In spite of the long journey he had made through fantasy when he first lay down—"What if," his mind had asked, and then the screen had lighted up and the projections had begun—at some point there had been a halt and sudden darkness, and, although he had not slept very long, because it was still scarcely later than dawn, he felt surprisingly lively. It could of course be the false energy that sometimes manifests itself at the moment of awakening after a short night's sleep, only to change to lassitude after the first hot cup of coffee. As he stretched and yawned voluptuously, he suddenly remembered that he had slept all yesterday afternoon; the idea of this encouraged him to think that perhaps he had had enough sleep after all, and could risk looking at his watch, which in effect meant getting up, since once he knew the hour he almost never fell asleep again.

It was a few minutes before ten; the gray, unaccustomed light above the Medina was that of a dark day—not of dawn. He sat up and rang the bell. It was Abdelmjid who knocked in answer. He ordered his breakfast by shouting from bed, without opening the door. Then he crossed the room to the washstand, dashed cold water over his face, and combed his hair. On his return to the bed he unlocked the door. He lay back against the pillows, waiting, looking out over the further edges of the city to the dim hills behind. The light rain falling blurred the air and removed the color from the landscape, giving it instead a gray luminosity which blotted out the familiar landmarks.

Abdelmjid was a long time coming with the tray. When he entered, his face was set in a rigid mask which announced as well as words could have that he did not want to talk. And Stenham realized, when he looked at him, that as a matter of fact neither did he. They exchanged the brief commonplaces appropriate to the time of day, and Abdelmjid went out.

It was as he was finishing his breakfast that Stenham always began to plot the course of his work for the morning. Today it was not even to be considered. It was impossible to spin fantasies about the past when the present was like a bomb lying outside the window, perhaps ready to explode any minute. This was the most cogent argument for leaving the place—not the warnings of the Nationalists or the threats of the French. If all prospects for work were withdrawn there was no point in staying; the only sensible thing was to move on to another place, in the Spanish Zone this time, where he would still be in Morocco, but in a Morocco not yet assailed by the poison of the present. He did not want to leave; he dreaded going to Moss and discussing it, but there was the undeniable fact in front of him. This was the moment of the day when he saw things most clearly, while his breakfast tray was still across his lap. A judgment reached later in the day could go wide of the mark because then he had the use of his equipment for self-deception, whereas at this hour it had not begun to function.

"Good. Then it's decided. I get out." Moss could stay or go as he liked; his own mind was at rest. When, as he was dressing, he looked out the window at the grayness, he was thankful for the rain, for it made his decision seem less painful. It was easier to renounce the city when it was color-less and wet, and the outer hills were hidden from view, and he knew that the mud was in the streets.

He packed methodically for about an hour, putting the filled valises one by one at the door, ready to be carried downstairs. Instead of notifying the desk to prepare his bill he decided to demand it in person at the last possible moment: they would have less time to work out the false extras with which they so loved to pad their *factures*. As he was stuffing some soiled shirts into a duffle bag full of books, the telephone rang.

"Hi," said a lively, matter-of-fact voice.

He opened his mouth to speak, but said nothing—merely held the receiver in his hand and looked at the wall a few inches in front of him.

Then the voice said: "Hello?"

"Lee?" he asked, although there was no need for that.

"Good morning."

"Well, my God! Where have you been? Where are you now?"

"I've been everywhere, and I'm in my room here at the hotel, this hotel, your hotel, the Mérinides Palace, Fez, Morocco."

"You're here in the hotel?" he said. "When did you come?" He had almost said: "Why did you come?" turning his head to look at the row of valises by the door. "When can I see you? I want to see you right away. We can't talk on the phone."

Her answer was a short, satisfied laugh. Then she said: "I'd love to see you. Suppose I meet you in the writing room, that room upstairs with the big window."

"When?"

"Any time. Now, if you like."

"I'll be right down."

He got there first, but she came in half a minute later, looking just as he had remembered her, only better. She was deeply tanned, and in places the sun had lightened the brown of her hair to gold. They sat down on the cushions against the window. He made her do most of the talking. She had simply decided to go to Meknès, she said, and from there she had gone on to Rabat, and then she had wired a friend of hers from Paris, a French girl who had married an army man, stationed down in Foum el Kheneg, on the edge of the Sahara, and they had invited her down there, and so she had gone, and everything had been marvelous. Why she had left Fez, and above all, why she had returned—when he came to ask her those two questions, he found he could not.

"You know," he told her, "I nearly went to Meknès after you did."

"You did?" she said curiously. "Why?"

He brought out his wallet and pulled the folded telegram from it. "Look at this wire you sent me," he said, spreading it on the cushion in front of her. "Look. Doesn't it say: JOING MEKNES? For a while I was sure it was the final 'G' that was the mistake. Wistful thinking."

She laughed. "It's lucky you didn't come. You'd never have found me."

"I'll bet I would. Weren't you at the Transatlantique?"

"I was not. I was in a little native hotel called the Régina. It was pretty grim, too."

He looked at her incredulously, and felt all the uncomfortable suspicions surge again in him. This time, even if it destroyed their friendship, he would find out.

"I don't know," he said unhappily. "I think you're crazy."

Apparently she was aware that something was amiss with him, for she was studying his face with an expression of curiosity. "Why, do you think it's improper or something for me to put up at cheap hotels? Moving around costs money, you know. We can't all stay in the Mérinides Palaces and Transatlantiques *all* the time."

It was not good enough. "Lee, you know damned well what I mean." But of course he could not go all the way. "There's an undeclared war on here, people are being shot and blown up every day all over the place, and you calmly wander around in a way nobody would do, even in normal times. What's the answer?"

Again she laughed. "The answer is that you only live once."

"Haven't you got a better one than that? I mean, a more truthful one?" he said, staring at her intently.

"More truthful?" she repeated, puzzled.

He was assailed by doubt, decided to laugh. "Now I'm in deep," he said ruefully. "I mean, are you sure you're not snooping around down here for somebody?"

"What a peculiar thing to say!" she exclaimed, drawing her head up and back in surprise. "What a funny man you are!"

His laughter continued, lame and unconvincing. "Just skip it. It was just an idea that came to me."

But now she was indignant; her eyes blazed. "I certainly won't skip it! What did you mean? You must have meant something. Why would such an idea just 'come' to you?"

"Consider it unsaid and accept my sincere and profound apologies," he suggested with mock contrition. And before she could answer again: "Look!" he cried, pointing out the window, "the rain has stopped. The sun's coming out. Let's hope it's a good omen."

"For what?" Her voice sounded angry still, and instead of heeding his exhortation to look out into the garden, she had opened her compact and was studying herself in its mirror.

"For today. For the trouble here."

"Why? Is it so much worse now? Is it really bad?"

"What do you mean, is it bad? It's terrible! Didn't you see anything at the station when you came in? Soldiers or crowds?"

"I didn't come by train. I hired a car in Rabat and came straight through."

He was delighted to have found a way out of the impasse of an instant ago, and he went ahead to recount the story Moss had told him last night, leaving out the visit of the two young men to the hotel. She listened, an increasingly horrified expression on her face. When he had finished, she said: "I wondered why Hugh had suddenly left like that. It wasn't like him not to leave at least a note."

"You mean for you? But how would he know you were coming back to Fez?"

"I wired him from Marrakech," she said.

"Oh. I see." For the moment he had forgotten that she was Kenzie's friend, that it was he who had introduced them. "Yes."

After a pause he said: "Are you sure he didn't leave some word for you? They might easily have mislaid it in the office."

"No, he didn't."

"Are you very much upset to have missed him?"

"Oh, it's too bad. But perhaps I'll see him in Tangier on my way up. I'm only going to stay a day or so here. I've got to get back to Paris."

He was thinking: You may not find it that easy. She seemed still not to have envisaged the possible effects of the conflict should it break out into violence, and this puzzled him; however, he did not feel that it was his duty to try to make her aware by alarming her.

They went down to lunch. The empty dining-room astonished her. "You mean there's not a soul in the hotel but you and Mr. Moss?" she exclaimed.

"And you and the staff. That's right."

Their table was by the window; they watched the sun slowly devour the mist that steamed upward from the Medina.

"This may be a historic day in the annals of Fez," he said. "I'm damned if I'm going to sit here in the hotel all afternoon. I'd like to get out and see something. At least see if there's anything to see."

"Well, then, let's go out."

"Fine. Let's. But first I've got to leave a note for Mr. Moss. We'd been more or less planning on leaving if things got bad" (he thought with surprise, almost with disbelief, of the luggage stacked inside his door upstairs) "and we were going to have a sort of council of war today at some point."

"Don't you think you ought to go and see him?" she suggested.

"I'll drop in later, when we get back. I don't think he's all that eager to go. He's very conscious of the whole situation, as far as any outsider can be, and I don't think he thinks it's too dangerous. The trouble is, nobody really knows anything except a handful of Arabs and maybe a still smaller handful of French."

She told him about her trip to Foum el Kheneg—the difficulties of getting there, the unbelievable heat, the desolation of the landscape, the delightful home that Captain Hamelle and his wife had made for themselves in the hostile wilderness, and the trips they had taken in a jeep through the mountains to the Berber *casbahs* roundabout.

"I've never been in that particular valley," he said, "but I've been in country like it. It's magnificent."

"Magnificent country," she agreed, "but a pretty terrifying civilization, completely feudal. Those *caïds* have the power of life and death over their subjects, you know. Think of the gap those people have got to get across before they can hope to be anything."

He felt the anger rising to his lips; fighting it back, he said: "I don't think I know what you mean. What would you like them to be, other than what they are, which is perfectly happy?"

She looked at him carefully, as if she were measuring his intelligence. "Will you please tell me what makes you think those helpless serfs are *happy*? Or haven't you ever given it a thought? Are they just happy by definition because they're absolutely isolated from the world? They're slaves, living in ignorance and superstition and sickness and filth, and you can sit there and calmly tell me they're happy! Don't you think that's going a little far?"

"It's not going nearly as far as you. I say leave them alone. You say they've *got* to change, they've got to *be* something." He was excited; this was what had been standing between them. Perhaps they could get to it this time.

She tossed her head in a gesture of impatience. "They'll change," she said, with the air of a person who has access to private sources of information.

"You and the Istiqlal," he murmured.

"Look, Mr. Stenham. I don't think we know each other well enough to get into an argument. Do you?"

He was silent; the *Mister Stenham* had indicated the distance between them which doubtless had been there all along, only he had not been conscious of it. She was infinitely less approachable than he had thought; indeed, at the moment it was difficult to imagine what it would be like to be on intimate terms with her. He looked away from the table: the two rows of waiters, Moroccan and European, stood against their respective walls watching them discreetly.

"Smile," he told her.

She hesitated, drew back her upper lip in a tentative momentary grimace that was a sketch of a smile.

"Your teeth are too sharp," he said. "When I was a kid I once had a baby fox. It had fluffy fur and a big bushy tail and everyone who saw it used to make a dash for it and try to pet it. You can imagine the rest."

Now she smiled. "As far as I know, Mr. Stenham, I haven't got either a big bushy tail or fluffy fur."

"Don't you think it might help our struggling friendship if you called me John, instead of Mister Stenham?"

"It might," she admitted. "I'll try to remember. I'll also try to remember that you're a hopeless romantic without a *shred* of confidence in the human race." She was staring at him fixedly, and he resented the deep sensation of uneasiness her expression was able to awaken in him.

"You're a bright girl," he said with irony.

"You remind me so much of a friend of mine," she went on, still watching him. "A nice enough boy, but all tied up in knots by his own theories about life. You even look a little like him, I swear! He wrote pretty good poetry, too. At least, it seemed all right until you took time off and suddenly asked yourself what it meant."

"I'm not a poet." His voice was sour, but he smiled at her.

She continued, impervious. "And I'll bet your life histories have a lot in common. Did you ever join the Communist Party? *He* did; he used to put on a special outfit and go and stand on corners and sell the *Daily Worker*. Later he went in for Yoga, and the last I knew he'd become a Roman Catholic. That didn't stop him, though, from getting to be an alcoholic."

Stenham, whose face had briefly shown traces of alarm, now smiled. "Well," he said, "I think you've drawn a pretty complete picture of somebody who's about as different from me as he could get."

"I don't believe it," she announced in a firm voice. "I can

feel the similarity. Intuition," she added, as if to keep him from saying it with sarcasm.

"Have it your own way. Maybe I am like him. Maybe the first thing I know I'll be standing on my head or going to Mass or joining Alcoholics Anonymous, or all of them at once. Who knows?"

"And another thing," she pursued. "Now that I think of it—of course!—it was after he left the Party that he began to have delusions. He suspected everybody else of belonging to it. You had to be practically a Swami for him not to challenge whatever you said. He smelled propaganda everywhere."

"I see," Stenham said.

"You may be unconscious of it, but twice since we've been sitting here *you've* practically accused *me*. You think back a minute."

He sat quietly until the waiter had left the table. Then he leaned forward, speaking intensely. "But, Lee, I don't make any bones of the fact. Of course I was in the Party. Exactly sixteen years ago. And I stayed in, officially, exactly twenty months and attended exactly twenty-four meetings and so what? I wasn't even in the United States most of the time—"

She was laughing. "But you don't have to defend yourself! I don't care how long you were in the Party or why you joined or what you did in it. I'm just delighted to see I was right, that's all."

"Do you want coffee?"

"No, thanks."

"I think we'd better go, don't you? The mud'll be pretty well dried by now."

"Just a minute," she said with mock sternness. "You *did* accuse me, didn't you?"

"All right, I did. But you brought it on yourself with your remarks."

"I think you're crazy."

"No, I mean it."

"Let's go," she said, rising.

The head waiter bowed them out and closed the door after them. Stenham walked behind her along the damp corridor with its straw-paneled walls, thinking that the conversation had been completely unsatisfactory. What he had wanted to say was: You brought it on yourself with your half-baked, pseudo-democratic idealism. But he knew she would not accept criticism from him; she was an American woman, and an American woman always knew best. She assumed the role of a patient and amused mother, and with gentle ridicule reduced you to the status of a small boy. But if you spoke up in your own defense, which necessarily meant attacking the falseness of her position, she swiftly invoked the unwritten laws of chivalry. Too, he envied Lee for being able to speak in so jaunty and offhand a manner of a thing about which he felt such a profound, if irrational, guilt.

The mud had been dried into an inoffensive paste that crumbled underfoot, the sky was clear, and the glare that had accompanied the rising of the mist had been dissipated. For Stenham the act of stepping out into the street constituted an automatic leaving behind of rancor; he observed this and rejoiced, for it would have been an ordeal to wander through the town carrying the weight of his bad humor. As they followed the zigzagging street between the walls, he wondered whether coming out here had performed the same catharsis for her, or whether she even needed such a thing, seeing that she could not very well consider herself in any light save that of victor in the recent verbal bout. Apparently she had nothing at all on her mind save the things she was seeing around her. Every little while she hummed a tune to herself as she carefully picked her way around the places that might still be slippery. He listened: it was *On the Sunny Side of the Street*, phrased arbitrarily, according to her breathing.

They came to the pigeon market below the old mosque at Bab el Guissa. There was certainly something abnormal about the day, but he could not discover what it was that made him think so. Work was going on as always in the quarter, which was devoted largely to oil presses and carpenters' workshops. There were the usual numbers of donkeys being driven and ridden back and forth, of small children bearing trays of unbaked and baked bread on their heads going to and from the ovens, of girls and old women carrying vessels of water from the public fountains. At the same time there was a definite if subtle difference between today and other days, one which he was convinced was not imaginary, and yet he could not tell where the difference lay. Could it be in the expressions on the faces? He decided not; they were inscrutable as always.

They got to the blind passageway just beyond the Lemtiyine school, a long narrow alley leading downward to an arched door whose gate was always open. Split banana-leaves waved across the top of the wall like the battered paper decorations of a festival long past. Suddenly he knew what was amiss; seeing this empty corridor had told him.

"Ah!" he said with satisfaction.

"What is it?"

"I'd been thinking that there was something strange about the place today, but I couldn't put my finger on it. Now I know what it is. All the boys and young men are missing. We haven't seen a boy over twelve or a man under thirty since we left the hotel."

"Is that bad?" she asked.

"Well, it's been known to be bad, all right. The crazy French think if they can get that age group behind bars they automatically remove most of the sources of trouble. But probably today it's a case of something big going on down in the town, and they're all there to see it. What's going on is anybody's guess."

"I don't want to get into any crowds," she declared. "It's all right with me where we go and what we do, as long as we steer clear of the mob. I have a thing about getting caught in a crowd. I don't think there's anything more terrifying."

They walked more slowly. "I'm inclined to agree with you," he said. Suddenly he stopped. "I'll tell you what. If you don't mind walking a little more, it might be the better part of valor to go back and out Bab el Guissa, and do the whole thing outside the walls. That way we're sure of avoiding getting hemmed in down in the Talâa. We'll get to Bou Jeloud a little later, that's all."

She looked at him as if she were wondering why he had not suggested this in the beginning, but all she said was: "Fine."

For ten minutes or so they retraced their steps, until they came to the mosque. The massive arch of Bab el Guissa was behind, a short distance up the hill, a small fortress in itself, the interior of which had been rebuilt by the French to house a police office. They went through the first gate into the cool darkness. The passage made a turn to the left, then to the right, and they saw the trees and hills ahead. As they walked through the outer arch, two French policemen standing along the wall conferred briefly, and then one of them called out.

"Where are you going, monsieur?"

Stenham said they were taking a walk.

"You are from the Mérinides Palace?"

Stenham said they were.

"When you go back into the Medina to return to your hotel, you will use the other gate, not this one," the policeman told him.

Stenham said they would.

"And when you have finished your walk, you will take no more walks until you are told. They should have warned you at the hotel. There are disorders in the native quarter."

Stenham thanked him and they walked on.

"We'll have to go a little out of our way now," he told her presently, "or they'll see we're turning in the wrong direction and call us back."

They walked straight ahead toward the hills until they came to the main road. Then they stopped and looked back. Behind them stretched the blank face of the ramparts, broken only by the single arch of Bab el Guissa. The two policemen were still visible, tiny blue spots against the darkness of its opening.

When the road curved, they set off across the cemetery, cutting back toward a path that ran more or less parallel to the ramparts, but along extremely uneven terrain. First they were at a level with the top of the ramparts, and could see the further side of the Medina, then they were in a deep hollow where the path wound between rows of cactus and aloes, with nothing beyond but the steep dust-colored slopes rising on both sides toward the sky. Then the land dropped away, and the narrow lane which had been at the bottom of a ravine followed the spine of a twisting hill. Goats wandered and cropped the dwarf thistles under the olive trees on the hillside below. They skirted the bases of perpendicular cliffs, where dogs barked to protect the caves that men had dug with their hands out of the clay, and where babies now squalled and occasionally a drum was being beaten. Then they were in a dried-up meadow where the earth was veined with wide dark cracks.

"Whew! It's like walking inside an oven," she said.

"We'll take a cab back."

"If we ever get there. How much further is it?"

"Not far. But you're going to have to hold your nose pretty soon. I warn you."

From the top of an absurd little crest of land across which the path led them, they could see over the ramparts into the Casbah en Nouar near by; its roofs and gardens hid the center of the Medina. They stood still a moment and looked at the panorama of strange formations around them. The earth's configurations here were like those of an unruly head of hair. The land whirled up into senseless peaks and dropped off vertically into mysterious pits and hollows.

"Listen," Stenham told her. Like the shrilling of insects came the distant sound of prolonged shouting from many throats. "There's whatever's going on," he said.

"Well, thank heavens we turned around. I wouldn't be down in there for anything in the world."

The stench began before the village came into view. Then they passed the first dwellings, made with packing cases, thorn bushes and oil cans, tied together with rope and strips of rags. A more intense squalor would have been inconceivable. Children, naked or with mud-colored pieces of cloth hanging to them, played on the refuse-strewn waste land between the huts, where the ground glittered with tin and broken glass.

"This is all new," he told her. "None of this existed a few years ago."

"God," she said with feeling.

The mud had not dried here; they were obliged to walk at the sides of the path. The ground crawled with countless flies; at each step a small swarm rose a few inches into the air, only to settle again immediately. As they passed through the village the people stared at them, but with no expression beyond that of mild curiosity. The way now led up a steep hill toward the ramparts. Tons of garbage and refuse had been dumped at the top and, sliding down the long slope, threatened now to engulf the improvised dwellings below; along the side of this encroaching mountain half-starved dogs wandered like hopeless ghosts, feebly nosing the objects, occasionally dislodging a tin can which rolled a bit further down. There were people here, too, carefully examining the waste, and from time to time putting something into the sacks they carried slung over their shoulders.

When they reached the top of the hill, panting, they did not stop and turn to see the village behind them, but continued to walk until the stink had been left behind and they had gone through Bab Mahrouk's two portals. Then, beyond the shadow of the ramparts, in the wicker market, they stood still a moment to catch their breath.

"I'm going to say something that's almost worthy of a John Stenham," she told him. "And that is, that I wish you hadn't taken me through there. It somehow spoils the rest of the place for me."

"That's about one twentieth of what there is outside the walls," he said. "Don't you take slums for granted, yet? Have you ever seen a city that didn't have them?"

"Oh, but not that kind! Not quite that hopeless. My God, no!"

"I should think you'd be glad to have seen it. It's one more thing to be changed."

Ignoring his sarcasm, "That much it certainly is," she said grimly.

He pointed back at Bab Mahrouk's wide arch. "One reform they've made recently," he went on in the same mock-innocent fashion, "is that now there are no heads decorating that beautiful gate. They used to have a row of them on pikes for people to admire as they went out. Enemies of the Pacha and other evil-doers. Not in the Middle Ages, I mean, but in the twentieth century, just a few years ago. Don't you think it's an improvement without them?"

"Yes," she said with exasperation. "It's an improvement without them."

It was a pleasure to walk in the shade of the plane trees along the avenue that led back toward Bou Jeloud. When they got to the square where the buses waited, policemen were lined up in front of the gaudy blue gate; it looked like a scene in a lavish musical comedy. They waited at the far end of the open space, studying the array of men in uniform. Framed by the arch of Bab Bou Jeloud among the squat mud buildings was a low minaret with a huge mass of straw atop it, and in the middle of the straw stood a stork with one leg raised and bent against its body; it looked very white in the strong sunlight.

"I think this is the end of our excursion," he said to her. "If we go through the gate we'll be in the Medina, and we don't want that. And anyway, it doesn't look to me as though they'd let us through. There's a nice little café here. Are you game for a mint tea?"

"I'm game for anything as long as I can sit myself down," she said. "Just to sit would be a terrific luxury at this point. But let's make it inside, out of the glare."

CHAPTER 23

There were four cafés on the square, and each one had a large space in front of it which was ordinarily full of tables and chairs. Today, these had prudently not been set out, so that the sides of the square presented a deserted aspect which was emphasized by the fact that the center also was empty, for no one was walking in it. True, it was hot, and there would have been few strollers at this hour in any case, but the absence of people was so complete that the scene—even if the line of police could have been disregarded—had no element of the casualness which ordinarily gave the place its character.

"*Very* strange," Stenham muttered.

"Am I wrong," she said, "or does this look sort of sinister?"

"Come on." He took her arm and they hurried across to the café nearest the waiting buses. One of the *mokhaznia* standing by the footbridge across the stream looked at them dubiously, but did not stop them from passing. In the café, a group of thirty or forty men sat and stood quietly near the windows, peering out through the hanging fronds of the pepper trees at the emptiness of the sunny square. More than by the unusual tenseness of these faces, Stenham was at once struck by the silence of the place, by the realization that no one was talking, or, if someone did speak, it was in a low voice scarcely pitched above a whisper. Of course, without the radio there was no need to shout as they ordinarily had to do, but he felt that even had the radio been playing, together with all its extra amplifiers for the smaller rooms, they still would only have murmured. And he did not like the expressions on their faces when they looked up and saw him. It was the first time in many years that he had read enmity in Moroccan faces. Once more than twenty years ago he had ventured alone inside the *horm* of Moulay Idriss—not the sanctuary itself, but the streets surrounding it—and then he had seen hatred on a few faces; he had never forgotten the feeling it had given him. It was a physical thing that those fierce faces had confronted him with, and his reaction to it had likewise been purely physical; he had felt his spine stiffen and the hair at the back of his neck bristle.

He began to speak with Lee in a loud voice, not paying much attention to what he was saying, but using what he thought would be an unmistakably American intonation. He saw her glance at him once with surprise.

"There are a lot of little rooms out in the back," he went on. "Let's get one that's not so crowded." She was annoyed; he could see that. He could also see that the only result his bit of play-acting had brought him was that a good many more of the bearded, turbaned and *tarbouched* individuals had looked away from the window and were staring at them with equally hostile countenances.

"Let's just sit anywhere and stop being so conspicuous," she said nervously; at the same time she took several steps toward an unoccupied table by the wall opposite the entrance. But Stenham wanted, if it were possible, to get out of the range of these unfriendly faces. In the next room they found a party of elderly men from the country sprawled out, smoking kif and eating. A boy stood in the doorway to a further room. Behind him the room appeared to be empty. Stenham stepped across and peered in; the boy did not move. There was no one in there at all. Through a back window he caught sight of a sheet of water shining in the sun.

"Lee!" he called. She slipped through the doorway and they sat down.

"Are you yelling so they'll think you're an American? Is that it?" she demanded.

"It's very important they shouldn't think we're French, at least."

"But you sounded so funny!" She began to laugh. "It would have been so much more effective if you'd just roared: 'O.K., give money, twenty dollar, very good, yes, no, get outa here, god damned son of a bitch!' Perhaps they'd have gotten the point then. The way you did it, I don't think you got it across to them for a minute."

"Well, I did my best." Now that he was in the inner room out of sight of the inimical faces, he felt better.

Presently the waiter came in with a glass of tea for the boy at the other table. Stenham ordered tea and pastries.

"Damnation!" he said. "I forgot to leave a note for Moss."

"It's my fault," she declared.

"Very sweet of you, but completely untrue."

"You could phone him."

"No. There's no phone here. I don't know. Sometimes I wonder what's wrong with me. I know just how to behave, but only before or after the fact. When the moment's there in front of me, I don't seem to function."

"You're no different from anybody else," she said.

He suspected that she was waiting for an adverse reaction to this statement, so he said nothing. They were both silent for a minute. The Arab boy was sipping his tea with the customary Moslem noisiness. Stenham, in good spirits, did not mind his presence; he was a bit of native decoration. He would not have objected even if the boy had begun to make the loud belches that polite Moroccans make when they wish to show their appreciation of what they have eaten or drunk. The boy however did not belch; instead he rose from his table and taking up a good-sized stone from the floor, started to pound on the bolt of the door that led to the little garden outside. Stenham leaned across the table and took Lee's hand. He had never noticed the wedding ring until this minute—a simple gold band. "It's good to see you," he told her, and then immediately wished he had sat still and said nothing, for at the contact of his hand her face had clouded. "It's always good to see you," he added with less buoyancy, watching her closely. For a time she seemed to be trying to decide whether or not to speak. Then she said: "Why do you do that?"

"Why shouldn't I?" He spoke quietly because he wanted to avoid stirring up another argument.

Her expression was one of utter candor. "Because it puts me in a false position," she told him. "It makes me so uncomfortable. I can't help feeling that something's expected of me. I feel I should either go coquettish or prudish on you, and I don't want to be either one."

"Why don't you just be natural?" he suggested gently.

"I'm *trying* to be natural now," she said with impatience, "but you don't seem to understand. You put me in a position where it's next to impossible to be natural."

"Is it that bad?" he said, smiling sadly.

"They say you can't tell any man that you don't find him sexually attractive, that a woman's whole success in life is based on the principle of making every man feel that given the right circumstances she'd rush to bed with him. But I think there must be a few men bright enough to hear the news without going into a fit of depression. Don't you think so?" She smiled provocatively.

He said slowly: "I think you know that isn't true. What's being bright got to do with it? You might as well say an intelligent man won't mind being hungry as much as a slow-witted one will."

"Well, maybe that's true," she said gaily. "Who knows?"

He was hurt; to keep her from knowing it he held her hand tighter. "I'm not that easy to discourage," he assured her lightly. She shrugged and looked down at the table. "I was just being friendly," she pouted. "Because I really like you. I like just being with you. If that isn't enough—" she shrugged again— "well, then, the hell with it."

"Fine, fine. Maybe you'll change."

"Maybe I will. I like to think I have an open mind."

He did not answer, but sat back and looked out the window. The boy had taken off his shoes and was wading in the pool, a sight which, because of his state of mind, did not at once strike him as peculiar. When he saw him bend over and fish a large, bedraggled insect out of the water, he became interested. Now the boy held his hand very close to his face, studying his prey, smiling at it; he even moved his lips a few times, as though he were talking to it.

"What is it? What are you staring at?" she asked.

"Trying to make out what that kid's doing out there, standing in the middle of the water."

Suddenly the insect had flown away. The boy stood looking after it, his face expressing satisfaction rather than the disappointment Stenham had expected to see. He climbed out of the pool and sat down at its edge where he had been before.

Stenham shook his head. "Now, that was a strange bit of behavior. The boy made a special trip into the water just to pull out some kind of insect."

"Well, he's kind-hearted."

"I know, but they're not. That's the whole point. In all my time here I've never seen anyone do a thing like that."

He looked at the boy's round face, heavy, regular features, and curly black hair.

"He could be a Sicilian, or a Greek," he said as if to himself. "If he's not a Moroccan, there's nothing surprising about his deed. But if he is, then I give up. Moroccans just don't do things like that."

Lee stood up briefly and looked out the window; then she sat down again. "He looks like the model for all the worst paintings foreigners did in Italy a hundred years ago. *Boy at Fountain, Gipsy Carrying Water Jar*, you know?"

"You want another tea?"

"No!" she said. "One's plenty. It's so sweet. But anyway, I don't believe you can make such hard and fast general rules about people."

"You can in this case. I've watched them for years. I know what they're like."

"That doesn't mean you know what each one is like individually, after all."

"But the whole point is, they're not individuals in the sense you mean," he said.

"You're on dangerous ground," she warned him.

For fear that she might take exception to his words, he was quiet, did not attempt to explain to her how living among a less evolved people enabled him to see his own culture from the outside, and thus to understand it better. It was her express desire that all races and all individuals be "equal," and she would accept no demonstration which did not make use of that axiom. In truth, he decided, it was impossible to discuss anything at all with her, because instead of seeing each part of total reality as a complement to the other parts, with dogged insistence she forged ahead seeing only those things which she could twist into the semblance of an illustration for her beliefs.

From somewhere outside there came a faint sound which, if he had not known it was being made by human voices, he might have imagined sounded like the wind soughing through pine branches. The boy, who sat by the pool as though he were the express reason for the sun's existence at that moment, seemed to hear the sound, too. Stenham glanced at Lee: apparently she heard nothing. There were only two bits of stage business, he reflected, of which she was capable. One was to pull out her compact and occupy herself by looking into its mirror, and the other was to light a cigarette. On this occasion she used the compact.

He watched her. For her the Moroccans were backward onlookers standing on the sidelines of the parade of progress; they must be exhorted to join, if necessary pulled by force into the march. Hers was the attitude of the missionary, but whereas the missionary offered a complete if unusable code of thought and behavior, the modernizer offered nothing at all, save a place in the ranks. And the Moslems, who with their blind intuitive wisdom had triumphantly withstood the missionaries' cajoleries, now were going to be duped into joining the senseless march of universal brotherhood; for the privilege each man would have to give up only a small part of himself— just enough to make him incomplete, so that instead of looking into his own heart, to Allah, for reassurance, he would have to look to the others. The new world would be a triumph of frustration, where all humanity would be lifting itself by its own bootstraps—the equality of the damned. No wonder the religious leaders of Islam identified Western culture with the works of Satan: they had seen the truth and were expressing it in the simplest terms.

The sound of shouting suddenly increased in volume; it was obviously coming from a moving column of men. How many thousand throats did it take, he wondered, to make a sound like that?

"Listen," said Lee.

The progress through the streets was slow, and the acoustics, changing from moment to moment, brought the sound nearer, then removed it to a more distant plane. But it was clear that the crowd was on its way up toward Bou Jeloud.

"Here comes your trouble," he said to her.

She bit her upper lip for a second, and looked at him distraughtly. "What do you think we ought to do? Get out?"

"Sure, if you like."

The boy came through the door, glanced shyly at them, and turned to sit down at his table. Stenham called out to him: "*Qu'est-ce qui se passe dehors?*" The boy stared at him, uncomprehending. So he was a Moroccan, after all. "*Smahli,*" Stenham said. "*Chnou hadek el haraj?*"

The other looked at him with wide eyes, clearly wondering how anyone could be so stupid. "That's people yelling," he said.

"Are they happy or angry?" Stenham wanted to know.

The boy struggled to keep his sudden suspiciousness from becoming visible in his face. He smiled, and said: "Maybe some are happy, some are angry. Each man knows what is in his own heart."

"A philosopher," Stenham laughed in an aside to Lee.

"What does he say? What is it?" she asked impatiently.

"He's being cagey. *Egless.*" He indicated the third chair at their table, and the boy sat down carefully, never taking his eyes from Stenham's face. "I'd better offer him a cigarette," Stenham said, and did so. The boy refused, smiling. "Tea?" asked Stenham. "I've drunk it. Thank you," said the boy.

"Ask him what he thinks about staying here," Lee said nervously.

"You can't hurry these people," he told her. "You get nothing out of them if you do."

"I know, but if we're going to go we should go, don't you think?"

"Well, yes, if we are. But I'm not sure it's such a good idea to go out there running around looking for a cab now, do you think?"

"You're the expert. How should I know? But for God's sake try and make sense at this point. I don't feel like being massacred."

He laughed, then turned his head to face her completely. "Lee, if I thought there were any serious danger you don't think I'd have suggested coming here, do you?"

"How do I know what you'd have suggested? I'm just telling you that if there's any question of a mob smashing into this café I want to get out now, and not wait until it's too late."

"What's this sudden hysteria?" he demanded. "I don't understand."

"Hysteria!" She laughed scornfully. "I don't think you've ever seen a hysterical woman in your life."

"Listen. If you want to go, we'll go now."

"That's just what I *didn't* say. I merely asked you to be serious and realize that you've got the responsibility for us both, and act accordingly. That's all."

What a schoolmarm, he thought angrily. "All right," he said. "Let's sit right here. This is an Arab café. There are about fifty police outside and there's a *poste de garde* right across the square. I don't know where we could be safer, except in the Ville Nouvelle. Certainly not in the hotel."

She did not answer. The noise of the crowd had become much louder; it sounded now like prolonged cheering. He turned to the boy again.

"The people are coming this way."

"Yes," said the boy; it was evident that he did not want to discuss the subject. Another tack, a different approach, thought Stenham, but not a personal one, either. "Do you like this café?" he said after a moment, remembering too late that statements were better than questions in the task of trying to establish contact with the Moroccans.

The boy hesitated. "I like it," he said grudgingly, "but it's not a good café."

"I thought it was a good café. I like it. It has water on both sides."

"Yes," the boy admitted. "I like to come and sit. But it's not a good café." He lowered his voice. "The owner has buried something outside the door. That's not good."

Stenham, bewildered, said: "I see."

The noise now could not be disregarded; its rhythmical chanting had grown into a gigantic roar, unmistakably of anger, and it was at last possible to hear details in its pattern. It had ceased being a unified wall of sound, and become instead a great, turbulent mass of innumerable separate human cries.

"*Smahli,*" said the boy. "I'm going to look." Quickly he rose and went out of the room.

"Are you nervous?" Stenham asked her.

"Well, I'm not exactly relaxed. Give me a cigarette. I've run out."

While he was lighting her cigarette there came the sound of one lone shot—a small dull pop which nevertheless carried above the roar of voices. They both froze; the roar subsided for a second or two, then rose to a chaos of frenzy. Their wide eyes met, but only by accident. Then from what they would have said was the front of the café there was a phrase of machine-gun fire, a short sequence of rapidly repeated, shattering explosions.

They both jumped up and ran to the door. The other room was empty now, Stenham noticed as they went through it, save for one old man sitting on the floor in the corner, holding a kif pipe in his hand. They went only as far as the doorway of the large front room. There men were still falling over each other in their haste to get to the windows. Two waiters were sliding enormous bolts across the closed entrance door. When they had finished doing that they hurriedly pushed a large chest in front of the door, and wedged tables between it and a pillar near by. They did the work automatically, as though it were the only reaction conceivable in such a situation. Then they went behind a wall of bottle cases and peered worriedly out a small window there. From where they stood in the inner doorway Lee and Stenham could see, through the florid designs of the grillwork in the windows, only a series of senseless vignettes which had as their background the hard earth of the square: Occasionally part of a running figure passed through one of the frames. The noise at the moment was largely one of screaming; there was also the tinkle of shattering glass at intervals. Suddenly, like so many huge motors starting up, machine-guns fired from all around the square. When they had finished, there was relative silence, broken by a few single revolver shots from further away. A police whistle sounded, and it was even possible to hear individual voices shouting commands in French. A man standing in one of the windows in front of them began to beat on the grillwork like a caged animal, shrieking imprecations; hands reached out from beside him and pulled him back, and a brief struggle ensued as he was forced to the floor by his companions. Stenham seized Lee by the wrist and wheeled her around, saying: "Come on." They returned to their little room.

"Sit down," said Stenham. Then he stepped out into the sunlight, looked up at the walls around the patio, sighed, and went back in. "No way out there," he said. "We'll just have to sit here."

Lee did not reply; she sat looking down at the table, her chin cupped in her hands. He observed her: he could not be certain, but it seemed to him that she was shivering. He put his hand on her shoulder, felt it tremble.

"Wouldn't you like some hot tea, without the sugar?" he asked her.

"It's all right," she said after a pause, without glancing up. "I'm all right."

He stood there helplessly, looking down at her. "Maybe—"

"Please sit down."

Automatically he obeyed. Then he lighted a cigarette. Presently she raised her head. "Give me one," she said. Her teeth were chattering. "I might as well smoke. I can't do anything else."

Someone was standing in the doorway. Swiftly Stenham turned his head. It was the boy, staring at them. Stenham rose and went over, pulling him with him out into the next room. The old man still sprawled in the corner in a cloud of kif smoke.

"Try and get a glass of tea for the *mra*," he told the boy, who did not appear to understand. "The lady wants some tea." He's looking at me as though I were a talking tree, thought Stenham. He took the boy's arm and squeezed it, but there was no reaction. The eyes were wide, and there was nothing in them. He looked back into the room and saw Lee hunched over the table, sobbing. Pulling the boy by the arm, he led him to the chair beside her and made him sit down. Then he went out to the main room to the alcove where the fire was, and ordered three teas from the *qaouaji*; he too seemed to be in a state bordering on catalepsy. "Three teas, three teas," Stenham repeated. "One with only a little sugar." It'll give him something to do, he thought.

The feeble chaos outside was now almost covered by the voices of the onlookers within the café. They were not talking loud, but they spoke with frantic intensity, and all together, so that no one was listening to anyone else. Happily, this occupied them; they paid him no attention. He felt that if he left the *qaouaji* to prepare the tea and bring it by himself, he would be likely to fall back into his lethargy; he determined to remain with him until it was ready. From where he stood, through the small window in front of him, he could see only a part of the center of the square. Usually it was empty, but when a figure appeared, moving across the space made by the window's frame, it was always a policeman or a *mokhazni*. What had happened was fairly clear: the crowd had attempted to pass out of the Medina through Bab Bou Jeloud, and had been stopped at the gate itself. Now there were small skirmishes taking place well within the gate as the marchers retreated. When he heard a cavalcade of trucks begin to arrive, he knew it would be safe to go and look out the window, and so he squeezed himself into the narrow corridor between the piles of cases of empty bottles and the wall, and went to peer out. There were four big army trucks and they had drawn up in a line behind the two abandoned buses. Berber soldiers in uniform, their rifles in their hands, were still leaping out of the backs of the trucks, running toward the gate. There must be about two hundred of them, he calculated.

Now a slow massacre would begin, inside the walls, in the streets and alleys, until every city-dweller who was able had reached some sort of shelter and no one was left outside but the soldiers. Even as he was thinking this, the pattern of the shooting changed from single, desultory shots to whole volleys of them, like strings of fire-crackers exploding. He stood there watching tensely, although there was nothing to see; it was like seeing a newsreel of the event, where what is presented is the cast of characters and the situation before and afterward, but never the action itself. Even the gunfire might as well have been a sound-track; it was hard to believe that the rifles he had seen two minutes before were at this moment being used to kill people; were firing the shots that he was hearing. If you had had no previous contact with this sort of violence, he reflected, even when it was happening where you were, it remained unreal.

He went back to the alcove where the fire was, and was pleasantly surprised to see that the *qaouaji* had nearly finished making the tea. When it was done, he followed the man as unobtrusively as he could to the back room. When he looked at the table he did not know whether he was annoyed or delighted to find Lee and the boy engaged in a mysterious bilingual dialogue.

"Have some hot tea," he told her.

She looked up; there was no sign on her face that she had been crying. "Oh, that's sweet of you," she said, lifting the glass, finding it too hot, and putting it down again. "These people are really amazing. It took this child about two minutes to get me over feeling sorry for myself. The first thing I knew he was tugging at my sleeve and turning on the most irresistible smile and saying things in his funny language, but with such gentleness and sweetness that there I was, feeling better, that's all."

"That *is* strange," Stenham said, thinking of the state the boy himself had been in when he had left him. He turned to him and said: "*O deba labès enta?* You feel better? You were a little sick."

"No, I wasn't sick," the boy said firmly, but his face showed three consecutive expressions: shame, resentment, and finally a certain trusting humility, as if by the last he meant that he threw himself upon Stenham's mercy not to tell Lee of his weakness.

"When can we get out of here? We want to go home," Stenham said to him.

The boy shook his head. "This isn't the time to go into the street."

"But the lady wants to go to the hotel."

"Of course." The boy laughed, as though Lee's desires were those of an unreasoning animal, and were to be taken no more seriously. "This café is a very good place for her. The soldiers won't know she's in here."

"The soldiers won't know?" echoed Stenham sharply, his intuition warning him that there was more import to the words than his mind had yet grasped. "What do you mean? *Chnou bghitsi ts'qoulli?*"

"Didn't you see the soldiers? I heard them come when you were getting the tea. If they know she's in here they'll break the door and come in."

"But why?" demanded Stenham idiotically.

The boy replied succinctly and in unequivocal terms.

"No, no." Stenham was incredulous. "They couldn't. The French."

"What French?" said the boy bitterly. "The French aren't with them. They send them out alone, so they can break the houses and kill the men and take the girls and steal what they want. The Berbers don't fight for the French just for those few francs a day they give them. You didn't know that? This way the French don't have to spend any money, and the city people are kept poor, and the Berbers are happy in their heads, and the people hate the Berbers more than they hate the French. Because if everybody hated the French they couldn't stay here. They'd have to go back to France."

"I see. And how do you know all that?" Stenham asked, impressed by the clarity of the boy's simple analysis.

"I know it because everybody knows it. Even the donkeys and mules know that. And the birds," he added with complete seriousness.

"If you know all that, maybe you know what's going to happen next," Stenham suggested, half in earnest.

"There will be more and more poison in the hearts of the Moslems, and more and more and more"—his face screwed itself up into a painful grimace—"until they all burst, just from hating. They'll set everything on fire and kill each other."

"I mean today. What's going to happen now? Because we want to go home."

"You must look out the window and wait until the only men there are French and *mokhaznia*—no partisans at all. Then you make the man open the door and let you out, and go to a policeman, and he'll take you home."

"But we don't like the French," objected Stenham, thinking this was as good a moment as any to reassure the boy as to where their sympathies lay; he did not want him to regret his candor when the excitement of the instant had passed.

A cynical smile appeared on the young face. "*Binatzkoum.* That's between you and them," he said impassively. "How did you get to Fez?"

"On the train."

"And where do you live?"

"At the Mérinides Palace."

"*Binatzkoum, binatzkoum.* You came with the French and you live with the French. What difference does it make whether you like them or not? If they weren't here you couldn't be here. Go to a French policeman. But don't tell him you don't like him."

"Look!" said Lee suddenly. "I don't feel like sitting here while you take an Arab lesson. I want to get out of here. Has he given you any information at all?"

"If you'll just have a little patience," said Stenham, nettled, "I'll get all the details. You can't hurry these people; I've told you that."

"I'm sorry. But it *is* going to be dark soon and we *have* got to get all the way back to the hotel. What I meant was, I hope you're not just having an ordinary conversation."

"We're not," Stenham assured her. He looked at his watch. "It's only four-twenty," he said. "It won't be dark for a long time. The boy doesn't think we ought to go outside quite yet. I'm inclined to think he's right."

"He probably doesn't know as much about it as you do, if you come down to that," she said. "But go ahead and talk."

The sounds of shooting had retreated into the distance. "Why don't you go and look out the window?" Stenham suggested to the boy, "and see what's happening."

Obediently the boy rose and went out.

"He's a good kid," said Stenham. "Bright as they come."

"Oh, he's a darling. I think we should each give him something when we go."

It was a long while before he returned, and when he came in they saw immediately that he was in a completely different state of mind. He walked slowly to his chair and sat down, looking ready to burst into tears.

"*Chnou?* What is it?" Stenham demanded impatiently.

The boy looked straight ahead of him, a picture of despair.

"Now *you* be patient," Lee said.

"You can go," the boy said finally in a toneless voice. "The man will open the door for you. There's nothing to be afraid of."

Stenham waited a moment for the boy to say more, but he merely sat there, his hands in his lap, his head bent forward, looking at the air. "What is it?" he finally asked him, conscious that both his experience and his Arabic were inadequate for dealing with a situation which demanded tact and delicacy. The boy shook his head very slowly without moving his eyes. "Did you see something bad?"

The boy heaved a deep sigh. "The city is closed," he said. "All the gates are closed. No one can go in. No one can come out."

Stenham relayed the information to Lee, adding: "I suppose that means going through hell to get into the hotel. Officially it's inside the walls."

She clicked her tongue with annoyance. "We'll get in. But what about him? Where does he live?"

Stenham talked with the boy for a bit, drawing only the briefest answers from him. At the end of a minute or so, he said to Lee: "He doesn't know where he's going to eat or sleep. That's the trouble. His family lives way down in the Medina. It's a mess, isn't it? And of course he has no money. They never have any. I think I'll give him a thousand. That ought to help some."

Lee shook her head. "Money's not what the poor kid needs. What good's money going to be to him?"

"What good is it!" exclaimed Stenham. "What else can you give him?"

Lee reached over and tapped the boy's shoulder. "Look!" she said, pointing at him. "You. Come." She waggled her fingers like two legs. "Him." She indicated Stenham. "Me." She pointed her thumb at herself. "Hotel." She described a wide arc with her hand. "Yes? *Oui?*"

"You're crazy," Stenham told her. A flicker of hope had appeared in the boy's eyes. Warming to her game, Lee bent forward and went on with her dumb-show. Stenham rose, saying: "Why get him all worked up? It's cruel." She paid him no attention.

"I'm going to take a look into the other room," he said, and he left them there, leaning toward each other intently, Lee gesticulating and uttering single words with exaggeratedly clear enunciation—like a schoolteacher, he thought again.

"What does she want? Gratitude?" He knew how it would end: the boy would disappear, and afterward it would be discovered that something was missing—a camera, a watch, a fountain pen. She would be indignant, and he would patiently explain that it had been inevitable from the start, that such behavior was merely an integral part of "their" ethical code.

The other room was quiet. Only a few men stood in the windows looking out. Of the rest, some talked and the others merely sat. He went to the little window where he had gone before, and peered out. In the square there was activity: the soldiers were piling sandbags in a curved line across the lower end, just outside the gate. A large calendar hung on the wall beside the window; its text written in Arabic characters, it showed an unmistakably American girl lifting a bottle of Coca-Cola to her lips. As he went back across the room two or three men turned angry faces toward him, and he heard the word *mericani,* as well as a few unflattering epithets. He was relieved: at least they all knew he was not French. It was unlikely that there would be any trouble.

In the middle room the old man had slumped to one side and closed his eyes: so many pipes of kif in one afternoon had proven more than he could manage. When Stenham stepped through the further doorway Lee stood up, smoothed her skirt, and said: "Well, it's all settled. Amar's coming with us. They can find somewhere for him to sleep, and if they won't, I'll simply take a room for him tonight."

Stenham smiled pityingly. "Well, your intentions are good, anyway. Is that his name? Amar?"

"Ask him. That's what he told me. He can say my name, but he pronounces it Bali. It's rather nice—certainly prettier than Polly."

"I see," said Stenham. "It means old, applied to objects. If you want to lug him along it's all right with me."

The boy was still seated, looking up at them anxiously, from her face to his and back again.

"Suppose he hadn't happened to meet us," Stenham suggested. "What would he have done then?"

"He'd probably have gone back into the town before the trouble started and gotten home somehow. Don't forget it was you who spoke to him and asked him to sit down with us."

"You're sure you wouldn't just like to give him some money and let it go at that?"

"Yes, I'm sure," she said flatly.

"All right. Then I guess we'd better go."

He handed the boy five hundred francs. "*Chouf.* Pay for the tea and *cabrhozels*, and ask the *qaouaji* to open the door for us." Amar went out. It was perfectly possible, thought Stenham, that the proprietor of the café would refuse to run the risk of opening the door; they had no one's word but the boy's to the contrary. He stepped to the back door and looked out once again at the pool. The sun had gone behind the walls; in the afternoon shade the patio had taken on an austere charm. The surface of the water was smooth, but the plants along the edges, trembling regularly, betrayed the current beneath. A swallow came careening down from the ramparts toward the pool, obviously with the intention of touching the water. Seeing Stenham, it changed its direction violently, and went off in blind haste toward the sky. He listened: the shooting was not audible at the moment, there were no street-vendor's shouts, no watersellers' bells jangling, and the high murmur of human voices that formed the city's usual backdrop of sound was missing. What he heard was the sharp confusion of bird-cries. It was the hour of the swallows. Each evening at this time they set to wheeling and darting by the tens of thousands, in swift, wide circles above the walls and gardens and alleys and bridges, their shrill screams presaging the advent of twilight.

So, he thought, it's happened. They've done it. Whatever came to pass now, the city would never be the same again. That much he knew. He heard Lee's voice behind him.

"Amar says they've unlocked the door for us. Shall we go?"

BOOK FOUR

The Ascending Stairways

*A questioner questioned concerning the doom about to fall
upon the disbelievers, which none can repel, from Allah,
Lord of the Ascending Stairways.*

—THE KORAN

CHAPTER 24

THE MAN and the woman stood there for a moment while
the *qaouaji* closed and bolted the door behind them. A
pall of dust over the square, raised by the boots of the soldiers as they hurried back and forth from the trucks to the
barricade they were building at the foot of the gate. In his
head Amar was thinking: "Allah is all-powerful." Once more
He had intervened in his favor. Now that he reviewed the
events of the past two or three hours, it seemed to him that
at the first moment when the man had come into the café he
remembered having noticed a strange light around his head.
A second later he had seen that it was only the glint in his
blond hair. But now that their two fates were indissolubly
linked, he recalled the brightness that had moved in the air
where the man's head was, and preferred to interpret it as a
sign given him by Allah to indicate the course he must follow.
It was his own secret power, he told himself, which had made
it possible for him to recognize the sign and behave accordingly. From the moment he had seen the man's grave face
looking out the window at him as he sat by the pool he had
known that he could, if he wanted, count on his protection.
It was even possible that in addition he might be able to add
enough to his savings to buy a pair of shoes. But that was a
secondary consideration of which he was ashamed as soon as
it occurred to him. "I don't want the shoes," he told Allah,
while they were crossing the square. "All I want is to stay with
the Nesrani and obey his commands until I can go home
again."

The fact that it was the woman who had made the actual suggestion of taking him to the hotel counted for nothing: the pattern of life was such that women were on earth only to carry out the bidding of men, and however it might look as though a woman were imposing her desires, it was always the will of men that was done, since Allah worked only through men. And how rightly, he thought, gazing with distaste at this woman's scanty clothing and her shameless way of walking along jauntily beside the man, as though she thought it perfectly proper for her to be out in the street dressed in such a fashion.

They had come to a row of policemen who stood in the way of the exit from the square. The man was talking to them. One of them designated Amar. He supposed the man was explaining that this was his servant, for presently whatever difficulties had existed appeared to have been smoothed out, and the Frenchmen seemed satisfied. Two of the uniformed men began to walk with them, so that they were now a party of five, going up the long avenue between the walls toward the sunset.

There were soldiers everywhere; they walked in the public gardens under the orange trees, leaned against the wall along the river, strutted among the overturned deck-chairs of the cafés in the park, and stood glowering at attention on either side of the high portal that led into the old Sultan's palace. A few were French, but most of them were grim-faced Berbers with shaved heads and narrow slanting eyes. They had helped the French in Indochina, and now they were helping them once more in their own land, and against their own countrymen. Amar felt his heart swell with hatred as he walked past them, but then he tried to think of something else, for fear the Frenchmen going along beside him would feel the force of his hatred. The man and the woman were talking together in a lively fashion as they turned into the long street of Fez-Djedid, and occasionally they even laughed, as though it had not occurred to them that death was everywhere around them, behind the walls of the houses and in the twilit alleys to their left, to their right. Perhaps they did not even know what was happening: they belonged to another world, and the French had respect for them.

About halfway to Bab Semmarine the street took on a somewhat more usual aspect. Here the large Algerian cafés were full, the flames of the lamps flickered on the tea-drinkers' faces, certain clothing shops were open, throngs of men and boys walked back and forth talking excitedly, being prevented from stopping by the police who constantly prodded them, saying gruffly: "*Allez! Zid! Zid! Vas-y!*" It was along here that Amar suddenly became aware of someone walking behind him, softly saying his name: "*Amar! Yah, Amar!*" The voice was deep, mellow, resonant; it was Benani. But remembering Benani's warning of the night before, that he must not step outside the walls of the Medina, he decided to pretend to hear nothing, and walked along as close to the Christian man as he was able. Still the voice continued to call his name discreetly, perhaps two meters behind him, through the hubbub and chaos of the crowd, never increasing in volume or changing its inflection.

"So that's what they're like," he thought cynically. Amar was supposed to stay inside the Medina and wait for the French to shoot him or carry him off to jail, while the members of the Party, once they had made the trouble, took care to remain outside, so that they might enjoy complete freedom.

In a café on their right several Algerians were singing, grouped around a young man playing an *oud*. The two tourists wanted to stand still a moment and listen, but the police would not let them, and instead hurried them along toward Bab Semmarine. It was only when they had gone beneath the first arch, and were holding their breaths against the onslaught of the urinal's stench inside, that the insistent voice became more pressing. "Amar!" it said. "Don't turn around. It's all right; I know you hear me." (Amar glanced slyly first at the policeman on his left, then at the other. Apparently neither one of them understood Arabic, and even if they had, it was unlikely that they would have been able to notice and single out that one voice in the tumult around them.) "Amar! Remember you have no tongue. We—" The echoing sound of a carriage passing through the vaulted tunnel covered the rest of the message. When they had come beneath the further arch out into the open once more, the voice was gone. The bad dream had been dispersed by the admonition to keep silence; Benani imagined that he and the two foreigners were under arrest.

The Rue Bou Khessissate was virtually deserted, the shop-fronts had been battened down, and the windows of the apartments in the upper stories, where the more fortunate Jewish families lived, were hidden behind their shutters. Here and there, as they went briskly down the long, curving street, Amar saw, in back of a blind partly ajar, a stout matron in her fringed headdress, holding a lamp and peering anxiously out, doubtless asking herself vaguely if the thing which every Jew feared in times of stress might come to pass—if the infuriated Moslems, frustrated by their powerlessness to retaliate against the Christians, might not vent at least a part of their rage in a traditional attack upon the Mellah. For there was certainly nothing to stop them, if the desire came to them: a token detachment of police, most of them Jewish themselves, and one little radio patrol car, stationed just inside Bab Chorfa, which the mob could have turned over with one hand if it had felt like it. He wondered whether the young Arabs would be coming tonight to kill the men and violate the girls (for although it was not a very great triumph to have a Jewish girl, still it was a fact that a good many of them were actually virgins, and this was an undeniable attraction in itself); his intuition told him that this time would not be like the other times, that the Istiqlal would issue special directives forbidding such useless excesses. For the moment he felt magnificently superior: he was walking with four Nazarenes, and he could count on their protection. Then he thought of the old adage: "You can share the meal of a Jew, but not his bed. You can share the bed of a Christian, but not his meal," and he wondered if he would have to share the man's bed. It was well known that many Christians liked young Arab boys. If the Christian attacked him, he would fight; of that he was certain. But he did not really believe in the likelihood of such a thing.

When they came to the Place du Commerce, he saw that the fair which had filled the square the night before was now almost entirely dismantled. Even in the dark, with the aid of flashlights and carbide flares, workmen were hastily folding the flimsy partitions, crating the mechanical apparatuses, and

piling everything into the trucks that had been standing behind the booths. There were several taxis at the far end of the
square. The policemen led them to the first car, and when
Amar and the two tourists were inside, one of them got in
front beside the driver. The other stepped back, saluted, and
told the man at the wheel to go to the Mérinides Palace.
Amar was elated. He had never before been in a taxi, nor, indeed, in any ordinary automobile—only in buses and trucks,
and there was no denying that these small vehicles went much
faster. The little suburban villas sped past, then the stadium
and the railway crossing, and then there were, on one side,
the long unbroken ramparts enclosing the Sultan's orchards,
and the open desolate plain on the other.

So far, the man had studiously avoided speaking at all to
Amar, and Amar guessed that he did not want the police to
know he understood Arabic. Occasionally the woman flung
an encouraging smile at him, as if she thought he might be
afraid to be with strangers. Each time she did this he smiled
back politely. They were talking about him now, he knew, but
it was in their own language, and that was all right.

Outside Bab Segma there was great activity. In the dust
raised by moving vehicles the beams of several powerful
searchlights crossed each other, making a design that was
complicated by the headlights of trucks and camionettes. As
the taxi approached the gate, Amar saw a row of small tanks
lined up against the wall. A sudden, enormous doubt surged
within him. It was perfectly useless, this absurd flight he was
making from his own people into a foreign precinct, with foreigners. Even if the police did not pull him out of the car here
at Bab Segma, or further along the road, or at Bab Jamaï,
they would surely take him from the hotel. And even if the
kind lady and gentleman managed to protect him for a certain
length of time, sooner or later there would come an hour
when he would be alone momentarily, and that was all the
French needed. Certainly in their eyes he would be more suspect for having been with these two outsiders.

The taxi swerved to the left, climbed the hill that led past
the entrance to the Casbah Cherarda where the Senegalese
troops were quartered. There were tanks there, too, and it
was evident that tonight the guards were not the customary

tall black men with their faces decorated by knife-scar designs, stiffly holding their bayonets at their sides; in their place stood red-faced Frenchmen with tommy-guns. At the top of the hill the car turned right, and went along the barren stretch where the cattle market was held on Thursdays. The policeman lolled beside the driver, one arm over the back of the seat, smoking a cigarette. Now that they were out in the country, and Amar's fear had subsided somewhat, he was again able to view things rationally, and to be ashamed of his emotions of a minute ago. Allah had provided him with a means of escape from the café, without which he would no doubt have remained in there indefinitely, for no one else would have stirred outside, with all those soldiers in the square. And it was probable that he would eat tonight, and sleep quietly until morning. No man could righteously ask for more than that. When morning came, it would be a new day with new problems and possibilities, but of course it was sinful to think about a day that had not yet arrived. Man was meant to consider only the present; to be preoccupied with the future, either pleasantly or with anxiety, implied a lack of humility in the face of Providence, and was unforgivable.

All at once the car was filled with a sweet smell, like flowers, as the lady opened a small bag she carried with her, and pulled out a pack of cigarettes. Fez lay far below, wrapped in darkness, its presence betrayed only here and there by a feeble reddish gleam—a lamp in some window or a fire in a courtyard, visible for the fraction of a second as the taxi moved ahead, following the sinuous course of the road along the edge of the cliffs.

They came to the summit, where the ruined tombs of the Merinide royal family looked down across the olive groves and the eastern end of the city. The broken domes stood out black and jagged against the limpid night sky. Amar recalled the last time he had come down these slopes and rounded these curves: he had been on his way home to a beating. He smiled as he remembered how the boy steering the bicycle had misunderstood his query about the brakes, had imagined Amar was afraid it might go off the road, when actually he had been hoping that it would do just that, catapulting them both into a ravine. And he smiled again when he thought of how very seriously he had taken the prospect of that beating, whereas now, he decided, it would mean nothing to him, save the sadness he would feel at being the object of his father's displeasure, for he had grown up a good deal since then. But had he grown up entirely? For an instant he was sufficiently detached to be able to pose the question. In his pocket was a paper of kif, part of a long-term project of vengeance against Mustapha, in retaliation for that very beating. Would it not be pleasing to Allah if he should suddenly toss it out the window at this moment? But Bab Jamaï then appeared below in a confusion of moving lights, and the thought slipped out of his head to be replaced by the more real preoccupation with what might happen if the police should insist on pulling him from the taxi. This was the most dangerous spot, because it was here that they had to go into the Medina. They had arrived at the gate. The driver came to a halt and shut off the motor. A flashlight was played into their faces and then around the interior of the taxi, and a French soldier poked his head through the back window, exchanging a few words with the man and the woman. "*Et cet arabe-là,*" he said, indicating Amar with the faintly contemptuous familiarity of proprietorship, "he is your personal servant?" And although Amar did not understand the words, he knew perfectly well what the soldier had said. Both the foreigners replied yes, that was the case. "*Vous pouvez continuer à l'hôtel,*" he told them, and the car started up and went ahead the hundred yards to the hotel gateway.

And then began for Amar a strange series of confused impressions. Led by his new friends, he passed through two small courtyards and up two flights of carpeted stairs to an endless corridor, also carpeted, so that their footsteps made no sound. And there was expensive reed matting covering the walls all along the way, and lanterns overhead such as were found only in the Karouine Mosque or the Zaouia of Moulay Idriss. And then they opened two great doors of glass and went down a few steps into a room which was like nothing he had ever seen, but which, he decided, could not have been made for anyone but a sultan. The intricacies of the high domed ceiling were only faintly illumined by the many-colored rays of light that streamed from the colossal lanterns overhead; it was like being in a vast and perfect cave. He had only a short moment to look around as they crossed the room, and then they were out in another corridor climbing another flight of stairs, this time very old ones of mosaic, and without carpeting—rather like the stairs in his own house, except that the edges of the steps were of white marble instead of wood. The man and woman spoke in low voices as they climbed, Amar behind them. At the top of the stairs there was another corridor, less beautiful than the one below.

Then the man opened a door and they were in the room. "Go in," he said to Amar, breaking the long silence that had been between them. He spoke to the woman, urging her to enter, too. After some hesitation she finally agreed, and she and the man sat down in two large chairs. Amar remained standing by the door, looking at the magnificent room. "Sit down," the man said to him. He obeyed, seating himself on the floor at the spot where he had been standing, and continued his careful examination of the carvings on the beams overhead and the fancy painted plaster frieze of geometric designs. The rugs were thick, the heavy curtains hid the windows, and on the bed the covers had been pulled back to reveal the whiteness of clean sheets.

Now the man looked at him closely for the first time, took out a pack of cigarettes, and after offering the woman one, tossed the pack to Amar. "What's the matter with your nose and eyes?" he asked him. "Have you had a fight?" Amar laughed and said: "Yes." He was embarrassed, and he longed to get up and look into the mirror over the washstand, but he sat still and smoked. The man's manner of casual familiarity with him was assuredly designed to put him at his ease, and he was grateful to him for it; however, the presence of the woman made him nervous. She kept looking at him and smiling in a way that he found disconcerting. It was the way a mother smiles at her small child in a public place when many people are watching and she hopes that it will continue to behave properly. He supposed she meant it to be friendly and reassuring, perhaps even an encouragement, a promise of future intimacy if ever they should find themselves alone. But to him it was a shameless and indecent way for her to behave in front of the man, now that they were all three seated in his bedroom, and he felt that out of deference to his host he should pretend to ignore her smiles. Unfortunately she would have none of this; the less attention he paid her, the more determinedly she kept at him, grimacing, wrinkling her nose at him like a rabbit, blowing smoke toward him as she laughed at things the man said, and generally behaving in an increasingly shocking fashion. And the man went on talking, as if he were completely unaware of what she was doing—not pretending, not indifferent, either, but truly unaware.

Amar was embarrassed for them all, but particularly for the man. He disapproved likewise of the fact that the man and the woman presently embarked on a long and occasionally stormy conversation regarding him; he knew he was the subject by the glances they gave him while they were talking. Being with them was going to be difficult, he could see that, but he was determined to show a maximum of patience. It was the least he could do in return for having been offered protection, shelter and food in this time of hardship. The discussion appeared to be one concerning food, for suddenly without any pause or transition the man said to him: "Would you mind eating alone in this room?" He answered that he would not mind at all—that, indeed, he thought it the best idea. The man seemed relieved upon hearing his reply, but the woman began to make silly gestures meaning that he ought to go downstairs and eat with them. While she did this the man glowered. Amar had no intention of accompanying them to any public room where he would be on view to the French and the Moroccans who worked in the hotel. He smiled amiably and said: "This is a good room for eating." For a while the conversation between the two became more animated; then the woman got up petulantly and walked to the door, where she turned and waved coyly at Amar before she went out. The man stepped into the corridor with her for a moment, came back in, and shut the door. His expression was one of annoyance as he took up the telephone and spoke briefly into it.

Amar had been studying the patterns in the rug beside him; he had decided it was the most beautiful object in the room.

When he had hung up the receiver, the man sat down again, heaved a deep sigh, and lit another cigarette. Amar looked up at him.

"Why do you talk so much with that woman?" he said, the expression of his voice a mixture of shyness and curiosity. "Words are for people, not for women."

The man laughed. "Aren't women people?" he asked.

"People are people," Amar said stolidly. "Women are women. It's not the same thing."

The man looked very surprised, and laughed more loudly. Then his face became serious; he leaned forward in the chair. "If women aren't people," he said slowly, "how does it happen they can go to Paradise?"

Amar looked at him suspiciously: the man could scarcely be that ignorant. But he could discern no mockery in his face. "*El hassil,*" he began, "they have their own place in Heaven. They don't go inside where the men are."

"I see," the man said gravely. "It's like the mosques, is that it?"

"That's it," said Amar, still wondering if the man might not be making fun of him.

"You must know a lot about your religion," the man said dreamily. "I wish you'd tell me something about it."

Now Amar was convinced that he was being baited. He gave a short, bitter laugh. "I don't know anything," he said. "I'm like an animal."

The man raised his eyebrows. "Nothing at all? But you should. It's a very good religion."

Amar was displeased. He studied the face of this patronizing infidel for a moment. "It's the *only* one," he said evenly. Then he smiled. "But now we are all like animals. Just look in the streets, see what's happening here. Don't you think it's the Moslems' fault?"

The man's swift glance told him that he was awakening some sort of respect. "The Moslems have some blame," he said quietly, "but I think the great blame goes to the French. You don't judge a man too harshly for what he does to an intruder he finds in his house, do you?"

Now Amar was about to reply: "Allah sees everything," but a voice in his head was whispering to him that it was not the sort of remark the Nazarene would really hear. If he wanted to keep alive the spark of respect he felt he had kindled, he must work hard inside himself. "The French are thieves in our house, you're right," he agreed. "We invited them in because we wanted to take lessons from them. We thought they'd teach us. They haven't taught us anything—not even how to be good thieves. So we want to put them out. But now they think the house is theirs, and that we're only servants in it. What can we do except fight? It is written."

"Do you hate them?" the man asked; he was leaning forward, looking at Amar with intensity. There was no one there but the two of them; if the man turned out to be a spy he would at least have no witnesses. But that was an extreme consideration: Amar was positive he was only an onlooker. "Yes, I hate them," he said simply. "That's written, too."

"You have to hate them, you mean? You can't decide: I will or I won't hate them?"

Amar did not completely understand. "But I hate them *now*," he explained. "The day Allah wants me to stop hating them, He'll change my heart."

The man was smiling, as if to himself. "If the world's really like that, it's very easy to be in it," he said.

"It will never be easy to be in the world," Amar said firmly. "*Er rabi mabrhach.* God doesn't want it easy."

The man did not answer. Soon he rose, went to the open window, and stood looking down at the dark Medina below. When he turned back into the room, he began to speak as though there had been no break in the conversation. "So you hate them," he mused. "Would you like to kill them?"

This immediately put Amar on his guard. "Why do you ask me all these questions?" he said aggrievedly. "Why do you want to know about me? That's not good at a time like now." He tried to keep his face empty of expression, so that it would not look as though he were indignant, but apparently his effort was not completely successful, for the man sat back and launched into a long apology, making a good many errors in Arabic, so that Amar often was not certain what it was he was trying to tell him. The recurrent motif of this speech, however, was that the Nazarene was not attempting to pry into Amar's life in any way, but only to learn about what was happening in the city. To Amar this was a most implausible explanation; if it were the truth, why did the man keep asking him for his personal opinion?

"What I think about the trouble is less than the wind," he finally said with a certain bitterness. "I can't even read or write my own name. What good could I be to anybody?" But even this confession, with all it cost him to make it, seemed not to convince the man, who, rather than accepting it and letting the matter drop, seemed positively delighted to learn of Amar's shame. "Aha!" he cried. "I see! I see! Very good! Then you have nothing to fear from anyone."

This remark Amar found particularly disturbing, for it must mean that he was going to send him away. The Nazarene had understood nothing at all; Amar's spirits sank as he perceived the gap that lay between them. If a Nazarene with so much good will and such a knowledge of Arabic was unable to grasp even the basic facts of such a simple state of affairs, then was there any hope that any Nazarene would ever aid any Moslem? And yet a part of his mind kept repeating to him that the man could be counted on, that he could be a true friend and protector if only he would let himself be shown how.

They continued to talk, but the conversation was now like a game in which the players, through fatigue or lack of interest, have ceased to keep the score, or even to pay attention to the sequence of plays. The point of contact was gone; they seemed to be looking in different directions, trying to say separate things, giving different meanings to words. Mercifully, a knock came at the door, and the man sprang to open it. The woman stood there, dressed in a more seemly manner this time, and looking very pleased with herself. In she came, down she sat, and then on and on she talked, while Amar's boredom and hunger grew. When there was another knock at the door, he rose, swiftly crossed the room, and managed to be at the window, leaning over the balcony, when the servant came in carrying his tray, and he remained there until he had heard him go out and shut the door behind him. His eyes having grown used to the dark as he stood there, he was able to find, among the thousands of cubes which were the houses in the dimness below, the mosque that stood on the hill at the back of his house. And off in the east, behind the barren mountains, there was a glow in the clear sky which meant that the moon would shortly be arriving.

In the room the man and the woman made clinking sounds

with their glasses, and talked, and went on talking. He wondered how the man found the patience to go on making conversation with her. After all, he reflected, if Allah had meant women to talk to men, He would have made them men, and given them intelligence and discernment. But in His infinite wisdom He had created them to serve men and be commanded by them. The man who, forgetting this, allowed one of them to addle his brain to such an extent that he was willing to meet her on equal terms, sooner or later would bitterly regret his weakness. For women, no matter how delightful they might seem, were basically evil, savage creatures who desired nothing better than to pull men down to their own low state, merely to watch them suffer. In Fez it was often said, half jokingly, that if the Moroccans had been really civilized men, they would have devised cages in which to keep their women. As it was, the women enjoyed far too much freedom of movement; and yet the Nationalists actually wanted to give them more, wanted to allow them to walk alone in the street, go to the cinema, sit in cafés, even swim in public places. And most unthinkable of all, they hoped to induce them to discard the *litham*, and show their faces openly, like Jewesses or Christians. Of course this could never really happen; even the prostitutes wore veils when they went out to shop, but it was characteristic of the times that some Nationalists dared speak openly of such things.

Soon the man called: "*Fik ej jeuhor?* Hungry?" Amar turned. On the tray there was a plate with pieces of white bread on it. "These are for you," the man said. "That's your dinner."

Determined not to show his disappointment at finding that the man held him in such low esteem as to offer him nothing but these few mouthfuls of bread, he smiled, went over to the table, and took a piece. Then he discovered that each one was two pieces, and that they had butter and chicken inside. This was partly consoling. The tray also held a bottle of Coca-Cola. He sipped a little, but it was too cold. "We're going down and eat," the man said. "This is enough for you?"

Amar said it would be. He was now terrified that someone might come to the room while he was in it alone. "Please lock the door," he said.

"Lock the door?"

"Lock the door, please, and take the key with you."

The man repeated this to the woman; he seemed to think it an amusing request. When she heard the words her face assumed a bewildered expression, as though it were an unheard-of idea to lock anyone into a room. Then the man, in passing him, tousled his hair, saying: "*Nchoufou menbad.*" Amar's mouth was full of bread and chicken, but he nodded his head vigorously. After the man had shut the door, he went over and tried the knob, just to be sure. Then he set the tray on the floor, sat down beside it, and began to eat in earnest.

CHAPTER 25

They sat opposite each other at a small table in the farthest corner of the bright dining-room. Lee was thinking: How white the French waiters look, and how dark the Moroccans. But it was more than that. The French stood in apathetic postures, without even whispering among themselves, staring morosely or self-consciously at the floor, and the Moroccans were stiffer than usual, with set, inexpressive faces. The room seethed with an abnormal silence; it was difficult to talk above it.

Suddenly she laughed. Stenham looked inquiringly at her. "This is really very funny, I think," she said, aware that it was a lame explanation; but she could find no other immediate one. She knew he was going to say: "What is?" which was exactly what he did say. And then of course she had nothing to answer, because if he didn't see it, nothing could make him see it.

"You know you never called Mr. Moss," she told him, as though she had just thought of it, although it had occurred to her nearly an hour before, while they were having soup.

"There's no point in calling him now, because he's out."

This was typical of Stenham; she was faintly piqued without knowing exactly why.

"He is! But how do you know?"

"They gave me a message from him when I phoned down for the drinks."

"Oh? You didn't tell me."

"I didn't think you'd be interested."

"But what's he doing out, tonight of all nights?"

"He could get in and out of the Medina during a full-scale war, that one. He could see the leader of the Istiqlal for tea and have the Résident for dinner."

She was amused at his evident resentment. "You don't like that, do you?" she said.

"What man does like to see another enjoying privileges he'll never have?"

"Well!" She laughed. "You'd better be careful with that subversive talk! You sound almost like me."

"After all," he continued, pretending to ignore her sarcasm, "he's got millions, so his motives are above suspicion. While who knows what we might be up to? We might be seeing the wrong kind of native. Like the kid upstairs, who'd never join any group, but would do anything at all if the right person gave the order. And that right person could be anybody he chanced to meet and admire. Those are the dangerous ones—not the joiners. You can keep tabs on the joiners easily enough. I can see why the French are going crazy. The only natives under control are the few thousand party members. The other nine million fanatics are anybody's guess."

Now Lee's voice became thin and sharp, her accent a parody of the accent of the typical New York stenographer: "Is there any comment on Comrade Stenham's report? If not, we will proceed to the next point on the agenda. In the absence of Comrade Lipschitz—" He stopped her with a well-aimed snap of his napkin in her face. The Moroccans stared in astonishment; the French remained sunk in their collective lethargy. Lee snickered. She was in a good mood. The day had not been without its adventure, and the future was just unpredictable enough to be exciting. Then, the dinner had been better than usual, since, with only two guests to cook for, the chef had not bothered to attempt any of his more complex creations. In addition, she was just a little tipsy from the wine, to which she had kept helping herself because it was so good, being chilled to exactly the right temperature. She had just ordered another half bottle, and was looking forward to having coffee on the terrace.

"I don't know what I'll do when I leave Morocco and have to give up this marvelous Algerian rosé," she said.

"You can get it in France," he told her.

It was at that instant that the lower garden sneezed. They looked at each other as the echoes shuddered from wall to wall; in another second there was only the sound of a fine rain of earth and stones falling. Now they were on their feet, running to the window, but there was nothing to see below save the dark interlacing of branches and the tile walks reflecting the early moonlight.

"Why would they do that?" Stenham said, his voice sounding unrecognizable after that racket; or perhaps it was his imagination.

"It's a French hotel," she answered, her teeth together, as though she had a gun in her hands and were saying it over her shoulder between shots.

He laughed briefly. "Let's go back and finish dinner." The waiters had rushed out onto the balcony and were peering over the railing down into the garden, French first, and Moroccans craning to see over their heads.

The rest of the meal was not a success. In some indefinable manner one would have said that the air had changed in density, that the room had altered its proportions. The acoustics seemed different, the lights shone too brightly and the shadows were too dark. And the mechanism of the service appeared to have been thrown hopelessly out of order. They were each brought two custards by mistake, but no spoons with which to eat them. The waiters gave the impression of being in a great hurry, but they had forgotten where things were.

"Did it upset you?" he asked her.

"No more than any other sudden noise would have," she said. "I hate sudden noises. You're always waiting for them to repeat themselves."

"I know. Why don't we have coffee in the bar? I think it'd be a little *too* reckless to have it on the terrace at this point."

"Let's have it up in your room. We ought to get back to that poor kid."

They found him sitting in the middle of the floor facing a semicircle of shoes; he had a shoe in his hand, and was examining it.

"These are good shoes," he announced, pointing to the

one he held. "You should always give them polish. The leather is going to crack, and then they'll be finished. *Safi!*"

"If I'm not mistaken, he's found my shoeshine and rag, and polished all these shoes before he put them out to admire," Stenham said. "It's the sort of thing I never have time to do, and would never remember if I had."

"Ask him what he thought of all the noise."

A moment later, Stenham told her: "He doesn't seem to have given it much thought. He says the boys in Casablanca make the bombs, and they're not much good, and they throw them haphazardly. What the French call *des bombes de fabrication domestique*. In any case, he says it's a new thing here in Fez. It's been mostly individual stabbings and shootings."

Even as Stenham spoke, there was another loud explosion below in the Medina, not very far away. Amar ran to the window, stood there awhile looking down. When he turned his head back toward the room he said: "I think that was at the bank."

"He's so calm about it," said Lee. "You'd think it happened every day of the year."

"It's all a game to them."

The coffee came, Stenham taking the tray from the waiter's hands in the doorway to prevent his entering the room. Then they sat discussing the trouble, while from time to time Stenham, in a manner slightly more oblique, made further efforts to elicit information and personal reactions from Amar. But it was clear even to Lee, on the outside of all this, that the boy was not in a confiding mood. Under his mask of polite reserve he was hesitant and reluctant to answer Stenham's questions, and, she thought, at times even outraged by them. Finally she decided to interrupt, for the boy was looking increasingly confused and unhappy.

"Oh, let the poor kid alone!" she exclaimed. "He'll end up thinking we're as bad as the French. I don't think it's right to grill him that way."

Stenham did not seem to have heard her. "This kid is split right down the middle," he said. "You've got all Morocco right here in him. He says one thing one minute and the opposite the next, and doesn't even realize he's contradicted himself. He can't even tell you where his sympathies are."

Lee snorted. "Don't be ridiculous. I never saw a face with more character. If he doesn't talk, it's only because he's decided not to."

"What's character got to do with it? He's in a situation. He's on the spot. It has nothing to do with him. Whether he manages it one way or another, it'll be the same for him."

She got up, walked to the window, and walked back again. "I'm awfully fed up with that kind of mysticism," she declared. "It's such a bore, and it's so false. Every little thing makes a difference, whether you decide it yourself or whether it's pure accident. So many people have had the whole course of their lives changed by something perfectly simple like, let's say, crossing the street at one point instead of another."

"Yes, yes, yes, I know," Stenham said with exaggerated weariness. "As far as I'm concerned that's just as boring, and a lot more false, by the way. The point I'm trying to make is that he loves his world of Koranic law because it's his, and at the same time he hates it because his intuition tells him it's at the end of its rope. He can't expect anything more from it. And our world, he hates that too, just on general principles, and yet it's his only hope, the only way out—if there is one for him personally, which I doubt."

Lee poured herself half a cup of coffee, sipped it, and finding it cold, set it down. "You talk as though it were his own private little set of circumstances, something that had to do with him as a person. My God! I'd like to know how many millions of people there are in that identical situation at this minute, all over the world. And they're all going to do the same thing, too. They're all going to throw over their old way of thinking and adopt ours, without any hesitation. It's not even a problem. There's simply no question about it in their minds. And they're right, right, right, because our way happens to work, and they know it."

For an instant his anger was so great that he could not trust himself to speak.

"My dear little friend," he finally said, and his voice grated unpleasantly, "the worst fate I can wish for you is that you'll still be around when the horror you want is here."

"I'll be around," she said calmly, "because it's not going to take long."

It was too bad she had to have opinions; she had been so agreeable to be with before she had started to express them. And then, the terrible truth was that neither she nor he was right. It would not help the Moslems or the Hindus or anyone else to go ahead, nor, even if it were possible, would it do them any good to stay as they were. It did not really matter whether they worshipped Allah or carburetors—they were lost in any case. In the end, it was his own preferences which concerned him. He would have liked to prolong the status quo because the décor that went with it suited his personal taste.

There was not much more conversation that evening. When the moment came for Lee to go to her room, the question of Amar's sleeping-place arose. She wanted to call downstairs and arrange for the management to give him a servant's room or a bed in some corner, but Amar, when Stenham relayed this idea to him, began a frenzied plea to be allowed to remain where he was and simply stretch out on the rug.

Lee shrugged. "The only thing is," she told Stenham, "I don't want you to be bothered. I brought him, and now you seem to be getting stuck with him. I'm afraid he may interfere with your work."

"It makes no difference at all," he said brusquely; he was still exceedingly angry. When she had gone, and he had heard her lock her door, he took the boy down the stairs to the lavatory, and waited in the big, dark ballroom to show him the way back.

A cricket had installed itself somewhere in the matting, and was singing happily. Its repeated silvery note was like a tiny bell being tolled there in the darkness. The huge moon was high in the sky, and its light entered the room through the shifting screen made by the leaves of the poplars in the garden. He stood there listening and looking, wondering whether he would ever see the big room again by moonlight, as he had seen it night after night for so many years, passing through on the way to his room in the tower. Perhaps never again moonlight after this minute, he thought, as he heard the flushing of the toilet behind him, and the opening of the door. The boy came out, and in a penetrating stage-whisper began to call: "*M'sieu! M'sieu!*" "My God! I can't have him calling me that," he said to himself, glad for something to

seize upon, to take his mind away from its melancholy speculations. Saying "Shh!" he led the way back up the stairs to his
room, pushed him inside, and locked the door.

Immediately the boy seized a cushion from the seat of a
chair and tossed it onto the rug in the center of the room.
Then he took the spread from the foot of the bed, and wrapping it around him, lay down on the floor. " *'Lah imsikh
bekhir,*" he said dutifully to Stenham, whereupon he whispered a few words of prayer and was quiet.

Stenham read for a half hour or so before turning off his
bed-lamp. He was in an unpleasant frame of mind over the
way the evening had turned out. It was getting mixed up
with this boy that had done it all; without him there would
have been a way, in spite of Lee's coolness and candor at the
café. He even suspected her motives in insisting upon bringing the boy along to the hotel: mightn't she have guessed
that he would prove useful by providing a convenient ob-
struction to any possible intimacy? Twice in the night he
awoke and saw the shrouded form lying there in the moonlight.

The next time he opened his eyes, the sun was very bright,
and the boy stood in one of the windows looking out. One
thing he did not want was to get involved in talk before he
had had coffee. Surreptitiously he felt around behind the pillows for the bell, pushed the button, and pretended to be
sleeping. The ruse worked so well that he was actually almost
asleep again by the time there was a knock at the door. As he
opened his eyes, he realized that the boy was trapped, in full
sight of whoever was to come into the room. He jumped out
of bed and opened the large mirror door of the armoire, signaling to the boy to step behind it. The knocking was repeated with added force.

A stout Frenchman stood there with his breakfast tray. "I'll
take it," he said nonchalantly, reaching out for it. It was not
until he had the tray in his hands that he felt free to go on
talking. "What's happened to the Arabs?" he asked; no one
but Rhaissa or Abdelmjid had ever brought him his breakfast.
"*Tous les indigènes sont en tôle.*" The man was grinning. "The
major domo has locked them all in their rooms and put the
keys in the office safe. That way we're sure of *those* natives, at

least." Changing his tone, he went on: "It's very serious, what's happening, you know."

"I know," said Stenham.

"I'm surprised you stay."

"And you?"

The big man shrugged. "*C'est mon gagne-pain, quoi!* We all have to earn our living."

"Ah, you see?" Stenham exclaimed. "That's why I stay, too."

The man nodded, making it obvious that he did not believe this for a moment. Stenham shut the door, and the boy's head appeared around the side of the wardrobe, his eyes large with excitement. Probably his imagination was still ablaze with images of police tortures.

"*Sbalkheir.* Good morning."

"*Sbalkheir, m'sieu.*"

Stenham poured half the coffee and half the hot milk into a tumbler, sweetened it, and handed it down to the foot of the bed where the boy stood. It was this gesture, together with the consciousness of exactly how many francs it represented, which made him smile at the absurdity of having this primitive youth, whose name he did not even know, sharing his room and breakfast with him. The mechanics of ridding himself of him were nothing; on the other hand, the moral responsibility involved was enormous, or so it seemed to him. And each hour that the boy spent with him would increase its weight.

Suddenly he asked the boy his name. "Of course, now I remember." He took another swallow of coffee and finished eating a slice of toast. "What would you do, Amar, if I should put you out?" The boy focused his piercing gaze upon him. His eyes were those of a wild animal, but at the same time they were human, compelling and extraordinarily expressive.

"I am in Allah's hands. If I go, that will be His will."

"Then you're not afraid?"

"Yes, I'm afraid. And I want very much to see my father and mother." He seemed about to say more, then to think better of it.

There was a knock at the door, and the stout waiter came in. "*Ah, pardon!*" he exclaimed, looking at Amar in surprise. "I thought monsieur had finished."

"Bring the same order again, will you? I'm still hungry. I've shared my breakfast." It was a moment that demanded brazenness.

The waiter smiled. "*Une petite causerie matinale?* A little morning chat over the coffee cups is always agreeable." Still smiling, he went out.

I suppose he's on his way down to the manager to report the presence of the enemy in the fort, thought Stenham, but he said nothing. A few minutes later the waiter reappeared with another tray, which he set on the bed between them. "*Et voilà!*" He stepped back, flourishing his napkin. "*Votre serviteur discret!*" His pink face beaming, he stood an instant looking at them. Then he went out.

"More coffee?" Stenham held the spout of the pot over the boy's cup. But Amar had once more fallen into a state of frightened melancholy. It took Stenham a half hour to convince him that the waiter almost certainly was not going to report his presence to the police.

Outside the window the burning sun climbed slowly to a higher position over the city. It was a cloudless day, so clear that each ravine on the distant mountain-slopes was visible in painstakingly etched detail. And the ten thousand flat rooftops below were beginning to collect the heat and to send it back up into the air, where it would gradually take on intensity and substance, and remain until long after dusk.

It was about nine o'clock when the disorders began. Stenham was standing before the washbasin, shaving, and in the mirror he saw the boy move soundlessly to the window. At first there was only shouting, from one part of the town directly below, and then from a more distant quarter to the west. But shortly there came the nervous and formless phrases of gunfire, and this seemed to issue from all regions of the city, more or less at the same time. Stenham made no comment, continued to shave, imagining the conflict that must be going on inside the watching head at the window. On and off, all morning long, the shooting continued. Occasionally Stenham tried to engage the boy in conversation, but his replies were monosyllabic.

The packed valises still stood by the door. "Am I staying or leaving?" The answer seemed to be that he certainly was not leaving at the moment, in any case. Yesterday he had been ready to get out; her arrival had made him willing to stay, even without the possibility of work. There was the point at which he had gone off the track; that was clear enough, now that he was no longer free to go, now that nearly twenty-four hours later he was still there. But this morning he did not feel that he *was* here; he could have been anywhere. The room was not the same room that it had been, nor was the hotel the place that had been his home for so many seasons. It was all vaguely like an innocuous dream whose only meaning lies in the sleeper's awareness that at any moment it can become a nightmare. Of course there was no question of working again; the idea was ludicrous. Nor would he be able to sit and read. All he could do was to wait for the drama to play itself out, except that because he had no part in it, it would not even do that—at least, not in a way that could be satisfactory to him.

The boy did have a part in it; there he was, fingering the curtain at the window, looking out through the heat at the city where he had been born, listening to his people being murdered, feeling God only knew what emotions as he stood there. Inextricably involved, he still could do nothing which might conceivably change the smallest detail—perhaps not even within himself.

If he had any character, Stenham reflected, he would give the boy some money and turn him out, letting him take his chances in the street like the rest of his countrymen. Then he would telephone Moss and see if he wanted to leave, do the same with Lee, and just start going, with or without the other two. That would make a kind of sense that no other action could. And now he wondered why he had ever expected it to be anything but overwhelmingly depressing to watch the city being destroyed. Perhaps (he could no longer remember) he had imagined that somehow an occasion would present itself in which he could perform some positive act, could be of help. But of help to whom? The two adversaries shooting one another down there were equally hateful to him; he hoped each side would kill as many of the other as possible.

When it was about eleven, the telephone rang: Moss was speaking from his room.

"I say, John, I'm frightfully sorry about yesterday. I had some business that needed attending to. I couldn't let it go on any longer. You know, this thing has got quite out of hand. I think the time has come to take action."

"What action?" Stenham's inflection was more derisive than interrogatory.

"Could we meet shortly for a little talk?"

"That'd be fine. That's just what I feel like, myself."

Moss came to Stenham's room a quarter of an hour later. Seeing Amar standing at the window, "Who's that?" he demanded, as if he had discovered him in his own room.

"It's a long story. I'll tell you in a minute. Sit down."

Moss sat in the large easy chair, folded his hands in front of him, and looked up at the ceiling. "This is all so distressing," he said.

Stenham regarded him suspiciously. "You look very pleased with yourself," he told him. "My guess is that you made some money yesterday."

Moss showed astonishment; then a veiled smile spread across his face. "I made a small profit. Yes. Not nearly so much as I'd counted on, naturally. By waiting I might have doubled it, and then again it's possible I'd have found no market at all. My personal feeling is that it's time to move on to calmer waters. Which is what I wanted to discuss with you. Don't you think we could organize a joint exodus between us, rent a car, I mean, this afternoon, and go?"

"Go where?" said Stenham, immediately suspicious at hearing the words: "we could rent." If such a mode of travel was to be used, he did not intend to share in its expense.

"Practically anywhere. I'd thought of Rabat, because I have friends there" ("And probably a garage to sell," Stenham added mentally) "but it could just as easily be Meknès or Ouezzane, if you like, I suppose. I'm very keen on not being in Fez tomorrow. It's the Aïd, and practically anything may happen. Surely you agree there's no point in having trouble if we can avoid it."

"Madame Veyron's back, you know."

"Oh, no! How really extraordinary! What on earth for?"

"I think it's just inquisitiveness."

"Ah, your great plot proved not to have her in it?"

Stenham frowned. "No, I'm afraid she's innocent." But he was thinking: Where's the difference between innocence and guilt, in cases like hers?

"I'm delighted to hear you admit it," Moss was saying patronizingly.

"And then there's Amar." He pointed to the window.

"So I see. But who is he? What's he doing here?"

When Stenham had finished telling him, Moss exclaimed: "Oh, come! Now what's this nonsense? I haven't understood a word of what you've said. It's all very commendable and romantic to take in a waif, but surely you don't intend to keep him."

"No, no, no!" Stenham cried. "Of course not! I don't know what I intend. I don't intend anything. I've just got to have time to think a little, that's all."

"Time! There isn't much of that at the moment, you know. I suggest you turn the institution of oriental cupidity to your advantage for once, hand the young man a five-thousand-franc note, and then set him free. It's astonishing what an excellent safe-conduct money can be."

"Yes, I've thought of that," Stenham replied distraughtly. "I don't know."

"Really, John! I can only look at you and marvel at the inscrutability of the human soul."

He's warming up for a round of the old game, thought Stenham. But I haven't got the energy to play. He did not answer.

Moss was silent for a moment. Now and then, in the confusion of rifle and machine-gun fire, there came the heavier sound of a grenade bursting. "With or without waifs and Americans," he resumed, "I have my eye set upon being far from Fez before tomorrow's dawn. And I'm dead serious about this, John. It's not a little fantasy of mine."

"You think tomorrow's the bad day, and after that it'll be better?"

"I think tomorrow will be the climax. It's going to be a thwarted Aïd el Kebir, don't forget. After that I think passions will slowly subside. Nothing can stay at fever pitch indefinitely."

Stenham, without replying, had begun to talk with Amar.

"Oh, that accursèd dead language that refuses to die!" Moss wailed, raising his eyes heavenward. "In order to say good morning one must use eighty-three separate words, each one with more hideous sounds in it than the last. Now, John, stop being difficult and talk to me, will you, please?" For a time he sat silent, in an attitude of mock resignation, looking very sorry for himself.

Presently Stenham looked up. "I've found a solution," he announced. "Amar will take us to Sidi Bou Chta."

"Very kind of him, I'm sure. If anyone wants to go. And would you like to tell me where this place is, and why we should go there, instead of somewhere that we've heard of?"

"It's a pilgrimage spot in the mountains, miles from anywhere. The great advantage is that there are no French. That means there's no trouble, either for them or for us. And they'll really observe the feast. I'd like to see it."

"Hotel?" said Moss.

"We'd sleep on mats, in the shelters."

Now Moss stood up and recited the lengthy tirade he had evidently been preparing. Its organization, phrasing and delivery were all admirable. When he had finished, "I enjoyed that," Stenham told him. "You're still *en forme*. I suppose you mean you won't come."

Moss yawned and stretched, reassumed his normal voice. "I'm afraid not, John. It's just not my cup of tea. You should know me well enough to understand that. What would you do: stay a day or two, and then come back here?"

Wearily Stenham said he did not know, that the idea had only now occurred to him, that how it was carried out would depend upon the boy, and whether it were put into effect at all would probably be decided by Madame Veyron. "It doesn't matter to me one way or the other," he concluded. "But I think you're right about not being here tomorrow."

"Well, John, it looks like the parting of the ways for a time."

"It's awful," said Stenham, for whom any leavetaking had a faint savor of the deathbed. "So sudden."

"I shall miss our expeditions. Into the Medina, I mean. Not those into the labyrinths of polemics."

Stenham smiled feebly. "Where will you be?"

"I think I'll visit some friends in Cintra. It's very charming there. I don't think you'd like it. You can reach me at the British Consulate in Lisbon. Three or four days ought to see me through my business and out of Morocco. I must say I hope so. All this excitement is fatal for my painting. And you, how can you concentrate on your work in a place that's like an overturned anthill?"

Stenham heard the phrases and understood them, but a part of his consciousness was perversely working to distract his attention. Morocco, Moss, motor, moustache, moving, mow, sometimes my mind runs away with me like this, but it's usually only in moments of stress. So, this must be a moment of stress. He's the last link with the way things used to be. Moxie, it went on, Moylan ("That's not allowed; nobody ever heard of it.") "It's where the Hedgerow Theatre is, outside Philadelphia. Objection overruled.") *Mozo.* ("This is *my* game. No holds barred. Foreign languages accepted.") *Mozo* was certainly the boy in the window. But thank God that's the end of the alphabet. Thank God his name was Moss, and not Moab. Now he looked at Moss, and thought how sallow his complexion was, and how unusually long his eyelashes were; he had never noticed either of those details before. Perhaps it was the angle at which the thick lenses of his glasses struck the lashes, but he doubted it.

"Or probably the idea appeals to you, staying on here and seeing it all with your own eyes."

"No, it doesn't," he said simply.

Moss shifted his feet with impatience. He sighed. "Oh, well, John, it's all too mysterious and complicated. We do what makes us happy, and there's no point in going further into it."

"That's right." It was a completely erroneous summing-up of all the understandings they thought they had reached in the years they had known each other, but the world was the way it was. "That's absolutely right," Stenham said again, with more feeling.

After a few more exchanges of words, they shook hands, and Moss left.

CHAPTER 26

When Polly Burroughs arrived back in her room, she put on
a clean pair of shantung pajamas, got into bed with her tiny
typewriter, and set to work writing letters. Her correspondence was a lusty one; most days she sent off a dozen or so
missives, some short and some surprisingly lengthy, all of
which she typed with great speed and gusto. It often happened that she could not be sure what she thought about a
thing until she had written a letter to someone about it; in the
spontaneous sentences that flowed from her fingertips as she
ran them over the keyboard, her ideas were crystallized, became visible to her. She was not one to be concerned with
profundities, for she was well aware that there are too many
different angles, all of them more or less equally valid, from
which to look at a simple truth; what she strove for was a neat
arrangement of her own personal opinions and reactions to
outward phenomena, and she possessed an over-all formula
which greatly facilitated the achievement of this. By keeping
in her mind's eye the face, the sound of the voice, and the
temperament of the individual to whom she was writing, she
managed to speak directly to that person and to no one else.
She had no one mode of expression, no style, which could
properly be identified as hers. The letters were considered
breezy and original, and were much admired (and carefully
collected) by almost everyone who received them; the steady
production of them had come to be one of her principal
raisons d'être. "Wonderful? I don't know what you mean. And
anyway, I don't write them; they write themselves. It's just a
state of mind you have to get into."

Polly belonged wholly to her time. Alert to its defects and
dangers, she nevertheless had reached what she herself called
an "adjustment," and she was very firm in her belief that
without the attainment of a state of conscious harmony with
the society in which he functioned, no individual could hope
to accomplish much of anything.

She had understated the facts in telling Kenzie that she had
"heard of" Stenham. Actually she had read all his books and
was something of a fan of his. She liked his style, an important by-product of what seemed to her an unusually vigorous

mind in a healthy state of controlled, and therefore construc-
tive, rebellion. Particularly the way he wrote about love
pleased her: the passages had a militant detachment that bordered on the clinical, and yet were saved from that kind of
shallowness by what she felt to be an underlying and ever present sense of inevitability. These sections of his books were
the very antithesis of what commonly is considered "romantic," yet to her they were all of that and much more: she had
gone so far as to call them "sheer poetry." She had even
known he was in Morocco when she had decided to come.
There were Marrakech and the political situation and the
Grand Atlas and native festivals, certain of which would take
place during her stay, and Fez and Stenham and the Sahara,
plus whatever might present itself in between. For Polly Burroughs had the makings of a good journalist. She believed
that, assuming one had open eyes and an open mind, one
needed only to be on the spot in order to capture the truth.
If anyone had discussed it with her, she would have maintained that a photograph was nearer to reality than a painting,
because it was objective. For her there was either the garden
of facts or the wilderness of fantasy, and because Stenham's
florid ramblings appealed to her imagination, she had decided
they were actually a variety of fact—symbolic fact, it was true,
but still fact.

". . . I finally met your favorite writer," she had written
weeks back, the day they had all had lunch at the Zitoun, "or
isn't John Stenham your favorite? It seems to me I remember
words to that effect from you, one day when we were sitting
on the Brevoort terrace, at least five years ago. I'm a little disappointed because he's not in the least as I had expected.
Probably that's my fault, because he's a true writer, and the
best of any true writer is in his books, where it belongs. There
were also some real British drips present. They were useful as
atmosphere, of course, along with the storks and Arab waiters
in costume, but at least the last two didn't try to make conversation, thank God."

To a different friend the next night she had written: "As
you probably know, John Stenham lives here in Fez. We went
for a long carriage drive together today. I don't recommend
ever meeting an author whose books you admire. It spoils

everything, but everything. I had imagined someone so utterly different, someone more decided and less neurotic, more understanding and less petulant. I feel terribly let down. You could say he means well, I suppose, but he's so clumsy and moody and calculating, all at the same time, that a little of him goes a long way. The most embarrassing moment came when it got dark and he decided that I expected him to take an interest in me. It was all very sad. He does know the country and speak the language, *mais à quoi bon?*, I keep thinking, since he couldn't be more apathetic regarding the struggle for independence. That of course is the big thing here. You feel it in the air, something colossal and heroic and potentially tragic, and in any case very exciting. . . ."

Tonight her work was cut out for her: to report to as many stay-at-homes as possible the events of the afternoon. ". . . I only got back to Fez last night, and during my absence things have moved swiftly to a crisis. . . ." ". . . The city is without electricity, and in a virtual state of siege. . . ." "Today there was a wholesale massacre of demonstrators at one of the gates. God knows how many hundred were slaughtered. . . ." ". . . Here I am, in the middle of a real war. You won't read about it, or if you do, it will be a perfunctory and watered-down version, since all news is strictly censored by the French. (As a matter of fact, you may never even get this, but anyway, I'm doing my best.)"

It was only in her fourth letter of the evening, which was to a friend in Paris, and therefore, she thought, less likely to be destroyed by the French authorities than those going to America, that she allowed herself to divagate sufficiently from her theme to reach the subject of Stenham. ". . . One person who could if he wanted give me a satisfactory breakdown on the whole situation is John Stenham, but God forbid that I should have to go to him for it. If he were standing in the middle of the railroad track and the crack express were coming around the curve, he would begin to ask himself which side of the tracks it would be better to stand on while the train passed. It's that kind of mind, a little like Dr. Halsey, but even more ineffectual and soft. At the same time he's the most reactionary and opinioned man I've ever met, bar none—a typical disillusioned liberal. (I might add I just had

an argument with him, so you won't think we're on quite
such bad terms as this might sound.) The mystery to me is
where the books come from. It's hard to believe they could
have come out of that flabby, selfish mind. If I had several
lives I'd read them again out of curiosity, just to try and tie
them up with the man, and see what ever made me think they
were alive, because *he* certainly isn't. . . ."

When she reread this passage, it seemed a little excessive,
because she did not feel so strong an antipathy to Stenham as
its words suggested, and so she immediately added: "At the
same time, there's something vaguely saintlike about the man,
but it's as though he had only the mind of a saint and not the
soul, and were quite conscious of the fact that he could never
come any nearer to it than that. Very unsatisfactory for him,
I should think. The awful thing is, and this is confidential,
he's definitely interested in *me*, and as far as I'm concerned
it's like having a two-toed sloth interested. *Rien à faire.* But
one of these days, if I get out of this country in one piece, I'll
be back at the *rue* St. Didier, and I'll call Élysée 53-28 and tell
you everything. . . ."

When she had finished her letter-writing, she set the typewriter on the night table, turned out the light, and at the end
of five minutes of darkness, during which she was conscious
of the mildewed smell of the bed and the intense silence
around her, a silence changed only by the sound of a few
leaves rustling outside her window when a faint breeze moved
them, she fell asleep. There were almost no interstices in her
life. When she was awake she was busy, and when she ceased
being busy she went to sleep. It was seldom that she made
room in her day for thought or conjecture: anything of an indefinite nature, not immediately soluble, made her uneasy.
And so, untroubled by interior difficulties, she slept well; it
was a habit of long standing.

The following morning about nine o'clock she began to expect a telephone call from Stenham. The hysteria in the city
below had irrupted then, and she thought it unlikely that he
would be either sleeping or working through such an uproar.
When time passed and he did not call her, she felt neglected
and consequently resentful, although she told herself that she
had every reason to rejoice at being left to her own devices. As

the commotion down in the Medina increased, even though only slightly, she grew unaccountably nervous, her letter-writing mechanism jammed, and then she furiously typed: "Can't go on now. The noise is too much." She hesitated as to whether to add: "It sounds as though the mob had started up the hill toward the hotel," decided it would look melodramatic (and in any case the noise did not really sound any nearer—merely louder and more general). She finished, "In haste and with love," and signed her name with a fountain pen.

Downstairs in the office she stood at the desk awhile, waiting for someone to come to sell her stamps. Here the sounds of disorder were almost shut out by the high walls that surrounded the garden, and in an adjacent room a subdued radio played Hungarian gypsy music.

It was the manager himself who finally appeared. "*Bon jour, madame,*" he said ceremoniously. Then, abruptly changing his tone, he continued. "I meant to ask you, have you made arrangements for leaving Fez? We have received orders to close the hotel."

She was shocked. "You're going to close? When? I don't understand. Of course I haven't made any arrangements." Her voice sounded indignant and querulous, in spite of her efforts to keep it normal.

"*Ah, mais il faut faire des démarches,*" he announced, as if she had told him she had known it all the time, but hadn't bothered to do anything.

"But what steps?" she cried. "You can't put me out until I have somewhere to go."

The manager's eyebrows went up. "You are not being *put out*, madame," he said, enunciating with great clarity. "These are circumstances beyond our control."

She looked at his immaculate clothing, his supercilious face, and hated him. "And where am I supposed to go?" she demanded, knowing in advance that he would have an answer to everything, that she could not possibly win.

"I can scarcely be of use to you on that score, madame. But if my personal opinion interests you, I should advise you to leave Morocco altogether. One can expect to encounter disorders of this kind in every city. Shall I order a car for you at three, after you have had lunch?"

"*Mais c'est inouï,*" she protested feebly, "it's unheard-of to send a woman off alone like this. . . ."

"The police will see to it that you are in no danger," he said wearily. "You will be escorted."

She decided to temporize. "What about Monsieur Stenham? What time is *he* going?"

"One moment. I have not yet apprised him of the official decision." And while she stood there, drumming her fingers on the desk, he turned and in funereal tones telephoned Monsieur Stenham and informed him that he too must prepare for an immediate departure.

Apparently the recipient of this news was no more pleased to get it than she had been; she heard insect-like buzzings issuing from the earphone, and the man's face assumed a martyred expression. "Let me speak to him," she said, reaching out for the instrument.

"Good morning!" she cried, her eyes on the wall clock above: it was ten minutes to noon. "Isn't this incredible?"

His voice sounded like the first phonograph record. "I guess it is." This insufficient reply disappointed her; she felt somehow betrayed. "Would you mind coming down so we can talk about it?"

"Be right down."

When he arrived, he said: "*Bon jour,*" in a peremptory fashion to the manager, took her arm and led her out and across the terrace to the court where the high banana plants grew. The sunlight burned the skin of her bare arm like an acid, and she took a step in order to be completely in the shade. He described his project for going to Sidi Bou Chta. She listened patiently, feeling all the time that it was a harebrained idea, but without a counter-proposition with which to meet it. "I see," she said from time to time. "Oh."

"And afterward?" she finally asked. "When we've finished there and seen the festival. Where do we go?"

"Well, we come back here and start out fresh from here, wherever we're going. I'm going to the Spanish Zone."

"Why not just go to the Spanish Zone today and have done with it?"

"Because I'd like to see what goes on up there at their festival."

"That's ridiculous," she said nervously. "It's much more important to get out while it's still possible."

"Well, there's no point in arguing about it," he sighed, seeing that they were on the verge of doing just that. "I'll be going in a native bus anyway. I don't think it would be very comfortable for you."

"You don't know anything about me," she declared, snapping up the bait. "But the point has nothing to do with whether you go in a bus or on a mule."

Then they did enter into a long argument from which they both emerged hot and ill-tempered. "Let's go and sit down," he suggested finally.

"I've got to see the manager about getting a car. And I'm not packed. Perhaps I'll see you at lunch." She stepped back into the searing sun and strode across the terrace, furious at herself for having displayed even a little emotion. He would think it mattered to her whether he was with her or not. And to be perfectly honest, she admitted to herself, it did matter quite a lot. In a crisis like this she would expect any American man to do his utmost to see that she got out in comparative safety. And any other American man *would* have done his utmost. Each step she took across the terrace's blistering mosaic floor was like another note in a long crescendo passage of rising fury, so that by the time she got to the office she was nearly beside herself with anger. "Selfish, egotistical, conceited monster," she thought, vaguely eying a travel poster that showed a nearly naked Berber with a pigtail holding up a huge black cobra toward the cobalt sky, through which rushed a quadri-motored plane. MOROCCO, LAND OF CONTRASTS, ran the legend beneath. When she had ordered a car for three o'clock she went up to her room and packed. It seemed to her that the heat had increased to a fantastic degree in the past half hour. When she breathed she had the impression that she was not breathing at all, because the air was so warm she could not feel it entering her lungs, or even her nostrils. Then she breathed too deeply and violently, and that made her dizzy. And all the objects she touched seemed to be warmer than her hands, which was disconcerting. "How can it be so hot?" she thought. It was half past one when she finished her packing, and she telephoned down for a porter.

"Ah, madame, I regret. There are no porters," said the manager.

"I don't know what you mean," she shrilled. "It's absurd. There must be someone who can carry my things down."

The noise in the town still continued; she had forgotten about it for at least an hour, but there it was.

"I regret."

"And lunch. I suppose there's no one to serve lunch, either?"

"The *maître d'hôtel* will prepare you an omelette and an *assiette anglaise*, madame."

"Why can't one of the waiters carry my luggage?"

The manager seemed to be losing patience. "He cannot, madame, because all the native servants, including the waiters, are locked in their dormitories, and Europeans do not carry luggage in Morocco. *Vous avez compris?* The hotel regrets profoundly that it is unable to accommodate you, but as I pointed out to you earlier, these are circumstances which go beyond us. I suggest you ask Monsieur Stenham to assist in transporting your valises to the taxi." He hung up.

She sat on the bed and looked out at the glaring, barren hills. A little fire of cosmic hatred had begun to burn inside her, a hatred directed at everyone and everything, at the idiotic poplar trees in the garden, whose leaves were stirring when there was not a breath of air, at the hideous satiny tenor of the manager's voice on the telephone, at her rumpled linen dress, already soaked at the armpits, at the evasive geometrical designs so carefully painted on the beams over her head, at her red fingernails, at the popping of the deadly fireworks out there, and directed above all at her own weakness and carelessness in allowing herself to fall into such a state. Then she decided to blame it all on the heat. "It's suffocating in here," she thought. She took a deep breath and stood up. By herself she carried the bags out into the corridor. But then she realized that she would never be able to lug them through the hotel and out to the taxi. Perhaps when it arrived if she described her plight to the driver he would offer to help. However, long association with the French had taught her that they could be the least chivalrous of men when they chose, and so she did not have too much hope. "I *won't* ask that son of a bitch," she kept telling herself, as if it were a consolation, looking down the hall toward Stenham's door.

Suddenly she thought of Amar. If she could get to the boy without seeing Stenham, he would surely help her. It occurred to her that perhaps Stenham had already put him out; they had not mentioned him during their conversation. She decided to go down to lunch now; possibly then she could leave the dining-room while Stenham still was eating. Outside his door she stopped to listen; she heard nothing. The windowless hall was very still. No sounds came up from the hotel. Then she did hear an exchange of mumblings from the room. She passed silently along and down the stairs.

The omelette came in almost cold, and the *assiette anglaise* consisted of two very thin slices of ham, a piece of cold liver and some extremely tough roast beef, which she suspected of being horsemeat. When she had nearly finished, Stenham came into the dining-room, saw her, and approached the table. "Sit down," she said, giving a ring to her voice that would make it sound as though she were trying, against great odds, to be pleasant.

He sat opposite her. "This is the worst meal I've ever eaten, I think," she told him. He was staring beyond her head, out the window into the sky, and did not seem to have heard her. However, an instant afterward he said: "Is it?" The *maître d'hôtel* approached. "A bottle of beer," she announced. "Tuborg." When he had moved off, she said: "What's happened to our orphan? Is he still upstairs or is he gone?"

Stenham looked at her almost as if he were surprised that she knew of the boy's existence. "Why, no. He's up there. He's having his lunch."

They made perfunctory conversation while she drank her beer, avoiding the topic which, proclaiming its presence afresh each instant with a new burst of bullets, filled their minds completely with itself and its corollaries. It could not be discussed because she hoped for an Istiqlal victory, and he did not.

"I've ordered a car for three o'clock. Did you say you were coming back here after your festival? How can you? I don't understand."

"Back here to Fez, to the French town, I mean."

"Oh." She laid her napkin on the table and got to her feet. "Will you excuse me? I've got a few more things to finish up."

Climbing the stairs she wondered why she had gone to the trouble of such elaborate subterfuge in order to ask the boy to carry her bags. It would have been simple enough to go and knock on the door and say to him: "Come with me," Stenham or no Stenham. But then Stenham very likely would have insisted on helping, which, since she wanted to keep her image of his supreme selfishness intact, was not at all desirable.

Unfortunately she had not counted on Stenham's small appetite. He had found the food so bad that he had not bothered to eat it, and was back upstairs standing in the doorway while she was still trying to explain to Amar what it was she wanted.

"Is there something wrong?"

She jumped, startled, hoped she did not look as guilty as she felt, and turned to face him. "Nothing at all," she said, flushing with annoyance. He was really incredible, to have followed her upstairs this way. "I'm just trying to get some help with my luggage. There's no one in the hotel to carry it. I thought Amar might be willing."

"We'll have it out there for you in two minutes. Where is it?" He glanced down the corridor, saw the bags, and calling: "*Amar! Agi! Agi ts'awouni!*" started in the direction of her door.

"You go back and finish your lunch," she said coldly. "He can do it perfectly well." The boy ran past her.

Stenham laughed without turning his head. "What lunch?"

At that moment she heard someone coming up the stairs, and she stepped to the door so she would not actually be in Stenham's room when the person passed. It was the fat waiter who had brought her breakfast. He smiled, said: "*Pardon, madame,*" and pushed by her into the room. As he returned, bearing Amar's empty tray, he said: "It's really hot, isn't it?"

"*Affreux,*" she agreed.

"Ah, yes," he said philosophically. "*La chaleur complique la vie.*"

She stared after him, feeling that he had been insolent, that he had somehow had his mysterious joke at her expense. This was what she so hated about the French: when they wanted to be subtle it made no difference to them whether they were understood or not. The mere voluptuous pleasure they got from making their hermetic little phrases seemed to suffice; they imagined they became superior by shutting you out. It could be perfectly true that, as the waiter had said, the heat complicated people's lives; it had even complicated hers this morning, but why should he make the observation to her at that particular moment?

By the time she had ceased trying to define the insult, all her luggage had been carried out. Stenham joined her in her room; Amar had remained at the back entrance with the bags.

"The hotel's empty, deserted," he informed her. "I was a little worried that somebody might see the kid and ask questions, but there's not a soul, there's nobody at all."

The telephone rang. "*Oui?*" she said. Once again the manager's doleful voice spoke. "We have been requested by the authorities to inform our guests" (Even as he talked, *Now* what's coming? she thought.) "that vehicles will be permitted to circulate only along the highway to Meknès-Rabat-Casablanca, where adequate protection will be afforded them."

"What?" she cried. "And if one wants to leave the country?"

"It is no longer possible, madame."

"But you yourself advised me this morning to leave."

"The frontier has been temporarily closed, madame."

"But where will I go? What hotel can I find?"

"The Transatlantique in Meknès is not operating as of today. In Rabat the Balima and the Tour Hassan are full, of course. However, there are many hotels in Casa, as you know."

"Yes, and I know they're always full too, unless one has a reservation."

"Perhaps madame has influence at the American Consulate. Otherwise I should advise her to stay here in Fez, in the Ville Nouvelle."

She was shouting now. "*Mais ça c'est le comble!* This is the last straw!"

"Doubtless it is most disagreeable for you, madame. I have communicated to you the orders issued by the police. Your bill has been prepared. You will pass by the office to settle it?"

"I usually do," she said furiously, and slammed the telephone into its cradle. She turned to Stenham. "It's really too much." She repeated the manager's message.

Stenham's face assumed a pensive expression. (If she had not been there, she decided, he would have been as indignant as she.) His mind raced ahead through likelihoods and possibilities. "The border's closed. That's bad," he said slowly. "But they'll probably reopen it in a day or two. It's obviously to keep the Nationalists from getting out. They've been combing all the cities, street by street and house by house. It's a *râtissage*."

She had gone to the window. "I just hope the Arabs raise holy hell with them, and make them wish they'd never set foot here." She walked back toward him. "Why, if I spoke the language I'd be down there day and night working for independence. Nothing would give me greater pleasure at this point." Without transition she continued. "Where am I supposed to go? Where am I supposed to sleep tonight? In the street?"

"There's only one place for you to go, and that's the Ville Nouvelle here in Fez. There are hotels."

"Well, *that* I *refuse* to do. After all, the whole point of being here is to be where the natives are."

He was about to tell her not to be childish, but he decided not to. "Then come with me," he said, smiling and shrugging. "I'm going to be where natives are."

"All right, damn it, I will!" she exclaimed. "And it had better be good."

CHAPTER 27

Almost from the outset she found herself in a better humor. Perhaps it was the fact that upon leaving the city the bus had begun at once to climb, threading its way back and forth across the southern slope of Djebel Zalagh, and the air was growing increasingly fresher. Or perhaps it was purely emotional: the bus without glass in its windows, the excited chatter of the people in their mountain clothing, and the relief she felt that no policeman or soldier had prevented their departure at the last moment before the crazy old vehicle finally had moved out of the shabby side street in the Ville Nouvelle.

They had used her taxi only to transport their luggage to a sad little hotel where they had engaged one desperate room, piled it all in, and locked the door. The proprietress, sour-faced but not really unpleasant, had demanded to see their passports, and upon examining them had insisted Stenham pay her three days in advance.

The passengers were almost all country folk from the mountains to the south who had gone to Fez solely because the road passed through and they had to change buses there. They were beautiful people, clean and with radiant faces, and she wondered vaguely if it were possible that they had heard nothing about the disturbances. She would have asked Sten-ham his opinion if he had been sitting near enough to her, but although they were occupying the same bench, they were separated from each other by three women, he near the left end of the bench and she at the extreme right, beside the glassless window.

And Amar, mysterious youth, had brought along a friend— or, rather, an enemy, she would have sworn, judging from his expression when the other had accosted him on the sidewalk beside the bus. She had happened to be near the scene, and was positive she had noticed a grimace of distaste or even some stronger emotion when Amar had turned to see who had tapped on his shoulder. Why then had he presently sought out Stenham and asked his permission to invite the newcomer to accompany them on the journey? She did not know, but she was not averse to his presence: he was well brought up, polite, a good deal cleaner than Amar (whose clothes were in a shocking state), and he spoke French flu-ently. The two boys had managed to get a small strip of seat together in the back of the bus; the last time she had looked around they had appeared to be conversing amiably.

The late afternoon light illumined the countryside. It was a characteristic of Moroccan mountain roads that they very sel-dom passed through a village; the villages could be seen, cow-ering against the flanks of distant side-hills, or standing like crest-feathers at the tops of cliffs, or spread out sparsely along the sinuous ridges of lesser mountains, always with a valley lying between the road and them. In spite of the heat the air was pungent with the scent of mountain plants, and its utter dryness, after the vapors of the ubiquitous river-waters of Fez, was a tonic in the nostrils. Whenever the bus passed through a wooded spot, the frantic shriek of the cicadas came in from both sides of the road. A curve, a bank of pink clay, the swaying and rattling of the chassis, the ceaseless sound of the heated motor laboring in second, a green-gray cactus at the edge of the abyss ahead, a curve, a hundred miles of granite mountaintops against the enamel sky, the explosive shifting of gears and the altered sound and speed that came after it, the sleepy sobbing of a baby somewhere behind her in the bus, a curve, a savage ravine below, with the twilight already welling up from its depths. And on a slope beside her, still glowing in the calm late sunlight, a grove of ancient olive trees, their great twisted trunks as if frozen in the attitudes of some forgotten ceremonial dance. She remembered what Stenham had told her before they had started out: that they would be going through a region where the cult of Pan was still alive, its rites still observed with flutes and drums and masks. She had neither believed nor disbelieved it; at the time it had sounded merely like a rather improbable statistic. But now as she looked, it seemed for no good reason entirely credible. The wild land lent itself to such extravagances.

What she found astonishing about these people was the impression of cleanliness they gave her. It was not only their bodies and clothing that seemed clean (the interior of the bus smelled like laundry drying in the sun); it was as much the expressions on their faces, the aura of their collective spirit; they made her think of the purity of mountain streams, untouched regions. She determined not to discuss any of her reactions with Stenham, because he would make analytical remarks which, false or correct, would only end by infuriating her.

Yesterday afternoon in the café, for instance, he had said: "The intellect is the soul's pimp." She had not wanted to know what he meant, but of course he had gone on and explained that the intellect was constantly seducing the soul with knowledge, when all the soul needed was its own wisdom. The only way to enjoy this excursion, she decided, was to refuse to discuss anything at all with him, and not even to

comment on what was before their eyes, save perhaps to exclaim now and then if an exclamation seemed in order. She
knew that such a plan would prove at least partially unen-
forceable, but if she persevered, she thought, it was just conceivable that he might become aware of what she was doing
and follow suit.

They stopped at a spring for water. The sudden lack of motion and the silence broken only by occasional murmurs (for
most of the voyagers had long ago fallen asleep) made her feel
faintly nauseated; she longed for the bus to start again. A few
people wanted to get down, but the driver, who had stayed at
the wheel while his assistant filled the radiator, objected. Stenham leaned forward, looked across the three white bundles
who slept between him and her, said: "It's a relief to be up
here, isn't it?"

"It's marvelous!" she agreed, startled by the unnaturally
heartfelt enthusiasm in her own voice. Her ears sang, and she
was a little giddy from the altitude. But now she knew, as the
door slammed shut and the comforting sound and motion resumed, *why* it was a relief. It was not only the pure air and the
slowly increasing coolness; much more than those things it
was being away from the vaguely sinister sense of expectancy
and apprehension with which she had been living for the past
two days. Those two days had been endless. The city had
been there, right under her eyes the whole time, and she had
been able to stand in her window and examine it roof by roof,
but it might as well have been invisible, like a snake hidden in
the bushes, waiting. At the moment she felt she never wanted
to see Fez again. However, it was extremely important to
keep *that* from Stenham: if he guessed how she felt he would
make capital of it, taunt her with her inability to accept the
physical concomitants of the social change she advocated.
"Ah!" he would say triumphantly, "at last you're beginning to
understand what it means, this business of destroying faith."
And she would only become querulous and invent a series of
bad-tempered rejoinders, instead of telling him simply that
even though every detail of the transition were hateful to her,
she would still wish it wholeheartedly because it meant life,
whereas if the metamorphosis failed to take place, there were
only decay and death ahead. So she would be very careful

about it, and if she could not keep him from noting an added glint of health in her eyes which had not been there before (for he was observant), she would tell him that Fez had been damper than she had realized, because now upon having left it her sinus pains had completely vanished.

At first she dozed, as if exploring that first ledge of nonbeing, then she slipped and fell into the chasm of sleep. The early night came, blue and not dark under the clear sky. The bus had turned on to a side road and was navigating the edge of a precipice. Only the driver and his helper could appreciate the skill that was required to keep its shuddering old carcass upright, out of the ditch on the one side and yet at a safe number of inches from the brink on the other. Far ahead and below, Stenham caught sight of a pair of headlights rounding a curve, and he thought: There's going to be trouble when that car gets here; one of us will have to back up. But the other car never arrived, and he realized that it was moving ahead of them, another bus filled with pilgrims, very likely.

When they had come to the bottom of the descent they crossed a rushing stream, and set off in another direction over a plain. Here it was warmer, and they raised clouds of dust, some of which came up between the floorboards and set people to sneezing. Then once again they began to climb, this time on a trail which was so bad that several sleeping forms rolled off their seats. Lee had awakened and was holding on to the bench ahead for support. He caught her eye and grinned. She shook her head, but she did not look unhappy. The score or so of men traveling on the top of the bus began to pound violently on the metal roof. At first he thought that someone might have bounced off, but presently he heard them singing, and the banging resolved itself into a rhythm. The mad climb with its incredible jolting and swaying lasted for nearly an hour. Then what looked like a city of pink lights came into view ahead. A moment later the bus drew to a halt. The city was several thousand tentlike shelters improvised of sheets and blankets that had been stretched between the trunks of a vast olive grove covering the slopes of two hills, and against each square of cloth the flames that flickered inside threw shadows. That much they saw while they were still in their seats. In the confusion of getting down (for each passenger had innumerable bundles of food and cooking utensils, and there were loose babies and live fowls scattered about among the bundles) they forgot about it, and it was only an hour or so later, when they had climbed up out of the hollow where the trucks and buses were ranged, and sat, all four of them, on a log watching the moon rise, that Stenham commented on the strange aspect of the place.

"It's wonderful," she answered in a low voice, hoping to keep him from saying more. He appeared to have understood, for he began to talk to the two boys, leaving her to think her thoughts. Of course it was wonderful, with the shadows and the flames and the great circles of men, hundreds of them, dancing arm in arm, and the orchestras of drums like giant engines pulsing. But it was wonderful only as a spectacle, since it meant nothing. That was what she must remember, she told herself, because she felt that the place represented an undefinable but very real danger. It meant nothing, never could mean anything, to Polly Burroughs. For that to happen, she would have to go back, back, she did not know how many thousands of years, but back far enough for it to denote some sort of truth. If she possessed any sort of religion at all, it consisted in remaining faithful to her convictions, and one of the basic beliefs upon which her life rested was the certainty that no one must ever go back. All living things were in process of evolution, a concept which to her meant but one thing: an unfolding, an endless journey from the undifferentiated toward the precise, from the simple toward the complex, and in the final analysis from the darkness toward the light. What she was looking down upon here tonight, the immense theatre full of human beings still unformed and unconscious, bathed in sweat, stamping and shrieking, falling into the dust and writhing and twitching and panting, all belonged unmistakably to the darkness, and therefore it had to be wholly outside her and she outside it. There could be no temporizing or mediation. It was down there, spread out before her, a segment of the original night, and she was up here observing it, actively conscious of who she was, and very intent on remaining that person, determined to let nothing occur that might cause her, even for an instant, to forget her identity.

As time passed, she could feel Stenham growing restless, but it had not occurred to her that he might be hungry until he suddenly rose and announced that he was going down to see what sort of food was on sale at the stands. "Anything special you want?" he asked her. She replied that she was not very hungry. "I'll bring back something. *Nimchiou?* Shall we go?" he said, turning to Amar, who jumped to his feet.

When she and the other youth were alone, she asked him his name. "Mohammed," he answered, flattered by her question, but particularly because she had said *vous* to him instead of *tu*. "And have you known Amar for a long time?" "*Oui*," he said vaguely, as if the subject were of no possible interest. They were silent for a while. Then he asked her where her husband had gone; she burst into laughter and immediately felt a wave of disapproval emanate from him. Bending toward him, she saw his stern young face in the moonlight; swiftly she grew very serious, and committed the even graver error of telling him that Stenham was just a friend. "A very old friend," she added, hoping that this might in some way save her from worse opprobrium. Apparently it was not a mitigating circumstance in his eyes, for he merely grunted, and soon burst out indignantly: "You shouldn't have come here with him if he's not your husband. Where is your husband?"

"He's dead," she told him, not being sure of the Moslem attitude toward divorce.

"How long ago did he die?" he wanted to hear. Now she began to improvise wildly. He had been killed in the War, leaving her with three children. (She did know that they approved of a woman's bearing as many children as possible.) This was not well received, either; he obviously thought she should be with them, and not consorting with a strange man. "This is a holy place, you know," he informed her; his words were a reproach and a warning. "*Ah, oui, je sais,*" she agreed feebly.

The music and dancing went on; it must go on without a break for at least twenty-four hours, Stenham had told her. Occasionally the singing in one circle or another would disintegrate for a time into a series of savage rhythmical cries, vomited from a hundred throats at the same split second, with a simultaneity which gave the sound an extraordinary solidity.

She sat listening to the senseless noise rather in the way one looks down into a tank full of crocodiles, her principal emotion one of thankfulness at being where she was, at not having accompanied Stenham to the food-stands, which were in the center of a constant throng. To her it seemed that he had been gone for well over an hour; she could not understand how buying a little food could take so long. In the tent nearest to where she and the silent Mohammed sat, the flames were unusually bright, women were laughing behind its slightly waving walls, and outside, a few paces higher up the hill, a tethered horse stamped its hoof on the earth. The astringent smoke from the numberless fires of thuya branches curled lazily upward, sometimes sweeping suddenly back down and making a flat screen above the hillside as a breeze gave chase to it. Then the screen would move out over the furthest fires into the deserted countryside and be dissipated, and again the casual spirals would form. Each turban, donkey, and olive branch was needle-clear in the powerful moonlight. (If she had had a newspaper she could have read it easily, she was certain—even the fine print.) The moonlight was hard; it gave the impression of having converted all the elements of the landscape into one substance, not blue, not black, not green, not white, but a new color whose thousand gradations partook of the essences of all those colors. And everywhere in this world made soft by the hard light from above, the fires burned, looking redder than fire should look.

Out of the shadows beside her Stenham appeared, startling her. A second later Amar was there behind him. "Did you get anything?" she asked.

"I did. Two dozen skewers of lamb. Shish kebab. Amar's got the whole lot. Sorry to be so long. The crush was terrific."

They sat eating, the two Moroccans at one end of the log and the two Americans at the other. The meat had a peculiar flavor, not spicy but herbal. "We can't drink the water," Stenham said, "so we'll have to go down and have tea afterward in one of the cafés."

She was surprised that there should be cafés here, but her mouth was full and she said nothing. Presently, "It seems I ought by all rights to be your wife," she told him, laughing.

"Mohammed thinks it's indecent of me to be here, an unattached woman."

"It is," he agreed. "Very indecent. If you're unattached, it can only mean you're potentially attached to anyone and everyone. You shouldn't have told him."

"I don't think it would have helped much not to. Amar certainly knows we're not married."

"Oh, Amar! He's different."

She reached for another skewer. "I can feel that, but I don't quite know where the difference lies."

"It's everywhere, everywhere," Stenham said absently.

"And anyway," she pursued, making her voice jovial again, "I believe you already have a wife in some part of this world, haven't you?"

"*Yes*, I have a wife." He laughed shortly. "What part of this world she's in, though, I couldn't tell you. Last I heard she was in Brazil. But that was quite a while ago."

"If I were your wife and I heard you talk about me in that offhand manner, I think I'd kill you. Assuming, of course, that I were and you did. If and if."

"My dear Lee," he said with mock courtesy, "those two ifs are mutually exclusive. But in the case of my true wife—I was almost going to say her name aloud and risk seeing Sidi Bou Chta vanish in a puff of smoke—she knows damned well how I talk about her, and I hear that when she mentions me it's a lot worse. There's no love lost, I can tell you."

"I don't know whether to sympathize with you or with her. What's she like? Not that a description coming from you would—"

He cut her short, rather rudely, she thought, saying: "There are two more skewers. You want one? The two kids have eaten sixteen between them. I've counted."

"No, I don't. I'm finished."

"Well, then, if you'll excuse me, I'm going to eat both of them. I had no lunch. And then let's go down and have our tea and see something. The whole thing is magnificent."

"Good," she said, rising and making a silent resolution to be amenable here; even if it proved terribly difficult, it would be more satisfying in the end than finding objections at every

turn. She wanted to take the maximum of remembered tro-
phies back to Paris with her, and she knew herself well
enough to realize that her shell of recalcitrance, if she in-
dulged herself to the point of donning it, would impede her
receptivity.

When they had stumbled down the hill over stones and
bushes that lay hidden in the shadow of olive leaves, they
stopped for a while on the fringe of the nearest ring of spectators, and gradually wedged their way in toward a position
from which they could see the dancing. Well over a hundred
men participated, all of them in white *djellabas* and turbans,
chanting breathlessly as they heaved and dipped. Their movements were rather like those of horses, she decided. Sometimes they pawed the earth with a certain spiritedness and
nobility; then they went back to being work-horses, straining
to pull their invisible loads as they all bent in one direction
and then in another. "How strange," she said to Stenham, because it was like nothing she had ever seen or imagined. She
could not see his face, but he pushed her toward the fore, saying nothing, and stationed Amar on her left and Mohammed
on her right, he standing directly behind her. This solicitousness annoyed her: it made her feel like a piece of property
being guarded against thieves, and, which was worse, she
suspected it to be a maneuver, very probably unconscious,
aimed at influencing her reactions to what she was seeing—an
attempt, as it were, to establish a sort of mesmeric control.
And, in any case, there was an extremely tall man directly in
front of her. She moved ahead, the men politely yielded and
allowed her to step into the front ranks facing the circle of
dancers. Now she was able to see that the circle was really an
ellipse; at one end of the enclosed space was a huge bonfire
whose flames shot up to the height of her face, and at the
other was a smaller ring of a dozen or so seated men playing
drums. "It's quite a show," she said to herself contentedly,
and she became interested in the pattern of the dance. From
time to time she looked back to be sure Stenham and the
boys were there. Once Amar waved to her, his face beaming
with delight.

It was not long before she became aware that something
absurd had begun to happen inside her. It was a little as

though she were living her life ahead of time. It had started, she thought, while she was sitting up there with Mohammed. Observing the phenomenon from the outside, she came to the conclusion that it might be because no one had ever before made her feel quite so unwanted. She had seen herself back in Fez in the horrible little Hôtel des Ambassades, separating her valises from those of Stenham, alone in a cab riding to the station (as if there were trains running now, she thought with a sudden wry grimace). She was in the train with the new issue of *Time* and a copy of the Paris *Herald* on her lap; she was on the Algeciras ferry watching the gray, lumpy mountains of the African coast slowly fade into the distance; she was eating shrimps under an awning in a waterfront café, being brushed against by the newsboys passing among the tables; she was sitting with the Stuarts at Horcher's in Madrid with the treasure of her Moroccan trip stored away in her memory, a treasure which would seem the richer for being kept hidden, with only a piquant detail divulged here and there—just enough to suggest the solid mass beneath the surface. "I have so many things to tell you, but I don't know where to begin. My mind is so disorderly." "Don't be silly, Polly. I've never known anyone with a clearer mind, or such a gift for telling experiences."

The insistent drums were an unwelcome reminder of the existence of another world, wholly autonomous, with its own necessities and patterns. The message they were beating out, over and over, was for her; it was saying, not precisely that she did not exist but rather that it did not matter whether she existed or not, that her presence was of no consequence to the rest of the cosmos. It was a sensation that suddenly paralyzed her with dread. There had never been any question of her "mattering"; it went without saying that she mattered, because she was important to herself. But what was the part of her to which she mattered?

She pulled out a cigarette and lighted it with impatient gestures. Unreasonably enough, she felt that she had already seen whatever the festival might have to offer. If one man went into a trance and beat his breast and tore out handfuls of hair during his seizure, as was now happening in front of her, it was the same as if a score of men were to do it, one after the other or all together. There could be no progression: she refused to slip into the hypnotic design. If all the members of this particular circle of leaping figures became possessed, took out their souls and threw them onto the pile in the middle (they were doing it; she knew it) so that there was only one undifferentiable writhing mass in there and no one was sure of getting his own back when it was finished, and, moreover, no one cared, then she had seen that, too, and she did not need to go on to another group to see the same thing done again, this time to a slightly different drum rhythm and with the addition of oboes and occasional gunfire. But Stenham was succumbing, she was positive of that; certainly he never had intended any resistance. He was going to let his enthusiasm for the *idea* of the thing carry him off into a realm whose atmosphere was too thin for rationality to exist in it, and where consequently everything could be confused with everything else—a state of false ecstasy, false because self-induced. That was why she would have none of it, she insisted to herself; she wanted no counterfeit emotions.

The glare of fire before her face, the long white robes catching its redness in their folds as the men crouched and leapt, and the darkness pressing in from left and right! But it was not darkness, since darkness has no breath and hands. "Mr. Stenham," she called, looking back past the bearded faces, the tightly wound turbans, the shining black eyes, and mouths stretched (in a monkey-like, frozen smile that had nothing to do with smiling) to reveal the rows of white teeth ("wild animals"), heads tilted upward to see over other heads, and panic began to pour in upon her from all sides. "Mr. Stenham!" She was with her back to the fire now, her eyes running over the rows of fascinated faces, looking desperately for the lighter face. "Nonsense," she said aloud, horrified that the panic had been able to get in so easily. It simply wasn't possible, she knew herself too well. But there were her knees, feeling like paper tubes. She turned around and called his name again into the uproar, like a pebble being tossed against an onrushing locomotive. And then she caught sight of him for a flash, between two cavorting figures as they gyrated. He had moved all the way around to the other side of the circle. Rage exploded in her; she could feel its heat just beneath the skin of her throat and cheeks and forehead. But now at least she knew where he was, and she turned and pushed her way toward the outer edges until she was free to walk normally. It was dark here after the fire's glare, and she bumped blindly into several astonished strollers before she regained her vision.

"Well, that was an unpleasant experience," she thought, to help her to believe it was over. When she had worked her way around to what she thought was the place where she had seen Stenham, she had to look for rather a long time before she located him. Then she took up a position behind him and concentrated on regaining complete command of herself. To do this she tried to get back into the stream of fantasy in which she had been swimming a while ago, but it was no good—the sober brown interior of Horcher's would not come alive. It might as well have been the Hanging Gardens of Babylon she was striving to evoke. The act of walking had partly calmed her, and rather than risk losing the solace of even that meager control, she decided to speak to him now. She called his name as loud as she dared, and, miraculously, he heard and turned. Now she smiled, put on as natural an expression as she could muster. He came slowly back toward her, pushing his way past the transfixed onlookers. "It's better from this side," he remarked. "Yes," she said, then after waiting what she thought was a normal interval, she suggested they go and have their tea. "Ah, of course!" he cried. "Amar! Mohammed!" he called. They appeared from different sides, and together the four wandered away from the light, into the dark.

The café consisted of several strips of matting placed on uneven ground, fenced in by bunches of green branches wired together. Long stakes had been driven into the earth at arbitrary points and blankets suspended by their corners from them, but in a completely haphazard fashion. Near the entrance, behind a little counter of rocks, the *qaouaji* and his assistants crouched; the remainder of the space was fairly well filled with seated and reclining men. Even beside the center pole the draped ceiling was not high enough to stand up under; they had to advance with their heads bent far forward.

Once they were installed on the mat and had been given glasses of tea, she said to Stenham: "You know, I thought I'd lost you for a while."

"Oh, no," he said lightly. "I had my eye on you. I knew just where you were."

"Oh, you did!" She wanted to ask him why he had gone around to the other side and left her alone, but she suspected she could not go into the subject without losing her temper.

"Anyway, this'll be our headquarters, this café," he went on. "We can always find each other back here. When we want to sleep, they'll clear out the people from this whole end, and we'll have it to ourselves. The *qaouaji* seems all right."

When they had drunk the tea, Stenham suggested they go out again. Amar and Mohammed had already risen and were standing outside the entrance.

"Why don't you go, and I'll stay here and rest," she said. "Come back in a half hour or so and maybe I'll feel like going out with you again. I'm a little tired." What she meant was: "Stay here with me awhile," and she thought surely he would interpret her words thus.

"But how can you stay alone?" he exclaimed. "I don't like to leave you here all by yourself."

"Why not?" she demanded sourly. "At least I can't get lost in here."

"I'll be back in a few minutes." His voice sounded uncertain. "Shall I order you another tea before I go?"

"No, thanks. I'll order one if I want it."

He glanced at her oddly. "Well, so long." Then he stooped and said a few words to the *qaouaji*. When he had gone out, she counted to ten slowly, then sprang up, ramming her head against the blankets above, which she had forgotten. Quickly she stepped across the café and out through the opening, turning in the opposite direction to the one Stenham had taken. The wind had come up stronger. She looked back for a second, to fix the place in her mind; the shape of the olive tree above the café was unmistakable. Then, in a turmoil of rage and self-pity, she strode ahead up the hill, at first oblivious and afterward indifferent to the men who gazed at her.

The women in the tents were cooking the evening *tajine*; the smell of the hot olive oil mingled with the wood smoke. She kept on climbing, telling herself that she should have expected all this to happen, that it was her own fault for having come, since she had known from the start that he was a selfish clod. Her initial reaction had been the correct one. "I won't go," she had said, and then her anger with the French had blunted the edge of her common sense.

Up here the tents were sparsely strewn among the trees, and ahead there was only the empty countryside. The sound of the drums still came up from below, but it was mixed with the hissing of the olive leaves in the rising wind. Some distance away a native dog barked; the high sound was like the hysterical laughter of a woman. When she had gone beyond the last tent and its light was no longer visible, she stopped, a little sobered by the solitude, and stood leaning against a low-swung bough. The wind's force increased by the minute. She was out of breath, and she would have liked to sit down, but memories of scorpion and snake stories she had heard kept her standing, and she remained as she was, breathing hard of the pure air that came rushing across the hillside toward her. It was a strange wind, she decided; it blew as if it were determined not to allow itself to abate for a single second. It was not like a wind at all, but like the breeze from a monstrous stationary fan, or like a huge draught steadily increasing in force. The noise it made in the trees was like the ocean now, or like the sound of an approaching storm. Instinctively she looked up into the sky: the calm, coldly burning moon stood above, and no cloud existed. But that was what it was; the noise like the sea out there on the mountain was a windstorm that had not yet arrived, a crazy nocturnal gale on its way. She listened for a trace of the festivities behind her and could hear none. Still, she knew she had only to go over the hummock beyond that fat-trunked tree to see the flickering pink walls of the last tent.

When the full force of the wind struck, she flung out her arms and let it push her against the tree, and she breathed deeply of it until she was giddy and would have had to sit down had she not been pinioned there by it. It had an amazing smell, like the smell of life itself, she thought; but after a moment it reminded her of sun-baked rocks and secret places in the forest. Then it grew very strong indeed, and she decided she would have to go back. A few more breaths, she said, filling her lungs completely with it, breathing out, and in.

Her head swam. Cataracts of wind rushed down the polished channels they had gouged across the sky, spilling out against the mountainside. Dust and dry bits of plants dancing upward in spirals smote her face. Carefully she sat down on the ground and leaned against the tree. Now she felt momentarily ill, but much happier. The wind roared; something touched her shoulder. She looked up, catching her breath, frightened for one instant, relieved for the next, and vexed immediately afterward. It was Stenham, standing over her, saying nothing, about to crouch down beside her. She made a great effort and got to her feet.

"Hello," she said, feeling like a guilty child, but only because he would not say anything. Now he did speak. "What's the idea?" His voice was angry.

"What idea?" she asked, and spat out the dust that had blown into her mouth.

He seized her arm. "Come on," he said, trying to pull her along.

"Stop. Wait." She was not ready to leave the hilltop.

"How'd you get way up here?"

"I walked. Would you mind letting go of me?"

"Not at all. That's quite all right with me."

"Do you have to be insulting, too?"

"What's the matter with you?" He took her arm again, impatiently.

"Please. I can walk perfectly well. Let *go* of me!"

"Oh, well, God damn it, *fall* down, then, if that's what you want."

It was like a command: she stumbled against a rock, tried to go on, and sank to the ground. He stooped, was beside her, trying to comfort her, being ineffectual, saying: "Where does it hurt?" and "I'm terribly sorry" and "I feel as though it were my fault," at which she made a silent gesture of denial, although he probably did not interpret it as such. "Do you think you can walk?" he inquired. She said nothing; all she wanted to do was push against the pain. If she relaxed the pressure an instant she would burst into tears, and that could not happen, must not happen. But after he had grown used to her muteness, sitting back helplessly to watch her, he came nearer again and put his arm around her, caressed her shoulder tentatively. It was not what she wanted. She shivered, and moaned inaudibly once. Then he tried to draw her to him, both of them squatting there in that ludicrous position.

At all costs this must be stopped, she told herself, even at the risk of having him see her weep, which she felt would certainly happen if she moved or spoke. And anyway, she thought, as she felt his hands moving softly along her flesh (as if she were a tree and they were the tendrils of a creeping parasitic plant), what sort of man was it who would take such a blatantly unfair advantage? With this pain how could she be expected to defend herself against his unjust tactics? The tears began to flow; it had required only that last reflection to loose them. She sobbed, and with all her might tore his hands away.

She was free, but now she was in the grip of her tears, and the shame of having him see her this way, even in the moonlight and with the vast wind sweeping by, increased them. Hatred for him welled up within her; if she had had the strength she would have hurled herself upon him and tried to kill him. But she did not move, doubled up there on the earth, pressing and rubbing her ankle as she wept. "What a *fool* you are! What a *fool* you are!" she heard her own voice repeating inside her head, and she did not know whether she was saying that to him or to herself. He had risen, and remained aloof now, looking down at her. After a long time, she slowly got to her feet, and with his help (it made no difference, now that she hated him) limped painfully all the way back down to the café.

And then she sat there in the smoke and dimness, with the hubbub of voices and music around her, and began to live the next hours of her own bland hell. Stenham sat near by, breaking his silence only now and then to say a few words to the two boys, both of whom looked exceedingly glum and sullen. Once she found herself thinking: Thank God nothing happened up there, and was furious that she should have such a thought; there had been no question of it. But she could not look at Stenham. She passed the time massaging her ankle and smoking furiously, not planning the details of her vengeance, but reinforcing her determination to have it, one way or another. About midnight, when the pain had subsided somewhat and she was beginning to feel exhausted and a little sleepy, perhaps because of the pall of kif smoke that lay in the tent, he turned and said to her: "The wind has died down." She did not answer for a moment; then she said: "Yes." That was all. Then he began to talk seriously and at great length in Arabic with the boys. Once again, a good deal later, he spoke to her, his voice enthusiastic, almost tremulous, as if he had for the moment completely forgotten that a state of hostility existed between them. "This boy sees an untainted world," he exclaimed. "Do you realize that?" Her mumbled reply apparently was inaudible to him. "What'd you say?" he asked.

"I said I couldn't say," she replied, raising her voice. She did not know whether the world that Amar saw was still in a pristine state or far advanced in decay; she suspected it was the latter, but in either case, the speculation was one of distinctly minor interest to her at the moment. Her mind was occupied with thoughts of herself and her mistreatment; because she felt she had been humiliated, she also believed that Stenham must be triumphant, must imagine he had gained some perverse sort of victory over her. For the time being she saw her whole Moroccan adventure as a ghastly fiasco, and she herself as having failed in some mysterious but profound manner.

In the first place, she argued, getting back to inessentials, which were the only things she could manipulate in her present state, her first meeting with him should have persuaded her that he was not a man she could ever want to know, for he was not physically attractive to her. Of that she had been aware in a flash. She could tell immediately what was for her and what was not, and Stenham had straightway fallen into the latter category: he had failed the test. (The test consisted of imagining a man lying in bed asleep in the morning; if the thought of his inert form sprawled out there among the sheets in their disorder could be entertained without revulsion, then she knew there was a possibility, otherwise he simply was not for her.) The test had always worked, and she had always sidestepped getting to know too well those who had failed to pass it, precisely in order to avoid just such circumstances as these. But her weakness and carelessness this time by no means excused a jot of his behavior, nor, when the moment of reckoning came, would she even consider her own shortcomings.

She dozed, awoke, dropped off again, returned to hear always the same eternal conversation: Stenham, Amar and the other boy, whose voice came in only now and then, like a *compère*, with the chorus of tea-drinkers and kif-smokers in the background. Tomorrow would be unbearable from all points of view; she contemplated its confusion and endlessness with dread. But she would escape in the first bus or truck that moved out of Sidi Bou Chta, even if it meant spending a day, two days, in the filthy little room at the Hôtel des Ambassades.

Again, a long time afterward, she awoke to find all three of them gone. "So much the better," she thought grimly. The chaos of drums and shouting still went on, with added vigor, if anything, and guns were being fired into the sky at short intervals. In an hour or two it would be light; the dawn of the Aïd el Kebir would have broken, and the already sharpened knife-blades would be thoughtfully thumbed once again in anticipation of the mid-morning hour of sacrifice.

CHAPTER 28

They sprawled on the matting, Stenham, Amar and Mohammed, involved in a discussion which had been going on for at least two hours. As far as Stenham was concerned, its subject was religion, and Amar seemed content to let it remain on that plane. Mohammed, however, felt constantly impelled to give it a political direction; indeed, one would have said he was incapable of keeping the two things separate. Religion to him was a purely social institution, and the details of its practice were a matter of governmental interest. Stenham was irked by the boy's thick-headedness; he wondered why Amar had wanted to bring him along.

Most of the men who were not asleep had by now gone out to pray and to be present when the dawn came. A few still engaged in aimless conversation; the rest slept. Lying on this ground, thought Stenham, was like being astride a starved horse: no matter what position he took, he could not make himself comfortable. There seemed to be rocks everywhere under the smooth mat. Lee at last lay unmoving. For a long time she had been in a half-sleep, turning repeatedly from one side to the other. The two boys had been upset when she had come limping in, leaning on Stenham's arm, but she had looked at them with such animosity that their expressions of sympathy had died on their lips. As the time had passed and she had refused to address even a word to any of them, Amar had remarked to Stenham that the lady was unhappy. "Of course. She's in pain," Stenham told him. "No, I mean she's always unhappy. She's always going to be unhappy in her head, that lady." "Why?" Stenham had asked, amused. "Do you know why?" "Of course I know why," Amar had replied confidently. "It's because she doesn't know anything about the world."

This had seemed a pointless enough reply, and Stenham had let the subject drop. But during this long discussion, which had provided him with his first true opportunity for going even a little below the top of Amar's mind, he had been struck again and again by the boy's unerring judgment in separating primary factors from subsidiary ones. It was a faculty which had nothing to do with mental alertness, but derived its strength rather from an unusually powerful and smoothly functioning set of moral convictions. To have come upon this natural wisdom in an adult would have been extraordinary enough, but in an individual who was little more than a child, and illiterate as well, it was incredible. He sat watching the changes of expression on Amar's countenance as he spoke, and began to feel a little like the prospector for gold who in spite of his own prolonged lack of hope suddenly finds himself face to face with the first nugget. And he marveled at the mysterious way in which the pieces of the world were tied together, that it should have been a purely sentimental detail like a dragonfly struggling in a pool of water, a thing exterior to any conceivable interpretation of Moslem dogma, which had made it possible for him to suspect, even unconsciously, the presence of hidden riches.

When a silence arrived, he said to Amar: "So the lady knows nothing about the world? What makes you think that?"

"*Hada echouf.* You can see she wants to be something

powerful in the world. She thinks she can, but that's because she's never surrendered."

"Surrendered? What do you mean?"

"Of course. What is the first duty of everyone in the world? To surrender. *Al Islam! Al Islam!*" He thrust his arms forward (the mud of the Medina was still on his sleeves from his encounter with the police) and bent his head downward in the beginning of a gesture of prostration. Then, continuing, he sketched a series of imaginary instances where the persons involved had or had not submitted to divine authority. In each illustration the accursed person—that is, the unhappy one—saw himself as a being of importance, whereas the blessed and joyous ones had understood that they were nothing at all, that whatever strength they were able to wield existed only in direct proportion to the degree of their obedience to the inexorable laws of Allah.

To be happy, cease striving and admit you are powerless. Islam, the religion of surrender. It had never occurred to Stenham that the word "Islam" actually meant "surrender." "I see," he said aloud.

"Every man you see in the street thinks his life is important," pursued Amar, warming to his subject, for his own life still seemed terribly important to him, "and he doesn't want it to stop. But Allah has decreed that each one must lose his life. *O allèche?* Why? To convince men that life isn't worth anything. No man's life is worth anything. It's like the wind." He blew his breath into the air and made a single clutching motion with his outstretched hand.

"Now, wait," said Stenham. "You say—"

But Amar would not wait. "Why are we in the world?" he demanded.

Stenham smiled. "I'm afraid I can't answer that."

"You don't know why?" asked Amar sadly.

"No."

Mohammed yawned ostentatiously. "I'll tell you," he volunteered. "To talk all night long, while real men are being shot."

Stenham would have said that a shadow of pain flickered across Amar's face, but in an instant it was gone, and he continued. "We're in the world for only one reason, and that's to act out what was written for us. The man whose destiny is bad, he's lucky, because all he has to do is give thanks. But the man whose destiny is good— Ay! That's much harder, because unless he is a very very good man he'll begin to think he had something to do with his good luck. Don't you understand?"

"Yes, but perhaps he *did* have something to do with it." (In such arguments Stenham often found himself unexpectedly extolling the bourgeois virtues.) "If he was good himself, and worked hard—"

"Never!" cried Amar, his eyes blazing. "You're a Nazarene, a Christian. That's why you talk that way. If you were a Moslem and said such things, you'd be killed or struck blind here, this minute. Christians have good hearts, but they don't know anything. They think they can change what has been written. They're afraid to die because they don't understand what death is for. And if you're afraid to die, then you don't know what life is for. How can you live?"

"I don't know, I don't know, I don't know," Stenham droned amiably. "And I don't think I ever will know."

"And the day you do know you'll come to me and tell me you want to be a Moslem, and we shall all have a great festival for you, because a Nazarene who has become a Moslem is worth more to Allah than a Moslem who was always a Moslem."

Stenham sighed. "Thank you," he said. He always thanked them when this point had been reached, for it was a proof of friendship when someone broached the subject of conversion. "I hope some day all that may happen."

"*Incha'Allah.*"

"Let's go out and watch the dancing," suggested Stenham, who suddenly felt like cutting the conversation short. It would be a good way, since the noise of the drums and chanting was so loud that talking became an impossibility once one had pushed one's way into a circle. The two boys jumped up and slipped into their sandals. Stenham rose, stretched, and glancing quickly at Lee to be sure she was still asleep, took his shoes in his hand and tiptoed over to the opening in the tent. "*Nimchi o nji,* I'll be back," he told the *qaouaji.*

It was the coldest hour of the night. The moon had gone

behind the mountain that lay to the west, but a part of the
sky there was still bright, and the more distant parts of the
countryside continued to bathe in its radiance. The two boys
stamped their feet and kicked up their heels in the steps of an
improvised dance; this took them along the ground more
quickly than Stenham could walk. When they had got ahead
some distance he saw Mohammed glance swiftly back, and
then put his hand on Amar's shoulder and say a few words
into his ear. He watched Amar to see his reaction, but as far
as he could tell there was none. However, he did reply briefly.
When they reached a more crowded crosspath they stood still
and waited for Stenham to come abreast of them. He turned
his face toward the eastern sky, hunting for a sign of daybreak,
but it was not yet due.

"What are they up to?" he wondered with a faint uneasiness. He could not believe that Amar would take part in any
sort of craftiness directed at him, but of course Mohammed
was an unknown quantity, probably a typical *harami* of Fez,
and he did not know the extent of his influence over the
other.

It was as if the night, in her death agony, were making a
final, desperate effort to assert herself by creating as much
darkness as she could. The fires and flares in most of the circles had died, and the sound of the drums coming out of the
gloom seemed much louder. Down here in the crease between the two hills, the chill in the air was intense; those who
walked had the hoods of their *djellabas* up, so that the principal thoroughfare looked like a dim procession of monks. The
smoldering fires gave forth much more smoke than when they
had been blazing; one heard constant coughing.

Several smaller circles had formed since he had last come
this way. It was difficult to tell what was going on in their
midst, or why people crowded in to watch. In one a woman
stood perfectly still, her long hair almost completely covering
her, making a faint and rhythmical moaning sound; occasionally she seemed to shiver imperceptibly, but Stenham could
not be sure. In another, there was an old Negro leaning far
forward, his chest propped against a stake that had been driv-
en into the ground. Beside him lay an earthen pot of coals
from which rose a sluggish smoke with a foul stench. "What

is it?" asked Stenham in a scandalized whisper. "*Fasoukh*. Very good," Amar told him. "If you wear that in your shoe, even though there's something buried at the entrance of a house or a café, you're safe." "But why do they burn it?" he insisted. "This is a bad hour," said Amar.

He looked at the old man, and found him vaguely obscene. "What's he doing?" he whispered. "He's trying to remember," Amar whispered back. The man's eyelids were half open, but his pupils had rolled quite out of sight, and from time to time his ancient, soft lips moved very slightly to form a word which never came out; instead, a bubble of saliva would slowly form and break. In the front row of spectators, seated, was another very black man wearing a jacket and skull-cap entirely sewn with white cowrie-shells. The sounds that came from the flat drum he was languidly beating were his only interest; he listened with complete attention, his eyes closed, his head to one side. "*Nimchiou*," Stenham muttered, eager to escape the fantastic odor of the smudge rising from the pot of coals. There was a sweet aromatic gum in the substance, but there was also a greasy smell as of burning hair; it was the mixture that was offensive. Even when they had gone well out of its range, the membrane of his throat and nose seemed still coated with the viscid fumes. He spat ferociously. "You don't like *fasoukh*," said Amar accusingly. "That means you're in the power of an evil spirit. No! By Allah!" he cried, as Stenham protested laughingly. "I swear that's what it means." "All right," said Stenham. "A *djinn* lives in me."

They had come upon another small circle. Here two girls spun silently round and round, their heads and shoulders entirely hidden by pieces of cloth which had been laid over them. No grace was in their movements, no music accompanied them. One would have said that two children had taken it into their heads to see how many times they could turn before they dropped, and that the people had gathered to watch out of sheer inanition. "What is this?" Stenham inquired. "*Zouamel*," said Amar softly. So they were not girls at all; they were merely dressed as girls.

They turned to go back to the flatter part of the valley where the large groups were gathered. The exhibits had left Stenham with a faint nausea. The combination of meaning-

lessness and ugliness bothered him. There had been something definitely repulsive about those little rings of unmoving
people. It was not the long-haired woman herself, nor yet the
old Negro, and certainly it was not the spectators; the mindless watching of a thing which he felt should have been going
on in the strictest privacy, that was what was upsetting. The
world had suddenly seemed very small, cold, and still.

Amar raised his arm and pointed. "The day's coming," he
said. Stenham could see no light in the sky, but Amar was insistent that it was there. They edged into what looked like the
largest of all the circles. In the center, by the light of what
remained of a fire, stood a woman all in white, singing. And
the chorus of men surrounded her, their arms interlocked, answering at the end of each strophe with a cry like a great gush
of water, but one which ended miraculously each time in the
same long channel of accurate musical sound, that led to the
first note of her next strophe. At this moment it seemed always that they were about to rush in upon her and crush her.
Lowering their heads, they would push forward like charging
bulls, take three long steps, so that the circle, receding inward
from the spectators, became very small; then, while the
woman slowly turned like a stately object on a revolving
pedestal, they would catch themselves up and pull backward
and outward. The very repetitiousness and violence of the
dance gave it a hieratic character. The woman's song, however, could have been a signal called by one mountain way-
farer to another on a distant hill. In certain long notes which
lay outside the passage of time because the rhythm was suspended, there was the immeasurable melancholy of mountain
twilights. Telling himself it was a beautiful song, he decided
to stand still and let it work upon him whatever spell it could.
With this music it was senseless to say, because the same thing
happened over and over within a piece, that once you knew
what was coming next you did not need to listen to the end.
Unless you listened to it all, there was no way of knowing
what effect it was going to have on you. It might take ten
minutes or it might take an hour, but any judgment you
passed on the music before it came to its end was likely to be
erroneous. And so he stood there, his mind occupied with
uncommon, half-formed thoughts. At moments the music

made it possible for him to look directly into the center of himself and see the black spot there which was the eternal; at least, that was the way he diagnosed the sensation. *Cogito, ergo sum* is nonsense. I think *in spite* of being, and I *am* in spite of thinking.

The dark died slowly, fighting to remain, and the light came, at first gray and hideous, and then suddenly, once the sky existed, beautiful and new, and people began surreptitiously to look at one another, to see who had been standing next to them, and the lone woman in the middle became a real woman, but somehow less real for being more than a mask made red by the fire's light. And as all these things came about, and the sum of the drumming grew less urgent (because so many of the drummers, suddenly realizing that something had changed, and it was daylight now, had ceased pounding on their drums), a strange new sound rose up on all sides to meet the dawn. It was like cockcrow, but it was the voices of the thousands of sheep roundabout, inside the tents, calling to each other, greeting the day on which they were to die for the glory of Allah.

The piece had finished, although there was never any clear-cut end, because the drumming always went on in a desultory fashion through the interlude, until a new piece had begun and had swept it along with it, back into the stream. The woman quietly stepped through the circle of men and disappeared. Stenham glanced at Amar, looked away, and then looked again carefully. There was no doubt about it: tears had wet his cheeks. Out of the corner of his eye he watched the boy become conscious of his surroundings, rub his face with his sleeve, harden his expression, turn a quick hostile glance at Mohammed to reassure himself that the other had not noticed his weakness, and then spit loudly on the ground behind him.

Inwardly Stenham sighed. Even here there existed the unspoken agreement that to be touched by beauty was shameful; one must fight to keep oneself beyond its reach. Nothing was really what he had imagined it to be. In the beginning the Moroccans had been for him an objective force, unrelieved and monolithic. All of them put together made a *thing*, an element both less and more than human; but any one of them alone existed only in so far as he was an anonymous part or a recognizable symbol of that indivisible and undifferentiable total. They were something almost as basic as the sun or the wind, subject to no moods or impulses started by the mirror of the intellect. They did not know they were there; they merely were there, at one with existence. Nothing could be the result of one individual's desire, since one was the equivalent of another. Whatever they were and whatever came about was what they all desired. But now, perhaps as a result of having seen this boy, he found himself beginning to doubt the correctness of his whole theoretical edifice.

It was not that what Amar said was different from what so many others had said before him. Probably it was that he said it with such a degree of certainty, and had been so unaffected by the presence of the other culture, rational and deadly, at his side. Stenham had always taken it for granted that the dichotomy of belief and behavior was the cornerstone of the Moslem world. It was too deep to be called hypocrisy; it was merely custom. They said one thing and they did something else. They affirmed their adherence to Islam in formulated phrases, but they behaved as though they believed, and actually did believe, something quite different. Still, the unchanging profession of faith was there, and to him it was this eternal contradiction which made them Moslems. But Amar's relationship to his religion was far more robust: he believed it possible to practice literally what the Koran enjoined him to profess. He kept the precepts constantly in his hand, and applied them on every occasion, at every moment. The fact that such a person as Amar could be produced by this society rather upset Stenham's calculations. For Stenham, the exception invalidated the rule instead of proving it: if there were one Amar, there could be others. Then the Moroccans were not the known quantity he had thought they were, inexorably conditioned by the pressure of their own rigid society; his entire construction was false in consequence, because it was too simple and did not make allowances for individual variations. But in that case the Moroccans were much like anyone else, and very little of value would be lost in the destruction of their present culture, because its design would be worth less than the sum of the individuals who composed it—the same as in any Western country. That, however, he could not allow himself even to consider; it required too much effort to go on from there, and he had not slept at all during the night.

Now he had to go back and face Lee. If I know her at all, he thought, she'll still be angry. She was not the sort to wake up in the morning having decided to forget the night before. "*Yallah!*" he said roughly, and the two boys followed him. On the way back to the café he turned to see if they were in his wake, and again he found Mohammed engaged in surreptitious conversation with Amar; its conspiratorial nature was confirmed when they saw Stenham looking back at them and quickly drew apart. He stopped walking, to wait for them to catch up with him. Mohammed immediately slowed his pace, obviously in the hope he would go on, but he stood still and waited. Amar came first; his face wore a determined expression. Before Stenham had an opportunity to speak, he said: "M'sieu! Mohammed and I want to go back to Fez."

Stenham was both relieved that Amar should have spoken out, and troubled by his request. "Oh," he said. "That's what you've been whispering about together all night."

"*Sa'a, sa'a.* Once in a while. Mohammed says the French let everyone come here so it would be easier for them to kill the ones who stayed behind."

Mohammed, guessing the subject of their dialogue, loitered even more shamelessly.

"I thought you had some brains," Stenham told Amar disgustedly. "How many people do you think have come here from Fez? Probably about fifty. How are the others going to get out of the Medina and come here when it's all closed and the soldiers are at every gate? Tell me that."

Amar did not reply. At last Mohammed had arrived within speaking distance.

"What's this about going to Fez? Why do you want to go?"

Assuming an aggrieved air, Mohammed enumerated a list of utterly unconvincing arguments for their being in Fez that day, rather than here in the mountains. At first Stenham had intended to reply to each point, demolishing them one by one, but as the number and absurdity of Mohammed's reasons increased, he despaired, and then grew angry. "Just tell me one thing," he finally demanded. "Why did you come?"

This question presented no difficulties to Mohammed. "My friend asked me." He pointed at Amar.

"You can go back again if you want to. It has nothing to do with me."

"The bus ticket." He looked reproachfully at Amar.

"None of it has anything to do with me. I'm not going to buy your bus ticket. I invited you both here, and you're here. I haven't invited you back to Fez yet. When I do, I'll buy your bus tickets. But it won't be today. You're lucky to be here out of trouble. If you had any heads, you'd both know that." As he spoke he watched Amar, whose changing countenance convinced him that he was voicing what were more or less Amar's opinions, and that it was only Mohammed who was bored and wanted to get back to the city. Mohammed was a troublemaker; there was no doubt of it. But it was out of the question that he should be sent back alone: he would not have gone without Amar, nor would Amar have allowed him to go by himself. The shame attached to such behavior would be overwhelming. If Amar had invited Mohammed to Sidi Bou Chta, Mohammed was Amar's guest, and Amar was responsible for his well-being and contentment while he was there. Now Mohammed wanted to go to Fez, therefore Amar must take him to Fez.

"If Amar wants to buy your bus ticket, that's all right." But Amar looked woebegone upon hearing this. Now I'm in the act of becoming the wicked Nazarene, Stenham thought. They always have to have one around, and I might as well be it. He began to walk again.

In the café Lee was sitting up, smoking, and looking even more dour than he had expected. "Good morning," he said jovially. "Good morning," she said quickly, like a machine, and without glancing at him.

A wave of rage swept over him; he wanted to say, with the same pleasant heartiness: "How's the martyr this morning?" but of course he said nothing. The two boys came in, removed their sandals, and sat down, still muttering to each other. Then Amar remembered Lee and looked toward her, saying: "*Bon jour, madame*," and Mohammed followed suit. Her acknowledgment of their greeting was slightly more cordial.

Most of the men in the café were the same ones who had been there the night before, but there were also two or three new faces among them, noticeable because they were obviously from the city. Having nothing else to do, he watched them, comparing their city gestures and postures with the noble bearing of the country folk. Decadence, decadence, he said to himself. They've lost everything and gained nothing. The French had merely daubed on the finishing touches at the end of a process which had begun five hundred years ago, at least. Their intuitive moral desires coincided with the ideals embodied in the formulas of their religion, yet they could live in accordance neither with those deepest impulses nor with the precepts of the religion, because society came in between with all the pressure of its tradition. No one could afford to be honest or generous or merciful because every one of them distrusted all the others; often they had more confidence in a Christian they were meeting for the first time than in a Moslem they had known for years.

Now, that foxy-looking one there in seedy European clothes, he thought, with the thick lips and the heavy fuzz on his cheeks and the boil on his neck, talking so secretively to the enormous mountain man with his silver-handled dagger stuck in its scabbard at his hip—what could a miserable young purveyor of the *souks* like that have of interest to tell a man who looked like a benevolent king? Something of vital concern, to judge from the way in which the man presently reacted, for his eyes gradually opened very wide, as an expression of consternation spread across his face. The younger one sat with narrowed eyes, rubbing his hand over his unshaven chin, and leaned even closer, whispering urgently.

Seized with a sudden suspicion, Stenham rose and left the tent. At random he chose another café a little further down the hill, went in, and ordered a glass of tea, disregarding the glances of suspicion that were leveled at him. Such glances were an old story and he was used to them. This café differed very little from the other, save that it was somewhat larger, and had a second room, more symbolic than actual, the division being marked by a length of matting tacked onto some upright poles. In the larger space where he had seated himself very little seemed to be going on: the men smoked their kif pipes and sipped their tea. Soon he rose and entered the second room, where he chose a corner and sat down to wait for his tea. Here again were the same peculiar and unexpected circumstances, only more strikingly presented than in the other café, in that here the city youth, this one wearing glasses, was speaking to six important-looking rustics, instead of only one. It was difficult for him to feign nonchalance in the face of the sudden silence and the frankly hostile glares that followed his entry into this little chamber. He decided to play the innocent tourist, in search of atmosphere; not that they would recognize the part he was playing, but it was the only way he could be sure of being able to carry it off. He smiled fatuously at them all, and said: "Good morning. *Bong jour. Avez-vous kif? Kif foumer bong.*" I hope I haven't overdone it, he thought. Two of the men had begun to smile; the others looked confused. The city man sneered, said contemptuously: "*Non, monsieur, on n'a pas de kif.*" Then he turned and said to the mountain men: "How did that foreign pig find his way to Sidi Bou Chta? Even here, and on the Aïd, we have to look at these sons of dogs." One of the men smiled philosophically, remarking that last year there had been three Frenchmen at the Moussem of Moulay Idriss, and they had taken photographs. "This one's not even French," the young man told him disgustedly. "He's some other kind of filth from England or Switzerland." Again he let his gaze of hatred play over Stenham's face for a moment; then he turned away with an air of finality and resumed his monologue, but now in a very low voice which kept Stenham from hearing all but an occasional isolated word or phrase. However, the young man, forgetting, soon raised his voice a shade, and this difference made it possible for Stenham to hear most of the words. When the tea came he drank it as quickly as he could without the risk of attracting attention to himself, then, bidding a clumsy good-bye to the men in the room, he went outside once more. There was no possible way of believing that one or two stray young men from Fez had come up and happened to be telling friends of the recent turn of events there, but he wanted the pleasure of knowing, instead of merely entertaining a suspicion. He determined to try a half dozen more cafés, to see on how large a scale the campaign was being waged. In the event anyone asked him what he was doing, he would pretend to be looking for Amar. And so, one after the other, he stopped and went in, glancing about in a preoccupied manner, and retiring after scanning the faces of the occupants.

Only in one did the *qaouaji* ask him what he wanted. The man's voice was unpleasant, and he did not give himself the time to look with care. In one other he could not be sure: the type he had singled out was not well enough defined. But in the other four there was not the least doubt. The Istiqlal had sent an entire committee up here to make contact with the *cheikhs*, *caïds* and other notables, and attempt to dissuade them from carrying out the sacrifice. Furthermore, they were spreading the story, very likely true in its general outlines, that the girls and women of the Medina in Fez were being systematically raped by the tens of thousands of native soldiers the French had turned loose inside the city. Houses and shops were being looted, great numbers of men and boys had been shot, and fires had started all over the city. That much he had heard in the second café while he waited for his tea, and the expressions on the faces of the listeners in the other places had been identical in each case.

He stood in the hot morning sun, hearing the chorus of bleating sheep all around him, and because he was tired and hungry, had a little imaginary conversation inside himself. Well, now are you satisfied, or do you have to see another ten cafés? No, there's no need. And now that you know, what are you going to do about it? Nothing. I just wanted to know. You thought there was a place that might still be pure. Are you satisfied?

But he did not want to go back to the café and see the two boys, and be forced to feel that he was standing in judgment before them. For, absurd as it might sound, it was inevitable that he should feel a certain guilt when he thought of the disparity between their childish hopes and his own, which were scarcely to be formulated because they were purely negative. He did not want the French to keep Morocco, nor did he want to see the Nationalists take it. He could not choose sides because the part of his consciousness which dealt with the choosing of sides had long ago been paralyzed by having chosen that which was designed to suspend all possibility of choice. And that was perhaps fortunate, he told himself, because it enabled him to remain at a distance from both evils, and thus to keep in mind the fact of the evil.

He stopped at the food stalls and got himself half a disk of bread and some skewers of lamb. Then, eating as he went, he set out for the hill that lay behind the eminence where the sanctuary was built. There was a constant coming and going of people on their way down from and up to the shrine, but the route they used was to his left, and his path, made by goats most likely, was unfrequented. For the only permanent building in the region was the little *marabout* which had been constructed around the tomb of Sidi Bou Chta himself. When there was no pilgrimage, no one happened by but individuals who had come to fulfill their vows, plus whatever shepherd chanced to stray within the precinct with his goats.

From the very top he looked down upon the whole bright panorama, the barren ochre earth to the south, the rows of mountain ranges to the north, and in front of him to the west the wooded gray-green slopes with the open spaces, where the thousands of tiny white figures were. Whatever movement these last made was so dwarfed from this height that they seemed frozen and stationary objects in the landscape; it was only if he watched carefully for a while that he could convince himself that they were actually moving about. Here in the joyous morning sun he felt very remote, and he wondered vaguely if it might not be better to witness the sacrifice from here—see it while not seeing it. The Istiqlal agents could never succeed in preventing all the people from killing their sheep; that was not their purpose, in any case. They would manage just well enough to see that the elements of confusion, uncertainty and suspicion were injected into the proceedings, in such a way as to divide the people among themselves and ruin any sense of satisfaction which could have resulted from a well-performed ritual. This sort of destruction had to be carefully planned, and then allowed to work by itself. If the young men were clever, the people would go away from Sidi Bou Chta this year in a disgruntled mood, and many of them would fail to come back next year. One break, one year without the ritual, and the chain was sundered; the young men knew that. Any kind of change in their rhythm disorientated the people, because their lives were entirely a matter of rhythmic repetition, and failure to observe a prescribed ritual brought its own terrible psychological consequences, for then the people felt they were no longer in Allah's grace, and if they felt that, very little mattered to them—they would do whatever was suggested to them. He wondered if all the young Istiqlal agents had come up in one bus. If they had, he thought, what a blessing it would have been for it to have plunged off the road over a cliff on its way up! The people would have carried out the directions of Allah with rejoicing, and happiness during the coming year would have been assured for the countryside roundabout. A little sentence he had once read came into his head: *Happy is the man who believes he is happy.* Yes, he thought, and more accursed than the murderer is the man who works to destroy that belief. It was the unhappy little busybodies who were the scourge of mankind, the pestilence on the face of the earth. "You dare sit there and tell me they're happy," Lee had said to him, the self-righteous glow in her eyes. Surely the intellectuals who had made the French Revolution had had the same expression, like the hideous young men of the Istiqlal, like the inhuman functionaries of the Communist Party the world over.

In the mouth of any but the most profound man the words: "All men are created equal" were an abomination, a clear invitation to destroy the hierarchies of Nature. But even his closest friends, when he suggested this to them as one of the reasons why the world became worse each successive year, smiled and said: "You know, John, you should be careful. One of these days you're going to grow into a real crank." The lie had been too firmly planted in their minds for them to be able to question it. Besides, he had no compulsion to save the world, he told himself, lying back to see only the sky. He merely wanted to save himself. That was more than enough work for one lifetime.

The morning wind had come up from the east behind him; it carried off the faint thumps of the drums down there, so that he heard only the light whistling sound it made in the thorn bushes as it passed. He fell gradually into a mindless reverie, a vegetative state in which the balance between the heat of the sun and the cool of the wind on his skin became his entire consciousness. His last clear thought was that there would be many more mornings somewhere on the earth for him to lie thus, spread out under the sky, considering these meaningless problems.

CHAPTER 29

For a long time Polly Burroughs had been banging along the rough roadbed of her dreams, vaguely aware that something was wrong, but without the power to know that she was only desperately uncomfortable, her body twisted there in one tortured position after another, all of them dictated by the bumpy contours of the matting beneath her. And little by little, painfully, through a world of dust and Arabic words, her mind began to climb up from the place where it lay. Eventually a loud burst of laughter from the *qaouaji's* corner roused her, and she sat up suddenly, feeling as though every muscle in her body were about to snap in two. A few boys looked at her with curiosity; she refrained from stretching, which was what she desired more than anything. Foregoing that voluptuous pleasure made her sorry for herself; it would have been so satisfying. However, she did push forth her arms, wriggling her fingers, and yawn discreetly, and even this was agreeable enough to remind her that she had scored a victory.

It was almost like a dream now, that short interval between two sleeps when she had been so wide awake. The boy had come into the tent with his friend, had had the audacity to wake her, and in her anger she had seen him in his true light, clearly. Clearly, that is to say, in that for the first time she had understood just what he signified to Stenham. (What the boy meant to himself she did not assume the possibility of knowing, nor was she interested.) She sat there, momentarily incapacitated by fury, and stared at him. A boy with smooth, weather-tanned skin, huge eyes and black hair, and with the basic assurance of a man but not by any means the manner of one. A complete young barbarian, she thought, the antithesis of that for which she could have admiration. Looking at him she felt she knew what the people of antiquity had been like. Thirty centuries or more were effaced, and there he was, the alert and predatory sub-human, further from what she believed man should be like than the naked savage, because the savage was tractable, while this creature, wearing the armor of his own rigid barbaric culture, consciously defied progress. And that was what Stenham saw, too; to him the boy was a perfect symbol of human backwardness, and excited his praise precisely because he was "pure": there was no room in his personality for anything that mankind had not already fully developed long ago. To him he was a consolation, a living proof that today's triumph was not yet total; he personified Stenham's infantile hope that time might still be halted and man sent back to his origins.

The other youth crouched near by, gnawing on a stick, surveying her with a calm and detached air of amusement.

"What is it?" she said evenly to Amar, quite forgetting that he could not understand her.

"He wants to say good-bye to you," the other explained.

(He's not going to get away that easily, her mind remarked, but by "he" she meant Stenham.)

"*Mohammed*," she said, "*tu ne veux pas faire quelque chose pour moi?*"

He sat up straight.

"I wonder if you'd go down and buy me a pack of Casa Sport?"

She opened her handbag and took out some change. He was on his feet, his head bending forward so it would not rub against the blanket above. He took the money and went out. She waited half a minute to be sure he had really gone. Then she turned to Amar and without hesitation handed him all the banknotes that were in her purse. They were neatly folded.

"Of course, he doesn't understand anything," she thought, as she saw his eyes become even larger, opening wide at the sight of the money in his hand. And even as she started to sketch the gestures of explanation he was trying to give it back to her. "Boom," she whispered in his ear. "*Révolver, pistolet.*" She did not know whether he understood or not; she glanced around the tent. So far, no one was looking at them.

She directed his attention to her right hand in her lap, and carefully raising it to the level of her face, crooked her index finger and shut her left eye, sighting with the other along an imaginary barrel. Then she pulled the trigger and pointed swiftly to the bills he held.

"Thank God," she thought: he did understand. She could tell that by the new expression on his face. She frowned and looked worried, indicating that he must quickly hide the money. He slipped it into his pocket. All was well.

When Mohammed returned, she was lying back, her arms folded behind her head, staring vacantly upward. To be civil, she talked awhile with him, and then the two boys rose to take their leave. When Amar shook hands with her, she looked meaningfully at him, as if to warn him against displaying any sign of gratitude, and merely said: "*Bonne chance*," as she released his hand. They went out, and she lay back, wondering why she felt that she had accomplished a particularly difficult piece of work.

Suddenly she smiled ruefully. Until now, she had had the firm intention of returning to Fez in the first vehicle that moved out of Sidi Bou Chta. That way she would not have to see Stenham again, unless he happened to come back and catch her in the act of leaving. But now it occurred to her that she had not finished with him. It was absurd, but unthinkingly she had made seeing him again a necessity. She had no money, and it was not likely that any bus-driver could be persuaded to take her to the city for nothing, merely because she gave him the address of the little hotel where she had left her luggage. The situation was more than absurd, she told herself; it was abject. "What the hell could have been in my subconscious?" she asked herself with astonishment and indignation.

She sent the *qaouaji's* assistant out for some skewers of lamb, and paid for them with her last coins. Then, feeling tired again, she stretched out and promptly fell asleep.

All that had surely been several hours ago. Now she sat blinking, staring out through the flap of the tent at the trunks of the olive trees in the hot light of what must be mid-afternoon. She glanced at her watch. "Ten past three," she murmured with a qualm of uneasiness. The drums still continued; they had not stopped once since she had got out of the bus the night before.

And the faces in the tent were new; she did not recognize any of them. With relief she saw that the *qaouaji* had not changed. She beckoned him over and asked him if Stenham had returned and gone out again, but his French was so rudimentary that it took a good deal of gesturing to get him to say that he had not seen the Nazarene gentleman all day. She thanked him and began to feel a little apprehensive.

She lay back, thinking that maybe she could lose herself in sleep once again: it was such a convenient way of making time pass. But there seemed to be no possibility of it, and she realized that she wanted to go outside and walk about. Her muscles ached, she felt nervous; to lie still any longer would be agony.

The dry, dust-laden air smelled of the horses and donkeys that stood among the tents, and the sun shining on the millions of tiny silvery olive leaves made her long for a drink of cool water. Down below, half-hidden by the curtain of white dust they were raising as they stamped, the dancers still moved mechanically, and the watchers still crowded around them. She turned and climbed upward in the direction of the open country.

It was easy to walk up here in the sunlight, and it had been so difficult in the dark. She went much further than she had gone the night before, until the trees had all been left behind and there were only wiry, stunted bushes and great rocks. She felt better: the muscular pains were nearly gone now, and the pure air had washed away her uneasiness. She leaned against a big boulder, first scrutinizing it for scorpions, and looked across the valley at the hill opposite. A tiny, lone figure was making its way slowly downward across the curved tawny expanse of countryside. A shepherd? She strained her eyes to sight the goats or sheep, but there were none.

She watched it awhile, and all at once she decided that it was Stenham: no Moroccan would wander so far alone. She stood a long time staring across the valley as the figure came lower and lower, finally leaving the sunlight and entering into the shadow thrown by the heights behind her. She could not be certain that it was actually Stenham, nor, she told herself, did she care in the least, but still, she was almost sure it was he, and she felt a pang of eagerness at the prospect of breaking her triumphant news, of announcing to him the manner and extent of his defeat. She took her time in going back down to the café, dallying where she wished, stopping to snap off the leaves from plants, sometimes leaping from rock to rock, and, when she got within sight of the outer tents, even sitting down to smoke a cigarette.

When she reached the café, she looked in and found he had not yet returned. She decided to walk among the trees to a place from which she could see the entrance, so that when he went in he would not find her; that would give her an immediate moral advantage. Over toward the left she went, through the wood smoke and dust, and stood like a conspirator, leaning against a tree, watching around its trunk for his arrival. People came out of the tents and stared at her with surprise and distrust, but not, as far as she could tell, with hostility. It seemed to her that he was very long in coming; he must have stopped to watch the dancing. But suddenly she saw him trudging up the hill toward the café. When he had gone in, she began to walk.

This morning she had been surly and uncommunicative, and she felt she must go on with it, take it up where she had left off. At the same time, such behavior did not suit her present purpose. She entered the tent.

He was sitting in the corner, looking rather glum, she thought. When he saw her his face brightened.

"Hello," she said without expression. "I was outside."

"How are you?" he asked, looking up at her, and then he moved over so she could sit down.

"All right," she said noncommittally; too obvious a show of truculence might stifle the conversation altogether. He held out a pack of cigarettes to her; she shook her head.

"I was afraid you might have gone," he said uncertainly.

"I intended to. But I was so sleepy. Besides," she added, as if it were an afterthought, "I haven't a penny. You'll have to lend me some money, I'm afraid. I gave all mine to Amar to buy a pistol with."

"You did what?" he said, as if she had been speaking a language he scarcely understood.

"I simply gave him all the money in my purse, and told him to go and buy a gun. And the important thing is, he took it. What he does with it's immaterial." She was about to add: "So there's your purity," but then suddenly she was no longer sure of the extent of her own intelligence. Everything she had said sounded absurd; she had done it all wrong. She closed her mouth and waited.

He had passed his hand over his eyes as though to shield them from too bright a light, and now he held it there loosely. There was no decipherable expression on his face. When he finally spoke, he said slowly: "Let me get this straight." Then he continued to sit without speaking. Finally his hand came down, and looking away from her, he said: "I don't think I understand, Lee. It's too complicated for me."

"Don't be silly," she said gaily. "You're just *making* it complicated. If you had even a grain of poetry in you, you'd understand. The boy wanted action. At his age he has to have it. This is the crucial point of his whole life. He'd never have forgiven himself later if he'd sat around moping now. Can't you see that?"

Stenham looked at her, but not as though he were listening to her. The mask of preoccupation he wore contrasted strangely with his violence in suddenly crying: "Leave all that!" Now he turned to face her. "I'm not thinking of him. He's gone. One little life, another little life. What's the difference?" (She studied his face briefly, and found that she was unable to tell whether this last was irony or whether he was speaking sincerely. Now he seemed to be waiting for her to answer, but she said nothing.) "What I don't understand is you." He stopped, hesitated. "As a matter of fact, I do understand it. I just want to hear you say it in your own words. What did you think you were doing? What in the name of God would make you decide to do a thing like that?"

She was disappointed: where was the rage? "It's *something* to make a person happy," she began tentatively.

"Agh!" His voice was harsh. "There's a four-letter word for that. You guess which one and tell me. It'd mean more coming from your lips. You could give it its money's worth."

She had been lighting a cigarette to cover her nervousness, and she had discovered that her hand was trembling. Of course, she told herself, he would show his anger in this icy, abstract fashion. She had been foolish to expect a normal, simple quarrel.

"Your venom isn't really insulting, you know," she told him. "It has no focus. If you want to be really nasty, at least you've got to be conscious of the other person."

At this point she thought he was going to say: "I'm sorry," but he merely looked at her.

"I believe in what I did," she went on. "There's no reason—"

"I know," he interrupted. "That's the tragic part of it. You have no sense of moral responsibility. As long as you get your vicarious thrill you're fine. This time you had two thrills. The little one was Amar and the big one was me."

She laughed uncomfortably. "It could be. I haven't an analytical mind."

He glanced toward the entrance of the tent. The light outside was fading, the drums still went on, and the café was being slowly filled by older men who talked quietly.

"What does it feel like to have the power of life or death over another human being?" he asked her suddenly. "Can you describe it?" And because he looked truly angry now for the first time, she felt her heart leap up and light a corresponding flame within her.

"It must be exhausting to see everything in terms of cheap melodrama," she said with feigned solicitousness. "I wonder you have the vitality."

Now he said the four-letter word he had not said a few minutes earlier, got to his feet, and stalked out of the tent. She sat on, smoking, but she did not feel calm.

Almost immediately he came back in, clearly having been debating with himself outside the entrance; his expression was determined, a little embarrassed, and he was shaking his head. He walked over to her. "God damn it," he said, sitting down again beside her, "why do we have to act like two six-year-olds? I'm sorry if I've behaved badly." He waited for her to speak.

She could feel herself growing more nervous by the second. "If you mean just now—" she began. Then she stopped; she had been going to refer to his behavior last night, but she was quiet an instant.

"Oh, it doesn't matter," she heard herself saying with a vast, incomprehensible relief, as if this were solving everything.

He was looking at her with great seriousness. "After all, we got on all right with our differences of opinion before we saddled ourselves with that kid. I don't know why we shouldn't be able to pick up where we left off. Nothing's changed, has it?"

"That's true," she said thoughtfully. But in her mind she was aware that something *had* changed, and because she did not know what had made this difference or in what it consisted, she postponed complete agreement with his thesis until some later time. Then she said, with a sudden vehemence which made him look at her curiously: "I don't know. I don't think the boy had that much to do with it. I think it's this place that's got us down. I know if I have to sleep here again tonight, I'll go into a decline, that's all. Can't you find *some* way out of here?"

She had spoken without thinking, and now she expected resistance. But all he said was: "It won't be easy. And don't forget, we came up here so as not to be in Fez today. It's still the big day."

"I haven't forgotten," she protested. "They can come and murder me in my bed, but at least it'll be a *bed*, and not a pile of rocks." She patted the matting beside her, and glanced up quickly to catch his expression; did he understand, or was he merely disgusted with her? ("Nothing's changed," he had said an instant ago.) And now, when she saw his smile, she knew in a flash what had changed; she knew that even though she still thought that smile faintly fatuous, it did not repel her. With her gesture of hostility she had brought herself within his orbit. But it was not only she who had changed, for, otherwise, why was he smiling?

"We can't do more than try," he said, still smiling, and got up to go out.

Later, when the passage back was all arranged, and the truck would be leaving in an hour or so, and they had finished their evening meal of soup, bread, lamb and tea, they took a stroll, climbing to the top of the hill behind, to watch the panorama once again. "Back to the scene of the crime," she thought, feeling the pressure of Stenham's fingers on her arm as he guided her between the dim bushes, around the dark rocks, to a spot from which the valley of flame, smoke and moonlight was entirely visible. Up there they sat quietly, and when he drew her to him, implanting a kiss first on her forehead, then on each cheek, and finally (so beautifully), on her lips, she knew it was decided, and she realized with some surprise that however eagerly he might be looking forward to the intimacies of love, she herself hoped for that moment with no less impatience.

She stretched out her hand, wonderingly touched first the hard stubble on his chin, and then the smoothness of his lips, and thinking: "Why now, and not before?" pulled him to her again.

CHAPTER 30

The convoy of buses sped around the curves, each one bathing in the dust raised by the one ahead. In the first vehicle sat all the young men from the Istiqlal, who had planned with the drivers of the other buses that as part of the strategy they would stop at a certain point on the road before they arrived back at the junction of the main highway, and rearrange the seating in such a way that when they drew near to Fez there would be two or three party members in each bus. They were also not to drive into the town all together, of course, but were to time the entry of each vehicle at alternate ten- and fifteen-minute intervals. From the first moment when he had heard the terrible news, Amar had begun to tremble; they must be halfway to Fez now, and he was still trembling. An image haunted his mind: he stood just inside the door of the large room in his house, seeing his mother pinned to the floor by the point of a bayonet, but struggling to rise, while a shadowy form engaged in the deflowering of Halima on the cushions in the corner. Doubtless his father and Mustapha lay dead outside in the courtyard, which explained the fact that they did not figure in the fantasy.

Mohammed sat beside him trying to make conversation, but Amar could not hear what he was saying. Surely this was the day of reckoning, the day of vengeance—perhaps his last day on earth! The other men in the bus sat stiff and grim, without speaking, some of them with their faces covered against the dust. Suddenly there was a loud report, above the clanking and rattling. Hands went to daggers as the bus slowed and stopped, but it was a punctured tire. Everyone got out and wandered up and down the road, while the other buses went by one by one, leaving storms of white dust in the air behind them. Ordinarily the men in the buses passing would have called and waved with glee, because it was always amusing to see one's friends suffer a slight misfortune, but today they scarcely looked out. Mohammed was disgusted. "The sons of whores!" he grumbled. "Suppose we need something to change the tire with. Who's going to give it to us? Nobody! They've all gone by."

Amar returned slowly from his scenes of carnage. He and Mohammed were sitting on a boulder looking down at the bus; he was surprised to find himself nibbling sunflower seeds. It seemed to him that Mohammed had been talking for hours, and he had heard scarcely a word. Now he was again on the subject of the money he thought Amar should have given him for the bicycle three days ago. When he had taken it back to the Frenchman, he had not been able to pay for its rental; with great luck he had managed to borrow enough from a friend who worked in the lumberyard down the street. But now it was the Aïd and the friend wanted to be repaid, and anyway, whose fault was it that they had gone to Aïn Malqa, and who had promised to pay for both the bicycles?

Amar had every intention of giving him the money, but he found Mohammed's insistence annoying, above all at this moment. "With everyone dying you're worried about a few francs," he said scornfully. The Nazarene lady had given him an enormous amount of money; how much, he did not know, because he had not yet had an instant's privacy in which to count it. At all events, now he was very rich, and the little he owed Mohammed did not trouble him. However, he thought it shameful on Mohammed's part to keep talking about it. Suddenly he turned his entire attention to what Mohammed was saying. "And the thirty rial I had to spend for medicine after you hit me, let them go; they don't matter." His apology had thus counted for nothing, or Mohammed would not be reminding him of their fight. What was the good of trying to make a friendship with a boy like this? "*Yah*, Mohammed," he said. "You don't trust me, but that's only because you think everybody's like you." He wanted very much to take out his money and hand over every franc he owed him, just to have done with it, but of course it was out of the question to let him see how much money he had. Mohammed turned a withering glance upon him, saying in disgust: "You have a head like an owl, or a scorpion, or a stone. I don't know what kind of a head you have." "*Majabekfia*," retorted Amar. "Don't worry about me." They sat a long time, perhaps an hour, without speaking, before the tire was finally changed and the bus ready to leave.

Now that theirs was the last bus, once they had started up, the driver felt impelled to go like the wind. They skirted the edges of the abyss at terrific speed, the brakes squealing as they rounded curves, the old motor roaring like a demon when they were not coasting. If Allah had not been with them, Amar thought, on several occasions the bus would surely have hurtled into space. When they approached the place where it had been agreed that they would all stop so that the Istiqlal men could spread out, there was nothing but the empty road. This seemed a bad omen; the men shook their heads and grumbled. For they wanted the learned young men to be with them when they arrived in the city. All the other buses had their quotas of them by now; only this one, through the stupidity of the driver (for they now held him responsible for the delay occasioned by the blowout), remained without its commanders. But as they came almost in sight of the paved road, a small truck loaded high with watermelons appeared around a curve, coming toward them, blowing its horn in an imperative manner; dark arms emerged from both sides and wigwagged furiously. The bus driver slowed, stopped, and everyone stared at the wild faces of the four men in the truck.

"Brother! Brother!" all four cried at once. "Don't go! They got them all! They killed them!" The four men jumped up and down on the seat, waved their arms and struck each other in their excitement, and the truck driver sketched a dramatic, sweeping semicircle to suggest a machine-gun firing. "By the railroad crossing!" At this news there were groans and curses in the bus, together with the uttering of the names of unfortunate relatives and friends who had left Sidi Bou Chta in the other buses. As the first explosion of frenzy died down and words began to be spoken in more nearly normal tones, it appeared that only a few men had actually been killed by gunfire, the others having been carted off to jail in military trucks; as each bus had arrived, its occupants had been transferred under guard to trucks manned by French soldiers, and had been driven away. The important thing now, if they wanted to get to the Ville Nouvelle, cried the four men, was to bypass the road where the trouble had occurred, take the Meknès road and double back, stopping at a point which they would indicate, having just come from there.

"It's a police trap," murmured Mohammed into Amar's ear; this was the first word to pass between them since the disagreement on the boulder. "Who knows? Maybe they're *chkama*. Maybe the others all got through."

Amar had studied the faces of the men in the truck, and he would have staked his entire future on the veracity of their story. "You're dizzy," he told Mohammed, reflecting at the same time that there was one so crafty that he distrusted everyone, which was almost as foolish as trusting everyone.

At all events, the bus driver seemed not to doubt the truth of their account. He waited while the truck backed and turned, and then he began to follow it at a distance of about fifty meters. This was a terrain closed in by steep slopes of bare earth; in the midday sun it had become a little inferno. When they got onto the highway the truck increased its speed, as did the bus, and so there was some breeze inside. The driver shouted to the men sitting silent behind him: "Pray! You're coming from Sidi Bou Chta!" This seemed an excellent idea. If they passed a police car at Bab el Guissa a pilgrims' prayer might possibly allay suspicion.

> *"Oua-a-l ach f'n nebbi,*
> *selliou alih.*
> *Oual'la-a-ah m'selli alih,*
> *karrasou'llah!"*

they chanted, as the bus sped along the flat highway across the bridge, frightening two white herons in the river below, and then started to wind its way upward through the tangles of cane-brake. This was scarcely the usual moment to invoke divine protection for the voyage, when everyone had returned safely from the pilgrimage, and the bus driver was fully aware of it; the cynicism of his suggestion resided in the fact that he also knew there were probably not more than two Frenchmen in all of Fez who would be aware of it, and neither of them was a policeman. The Moroccans could count on a certain degree of obtuseness in the observational powers of the French.

Since the servant always gains more knowledge of the master than the master can hope to gain of him, the Moroccans knew they could afford imprecisions without being detected, while the French had no such advantages; it was virtually impossible for them to deceive anyone. The Moroccans who had any contact at all with the French knew where their masters went, whom they saw, what they said, how they felt, what they ate, when and with whom they drank and slept, and why they did all these things, whereas the French had only the most sketchy, mechanical and inflexible understanding of the tastes, customs and daily life of the natives in whose land they lived. If an officer in the cavalry showed less skill than usual one day in mounting his horse, his orderly saw it, began to speculate as to the reason, and secretly spied on him. If a functionary were smoking a cigarette which was not one of his accustomed brand, the shoeshine boy noticed it and commented upon it to his colleagues. If the mistress of the house drank only one cup of *café au lait* when on other mornings she habitually drank two, the maid's curiosity was aroused, and she mentioned it to the scrubwoman and the laundress. The only way the French could preserve even the illusion of privacy was simply to pretend the natives did not exist, and this automatically gave the natives an enormous advantage. Thus it did not seem likely that the police would see anything strange in their chanting at this moment; on the contrary, it might give the bus an inoffensive air, for they had found that if they appeared to be occupied with religious matters, the French generally let them alone.

Where were they going and what did they intend to do when they got there? Not one of them could have answered the question, nor could the question have been posed; it would not have been in key with the prevailing temper, more suited to the chanting of prayers than to the elaboration of projects. They knew that if an angel were to appear suddenly in the sky above the fruit orchards they were passing, and were to give them the clear choice between renouncing their vows of vengeance and dying, they would gladly give up their lives then and there, rather than betray their brothers in Islam. But no angel came, and they were not far from the city walls.

Alone among all the passengers Amar was working out a plan of action: no one but he had a mother and sister in the Medina. The mountain men's vested interest in the holiness of the city provided them with excitement, but it was excitement of the sort that comes when many people make a common decision to defend a cause, and it awakened none of the desperate intelligence of the individual who finds himself in extremities. Mohammed's family had gone to Casablanca to pass the Aïd there with relatives, and he was staying with a married sister in Fez-Djedid outside the walls, which meant that not only was he free from worries about the possible fate of his mother and sisters at the hands of the partisans, but could come and go as he pleased. This explained, even if it did not excuse, his obvious lack of interest in Amar's predicament. All he wanted was his bicycle money, and that Amar intended to give him as soon as he had a minute to hide himself and count it out; he would hand it to him and say good-bye, for he wanted to get rid of him before he set to work.

They were approaching the big curve by Bab Jamaï, which brought the road up out of the orchards to within a few meters of the walls, and then swung it immediately away again, out onto the stony mountainside. Several hundred soldiers were there, moving about among the tents that had been hastily set up along the outside of the ramparts. But the pilgrims looked straight ahead, chanting with ferocity, and pounded the sides of the bus and the seats. On up the hill they went, their clear voices floating out over the empty cemeteries. When they got to the top, Amar could not keep from stealing a glance down at the Medina. No columns of smoke rose from its midst; it looked the same as every other day. The Nazarene gentleman had told him that the Istiqlal spread many lies. He knew that; everyone told lies. It was for the intelligent man to distinguish truth from lies, just as it was only the intelligent man who knew how to lie in a way that made it next to impossible for others to find his lies and identify them as such. As he looked at the Medina stretched out down there in the glaring sun, unchanged, it occurred to him to question the truth of what they had said, but only for an instant. If it were not yet true, it soon would be. His problem was to get home, if possible before it was too late, but in any case to get there.

The road now straightened out; the little truck ahead with its load of watermelons went faster. Again there were tents along the walls, between Casbah Cherarda and Bab Segma. The men from the mountains sang out into the surprised, slow faces of the Senegalese soldiers. No one halted the bus, and it sped ahead toward the west, along the Meknès road.

They stopped a few meters off the side road in a lane with high cane on either side. Quickly everyone got out. The four men of the truck were in a frenzy of anxiety. "Hurry! Hurry!" they cried, suddenly having exhausted the courage which had made it possible for them to go to the rescue of the lost bus. Without thinking, they had driven into the lane to show the way; now they were obliged to wait until the bus had backed out to the road, before they themselves could get out. "Quick!" And it was a bad moment when an old man fell flat on his face and had to be helped up, dusted off and set straight.

When Amar's feet touched the ground and he became aware of the familiar odor of the river, he felt all at once as though he had been away from home a very long time, and his sense of urgency redoubled. It was as if he had been asleep, and had awakened. His patience with the pilgrims was at an end; they were moving ineffectually around the bus in a dazed fashion because the chanting was over and their minds were still in it, but at any moment someone might come along the road and turn into the lane. "Come on," he said to Mohammed, and they started back to the road.

"But where are we going?" Mohammed wanted to know.

"I'm going to see a friend of mine, and I'm going alone."

"And my money?" cried Mohammed.

Amar was delighted. It was exactly the reaction he had been hoping for. This would make it easy to pay him off and dismiss him without ceremony. "*Ah, khlass!*" he said, making a show of disgust. "Your money! All you have in your head is your money." He was looking for a stretch of wall or cactus fence, something to go behind for a moment, and until he found it he would have to improvise a critical lecture on Mohammed's cupidity. Finally he caught sight of an abandoned hut ahead; when they had reached it, he said: "Wait a second." He could see that Mohammed was loath to let him out of his sight, for fear he would bolt without paying him, but he could scarcely follow him into the hut, where he was going ostensibly to relieve himself. There was daylight inside: long ago the roof had fallen. He pulled out his money and counted it. The Nazarene lady had been generous even beyond his expectations: there were eight thousand-franc and two five-hundred-franc notes. He looked down at them with love. "Mine," he thought, and then he corrected himself. "*Jiaou.* They came. It was written." It was for this that Allah had decreed the man should take him away from the café, feed him and protect him. True, there was another part to it somewhere, that had to do with friendship and the man's own understanding of him, but it was too difficult to reach with his mind now, and he did not insist upon it. He folded the money carefully and put it away again. Then he took two hundred francs out of the handkerchief in which his own money was tied and put it loose into his other pocket. When he came out, Mohammed was standing there, looking anxiously toward the door, as if he were afraid Amar might simply vanish. This was a mystery Amar had never been able to fathom. The rich were not ashamed to let it be seen that they cared about money. Where a man with only twenty rial in the world would as a matter of course use those twenty rial to pay for all the teas at the table, another with a thousand rial in his wallet, when the time came to leave the café, would begin to fumble inside his clothing and murmur aloud: "Let's see, there are six people at fifteen francs each, that's eighteen rial. I have only fifteen francs change, which is exactly my share. Each one had better pay his own." For the poor man such behavior was unthinkable: his shame would be so great he could

never face his friends again. But the rich gave it no importance. "That will all change when the French leave," Amar
was fond of thinking. The concept of independence was easily confused with that of social equity.

They walked along briskly, Amar apparently having forgotten the monologue he had been delivering. To Mohammed
this meant he had forgotten the money once more, and he
was rash enough to mention it. Amar stopped walking,
reached into his pocket, and pulled out the two hundred
francs. Without saying anything he put it into Mohammed's
hand. They took a few more steps. "Happy?" asked Amar
with what he considered delicate irony. Mohammed seemed
shamed into silence.

When they came to a dirt road leading off across the fields
to the south, Amar stood still again and said firmly: "I'll see
you some day soon. *B'slemah.*" Mohammed merely looked at
him. That was the world, Amar thought as he walked away.
He had been willing to make him his friend, and Mohammed
lacked the sense to realize it. He had even given him a second
chance, which Mohammed had likewise disregarded. It was
all really very fortunate, he reflected, for now he had complete freedom of movement, whereas Mohammed's presence
would surely have hampered him.

He looked back twice, just to be sure Mohammed had
really continued along the other road; the first time he was
still standing there, as if he were debating whether to follow
him and try to get more money, but the second time he had
already gone some distance down the road toward the city.

The fields were parched; only a dead yellow stubble covered
their cracked earth. But insects whirred and buzzed in the
weeds that edged the lane, and where there was a tree there
were birds. When a man was extremely thirsty the sound of a
bird singing was like a little stream of water trickling from the
sky. His father had told him that, but he could not see that the
birds were of any help now. Or perhaps they were; perhaps his
thirst would have been stronger without them.

An hour or so later he came upon the cut-off he had been
looking for—a path that led straight across the open plain between stiff-speared agaves, to the Aïn Malqa road. The distances were big out here; things looked near and small, but

they were always larger and further away than one thought. It was the golden hour of the afternoon where he reached the olive grove. This time no motorcycle appeared, and he arrived at the house without disturbing the fabric of cricket-songs through which he walked. For a moment he stood by the door doing nothing, reluctant to bang the knocker. But having come all the way here, he was unable to think of anything else to do, and so he lifted the iron ring and let it fall, twice. The sound was surprisingly loud, but immediately after it the calm was there again, unchanged. He listened intently for voices inside. The crickets were too loud.

He waited a long time. If no one answered, he was prepared to sit at some distance from the house in the bushes and go on waiting there, until Moulay Ali returned. From where he stood, he surveyed the overgrown garden, selecting and rejecting vantage points. There was a click behind him, and he wheeled about. The door was open just far enough to let a nose and mouth be seen in the aperture. "Mahmoud?" he asked hesitantly, his voice breaking on the second syllable, as it still did sometimes when he put insufficient force behind it. The name had come to him that instant, as he had said it. But whoever it was softly closed the door, and he was alone again. And now he waited even longer, but with the knowledge that at least someone was in, even though there was no more sound inside or out of the house than as if it had been a ruin. In the grove a bird called repeatedly, two clear notes, a silence, two clear notes.

CHAPTER 31

This time the door really opened, very quickly, and a tall man with a gray *tarbouche* and one white eye stood there, holding a large, bright revolver which was leveled straight at Amar's chest.

"Good afternoon," said the man, and on hearing the deep voice Amar remembered his name, too.

"*Yah, Lahcen, chkhbarek?* How are you?" he began, a little too familiarly, he realized, as the big man's expressionless face did not alter.

"Come in," Lahcen said, stepping aside, following Amar's movements with the gun. "I wonder if he thinks I'm afraid of that," Amar was asking himself. He heard Lahcen bolting the door as he started up the stairs. When they were up on the gallery they did not go into the large room where he had been before, but walked its battered length, the droning of bees above their heads, to a small door at the far end. "Open it," said Lahcen.

There were three steps leading down onto another gallery which ran at right angles with the first. This part of the house was even more dilapidated than the other: the floor tiles were almost all missing, the walls had partially crumbled and fallen, and some of the ceiling beams, rotted away at the outer edge, sagged so low that they had to bend their heads as they passed. Now Lahcen stepped ahead and opened a door on the right. It was dim inside; there was only one small window which had been covered over with a sheet of yellowed newspaper, and in the air was the still heat of a closed-up room in summer, the dry, blind smell of slowly accumulating dust. Lahcen shut the door and Amar heard his slightly labored breathing as he brushed past him.

Suddenly there was light. A door directly in front of Amar had opened. Moulay Ali stood there in a green silk dressing gown, his hand on the doorknob. Behind him was a flight of narrow wooden stairs leading up, or so it looked, to the sky.

"*El aidek mebrouk*. Holiday greetings," said Moulay Ali pleasantly, with no trace of irony. "Come up." He turned and mounted the stairs ahead of Amar, and Lahcen came behind him.

It was the sky that Amar had seen; the sky was all the way around the room, because the walls were made entirely of windows. Some were open and some were shut, and there in the dying sunlight were the mountains, the plain, the tops of the olive trees below, and on the front side only the roof of the house, which was built up higher than the room. Amar looked around delightedly, very much impressed. Moulay Ali watched him. The only furnishings were a large table and some heavy leather hassocks to sit on. The table was littered at one end with books, magazines and newspapers; at the other end there was a typewriter.

"Sit down. How do you like my workroom?"

"Never in the world have I seen such a room," Amar told him, glancing sideways toward Lahcen, who had sat leaning against the door, his revolver still in his hand. Moulay Ali noticed his wandering gaze and laughed.

"Lahcen's my bodyguard this afternoon. For once I think I have one I can trust." Lahcen grunted complacently. "The others all went singing their little songs to their friends."

"You mean to the police?" said Amar, scandalized.

Still Moulay Ali studied him, his head slightly to one side. He smiled. "No," he said calmly. "But they talked too much, and that's almost as bad. You see, I'm not here today. You think you see me, but I'm really in Rabat." Suddenly he changed the tone of his voice and said, somewhat menacingly, Amar thought: "But what's all this about the police? Why would anyone go to the police? Why did you say that? You'll have to explain that to me, I'm afraid. I don't understand."

The fresh twilight breeze was beginning to move across the plain from the mountains; it came through the open window and touched Amar's cheek. If Moulay Ali had really intended to play the game of innocence with him, he would not have told him what he had just told him about Rabat. "I don't know," he said simply. "I suppose the French would like to catch you. Wouldn't they like to catch everyone who works for freedom?"

Moulay Ali narrowed his eyes. "I think you're right," he said, gazing out across the countryside. "I think they would like to catch me. That's why it's not good to have people know where I live." He turned back and looked thoughtfully at Amar.

Amar was silent, wondering whether he should explain to him now why he had come, or wait a bit. So long as they spoke at cross purposes, he decided, with Moulay Ali wondering how much he knew, and he wondering what Moulay Ali was suspecting about him, it was hopeless. And he had an uncomfortable feeling that each minute which passed without the situation's being clarified held the danger of bringing forth some irreparable decision on Moulay Ali's part.

"I saw Benani," he said suddenly.

"I see," replied Moulay Ali; he seemed to be waiting for Amar to go on. (At least he had not said: "Who's Benani?")

After a pause, Moulay Ali said evenly: "Who else did you see?"

"I don't know their names, the ones who were with him."

"I'm not talking about them," Moulay Ali said quietly. "I know who they were. I meant who else have you seen since you were here three days ago?"

Only three days, thought Amar; it seemed a month. In the pink light that came from the setting sun a large round sore on Lahcen's leg looked as though it were full of fire. He sighed. This was going to be like Benani's grilling, all over again. "I saw my family, and Mohammed Lalami."

"Who?" said Moulay Ali sharply. Amar repeated the name. "Who's that?" he wanted to know. "A *derri* who lives in the Medina. The one who hit me in the nose the other day," he added brightly. "Who went to Aïn Malqa with me."

"Who else?" pursued Moulay Ali.

It simply did not occur to Amar to mention the two tourists; they and the time he had spent with them were part of another world far away, that had nothing to do with the world they were living in and discussing at the moment. "Well, I didn't see anybody else," he said.

"I see." All at once Moulay Ali's face became extremely unpleasant to look at. It twisted itself up into a knot and twitched, like a snake that is dying, and then for the fraction of an instant he seemed to be about to shed tears, but instead he took a deep breath and his eyes opened very wide, and Amar was frightened, because he realized that Moulay Ali was exceedingly angry. He exploded into a yell of rage, jumped to his feet, and began to talk very fast.

"Why haven't you any respect for me?" he shouted. "Respect! Respect! Just simple respect! Only a little respect would put enough sense into your donkey's head so you'd know you can't lie to me. Where'd you sleep last night?"

He towered above Amar, his body shaking slightly as he spoke. Instinctively Amar got to his feet and stood a little further away on the other side of the hassock.

"I didn't sleep at all," he said with an air of wounded dignity. "I was at Sidi Bou Chta watching the *fraja*."

Moulay Ali looked to the ceiling for support; the thought passed through Amar's head that the angrier he got, the less respect he inspired, because he became just like any other man. "The master of lies! Listen to him!" He turned and thrust his head forward at Amar. "Do you want to know where you slept?" he roared. "You slept at the *Commissariat de Police.* That's where you slept; I can tell you, since you've got such a bad memory." He reached out and yanked Amar roughly to him, felt in his pockets until he had found all his money; then he let go of him, and with the packet of bank-notes slapped his cheek smartly. It certainly did not hurt, but as an insult it was unbearable. Without any regard for the possible consequences Amar drew back and delivered a good blow with his fist to Moulay Ali's prominent chin. Lahcen was on his feet; the pistol was suddenly waving in front of Amar's face, and at that moment Moulay Ali dealt him a blow which sent him to the floor. Now he sprawled there, leaning obliquely against the hassock where he had been sitting, and rubbing his face automatically, but watching Lahcen.

Moulay Ali counted the money, threw it on the table. The handkerchief with Amar's own money in it he still held in his hand, winging it around and around.

"Nine thousand francs! I didn't know I was worth so much to them," he said with quiet sarcasm and a faint air of surprise.

Amar was beside himself. To be innocent and to be treated as though he were guilty, that was something he could not accept. This man was not his father; he owed him nothing. Lahcen could shoot if he wanted. It did not matter. "You mean you didn't know *I* was worth so much to them!" he cried.

Lahcen growled menacingly, but Moulay Ali pushed him back toward the door. "Sit down," he said. "I can manage this *ouild*. He's very interesting. I've never seen an animal quite like him." He began to walk back and forth, a few steps one way and a few the other.

"I've seen a lot of *chkama* in my life, practically nothing but *chkama*. Most of the *drari* like you end up by turning informer; that's not unusual," he added with a short laugh. "But I admit I've never yet seen one anything like you."

"Then look carefully," Amar retorted, nearly weeping with

emotion (what emotion he did not know); "because you'll never see another. A man like you who's used to blacksmiths doesn't meet spice-sellers. May Allah give you some brains. I swear I'm sorry for you."

Moulay Ali snorted, turned to Lahcen. "But listen to him!" he shouted, astounded. "Have you ever heard anything like that?" To Amar he said: "I think I can manage with the brains I have, without Allah's further help."

These last words were sheer blasphemy. Amar looked at Moulay Ali, turned his head away and spat ferociously. Then he turned back and spoke in a low, intense voice. "I came here happy in my head to see you, even though I know you're not a Moslem." Moulay Ali opened his mouth, closed it again. "I did have respect for you, much respect, because I thought you had a head and were working for the Moslems. But whatever you make for us will be a spiderweb, an *anka-butz*, and may God who forgives all hear my words, because it's the truth." He sobbed, and having done it that once, buried his face in the hassock and continued.

At one point Moulay Ali had ceased pacing the floor, to stand merely looking at Amar in fascination; now he resumed walking back and forth, perplexedly rubbing his chin. The sunset was over; the light in the room was swiftly fading. "Tell Mahmoud to bring a lamp," he said to Lahcen, who rose and handed him the revolver before he went out. Moulay Ali laid it quietly on the table beside the typewriter and stood watching Amar. He picked up the money and flicked it several times with his fingernails. Then, apparently having made a decision, he crossed to where Amar was, knelt, and touched his shoulder. Amar lifted his head, but turned away miserably and remained silent.

"When you feel like talking," Moulay Ali told him gently, "tell me the whole story."

Amar sighed deeply and shook his head. "What good will it do?" he murmured.

"That's for me to decide when I hear it," said Moulay Ali somewhat less gently. "I want to hear everything, everything you've done since you left my house."

Still sighing, Amar picked himself off the floor and sat again on the hassock. He described his trip back to the Ville Nouvelle, the storm, the bus ride, the fair, the sailor doll, and all the other details of that evening. Once or twice he heard Moulay Ali chuckle; this gave him a little incentive to continue. The part about his meeting with the two tourists seemed to interest his listener considerably; he asked a good many questions about them, but finally let the story get on to hearing Benani's voice behind him in the street when he was walking with the tourists and the police. At this point the door opened, and Mahmoud came in carrying a large oil lamp which he set on the table. He was about to go out again, but Moulay Ali stopped him.

The light of the lamp shone into Amar's face. "I think you want something to eat," said Moulay Ali, looking at him carefully. To Amar it seemed a long time ago that hunger, and even thirst, had existed in the world. And so if he said yes, it was only out of politeness toward his host.

Mahmoud shut the door behind him. "Go on," prompted Moulay Ali. "Did you know Benani thought you had been arrested, or didn't you?"

"Yes, I knew it," Amar answered, and he went on with his recital, too tired to choose between relevant and extraneous detail and thus including everything that came into his head—the carving on the beams in the tourist's room, the lady's loquaciousness, the mechanism of the flush toilet, the fat French waiter who, once the tourist was out of the room, would keep bringing him more food every two minutes and pinch his cheek while he ate it, how he had manged to persuade Mohammed Lalami to go with him to Sidi Bou Chta by telling him the Nazarene lady was eager for love and had slept with him the night before, and how Mohammed, once he was alone with her, had been so nervous that he had said all the wrong things. "And then we watched the Aïssaoua and the Haddaoua and the Jilala and the Hamacha and the Derqaoua and the Guennaoua and all that filth, because the Nazarene liked to see the dancing." He made a wry face at the memory. "It makes you sick to your stomach to look at it, all those people jumping up and down like monkeys."

"Yes," agreed Moulay Ali. "And then?"

"Then I heard what they were all saying about the partisans in the Medina, and I wanted to go home."

"So you came to me instead. Why? Did you think I could get you into the Medina?"

Amar admitted he had thought that, and Moulay Ali laughed, amused and a little flattered by his ingenuousness. "My friend," he told him, "if I could get you into the Medina I could make every Frenchman leave Morocco tomorrow morning. Go on."

But Amar seemed not to hear. The full import of what the other had said was only now reaching him; he looked into Moulay Ali's face desperately. It was useless to say: "My sister, my mother." There were thousands of sisters and mothers. But he said it anyway. Moulay Ali smiled sadly.

The tray that Mahmoud brought had bread and soup on it. "*Bismil'lah*," murmured Amar, and he began to chew a piece of bread mechanically. Moulay Ali, his bowl of soup tilted in front of his face, observed him carefully over its rim, saw hunger slowly fill the boy's consciousness as he tasted food. He said nothing until Mahmoud had returned with a second tray, this time with a large earthenware *tajine* of lamb, eggplant and noodles.

"Perhaps I can help you," he said finally. "I have a few contacts at different spots. I might be able to get news from your house."

Amar stared. The idea of finding out about his family without going home himself had not occurred to him.

"Would you like that?" said Moulay Ali. Amar did not answer. What good was hearing about his family if he could not be there to see them with his own eyes? And how could he believe whatever news came to him, good or bad? But he saw that Moulay Ali was doing his best, was trying to be helpful, and so he said: "I'd be very happy, Sidi."

"I'll see what I can do. Now tell me the rest."

There was not very much more to tell, said Amar. Mohammed and the lady had been talking in French about the fighting in the Medina. He had been too unhappy to listen to what they were saying. The lady had waited until Mohammed had stepped outside, and then she had called Amar over to her, opened her pocketbook and, making sure that no one was looking, put the folded bills into his hand. When he described the gestures she made to indicate an imaginary gun,

Moulay Ali interrupted, exclaiming delightedly: "Ah, a woman with a head!" And when he came to the episode of the buses and the carrying off to jail of all the mountain men, Moulay Ali, looking very grim, said: "Good! Good! The more the better." Amar was startled, because he had expected quite the opposite reaction from him. Perhaps his mystification showed in his face, for a moment later Moulay Ali elaborated. "When they get back to the mountains not one of them will be able to hear the word *France* without feeling his heart ready to burst with hatred." Amar thought a bit. "That's true," he agreed. "But some of them were killed."

"They died for freedom," said Moulay Ali shortly. "Remember that."

They did not speak for a moment. Through the open windows, along with the constantly increasing night wind, came the sound of a dog howling, from some distance away. Amar looked up, and saw in the shining glass panes distorted reflections of their movements against the blackness beyond. Mahmoud had brought a big bowl of sliced oranges prepared with strips of cinnamon bark and rose water. When they had finished Moulay Ali sat back, wiped his face with his napkin, and said: "Yes. They died for freedom. And that's why I'm not going to ask your pardon for being rough with you. It would be an insult to them. I was suspicious, and I was wrong, but I wasn't wrong to be suspicious. Do you understand? At first I thought: No, he couldn't have gone to the French, because if he had, he certainly wouldn't come back here."

"Ah, you see?" Amar said, pleased.

"But then I thought: Wait. They've used him as a guide, and sent him in alone, and they're outside waiting."

"Oh!" said Amar. He was thinking that now if by some terrible misfortune the French did manage to find Moulay Ali, he would be certain to suspect that Amar had had something to do with it; he decided to let Moulay Ali know what was in his mind.

"No, no, no," replied Moulay Ali consolingly. "They'd have been in the house long before this if they'd come with you. The day a Frenchman learns patience the camels will pray in the Karouine."

These reassuring words set off a whole series of mechanisms inside Amar which resulted almost immediately in an overpowering desire to close his eyes; he could feel his head being turned to stone, and his body being rapidly immured in the paralysis of sleep. Moulay Ali was talking, but he heard only the sound of his voice.

"Come, come," the voice said sharply. "You can't just fall asleep like that."

Moulay Ali had risen, and was standing above him. "Get up, and come with me," he said. With a flashlight in one hand he led him down the stairs through the hot little room, to the back gallery, where a man lying on a mat in front of the door grunted and sat up as Moulay Ali stepped over him, saying softly: "*Yah, Aziz.*" They picked their way along the uneven floor.

Another door was opened; the inquisitive beam of the flashlight played briefly around its walls. There was the mattress. "I think that will take you through to morning," said Moulay Ali. "*Incha'Allah,*" Amar replied. Then he thanked Moulay Ali with what sense and force he had left, and let himself drop onto the mattress. "*'Lah imsik bekhir,*" said Moulay Ali as he closed the door. The crickets were singing outside the window.

CHAPTER 32

There are mornings when, from the first ray of light seized upon by the eye, and the first simple sounds that get inside the head, the heart is convinced that it is existing in rhythm to a kind of unheard music, familiar but forgotten because long ago it was interrupted and only now has suddenly resumed playing. The silent melodies pass through the fabric of the consciousness like the wind through the meshes of a net, without moving it, but at the same time unmistakably there, all around it. For one who has never lived such a morning, its advent can be a paralyzing experience.

Amar awoke, heard the cackling of geese against a soft background of bird song, listened for a moment to the unfamiliar sounds about the house—the closing of a door,

words exchanged between servants and the noises they made
in their work—and without even bothering to open his eyes,
sank into a melancholy but comfortable state of nostalgia for
his childhood, that other lifetime finished so long ago at
Kherib Jerad. He remembered little events that he had not
thought of since the day they had happened, and one big
event: the time he had got into a fight with Smaïl, his only
friend among the boys of the place, who instead of hitting
him had all at once sunk his teeth in the back of Amar's
neck and refused to open his jaws until the men had come
and beaten him. He still had the marks of those sharp white
teeth; if the barber shaved his neck a little too high they
were visible. And that night a delegation of the elders of the
village had come with lanterns and torches to see his father,
to apologize, and, which was much more important to them,
to try and exact a word of forgiveness from Amar, for if
Amar refused, everything would go badly for them until they
brought an offering to the young Cherif who had been
wronged by one of their number. And Amar did refuse, being still in a good deal of pain, so that the next day they
came again with a beautiful white sheep which they gave his
father in order that their crops and homes might be spared
the displeasure of Allah. His father had been unhappy about
it. "Why wouldn't you forgive Smaïl?" he asked him. "I hate
him," Amar had replied heatedly, and there was no more to
be said about it.

He remembered the river and the coves between its high
clay banks where he had played; and the fine clothes he always
had worn on the bus trip to Kherib Jerad, for in those days
there had been money, and his mother had spent a great deal
of it keeping Amar in capes and trousers and vests and slippers
made for him by the best tailors and cobblers in Fez. He remembered, and he listened to the birds singing near by and
farther away, and it seemed to him that the sweet sadness he
felt would never stop as long as he lived, because it was he; he
had ceased being himself by having been cut off from his
home. Now he was no one, lying on a mattress nowhere, and
there was no reason to do anything more than simply continue to be that no one. Occasionally he slept for a moment,
dipping softly downward, so that the horizon of being dis-

appeared; then he came up again. It was like floating on a gentle ocean, following the will of the waves.

At one point, toward mid-morning, the door opened quietly and Moulay Ali looked in at him, on his way to his office in the tower, but it happened to be a moment when he slumbered; Moulay Ali shut the door and left him alone. Again when it was nearly noon he returned, and seeing him still lying there, decided to awaken him. Unceremoniously he shook him by the shoulder and told him it was very late; then he went and called Mahmoud, who came and led him, still more asleep than otherwise, to a room where there was a pail of cold water and a cake of soap. By the time he had washed thoroughly he was wide awake. When he re-emerged onto the gallery Mahmoud was just arriving with a huge copper tray which he set on its legs outside the bathroom door. "Eat here," said Mahmoud. "It's cooler."

While Amar was eating his breakfast Moulay Ali came along the gallery. He looked weary and unhappy. "Good morning. How did you awaken?" he inquired, and without waiting for a reply he walked on toward his office. At the door he turned and said: "I may have news for you later." Then Mahmoud came by to see if Amar had finished; since he had not, he stood looking down at him, watching him eat. "You can't go out of the house, you know," he told him suddenly. This information was not a surprise to Amar, nor did it interest him. There was nothing he wanted to do outside, in any case, no one to see, nowhere to go—only the olive trees, the hot sunlight and the cicadas shrilling. He was quite content to sit in the house and bask in the listlessness that the day had brought.

Apparently Mahmoud sensed the apathy in which he was submerged, for when he lifted the tray to carry it away he said: "Come," and led him to the big room where he had sat with the boys the other day. Now it was in even greater disorder, with newspapers lying open on the cushions, unemptied ashtrays here and there in the middle of the floor, and in a corner a small table holding a disemboweled radio, its parts spread out in confusion around its empty case. On one couch there were several copies of an Egyptian illustrated review. He sat down and began to thumb through them; in each one there were some pictures of Morocco. French policemen pointed to a long table laden with pistols and daggers, wounded Moslems were helped along a street by their countrymen, a child wandered in the ruins of a bombed-out building, five Moslems lay in the twisted postures of death in a Casablanca street, the traffic going by at only a step from their bodies, while a French soldier delicately indicated them for the photographer with the tip of his boot. It was hard to understand why these publications should be so strictly prohibited, when they had exactly the same photographs in them as the French magazines that were on sale outside the shops of the Ville Nouvelle. But then, was there any way of comprehending the laws made by the French, save to assume that they all had been made with the same express purpose, that of confusing, harassing, insulting and torturing the Moslems? On other pages there were pictures of Egyptian soldiers in smart uniforms driving tanks, inspecting machine guns, demonstrating to students the technique of throwing hand grenades, watching army maneuvers in the desert, and marching through the magnificent streets of Cairo in their khaki shorts. Everyone looked happy and healthy; the women and girls waved from the windows of the apartment houses. He turned back to the pictures of Morocco and studied them, taking a masochistic pleasure in remarking the contrast between the scenes of wreckage and death and the platoons of triumphant young soldiers.

He looked around the room; it seemed to him the very essence of the sadness and remoteness of Morocco. *Maghreb-al-Aqsa*, that was the name of his country—the Farthest West. Exactly, the extremity, the limit of Islam, beyond which there was nothing but the empty sea. Those who lived in Morocco could only look on with wistfulness and envy at the glorious events which were transfiguring the other Moslem nations. Their country was like a vast prison whose inmates had almost relinquished all hope of freedom, and yet Amar's father had known it when it was the richest and most beautiful land in all Islam. And even Amar could remember the pears and peaches that had grown in the orchards outside the walls of Fez near Bab Sidi bou Jida before the French had diverted the flow of water to their own lands and left the trees to wither and perish in the summer heat.

The room smelled strongly of kerosene: someone had been careless in filling the lamps. He got up and wandered about listlessly. Yes, the room was Morocco itself; there was not even any way of seeing out, because the windows were all high above the level of anyone's head. He walked to the door and stood listening to the long sound of the bees, wondering vaguely whether, if a man were to smash their nests and be stung, their poison would be powerful enough to kill him.

Presently Moulay Ali appeared in the doorway coming from the back gallery, and seeing Amar, approached and took him by the arm. "You shouldn't have come here," he told him. "I can't let you go, and you'll get very tired of being shut up here." He led him back into the room and closed the door. "But the world's very bad this day, very bad." From his pocket he took Amar's handkerchief with the money in it, the packet of notes the Nazarene lady had given him, and the little paper of kif he had bought for Mustapha at the Café Berkane. This last he dropped into Amar's hand quickly and with great distaste. "What are you doing with that filth?" he demanded. "I thought you were a *derri* with some sense."

Amar, who had forgotten the existence of the tiny bundle, was horrified to see it lying there in his own hand. "That's not mine," he exclaimed, looking down at it.

"It was in your pocket."

"I mean, it's for my brother. I got it for him."

"If you loved your brother you wouldn't put chains on his legs, would you?"

Amar had no answer. Moulay Ali had just put into clear words what he had only vaguely hoped: that the kif might indeed be a chain to bind Mustapha. If he pretended innocence he would seem abysmally stupid in the eyes of Moulay Ali; if he did not, he would probably think him incredibly wicked. Moulay Ali stood looking at him expectantly.

"We don't get on very well," Amar finally murmured.

But now Moulay Ali's face was rapidly changing. "You mean," he said incredulously, "that he likes kif and you give it to him to ruin his health and weaken his mind, so he'll never be worth anything? Is that it?"

Amar admitted miserably that such had been his intention. Since he had told Moulay Ali the truth about everything else, he might as well tell it here too. "But he's already not worth anything," he added by way of explanation, "and besides I didn't give it to him."

Moulay Ali whistled, a long low sound. "Well, my friend, you're just a young Satan. That's all I can say. Satan a hundred percent. But here's your money. Otherwise I may forget it."

As he was about to go out, he spun around and raised his forefinger threateningly. "And don't buy a gun with it, *smatsi?* Unless you want to spend the rest of your life in Aït Baza." Seeing Amar's forlorn expression, he turned all the way around. "Some friends will probably be coming tonight, if they don't get killed or arrested first, and they'll sing you a song. Do you know the one about Aïcha bent Aïssa?"

"No," said Amar, for whom the prospect of arrivals gave the day a sudden slight glow.

"It's a very important song for you to hear." Moulay Ali went out and shut the door.

Somewhat later an unkempt-looking boy brought in a tray of fruit and bread and honey, grinned at Amar, and went away again. Amar ate without appetite. "*Ed dounia mamzianache,*" Moulay Ali had said—the world was very bad today. It could scarcely be worse than yesterday, he told himself, yet forebodings of gloom filled his mind, and he was afraid. After he had eaten, he removed all the newspapers and magazines from the most comfortable mattress, and curled up there, staring for a long time at the blue sky through the window opposite, and finally closing his eyes. He stayed there all afternoon, sunk in a melancholy whose only antidote was the occasional memory of Moulay Ali's promise that the evening would bring company and there would be someone to talk to.

And at the end of the afternoon, as the light faded from the squares of sky above, and life ebbed from the airless room, his sadness grew, became a physical pain in his heart and throat, and he felt that nothing could ever mitigate it—not whole days of weeping, and not even death. One day, years ago, when he and his father had been walking in the Zekak al Hajar where the beggars sat chanting, holding up their stumps of arms and displaying their disfigured bodies, his father had said to him: "When a man dies and is buried, he is finished with this world, and his friends give thanks that he has had the good luck to escape. But when a man crawls in the street without friends, without clothes, without a mat to lie on, without a piece of bread, alive but not really alive, dead but not even dead, that is Allah's most terrible punishment this side of the fires of Jehennam. Look, so you will understand why charity is one of the five duties." They had stopped walking and Amar had looked, but really only with fascinated repulsion at a man whose lips had grown out into an enormous purplish pouch as big as his whole head, and he had thought in his childish brain what a strange being Allah must be, to play such odd tricks on people.

Now he remembered what his father had said. This misery was what would soon be happening to him and to everyone else, but there would not be between them even the bond forged by suffering which made the beggars help one another to get through the streets (the ones with twisted legs creeping ahead like sick dogs, leading the blind ones), because each one would hate and fear his fellow, and no one would know which were the spies and which were not, for the simple reason that any one of them, given the appropriate inducement, or subjected to the proper torture, was capable of betraying the others.

For a while the objects in the room remained visible, held together by the lingering light, then the texture of things disintegrated, turned to ash, darkened, and finally dropped into total obscurity. Amar lay still, devoured by self-pity. To be a prisoner in a lonely house in the country was bad enough for anyone used to the Medina and its crowds, but to be left alone in the darkness without even the possibility of making a light, that was really too much. But now he heard footsteps approaching along the gallery, and an instant later someone opened the door. A flashlight played across the mattresses, picking him out where he lay. There was an exclamation of surprise from Moulay Ali. "Are you asleep in there?" he cried. Amar said very clearly that he was not. "But what are you doing in the dark? Where's Mahmoud? Hasn't he brought a lamp?" Amar, for whose wounded ego this solicitousness was balm, replied that he had not seen Mahmoud for several hours—not since his breakfast, to be exact.

"You must forgive him," Moulay Ali said, still standing in the doorway. "He's been very busy today. Everyone in the house has been very busy."

"Of course," said Amar.

It was Moulay Ali's suggestion that they go up to the office and watch for the arrival of the guests, who would be coming by a back lane from the Ras el Ma road. As they went through the dusty little antechamber toward the foot of the stairs he told Amar: "This will be just a small gathering of a few friends. Even in the middle of a war one must laugh." It was the first time Amar had heard the trouble referred to as a war; the word excited him. Perhaps among those who were to arrive there would be men who that very day had killed Frenchmen with their own hands—heroes such as one sees only in the cinema or in magazines.

The shaded lamp on the table had been turned down so that it gave only a dull yellow glow. They sat on the hassocks and talked, Moulay Ali running his eyes unceasingly over that particular region of the blackness outside in which he expected to see lights appear. "It's very bad to be impatient," he remarked at one point, "but tonight I'm more than that. In this work, at times like this, every day is like a year. You know the situation in the morning; by evening it's all different, and you have to learn it all over again. But the one who wins is the one who studies it most."

Amar looked at the well-nourished flesh of Moulay Ali's face. He was talking because he was nervous, that much was evident. It was also clear that he thought of himself as a kind of general in this struggle he called a war, and the men who surrounded him accepted him as such. But a general does not live in a comfortable house attended by servants, nor spend his time sitting at a table typing and reading, Amar reflected; he has the finest horse and sword of all, and he rides at the head of his troops, spurring them on to greater daring and more complete disregard of life. That was what generals were for; they were to set the example. However, instead of giving voice to the things that were on his mind he merely sat quietly, until he heard Moulay Ali give a little grunt of satisfaction. "Aha, at last," he said, sitting up straight and peering out into the night. Amar looked, saw nothing, continued to look, and eventually did see some small lights moving along irregularly, disappearing, re-emerging and gradually coming nearer. "It's not an automobile," he said in surprise. "Of course not," said Moulay Ali. "They're coming on donkeys. It's a very narrow path." He rose to his feet. "Excuse me a moment. They'll be here in a little while. I want to be sure the big room is ready."

In the dim room, sitting alone, Amar felt his doubt grow more intense. Moulay Ali might be a very good man, but he was not a Moslem. He never said either "*Incha'Allah*" or "*Bismil'lah,*" and he drank alcohol and almost certainly did not pray, and Amar would not have been at all astonished to hear that on occasion he had eaten pork or neglected to observe Ramadan. How could such a man take it upon himself to lead Moslems in their fight against the injustices of the infidels?

As he was thinking about this, there came to him the unformulated memory of another personality; it was only a flavor, a suggestion, a shadow, like the premonition of a presence that had been with him and mysteriously still was with him, and a part of his mind compared it to the flavor of Moulay Ali, and found it better. All this taking place in the lightless depths of himself, he was aware only of a troubled feeling whose source he would not attempt to locate. But, as a whiff of smoke can whisper of danger to a man buried in the depths of sleep, this other presence, which he felt only as an unquiet place within him, was murmuring a message of warning—against what, he did not know.

CHAPTER 33

The dinner had been very good. They sprawled on the mattresses around the sides of the big room, talking and laughing. There were ten of them, including Lahcen, who had arrived late, having come by the main road on a bicycle. At the beginning of the meal, when one of the guests, a student from the Medersa Bou Anania, had tried to bring politics into the conversation, Moulay Ali had turned to him and announced loudly that he for one wanted to forget work and trouble for a while, and that he thought it would be a good idea to shelve the issues of the day while they ate. Everyone had approved vehemently; as a result the student had adopted a sour expression and refused to say a word to anyone during the remainder of the meal. Several bottles of wine had already been emptied, and more were on the way.

"That lamp," said Moulay Ali suddenly to Amar, who sat next to him. "Turn it down. It's smoking." Ever since the arrival of the guests he had been using Amar as a sort of orderly, a position which Amar was not at all loath to occupy, since it implied a certain intimacy between them. And then, he had noticed that it annoyed Lahcen, which gave him great pleasure, for he had no friendly feeling left for him, after all the gun-waving the big man had done in his face last night. Lahcen kept glowering in his direction, making it obvious that he disapproved of the whole game. Having heard Amar's denunciation of his idol, he had decided once and for all that the boy was an enemy, and that it was very unwise of Moulay Ali to keep him in the house; in his uncomplicated mind there were no mitigating circumstances for behavior such as Amar's.

Occasionally, as if they all had decided beforehand at what instant it should be, there would come a silence, a gap in the sound of talking through which the hostile night around them was clearly perceptible, and they heard only the deceptively reassuring music of the crickets outside. Then swiftly, a little recklessly, someone would begin to talk, about anything at all—it did not seem to matter—and his words would be welcomed with an enthusiasm completely disproportionate to the interest they had evoked.

Mahmoud now brought a tray of bottles, most of which contained beer. But there was also the same decanter of green chartreuse from which Amar had been served the other day. Moulay Ali tried to give him a bottle of beer. When he refused it, he offered to pour him a little of the liqueur. Amar wanted to say: "I'm a Moslem," but all he said was: "I don't drink." "But you drank some of this the other afternoon," said Moulay Ali, looking at him in astonishment. "That was a mistake," Amar told him.

When everyone had been served, Moulay Ali leaned toward

him and said in a low voice: "The news I promised to try and get for you is good." Amar's heart leapt. "Don't talk about this," he went on. "I don't want all the others to hear. You have an older sister?" Without letting Amar reply, he continued. "Your mother and young sister went to Meknès three days ago to stay with her and her husband. That's all I know." Raising his voice, he called across to a thin little man with glasses and a tiny moustache: "*Eh! Monsieur le docteur!*" (Amar stared at him in horror at the sound of the hated language.) "Come and sit here and tell me a few things." To Amar he said: "You don't mind moving down that way." Amar walked to the other end of the room and sat on a fat cushion by himself, facing the whole assemblage. The two young men nearest him, seated at the end of the mattress, sipped beer and discussed the party newspaper.

Presently one of them shouted to Moulay Ali: "Felicitations, master! I hear your bubonic plague story made the placards in the students' manifestation in Rabat yesterday. 'Moroccans in the Concentration Camps Aren't Dying Fast Enough to Suit the French. What's the Remedy? Introduce Bubonic Plague into the Camps, and Make Room for More Prisoners.' That was what they said. It made a number one scandal."

Moulay Ali smiled. "I should hope it would," he said.

Amar paid no attention to the talk, which seemed to grow louder as it progressed. He was occupied in giving repeated thanks to Allah for having saved Halima and his mother. As he began to listen once more to the words being said around him, he realized that this time Moulay Ali must have told his friends that it was safe to speak in front of him, for they were making no attempt to veil the meaning of anything they said. He could afford to feel delight over this, now that the worst tension was eased. Three days ago, Moulay Ali had said. That was the day he had gone to the Café Berkane and met the two Nazarenes, the very day he had walked out of his house to take a stroll, and his mother had said: "I'm afraid." They would have had to leave the house very shortly after he had, to have got out of the Medina before the shooting had closed it entirely. What could have decided his father to get them out so suddenly? Perhaps Allah had simply sent him a message.

"No chance of negotiation," said the doctor. "They can send a new Résident from Paris every morning if they like. It won't get them anywhere. It would still have been possible last week. Even yesterday, perhaps. Now, never." He seemed to be speaking to the room at large; everyone was listening. "It was a master stroke to get them all in there at once."

"But will the people really take it as hard as we imagine?" This was said rapidly in a high voice by a young man in a blue business suit. "Is the *horm* really so important to them? That's very necessary to know."

"*Skské huwa,*" said Moulay Ali shortly, pointing at Amar. "There's your people. Ask him."

Everyone but Lahcen turned and looked at Amar eagerly, with a strange expression almost of greed, he thought, as if he were a new kind of food which they were about to try for the first time. Moulay Ali merely smiled like a contented cat, while the doctor said to Amar: "Do you know what happened today in the Medina?"

"No, *sidi,*" Amar replied, new dread being born within him.

"The French swore they would put all the *ulema* of the Karouine in prison."

"They couldn't do that," said Amar. "The *ulema* are holy."

"Ah, but they could if they wanted! But the *ulema* went and took sanctuary in the *horm* of Moulay Idriss."

In spite of himself Amar was relieved. "*Hamdoul'lah,*" he said with feeling. The others watched, fascinated.

The doctor then leaned forward a little as he said: "But the French broke into the *horm* and beat them and pulled every one of them out. By now they're all in Rabat."

Amar's eyes had grown huge. "*Kifach!*" he cried. No one spoke. "But what's going to happen? Haven't we begun yet to burn the Ville Nouvelle?"

"Not yet," said Moulay Ali. "We will."

"But we mustn't wait!"

"Remember that the only people who can move around at all are the ones who live in Fez-Djedid. Everyone else is locked into his house. Don't forget that." Now he turned back to the doctor. "Brahim's suggestion would be sound if it weren't unrealistic at the very beginning. A thing like that takes time." They talked, but Amar retired once more into himself, with a faint feeling of having been tricked. Not that he did not believe what the doctor had told him, but he resented the way in which they all had wanted to see how he took the tragic news; it was as if they themselves did not really care at all what had happened, as if they were outsiders in the whole affair.

"*B'sif,*" a man with a black beard was saying. "The sooner you begin, the better. And you have to keep at it. Over and over. America sends France two hundred billion francs. America gives France a hundred billion more. France would like to leave Morocco, but America insists on her staying, because of the bases. Without America there would be no France. And so on. *Sahel, sahel.* All we need is one good attack on each American base. That shouldn't be so hard to work up. Do you think so, Ahmed?" The man turned to the student who had sulked at dinner.

"I think it would be easy, at least among the students." He was more out of sorts with Moulay Ali than with the others.

"Even with the faces of the French dogs in front of them everywhere, and the Americans hidden?" said Moulay Ali with delicate scorn. "*Soyez réaliste, monsieur.*"

"We're not all *djebala,* straight from the mountains," the student retorted haughtily.

"And once we've had a few incidents directly involving American lives and property, maybe the Americans will know there's such a country as Morocco in the world," went on Brahim of the black beard. "Now they don't know the difference between Morocco and the Sénégal. You can all sit there and say it's unrealistic. But I'll wager you that within a year it'll be an official directive. The target will be shifted from the French to the Americans." No one said anything; apparently they had been impressed into silence. The crickets sang: "Ree, ree, ree, ree."

"Even if it's only for propaganda purposes," continued Brahim, encouraged by their stillness and by the wine he had drunk, "it would be useful. But it's also true, which makes it much more powerful as propaganda."

"The value of propaganda has no relationship to the degree of its truth," intoned the man in the blue business suit, pouring himself another glass of beer. "Only with its credibility to the section of the people at which it is aimed."

Moulay Ali looked surreptitiously at the doctor and raised his eyebrows; the doctor winked. Brahim, not to be discouraged, paid no attention. "It's the truth that America furnishes France with money, and that some of that money is spent for arms which are used against us. That may not make propaganda—I don't know. But it's the truth."

Amar listened; this was something new. He had not known of the Americans' secret villainy. But then, of course, there were a great many things that he was hearing for the first time. This word propaganda that they all kept using—he had never heard that before, but obviously it was a very important thing. The story of the evil Americans fascinated him; he longed to see one, to know what they looked like, what color their skin was, what language they spoke, but everyone else in the room knew the answers to those questions, and so he could not ask them. Now there seemed to be three separate conversations going on at once among the guests; some of them were shouting in their excitement. The room had grown smaller with their obstreperousness. A fat man had pushed the doctor out of the way and sat beside Moulay Ali, reading him a newspaper clipping. Moulay Ali leaned back, his eyes closed, now and then opening them to take a puff on his cigarette, and watching the smoke curl upward for a moment before he closed them again. Only he, of all of them, appeared able to maintain a wholly calm exterior. But even he, Amar thought with sadness, was not a Moslem and thus could not be relied upon to lead the people. A half-emptied glass of beer lay at his feet, and soon he would bend forward to pick it up.

Gradually Amar fell into a contemplative state, just sitting and watching the men slowly become drunk. No one paid him any attention. Their voices grew louder constantly, and they had ceased to stop and listen to the crickets outside, even for an instant. There was no silence any more in their world. Each one talked to impress the others with his intelligence and erudition. Even Lahcen was arguing with a thin, bald young man who obviously had no desire to be talking to him, and kept trying to get into the conversation which was going

on opposite him. These men had no understanding of, no love for, either Allah or the people they pretended to be helping. Whatever they might manage to build would be blown away very quickly. Allah would see to that, because it would have been built without His guidance.

He sat there alone, looking at them, and it was as if he were far away on the top of a mountain, seeing them from a great distance. Sins are finished, the potter had told him. That was what people believed now, and so there was nothing but sin. For if men dared take it upon themselves to decide what was sin and what was not, a thing which only Allah had the wisdom to do, then they committed the most terrible sin of all, the ultimate one, that of attempting to replace Him. He saw it very clearly, and he knew why he felt that they were all damned beyond hope of redemption.

Suddenly Moulay Ali had brought out an *oud* from behind the cushions stacked in the corner near him, and was tossing it across to the doctor, who removed his glasses and began to tune it. For a while he plucked at the strings tentatively, perhaps not wanting to start a song until the conversation had worn itself down a bit. This did not happen; almost everyone continued to talk. Finally Moulay Ali clapped his hands impatiently for silence, and little by little the words stopped flowing.

"*Aïcha bent Aïssa,*" said Moulay Ali. "Now, listen to this, Amar. Listen carefully. This is for you. He wants to do big things," he confided jovially to the others. "I promised him this song."

It was not true, Amar thought. He wanted nothing. Not to do big things for the Party, not to hear music, not to speak to anyone. He felt absolutely alone in the room, alone in this alien world of Moslems who were not Moslems, but he would sit and listen, for the song had begun. It had a simple tune and simple words, and, he thought at first, a simple story about a woman whose son was sixteen years old and belonged to the Party. When his number came up, and it was his turn to go out and commit the murder assigned to him, and they came and knocked at the door of his house, the mother told the men to come into the house for a moment. They went in, and she said: "Where is the gun?" and they handed it to her.

Then she shot her son. But with the advent of this brutal and unexpected act, the song passed beyond his comprehension. He still listened, but the song, having shocked him, had ceased thereby to make sense. Then, sang the doctor, she handed back the gun to them, saying: "Get a man for your work—not a boy." That was all there was to it."

"She really exists, you know," murmured the student. "She lives in Casablanca, and the story is perfectly true." Lahcen, greatly touched, sniffed and rubbed his eyes with his sleeve. "He'll cry at a song," thought Amar disdainfully, "but if he saw the woman shoot the boy, he'd just stand there like a stone."

"Well, what about it?" cried Moulay Ali to Amar. "What do you think of it?"

Amar was silent, not knowing what was expected of him. Still Moulay Ali waited; in the end Amar said exactly what he was thinking. "I don't understand why she killed her son."

Moulay Ali was triumphant. "I didn't think you would. That's why I wanted you to hear it. She shot him because she knew he wasn't ready, and the Party was more dear to her heart than her own son." Amar looked confused. "She saw that when the French caught him he wouldn't die like a man, his lips closed tight, but like a boy, crying and telling them whatever they wanted to know. That's why she shot him, my friend."

Now Amar understood, but still he did not feel the truth of it, or even believe it, for that matter. "And you say there really was such a woman?"

Everyone began to speak of friends who claimed to know the legendary Aïcha bent Aïssa. Some declared she lived in Fedala, the doctor insisted she ran a *bacal* in the quarter of Aïn Bouzia, and the bald young man seemed to think she had been made one of the leaders of the Party and sent, he believed, to Boujad or Settat or some such place. In any case, they all adhered firmly to the theory of her flesh-and-blood existence. All, save perhaps Moulay Ali, who merely said: "The Party used to have a lot of young boys in it. They won't take them any more, except very special ones, and the new policy's largely due to that song."

This time Mahmoud brought a tray of smaller glasses and

two freshly opened bottles of cognac. His arrival was greeted by a certain amount of discreet applause by several of the guests; this in itself was proof to Amar, if any were needed, that they were no longer completely sober. The doctor sang several more songs, from which the attention of the others gradually strayed, so that in the end he was singing and strumming for his own pleasure. Amar sat for a long time watching them, not taking any part in their jokes and arguments, and feeling more and more solitary and miserable. At one point Moulay Ali called over to him, saying: "*Zduq*, Amar, it looks as though you'd be staying on awhile here with me."

Amar smiled feebly, hoping the other would not suspect what was passing through his mind as a result of that remark: a conscious determination to escape, in one way or another. Even the open fields, he thought, would be preferable to being shut into this house. He had money in his pocket now, and although he did not know his sister's address in Meknès, he was certain that he could find her house somehow. He put his hand into his pocket and felt the money there; the notes between his fingers excited him. He would buy a pair of real shoes, and some new trousers. For the first time, he thought of the money in terms of its buying power. But where would he buy the shoes? Perhaps in Meknès, *incha'Allah*. He was very sleepy; his eyes could scarcely stay open. Being near the door, he waited until the next time Mahmoud entered with more bottles and more glasses, and slipped out behind him just as he made his entrance. The gallery was dark, but the moon overhead shone down into the courtyard. Until he got to the back gallery he could hear the raucous laughter and the high thin notes of the *oud*, but once he was there the silence was complete, save for the countless little songs of the crickets. He felt his way cautiously to the door of the room where he had slept the night before, went in, and said a lengthy prayer because of the darkness. Then he lay down and instantly fell asleep.

He had been traveling great distances, and he did not want to come back, but a light shone in his face. He opened his eyes. A monster stood over him. He sprang up, crying out: "Ah!" but lost his balance and fell back down onto the mattress, and as he fell he knew it was only Moulay Ali standing there with a lantern. But the light shining from beneath made his face look like the face of a fat white devil, and his eyes were two round black holes. Amar laughed apologetically, and said: "*Khalatini!* You frightened me!"

Moulay Ali paid no attention, but held the lantern up higher, and whispered: "Come." The urgency with which he had uttered the one word did not strike Amar until he was already on his feet; then the relief he had felt after his initial fright began to give way to a new uneasiness, more rational but also very disturbing. "He's drunk," he told himself, as they went along the gallery, their shadows mingling on the ruined wall. Then he heard the voices of the others, and they all sounded like madmen. Some were whispering, some were laughing senselessly, in that their laughter had the sound but not the meaning of laughter, and some were talking, but about nothing at all. "Yes, very nice." "I thought that if she said it was like that we would go." "And do you like cigarettes?" "Oh, I, yes, I smoke. I like to smoke." "It would be better up there, if you knew what you have to know." "We came back, and, and, it was very hot." The intonations and rhythms were somehow wrong, too, and he had the impression that if the men had been asked what they had said, not one of them could have told, because the words had been merely the first words to come into their heads. Then someone—the doctor, he supposed—began to play on the *oud*, and these slight sounds, making a recognizable melody, mysteriously succeeded in giving the scene he had been listening to a semblance of sanity.

When they had reached the doorway to the large room, Amar saw that the guests were all standing. "My friends were about to go," explained Moulay Ali. (Where to, at this time of night, on the backs of donkeys? Amar wondered, but only in passing.) "And then I mentioned that you played the flute, and they all want to hear you."

"Oh!" Amar exclaimed, very much taken aback.

"Just one piece," urged Moulay Ali in a voice of velvet, pinching his arm. Amar stared at him: he seemed very odd indeed, and his eyes, even in this light, still looked like enormous black holes. He gazed around at the others in the room; they too had something extremely strange about them.

Again he wondered if it could be the effect of alcohol, or hashish, perhaps, but he had seen plenty of men under the influence of one or the other, and their behavior had been completely different. The idea passed through his mind that Moulay Ali had not really come at all and wakened him. In that case he was still lying there in the comfortable dark of the little room; it was one of those dreams where all things—the people, the houses and trees, the sky and the earth—are doomed at the outset to be merged in one gigantic vortex of destruction. Doomed from the start, but unless the dreamer is on the lookout he may not realize what is going to happen, because it is a maelstrom which begins to move only after a long while, declaring its presence in its own good time. In the end, very likely, everything would begin going around, one thing becoming another, and they would all be sucked down into emptiness, silently screaming, and clawing at one another with gestures of the most exquisite delicacy. In the meantime he had to pretend to be Amar being awake.

"I have no *lirah*," he said, certain that Moulay Ali would produce one that very instant, which he did, taking it up from a hassock behind him.

"But I play very badly. Only a little," he protested. Moulay Ali stroked his arm eagerly. "*Baraka'llahoufik. Baraka'llahoufik*," he murmured. Was it really Moulay Ali, and was any one of these men the person he had been before? Or was it Amar who had changed while he slept, that now everything should be so different?

"*I'll* play a piece," said Moulay Ali. He lifted the little reed flute to his mouth. Straightway everyone was utterly silent; the words that had no meaning, the strained and vacant laughter, the frantic whispered monosyllables, which of all the sounds they had been making seemed the only valid ones, all were suspended in a flash, and only the small windy voice of the flute remained to take their place. Moulay Ali executed a few warming-up phrases, and then, walking alone out onto the gallery, began to play, without any particular virtuosity, a slightly altered version of a song called *Tanja Alia*. Amar watched the guests: they looked straight in front of them, as if they were not listening, but were imagining how they would look if they were really listening. "*Yah latif!*" he thought. "They're all bewitched." That was what was wrong with them; at least, it seemed a more reasonable hypothesis to Amar at this moment than any other he could invent. A moment before, they had been turning around and bumping into each other. Now they all stood completely still, close together, intent on the music that managed, weak as it was, to fill the emptiness of the night. When Moulay Ali had stopped, even before he reappeared in the doorway, they began to move around again distractedly, staying close together, as if no one of them could bear to think of being at more than an arm's length from at least two others.

"Here," said Moulay Ali, handing him the flute. "Now you've got to play. Come." He led him over to the cushions where they had sat together at dinner. "Now, make yourself comfortable, and show me how *you* play *Tanja Alia*."

The more quickly he complied, thought Amar, the sooner he could go back to bed. He lay back on the cushions, put one leg up over the other, and began to play. After a few phrases, Moulay Ali smiled tautly, said: "Good. Beautiful," and walked back to the other end of the room. The guests had gone out the door onto the gallery. "Listen from there," he heard Moulay Ali murmur to them, while he breathed to start a new phrase. And a moment later he heard him whisper something else, something very curious indeed, that is, if he had not been mistaken. What he thought he had heard, behind and between the reedy sounds the flute made around his head, were the words: "It's Chemsi; don't forget. I know his walk. Don't forget."

Each time he opened his eyes he was aware of Moulay Ali's form standing over there beside the door, listening. It pleased him that he should want to hear him play, although he would rather have played for him alone than with all the others listening, too.

Chemsi. Who was Chemsi? Amar thought, as he brought to earth a long, slowly descending cadence that fluttered, quivered, tried to rise, and finally settled and lay still. Chemsi, of course, was the boy to whom Moulay Ali had handed all the newspaper clippings that first lost afternoon so long ago. But he was not interested in Chemsi, or in whether or not he had truly heard his name pronounced a few minutes back; he was bent on fashioning the most beautifully formed phrases of notes he could devise. Sometimes Allah helped him; sometimes He did not. Tonight he felt that there was a possibility of such help. When he himself became the music, so that he was no longer there, save as a single, advancing point on the long thread that the music spun as it moved across eternity, that was the moment when the music became a bridge from his heart to other people's hearts, and when he returned to himself he knew that Allah had lifted him up out of the world for an instant and that for that short space of time he had had the *h'dia*, the gift.

He played until he was alone in distant places. Allah did not help him, but it did not matter. The loneliness that was in his heart, the longing for someone who could understand him if he spoke, these came out in the fragile strings of sound he made with his breath and his fingers. Thinking of nothing, he played on, and slowly the person for whom he played ceased being the figure by the door, became that other presence he had become aware of back in the tower early in the evening, someone whose existence in the world meant the possibility of hope. He stopped for an instant, and in his head, indissolubly a part of that happiness liberated by the idea of the other being, he heard a second music—like singing coming from a far-off sunlit shore, infinitely lovely and inexpressibly tender, a filament of song so tenuous that it might be only the mind remembering a music it had never heard save in dreams. He lay still, hearing it, unable to draw the breath that would destroy it, perhaps forever. It was not from Allah, it was here, and yet he had not known that this world had anything so precious to offer. And when he finally had to breathe, and the other music ceased, as he had known it would, as naturally as if he had been thinking of him all the time, he saw in his mind the Nazarene man, a puzzling smile on his lips, the way he had looked in the hotel room the first evening.

At any moment Moulay Ali would say: "Go on," or "Thank you," and Amar wanted to think of the Nazarene. He had been a friend; perhaps with time they could even have understood one another's hearts. And Amar had left him, sneaked away from Sidi Bou Chta without even saying goodbye. He opened his eyes and glanced toward the end of the room. The dark form was still there, unmoving. He sat up suddenly and looked at it. It was a jacket hanging on a nail in the shadows beyond the door.

CHAPTER 34

The *lirah* rolled down between two cushions where he had dropped it. Almost as soon as he was off the mattress, he was at the door, looking up and down the empty gallery. He knew exactly what had happened, and he went over it all in his mind as he ran, checking each point. And he knew what would come next, unless he was unbelievably lucky. It was to look for that luck that he raced now to the stuffy little antechamber and up the moonlit stairs to the tower room, deserted save for the night wind that came through the open windows. There was only one side of the tower that interested him, and that was the side with the view of the roof; fortunately one of the windows on that side was ajar, so he would not have to run the risk of making a noise in pushing it open. He looked down, judged the distance to the top of the gable, a difficult calculation to make in the moonlight, for it seemed further as he sat on the window sill gauging it than it proved to be an instant later when he landed on it. He had thrust his sandals into his pocket, and his bare feet made almost no sound as he hit.

There was no place to hide on the roof where he could not be picked out by a flashlight either from below or from the tower; that he ascertained very quickly. What he wanted to know, however, was whether the tower itself, which he had never seen from the outside, had a flat roof or a dome, and now he saw, and gave thanks, for it was flat. The problem for the moment was to lift himself back up to the window sill and from there to the very top, managing on the way to close the window so as to put them off the scent as much as possible. They were looking first of all, of course, for Moulay Ali, a plump, unathletic middle-aged man, and it would not be reasonable to expect him to have climbed out the window and swung himself up to the top of the tower. In fact, Amar thought, as he worked at the feat, he did not know any boys of his age who could do it, either. The last part had to be done with faith that the tiny concrete cornice to which his fingers clung up there above his head would not detach itself as he hung his entire weight upon it. On his way up he had shut the window without being really able to shut it, since the only handle was on the inside. But if a strong gust of wind did not suddenly blow in through the tower from the west, it would stay as it was.

When he got to the top, he crawled on his belly to the center, flopped over onto his back, and lay looking up at the round moon almost directly above him. If he remained lying flat like this they could not catch him in any conceivable beam of light thrown from below. He wondered how many police there were down there with Chemsi, how much money they had given him, and whether Chemsi, as he stood hiding among the bushes with the French, and listening to the music of the flute, had been aware of any difference in the sound when Moulay Ali had ceased to play and Amar had begun. Very likely not, or there would have been a concerted attack on the house then and there; the police would have realized that this was the moment when Moulay Ali was getting away. He could very well imagine Chemsi standing out there, terrified, some petty grievance against Moulay Ali in his throat, so that all the friendship he had felt for him only a few days ago counted as nothing, whispering to the Frenchmen: "That's Moulay Ali playing now! He always plays that piece when he's drunk." And the extra few minutes that Moulay Ali had thus induced the French to take in making their preparations, those precious minutes that had saved him (for still there had been no sound, and a silent capture was inconceivable) had been supplied by Amar as he lay there like a donkey, making music which he hoped Moulay Ali might admire. He smiled, twisting his head around, trying to see the rabbit in the moon, wondering why he felt no hatred for Moulay Ali for having tricked him—only admiration for the psychological accuracy with which the idea had been conceived and executed, and extemporaneously, too. There was true Fassi cleverness. And then, he felt a little sorry for Moulay Ali, because he would surely be caught sooner or later, and that was not a pleasant thing to look forward to. Even if the present trouble died down, the French would never rest until they had brought him to earth. The idea of being hunted day and night, of never having a really peaceful moment, struck him as particularly terrible. And Chemsi! He would not want to be Chemsi for everything in the world. "Don't forget!" Moulay Ali had said as he went out, in case some were caught and some were not, in the flight they were about to make. Whoever was left free or could get a message to the outside would see to it that Chemsi was taken care of. For the Istiqlal was efficient above all at exterminating its own renegades. And they would find him eventually; he did not doubt that for a minute. The French would offer him only a token protection; they were at least sufficiently human to have only contempt for informers, even if it was merely because informers were so plentiful (and besides that, it was much more expedient to let the old ones be got out of the way and take on new ones whose identity was not yet suspected). It was not likely that Chemsi would live to see the Feast of Mouloud.

The moon was so bright that the stars were invisible. The warm wind carried the faint odor of summer flowers that open at night. Apart from the crickets, were there any other sounds to be heard? He thought so: vague stirrings below, on the other side of the house. Soon he was certain; a slight rasping noise came up, and then, unmistakably, a voice. A moment later, many voices: they had got into the house. He smiled, amused by the mental image he had of the rage that would be on the Frenchmen's faces when they discovered their quarry gone. They would run about like furious ants, along the galleries and into the rooms, up and down the stairs, shouting orders and curses, ripping open the mattresses and cushions, and smashing the tables—but carefully collecting all the papers. Not that it would do them any good, he thought; Moulay Ali was not the man to be careless with anything which could be compromising to members of the Party. If I'd been in the Party, he said to himself wistfully, he'd never have done this to me.

They were calling to each other in their harsh, hateful language, banging doors, stamping up and down. Now they had found Mahmoud and the other servants, and were bellowing at them in what they supposed was Arabic. "Which door did he go out?" roared one, and a second later, mimicking the inaudible reply: " 'I don't know, monsieur!' Maybe you'll know in the commissariat." He lay completely still, listening to each sound, wondering how far away Moulay Ali and the others had got by now. He hoped neither for their escape nor for their capture. It could not make much difference to Morocco one way or the other, nor could it be important how many other Moulay Alis there were and whether they failed or succeeded. By having lived with Christians they had been corrupted. They were no longer Moslems; how could it matter what they did, since they did it not for Allah but for themselves? The government and the laws they might make would be nothing but a spiderweb, built to last one night. His father had told him that the world of *politique* was a world of lies, and he in his ignorance and stubbornness, pretending to agree, privately had gone straight ahead believing that the old man, like all old men, was out of touch with everyday truths. Thinking of his father made him want to cry; he clenched his fists and hardened all the muscles of his face.

The sounds of shouting and banging had come very near. He heard the men climbing the stairs to the tower; he could even catch their little exclamations of satisfaction. Suddenly convinced that now they were going to find him, he abandoned precautions, and rolled over onto his side to press his ear against the concrete floor of the roof. The word "*machine*" figured in their comments. It was the typewriter whose discovery pleased them so much. Now he stared at the side from which they would appear. A thick hand, white in the moonlight, would come feeling its way up over the edge, then grasp the ridge, and then another hand would come up, and then a head with eyes.

All at once they were breaking the windows. In rapid succession they pushed out the panes. The sheets of glass hitting the ground below made a brittle music. He wondered if Moulay Ali were still within hearing distance, and if so, what were his reactions when these sounds reached his ears. Would he think that Amar had been caught and that a struggle was in progress? Above all, would he think that Amar was going to tell them what innocuous facts he knew? But then he sighed: Moulay Ali surely had gone so far by now that he

could hear nothing. Such tiny tinkling crashes would die on
the night breeze even before it had carried them as far as the
olive grove.

It was only now that he discovered and verified an astonishing fact: with the police only three or four meters below
him, he became aware that it was largely a matter of indifference to him whether they found him or not. He even had a
crazy momentary impulse to bang on the roof and shout:
"Here I am, you sons of dogs!" They would try to climb up
to get him, and he would simply lie still and watch. And when
they did have him finally, they would beat him and carry him
off to the torture room in the police station where they
would attach electrodes to his *qalaoui*, and the pain would be
more terrible than anything he had ever known or imagined,
but he would keep his lips closed tight. It would serve no
purpose at all, beyond that of giving him at last the wonderful satisfaction of feeling a part of the struggle. Perhaps if he
had had a secret to withhold, the temptation to announce his
presence would have become too strong to resist. But he
knew nothing; it would have been only a silly game. And it
occurred to him that no one cared whether there was an
Amar or not, that if anyone but his family should care, it
would not be because he was he, but because, as he moved
blindly along the orbit of his life, he had accidentally become
the repository of some scrap of information.

He listened: they were going back down the stairs, back
along the galleries, back through the house, and away. They
had parked their jeeps somewhere far out in the fields, for he
waited an interminable time before he heard the faint sound
of doors being shut and motors starting up. When they were
gone he turned over and sobbed a few times, whether with
relief or loneliness he did not know. Lying up here on the
cold concrete roof he felt supremely deserted, exquisitely conscious of his own weakness and insignificance. His gift meant
nothing; he was not even sure that he had any gift, or ever
had had one. The world was something different from what
he had thought it. It had come nearer, but in coming nearer
it had grown smaller. As if an enormous piece of the great
puzzle had fallen unexpectedly into place, blocking the view
of distant, beautiful countrysides which had been there until

now, dimly he was aware that when everything had been understood, there would be only the solved puzzle before him, a black wall of certainty. He would know, but nothing would have meaning, because the knowing was itself the meaning; beyond that there was nothing to know.

After a long time he crawled over to the edge and climbed down into the tower, slipping his feet into his sandals to protect them from the slivers of shattered glass that reflected the moon's light. His silent passage through the dark house was not even frightening: it was only infinitely sad, for now the house belonged completely to what had been and never would be again. He went straight to the broken front door and stepped outside. There were no sounds at all. The night had reached its furthest point: no crickets strummed in the grass, no night birds stirred in the bushes. In another few minutes, although it still was far away, the dawn would arrive. Even before he reached the olive trees, he heard the melancholy note of the first cockcrow behind him.

CHAPTER 35

And here he was in the Ville Nouvelle, and it was the middle of the morning. The sun hammered down upon the pavements that covered the earth of the plain, and the pitiful little trees that were meant to give shade slowly withered in its heat. He kept to the quiet back streets where few people passed. It was a painfully hot day. An old Frenchwoman was approaching, dressed all in black, carrying her shopping bag full of food home from the market. She looked at him with suspicion, and crossed the street slowly before he got to her, so as not to have to meet him face to face. Not a single child played outside the houses, no traffic passed, and no radios played; possibly the electricity was still cut off. The city seemed nearly deserted, but he knew that behind the curtains of the windows were a thousand pairs of eyes peering out into the empty streets, following the passage of whoever ventured along them. Every sign was bad: when the French were frightened there was no knowing what they might do.

Beyond the small park with the iron bandstand was the be-

ginning of the street that led to the hotel where he had gone
with the Nazarene man and woman. He did not know how
he was going to get to see the man (nor did it even occur to
him that he might not yet be back from Sidi Bou Chta, or
that he might already be gone); he knew only that he had to
see him, to set things straight between them, to hear him talk
a while in his halting but learned Arabic, saying things that he
knew would in some way comfort him in his unhappiness.

He went around the end of the park instead of crossing it:
often there were policemen in there walking along its paths. At
the end of the long avenue on his right a few cars were parked,
but no person was in the street; it was like a flat stretch of stony
desert shimmering in the sunlight. Before he got to the hotel
a truck laden with cuttings of rusty tin drove slowly past. A
blond Frenchman at the wheel stared at him curiously and
yawned. The gray façade of the hotel looked as if it had been
boarded up and vacated a long time ago. Its six windows with
their closed shutters were like eyes asleep. In a loud voice he
said: "*Bismil'lah rahman er rahim*," and pulled the bell.

The woman who answered the door had seen him before,
the day he had come with the two tourists and had helped
them in with their luggage, but now she did not appear to
recognize him. Her face was like a stone as she asked him in
French what he wanted. A few paces behind her stood a large
red-faced man who stared over her shoulder at him threateningly. When she found Amar did not speak French, she was
about to shut the door; then suddenly something in her face
changed, and although her expression remained unfriendly,
he knew she had remembered him. She said something to the
man, and called in a shrill voice: "Fatima!" A Moslem girl appeared, dragging a broom behind her, and said to him: "What
is it?" The Frenchwoman seemed already to have known his
answer, for she said nothing, and walked over to where some
keys hung in a row against the wall. She examined them, exchanged a few words with the man, and spoke to the girl,
who said to Amar: "Wait awhile," and shut the door. He
walked to the curb and sat down. His knees were trembling.

After not too long a time he heard the door open behind
him. Quickly he stood up, but the long walk in the sun and
his stomach with no food in it had made him dizzy. He saw

his friend in the doorway, his arm raised in a gesture of welcome; then a cloud came swiftly across the sun and the street shot into its dark shadow. He leaned against one of the small dead trees to keep from falling. From a distance he heard the Frenchwoman calling abusive words—whether at him or at the tourist, he did not know. But then the Nazarene was at his side, leading him into the cool shade of the hotel, and although he felt very weak and ill, he was happy. Nothing mattered, nothing terrible could happen to him when he was in this man's care.

The man eased him into a chair and in no time had wrapped a cold wet towel around his head. "*Rhir egless*," he said to him. "Just sit still." Amar did, breathing heavily. The room held the sweet smell of flowers that the woman had always had on her clothing. When he finally opened his eyes and sat up a little straighter, he expected to see her, but she was not in the room. The man was sitting on the bed near by, smoking a cigarette. When he saw that Amar's eyes were open, he smiled. "How are you?" he said.

Before Amar could answer, there was a knock at the door. It was the girl called Fatima, bringing a tray. She set it on the table, went out. The man poured him a cup of coffee with milk, and handed him a plate with two rolls and some butter on it. As Amar ate and drank and looked around the dim room with its closed shutters, the man wandered back and forth, eventually coming to stand near him. Then Amar told him his story. The man listened, but he seemed restless and distraught, and twice he glanced at his watch. Amar went on until he had come to the end of his story. "And thanks to Allah you were here," he added fervently. "Now everything is well."

The man looked at him curiously and said: "And you? What can I do for you?"

"Nothing," said Amar, smiling. "I'm happy now."

The man got up and walked to the window as if he were about to open it, then changed his mind and went to the other. There was a crack in the shutter through which he peered briefly.

"You're lucky the police didn't see you here in the Ville Nouvelle today," he said suddenly. "Any Moslem in the street goes to jail. There's been big trouble."

"Worse than before?"

"Worse." The man went to the door. "Just a minute," he told him. "I'll be right back." He went out. Amar sat still for an instant. Then he stepped to the bed and carefully examined the pillow cases. Even in the half-light they were visible, the smears of red paint that whores and Nazarene women used on their lips, and the flower smell came up in a heavy invisible cloud from the bed. He went back and sat down.

The man opened the door, came in. It was only now that Amar saw the luggage stacked by the door.

"Well, I'm glad you came," said the man.

"I'm glad too."

"If you hadn't come now I wouldn't have seen you again. We're going to Casablanca."

It was all right, because the man was still there in front of him, and Amar could not really believe that having found him he would lose him so soon. If Allah had seen fit to bring them together once again, it was not so that they might talk for five minutes and then say good-bye. A car door slammed outside in the quiet street. "Here's the taxi," said the man nervously, without even going to peek through the shutter. "Amar, I hate to ask you again, but how about helping us once more with our luggage? This is the last time."

Amar jumped up. Whatever the man asked him to do, he would feel the same happiness in obeying; of that he was sure.

As he carried the valises downstairs one by one, the French woman and the big man stared out at him through a little window from where they sat in their room, observing a hostile silence. When all the luggage had been packed into the car, and Amar, a bit dizzy again from the exertion, stood on the curb with the man, the woman appeared in the doorway, looking prettier than Amar had ever seen her look, and walked toward them. She smiled at Amar and began to go through a pantomime of looking up and down the street fearfully, then pointed at him. Grinning back at her, he indicated that he was not afraid.

"Can I take you anywhere?" the man asked him. "We're going out the Meknès road. I don't suppose that will help you much—"

"Yes!" said Amar.

"It will?" said the man, surprised. "*Mezziane*. Get in front." Amar took the seat beside the driver, who was a Jew from the Mellah.

The woman was already sitting in the back, and the man got in beside her. When they had driven out to the end of the Avenue de France, the man said: "Do you want to get out here?"

"No!" said Amar.

They went on, past the service station and down the long road leading to the highway. The high eucalyptus trees went by quickly, one after the other, and in each one the insects were screaming the same tone. The man and the woman were silent. In the mirror before him, a little higher than his eyes, Amar could see the man's fingers caressing the woman's hand, lying inert in her lap.

As they approached the highway, the man leaned forward and told the driver to stop. Amar sat quite still. It was stifling in the car now that no breeze came in through the windows. The man touched his shoulder. "*El hassil, b'slemah, Amar,*" he said, holding his hand in front of Amar's face. Amar reached up slowly, grasped it, and turning his head around, looked at the man fixedly. In his head he formed the words: "*Incha'Allah rahman er rahim.*"

"I want to go to Meknès," he said in a low voice.

"No, no, no!" cried the man, laughing jovially and pumping Amar's hand up and down. "No, Amar, that won't do. Even here it's a long way for you to walk back, you know."

"Back to where?" said Amar evenly, neither shifting his gaze from the man's eyes nor letting go of his hand, which the man moved up and down again violently, trying to withdraw it. His face was changing: he was embarrassed, annoyed, growing angry. "Good-bye, Amar," he said firmly. "I can't take you to Meknès. There's no time." If he had said, "I won't take you with me," Amar would have understood.

Without the motor going, the one endless rasping note of the cicadas overhead was very loud.

"My mother's there," murmured Amar, scarcely knowing what he said.

The woman, who seemed not to understand anything, smiled at him, raised her arms, pretending to aim a gun, and cried: "Boom! Bam!" She shifted her position and was behind an imaginary machine-gun. "Dat-tat-tat-tat-tat!" she said very quickly. When she had finished, she pointed her forefinger at Amar. The man nudged her, raising an eyebrow at the back of the driver's head. Then he said something to the driver, who reached in front of Amar and opened the door for him, looking at him expectantly.

Amar let go of the man's hand and stepped into the road, his head lowered. He saw his sandals sinking slightly into the hot sticky tar, and he heard the door slam beside him.

"*B'slemah!*" called the man, but Amar could not look up at him.

"*B'slemah!*" echoed the woman. Still he could not raise his head. The motor started up.

"Amar!" the man cried.

The car moved ahead uncertainly, then it gathered speed. He knew they were looking out the rear window, waving to him, but he stood still, seeing only his feet in their sandals, and the black tar beside them. The driver turned into the highway, shifted gears.

Amar was running after the car. It was still there, ahead of him, going further away and faster. He could never catch it, but he ran because there was nothing else to do. And as he ran, his sandals made a terrible flapping noise on the hard surface of the highway, and he kicked them off, and ran silently and with freedom. Now for a moment he had the exultant feeling of flying along the road behind the car. It would surely stop. He could see the two heads in the window's rectangle, and it seemed to him that they were looking back.

The car had reached a curve in the road; it passed out of sight. He ran on. When he got to the curve the road was empty.

—*Taprobane, Weligama*
16/iii/55

CHRONOLOGY

NOTE ON THE TEXTS

GLOSSARY

NOTES

Chronology

1910   Born Paul Frederic Bowles on December 30 in Jamaica, Queens, New York City, the only child of Rena Winnewisser and Claude Dietz Bowles. (Bowles family immigrated to New England in the 17th century; Paul's grandfather, Frederick Bowles, fought for the Union in the Civil War and settled in Elmira, New York. Rena Winnewisser's grandfather was a German freethinker and political radical who came to the United States in 1848; her father owned a department store in Bellows Falls, Vermont, before moving family to a 165-acre farm near Springfield, Massachusetts.) Father is a dentist. The family lives at 108 Hardenbrook Avenue in Jamaica, the building where his father has his office and laboratory.

1911–15   Bowles learns to read by age four and keeps notebooks with drawings and stories, a habit that will continue throughout his childhood. His activities are strictly regimented by father. He spends summers with paternal grandparents in Glenora, New York, or the Winnewissers.

1916–18   Family moves to 207 De Grauw Avenue in Jamaica in summer 1916. Bowles begins attending Model School in Jamaica the following year, entering at the second grade level. Mother reads him stories by Hawthorne and Poe. Beginning in 1918, Bowles goes to Manhattan twice a week for orthodontic treatment, which will continue for ten years; makes monthly visits to New York Public Library on 42nd Street, where Anne Carroll Moore, a family friend, is head of the children's department. Receives books from Moore and visits her Greenwich Village apartment. Father confiscates notebooks in a fit of rage. (Bowles would write in his autobiography: "This was the only time my father beat me. It began a new stage in the development of hostilities between us.")

1919   Bowles and parents catch influenza but survive worldwide epidemic. Father buys phonograph, collects classical recordings, and forbids his son from bringing jazz records into the house. Bowles continues to buy "dance" records.

After family buys piano, Bowles studies theory, sight-singing, and piano technique. Writes "Le Carré: An Opera in Nine Chapters" about two men who exchange wives.

1920–21   Keeps diary filled with imaginary events and made-up characters. Writes daily "newspaper." Is promoted from fourth to sixth grade.

1922   Family moves to 34 Terrace Avenue in Jamaica. Bowles gives readings of his poems and stories after school. Buys first book of poetry, Arthur Waley's *A Hundred and Seventy Chinese Poems.*

1924   Graduates from Model School and attends public high school in Flushing, New York. Appointed humor editor of *The Oracle,* the school magazine.

1925–26   Writes crime stories with the recurring character "the Snake-Woman" and reads them at the summer home of Anna, Jane, and Sue Hoagland, friends of the family in Glenora. Meets the Hoaglands' friend Mary Crouch (later Oliver). Transfers to Jamaica High School. Reads English writer Arthur Machen. Is deeply impressed by a performance of Stravinsky's *The Firebird* at Carnegie Hall. Shows talent in painting.

1927   Performs with the Phylo Players, an amateur theatrical group. Reads André Gide. Buys an issue of the Paris-based literary magazine *transition,* which has a major impact on him. Is promoted to poetry editor of *The Oracle.*

1928   Graduates from Jamaica High School in January. The Hoagland sisters help him sell his paintings; when father refuses to support his artistic aspirations, mother pays for classes at the School of Design and Liberal Arts in New York. Bowles publishes poem "Spire Song" and prose poem "Entity" in *transition.* Spends summer working in the transit department of the Bank of Manhattan. Enters University of Virginia in the fall. Reads *The Waste Land;* discovers Prokofiev, Gregorian chant, Duke Ellington, and the blues. Experiments with inhaling ether. While home on winter break, attends one of the Aaron Copland–Roger Sessions Concerts of Contemporary Music, featuring music by Henry Cowell and George Antheil.

1929   Returns to University of Virginia in January and is hospitalized with conjunctivitis. Decides to move to Paris and obtains passport with the help of Sue Hoagland and Mary Oliver; tells virtually no one else of his plans. Arrives in Paris in April and works as a switchboard operator at the *Herald Tribune*. Mother refuses request to send money to Bowles made by a friend of Oliver's. Bowles receives 2,500 francs from Oliver and quits job; takes a short trip to Switzerland and Nice. Publishes poems in English and French in the Paris-based magazines *Tambour*, *This Quarter*, and *Anthologie du Groupe Moderne d'Art*. Visits northeastern France and Germany. Loses virginity on a camping trip with a Hungarian woman he had met the day before at the Café du Dôme; has sexual experience with Billy Hubert, a family friend. Accompanies Hubert to St.-Moritz and St.-Malo. Decides to return home and sails for New York on July 24. Works at Dutton's Bookshop and rents a room at 122 Bank Street. Begins writing "Without Stopping," fictional account of his travels in Europe.

1930   Meets Henry Cowell, who calls Bowles' musical compositions "frivolous" but writes a note of introduction to Aaron Copland. Moves to parents' home in order to use piano after Copland offers lessons in composition. Returns to University of Virginia in March. Hitchhikes to Philadelphia to attend Martha Graham's ballet *Le Sacre du Printemps* on April 11; meets Harry Dunham, who will become a close friend. Decides to leave college after finishing out the term in June. Spends September and October with Copland at the Yaddo Arts Colony in Saratoga Springs, New York. Asked by college friend Bruce Morrissette to edit an issue of University of Virginia magazine *The Messenger*, solicits submissions from William Carlos Williams, Gertrude Stein, and Edouard Roditi, who becomes a lifelong friend and correspondent. Quarrels violently with parents in December.

1931   Sails for Europe on March 25. Shortly after arriving in Paris, looks up Gertrude Stein, with whom a friendship develops. Meets Jean Cocteau, Virgil Thomson, Ezra Pound, and Pavel Tchelitchew. Goes to Berlin with Copland at the end of April. Meets Jean Rhys, Stephen Spender, and Christopher Isherwood, who will give

Bowles' surname to the heroine of his *Goodbye to Berlin*. Continues composition studies with Copland but dislikes Germany. Visits Kurt Schwitters in Hannover and is impressed with his studio; Bowles will soon incorporate one of Schwitters' abstract poems into his *Sonata for Oboe and Clarinet*. Writes to friend Daniel Burns that he feels his poems are "worth a large zero" and stops writing poetry for more than two years. Spends part of July with Stein and Alice B. Toklas in Bilignan, France, where they are joined by Copland; at Stein's suggestion, the two men visit Morocco, which enchants Bowles and frustrates Copland. They live in Tangier until early October. Bowles meets Claude McKay and the surrealist painter Kristians Tonny. After visiting Fez, Bowles writes to Morrissette, "Fez I shall make my home some day!" Bowles travels in Morocco with Harry Dunham after Copland leaves; returns to Paris via Spain. Attends final Copland-Sessions concert on December 16 in London, where his *Sonata for Oboe and Clarinet* is performed.

1932   Taken ill during a ski trip in the Italian Alps. Travels with literary agent John Trounstine to Spain and Morocco. Returns in May to Paris, where he is hospitalized with typhoid. Bowles' songs are performed at Yaddo. After leaving hospital in July, travels in France, seeing Gertrude Stein for the last time and meeting mother and Daniel Burns at Morrissette's house near Grenoble. Completes *Sonata No. 1 for Flute and Piano*. Goes to Spain with mother and Burns; after their departure, stays with Virgil Thomson and the painter Maurice Grosser. Visits Monte Carlo, where he becomes friendly with George Antheil. In December, finishes *Scènes d'Anabase*, based on the poem by Saint-John Perse. Leaves for Ghardaïa, a town in the northern Sahara recommended by Antheil.

1933   Arrives in Ghardaïa and settles in nearby Laghouat, where he uses the harmonium in the town's church to compose a cantata, using his own French text. Travels around the Sahara and North Africa with George Turner, an American. Goes to Tangier, where he shares house with Charles Henri Ford, surrealist poet and editor of *View* with whom he has been friendly since 1930, and Djuna Barnes. Returns to United States after a three-week visit to Puerto Rico en route to New York City. *Sonatina for Piano* performed on WEVD in New York on June 18. Bowles has difficulty adjusting to life in America; on June 24, writes Thomson, "Certainly nobody hates New York more than I do." Writes short story "A Proposition." Writes song cycle *Danger de Mort* and *Suite for Small Orchestra* and score for Dunham's film *Bride of Samoa*. Publishes "Watervariation" and "Message" in pamphlet *Two Poems*, his first separate publication. Sublets apartment from Copland at 52 West 58th Street. Founds music publishing company Editions de la Vipère and publishes *Scenes from the Door*, songs based on passages from Stein's *Useful Knowledge*. *Sonatina for Piano* performed in December at the League of Composers' Concert, where Bowles meets John Latouche, who becomes a close friend.

1934   Bowles meets George Balanchine and Lincoln Kirstein, who are interested in commissioning a score for American Ballet Caravan. Hired as a secretary by Charles Williams, director of the American Fondouk, a foundation in Morocco working for the prevention of cruelty to animals. Pays for Atlantic passage by working as a guide for a stockbroker vacationing in Spain. Buys records of North African music. His duties end in October and, after a brief stopover in Spain, he travels to Colombia; smokes marijuana for the first time while at sea. Falls ill from unpurified water and recuperates on a coffee plantation in the Colombian mountains. Returns to the United States, visiting Los Angeles and San Francisco, where he sees Henry Cowell; Cowell offers to publish Bowles' compositions in quarterly *New Music*.

1935   Accepts job as live-in companion to a wealthy Austrian invalid in Baltimore. Collaborates with painter Eugene Berman on an aborted ballet project. Quits job and returns to New York City. Receives commission to write score for Balanchine's *Yankee Clipper*. Allows his records of North African music to be reproduced for Béla Bartók. Writes music for Dunham's film *Venus and Adonis*, which is premiered at a screening and concert featuring several other works by Bowles. Scores two short films by Rudy Burkhardt and writes incidental music for *Who Fights the Battle?*, a play by Joseph Losey. Works as copyist for the Broadway composer Vernon Duke.

1936   With the help of Virgil Thomson, receives commission to
        write music for *Horse Eats Hat*, Edwin Denby's adapta-
        tion of a Eugène Labiche farce directed by John House-
        man and Orson Welles and supported by the Federal
        Theater Project. Helps to found the anti-Franco Com-
        mittee on Republican Spain. Article by Copland com-
        mends Bowles' music in *Modern Music* as "full of charm
        and melodic invention, surprisingly well-made in an in-
        stinctive and non-academic fashion." Bowles learns or-
        chestration and works on score for production of
        Marlowe's *Doctor Faustus* directed by Welles.

1937   *Doctor Faustus* opens in January; Thomson praises the
        score in *Modern Music* as "Mr. Bowles' definite entry into
        musical big-time." In February, Bowles is introduced to
        Jane Auer (b. February 22, 1917) by John Latouche. Sees
        Auer the following week at E. E. Cummings' apartment;
        when Bowles and Kristians Tonny propose a trip to Mex-
        ico, Auer asks to join them, and Bowles goes to meet her
        parents the same evening. Orders 15,000 anti-Trotsky
        stickers to distribute in Mexico. Travels to Mexico by bus
        with Auer, Tonny, and Tonny's wife, Marie-Claire Ivanoff.
        Auer falls ill with dysentery a week after arriving in Mexico
        and returns home without telling her companions. Bowles
        meets the composer Silvestre Revueltas, who leads an im-
        promptu performance of his *Homenaje a García Lorca* for
        him. Works on pieces influenced by Mexican folk music.
        Travels to Tehuantepec and helps prepare for the town's
        May Day Festival, then visits Guatemala. At Kirstein's re-
        quest, returns to New York to orchestrate Balanchine's
        Yankee Clipper. Auer invites him to spend a weekend with
        her in Deal Beach, New Jersey, after which they see each
        other regularly. *Yankee Clipper* premieres in Philadelphia.
        Bowles begins writing music for opera *Denmark Vesey*
        (now lost), with libretto by Charles Henri Ford. The first
        act of *Denmark Vesey* is performed at a benefit for *New
        Masses*.

1938   Bowles marries Auer on February 21. The couple honey-
        moon in Central America, then travel to Paris. Jane
        Bowles works on novel *Two Serious Ladies*. The Bowles
        meet Max Ernst and the painter and writer Brion Gysin,
        who will become a friend. Marriage is strained as Jane

spends much of her time apart from Bowles. Couple sep-
arates briefly when Bowles goes to the south of France;
Jane joins him after Bowles urges her by wire to do so.
The Bowles rent a house for the summer in Eze-Village
near Cannes. Returning to New York in the fall, they
move into the Chelsea Hotel. Bowles is commissioned to
write music for Houseman and Welles' production of
William Gillette's *Too Much Johnson*; finishes score but
when the production is canceled, transforms his music
into the piece *Music for a Farce*. Nearly broke, moves
with Jane to a cheaper apartment.

1939   Receives relief payments from the Federal Music Project.
Joins the American Communist Party. Writes score for the
Group Theatre's production of William Saroyan's *My
Heart's in the Highlands* and uses the money to rent a
farmhouse on Staten Island, where he works on *Denmark
Vesey* while Jane resumes writing *Two Serious Ladies*.
Writes short story "Tea on the Mountain." Mary Oliver
moves in and becomes Jane's friend and drinking companion, causing Bowles to move out. Bowles rents a
room in Brooklyn and invites Jane to live with him. Jane
refuses and moves with Oliver to Greenwich Village
apartment; the Bowles continue to attend parties and social events together.

1940   Bowles and Jane move to the Chelsea Hotel in March.
Bowles completes music for Saroyan's *Love's Old Sweet
Song*, which begins trial run in Princeton on April 6. After being hired by the Department of Agriculture to write
music for *Roots in the Soil*, a film about soil conservation
in New Mexico, travels to Albuquerque with Jane and
Jane's friend Bob Faulkner. Finishes score in June and
goes to Mexico with Jane and Faulkner. Meets Tennessee
Williams in Acapulco. Reluctantly moves to Taxco when
Jane rents a house there without consulting him; Jane
invites Faulkner to the house and begins a romantic
relationship with Helvetia Perkins, an American woman
working on a novel. Bowles returns to New York alone in
September to compose music for the Theatre Guild's production of *Twelfth Night*, which opens on November 19.
Bowles' score is a critical success; he receives a second
Theatre Guild commission for Philip Barry's *Liberty Jones*,

directed by Houseman. Jane arrives in New York on Christmas Day and rents a separate room at the Chelsea, where she is joined a few weeks later by Perkins.

1941   *Liberty Jones* opens on Broadway on February 5; the play and score receive negative reviews. Bowles writes music for Lillian Hellman's *Watch on the Rhine*. Attempts to quit Communist Party and is told that expulsion is the only means of leaving the organization. Writes *Pastorela*, an opera-ballet based on Mexican themes, for American Ballet Caravan. Lives with Jane at "artist's residence" on Middagh Street in Brooklyn Heights (other residents at the time include W. H. Auden and Benjamin Britten). Publishes obituary for Revueltas and essay "On Mexico's Popular Music" in *Modern Music*. Receives Guggenheim grant in March to compose an opera and travels to Taxco with Jane and Perkins. At the request of Katharine Hepburn, writes music for the play *Love Like Wildfire*, written by Hepburn's brother Richard. Meets Ned Rorem, who will become a friend and lifelong correspondent. *Pastorela* tours South America. Bowles meets Mexican painter Antonio Álvarez, who becomes close friend. Hospitalized with dysentery in September; recovers but falls ill with jaundice and recuperates at a sanitarium in Cuernavaca. Reads manuscript of Jane's *Two Serious Ladies* and suggests revisions.

1942   Works on light opera *The Wind Remains*, based very loosely on García Lorca's *Así que pasen cinco años*, in Mexico after Jane returns to New York to look for a publisher for *Two Serious Ladies*. Jane attempts suicide by slashing wrists but does not tell Bowles for many years. Bowles returns to United States with Álvarez, who is now partially paralyzed from a suicide attempt. Moves to apartment on 14th Street and Seventh Avenue and becomes acquainted with Marcel Duchamp, its previous occupant. Sees Jane often while maintaining separate household and finances. Debuts as music critic for the New York *Herald Tribune* on November 20; will contribute reviews regularly until 1946. Drafted for military service but dismissed after psychological examination.

1943   *The Wind Remains*, conducted by Leonard Bernstein with choreography by Merce Cunningham, premieres at

the Museum of Modern Art on March 30. Jane Bowles'
Two Serious Ladies is published on April 19 to mostly negative reviews. Composes incidental music for productions
of John Ford's *'Tis Pity She's a Whore* and a stage adaptation of James Michener's *Tales of the South Pacific.*
"Bluey: Pages from an Imaginary Diary," a section of his
childhood notebooks, is published in *View.* Bowles meets
Peggy Guggenheim, who organizes a recording of five of
his pieces. Meets Samuel Barber, Gian-Carlo Menotti,
and John Cage. Visits Canada with Jane.

1944   Writes music for Theatre Guild production of Franz
Werfel's *Jacobowsky and the Colonel* (adapted by S. N.
Behrman) and for *Congo,* a film directed by André Cau-
vin with script by John Latouche; receives recordings of
Congolese music from Cauvin that influence the score.
Composes music for ballet *Colloque Sentimental,* pro-
duced by the Ballet Russe de Monte Carlo with sets by
Salvador Dali, and incidental music for Williams' *The
Glass Menagerie.*

1945   Moves to an apartment on West 10th Street; Jane and
Perkins rent apartment in the same building. Edits special
issue of *View* on Central and South America and the
Caribbean, translating several articles and contributing an
anonymous story supposedly taken from a Mexican magazine; story will be revised four years later as "Doña
Faustina." Writes "The Scorpion," inspired by his reading
of indigenous Mexican myths, later writing that "the objectives and behavior of the protagonists remained the
same as in the beast legends. It was through this unexpected little gate that I crept back into the land of fiction
writing." Travels to Central America with set designer
and distant cousin Oliver Smith during summer. Publishes "The Scorpion" and writes "A Distant Episode."
Translates Borges' story "The Circular Ruins." Develops
close friendship with Australian composer Peggy
Glanville-Hicks, who will set Bowles' texts to music and
become a frequent correspondent.

1946   Writes music for *Blue Mountain Ballads,* with lyrics by
Tennessee Williams. Works on translation of Sartre's play
Huit-clos. Publishes "By the Water" in *View* and "The
Echo" in *Harper's Bazaar.* Completes *Sonata for Two*

Pianos and several theater scores. *No Exit*, Bowles' translation of *Huit-clos* directed by John Huston, opens on November 29 and is awarded Drama Critics' Award for the year's best foreign play.

1947   *Partisan Review* publishes "A Distant Episode." At a meeting with Dial Press about a possible collection of stories, Bowles is introduced to Helen Strauss, who agrees to be his agent. Hears from Strauss that Doubleday has offered an advance for a novel; Bowles signs contract and leaves for Morocco soon after. Writes "Pages from Cold Point" while at sea. Works on *The Sheltering Sky*, spending the fall in Tangier. Although he will travel frequently to Europe, Asia, and the United States, Tangier will be Bowles' home for the rest of his life. Contacts Oliver Smith in New York and they agree to buy a house in the Casbah of Tangier together, which upsets Jane. Meets Moroccan artist Ahmed Yacoubi, who will become a close companion during the 1950s. Begins taking *majoun*, a jam made from cannabis; tries kif, which he will begin smoking regularly and in large quantities from the 1950s through the 1980s, when health problems force him to reduce his consumption to one cigarette a day. Goes to Fez in December.

1948   Crosses into Algeria and travels around the Sahara. Jane arrives in Tangier with her new lover. Edwin Denby arrives and the four visit Fez. Jane has averse reaction to *majoun*, hallucinating and experiencing severe paranoia. Bowles finishes *The Sheltering Sky* in May; travels through Anti-Atlas Mountains with singer Libby Holman. Returns to New York alone in July. Doubleday rejects *The Sheltering Sky* and demands return of the advance. Several months later, English publisher John Lehmann reads *The Sheltering Sky* while visiting New York and agrees to publish it; James Laughlin of New Directions promises to bring out the American edition. Writes music for Williams' *Summer and Smoke*. *Concerto for Two Pianos, Winds, and Percussion* premieres in New York. Bowles becomes friends with Gore Vidal and Truman Capote. Jane develops an intense emotional attachment to a Moroccan woman named Cherifa that will last for many years. Bowles returns to Morocco, writing "The Delicate Prey" while at sea in December.

1949   Hosts Tennessee Williams and Williams' lover Frank Merlo. Travels in Sahara with Jane, who is impressed by the desert and writes her last completed story, "A Stick of Green Candy," in Taghit. Visits Paris for a performance of his *Concerto for Two Pianos and Orchestra*. John Lehmann publishes *The Sheltering Sky*. Bowles works on novel "Almost All the Apples Are Gone," never completed. In October, travels to England, where he is feted and introduced to Elizabeth Bowen, Cyril Connolly, and other British writers. New Directions publishes *The Sheltering Sky* in a small first printing on October 14, planning a second of 45,000 for the following year. Sails for Ceylon and begins writing a new novel, *Let It Come Down*.

1950   *The Sheltering Sky* enters the *New York Times* best-seller list on January 1; reviewing it for the *Times*, Tennessee Williams praises its "true maturity and sophistication." Bowles spends several months in Ceylon and southern India, working on *Yerma*, an opera for singer Libby Holman based on the García Lorca play. Joins Jane in Paris, where she is working on her play *In the Summer House*; Jane goes to New York, hoping to see the play staged, and Bowles returns to Morocco and receives visit from Brion Gysin. John Lehmann publishes *A Little Stone*, omitting "The Delicate Prey" and "Pages from Cold Point" because of censorship concerns. American version, *The Delicate Prey and Other Stories*, includes the two stories and is published by Random House in November.

1951   Bowles buys Jaguar and hires Mohammed Temsamany as chauffeur; travels with Gysin through Morocco and Algeria. Works on *Let It Come Down* during summer in the mountain village of Xauen; returns to Tangier in the fall and finishes the novel. Translation of R. Frison-Roche's *The Lost Trail of the Sahara* is published in August. Bowles leaves with Yacoubi for India in December.

1952   *Let It Come Down* published in February by Random House and by John Lehmann in England. Accused of spying by the Ceylonese government, Yacoubi and Bowles are detained for two days before being permitted to travel to Ceylon. Bowles makes offer to buy the island of Taprobane off the coast of Ceylon. Leaves with Yacoubi for Italy, where he plays a role in Hans Richter's film *8 x 8*. Agreement to buy Taprobane is sealed.

1953   Jane Bowles completes *In the Summer House*; having
            agreed to write music for the play, Bowles sails to New
            York with Yacoubi in March. Visits Jane at Libby Hol-
            man's house in Connecticut. Holman, infatuated with
            Yacoubi, convinces him to live with her, and Bowles re-
            turns to Tangier without completing score for *In the
            Summer House*. Writes *A Picnic Cantata*, with text by
            James Schuyler. Yacoubi returns to Tangier after quarrel-
            ing with Holman. Bowles and Yacoubi go to Italy, where
            Bowles collaborates with Tennessee Williams on English
            adaptation of Visconti's film *Senso*. Bowles goes to Istan-
            bul with Yacoubi to write travel essay for *Holiday*. They
            return to Italy in October and see Williams and Truman
            Capote before returning to Tangier amid rioting against
            the French. Bowles sails alone to United States, and com-
            pletes music (now lost) for *In the Summer House* in time
            for its December 14 performance in Washington and its
            six-week Broadway run.

1954   Returns to Tangier, where he is soon joined by Jane. Falls
            ill with typhoid and sees Williams and Frank Merlo while
            convalescing. Receives brief visit from William Burroughs,
            who will live in Tangier for several years. Bowles begins
            writing *The Spider's House*, inspired by political upheaval
            in Morocco; moves for the summer with Yacoubi to a
            rented house overlooking the ocean and maintains strict
            schedule of writing. Transcribes Moghrebi tales told to
            him by Yacoubi. Moves to Casbah in fall. Bowles and
            Jane refuse to visit each other because of Bowles' suspi-
            cion of Cherifa and Jane's distrust of Yacoubi. Hoping to
            ease tensions by leaving Tangier, Bowles sails for Ceylon
            with Jane and Yacoubi in December.

1955   Works on *The Spider's House* at house on Taprobane; Jane
            dislikes the island, is unable to write, and returns to Tan-
            gier in March. Bowles finishes *The Spider's House* on
            March 16. Travels with Yacoubi in East Asia before re-
            turning to Tangier in June. Works on *Yerma*. Writes text
            for *Yallah*, a book of Saharan photographs taken by Peter
            Haeberlin. Writes to Thomson in September that "the
            possibility of being attacked is uppermost in every non-
            Moslem's mind . . . I have taken an apartment until the
            first of October next year, but whether I'll be able to stick
            it out that long remains to be seen." Develops friendship

with Francis Bacon. At Jane's request, agrees to give Casbah house to Cherifa. *The Spider's House* is published by Random House on November 14.

1956   In Lisbon, Bowles writes anonymous article on Portuguese elections for *The Nation*. Morocco gains independence on March 2, with Tangier remaining under international control; Bowles writes in *The Nation* that "in fact, if not officially, the integration of Tangier with the rest of Morocco has already taken place" and that Europeans "know better than to wander down into the part of town where they are not wanted." Bowles' parents visit during the summer. German edition of *Yallah* published in October by Manesse Verlag in Switzerland. Bowles travels to Ceylon with Yacoubi, arriving in late December.

1957   Needing money, attempts to sell Taprobane. English edition of *The Spider's House* brought out by Macdonald & Co. Bowles travels to Kenya to cover the Mau Mau uprising for *The Nation*. Upon return to Morocco in May, discovers that Jane has suffered a stroke; rumors circulate of a violent reaction to *majoun* or poisoning by Cherifa. Receives visits from poets Allen Ginsberg, Peter Orlovsky, and Alan Ansen, who are drawn to Tangier in part because Bowles and Burroughs live there. Bowles posts bail after Yacoubi is arrested for alleged indecent behavior with an adolescent German boy. Takes Jane to London for treatment in August. Returning briefly to Morocco, Jane continues to have seizures and her psychological state deteriorates; she goes back to England and is admitted to a psychiatric clinic. Bowles and Yacoubi visit Jane in September. Bowles is hospitalized with Asiatic flu and writes "Tapiama" while suffering severe fever. Contracts pneumonia and pleurisy and is bedridden for three weeks; convalesces at the house of Sonia Orwell. Jane receives electric shock treatments. American edition of *Yallah* published by McDowell, Obolensky in October. Bowles convinces English publisher William Heinemann to bring out a story collection. Returns to Tangier with Jane and Yacoubi in November; Yacoubi is arrested and charged with "assault with intent to kill" the German boy.

1958   Police interrogate Bowles about Yacoubi and begin investigating Jane's relationship with Cherifa; the Bowles leave

Tangier and Temsamany is repeatedly questioned about them. Taprobane is sold but Bowles is unable to take any of the proceeds of the sale out of Ceylon. The Bowles travel to Madeira, where Jane's condition improves. Yacoubi is acquitted in a trial lasting five minutes. Jane flies alone to New York in April. En route to the United States in June, Bowles finishes score for *Yerma*, which premieres at the University of Colorado on July 29. Jane enters psychiatric clinic in White Plains, New York, in October. Bowles goes to Los Angeles and quickly writes score for Milton Geiger's play *Edwin Booth*, directed by José Ferrer. Returns to New York; with Ned Rorem and John Goodwin, tries mescaline for the first time. Seeks financial support to record Moroccan folk music. Jane is released from the hospital and leaves the United States with Bowles in December, arriving in Tangier by the end of the year.

1959   Bowles travels to New York after he is asked to write the score for Williams' *Sweet Bird of Youth*, which opens on Broadway March 10. Sees Ginsberg frequently. Awarded Rockefeller Grant to record North African music and returns to Morocco. Heinemann publishes the story collection *The Hours After Noon* in May. Accompanied by Canadian painter and journalist Christopher Wanklyn and driver Mohammed Larbi, Bowles makes four trips to record in remote areas and takes extensive notes that form the basis of essay "The Rif, to Music." Near the end of the project, the Moroccan government forbids further recording, calling the endeavor "ill-timed."

1960   The Bowles move into separate apartments in the same building, the Inmeuble Itesa in Tangier. Bowles refuses offer of a year-long professorship from the English Department at Los Angeles State College. Writes articles for *Life* and *Holiday* about Marrakesh and Fez.

1961   Tape-records and translates tales by Yacoubi, publishing "The Game" in *Contact* in May and "The Night Before Thinking" in *Evergreen Review* in September. Ginsberg returns to Tangier and encourages Bowles to write to Lawrence Ferlinghetti, publisher of City Lights Books, with a proposal for a collection of stories about kif-smoking that were written with the aid of kif; Ferlinghetti accepts enthusiastically.

1962   Bowles continues to record and translate stories told to him by Moroccans, a pursuit that will figure prominently in his later career. Meets Larbi Layachi, who tells Bowles autobiographical tales; under the pseudonym Driss ben Hamed Charhadi, Layachi's "The Orphan," transcribed and translated by Bowles, is published in *Evergreen Review*. Grove Press offers to publish Layachi's autobiography. When English publisher Peter Owen solicits a manuscript, Bowles collects essays and magazine pieces that will be published the following year as *Their Heads Are Green* (American edition is entitled *Their Heads Are Green and Their Hands Are Blue*); Peter Owen will be Bowles' primary English publisher for the rest of his career. *One Hundred Camels in the Courtyard* published by City Lights in September. Bowles returns with Jane to New York to write music for Williams' *The Milk Train Doesn't Stop Here Anymore*; visits parents in Florida and attends tryouts of *Milk Train* before returning to Tangier.

1963   Completes translation of Charhadi's *A Life Full of Holes*. Rents beach house at Asilah, a town south of Tangier, and spends several months there with Jane. Begins writing *Up Above the World*.

1964   *A Life Full of Holes* published by Grove Press in May. Working steadily, Bowles completes *Up Above the World* late in the year. Burroughs, Gysin, and Layachi leave Tangier for New York.

1965   Bowles and Jane visit the United States to visit his father, who has suffered a cerebral hemorrhage, and they consider buying a house in Santa Fe. Random House rejects *Up Above the World*. With Jane, Bowles returns to Tangier, where he learns that Simon & Schuster has accepted *Up Above the World*. Agrees to write book about Bangkok for Little, Brown. Begins to record and translate the spoken stories of Mohammed Mrabet, who becomes a close friend and regular visitor to Bowles' home.

1966   Film rights to not-yet-published *Up Above the World* are sold to Universal Studios for $25,000 in February; the novel is published by Simon & Schuster on March 15 to mixed reviews. Bowles receives word in June that parents have died within a week of each other. Travels with Jane to New York, then sails alone for Southeast Asia in July. Arrives in Bangkok in the fall and immediately dislikes the city. ("Most of Bangkok looked like the back streets of the nethermost Bronx relocated in a Florida swamp.") Goes to Chiengmai; records indigenous Thai music. Begins stage adaptation of story "The Garden."

1967　　*Jilala*, an album featuring recordings of the Jilala religious brotherhood made by Bowles and Brion Gysin, is released in January. Bowles returns to Tangier in March after being informed that Jane's condition has worsened, her depression so severe that she can barely sleep or eat. Takes Jane to a clinic in Málaga, where she is treated until August. "The Garden" is performed in April at the American School in Tangier. Bowles abandons Bangkok book and returns advance. Translation of Mrabet's *Love With a Few Hairs* is published by Peter Owen in London; book is adapted for the BBC and shown on September 22 (American edition is brought out by George Brazillier in 1968).

1968　　Peter Owen publishes story collection *Pages from Cold Point* in April. Jane returns to Málaga clinic for treatment. Bowles accepts teaching appointment in the English Department of San Fernando Valley State College in California, where he teaches a seminar on existentialism and the novel.

1969　　Returns to Tangier, bringing Jane; Jane loses weight excessively and returns to the hospital in Málaga. Signs contract to write autobiography for G. P. Putnam. Publication of Mrabet's *The Lemon* by Peter Owen (American edition, City Lights, 1972) and *M'Hashish* by City Lights, both translated by Bowles.

1970　　Poet Daniel Halpern, whom Bowles had met while teaching in California, starts the magazine *Antaeus*; Bowles is named founding editor. In May, Jane suffers stroke and her condition deteriorates, causing her to lose her vision. Premiere of Gary Conklin's film *Paul Bowles in the Land of the Jumblies* (retitled *Paul Bowles in Morocco* for English release and airing on CBS the following year) on December 10 in New York.

1971–72   Bowles begins translating the work of Mohamed Choukri, Moroccan writer, working from Choukri's Arabic texts. *Music of Morocco*, two-disc set taken from Bowles' recordings in the archives of the Library of Congress, is released. Black Sparrow Press brings out *The Thicket of Spring: Poems 1926–1969*. Autobiography, *Without Stopping*, is published by G. P. Putnam's Sons on March 15, 1972. Bowles discovers the stories of Swiss expatriate writer Isabelle Eberhardt (1877–1904) and begins to translate them.

1973   Jane Bowles dies in Málaga clinic on May 4 with Bowles at her side. In the years following Jane's death, Bowles will travel outside of Morocco infrequently and will be increasingly confined to the Inmeuble Itesa (in part because of health problems); receives many visitors and, choosing not to install a telephone at his home, maintains extensive correspondence.

1974   Bowles publishes three translations: Choukri's *For Bread Alone* and *Jean Genet in Tangier*, and Mrabet's *The Boy Who Set the Fire*. Resumes writing his own short stories after a hiatus of several years.

1975   Publishes translations of Mrabet's *Hadidan Aharam* and Eberhardt's *The Oblivion Seekers* in November. Stories "Afternoon with Antaeus," "The Fqih," and "Mejdoub" are collected in *Three Tales*, published by Frank Hallman in the fall.

1976–78   Black Sparrow Press publishes translations of Mrabet's *Look & Move On* and *Harmless Poisons, Blameless Sins* in 1976 and *The Big Mirror* in 1977; Bowles' story collection *Things Gone and Things Still Here* published in July 1977. Meets Millicent Dillon, who is working on a biography of Jane Bowles (*A Little Original Sin*, 1981).

1979   *Collected Stories 1939–1976* is published by Black Sparrow with an introduction by Gore Vidal. Publication of translations *Tennessee Williams in Tangier* by Choukri and *Five Eyes*, collection of stories by Abdeslam Boulaich, Mrabet, Choukri, Layachi, and Yacoubi.

1980   Translation of Mrabet's *The Beach Café & The Voice* is
             published. Bowles begins working on *Points in Time*,
             long essay about Morocco in a genre that he calls "lyrical
             history."

1981–82   Premiere of Sara Driver's film *You Are Not I*, based on
             Bowles' story, on May 12, 1981, in New York. Story collec-
             tion *Midnight Mass* is brought out by Black Sparrow Press
             in June 1981. *Next to Nothing*, collected poems, is published
             by Black Sparrow the same month. Bowles completes
             Points in Time, published August 1982 in England by
             Peter Owen (American edition, The Ecco Press, 1984).
             Teaches summer writing seminars in Tangier program of
             the School of Visual Arts in New York. One of his col-
             leagues in the program is Regina Weinreich, who will make a
             documentary about him. Bowles discovers the work of Guat-
             emalan writer Rodrigo Rey Rosa, one of his students, whose
             stories he begins to translate. Translation of Rey Rosa's
             The Path Doubles Back is published in November 1982.

1983–85   Bowles publishes unpunctuated "Monologue" stories in
             The Threepenny Review and *Conjunctions*. Translation of
             Mrabet's *The Chest* is published. Bowles travels to Bern,
             Switzerland, for medical treatment in summer 1984. Pub-
             lication of *The Beggar's Knife*, stories by Rey Rosa trans-
             lated by Bowles, and *She Woke Me Up So I Killed Her*,
             collection of translations from several authors.

1986–90   Translation of Mrabet's *Marriage with Papers* is pub-
             lished in 1986. Bowles suffers aneurysm in the knee and
             undergoes surgery in Rabat in September 1986. Meets
             the following year with director Bernardo Bertolucci,
             who is interested in adapting *The Sheltering Sky*. Begins
             keeping a diary (which will be published as *Days: Tan-
             gier Journal 1987–1989* in 1991). Concert of Bowles' cham-
             ber music is performed in Nice. Story collection
             Unwelcome Words is published by Tombuctou Books.
             Shooting of *The Sheltering Sky* on location in Morocco
             begins in 1989. Bowles plays role of narrator, which in-
             cludes on-screen appearance; becomes frustrated with
             Bertolucci's refusal to listen to his objections to the
             adaptation. Peter Owen brings out story collection *Call
             at Corazón* and Bowles' translation of Rey Rosa's *Dust
             on Her Tongue*. Bowles meets Virginia Spencer Carr,

who will become his biographer. Travels to Paris for premiere of *The Sheltering Sky*, calls the film "awful." Exhibition "Paul Bowles at 80" mounted at the University of Delaware. *The Invisible Spectator*, biography by Christopher Sawyer-Lauçanno, is published by Grove Press; Bowles objects to the book and writes in *Antaeus*, "I wonder if he knows how deeply I resent his flouting my wishes." Robert Briatte's biography, *Paul Bowles: 2117 Tanger Socco*, is published in France.

1991–94 Translations of Mrabet's *Chocolate Creams and Dollars* and Rey Rosa's *Dust on Her Tongue* are published in the United States in 1992. Limited edition of essay *Morocco*, with photographs by Barry Brukoff, appears the following year. Bowles' vision is impaired due to glaucoma. Scores written for synthesizer are performed at productions of Oscar Wilde's *Salome* (1992) and Euripides' *Hippolytus* (1993) at the American School in Tangier. In April 1994, Bowles attends concert of his music at the Théâtre du Rond-Point in Paris, which is recorded and released as *An American in Paris*. Spends a month in Atlanta for medical treatment at Emory University. Show of Bowles' photographs exhibited at the Boijmans van Beuningen museum in Rotterdam; *Paul Bowles Photographs: "How Could I Send a Picture into the Desert?"* is published. Canadian filmmaker Jennifer Baichwal visits Bowles and begins filming a documentary. *In Touch*, an edition of Bowles' letters edited by Jeffrey Miller, is published. Premiere of *Paul Bowles: The Complete Outsider*, documentary film by Catherine Warnow and Regina Weinrich.

1995 Premiere of *Halbmond*, adaptation of Bowles' stories "Merkala Beach" (alternate title of "The Story of Lahcen and Idir"), "Call at Corazón," and "Allal" by German filmmakers Frieder Schlaich and Irene van Alberti, with Bowles introducing the film in an on-screen appearance. For the first time in decades, Bowles visits New York City for three days of concerts devoted to his music and a symposium at the New School for Social Research, September 19–21. Receives standing ovation at concert at Lincoln Center. Reunion with Burroughs and Ginsberg at Mayfair Hotel is filmed by Baichwal. *Paul Bowles: Music*, a collection of essays relating to his career as a composer, is published by Eos Music Press.

1996–98   Contributes essay to monograph on Tangier-based artist
           Claudio Bravo published in 1996. Makes final visit to the
           United States for medical treatment in 1996. *The Music of
           Paul Bowles*, performed by the Eos Orchestra under the
           direction of Jonathan Sheffer, is released by BMG/Cata-
           lyst. *Paul Bowles: Migrations*, performed by members of
           the Frankfurt-based Ensemble Moderne, is released by
           Largo. Mohamed Choukri's *Paul Bowles wa 'uzla Tanja*,
           a book hostile to Bowles, is published in Arabic in Mo-
           rocco in 1996 and in French translation (*Paul Bowles, le
           reclus de Tanger*) the following year; in a 1997 interview in
           the Tangier weekly *Les Nouvelles du Nord*, Bowles says
           "there's no logic" to Choukri's accusatory assessment.
           Premiere of Baichwal's *Let It Come Down: The Life of
           Paul Bowles* at the 1998 Toronto International Film Festi-
           val. Millicent Dillon's *You Are Not I: A Portrait of Paul
           Bowles* is published in 1998. Edgardo Cozarinsky's *Fan-
           tômes de Tanger*, fictional film about post-war Tangier in
           which Bowles appears as himself, is released in France.

1999   Bowles transfers the majority of his literary papers to an
           archive at the University of Delaware. Owsley Browne's
           documentary *Night Waltz: The Music of Paul Bowles* is re-
           leased. Bowles is admitted to the Italian Hospital in
           Tangier for cardiac problems on November 7. Suffers
           heart attack in hospital and dies on November 18. Bowles'
           ashes are interred near those of his parents and grandpar-
           ents at Lakemont Cemetery in Glenora, New York.

Note on the Texts

This volume contains the first three novels written by Paul Bowles: *The Sheltering Sky* (1949), *Let It Come Down* (1952), and *The Spider's House* (1955). The texts of these novels are taken from the first American editions, since Bowles did not revise these books after their initial publication. Describing his working habits in an interview published in 1975, Bowles said: "The first draft is the final draft. I can't revise. I should qualify that by saying I first write in longhand, and then same day, or the next day, I type the longhand. There are always many changes between the longhand and the typed version, but that first typed sheet is part of the final sheet. There's no revision."

Bowles' short stories began to appear in magazines in the mid-1940s. Early in 1947, looking for a publisher to bring out a collection of stories, Bowles met with editors at Dial Press, who told him that most publishers would be reluctant to publish a collection by someone who had not yet written a novel. At the same meeting, Dial Press arranged an introduction to Helen Strauss of the William Morris Agency, who agreed to be Bowles' agent. Through Strauss, Doubleday offered Bowles an advance for a novel, which he began planning after signing a contract in the spring of 1947. According to Bowles' autobiography, *Without Stopping*, the novel's title came first: "Before the First World War there had been a popular song called 'Down Among the Sheltering Palms'; a record of it was at the Boat House in Glenora, and upon my arrival there each summer from the age of four onward, I had sought it out and played it before any of the others. It was not the banal melody which fascinated me, but the strange word 'sheltering.' What did the palm trees shelter people from, and how sure could they be of such protection?" Having decided that *The Sheltering Sky* would be set in the Sahara, Bowles left for North Africa in July. While living and traveling in Morocco, Spain, and Algeria, he wrote *The Sheltering Sky* during the second half of 1947 and the spring of 1948 and sent the completed typescript to Strauss in May.

After receiving Bowles' typescript from Strauss, Doubleday refused to publish *The Sheltering Sky* and demanded the return of the advance, claiming that they had "contracted for a novel" but he had written "something else." Several more rejections followed before *The Sheltering Sky* was read by John Lehmann, an English publisher, during a visit to New York. Lehmann responded enthusiastically to

the novel and decided to publish it in England; James Laughlin of
New Directions soon agreed to bring out an American edition. *The
Sheltering Sky* was published in England late in the summer of 1949
by John Lehmann. The American edition was published by New Directions in October 1949 in a small first printing that quickly sold
out; a second printing of 45,000 copies was issued in January 1950.
The John Lehmann and New Directions editions are the same except for changes to make the Lehmann edition conform with British
conventions of spelling and usage. This volume prints the text of the
1949 New Directions edition of *The Sheltering Sky*.

Bowles began *Let It Come Down* late in 1949 while traveling from
England to Tangier. He continued writing the novel throughout
1950 and 1951 while working on other projects, such as *Yerma*, an
opera he was composing for the singer Libby Holman. In the summer of 1951 Bowles moved to a house in the Moroccan village of
Xauen to focus on *Let It Come Down*; he finished the novel shortly
after his return to Tangier that fall. The book was published in February 1952 in England by John Lehmann and in the United States by
Random House. This volume prints the 1952 Random House edition
of *Let It Come Down*.

In the spring of 1954, as the Moroccan struggle for independence
from European rule intensified, Bowles visited Fez with the painter
Ahmed Yacoubi and his driver Mohammed Temsamany. Bowles recalled in his autobiography: "I wanted to see Fez in a time of political unrest. On the way we had to draw up alongside the road and
wait while French tanks and armored cars rolled by. There were
tanks stationed outside the walls at Bab Fteuh when we got there. A
startling change had come over the city. Each day the newspapers
published lists of the previous day's atrocities. No one knew where
the next dead body would be found or whose body it would prove
to be. The faces of passersby in the street showed only fear, suspicion, and hostility." After the trip to Fez, Bowles returned to Tangier and began writing *The Spider's House*. He worked steadily on
the novel through the summer and fall of 1954 before traveling with
Yacoubi and Jane Bowles to Taprobane, an island off Ceylon he had
purchased in 1952. He finished *The Spider's House* in Taprobane in
March 1955. *The Spider's House* was published by Random House on
November 4, 1955. An English edition was published by Macdonald
& Co. in 1957. The text of the 1955 Random House edition of *The
Spider's House* is printed here.

This volume presents the texts of the original printings chosen for
inclusion here, but it does not attempt to reproduce nontextual features of their typographic design. The texts are presented without

change, except for the correction of typographical errors. Spelling, punctuation, and capitalization are often expressive features and are not altered, even when inconsistent or irregular. The following is a list of typographical errors corrected, cited by page and line number: 40.32–33, metalic; 88.33, Lyle's; 140.31, wan't; 275.35, Just; 301.35, herself,; 322.27, Chaos",; 337.38, feet.,; 344.17, Taylor's; 348.37, *Allô*,; 350.15, folk; 364.13, I'm; 365.26, proceded; 366.20, Holland,; 367.7, asperity; 378.8, things!; 414.31–32, give to; 435.26, 01",; 440.25, delight; 516.21, his; 696.38, George's; 704.22, What; 720.34, lost.; 787.9, You'd.

Glossary

The Moghrebi Arabic words and phrases listed below take the form of Bowles' transliterations as they appear in the text.

Aabouches]   Leather slippers.

Aallem]   Muslim scholar.

Achrine]   Twenty.

Agi!]   Come! *Agi menah!*: Come here! *Agi ts'awouni!*: Come help me!

Aïd el Kebir]   Muslim festival commemorating Abraham's willingness to sacrifice Isaac in which a sheep is slaughtered after morning prayers and eaten throughout the day.

Allèche?]   Why?

Ana?]   Me? *Ana n'khallesik:* I'll pay.

Askout]   Shut up.

Assas]   Watchman.

Bacal]   Grocery shop.

Bache idaoui sebbatou . . .]   To cure his . . .

Balak!]   Watch out!

Baraka]   Blessedness; those with *baraka* are believed to enjoy divine protection.

Baraka'llahoufik]   Thank you.

B'd draa]   By force.

Bezef]   A lot.

Binatzkoum]   It's between you and them.

Bismil'lah]   In the name of God. Also *Bismil'lah rahman er rahim.*

Bordj]   Outpost, fort.

B'slemah]   Good-bye.

Cabrhozels]   A kind of pastry.

Caïd]   Local tribal ruler.

Ch'andek]   What's the matter with you?

928

Chechia]   Straw hat.

Cherif]   Or sherif. Muslim leader who is a descendant of the prophet Mohammed.

Chkama]   Informers, finks.

Chkhbarek?]   How are you?

Chkoun?]   Who?

Chnou?]   What? *Chnou hada?*: What are you doing? *Chnou hadek el haraj?*: What's that noise? *Chnou bghitsi ts'qoulli?*: What did you want to tell me?

Chorfa]   Class of the Moroccan aristocracy to which the cherifs belong.

Chouf]   Look.

Chta]   Rain.

Cirf halak]   Go away.

Deba, enta]   Now, you.

Derb]   Neighborhood.

Derri]   Child.

Djellaba]   A hooded overgarment with sleeves. Formerly a man's garment, but now worn by both sexes.

Djibli]   Peasant (perjorative).

Drari]   Children.

Drbouka]   Large ceramic hand drum used in traditional Moroccan music.

Echkoun?]   Who? *Chkoun entina?*: Who are you?

Egless]   Sit.

El hassil]   Anyway.

Enta m'douagh.]   You're crazy. Also *Enta hmuq bzef.*

Entina]   You.

Essbar]   Wait.

Essmah!]   Listen!

Fassi]   A person from Fez.

Fhemti]   Do you understand? *Fhemtek!*: I understood you!

Fondouk]   Hotel or inn.

Fqih]   Holy man.

Fraja]   Mass dancing.

Gandouras]   Long dresses worn by both sexes.

Guinbri]   Plucked lute-like instrument.

Gzara]   Butcher.

Habibi]   Beloved.

Hachouma!]   Shame!

Hada echouf]   This one sees.

Hak]   Take.

Hamdoul'lah!]   Praise be to God!

Hamqat]   Crazy. *Haquat, entina!*: You're crazy! *Ana hamqat?*: I'm crazy?

Harami]   Dishonest one.

Horm]   Shrine.

Huwa hada]   It is this one.

Ijbed selkha men rasou.]   He is going to be beaten up.

Inaal din]   An oath.

Incha'allah.]   God willing.

Istiqlal]   The Istiqlal (Independence) Party (PI), founded in 1944 and out-
lawed by the French in 1952, was the leading political organization
committed to the Moroccan struggle for independence.

Jilala cult]   Islamic confraternity named after the saint Abdel Qader Jilani
(1077–1166), whose itinerant musicians perform sacred music in small
ensembles. Jilala music often aims to call forth spiritual healing or to
induce a state of holy trance. Bowles recorded the music of the Jilala
brotherhood on several occasions.

Joteya]   Market.

Kabila]   Tribe.

Kafir]   Unbeliever.

Kerouine]   Religious university in Fez founded in the 9th century.

Khai]   Brother.

Khlass!]   Stop it. *Khlass men d'akchi*: Stop that.

Kif]   The fine leaves at the base of the flowers of the common hemp plant,
chopped and mixed (ideally in a ratio of seven to four) with tobacco
grown in the same earth.

Kifach?]   How?

Kuli!] Tell me!

La, khoya, la] No, brother, no.

'Lah imsik bekhir] Good night.

Lirah] Reed flute.

Litham] The cloth worn over the lower half of a woman's face.

Maallem] Master.

Maghreb] Sunset prayer.

Majabekfina] Don't worry about me.

Majoun] Literally, jam. In its special sense it refers to any sweet prepara-
tion eaten with the purpose of inducing hallucinations; its active ingre-
dient is the hemp plant.

Marabout] Shrine to a holy man.

Medersa] Religious school.

Mehari] Camel.

Mektoub] Destiny.

Mellah] Jewish quarters.

Menène jaou? O allèche?] Where did they come from? And why?

Meziane] Good.

Miehtsain] Two hundred.

Mokhazni] Soldier.

Mottoui] Leather purse for kif.

Moulana] God.

Moussem] Seasonal festival held at the tomb of a saint.

Mra] Woman.

Msalkheir] Good afternoon.

Naam, sidi] Yes, sir.

Nchoufou menbad] We'll see you later.

Nesrani] Christian.

Nimchiou] Let's go.

O deba labès enta?] You feel better?

Ouakha] OK.

Ouallah?] Swear to God?

Ouild] Boy; son. *Ouildi, ouildi*: My son, my son.

Ouled Naïl girls] Courtesans and dancing girls from a people of the Aurès Mountains of Algeria. Bowles visited a bordello with Ouled Naïl dancers while traveling in Algeria with friend George Turner in 1933.

Qaodi] Or qadi. A Muslim judge who rules on the basis of *Shari'ah*, Islamic law.

Qalaoui] Testicles.

Qaouji] Waiter.

Qoullou rhadda f'shah] Tell him tomorrow morning.

Rebab] Violin-like instrument with one to three strings, played with a bow.

Ronda] Popular card game played in North Africa and Spain.

Rhaddi noud el haraj man daba chovich.] I'm going to raise hell in a little while.

Rhaita] An oboe-like reed instrument. Bowles called it "the perfect out-door instrument, an oboe of stridency that permits it to be heard miles away, yet capable of executing the subtlest melodic features." ("North African Music I," New York *Herald Tribune*, December 27, 1942)

Sahel] Easy.

Sbalkheir] Good morning.

Sebsi] Long thin pipe for smoking kif.

Serouelles] Wide trousers worn beneath traditional clothing.

Skout] Shut up.

Sidi] Sir.

Skhoun b'zef] Very hot.

Smahli] I'm sorry.

Smatsi] Listen.

Smitsek?] What is your name?

Stenna, stenna. Chouia, chouia.] Wait, wait. Easy, easy.

Tanja Alia] The great Tangier.

Timshi] You walk.

Tlah] Go up.

Tskellem bellatsi.] Speak softly.

Trhol]   Enter.

Ulema]   Scholars trained in Islamic law (plural of *aallem*).

Wattanine]   Patriots.

Ya rabi]   Oh God.

Yah latif!]   My God!

Youca]   Owl.

Zaouia of Moulay Idriss]   Holy shrine dedicated to Moulay Idriss II, founder of Fez. *Zaouia*: Seat of a religious brotherhood, generally comprising a mosque, a school, and the tomb of the sect's founder.

Notes

In the notes below, the reference numbers denote page and line of this volume (the line count includes chapter headings). No note is made for material included in standard desk-reference books such as Webster's *Collegiate, Biographical,* and *Geographical* dictionaries. Foreign words and phrases are translated only if meaning is not evident in context. For Arabic terms, see Glossary on page 928. For further biographical information than is contained in the Chronology, see Robert Briatte, *Paul Bowles: 2117 Tanger Socco* (Paris: Plon, 1989); Gena Dagel Caponi (ed.), *Conversations with Paul Bowles* (Jackson: University of Mississippi Press, 1993); Millicent Dillon, *You Are Not I: A Portrait of Paul Bowles* (Berkeley: University of California Press, 1998); Michelle Green, *The Dream at the End of the World: Paul Bowles and the Literary Renegades in Tangier* (New York: Harper-Collins, 1991); Christopher Sawyer-Lauçanno, *The Invisible Spectator: A Biography of Paul Bowles* (New York: Grove Press, 1989).

THE SHELTERING SKY

5.5   EDUARDO MALLEA] Argentine novelist (1903–1982) whose books include *La bahia de silencio* (*The Bay of Silence*, 1940) and *Fiesta en noviembre* (*Fiesta in November*, 1949).

16.7   "*Qu'est-ce . . . là?*"] What are you looking for?

16.13   *Qu'est-ce ti vo?*"] What do you want?

17.6   "*Qu'est-ce . . . là?*] What are you doing here?

18.17   "*Je . . . soir,*"] I don't know if I want to go there tonight.

19.35   *Il faut rigoler.*"] You've got to laugh.

20.11–12   *C'est de la saloperie, ça!*] It's filth, that!

27.23   *Ci . . . dit!*"] She's not a whore, I told you!

50.28–29   "*Cell-là . . . en bas,*"] Put this one here below.

50.32   *Thé . . . gateau!*"] Only tea! No cake!

60.6   "*Dime . . . dejaste . . .*"] Tell me, ungrateful one, why did you abandon me, and leave me alone . . .

61.17   "*Je me suis trompée,*"] I made a mistake.

84.1–2   "*Ah, les salauds! . . . Krorfa!*"]   Ah, the bastards! We can see we're in Aïn Krorfa!

92.22   Abd-el-Wahab]   The Egyptian composer and singer Mohammed Abdel Wahab (1910–1991), a prolific and enormously popular songwriter and performer as well as an innovative orchestrator and pioneer in the development of the Arabic film musical.

112.18–19   *comme on a fait en Tripolitaine*"]   Like it's done in Libya.

132.17   *d'ailleurs.*"]   In fact.

139.33   "*Hassi Inifel!*"]   The name of the bordj.

147.33–34   "*Pourquoi . . . entrer?*"]   Why won't you let us in?

148.1   "*Peut pas,*"]   Can't.

148.25   "*Vous . . . propriètaire?*"]   Are you the owner?

148.27–29   "*Ah . . . ici!*"]   Ah, madame, go away, I implore you. You cannot come in!

156.31   "*Enfin . . . courageuse!*"]   Finally, madame, be brave!

172.23   "*Vous . . . pressé!*"]   You are in a hurry!

197.7   "*Pourvu qu'ils la trouvent là-bas!*"]   Hope they find her there!

205.37   Garamantic]   Or Garamantian, empire that flourished from 400 B.C. to A.D. 600 in the Fezzan (in present-day southwestern Libya).

241.32   "*Défendu!*"]   Forbidden.

245.25   "*Vous lui faites mal,*"]   You're hurting her.

246.12   "*Elle est costaude, cette garce!*"]   She's strong, this bitch.

LET IT COME DOWN

278.8–9   "*On peut entrer*]   Can I come in?

278.28   "*Estamos salvados,*"]   We're safe.

278.28–29   "*Qué gentuza más aburrida,*"]   Such boring people.

281.24   Lyautey]   Louis-Hubert Gonzalve Lyautey (1854–1934), French marshal and minister who served as the first Resident General of Morocco from 1912 to 1925.

296.6   *un machaquito*]   Alcoholic drink made with aniseed.

303.6–7   PIDIENDO . . . DIVINO]   Requesting divine protection.

307.38   "*Je suis navrée,*"]   I'm sorry.

307.39   "*Je . . . tout.*]   I'm not feeling well. It's not good at all.

308.25   "*No hay remedio,*"]   It's no use.

328.22–23   "*Υ pensábamos . . . hermoso!*"]   And we thought of going to Seville for the Holy Week. Oh, how beautiful!

328.25   "*Alors . . . toi!*"]   You're still making up your mind? You're funny, you!

328.28–29   "*Wunderschön . . . sein.*"]   Your love must be lovely.

328.30   "*Υ por fin . . . aquí.*"]   And at last we are staying here.

328.30   *que lástima!*"]   What a shame.

328.31   "*Ne t'en fais pas pour moi.*"]   Don't worry about me.

350.21   "*On va par-rtir.*"]   Let's go.

357.34   Crown Prince Rupprecht]   Heir to the Bavarian throne (1869–1955) and German military commander during World War I.

390.6–7   "*Je . . . savoir!*"]   I absolutely must know!

393.35–36   *Espérame . . . cinco,*]   Wait here for me. I will be back before five.

397.9   *Bastante!*]   Enough.

398.20   "*Je . . . suite,*"]   I'm coming down right away.

431.22–23   *Ili firmi . . . sbah.*"]   It's closed, sir. And then to Thami: Tell him tomorrow morning.

437.15   "DENTOLINE . . . EXCELLENCE,"]   Dentoline, the best toothbrush.

437.17   Om Kalsoum]   Egyptian singer (1904?–1975) known for her passionate virtuoso style; she began performing in Cairo in the 1920s and through recordings, radio broadcasts, and films became the most popular singer in the Arab world.

456.26–27   *Mann . . . sterben.*]   One only has to die. (German proverb)

500.19   Antaeus]   In Greek legend, the giant Antaeus, king of Libya, renewed his strength whenever he touched the ground. He challenged strangers to wrestling matches, then killed them when they became weak and exhausted. He was slain by Hercules.

524.29   "*Me . . . abajo.*"]   Can you wait here for me.

525.13   *carretera.*]   Road.

THE SPIDER'S HOUSE

531.2–6   *The likeness . . . but knew.*]   Chapter 29, verse 42.

549.1   El Mokhri]   Mohammed el-Mokri, Grand Vizier to Sultan Mohammed V.

549.9   an Alaouite from the Tafilalet] The Alawite dynasty has reigned in Morocco since the 17th century, when the first Alawite ruler Moulay Rashid conquered many principalities, captured Fez, and reunited the country. The Tafilalet, an oasis in southeastern Morocco, is home to the Filali clan, to which the Alawite rulers belong.

549.12–13   Drissiyine, descendants of the first dynasty,] The Arabian ruler Idriss I established the first royal line of sherifs after conquering Berber tribes in northern Morocco; his son, Idriss II, made Fez the capital in 808.

554.27–28   Si Kaddour] Algerian-born religious leader and playwright Kaddour ben Ghabrit (1873–1954).

555.3–4   "A . . . Français!"] Down with the French!

572.4   Ibn Saud] Founder and first king (ca. 1880–1953) of Saudi Arabia.

572.7   Sultan of the Hejaz] In 1924, Ibn Saud defeated his chief rival, Husayn ibn Ali, and annexed the Hejaz to the territory that would become Saudi Arabia in 1932. The Hejaz, the region where the holy cities of Mecca and Medina are located, had declared independence from Turkish rule in 1916.

572.17–18   carrion . . . throne?] Because of his resistance to French colonial policies, Sultan Mohammed V (Mohammed ben Youssef) was arrested on August 20, 1953, and sent into exile in Madagascar; he was replaced by his cousin Moulay Ben Arafa, an aging and widely unpopular monarch.

583.23   war of Abd-el-Krim] A rebellion by Rifian tribes that began in 1919. After a force led by the warlord Abd-el-Krim (1882?–1963) defeated Spanish troops at Anual in 1921, an autonomous region was established in the Rif. Abd-el-Krim's forces continued to advance into territory controlled by the Spanish and French until the uprising was suppressed in 1926.

608.5   Haroun er Rachid] Caliph of Baghdad (786–809).

614.39   Salim Hilali] Algerian-born singer (b. 1920) of North African and Spanish music.

616.1   *danse du ventre*] Belly dance.

616.4   Spahi] North African cavalrymen of the French army.

638.31   Si Allal] Allal al-Fassi (1906–1974), Istiqlal Party founder and leader.

638.37–39   Arafa . . . Youssef comes back.] See note 572.17–18.

639.7–9   *Hakim* . . . Alaoui dynasty] See note 549.9.

664.38   hands of Fatima,] Depictions of the hands of Fatima, the daughter of the prophet Mohammed, are believed to ward off evil.

666.24   Abd el Wahab] See note 92.22.

684.5–6   "*mais ce matin . . . compris?*"] But this morning I feel like drinking tea. With lemon. Do you understand?

690.19   "*Vous . . . chose,*] Would you like something.

717.16   *colon*] French settler.

735.26   "*Vous . . . pas?*"] You'll excuse me if I speak English, no?

736.37   *C'est . . . ça.*"] It's unfortunate, but that's how it is.

737.18   "*Oui . . . reconnaissants,*"] Yes, we are grateful to you.

738.2–3   *On . . . peuple.*"] One doesn't joke with the will of the people.

743.16   *factures.*] Bills.

761.14   "*Qu'est-ce . . . dehors?*"] What's happening outside?

773.3–6   *A questioner . . . Stairways.*] Chapter 70, verses 1–3.

792.38   "*Tous . . . tôle.*"] All the indigenous are in jail.

802.9   *mais . . . bon?*] But what good is that?

804.24   *mais . . . démarches,*"] But we have to take steps.

809.37–38   "*La chaleur . . . vie.*"] Heat complicates life.

846.22–23   "*tu . . . moi?*"] Don't you want to do something for me?

Library of Congress Cataloging-in-Publication Data

Bowles, Paul, 1910–1999.
  [Novels. Selections]
  The sheltering sky, Let it come down
  The spider's house
      p. cm—(The Library of America ; 134)
  Contents: The sheltering sky — Let it come down —
    The spider's house
  ISBN 1–931082–19–7 (alk. paper)
  1. Morocco – Social life and customs – Fiction.
I. Title: The sheltering sky. II. Title: Let it come down.
III. Title: The spider's house. IV. Series.

PS3552.O874   A6   2002
813/.54 21

                              2002019453

THE LIBRARY OF AMERICA SERIES

The Library of America fosters appreciation and pride in America's literary heritage by publishing, and keeping permanently in print, authoritative editions of America's best and most significant writing. An independent nonprofit organization, it was founded in 1979 with seed money from the National Endowment for the Humanities and the Ford Foundation.

1. Herman Melville, *Typee, Omoo, Mardi* (1982)
2. Nathaniel Hawthorne, *Tales and Sketches* (1982)
3. Walt Whitman, *Poetry and Prose* (1982)
4. Harriet Beecher Stowe, *Three Novels* (1982)
5. Mark Twain, *Mississippi Writings* (1982)
6. Jack London, *Novels and Stories* (1982)
7. Jack London, *Novels and Social Writings* (1982)
8. William Dean Howells, *Novels 1875–1886* (1982)
9. Herman Melville, *Redburn, White-Jacket, Moby-Dick* (1983)
10. Nathaniel Hawthorne, *Collected Novels* (1983)
11. Francis Parkman, *France and England in North America*, vol. I (1983)
12. Francis Parkman, *France and England in North America*, vol. II (1983)
13. Henry James, *Novels 1871–1880* (1983)
14. Henry Adams, *Novels, Mont Saint Michel, The Education* (1983)
15. Ralph Waldo Emerson, *Essays and Lectures* (1983)
16. Washington Irving, *History, Tales and Sketches* (1983)
17. Thomas Jefferson, *Writings* (1984)
18. Stephen Crane, *Prose and Poetry* (1984)
19. Edgar Allan Poe, *Poetry and Tales* (1984)
20. Edgar Allan Poe, *Essays and Reviews* (1984)
21. Mark Twain, *The Innocents Abroad, Roughing It* (1984)
22. Henry James, *Literary Criticism: Essays, American & English Writers* (1984)
23. Henry James, *Literary Criticism: European Writers & The Prefaces* (1984)
24. Herman Melville, *Pierre, Israel Potter, The Confidence-Man, Tales & Billy Budd* (1985)
25. William Faulkner, *Novels 1930–1935* (1985)
26. James Fenimore Cooper, *The Leatherstocking Tales*, vol. I (1985)
27. James Fenimore Cooper, *The Leatherstocking Tales*, vol. II (1985)
28. Henry David Thoreau, *A Week, Walden, The Maine Woods, Cape Cod* (1985)
29. Henry James, *Novels 1881–1886* (1985)
30. Edith Wharton, *Novels* (1986)
31. Henry Adams, *History of the U.S. during the Administrations of Jefferson* (1986)
32. Henry Adams, *History of the U.S. during the Administrations of Madison* (1986)
33. Frank Norris, *Novels and Essays* (1986)
34. W.E.B. Du Bois, *Writings* (1986)
35. Willa Cather, *Early Novels and Stories* (1987)
36. Theodore Dreiser, *Sister Carrie, Jennie Gerhardt, Twelve Men* (1987)
37. Benjamin Franklin, *Writings* (1987)
38. William James, *Writings 1902–1910* (1987)
39. Flannery O'Connor, *Collected Works* (1988)
40. Eugene O'Neill, *Complete Plays 1913–1920* (1988)
41. Eugene O'Neill, *Complete Plays 1920–1931* (1988)
42. Eugene O'Neill, *Complete Plays 1932–1943* (1988)
43. Henry James, *Novels 1886–1890* (1989)
44. William Dean Howells, *Novels 1886–1888* (1989)
45. Abraham Lincoln, *Speeches and Writings 1832–1858* (1989)
46. Abraham Lincoln, *Speeches and Writings 1859–1865* (1989)
47. Edith Wharton, *Novellas and Other Writings* (1990)
48. William Faulkner, *Novels 1936–1940* (1990)
49. Willa Cather, *Later Novels* (1990)
50. Ulysses S. Grant, *Memoirs and Selected Letters* (1990)

This book is set in 10 point Linotron Galliard,
a face designed for photocomposition by Matthew Carter
and based on the sixteenth-century face Granjon. The paper
is acid-free Domtar Literary Opaque and meets the requirements
for permanence of the American National Standards Institute. The
binding material is Brillianta, a woven rayon cloth made by
Van Heek-Scholco Textielfabrieken, Holland. The compo-
sition is by The Clarinda Company. Printing and
binding by R.R.Donnelley & Sons Company.
Designed by Bruce Campbell.